OF LOVE AND LIFE

OF LOVE AND LIFE

Three novels selected and condensed by Reader's Digest

CONDENSED BOOKS DIVISION

The Reader's Digest Association Limited, London

With the exception of actual personages identified as such, the characters and incidents in the fictional selections in this volume are entirely the product of the authors' imaginations and have no relation to any person or event in real-life.

The Reader's Digest Association Limited
11 Westferry Circus, Canary Wharf, London E14 4HE

www.readersdigest.co.uk

ISBN 0-276-42597-9

For information as to ownership of copyright in the material of this book, and acknowledgments, see last page.

CONTENTS

STOCK

THE DREAM CATCHER

Maria Barrett

Sarah, Roz and Janie: three women dreaming of a better life. Sarah is a single mother struggling to bring up her partially deaf son. Roz wants desperately to make her small farm financially viable. As for Janie, she's a GP's wife who dreams of escaping the ever-growing feeling of emptiness inside her. So, when Janie's brother Marcus suggests they start an investment club, the women jump at the chance. Soon they are making serious money; the sort of money that can make dreams come true . . .

Chapter One

SARAH PULLED HER OLD and rather battered Mini Metro into a parking space between two new, shiny four-wheel-drive vehicles and yanked up the handbrake. It made a rough, crunching sound as she did so and she had to hold it for a moment, then jerk it violently up into place. She switched the engine off and climbed out of the car, slamming the door hard because the lock was damaged and that was the only way to ensure that it closed properly. The car rattled in protest as she walked away.

Sarah was early today but, as usual, Janie Leighton was there already. Always the first: clean trousers, smart sweater, expensive handbag, hair brushed and lipstick on. She stood alone in the playground.

'Hello, Janie.'

Sarah crossed to her. They had been friends since their children had started at Wynchcombe Primary.

'Hi, Sarah. Did you finish early today?'

'No, I've been promoted.' Sarah worked for the local supermarket. It wasn't exactly a career, but it helped pay the bills.

'Have you? Gosh, that's great. Well done.'

'Don't get too excited.' Sarah gave a small, embarrassed laugh. 'I've been moved from check-out to customer services. It's more money, marginally, so I've cut down to four hours instead of five.'

'So you can put your feet up for an hour before you collect Rory?'

'I wish. No, I can get some shopping, load the washing machine, shove the Hoover round, and prepare some supper, so as to have a bit more time to spend on Rory's homework—when we're not doing speech therapy, special English or listening skills that is!' Again Sarah laughed, but falsely, and Janie gently patted her arm. Rory was partially deaf and sometimes the effort of it all seemed overwhelming.

'Come for tea,' Janie said, 'on Wednesday, or Thursday. Can you?'

'Yes, thanks, we'd like that.' Sarah looked towards the children waiting at the glass door. Little Katie Leighton was at the front; a gleaming, smiling, perfect child. Janie, Sarah thought, had no idea how hard life could be. Why should she? A GP's wife with a comfortable existence, needing nothing, happily married with a normal, healthy, charming little girl, But then Janie would touch Sarah with a comment just when it was needed most, and Sarah would wonder how she could have such intuition for sadness.

'Good. Ah, here they are.' Janie moved forward as Katie rushed out of the classroom door towards her. Sarah looked at Miss Meaney, who motioned for her to come over.

'I've been summoned,' she commented, walking past Janie. 'Again. See you tomorrow.' Sarah went on to the classroom.

'Mrs Greg, I wonder if I could have a word?'

Sarah smiled, and saw Rory at the back of the class, head in a book, oblivious to the fact that the classroom had almost emptied.

'I just wanted to say,' Miss Meaney began, as the last child went out of earshot, 'that we had a bit of an incident today.' She lowered her voice. 'The batteries went on his hearing aids and Mrs Perry thought he wasn't paying attention and told him off. I'm afraid that he got a bit upset because he said he couldn't hear and . . .' She broke off. 'Ah, hello, Rory. I'm just saying how well you've been doing recently and telling Mummy about your aids today in story time.'

Rory Greg smiled at his mother and Sarah's heart brimmed over with love. She bent, to put her face level with his, and spoke loudly and clearly. 'Hello, love. Did you have a good day?' He nodded.

'I'm not sure we put his aids in properly,' Miss Meaney said.

Sarah tilted Rory's face to the right, then the left, checking his ears. She stood straight. 'They're a bit skewhiff but I'll fix them in the car.'

'Can I go and play tag with Katie, Mummy?' Sarah looked outside at the playground and saw Katie Leighton playing with another little girl while Janie stood with the mother. 'Of course.' Rory ran off. Miss Meaney smiled after him. 'I'm sorry about today,' she said. 'I was worried it might mar his confidence.'

'He'll be fine,' Sarah replied. 'We have these little hiccups every now and then.' They both turned for a moment to watch Rory and Katie playing tag. 'Is Justin Betts still here?' Sarah asked.

Miss Meaney turned. 'Yes. It's the third time he's been picked up late this week.'

'Shall I take him for you? I'll hang on until Roz gets here if you like.'

'That would be very helpful indeed. Would you mind?'

'Of course not. Justin?' Sarah called out. 'D'you want to come and play with Rory until Mummy gets here?'

Justin Betts, a big child with a mop of unruly brown hair, nodded and ran to join Rory and Katie.

'Thanks, Mrs Greg,' Miss Meaney said. 'I'll see you tomorrow.'

Roz Betts was driving down School Lane too fast. Twice she had pulled up sharply to let other cars pass where the road became narrow, as she yelled at Kitty and Oliver in the back to keep the noise down.

'*Please* will you both stop arguing!' She waved as one of the mothers from Justin's class drove past. 'And if I hear that you've taken that guinea pig out of the box there will be *big* trouble! Understood?' She had one eye on the clock and one eye on the children. 'Bugger,' she muttered low under her breath. It was three forty-five, she had to collect Justin, drop the guinea pig off to the Walshes, and then get back to feed the pigs and do the pony. '*Oliver!* Leave that guinea pig where it is!'

She turned into the school drive not concentrating as well as she should have been, and as she swung round the corner, Kitty let out a scream and she jerked round to see what the matter was.

Rory was 'it'. He ran round the playground with Justin in his sight, but Justin was too fast. As he darted round the slide and ran to the gates, Sarah shouted for them to mind the road. Justin ignored her and ran out of the gate and across the road. 'Rory!' Sarah shouted, 'stay in the playground!' But Rory didn't hear her. He dashed out after Justin just as Roz rounded the bend.

Roz felt the thud of a small body against the car. She froze for a split second, then hit the brake. She thought she was going to be sick.

Sarah sprinted out of the playground and fell to her knees by her child. 'Oh God,' she cried. 'Oh God, Rory, please . . .'

Roz climbed out of the car. Her whole body was shaking and she thought her legs were going to buckle from under her. She knelt down by Sarah and Rory. There was the most terrible silence and even the air seemed to stop moving. Then Rory opened his eyes and said, 'It's OK, Mum, I think I'm OK,' and Roz started to cry.

Janie and Roz sat in silence in the A & E department of St Richard's Hospital in Chichester. Roz had her head in her hands, while Janie watched Katie read a book to Kitty, Oliver and Justin, and thanked God it hadn't been her daughter. Katie was her life; Katie was everything.

Roz stirred, looked up, and said, 'I just keep thinking, how could I have been so stupid? I honestly don't know what happened, Janie. It all happened so quickly!'

Janie didn't answer. There was nothing she felt she could honestly say that would help.

'God, I was in such a rush,' Roz went on. 'I've got so much on my plate, what with the small holding, the organic vegetables, the free range chickens, the pigs, the dogs, the cat, the pony, the kids and the eternal bloody struggle for money. No wonder I make mistakes.'

'You do too much,' Janie said. She felt she had to say something, that Roz expected some sort of comment.

But, sensitive and upset, Roz misinterpreted the remark as criticism. 'What d'you mean I do too much? How the hell can I do anything less?'

Janie's mouth dried up. It was in her nature to skirt issues, to disguise the truth if it was even the slightest bit unpleasant. 'I don't know,' she stammered, 'I just think that you need to slow down, that's all.'

'That's all! Jesus, Janie! Would you like to tell me how? How do I slow down and still manage to get everything done?' Roz's voice had risen.

Janie flushed. 'It was just a suggestion. I don't know how to do it.'

'Exactly!' Roz stared at Janie. She was feeling distraught, guilt-stricken and afraid, and she took it out on the person nearest to her. 'How *could* you?' she snapped. 'When the most stressful thing in your week is fitting in a hair appointment.'

The children stopped reading and stared at her. Roz knew immediately that she had gone too far. 'Oh God, I'm sorry, Janie, I . . .'

Janie looked down. The bloody awful truth of it was that Roz was right. 'It's OK . . .' She looked across at Katie. 'Don't stop reading sweetheart,' she said gently. Katie nodded, but didn't resume reading.

'I think I'll try and find Sarah,' Roz said. 'See what's happening. D'you want a coffee?'

Janie nodded.

'Milk, no sugar, right?'

'Yes.'

There was a moment of awkward silence, then Roz dug her hands in the pockets of her jeans and walked off.

'You'll need some change,' Janie called, holding out her purse.

'Oh God, yes, of course.' Roz shook her head and took the purse. Another mistake, they both thought.

Sarah sat by the side of Rory's bed in a curtained-off bay in A & E. They were waiting for the results of Rory's X-rays. She'd been told he had mild concussion and a broken rib, and the X-ray would show up anything more serious. He was, the nurse emphasised, extremely lucky; she couldn't stress enough the importance of road sense.

Sarah had replied that road sense was far easier if you could actually hear the cars coming, and she'd wanted to add that if Rory had had the digital hearing aids that he needed then he might have been able to do just that. But she hadn't said it. She was talking to a nurse who had been sent to comfort, not to take an ear-bashing about NHS funding.

She looked up as a houseman put his head round the curtain. 'Mrs Greg?' He sat on the edge of Rory's bed. 'Hi, I'm Dr Allen. I've been having a look at Rory's X-rays.' He made sure that Rory could see his face properly. 'How are you doing, young man?' he asked.

'Fine.'

'You gave everyone a nasty scare getting yourself run over like that!' He smiled and Rory smiled back. 'Still, not too much damage done by the looks of things, although your rib'll be sore for a while.'

He turned to Sarah. 'How long has he been without hearing?'

'Since birth. He's been aided since he was three.'

Dr Allen peered at Rory's ears and then looked back again to Rory's face. 'Cool aids. I bet they help, don't they?'

'Sometimes.'

'Perhaps you ought to use them along with these.' He pointed to Rory's eyes. 'Watch and listen, especially when crossing the road.' He flicked Rory's chin. 'You're dismissed.'

Dr Allen glanced back at Sarah. 'The skull X-ray was clear. I've got a head injury card here which gives you a list of the symptoms and signs to watch out for. Just keep an eye on him for forty-eight hours. If you're worried about anything, pop him down and we'll take a look. OK?'

'Yes, thanks.' She stood. 'Say goodbye please, Rory, and thank you.'

'Thank you, Dr Allen,' he said. The doctor smiled and left the cubicle.

Sarah reached forward to help Rory off the bed. 'Let's get you dressed.'

'Ouch!'

'I'll give you ouch!' Sarah said, then she gently hugged him. 'Oh Rory Greg,' she murmured, 'what are we going to do with you?'

An hour later, Janie swung her Land Rover into the space next to Sarah's car outside the school and stopped. She glanced over her shoulder at Roz in the back with Kitty on her lap, then she looked at Sarah in the front. 'Is everyone OK?' she asked. There was a murmur of assent and Roz opened the rear door and jumped down, sliding Kitty onto the ground. 'Oli and Justin, out now, please, we've got to get home.'

Both boys shuffled out of the car clutching their bags and the guinea pig, and Roz leaned back in for her bag. 'Thank you, Janie,' she said. 'I'm sorry, you know, for things earlier.'

Janie shrugged. 'Forget it.'

Sarah climbed out of the car. 'Are you all right?' she asked.

'I should be asking you that.' Roz stared at the ground. 'Sarah, I don't know what to say, I'm so sorry, I . . .'

Sarah touched Roz's arm. 'It's OK, he's OK. It was an accident.'

Roz looked up. 'Will you be all right on your own? D'you want me to come over tonight with a bottle of wine?'

'Thanks, but Rory and I will be fine.'

'Right.' Roz walked across to her car, hustled her children inside and strapped them in. 'Bye!' she called out before reversing out. Janie carried Rory to Sarah's car and carefully deposited him inside.

As she straightened, Sarah said, 'Why was Roz apologising? She upset you, didn't she? I can tell by your face.'

Janie shrugged. 'She spoke the truth, that's all. She said that my life was empty. It did upset me, but only because she was right and I don't know what to do about it.'

'Your life isn't empty, Janie. You're always busy. It probably seems empty to Roz because she's so snowed under. Roz always speaks too rashly. Take no notice.' Sarah smiled to try and reassure her friend.

Sarah leaned into the car and looked at Rory. 'All right, love?' she asked.

'Can we go home, Mummy? I'm tired.'

'Of course.' She turned back to Janie. 'I must go, he's had it. Thanks for bringing me home from the hospital.'

'If there's anything else I can do, just ring me, OK?' Janie said.

Sarah nodded, but she knew it was an offer she wouldn't take up. She had been a single parent for six years now and she had learned to be independent. People offered, but the reality was that nobody really wanted to be asked. 'Thanks.'

She climbed into her car and drove off, not for the first time feeling more than a little depressed.

Janie ushered Katie inside Bank Cottage and called out to Andrew. He appeared in the hall, a glass of wine in his hand.

'Hello, you look tired,' he said.

'Thanks.' Janie dumped their stuff by the door and Katie went across to give her father a hug.

'I didn't mean it like that,' he said. 'How's Rory? And Sarah?'

Janie went past him into the kitchen. 'Rory is fine,' she replied as he followed her in. 'A cracked rib and mild concussion; he was lucky.'

'Poor Sarah. God, what an awful fright for all of you. I've been worried ever since you rang.'

Janie began taking things out of the fridge. 'I thought I'd make Spanish omelette tonight; Katie can have hers now and we can warm it up later with some crusty bread and a salad.'

'I've ordered us a curry, Janie,' Andrew interrupted. 'I thought that the last thing you needed tonight was to cook. I . . .' His voice trailed off as Janie stared at him. There was a tense, injured silence while she struggled to control her sudden anger and disappointment.

'But I like to cook,' she said, her voice tight. 'It's what I do—cook and look after you and Katie, or hadn't you noticed?'

She took a red pepper and placed it on the chopping board, slicing it neatly down the middle. 'It would have been nice if you'd asked me whether I had anything planned for supper before ordering a takeaway.'

Andrew held his hands up. 'OK, OK, I'm wrong, again. I'm sorry for taking the initiative, but I really thought I was doing the best thing.'

Janie looked up. Andrew always thought he was doing the best thing—taking decisions, advising—and more often than not he was right. But every now and then she wished that he wouldn't just take control.

'I'll take Katie up for a bath,' Andrew said.

'Yes, yes, fine.' She had snapped again even though she hadn't meant to. He stared at her, then shook his head and walked out of the room. Janie continued to chop the pepper. Katie loved Spanish omelette so Janie would cook it just for her. Everything Janie did was for other people; perhaps, she wondered, that's why she had no life of her own.

Janie Leighton had once been Janie Todd. She had been independent, sure of herself, adventurous and full of potential. Then she'd met Andrew Leighton. He'd fallen in love with Janie, with her carelessness, her bravado and the dimples that she had on her back. He had been married before, had two small children who lived with their mother, and as a result he was cautious, sensible and wanted no surprises. He wanted to take care of Janie, to make sure that her carelessness didn't become recklessness, that her bravado didn't lead her into danger. He particularly wanted to make sure that no one else saw the wonderful dimples and so he asked her to marry him. And Janie, bowled over by the handsome, older man, was equally in love and so agreed.

It had been a happy marriage in the beginning and to some extent it still was. Andrew was a good, safe husband and they had a regular, predictable sex life, friends, ample income, conversation—albeit on the dull side—and Katie. But recently, Janie had begun to feel a space in her life that couldn't be filled with decorating or gardening or cooking and caring for her small family. She knew how to fill it but she knew that

Andrew would never agree. She wanted another child: he already had three. She was thirty-nine with two miscarriages behind her. He was a GP who knew the dangers to mature mothers who had difficulties carrying a child. She had a space to fill; he was complete.

'Is that omelette ready? Because here's one clean little girl who's starving,' Andrew said, coming into the kitchen. Janie glanced up from the frying pan and smiled at Katie—clear skin, fresh and gleaming; hair brushed and pale pink pyjamas on.

'Almost,' she said. 'Why don't you sit down at the table?'

Andrew pulled out a chair for Katie and she sat while he filled a glass with water and fetched her named cutlery from the drawer. Janie served the omelette and took it across to Katie. She pulled out a chair and sat down; Andrew poured her a glass of wine.

'If you really don't want a curry, I'll cancel it,' he said, sitting down.

'No, a curry will make a nice change,' Janie said, knowing that this was the right answer. Andrew smiled. He took her hand. 'You must be shattered. Why don't you pop up and have a bath and I'll get Katie into bed.' Janie nodded. How could she not be happy with such care and consideration? She got to her feet and picked up her wine. 'I'll drink this in the bath.' She ruffled Katie's hair. 'And I'll come and say good night when Daddy's read you a story. OK?'

Janie climbed the stairs and went into her bedroom. She glanced at herself in the mirror and the same image that she had always known stared back at her, only tonight, as had so often happened recently, she wasn't sure who it was.

Roz opened the front door to Chadwick farmhouse and two dogs came bounding out towards her. She greeted them and then reached for the light switch. Glancing down at the shabby hallway carpet she made her daily resolution—never fulfilled, to get the Hoover out that night.

'What's for supper? I'm starving!' Justin said behind her.

'Did you help Kitty and Oliver out of the car?' Roz replied. She glanced over his head and saw the two little ones straggling up the path. 'Well done, thanks, Justin.' She went back out, picked up Oliver, carried him inside, then returned for Kitty. 'Right,' she said, 'it's baked beans on toast for supper, but only after I've fed the pigs. You can watch a video until supper's ready. OK?'

'Hooray! I want to watch *Peter Pan*!'

'No, I want to watch *Cinderella*! Mummy, I don't want . . .'

'Either you agree or you don't watch anything! OK? Put a vid on for them will you, Justin, and then get your homework out?' Roz headed back out of the door and shoved her feet into wellies. Looking over her shoulder at all three children, she smiled. Despite all the hard work, the stress, the struggle, it was all right knowing that she had the children.

Roz and Graham Betts had bought Chadwick Farm, with its eleven acres, six years ago. It had been Roz's idea—a perfect way to bring up children, she had said, and a wonderful opportunity to work for themselves. She'd convinced Graham and they'd raised the money through a combination of Graham's redundancy package and a small inheritance. It had been their great white hope, their move from the city, their self-employed dream. They'd planned organic vegetables; hand-reared, home-cured pork; handmade chutneys and jams; asparagus, and sheeps' milk yoghurt and cheese. They would sell all this in markets across London. But one year into the project they had found themselves bogged down by the rules from the Soil Association, a steep drop in pork prices, impossibly strict EEC food and hygiene regulations and an unexpected pregnancy. To add to this they had problems marketing the goods and distribution was something that they just hadn't thought of.

In the second year they managed to eke out a meagre living, Roz doing everything with a second baby in a sling and a toddler on reins. But it was frustrating and exhausting. In the third year Graham went into antiques in an attempt to supplement their income, and by the time Oliver was born—after another unexpected pregnancy—the antiques business was making a small profit. The small holding, however, barely broke even. They juggled the two businesses, always in need of more cash and only just managing. They somehow got by. It wasn't easy, but as Graham often said, it was at least happy—well, for most of the time.

As she parked the old Mini Metro in the drive, Sarah was relieved to see her neighbour waiting for her. Sarah had rung Lindsay from the hospital and asked her to turn on the storage heaters.

'Hi.' Lindsay came across to her. She was a single woman twenty years older than Sarah, a retired teacher. Lindsay was often there, helping and reassuring, quietly and without any fuss. Sarah accepted the help because she knew that Lindsay really wanted to give it, and Lindsay enjoyed the company and the friendship that came as a result.

'Are you all right?' Lindsay asked.

'Yes, just.'

'Come on, let's get you inside. You look exhausted.'

Rory had climbed out of the car and walked into the house with Lindsay.

'It's nice and warm in here, Lindsay,' Sarah said. 'Thanks.'

'Not at all. I've got a lasagne next door if you fancy it. I made a bit extra this afternoon after you rang, and thought I could freeze it if you didn't want it. It wouldn't take a minute to heat up, I . . .'

'Thank you,' Sarah interrupted, 'we'd love it, wouldn't we, Rory?'

Rory turned and said, 'Pardon?' Sarah still made the mistake every now and then of talking behind him. She took a breath, suddenly irrationally irritated at having to repeat herself, and said slowly to his face, 'Lindsay has offered us a lasagne and I said we'd love it, wouldn't we?'

'Yummy! It's my favourite.'

Lindsay smiled. 'I'll go and get it. D'you fancy a glass of wine, Sarah? I've got a bottle open in the fridge.'

Sarah knew that Lindsay didn't have 'a bottle open' and that this was another gesture of friendship. She hesitated, but it was just for a moment. This was Lindsay. Sarah didn't have to refuse her help because she was the only one who offered and really meant it. 'I'd love some.'

Lindsay brushed past Sarah to pop next door. Sarah turned the lamp on, then ushered Rory upstairs. 'Let's get you into your pyjamas,' she said, 'and settled on the sofa. You can have your supper on your lap.'

'Can I watch TV?' Rory asked.

'It's good to see that your brain is intact,' Sarah said. 'No, you can't. Children's TV has finished and there's nothing else suitable on. You can watch a video, but there'll be no time for a story.'

Time was something that had dominated Sarah's life since Rory had been born. Two weeks overdue, Sarah had been carted off to hospital to be induced. 'The baby is in distress,' the consultant had said. 'We've got a high foetal heart rate, but I think we'll wait and see, Mrs Greg.'

This judgment proved to be nearly disastrous.

'Is she under yet?' the same consultant had shouted across the theatre twenty minutes later. 'Nearly,' the anaesthetist had replied, 'about five or six seconds . . .' Sarah opened her eyes. 'I haven't got six seconds,' the obstetrician shouted, 'I've got to go in now or that baby will be dead . . .'

Rory had had no pulse and had to be resuscitated, then intubated to try to clear his lungs and body of the thick, tar-like meconium that had almost suffocated him.

'We don't know the extent of the damage and won't do for some time', the consultant had said twenty-four hours later. 'There is a strong chance, however, that it could be severe.'

Sarah and Nick, her husband, took Rory home, and then began to watch and wait, monitoring every stage of his development, week after week, month after month. In and out of hospitals for tests, diagnoses, physiotherapy and operations, and finally, having overcome all those hurdles and come out with a child who seemed normal, they'd found out that Rory was partially deaf. And just three months after they had found out, Nick had left them.

He needed time, he had told her, to come to terms with what had happened. 'And I don't?' Sarah had screamed at him. 'I'm supposed to just take it, get on with it, cope, am I?' Then Nick had said, 'Don't shout, for God's sake, Sarah, Rory will hear you!' And Sarah had wept for a child who might never hear her scream, who would always be at a disadvantage, who would never quite fit in.

But she had got on with it and coped. While Sarah had been reading about hearing loss, lip-reading and sign language night after night, Nick had been out with Melanie, finding comfort in warm arms and a soft breast. They divorced a year later, Sarah keeping everything amicable, calm and friendly, when in truth she could have ripped the man's heart from his chest.

And here she was, struggling for money because Nick had another family and keeping up with maintenance payments was hard for him. Here she was, working hard, caring for Rory, who was, contrary to what she had worried most about in the beginning, immensely popular, and bright into the bargain. She wouldn't change him for the world.

'**H**ere.' Lindsay handed Sarah a brimming wine glass when she returned to the kitchen after settling Rory on the sofa.

'Thanks. Sorry about the background noise.' Rory was watching *Joseph and the Amazing Technicolour Dreamcoat.*

'Not at all, I might find myself singing along any minute. I know all the words. Forgive me if I suddenly burst into song.'

Sarah attempted a smile.

'Come on, he's all right—it could have been much worse.'

'That's just the point!' Sarah swallowed a large mouthful of wine. 'He was all right this time, but what about the next time? He just didn't hear the car, he . . .' Sarah put her hands up to her face.

'You have a good cry if you want to, God knows you deserve it!' Lindsay said. And that somehow made Sarah laugh.

'I deserve it, do I? That makes me feel a whole lot better, the fact that my life is so bloody awful that if anyone deserves a weep it's me!'

'I didn't mean it like that, I meant . . .'

Sarah touched her arm. 'It's OK, I know what you meant. But the thing is that today just showed me how much more work I've got to do with Rory to get him to be aware, for him to be streetwise.'

'Isn't there any way forward?' Lindsay asked. 'What about these cochlear implants? Haven't they had some success with those?"

'Not applicable to Rory; they're really only for the profoundly deaf. They have introduced digital hearing aids, which can apparently bring the quality of hearing right up to almost normal, but unless I'm prepared to buy them privately there's no hope of getting them.'

'And that's not an option, presumably?'

Sarah could have made a joke about her circumstances; that's what she usually did. But tonight she didn't have the heart. She simply said, 'I've got a bit saved up, Lin, but nowhere near enough.'

Lindsay glanced past Sarah to Rory on the sofa, singing away to the tape. 'He's a lovely boy,' she said truthfully. 'I'm sure he'll be OK. You know, lots of people don't even know he's deaf.'

'But I do.' Sarah followed Lindsay's gaze and smiled at Rory. 'And he does,' she said, and her smile dimmed.

CHAPTER TWO

LUCIE OPENED HER EYES the moment it was over and stared blankly up at the pale cream ceiling above her, its faux-Victorian ceiling rose an ornate affair of stuccoed leaves and fruit of the vine. It was yet another characterless hotel—hired for one night but used for just one illicit hour. Alex rolled off her, then he gently touched her face.

'That was wonderful. Did you . . .?'

She nodded and he nuzzled her neck, 'Good.' She sat up. He watched her, puzzled. 'Are you all right, Lucie? You seem a bit, well, distant.'

'Yes, fine,' she said, a little more sharply than she had intended, then felt immediately guilty. It wasn't his fault this wasn't working. 'I've got a lot on at work, that's all. I guess I'm a bit stressed.'

'Want to talk about it? I'm a good ear.'

'No, not really.' But she appreciated the offer; she couldn't remember the last time Marcus, her husband, had wanted to listen.

Alex sat up. 'Come here.' He pulled her to him and kissed her hair. 'You'll sort it out, Lucie, you always do, that's why you've got so far. You're very good at your job, so don't forget that, eh?'

Lucie let him embrace her and enjoyed the momentary comfort it allowed. Marcus almost never offered her any warmth or affection. 'I just feel under so much pressure at times,' she said. Suddenly the urge to unburden herself was overwhelming. 'I'm not sure I can cope.'

'Of course you can cope. What is it? A deal in the offing?'

She nodded. 'A merger; potentially a very big merger,' she said, then bit her lip. Alex was an investment manager; she headed up the corporate finance team at World Bank, and they both knew only too well the meaning of price-sensitive information.

But it seemed to go right over his head and he was interested in her, nothing else. 'You've pulled off some incredible deals before.'

'Yes, but this is so bloody complicated, and I just don't have the people to back me up. For example, I desperately need someone with specialist knowledge of cable franchise . . .' She stopped abruptly and looked at Alex. She had said too much. They both knew it, but neither wanted to acknowledge that fact.

There was a moment of uncomfortable silence. 'It'll work out, Lucie,' Alex said.

Lucie shrugged. 'I'm sure it will,' she replied. Getting to her feet, she picked up her underwear and turned towards the bathroom. 'I'd better have a shower and get going,' she said, but she was thinking, Oh God, I should have kept my mouth shut. What am I doing spouting off about work? It's this affair, it's this whole stupid bloody thing; I don't know what I'm doing.

At the bathroom door, Lucie stopped and looked back at him. 'I can trust you, can't I, Alex?' she asked.

'Of course,' he replied.

Lucie Croft—she was still known by her maiden name—had been married for three years, but they hadn't been particularly happy years. She was a bright girl, strong-minded and not used to compromise, and she had found the exchange of independence for domesticity difficult to take. She loved and respected Marcus, her husband, or at least she had in the beginning—but she didn't like being a 'wife'. She wondered briefly as she stepped out of the shower if that was where the problem had begun, with her reluctance to be what Marcus wanted her to be.

Lucie had been head girl at school and very ambitious. There was never any doubt that she would go through Oxbridge and then get herself a top job. Rising through the ranks of the corporate finance department she'd worked bloody hard and played as hard as she'd worked. Then she'd met Marcus.

Marcus Todd was also a high-flier. A top analyst, he was well and truly on the ascent. They'd met on a business trip and had dinner. Marcus had bought the most expensive wine in the restaurant at £250 a bottle, obviously to impress her. It had failed—anyone could take advantage of expenses—until he'd taken her to bed later and ordered another bottle to pour over her breasts and lick off. Both, she'd realised as he signed, were on his personal account. She had said, 'What an obscene waste of money,' and he'd replied, 'Who cares? The pleasure of tasting vintage 88 Clos de Vougeot Grand Cru on your skin is priceless.' Lucie had been torn then between thinking he was the most pretentious man she had ever met and the most attractive. The fact that the wine-tasting had taken four hours and had led to the best sex she had ever experienced tipped the balance. There was no looking back. Marcus was as energetic, dynamic and ambitious as she was. They had married within months.

Lucie dried herself and sat on the edge of the bath. She didn't want to go back out and face Alex. She had fallen into this affair. She had been seduced by the warmth and affection she found in Alex, warmth and affection that she didn't get from Marcus. Now she didn't know how to end it. She wasn't cut out for deceit, she hated herself for it and, besides, she *did* love Marcus. If only they could get it right and somehow both stop trying to take all the time—and start giving instead. She sighed and then put on her underwear and opened the bathroom door.

Alex was dressed when she came out. He was standing looking out of the window, waiting for her. He smiled and watched her dress for a few moments, enjoying the sight of it.

'When can I see you again?' He came across to her and took hold of her hand.

Lucie looked down at her hand. She liked Alex, she really did like him, but she no longer wanted to have an affair with him. She had never really wanted to, if she was honest.

'I'll ring you,' she said.

'Will you? You promise?'

Lucie hesitated. Despite the guilt, it felt good to be wanted so much. 'I promise.'

'OK.' Alex picked up his briefcase. 'I'll go first, shall I?'

Lucie nodded. He kissed her mouth. 'Bye, Lucie.'

She gave him five minutes, then left the room. She glanced at her watch in the lift and thought about the afternoon ahead. Her only saving grace in all this emotional muddle was work. With relief she pushed aside her problems and hurried back to it.

'Marcus? You coming, mate?'

'I've got a couple of calls to make so I'll meet you in the pub.'

John Daniels pulled on his jacket. 'Lighten up, man! You've just made this frigging bank two million quid in a morning! Don't be long.'

'Yeah, yeah, yeah.' Marcus Todd turned back to his desk and picked up the phone. He had to ring Lucie, but he dreaded hearing the tense, negative tone of her voice. He hated feeling the sinking disappointment and futile anger that things weren't right. Everything Marcus had ever done was a success. Except his marriage.

Lucie's mobile rang twice, then he heard the Vodaphone re-call service. Her phone was switched off.

'Lucie, hi, it's me. I'm going out tonight for a couple of drinks with a broker so I'll be in around eight thirty. Hope that's OK. See you later.' He hung up and sat staring blankly at his screen for a few moments. Then he sighed, stood up and grabbed his jacket off the back of his chair.

'Hey, Marco!' Someone from across the sea of screens called out as he crossed the room. 'There's a shift in the dot coms, they're on the up.'

'So?'

'You're not gonna leave this baby, are you? Marcus the invincible?'

Marcus held up his hands. Without Lucie, what was the point anyway? He said, 'BillyBob, I've just made myself fifty grand this morning. You take the dot coms.' And he walked out of the office.

Lucie was on the phone when Marcus arrived home. He opened the door and heard her voice. He stood tensely, just inside the door, and listened. He heard Lucie gasp, then say, 'God, Janie, how absolutely terrible for all of you.' It was his sister. He relaxed and walked into the apartment.

Lucie waved as he came in. She was sprawled on a sleek, modern sofa—upholstered in slate-grey linen—looking tired. Marcus went into the kitchen space to get a drink. He bent down to the state-of-the-art fridge, took out a bottle of beer and flipped the lid off on the edge of the granite work top. He saw Lucie scowl at him but he ignored her. They had had the place—a warehouse conversion in Notting Hill—completely 'done' by some designer Lucie had read about, and Marcus loathed it. He hated that it was someone else's choice, from the lighting right down to the knives and forks. And, deep down, he hated the fact that Lucie was so far removed from any kind of domesticity that she could leave the furnishing of her home to the latest It man.

Walking into the main living area, which was a huge expanse of window and tiled floor with the odd piece of very expensive and extremely uncomfortable designer furniture placed here and there, he slipped off his jacket and chucked it on a low table—chrome and marbled melamine—knowing that it irritated Lucie. He heard her say, 'Marcus has just come in, Janie, I'll put you on, shall I? Bye for now.'

He took the phone. 'Hello, Janie,' he said, 'how's things?' He watched

Lucie walk across to the kitchen area and switch the kettle on. *He wanted her*. At that moment he wanted her so much that he could have just thrown down the phone and taken her right there, on the hard, cold tiled floor. But it was impossible. He listened to his sister and the moment passed. Lucie mouthed the word 'bath' to him and he nodded. Then he said, 'You sound really down, Janie.' He watched Lucie, just visible in the bedroom. She took off her clothes, dropping her underwear on the floor. 'Why don't you come up for a night? Come on Friday. Do a bit of shopping, have supper with us, stay here and potter back on Saturday morning. Andrew can have Katie, can't he?' Marcus longed to get off the phone. 'You will? Oh good. Yes, ring me tomorrow to confirm. Listen, Janie, I've got to go. I'll talk to you tomorrow then. Bye.' He disconnected and dropped the phone on to the sofa. Loosening his tie he walked through the bedroom to the bathroom, to Lucie, wrapped in a towel.

'Poor Janie,' she said as he came in. She was sitting on the edge of the bath with a small mirror in her hand, plucking her eyebrows. 'Her friend's little boy is going to be all right though, thank goodness . . .'

'Not that you really care,' Marcus said.

Lucie looked up. She stopped plucking. 'No, I don't *really* care, you're quite right. How could I? I don't even know the people involved. But I am concerned—it's a pretty horrible thing to happen and Janie has my sympathy. OK? Does that clarify things for you?'

Marcus shrugged. 'Sorry, I didn't mean to be sarcastic.' He walked out of the bathroom. From just outside the door he said, 'I'll come in and we can start again, OK?'

Lucie stood and turned off the taps of the bath. She sighed. 'OK.'

He walked into the bathroom for a second time and sat down on a chair as she climbed into the bath. 'So, how was your day?'

Lucie closed her eyes. What could she say? Oh, it was all right; a couple of meetings, this merger isn't going too well and oh, by the way, I'm having an affair but the sex wasn't that good today. 'It wasn't brilliant,' was all she said. 'The merger is sinking and I'm supposed to be holding the whole thing afloat.' She looked at him. 'How was yours?'

'Not bad. I made a stack of money on one of the technology stocks.' He smiled. 'More investment into my pension plan.'

Lucie smiled back. 'You'll never retire,' she said. 'You'll die with a headpiece on shouting, Sell, sell, sell!"'

Marcus laughed. 'It's not only the money, you know.'

'Yeah, yeah, yeah.'

'It isn't, honestly. It used to be, but now . . .' He reached for the soap. 'Shall I wash your back?'

'Hmmm, please.' Lucie leaned forward and rested her head on her knees. 'So what is it then, if it isn't the money that drives you?'

Marcus had an overwhelming desire to tell her everything he'd ever thought, everything he knew, to unburden himself completely. But he didn't. He said, 'I don't know, I haven't worked it out yet.' Lucie laughed. Marcus stopped soaping and she relaxed back in the bath.

'Did I hear you ask Janie to stay?'

Marcus stood and dried his hands. 'Yes, she's coming on Friday. I thought we could have supper here, cook something maybe?'

Lucie pulled a face. 'Let's go out.'

'No, let's stay in.'

Lucie looked at him. She heard an edge to his voice. 'Why?'

'Because this is our home and I'd like to entertain in it.'

Lucie sat up. 'Marcus, I'll have had a tough week at work and the last thing I'll want to do is come home and stand over the bloody hob.'

Marcus was thinking that for once she might have just said, 'OK, I'll chuck some garlic and bacon in a pan, add some cream and wine and toss some pasta in it.' All it would have taken was that and a bag of salad. He stood up. 'We'll get a caterer in, I'll ask the girls in the dining room at work to recommend someone.'

'Oh.' Lucie finished washing and she too stood up. It never occurred to him that he could cook just as easily as she, but she didn't mention that. 'I don't see why we have to go to so much fuss. It's only your sister.'

Marcus walked out of the bathroom and took off his tie. 'No, it's not,' he called out. 'I asked the chap I had drinks with tonight. He's a broker for White Lowen. I think you'll like him. I thought we'd make up a party.'

Lucie came into the bedroom. 'You've not mentioned him before.'

'We only met a few weeks ago, at a brokers' lunch. His name is Alex,' Marcus said. He headed for the door. 'Alex Stanton.'

As he disappeared into the living area, Lucie sank down onto the bed. Her first feeling was panic, her second fear and her third terrible, suffocating guilt. Alex Stanton. Marcus was right, she did like him; she liked him so much she went to bed with him.

Sarah always waited in the playground until the bell had been rung and the children had all lined up for school. She felt better going to work knowing that Rory had gone in happy and content.

As she stood by the gate, she saw Janie arrive and waved to her. The bell rang, Janie dropped Katie off and hurried across to Sarah.

'You look smart,' Sarah said. 'Nice trouser suit. Giorgio Armani?'

Janie laughed. 'Marks and Sparks. I'm off to London, to stay with my brother.' She was looking forward to the trip. It made her feel that she had something constructive to do.

'Marcus and the power woman. What's her name?'

'Lucie. Lucie—I can't chat now because I'm in the middle of a multi-million-dollar deal—Croft?'

Sarah smiled.

'She's not that bad really, just a bit high-powered and self-important. Makes me feel like the dull old housewife that I am.'

'You're not old,' Sarah said, 'dull, yes, but . . .'

Janie laughed again and they both turned as Roz drove into the car park, late, with her exhaust pipe making a racket. She climbed out and ran Justin towards the school.

'Bloody exhaust fell off this morning!' she called across to them. 'More expense! Can you keep an eye on the little ones for me?'

'Of course!' Sarah called back. Janie made to leave.

'You have a great time,' Sarah said. 'And tell Andrew to ring me if there are any problems with Katie.'

Janie looked at her. Out of all the friends she had, Sarah probably had the worst deal and yet constantly remained the warmest and most giving. 'You've got enough on your plate,' she said. 'But thank you for the offer. I appreciate it.'

Roz came up and ran an admiring eye over Janie's suit. 'My word, this is a bit much for the school run, isn't it?'

'Janie's off to London for a well-deserved break,' Sarah said.

'Have a good time,' Roz said. 'Don't spend too much money.'

Janie smiled, with little sincerity, and hurried off to her car.

'Janie doesn't know how easy she has it, she . . .' said Roz.

'Yes, she does.' Sarah interrupted. 'And it's not always as easy as it seems.' She hooked her arm through Roz's and said, 'Come on, you never know, there's always the big win on the lottery.'

They walked together to Roz's car. 'That would solve all my problems,' Roz said. 'A couple of million would make me really happy.'

'Would it?'

Roz grinned. 'You bet!' She looked at Sarah. 'And don't tell me it wouldn't solve all your problems either, because you'd be lying.'

'It would solve some but there are some things I just can't change.'

Roz flushed, swamped with embarrassment. 'I'm sorry,' she mumbled. 'I didn't think . . .'

'It's OK.' Sarah smiled and patted Roz on the arm. 'Anyway, that's part of your charm; where angels fear to tread and all that.'

Roz suddenly laughed. 'Am I really that outspoken?'

'Yes.'

'Oh dear.' She opened the car door and peered inside. 'It's amazing what a Chupa Chup lolly will do for my peace of mind,' she said. Sarah peered into the car after her and saw Kitty and Oliver silent for once, a lolly stuffed firmly in each of their mouths.

Sarah laughed. 'Whatever it takes to keep you and them sane,' she said, and started for her own car. 'See you later Roz.'

Andrew was waiting for Janie when she got in from the school run. He had rearranged his day so that he could work during Katie's hours at school and had gone to a good deal of effort to accommodate this trip. He was snatching a glance at the newspaper when Janie came into the kitchen. He looked up as she crossed to the fridge.

'I've left a shepherd's pie in the fridge for tonight,' Janie said. 'All you have to do is heat it up on one-eighty degrees for forty minutes, but I've written that down on the list. And I've chopped some fruit for Katie—she can have it when she gets in from school. And then there's a home-made pizza in the freezer you could have for lunch with salad. I—'

'Janie, stop,' Andrew said sharply. 'Calm down, and just go, OK?'

'You're cross that I'm going,' she said. 'I knew you would be.'

Andrew folded the paper. 'No, I am not cross that you're going away, it has at least put you in a more positive mood than you've been in for months, but I am cross about this constant fretting. I do know how to chop fruit and heat a shepherd's pie. I am not a complete imbecile.'

'No, of course not, sorry, it's just that . . .' She wanted to say, it's just that I need to feel that there's some purpose to my life. This is my job and I'm good at it, I want you to know that. But she didn't see the point of starting an argument minutes before getting into the car. 'I worry, that's all,' she said.

Andrew sighed and came across to her. He held out his arms and she stepped into his embrace, not really wanting to be held.

'Now, you have a good time, Janie, don't worry about us and come back tomorrow feeling refreshed.' Andrew didn't understand the purpose of this trip, just as he didn't understand Janie at the moment either. He rarely went away on his own and when he did, to the occasional medical convention, he couldn't wait to return to his wife and child. He kissed Janie on the forehead, then said, 'Come on, you'd better get going. The sooner you start, the sooner you get there.'

'Obviously.' Janie smiled briefly up at him, then moved from his embrace and walked out into the hall to get her handbag. Andrew always said things that were so eminently sensible, and so predictable.

Andrew hurried across. 'Here, let me take that bag!'

Out on the drive, he placed her suitcase in the boot of the car and opened the driver's side door for Janie to climb in. He leaned in to kiss Janie on the mouth. 'Bye.' He touched her cheek for a moment, then stood back and slammed the door shut. 'Have a good trip.'

Janie pressed the window down. 'I will, thanks.' Then she accelerated forward and pulled out of the drive. She had expected to feel sad at leaving Katie and her home. All she felt as she started on her way was a wonderful, expanding feeling of relief.

Roz got her carrier bag out of the car and took it into the kitchen, with Oliver and Kitty trailing behind. She unpacked the shopping, looked at the sausages, potatoes, cabbage, cooking apples and tin of custard powder and thought, how sad. 'Glamorous,' she said to Oliver, 'my life is not.' What she wouldn't do to be going up to London for a snazzy lunch and dinner out.

Roz glanced up as someone knocked on the kitchen window. She shouted, 'Come on in, Cecil, the door's open.' Major Cecil Gorden, and his wife Daphne, owned the house at the end of the lane and the three fields to the right of Roz and Graham. The Major often called in for coffee, more for want of something to do than for friendship, Roz thought, but she never refused him a cup anyway. He was all right.

'Hello, Cecil. How are you?' Roz turned from the sink where she was filling the kettle. 'I'll get the kettle on, shall I?'

'No.

'No, thank you, Roz, my dear, I've just had a coffee with Daphne. It was she who suggested I come straight up actually, after we got the letter this morning.'

'Oh?' The Major was all right but Mrs G was most definitely not. Roz and Daphne didn't quite see eye to eye. 'What letter?'

'Well, it's something I've been meaning to mention to you, my dear. I thought I'd better come on over and get it straight.'

Roz spooned coffee into a mug and sat down at the table.

'You've lost me I'm afraid, Cecil. Get what straight?'

Major Gorden sat down opposite Roz.

'The four acres that border your small holding here. We've had a very good offer, Roz dear, from a developer . . .'

Roz heard the kettle come to the boil and switch itself off, but she didn't move. 'You told him where to go, I presume?' Even as she said it she knew that was the last thing the Gordens had done. 'It would ruin me, Cecil, an estate of houses all round us. There's the organic soil thing and the issue of contamination, and the very idea of houses either side of us, is just awful.' She stopped, suddenly aware that she was wasting her breath. There were a few moments silence, then she said, 'How much?'

'It's a great deal of money, Roz. Daphne feels, we both feel, that it's too good an offer to turn down.'

Roz walked across to the sink and held on to it for a while, her back to the Major. She was as tough as old boots, Graham said, but at this moment she was close to tears.

'I'm sorry, Roz dear, but you must see that Daphne and I can't really afford to let this sort of offer pass us by. It just wouldn't make sense . . .'

'Of course not,' Roz managed to say, turning round. 'I'm sure Graham and I would do the same if we were in your position,' she went on, to ease Cecil's embarrassment. She knew that she would never sell to a developer, never. She felt too strongly about carving up the countryside to build small, square boxes for no reason other than profit.

Cecil Gorden got to his feet. 'I won't keep you then, Roz,' he said, 'I'll say goodbye.'

Roz watched him go. She glanced down and saw Oliver and Kitty playing with the water in the dog's bowl, but instead of shouting she simply bent and removed it, saying nothing. She would fight, of course she would. She should tidy the house and then ring the council to find out who was in charge of planning and get an appointment to see them. She should ring the Gordens and ask for the name of the developer. But she didn't do any of that. She sat at the table, put her head in her hands and let a wave of self-pity wash over her.

Sarah was in the aisles the next morning, checking deliveries. They were short-staffed so she had been moved from the customer services desk and was back to regular supermarket duties until further notice.

She had just finished checking a delivery of tea when she heard a discreet cough and glanced to her right. A man stood with an empty basket and smiled at her.

'Sorry,' he said, 'to interrupt, but could you tell me if you stock Orange Pekoe tea?'

He had a great voice and he looked right at her, not just beyond her as most people who saw her turquoise-checked overall did.

'No,' Sarah said, 'that's a specialist tea and Earl Grey is about as specialist as we get. You might get it in the shop on the high street.'

'Right. Thanks.' He smiled again. It was an open, relaxed smile and it settled easily on his face. 'D'you only work mornings here?'

Sarah was taken aback. Not many customers talked to her.

'Yes,' she replied. 'I, erm, I work until one. I have to pick my son up from school at three thirty.'

'Of course. I've seen you up at school, at Wynchcombe Primary. How old is he, your son?'

Sarah glanced behind her. A few odd pleasantries were OK, a full-blown chat was not. She didn't want to get into trouble. 'He's six,' she said, glancing down at her list. 'Sorry, but I've got to get on.'

'Oh yes, right, of course you have. Thanks.'

Ten minutes later, having moved on to the bread section, Sarah noticed the man again. He seemed to be searching for something he couldn't find.

'Excuse me,' he said, 'I'm sorry to interrupt, but would you know if you have a part-baked ciabatta bread?'

Sarah handed him the loaf he wanted, then got on with her list. 'Thanks,' he said. 'You wouldn't know how long I bake it for, would you?'

Irritated, Sarah turned and he smiled at her again. It registered that he was an attractive man, but Sarah had no time for men, attractive or not. 'It's on the packet,' she said. 'Just read the instructions.'

'Right, thanks.'

Ten minutes later, as she finished taking a call on the customer services desk, he was there again and Sarah sighed as she saw him.

'I'm sorry . . .' he began.

'To interrupt,' she finished sharply for him. 'But . . .?'

He bit his lip, then said, 'It's OK, I've just spotted it.' He strode away and Sarah was embarrassed. It wasn't in her nature to be rude. She was wondering if she should apologise when the assistant manager appeared and said, 'You couldn't go on to four could you, Sarah?'

'Yes, no problem.'

Perhaps, Sarah thought, she could catch him on the way to the till, but the aisle was empty. Too late. He had gone and Sarah, not really sure why, felt disappointed.

Lucie sat in a meeting and tried hard not to drum her fingers on the table. Meetings were always too long and the men in them always said everything they needed to say at least twice. She glanced at her watch. It was three o'clock. She had to get hold of Alex before tonight. He would have to cancel; have an illness, anything except come for dinner.

In a moment of panic, she suddenly said, 'Will you excuse me, please? I have to make a call just after three, it's very important.'

Her client frowned, but there was a murmur of assent round the table and her colleague addressed the meeting. 'Let's take a five-minute break here, shall we? Can I get anyone coffee?'

In the next-door meeting room, Lucie dialled and waited. She heard Alex's voicemail message. 'Alex,' she said quickly, 'it's Lucie. Call me urgently, please. It's three o'clock on Friday.' She didn't say any more—she had no idea who picked up his messages. She dialled Alex's mobile, the message service answered and she left yet another voicemail.

'Fuck,' she said aloud. Chances were, she thought, that Alex had buggered off for the rest of the afternoon to the gym or the pub or God knows where. He'd probably switched off his mobile—he hated the thing anyway. She didn't know what to do.

It was Friday night, seven thirty, and Alex Stanton had been to the gym. He went on average four or five times a week, either to Cannons in the City or to the Riverside in Chiswick, a couple of miles from where he lived. By most people's standards he was extremely fit. He played tennis in the summer and squash in the winter and he ran at weekends. And it showed. He had washboard abdominals, well-defined pecs and rock-solid biceps. Alex Stanton worked in order to play. He liked his job, and was good enough at it to make the bank money, but he saw no point in doing more than was absolutely necessary. He was easy-going and unambitious. He was popular at work and highly thought of among friends. He had no plans other than to enjoy life and in that he was the complete antithesis of Marcus Todd.

As Alex sat in the bar at Cannons with an Isotonic drink, he wondered what Marcus's wife was like—that possibly she might be as driven and as high-powered as Marcus himself. Certainly Marcus gave the impression that he and his wife were too busy for much socialising. He also wondered about Lucie; where she was and what she was doing. He knew very little about her home life; she rarely talked about it, or about herself. But he liked the feeling that there was so much there that he had yet to find out.

His affair with Lucie had been going on for several months now, though where it was going he didn't know, or particularly care. They had met at a Christmas drinks party and had chatted all evening. The following week he had seen her again by chance at a lunch in the City and after that it just seemed to click. She was married, of course, but unhappily married and that made all the difference in his mind. Besides, it wasn't that sort of affair, not the deep-meaning sort. It was a laugh, great sex, and he liked the way they led their separate lives.

Alex finished his drink and looked at his watch. It was time to go. Getting to his feet, he collected his sports bag and found a taxi outside. He liked Marcus and was looking forward to tonight.

Lucie lay in the bath, soaking in perfumed water, her stomach churning and her mind in turmoil. She had been in there for forty minutes and just couldn't summon the energy to get out. She was dreading tonight. She had no idea how Alex would react and she had no way of even speaking to him alone because the house was so open-plan that there wasn't a square inch of privacy. At least Peter and Julie would be there, so there was someone to divert the attention if things got difficult.

Julie was an old friend of Lucie's from university and Peter was her husband. Lucie and Julie had once been close, but she had gone the way of most of Lucie's friends since she'd married Marcus and, despite denying it, kept her distance. Lucie had never asked any of her friends, but she thought it was probably to do with them not liking Marcus.

She wondered if Julie would sense that things were askew, but then they were no longer close. Perhaps, Lucie thought, it might actually be a relief if she did notice. She stepped out of the bath. Secrets, Lucie thought, ate away at the very core of a person, they destroyed integrity. She dried herself, then opened her wardrobe to look for something to wear. Secrets destroyed everything in the end.

Janie tipped the prepared salad into a large blue glass bowl and tossed the leaves briefly with her fingers. Reaching for the olive oil, she poured a generous measure into a screw-top jar.

'Balsamic vinegar? Lemon juice?' she asked Marcus.

Marcus looked up from the *Evening Standard*. 'Your guess is as good as mine, Janie. Try the fridge or the cupboard.'

Janie tried the cupboard first and found a jar of Marmite, some sachets of Cup-A-Soup and packet of pasta. She went to the fridge. 'Do you and Lucie ever eat anything?' she asked, peering inside.

'Yes, but nothing that has been prepared by our own hands.' He took a sip of beer, drinking straight from the bottle.

Janie laughed; she thought he was joking. 'Ah!' she cried, 'half a lemon.' She squeezed the juice into the olive oil.

'Thanks,' Marcus said, 'for doing all this.'

'I've only put what the caterer delivered into the oven, set the table and made a salad dressing. It's hardly "all this".'

'It's enough,' Marcus said. 'And we're supposed to be treating you. I think Lucie was right, she said we should have gone out to dinner. Perhaps that's why she's taken so bloody long in the bath, out of protest.' He drained his bottle of Becks. 'Either that or she's waiting to see if I get it together. Fat chance!'

Janie looked at him. She had always thought that Marcus and Lucie made an ideal couple. They were so alike; both driven, ambitious, wanting the same things, and in love. Now she wasn't so sure.

'What's a fat chance?' Lucie asked.

Both Janie and Marcus turned to look at her. She had changed from her suit into wide-legged black cashmere trousers and a sleeveless cashmere top. She had left her hair loose and it hung round her shoulders.

She looked sleek and expensive. Janie felt dowdy by comparison.

'Nothing,' Marcus said casually, throwing a look at Janie that warned her not to contradict him. 'Can I use the bathroom now?'

'Yes,' Lucie said coolly, picking up on Marcus's disgruntled tone. 'But if you were waiting why didn't you use the other bathroom?'

'My stuff is in our bathroom, we share it, remember?' Janie turned away. It wasn't bickering, more a restrained hostility.

Marcus said, 'Janie's been getting supper organised.'

'So I see,' Lucie replied. 'Thank you, Janie. The table looks lovely.'

Janie had bought Lucie a bunch of white lilies of the valley and had arranged them in a glass vase with a few blades of elephant grass and some grey pebbles. It looked good; it was in the exact style of the house.

'Janie did the flower arrangement herself,' Marcus said. 'You're not the only one with perfect taste around here.' Heading towards the bedroom, he smiled to indicate that he was joking, but Janie could see that Lucie was wounded by such unwarranted criticism.

'Sorry,' Lucie said, 'he's not in a very good mood.'

'Don't apologise,' Janie replied, 'he's my brother. I remember him as a spotty fifteen-year-old who didn't speak to my parents for six weeks once.'

'You got off lightly. He's been in a bad mood with me for quite a bit longer than that I'm afraid.' Lucie opened the fridge, took out a bottle of white wine and peeled the wrapping off the cork with the sharp point of a corkscrew. 'What did the caterer send for the main course?'

Janie frowned. 'Didn't you order it, Lucie?'

'Yes, but I just told them to deliver what they thought best. I didn't have time to discuss it with them.'

'I see.' Janie's life was dominated by all things domestic, and here was Lucie not even knowing the word.

Lucie handed Janie a glass of wine and said, 'Katie and Andrew well?'

'Both fine. Katie's growing up so quickly, she's quite independent at times.' Janie took a sip of wine. 'In fact I feel a bit redundant now.'

'You should get a job,' Lucie said. Janie was bright and articulate and wasted, in Lucie's view, on domesticity.

'Yes, maybe.' What could she do? She had been a freelance magazine stylist when she met Andrew. It had been fun, she'd had a sense of adventure then, a sense of future. But it had been hard work, with long hours in sweaty studios, little recognition and low pay. And besides, she wouldn't have a clue where to start now. In an attempt to change the subject, she said, 'Who's coming tonight?' Lucie immediately turned away, but not before Janie noticed her cheeks flood with colour.

'An old friend of mine called Julie Granger and her husband, Peter, and some friend of Marcus's, someone I've not met before.' Lucie was fiddling with the controls on the oven and Janie said, 'I put it on to one-eighty. It's a circotherm oven, isn't it?'

Lucie turned and Janie saw that her face was wretched. 'I haven't got a clue,' she said.

'Lucie?' Janie moved towards her, suddenly concerned that she was going to cry. 'Lucie, are you all right?'

The doorbell rang. Lucie started physically, then looked at her watch. 'God, it's twenty past eight!' She hurried over to the door, her heels clicking sharply on the tiled floor. I wish they'd get rugs, Janie thought, the whole atmosphere in this house is too cold.

Lucie put her hand on the door latch, took a deep breath, then released the lock. She saw Alex, saw his face register shock, then disbelief, and before he could utter a word she blurted, 'Hello, I'm married to Marcus.'

There was a brief silence. Alex was stunned. He managed to gather his wits sufficiently to realise that there must be other people close by and say, 'I'm Alex. Is this where Marcus Todd lives?'

'Yes,' Lucie replied, then again she said, 'I'm Lucie, I'm married to Marcus Todd. Please, come on in, Marcus is just taking a shower. Come and meet his sister, Janie.'

What an odd scene, Janie thought, moving out of the kitchen area. Alex walked towards her, but his mind was still reeling from the shock and he didn't really see her.

'Hello, I'm Janie Leighton. I'm Marcus's sister.'

Alex held out his hand and took Janie's. He forced himself to smile and say, 'Nice to meet you, Janie. D'you live locally?'

'Oh no, I'm up for the day from the country, on a bit of a jolly.'

Marcus came hurrying out of the bedroom.

'Alex! Sorry, mate, I was in the shower.' The two men shook hands and Alex struggled to recover himself. Marcus smiled and said, 'Glad you could come. You've met my wife, Lucie?'

Alex blinked, then said, 'Oh, yes, yes of course.'

'And she's getting you a drink?'

Lucie was in the kitchen area. 'What would you like, Alex?' she called. 'Wine, beer, or there's gin and tonic?'

'A beer, please,' Alex replied. He was sweating and hoped to God it didn't show. The doorbell rang again and Lucie said, 'That'll be Julie and Peter.' She hurried across to the door and let them inside.

Marcus kissed Julie, shook hands with Peter and introduced his sister and Alex. He was smiling a great deal and called out to Lucie to get more drinks. At least, she thought, pouring more wine, Marcus is enjoying himself. And studiously avoiding Alex's eye while plastering a smile onto her face, she took heart from this small mercy.

'So, Janie,' Peter said, turning to her on his left as Lucie handed him his starter. 'What do you do down in the country? Do you work at all?'

'No, no, I don't work. I've got a daughter of six and . . .'

'But you're thinking of working, aren't you, Janie?' Lucie said.

Janie shrugged. Actually it was Lucie who'd said that but she didn't want to disagree, there didn't seem any point.

Marcus refilled her wine glass. 'It isn't a job you want, Janie, it's some sort of small business or project that you can do in your own time.'

'I'm not really sure what I need,' Janie said, taking a gulp of wine.

'What about adult education?' Julie asked. 'A degree maybe?'

Janie laughed. She was beginning to feel a bit embarrassed, being the focus of the conversation. 'I don't think so, I'm not clever enough.'

'Nonsense,' Marcus cut in. 'But, you know, I did hear something on the radio last week about investment clubs, and that sort of thing might be exactly what you need.'

'What a great idea,' said Lucie.

'What's an investment club?' Janie asked.

'It's a number of people,' Marcus explained, 'each with a sum to invest, who get together and invest it as a group. They research and discuss their investments and also get a much better deal from the broker by doing one large investment rather than five or six smaller ones.'

'They're springing up all over the place,' Lucie said.

Julie turned to Alex. 'Have you come across any, Alex?'

'A colleague of mine invests for one group. They phone him every now and then for advice but do most of it themselves. They do a pretty good job on the whole, I think. He's quite impressed.'

'There you are!' Marcus said triumphantly. 'You could do it standing on your head, Janie. Get a few friends together, use me or Lucie or even Alex here for advice, and you're off! Easy peasy lemon squeezy.'

'I'll think about it,' Janie said, smiling.

'You should,' Julie advised. 'If you got in quick with some of these dot com companies you could make a killing. They'd be brilliant for a small investment club, wouldn't they, Alex?'

Alex had been surreptitiously looking at his watch and wondering how early he could get away. The situation was killing him. He hadn't been able to so much as look at Lucie and every time Marcus looked at him he wanted to cringe. 'Oh, um, yes. I've done quite a bit of work on the dot coms recently and I've made a colossal return. You have to watch the market closely, but yeah, they'd be a good place to start.'

'There you are,' Marcus cried, 'it's all sorted! Tomorrow morning you go home, organise some friends, then you get Alex to whack it into his favourite dot coms and you're away.' He stood up to clear the plates.

Lucie watched him. He seemed oddly animated tonight, drunk almost, but he'd hardly touched his wine.

Janie turned to Alex. The whole idea excited her. 'Would you mind getting involved?' she asked him. 'I mean, if I did manage to get some friends together with some money to invest?'

'Of course he wouldn't!' Marcus called from the kitchen area.

Alex forced a smile, and as Lucie got up to go to the kitchen she shot him a look that was narrowly missed by Marcus. He began to sweat again.

'Seriously?' Janie said. 'Would you?'

All eyes were on Alex. What excuse could he possibly give without sounding rude? 'Of course,' he mumbled. He heard Lucie bang down a dish in the kitchen and concentrated on looking at Janie. 'I'm not sure I could do it right now, I've got an awful lot on at work, but some time in the future, certainly I'd assist you.'

Marcus came back to the table carrying the salad. 'That's the boy! I'll give Janie your number.'

'I'll serve it in here,' Lucie shouted. 'Can someone give me a hand with the plates?'

Alex and Julie both stood up at the same time. 'I'll go,' Alex said. 'Please, let me do something to help.' Julie sat down not in the least bothered. She turned to Janie and asked her if she'd ever invested in the market before and the conversation switched to general investment.

In the kitchen area Lucie handed Alex a plate. He raised his eyes as if to say 'it wasn't my fault' and she shook her head. What was he playing at, agreeing to get involved with Marcus's sister? 'Sorry,' he mouthed at her. She shook her head again. It wasn't him who should be sorry. This whole thing was a mess and she realised, standing there dishing out pollo in porchetta, that the only person she had to blame was herself.

CHAPTER THREE

IT WAS AFTER NINE when Janie finally got up the following morning and, getting straight into the shower, she was surprised at how good she felt. She had drunk a great deal and deserved to be feeling terrible. She tried to identify the feeling she had. She ran through a list of words in her head and came to optimism. She smiled; yes, that was it. Marcus had got her thinking with his suggestion of an investment club, and for the first time in a long while Janie felt optimistic about the future. She stepped out of the shower, dried herself, and dressed. Then she went down into the kitchen area.

'Morning,' Marcus said from his seat at the dining table. The living area was immaculate. There wasn't a trace of the six people who had had dinner ten hours earlier. Marcus was drinking coffee, a half-full cafetière in front of him, the Saturday *FT* open.

'Hello. Have you cleared all this up this morning?'

'No, I did most of it last night. Coffee?'

'Thanks.' Janie went into the kitchen area and took a clean cup down from the cupboard. 'You should have waited for me to help,' she said, bringing her cup across to him.

'You did quite enough last night,' he said, putting the paper away and pouring her some coffee. 'I think this investment club thing is a really good idea. I think it would suit you perfectly, Janie.'

'It is tempting,' she said, 'I have to admit.'

'Of course it is. It would use your brain, and earn you some good money to boot. You could come up to London every now and then for meetings with Alex, have lunch with me, really enjoy it.'

'Do you really think I could manage something like this, Marcus? I mean, I'm not clever like you—I'm not really sure I could do it.'

Marcus shook his head. 'Hey! Where's your confidence?' He poured them both another cup of coffee. 'Janie, you could do it easily. You'd have Alex to help you as well as all my expertise . . .'

'But I'm not sure that Alex was keen to get involved.'

'Of course he's keen. If you get it right, within six months you could be making quite a bit of money, which is all commission for him.' Marcus smiled. 'Don't look so serious, Janie! What have you got to lose?'

'Nothing, I suppose, except my original investment.'

'You won't lose that, not with a team like us behind you.'

'How much would I need? I mean to start with?'

'I don't know, whatever you want, I guess. How many friends were you thinking of involving?'

Roz and Sarah immediately sprung to mind. 'Two others, maybe three?' She had no idea if they had any money to spare.

'Well, you could start with a thousand pounds each.'

'And how long would it take to set up?'

'You decide on the sum to invest, the stocks to buy, make your purchase and that's it. A day, a week? You might want to draw up some sort of legal agreement about who put up what and that would take some time, but it's entirely up to you.'

'You make it sound so easy.'

Marcus suddenly laughed. 'It is easy, Janie! That's why I told you about it.' He was still smiling when Lucie appeared, but it faded as she came toward them. 'You're dressed,' he said.

'Very observant,' Lucie quipped, but it didn't come out as a joke. Janie got up and took the coffee pot over to the kitchen. 'I'll make more coffee,' she said quickly, embarrassed by the change in atmosphere.

'Not for me,' Lucie said, 'I'm off to the club for a workout.'

Janie had her back to them but she could sense the tension.

'Good idea,' Marcus said.

'I shan't be here when you get back,' Janie said. 'I think I'll get off in half an hour or so. I'd like to be back for lunch.'

'Right, well, I'd better say goodbye now then,' Lucie said. She crossed to kiss Janie. 'Thanks for your help last night, Janie.'

'Not at all. Thank you for having me to stay.'

Lucie slung her sports bag over her shoulder.

'Are you taking the car?' Marcus asked. He made no attempt to get up and kiss Lucie and she didn't come across to him.

'No, I'll walk.' She headed towards the door. 'Bye then, bye, Janie.'

Janie watched Lucie glance behind her at Marcus as she left. But he missed her look; he had gone back to the paper.

Out in the street Lucie dug in her bag for her phone. Her hands shook as she pressed the buttons.

'Alex, it's me, Lucie.' She walked on and stopped at the end of the road. Alex was furious about the previous night.

'I tried to tell you,' she said, 'I've called you five times in the last twenty-four hours. I had no idea that you two knew each other.' She felt tearful, desperate almost. 'Listen, Alex, you haven't ever mentioned me to Marcus, have you? That you're having an affair?' She held her breath waiting for his answer. It came and she closed her eyes with relief. 'Thank God for that. No, no, I don't think he suspected anything. Look, you've got to get out of that investment club thing. You can't get involved with Marcus's sister. OK, yes, all right then, I'll leave it, if you're sure you can handle Marcus. He can be very persuasive.' She wished instantly that she hadn't said that. It was too disloyal talking about her husband to her lover. 'Look, I've got to go,' she said quickly and Alex immediately asked when he would see her again. 'I don't know,' she replied. 'I think it might be a good idea to break things off for a while . . .' He interrupted her. 'No, it's not like that. It's just that I need a bit of space, that's all, just a break. Yes, I will call, I promise.' She was lying; it was an empty promise. She said goodbye guiltily and suddenly felt exhausted and depressed.

Janie arrived home just before lunch. She hurried into the kitchen, looking forward to seeing Katie. She smelt pizza in the oven and saw two plates of salad laid on the table along with place mats, cutlery, linen napkins and two glasses. It looked like an intimate lunch party to which she hadn't been invited.

The weather was unexpectedly warm and sunny and the French doors onto the small terrace were open. She wandered across, standing in the doorway to look out at Katie and Andrew, who were weeding the border in the garden. Her first feeling was guilt—how could she have left them—and her second was jealousy. How could they get on so well without her? She stepped out, conscious of the stabbing ache in her chest, and called hello. Andrew looked round, shielded his eyes from the sun, saw her and stood up. Katie jumped up and ran across to her. Janie hugged her and some of the pain eased.

'We didn't expect you home so early,' Andrew said, coming across.

'I rang,' Janie replied. 'There's a message on the answerphone.'

'I told you I heard the phone,' Katie piped up, 'but Daddy said to leave it, the answerphone would get it.'

Andrew smiled. 'Sorry,' he said to Janie; then to Katie, 'You'll get me into trouble saying things like that. Never mind, there's plenty of pizza anyway.' He turned to Janie. 'Kiss?' Janie leaned forward and he kissed her mouth. 'We missed you,' he said, taking Janie's hand.

'It doesn't look like it,' Janie said as they went into the house. 'It looks as if you've managed perfectly well without me.'

Andrew looked at her. 'Do I detect a hint of pique in your voice?'

'No!' She dropped his hand abruptly and went across to switch the kettle on. How, she thought, would he feel if he went away and got back to find that the locum had done a better job than him?

'D'you think it's done yet?' Andrew asked, opening the oven door.

'Didn't you put the timer on?' Janie countered. Her voice had an edge of superiority to it that wasn't lost on Andrew.

'No, I've no idea how it works.'

'Good,' Janie said, 'at least I'm not completely redundant then!' And Andrew laughed. Only to Janie it hadn't been a joke.

'Oh, by the way,' he said, 'Sarah rang earlier. She said to ask you to ring her at Roz's house as soon as you got back. There's some kind of crisis apparently, only she wouldn't say what, except that it wasn't medical and that I needn't worry.'

'Oh? I'll ring as soon as I've got the lunch. I wonder what can have happened?'

'Ring now,' Andrew said, 'I can get lunch on the table.'

Janie didn't look at him. 'Right.'

'Are you eating with us?'

She moved towards the hall, 'No,' she said icily, 'I'm not hungry.'

Puzzled by her attitude, he watched her go, then he called Katie in to wash her hands. He really had no idea why she was so upset.

Sarah was on her hands and knees scrubbing the hall skirting board with a scourer pad and Jif when Roz came downstairs. It was one thirty in the afternoon, and she had been there since nine—cleaning, tidying, and keeping an eye on the children. She glanced up and said, 'Hello. You look better.'

'I slept for a couple of hours. God, Sarah, you didn't need to do all that!'

'Yes, I did, look at the difference. Anyway, it's nearly finished so just thank me and forget it.'

Roz smiled. 'I'm the outspoken one, not you. Thank you, Sarah.'

'Not at all. Come on, I'll make you a cup of tea.'

Roz followed Sarah into the kitchen. 'I really don't know what I'd have done without you.' Graham had had to go up to Newcastle urgently, so he'd rung Sarah to come and look after Roz. She had, he told Sarah on the phone, literally gone to pieces. It was as if all the stress of the last six years had suddenly erupted and left her helpless. She was constantly weeping, had been up all night unable to sleep, and she hadn't eaten for twenty-four hours. Sarah had come immediately and sent her to bed with two paracetamol.

'Blimey!' Roz stood amazed. 'I never knew the floor tiles were pale blue!' Sarah suddenly laughed. 'Seriously! I thought they were grey!'

Roz went across to the kettle, filled it and put it on to boil. 'I'd better get the kids some lunch. Have they been all right? Is Rory all right? He didn't mind having to spend the morning over here?'

'They've been fine and Rory was delighted to be able to watch three hours of uninterrupted TV. And I've fed them already. They had baked beans on toast.'

Roz found herself near to tears again and turned away.

'Oh, and Janie rang ten minutes ago and is on her way over.'

Roz turned back. 'Janie?'

'Yes.' Sarah looked at her. 'Graham was keen to get things moving. You need some sort of action group against the development, to get a petition going. Janie is a good organiser, Roz, and she's a good thinker.'

Roz's face was stony. 'I'm not happy about Janie getting involved, Sarah.'

'Well, it's too late,' Sarah said sharply. 'I've asked her and frankly you need all the help you can get.'

The kettle whistled and they both stood and looked at it for a moment. 'Janie is a good friend, Roz,' Sarah said gently, 'it's just that recently you've not been able to see it. She gets lonely and bored . . .'

'Ha! What I wouldn't give to be bored!'

'There you go again, you see?' Sarah went across to the kettle and took it off the boil. 'Janie has her own problems; she's as vulnerable as the rest of us, Roz. Don't let resentment ruin a good friendship.' Sarah made the tea. She brought the pot and two mugs over to the table, and said, 'Come on, let's see what Janie has to say when she arrives, all right?'

Roz nodded.

'Good.' Sarah sat down, poured tea into the cups and handed one to Roz. Just as she did so there was a knock at the door.

Roz got up. 'I'll go.' Then she disappeared and Sarah heard her say, 'Hi, Janie, thank you for coming over, I really do appreciate it.'

The three women had lunch before they did anything else. Janie had picked up a couple of big bunches of asparagus on the way over which she steamed and served with butter. It lifted Roz's morale.

When they had finished eating, Sarah said, 'Right, let's get down to business. Why don't we take our chairs out into the sunshine and let the children play in the garden?'

'I'll grab a pad and pen and see you out there,' Roz said. 'I'll gather the kids up, they're all upstairs playing.' Within minutes they had everything set up.

Then Sarah said, 'Let's make a note of ideas and draw up an action sheet.' She took up the pen and paper. 'Janie,' she offered, 'why don't you start?'

Janie leaned forward. 'I have had an idea,' she said. 'It's not directly related to the offer for the Gordens' land, but it would help to raise money to fund any action.'

Roz folded her arms and looked straight at Janie. For some inexplicable reason she had the odd sense that something important was about to be said. 'It involves all three of us,' Janie began, 'and if we do it right, it could become very big.' She took a breath. 'Very big indeed.'

At eight fifteen on Monday morning, Janie and Katie left the house. Janie carried her briefcase and a Thermos flask. Katie was delivered into the playground. Roz was already in her car waiting.

'Hello.' Janie knocked on the window and Roz climbed out. She looked smarter than she usually did, wearing a freshly ironed shirt and floral summer skirt. Janie said, 'Oh, where are Oliver and Kitty?'

'At home with Graham,' Roz said. 'He volunteered. I'm off to see the bank manager after this.'

'Come on, this morning's meeting is in my office,' Janie said.

Janie led the way across to her Land Rover. By the time they had climbed in and got settled Sarah had driven up and delivered Rory to school and was at the car.

'Jump in the back,' Janie said. Sarah did as she asked.

'I've made coffee. Shall I pour us a cup while Roz gives you a copy of what's in my file?'

'Hmm, please.'

Janie handed her briefcase across to Roz who took out a plastic folder and started sorting through sheets of paper.

'There's three for the Action Against Development group, now known as the AAD, and four for the investment club,' Janie said. 'Right, let's get on. Firstly, I've drawn up a list of what needs to be done as far as the AAD is concerned. I thought what we could do was think about it and then meet tomorrow to decide who's doing what. Secondly, I've done a draft for the letter to the local papers; read it later and tell me what you think. And, finally, there's a draft petition.'

'God, Janie,' Roz said, 'this is brilliant!' She speed-read through the bits of paper. 'It really is! It must have taken you ages.'

Janie shrugged. 'Not really. Now,' she said, 'moving swiftly on.'

Sarah smiled at the terminology. 'Very professional.'

'The other stuff,' Janie went on, too excited to be bothered with humour, 'is on the investment club. I spoke to my brother last night and he said he is certain that Alex Stanton, the broker I met at their house for dinner, will work with us.' She glanced up and saw that Roz was looking down at her sheet of lists and figures.

'Is the thousand pounds you mention here the minimum or the maximum investment, Janie?' Roz asked.

'I think it should be both. I think we should agree on a sum that we can all raise so that no one feels intimidated by numbers.'

'I agree,' Sarah said. She had thought long and hard over the weekend about Janie's idea. She had problems to solve and she had dreams, all of which needed money. It wasn't the answer to everything, but life would be a whole lot easier with a bit of cash to spend. And she could just manage £1,000. She had more saved, but she wanted to be sure that the sum she invested was money that she could afford to lose.

Roz read on and Janie sipped her coffee in silence, waiting for a reaction. In just forty-eight hours she had gone from feeling redundant and depressed to this—an ever-mounting sense of excitement, and a life that suddenly had direction.

'So?' She couldn't help herself, her impatience boiled over and she had to ask. 'What do you think?'

Roz was hesitant. She had talked it over at the weekend with Graham and he was sceptical. 'Janie, will we really have the time to commit to this? What with everything else going on.'

'Good point. I can only do evenings,' Sarah said. 'And they'll have to be at mine because I haven't got anyone to baby-sit. Is that OK?'

'Evenings are fine,' Janie replied. 'I can come to you.' She looked at them both. 'I'd thought that it might take us a couple of nights a week at first, to get set up, comparing our notes on companies and so on. And I thought that at the start of each evening we could spend an hour or so on the AAD.'

'Two nights a week sounds OK,' Roz said.

Sarah saw the sudden possibility of enjoying company without feeling like a burden. To be able to get together with married friends, without feeling that she was encroaching on their time with their partners would be a bonus. 'That sounds fine,' she said.

'How much work would we have to do on the stock market?' Roz asked. 'I don't know if I'm clever enough to be researching companies and stuff.'

'Don't worry about that. Just read the financial pages of the papers and keep your eyes open. I thought I'd get a basic list of stocks to look at from Alex and put in a lot of the legwork myself to start with.'

'Oh, Janie, are you sure?'

Janie smiled. 'I'd love it,' she answered honestly. 'I thought we could each of us take a sector of the market that we had an interest in. You, Roz, might like to look at food groups. And Sarah, I wondered about supermarkets, seeing as you work in one, and I thought I'd do pharmaceuticals, getting a bit of help from Andrew. I also thought we could all look at dot coms, seeing as they're on the up, and we can split the other sectors up between us. I'd be more than happy to take on the bulk, seeing as I'm the one who doesn't work.'

Both Sarah and Roz were silent for a few moments.

'Well?' Janie asked. 'How does it sound?'

Sarah was the first to speak. 'It sounds exciting, Janie.'

'Roz?'

Roz was wary of golden opportunities; she'd had one of those already in Chadwick Farm, and look where that had got her. 'Yes, I agree, it does sound interesting,' she said.

Janie stared out of the window, trying not to lose her composure. She couldn't believe how much she suddenly wanted this.

Roz stared at Janie. A thousand pounds was a lot of money and wasn't to be easily parted with, but there was something in Janie's face, something compulsive, dynamic and committed.

'Count me in,' Roz suddenly said. She wasn't going to stand on the side looking at the water, she was going to jump in.

Sarah added, 'Me too.'

Janie couldn't help the wide grin that broke out. 'Fantastic,' she said. There was a moment of conspiratorial silence, then all three women smiled.

Roz looked at her watch. 'Let's arrange the first meeting now, and then I'd better get going. I need to be at the bank at nine thirty.'

'Right,' Janie said, taking out her diary, more for show than use; she knew she was free all week. 'How does tomorrow night sound?'

'Sounds great,' Roz replied. 'Sarah?'

'Yes, tomorrow's fine. At my house?'

Roz and Janie nodded.

Sarah glanced at the clock on the dashboard. 'I must go,' she announced, 'life at Duffields supermarket goes on.' She opened the car door and climbed out. 'At least until I make my first million on the stock market,' she added. Janie laughed.

'Thanks, Janie,' Sarah said, rubbing her hands over her arms. 'I feel really quite optimistic about all this. I feel that life is about to change.'

Janie looked at her. 'It has already,' she said, 'for all of us.'

Five minutes late for work, Sarah steamed through her duties so as not to antagonise the manager even further.

She had finished the stocklists and was now back on customer services. It was quiet, so she decided to sort out some paperwork. She was halfway through this when she sensed a figure at the desk.

'Can I help you?' she asked pleasantly, while stapling two notices together. There was a discreet cough and she glanced up.

'Oh,' she exclaimed, 'it's you . . .' She stopped, aware that once again she had been rude, then stammered, 'I mean, erm, can I help you?'

The man she had upset last Friday stood in front of her in the same worn but impeccably clean jeans, and a loose wool sweater with a checked shirt underneath. 'I was wondering,' he began, not looking at her face but staring hard at something just above her right shoulder, 'if you'd like to have a quick lunch, a sandwich, or something at the pub, or whatever you like really, with me, erm, today, or tomorrow even or Wednesday, Thursday or Friday. It's just that . . .' he paused only to draw breath, 'erm, I thought, seeing as we're both parents at Wynchcombe Primary, that it would nice, I mean. . .' His voice trailed off.

Sarah blushed involuntarily. Lunch, drinks, anything at all to do with the opposite sex was an idea she just didn't entertain. She had never really got over Nick's betrayal, and certainly wasn't going to open herself up to that sort of risk again. So normally, if it had been an ordinary request for a date, she would have simply said no. But it wasn't an ordinary request. It was a sort of plea, a desperate attempt to make a friend, and she knew that she hadn't the heart to turn it down.

'OK,' she said. 'Today is fine. I finish at one, so how about a sandwich at Muffins across the road?'

He looked suddenly taken aback. 'Today? Really?' He smiled and again she noticed, as she had last week, how it lit his whole face from inside. 'Great!'

'I'll meet you in Muffins,' Sarah said, 'at about ten past one.' She picked up the stapler to indicate that she had work to be getting on with.

He took the hint. 'Right, OK, ten past one in Muffins.' He turned to go. 'Oh, erm, my name's Jack Lowe, by the way.'

'Sarah Greg.' She suddenly smiled; he was so wonderfully unassuming. 'Nice to meet you, Jack Lowe.'

He smiled back. 'See you later, Sarah Greg.'

Sarah was still smiling when he left the store, and completely amazed that for once the prospect of a date—however low-key—didn't fill her with dread.

Jack walked into his office above Dean & May Solicitors and picked up the post from the mat. He could smell coffee so he called out good morning to Dodi, his secretary, and went through to the little kitchen.

'Hiya, Jack. How's things?' Dodi was Australian, twenty-five, and saving wildly to get married; by working for Jack during the day and for the local pub every available evening and weekend.

'Things, my dear Dodi, are great. How about you? Nice weekend? Lots of tinnies and a barbie?'

Dodi thumped him playfully on the arm. A big girl, well-built, she had been with him since he started up a year ago and they had a good working relationship. She was quick-witted and ambitious with a shed-load of sense—her words, not his.

'So, what's new?' he asked. 'Any messages?'

'Two. Both enquiries from local lawyers for divorce cases.'

He pulled a face. 'For a small provincial town, there's an awful lot of adultery going on.' He took the pot of coffee and poured some into two mugs. 'Call them back,' he said, 'get the details.'

'No, you call them, Jack. They want to hear from you.'

'Oh God.' He walked out of the kitchen to his desk and sat down.

'I know you hate it but these cases pay the bills.'

'OK, OK.' He sighed. 'What would I do without you, Dodi?'

'You'd go out of business,' she replied sharply.

Jack Lowe was thirty-four, living alone in a small cottage with three acres of land on the outskirts of Wynchcombe. He had one son whom he adored and one ex-wife whom he didn't. She had left him two years ago, fed up with his inability to earn enough money to buy her all the things that she wanted, and moved in with a professional footballer. She now drove a Mercedes 80sl, wore designer clothes, and spent more money in an afternoon than he earned in a week. He supposed she was happy, but he had never asked. They were light years apart.

Jack cared little for material things. He earned enough money, from a business he didn't like, to pay maintenance for Jamie and to be able to treat him when he came to stay on alternate weekends and the odd week night. He spent the rest on his garden, for which his passion never faded. Indeed the gardening was possibly the root of all his problems.

Jack had inherited a business from his father at the age of twenty-three, a small but very lucrative private investigation agency in south-east London. At the time he had been doing an apprenticeship at the Royal Horticultural Gardens at Wisley and was loving it; then his father had died, leaving a business with four staff. Jack was the only one able to take it over, with a brother living in New Zealand and a mother who had been dead twelve years. He could have sold it, he realised later, but back then he had been young and inexperienced and grieving. It had been very hard to make the right decisions in the midst of all that mess.

So he took over the business and Sandra, who worked as his secretary, comforted him in the one way that she knew best. Within months they were an item and by the end of that year they were married. Sandra gave up work and they should have been happy. But they weren't.

The trouble was that Jack became almost obsessed with his garden. They had bought a terraced house in Putney and he had transformed the small bit of turf and shrub at the back of it. He created a hidden oasis of water and plants. He had put in a square pool filled with water lilies. He had put down gravel and brick and terracotta and filled the spaces with exotic plants and pots brimming with breathtaking arrangements. It had taken a year to finish and in that year he had neglected his business, his friends and, inevitably, his wife.

The business began to falter, Sandra began to stray and Jack found himself desperately trying to keep an ailing company afloat, and his wife in Prada handbags. To compensate for this he gardened in his every spare moment, creating gardens for friends. They had a baby; it was, Sandra said, the only way they would stay together. But when Jamie was two Sandra walked out, taking Jack's only real achievement with her. His son.

Sandra moved to Sussex with her boyfriend and married him. Jack followed them down in order to be near his son, closing the London branch of Lowe Investigations, and reopening in a very small way in Abbey Down. He cared very little for work, and spent all his time outside on his three acres of burgeoning garden.

'Whatchya doing for lunch?' Dodi asked, coming across to Jack's desk mid-morning. She was checking that he was writing the quotations for the calls he had made that morning and her casual glance at the notepad in front of him didn't fool Jack for one second. He held it out to her. 'No, not a garden plan. I've charged the one from Dean and May downstairs three-fifty, and Smith Album a nice round four hundred. OK?'

She did the diver's OK sign. 'So, what are you doing for lunch?'

'Actually,' Jack said, 'I'm, erm, meeting someone.'

He avoided her stare and flushed. Good Lord, he thought, I'm ten years older than this young woman and I'm acting like she's my teacher.

'Good for you,' Dodi said. And she meant it. Jack Lowe was far too good a bloke and far too much of a dish to spend his life on his own with a bunch of plants. 'I'll just get one sarnie then,' she said.

Jack was at Muffins at one o'clock exactly. It was busy with the lunchtime rush but he secured two seats at a table with a couple of elderly ladies and ordered himself a coffee. The coffee came, he took a sip, burnt his tongue and was in the act of holding his tongue out of his mouth between his teeth to cool down when Sarah came in. Embarrassed that she might have seen him like this, he jumped up suddenly and knocked into the old lady on his right, who spilt her tea all over her turquoise cardigan. Jack immediately began to mop the old lady's arm furiously with his handkerchief.

'I'm so sorry, madam, can I get you another tea?' He glanced up at Sarah. He thought she looked wonderful; fresh-faced, with brown hair cut short and unstyled and wearing jeans and a white T-shirt. Natural and cool, like a short burst of breeze. The lady pulled her arm away and said, 'I'm fine, thank you. Just watch what you're doing next time, young man.'

Jack nodded, blushed and glanced sidelong at Sarah. She caught his eye and smiled.

'Disastrous start,' he said, pulling out a chair for her. 'Sorry.'

The two ladies made to leave and Jack remained standing, helping them with their chairs and their coats, polite without being patronising, Sarah thought. Finally he sat down and smiled at her.

'What would you like to eat?'

'A tuna and cucumber sandwich on brown bread, please,' Sarah replied, 'and a cup of tea.'

'Right. I'll have . . .' Jack looked up at the board, but he hadn't brought his glasses, for reasons of vanity, and he couldn't read the writing. 'I'll have the same as you, then. I'll just go and order.' He went to the counter, gave their order and waited for the girl to put the sandwiches on a plate and pour Sarah's tea from a huge teapot.

He placed the sandwiches on the table and asked Sarah if she wanted anything else.

'No, no thanks,' she replied. 'This is lovely.'

'Is it?' Jack sat and lifted the corner of his sandwich. 'From the look and the smell of it I think my poor tuna probably died of something rather gruesome.'

'Mine is very nice,' Sarah said, widening her eyes and pulling a face to indicate there was someone behind Jack.

'Do you wish to make a formal complaint about your sandwich?' the lady behind Jack asked. Jack caught a glimpse of her badge which bore the word 'Manager'.

'Oh, no, I, erm . . .' Jack blushed, deeply embarrassed once again.

'He's got the most awful sense of humour,' Sarah chipped in, smiling at the lady. 'He was trying to be funny.'

The woman nodded, then smiled. 'I see,' she said, which clearly she didn't. She turned away and Jack put his hands up to either side of his burning face. 'If there was a big, gaping hole in the floor right now I could cheerfully jump in it,' he said.

'Actually,' Sarah said, 'it was quite funny.'

'Really?' Jack looked hopeful.

She smiled. 'No, not really, but I was trying to make you feel better.'

Suddenly he laughed. 'Thank you.' He took a bite of his sandwich, as Sarah took a sip of her tea and glanced at her watch.

'Jack,' she said, 'I'm really sorry, but I can't stop long. I've got to get home because tonight Rory's got listening therapy, and I like to have supper ready for when we get home or else it's too late to eat.'

Jack was silent for a moment. I've blown it, he thought, I've made a complete dick of myself and she can't wait to get away.

'That's fine,' he said. He felt let down and disappointed with himself. Why on earth, when he had been so bad at dating the first time round that he'd ended up marrying the only woman he had ever slept with, did he think he'd be any good at it ten years on?

'I'm glad I came,' Sarah said, finishing off her sandwich.

'Are you, or do you always eat this quickly?'

She blinked in surprise, then said, 'Actually I was being polite. I usually eat much quicker than this.'

Jack smiled. 'Touché.' He left his sandwich and dug his hands in his pockets. 'Right, erm, well, thanks for coming.'

Sarah stood. 'Thanks for lunch.' She braced herself, then said, 'Why don't we have a drink next time, in the evening? I can ask my neighbour to sit with Rory and, well, a glass of wine might relax us both.'

'OK,' Jack said, but he thought, I'm going to need half a bottle of gin to feel relaxed after this fiasco. 'I mean, that would be nice, really nice.'

'When?'

'Wednesday, not Thursday, because I have Jamie, but any night after that . . .'

'Wednesday then,' Sarah said. 'At the Anchor. I'll meet you there at eight thirty, and if there's a problem I'll send word via Jamie at school.'

Jack stood up. He felt odd, light-headed; he could hardly believe his luck. 'On Wednesday, really?'

'Yes, on Wednesday.' Sarah glanced at her watch. 'I must dash,' she said.

'Yes of course you must go. I'll stay and pay.'

She held out three pound coins but he shook his head. 'My treat,' he said.

'Thanks,' Sarah smiled. 'I've got to go.'

'Sure, see you Wednesday then.'

Jack opened the door for Sarah and watched her go off down the street, then turned back into Muffins and paid the bill.

Chapter Four

It was Wednesday afternoon and Sarah was standing outside the school, waiting until most of the other children had been collected before she went across to Miss Meaney. She caught sight of Janie hurrying across the playground and waved.

'Just waiting to see Miss Meaney. Again.' Sarah smiled but it did nothing to fool Janie, who stopped rushing and said, 'What's up?'

Sarah wished she could just brush over it, but she couldn't; she had to talk to someone. 'Rory got his radio aid today,' she said. 'It's a bit bulky, but supposed to make life in the classroom easier. Apparently he's refusing to wear it and hasn't spoken to anyone all day.'

'Oh.' Janie looked at her. 'He'll get used to it, Sarah,' she offered.

'I suppose so.'

Janie patted her arm. 'Try not to worry. Kids hate anything new but it won't be new for long.' She glanced at her watch. 'I must go.'

When Sarah got to the classroom Rory was sitting in the corner, withdrawn and sad.

He looked up and Sarah forced a smile, but he didn't move.

Miss Meaney took her arm. 'I think it might be a good idea to let Rory lead the way with the radio aid,' she advised. 'It's quite a big transition from hearing aids to that and he needs to come to terms with it. Let him decide when he wants to wear it, Mrs Greg, and maybe a chat with him about it might be a good idea?'

Sarah nodded. As if I haven't already had a chat about it, she thought. I've talked and explained until I'm blue in the face. But she just said, 'OK, we'll talk tonight.' She went across to Rory and squatted down. 'Come on,' she said, clearly and loudly, 'what say you we get an ice cream on the way to Ali's lesson?'

Rory nodded and Sarah could tell that he was close to tears. She held out her hand and Rory took it. Once inside the car, Sarah said, 'Can I have a look at your radio aid then?'

Rory sat silent.

She reached in the back for his school bag, opening it up to take out his radio aid receiver and transmitter. 'Wow,' she said, 'this looks pretty high-tech.' Still Rory said nothing, so Sarah examined the box and ear phones, then asked, 'Shall we try it?' He shook his head.

'You don't like it?' Sarah could see his eyes fill. 'Well, I think it's pretty cool,' she said, swallowing down the terrible hard lump that had come to her throat. If she could have taken the shame and the embarrassment for him she would gladly have done so. 'It's going to make a big difference to hearing things at school, things that you wouldn't be able to hear without it, like Mr MacIntyre's voice . . . Och de noo . . .' There wasn't even the faintest response on Rory's lips. 'I know it's a bit hard now, but you'll get used to it, love, I'm sure.'

'I hate it,' Rory said quietly. 'I hate being different. Everyone looks at me and I've got that pratty box round my neck like a deaf person and everyone thinks I'm stupid because I can't hear . . .' He sniffed and wiped his nose on his bare wrist.

'Well, pratty's not a very nice word and your radio aid certainly isn't pratty.'

'It is. It's pratty and stupid and I'm not wearing it.' Rory looked at her defiantly. 'I want to smash it to pieces,' he said.

'Well, you can't,' Sarah replied. 'It belongs to the Education Authority, and we would have to pay for it if you did that.'

'So?' He stared at her, the challenge on his face.

'So it would mean no sweets for a year.' She tried to smile, to lighten the situation. 'Or maybe two years.'

Grudgingly, Rory smiled back and Sarah leaned across and put her arms round him. She held him for a minute or so, then looked at his face. 'Come on, let's get off to the sweet shop before we go to speech therapy and buy the biggest and most expensive ice cream they have.'

As she reversed out of the parking space, she glanced sidelong at him with an aching heart. His expression was one of utter despondency.

It was five o'clock and Marcus was leaving the office early. He had arranged a game of tennis with Alex at the Riverside—not really his sort of thing, but he wanted Alex on board for Janie and her investment club and he thought tennis would go some way towards helping that along. Besides, it beat sitting in a dark bar on a warm sunny evening.

Jumping in a cab, Marcus made it to the Riverside at six fifteen, and waited for Alex. He watched the early-evening activity and attracted glances from the women to-ing and fro-ing from aerobic and step classes. Marcus was tall, well-built and gave off a sense of power; he had a brooding quality and an edge of secrecy that many found alluring. It was as if the dynamism of his personality pervaded his nice but ordinary looks and lifted them to another level. If he had wanted to be unfaithful to Lucie, he would not have had to look far for partners. But Marcus wasn't interested enough in other people to want to get involved with anyone else.

Marcus Todd wasn't interested in much really. He could do most things without much effort; play a decent game of tennis, swim, make witty conversation, charm friends, look good, speak French. The list was endless, which was probably why he couldn't be bothered. What was the point if everything could be done at a wink? Where was the challenge? Except in the stock market, of course. Except in pitching his wits against the never-ending risk of fluctuating share prices.

Marcus was a million-pound-bonus-earning creator of wealth. He regularly made hundreds of thousands of pounds in a single deal. He loved his job. He lived off the adrenaline, knowing that nothing else on earth gave him the same kind of buzz. He loved making money and he loved the fact that he could spend as much as he wanted to without even noticing the dent in his bank account. But it seemed, if not to him then to everyone else around him, that that was all he loved. Something in Marcus's life had gone awry. He had ceased working to live and begun living to work. He wanted money for the sake of money.

'Marcus. Hi!' Marcus turned as Alex approached, a sports bag over his shoulder. 'Shall we get on? I booked a court for six thirty,' Alex said.

'Great.' Marcus picked up his bag and followed Alex towards the male changing room.

The two men changed and Alex led the way on to the court.

'This investment club thing,' Marcus said, pulling the top off the can of balls. 'Janie is keen to get started and I've asked her and her two friends up to my office and then for lunch tomorrow. I said I'd speak seriously to you about it and let her know if you're interested.'

'I'm not sure, Marcus. I don't really think I've got the time . . .' Marcus waited for Alex to get into position at the other end of the court and then hit the ball across. Alex whacked it back.

'It wouldn't take much time,' Marcus called, 'an hour or two a week, max.'

'Why me?' Alex asked. 'Isn't there someone you work with who could do it for you?'

'I trust you, Alex,' Marcus said. 'You're an excellent broker. . .' He lunged forward and returned a low forehand. Alex missed it. 'I'd feel happy with you in on it.'

They continued to warm up, and ten minutes and a few serves later they were ready to start. Alex held his racket up. 'M or W?' he asked, with reference to the Wilson logo on the end of his racket.

'M,' Marcus said, then he continued, 'I've got a couple of good tips, too, for Janie to get going with, but I need a good broker, someone who can buy and sell at exactly the right moment.'

Alex twirled the racket and it fell on M. 'I'll serve,' Marcus said.

'Fine. What sort of tips?' Alex asked, unable to hide his curiosity.

Marcus bent to pick up a ball from the net and saw Alex watch him. He had Alex's attention.

'A couple of dot coms, a small industrial that's subject, I think, to a take-over.'

'I see.' Alex had to admit this was beginning to look good. Marcus was renowned for his skill and Alex saw a small opening to make a bit of easy cash for himself.

'Which end?' Marcus asked, content that he'd got as far as he needed to for the moment.

'I'll stay here,' Alex answered. 'Let's get on, shall we?'

'So will you be giving any more advice?' Alex asked in the changing rooms as they stripped for a shower.

'Well, I thought I'd keep my eye open for some good investment opportunities!'

Alex laughed and his brain went into overdrive. If Marcus gave his sister advice then what was there to stop Alex shifting a couple of grand on the back of that advice? He could do it through a trust, nobody had to know he was doing it except himself. He stepped into a hot shower and as the water gushed down over his body any concerns regarding Lucie went out of his mind. This was one hell of an opportunity, too good to turn down. If he could free up the cash there were likely to be several situations over the next few months where he could double, maybe even triple, his money.

Marcus was flattering him when he said he was a good broker. He was competent but he was never going to make a fortune; he didn't have the instinct for it. Now, if he was pointed in the right direction, who knows what he could achieve? He stepped out of the shower and saw Marcus already dressing.

'Where're you going for lunch tomorrow?' he asked.

'Soho, for dim sum. Come and meet them if you like.'

Alex hesitated, then glimpsed the label in Marcus's suit. I want one of those, he thought. I want to wear bespoke suits and handmade shoes, and he said, 'Why not? I'm happy to give it a go.'

Marcus smiled, a genuinely delighted smile. 'We'll be at the New World Restaurant in China Town at one tomorrow. Meet us there.'

Sarah opened her front door and glanced at her watch. It was seven fifteen and she was tense and upset. The speech therapy lesson had been terrible, and she had ended up getting cross. She spent a good deal of her hard-earned money on these extra lessons, she had told Rory on the way home, to make sure that he didn't ever feel behind. But if he couldn't even be bothered to answer Ali, there was no point in any of it.

Looking over her shoulder, she saw Rory sitting sulking in the car.

'Come on,' she called. 'Supper will be ready in five minutes.' Walking inside the kitchen, she smelt the food in the slow cooker and felt a rush of relief; dinner was ready.

Switching on the kettle, she reached for a packet of couscous and measured a cupful into a bowl. The kettle boiled, she covered the couscous with water and went outside.

'Rory,' she said, opening the passenger door, 'come in now. Supper is ready'. He made no acknowledgment. Irritated, she said, 'I am going to serve it up now and I won't wait for you.' She went back to the kitchen and had started to serve the food when she heard the front door slam.

'Rory?' He was on his way up the stairs and ignored her. 'Rory, supper's on the table,' she said, loud enough for him to hear. She took a deep breath. 'Please, you need some food. Come down and eat it.' Again he ignored her. Sarah had half a mind to ignore him and get on with her own supper, but in the end her maternal instinct won and she went upstairs to see if he was all right.

'Rory?' She knocked on his open door and walked into his room. He was lying in bed, the duvet pulled in tight around him. 'Rory, we can't have this sort of nonsense,' she said, clearly and loudly. 'Either tell me what's wrong or get up and . . .' Her voice trailed away as she saw his shoulders shake under the duvet. She knelt down beside his bed. Touching him, she felt the shudder of his weeping and her whole body ached. 'Rory?' He kept his face hidden as he sobbed. 'I hate it . . .' he managed to say, 'I . . . hate . . . being deaf . . .' And for all the world Sarah wished that it was she who was deaf instead of him.

Later, after he had sobbed himself quiet, Sarah took him downstairs and gave him some supper. He ate listlessly, toying with the food. Sarah glimpsed Lindsay at the back door and motioned to her through the glass that tonight was off. 'Come back in half an hour,' she mouthed.

When he was finally in bed, Sarah sat with him until he went to sleep, and at eight thirty she went downstairs and poured herself a large gin, drinking it neat. It wasn't very nice but it was all she had in the house, and tonight she certainly needed it.

Lindsay knocked on the back door. Sarah opened it and Lindsay said, 'God, you look ghastly! What on earth has happened?' Then she said, 'That's not neat gin, is it?' Sarah nodded. 'Hang on, I'll get you some tonic for it,' and she disappeared next door, returning just a few minutes later with an unopened bottle of tonic water. Lindsay opened the bottle and splashed some tonic into Sarah's glass. She propelled Sarah towards a chair beside the table. 'What happened?' she asked again.

Sarah shook her head. 'Rory,' she began, 'Rory can't cope and nor . . .' Her voice faltered. 'Sometimes, Lindsay, nor can I . . .'

Lindsay went to the cupboard, took down a glass and sat at the table, reaching across for the gin bottle to pour herself a drink. She added tonic, giving Sarah a chance to compose herself. Then she said, 'Sarah, you cope wonderfully. You never panic, you keep your worries to yourself and you let Rory be. Don't underestimate the power of that. What's happened?'

'The root of the problem,' Sarah said, 'is Rory's radio aid. It's awful, it says whoa guys, I'm deaf . . .' Her voice cracked and Lindsay reached across and patted her arm. 'No wonder he's so upset.'

'Isn't there an alternative?'

'Not really, nothing with the same reliability. Honestly, Lin, my heart could just break. He'll get lost at school—he's in a class of thirty-two and he's the odd one out. If he starts to go under, how can they spend time and resources on him when there's such demand from everyone else?' Sarah picked up her glass. 'It's not really this, it's everything. Him getting knocked down in the playground and feeling alienated at school, me not being able to afford the best for him, always feeling that if only Nick was here then it might be different.' She drained her gin and tonic.

'Another drink?' Lindsay said.

Sarah shook her head. 'No, thanks, Lindsay. You're a good friend. I appreciate all the food and wine and company.' Sarah looked up. 'I'm not going to go to London tomorrow,' she said. 'It's not fair to leave you with a distressed Rory.'

'Of course it is,' Lindsay said sharply, 'and you are going, full stop. You've paid for your train ticket and it's a good opportunity, Sarah. You are not going to cancel! I was a teacher, remember? I've seen more truculent six-year-old boys than you've had hot dinners and if I don't know how to handle them by now then I've wasted thirty years of my career.'

Sarah smiled. 'D'you really think it's a good opportunity?'

'I wish I'd had it.' Lindsay looked at her squarely. 'You are going and Rory and I will be fine. Which reminds me, what about that chap you were supposed to meet tonight?'

Sarah suddenly jumped up. 'Oh my God! I'd completely forgotten about Jack! I mean, I've forgotten to let him know that I couldn't make it . . .' She put her hand up to her mouth. 'Oh, Lin, how awful . . .'

'Phone the Anchor,' Lindsay said. 'Now.'

Sarah looked at her watch. 'I doubt he'll still be there, it's nearly nine o'clock. He wouldn't have waited half an hour.'

'Of course he would. Go on, phone now.'

Jack was sitting in a dark corner with a pint and was getting slowly but surely more and more depressed. He felt miserable and stupid. Of course she wasn't here. She'd just said it to make a quick getaway at Muffins; she'd said it to ease the situation. She'd had no intention of turning up. He looked at his watch. It was just after nine and she was half an hour late. He sighed. Be optimistic, he told himself, have some confidence. Maybe the baby sitter had been late or the traffic was keeping her. He took yet another gulp of beer and thought he'd give it till quarter past. If she hadn't arrived or rung by then, well, she'd obviously had no intention of coming in the first place. . . Jack's mind went off on another full circle and because of the noise in the pub, when the phone rang behind the bar he had no chance of hearing it.

A young girl—only her second night—took the call and, unable to raise the energy to shout over the din of the bar, said to the nearest few people, 'Jack Lowe? Does anyone know Jack Lowe?'

Several of the people right at the front heard her but no one looked even remotely interested. She went back on the line.

'Sorry,' she said, 'there's no Jack Lowe in the bar. I've asked around, but he's not here.'

Jack sat with his pint until nine fifteen, then he went up to the bar and said to the pub manager, 'Has anyone phoned here for me tonight? My name's Jack Lowe.'

The darts were about to start, the bar had gone crazy and the manager really didn't have the time or the staff to be acting as a message service. He shrugged. 'Sorry, mate,' he said, 'not that I know of.'

Lucie sat waiting for Alex in a Costa coffee bar in the West End, far enough away from where they both worked not to cause any rumours. She used the time spent waiting to look through some papers in her case on a forthcoming deal, but she had to make a conscious effort to quell her irritation. Alex was late.

'Hi, Lucie. Have you been here long?' Alex appeared at the table.

Lucie glanced up. 'Since eight fifteen, the time we arranged to meet.'

He looked at his watch. 'Blimey, it's almost eight thirty! Sorry!' He looked at Lucie's coffee. 'D'you want another one? What was it? Café latte?'

'Yes. I'll have another one.'

Alex ordered one café latte and one espresso, then came back. Lucie put her papers away and he placed the coffees on the table. He looked at her. 'It's good to see you, Lucie,' he said.

'I'm surprised you weren't on time then,' she replied tartly. Alex looked momentarily startled, then he frowned. He sat down. 'What's all this about?' he asked. 'It's obviously not us, is it?'

'No, it's about you. Marcus told me last night that you'd agreed to go in on this investment club thing.' She stared at him, her face pale with anger. 'I can't believe you'd do it, Alex. Why? Why are you hanging out with my husband? I just don't get it, Alex . . .'

'Whoa! Hang on a minute.' Alex held his hands up to stop her. 'It wasn't my idea to play tennis and Marcus is very difficult to say no to. I can't just drop him, he's a mate.'

Lucie shook her head. 'It's not as if you're old friends, you've only just met. You make excuses.'

'Stop telling me what to do!' Alex suddenly snapped. 'I'm not your puppet. Actually, I'll do what I think is right, OK?'

Lucie glared at him. 'No, it's not OK. This is my marriage you're talking about.'

'Well "your marriage" didn't seem to bother you that much in a hotel room last week, did it?'

'That was before . . .'

'What? Before you thought you might get caught?'

'Yes, all right then, before I thought we might get caught. Do you want to break up my marriage, Alex?'

'I think your marriage was broken before you met me, Lucie. If it had been whole you wouldn't have slept with me, would you?'

Lucie's face changed. He saw that it registered hurt—as if he had slapped her—then understanding and finally sadness. She bit her lip.

'I've got to go,' Lucie said. 'I've got a meeting.' Her voice wavered and he heard the catch in it. It surprised him; he had never imagined that Lucie Croft was the sort of woman to cry. 'I'll just go to the loo.' When she'd disappeared inside Alex stood up, but he knocked her folder off the table as he did so and the papers scattered all over the floor. Alex bent to pick them up, read the title of the first page and, unable to help himself, flipped through the remaining sheets. They were back in the folder and on the table when Lucie returned.

'Alex, look, I'm sorry if I sounded high-handed, it's just that I don't want either of us to . . . well, to get hurt. I honestly think that you getting involved with this investment club thing is not a good idea.'

Alex had the immediate urge to ask: for whom? As far as he was concerned, if he made money out of it then it couldn't be a bad idea.

'Lucie,' he said, placing his hand on her arm, 'relax, please. I know what I'm doing and it'll be fine. Trust me.'

'It won't be fine, Alex,' Lucie said. 'It will end in tears.' She didn't press her point. What was the use of saying any more? She tucked her folder under her arm. 'Bye, Alex,' she said.

'Can I see you again? Can we meet up next week?'

She shrugged. 'I don't know.' She began to walk away. 'I really just don't know.'

Marcus was waiting for them when Janie, Roz and Sarah arrived at his office. He asked reception to send them up and came to the lift to meet them.

'Hello.' They stepped out and, with the exception of his sister, they looked like tourists. He noticed that Roz's suit was much too tight and that her shoes were scuffed, and he wondered why Sarah, who was by far the most attractive of the three, didn't do more with herself and get some decent clothes. Janie at least had dressed well. She wore a long, fitted skirt that hung beautifully and a short jacket with a white silk T-shirt underneath. She knew how to make the most of herself. To Marcus, looking the part was just as important as playing it.

'How was your journey, ladies?'

'Fine,' Janie said. She turned to her friends. 'Marcus, let me introduce you to Roz Betts and Sarah Greg.' They shook hands.

'Come on down to my office. I want to have a quick chat about a stock I've caught sight of this morning before we do anything else.'

'What is it?' Janie asked. 'We've been discussing what we might buy on the way up.' They followed him down the corridor.

'It's a small dot com company launched this morning.' He opened a door and the women walked into a huge open-plan office space banked with screens, keyboards and phones. The noise was incredible.

'Here, look . . .' Marcus reached up and pulled one of the screens round to face them. 'Rightbuy dot com. There, the one in yellow. It's up two pence since I left the office.' Marcus held his finger under a line on the screen. 'It's risen eight pence since opening this morning.' Marcus grinned. 'It'll rise another forty or fifty pence over the next few days is my educated guess. There's a lot of hype about this one.'

'Really?' Roz glanced at Janie and could see that Janie was thinking exactly the same as she was.

'D'you think we should buy it, Marcus?' Janie saw the price move up another point. Her stomach started to churn with excitement.

Marcus looked at her. 'It's a risk, Janie, you've got to understand that. These dot com companies are all paper money based on future earnings, they've got very little else to recommend them.'

'So you're saying that it's too much of a risk?' Sarah asked.

Marcus shrugged. 'That's up to you.' That was the way Marcus worked. He highlighted a stock, gave the facts and left it at that; it was as far as his recommendation went. But it worked; not one of the stocks he'd ever highlighted had been a downer.

'Meeting,' Janie said. The three women moved together and Marcus stood back a pace.

'What d'you think? I hadn't expected to have to make a decision so quickly, but it looks like we've wandered into something pretty good.'

Roz was hooked on the whole atmosphere of the place. She loved the buzz, she loved watching the numbers move, knowing that they represented real money. 'I'm in,' she said quickly, knowing that if she thought about it she might change her mind.

'Sarah?' Janie was expecting Sarah to be cautious and was almost hoping she would be. She felt herself being swept away on a wave of investment fever.

'Let's do it,' Sarah said.

'Really?' Both women turned to look at her.

'How much?' Janie asked.

'All of it,' Sarah said and surprised even herself.

Janie stepped towards Marcus and said, 'We want to buy into Rightbuy dot com.'

'Right, I'll get Alex on the line.' He picked up a phone and dialled. 'Alex, hi, it's Marcus. Yeah, good, thanks, you? Great. Alex, can you buy . . .' He put his hand over the mouthpiece. 'How much?'

'Three thousand pounds' worth,' Janie said.

He went back on the line to Alex. 'Three thousand pounds' worth of Rightbuy dot com. Great, yeah, OK. Thanks, Alex.' Marcus hung up. 'He'll ring back,' he said, 'when he's bought the stock. Names for the certs?'

Janie glanced at Sarah and Roz and they all smiled. 'The Housewife Trust please, Marcus.'

Marcus's phone bleeped and he picked it up. 'Alex, hi. Yup, you did, great.' He pulled the screen round to face him. 'Top man, Alex! Yes, I do, it's the Housewife Trust please. Yup, thanks.' He disconnected the line, then turned to the women and said, 'Alex got in at twenty-nine and it's just gone up to thirty-one.'

'Great! We've made . . .' Janie got out her calculator and began to work it out.

'You've made two pence a share, which gives you a profit at the moment of two hundred and six quid, roughly,' Marcus said.

'Bloody hell.'

It had taken less than a quarter of an hour to put them in business and less than two minutes to put them in profit.

'Shall we move on for the tour?' Marcus asked.

'Oh, yes, erm, great,' Janie said. And the three women followed him down the office while he explained who did what and how things worked. But they were all so preoccupied with their own thoughts that none of them heard a single word he said.

Alex arrived half an hour late at the New World Restaurant in Soho, with the news that Rightbuy dot com was up to forty-four pence. It set the lunch off to a good start. They ate small parcels of oriental food—prawn with ginger wrapped in a slippery white skin and fried seaweed and chilli pork deep-fried in a won ton. While Sarah worried about how much it was all going to cost, Roz struggled with her chopsticks, twice dropping something onto her lap and privately thinking, I wonder if soy sauce stains? Janie was trying hard to commit to memory every word that Alex was saying. She was a businesswoman now, a professional, and she took it extremely seriously.

Both men's reaction to Sarah surprised Janie. It wasn't that she had never thought of Sarah as attractive. It was just that out of the dull, ordinary context of school she was unexpectedly taken by how uniquely lovely her friend was. Sarah had a manner which charmed, she was warm and soft and spoke with a wicked sense of humour. It seemed to draw Alex to her and Marcus was almost flirtatious.

At the end of the lunch Marcus offered to pay, but they all insisted that each pay their way. Sarah held her breath while Janie looked at the bill, then Janie burst out, 'Marcus, you toad! No wonder you wanted to pay—the bill is the princely sum of five pounds each.'

Everyone laughed. They paid, stood up, made their way to the exit and blinked as they walked out into the sunlight.

'Thank you, Marcus,' Janie said, reaching up to kiss his cheek. 'For organising this. It's been a good day.'

'It's been a pleasure,' he said.

Sarah looked at him and teased, 'Are you sure? Three country bumpkins plodding through your office, picking straw out of their teeth? You've been very patient with us, Marcus.'

Marcus leaned forward and kissed Sarah. She was a little unnerved. 'Of course I'm sure. It was fun,' he said. Sarah smiled and turned away. You old fool, she thought, it doesn't take much to flatter you.

Janie turned to Alex. 'So we'll hear from you, Alex, when you think it's time to sell Rightbuy dot com?' Marcus had advised not holding on to the stock for more than a week.

'Yup. Probably in the next few days or so. Right, Marcus?'

'Definitely. As we discussed, this is a short-term buy. Alex will keep a sharp eye on the price and as soon as it starts shifting he'll get out.'

Janie looked at Sarah and Roz and the expression 'hanging on to every word' sprang to mind. She nudged Sarah, who started, then said, 'Right, we should let you two go.'

They shook hands with both men and said goodbye. Marcus and Alex watched them walk off and then Alex held out his hand. 'Thanks for organising lunch, Marcus.'

They shook hands. 'I'll leave the Housewife Trust up to you then, Alex, and I'll be in touch the next time I think there's something good coming up.'

'Great.' Alex had invested £4,000 into Rightbuy dot com himself and was already pleased with the decision to get involved with the investment club.

The train was hot and stuffed to the last square inch with bodies when they got to Victoria. It was tourist season and it was also peak commuter time. Sarah, Roz and Janie squeezed themselves in among the office workers and the French exchange students, and waited for the train to move off. Janie's phone rang. She finally managed to get the phone out, answered it and said, 'It's Alex.' She listened for a few moments, then said, 'That's fine, Alex, whatever you think. Yes, OK, I'll speak to you tomorrow.' She turned to Sarah and Roz.

'Alex thinks we should probably move out of Rightbuy dot com tomorrow. He thinks it might have gone as far as it's going to go.'

Sarah and Roz looked disappointed. 'So how far has it gone?' Sarah asked. Two hundred pounds, she told herself, was better than nothing.

Suddenly Janie burst out, 'It's gone up to ninety-five pence a share!'

Roz let out a screech. 'Ninety-five pence!'

Sarah shook her head. 'My God, I can't believe it . . . we've made sixty-odd pence a share, that's almost . . .' She began to try to add it up in her head, but Janie got there before her. 'It's doubled our money in five hours,' she said. There was a moment's stunned silence, then—quite out of character—Janie threw her fist in the air and said, 'Yes!'

CHAPTER FIVE

JANIE WAS IN THE GARDEN when the phone rang. She was replanting a bit of the border that had been getting her down for years. Hurrying to the house, she answered the phone breathless, and Alex on the other end said, 'Is that Janie Leighton?'

'Yes, hello, Alex.'

'You recognised my voice, Janie, I'm impressed.'

Janie wanted to say, I don't know a single other well-spoken man who would ring me in the middle of the day, but she didn't.

'Janie, good news. I sold ten thousand, three hundred and forty-four shares in Rightbuy this morning at ninety-five pence a share. I hope that's OK? That means you've made a total gross profit of six thousand, eight hundred and twenty-seven pounds.'

Janie sat down.'Good Lord.'

'I will need to take my commission out of that, of course, which on the first twelve thousand pounds is almost two per cent.'

'Of course . . .' The numbers made very little sense to Janie; she was too overwhelmed with the words thousand and profit in the same sentence. She looked down at her muddy gardening trousers and suddenly jumped up off the chair. 'Oh, right. It all sounds, erm . . .' She began sweeping the soil off the cushion cover. 'Wonderful. Thank you, Alex.'

'Not at all, Janie.' He meant it too. He'd just made himself a gross profit of £9,000 on a small personal investment of £4,000. Not bad for one deal. 'I'll be in touch,' he said. 'Bye for now.' Janie stood motionless for a moment, then she let out a hoot and abandoned the dirty cushion cover. Sod it, she thought, with £2,000 I can buy six new chairs.

Sarah was stacking shelves when her name was called out over the tannoy. 'Sarah Greg to the supervisor please.' She hurried over to the supervisor's counter.

'There's a phone call for you, Sarah,' the supervisor said. 'It's personal.' She felt instant panic; this number was only for emergencies.The supervisor was a large, grey-haired woman of fifty with a frizzy perm, who rarely smiled and felt it her duty to run Duffields like a regimental sergeant major on her shift. She didn't approve of single mothers, they were a drain on society. She looked at Sarah and tapped her watch. 'Company time,' she said. 'Please be brief.'

Sarah nodded and took the receiver.

'Hello?'

'Sarah, it's Janie. Sorry to ring you at work, I'll be quick. Alex sold our shares this morning at ninety-five pence a share.'

'Wow!' Sarah burst out, then she caught the supervisor's eye and blushed. 'Janie, that's fantastic!' she whispered. 'I can't believe it.'

'Me neither. Meeting,' Janie went on, 'Monday night. Can you do it?'

'No problem. I'll have the drinks ready. I think this calls for a celebration.'

'Me too. Thanks, Sarah. See you later at school.'

'Bye.' Sarah replaced the receiver under the watchful eye of the supervisor and turned to go. 'I hope it was important, Sarah,' the woman said.

Sarah grinned; she couldn't help herself. 'Not really,' she replied.

Roz was up to her eyes in it. Kitty hadn't left her side since Roz's return from London, Oliver had a temperature and Justin had found a rat left by the cat in the playroom that morning. Graham had locked himself away in the box-room they used as an office, working on something he darkly called 'the mission'.

Standing at the sink washing the breakfast things with one hand, the other holding Kitty on her hip, Roz was just rinsing the last mug when the phone rang. She put Kitty in the pushchair by the back door, tucked a rug round her and wheeled her over to the phone. She reached for the receiver.

'Hello?'

'Roz? It's Janie. I rang to tell you that Alex sold Rightbuy dot com this morning at ninety-five pence a share. That's six thousand, eight hundred and twenty-seven pounds, split three ways, minus commission.'

'My God!' Roz stopped playing with Kitty and stood still for a moment. 'Bloody hell, that's more profit than I make in several months from this place.' Roz was speechless; almost. 'So what's next then?' she went on. 'When shall we meet up to discuss the next investment?'

'Monday,' Janie said, 'at Sarah's. Eight-ish?'

'Perfect,' Roz said. 'I'll be there. Oh and, erm, thanks, Janie.'

Roz hung up, wheeled Kitty, who was now fast asleep, into the hall, and then went up to tell Graham what had happened.

Roz tapped on the door of the box-room and heard Graham mutter something she took to mean come in. Graham let out a shout as she crumpled three piles of paper laid out on the floor with the door.

'I said hang on,' Graham snapped.

Roz bent to straighten the mess. 'Sorry.' She picked up one of the pieces of paper to look at it. 'What's this? "Local government corruption in town planning?"'She read the print-out of the news article, then looked up and said, 'It costs a fortune to surf the net in the middle of the morning, Graham. I hope you know what you're doing.'

'Not exactly,' Graham replied, 'but I'm starting to get more of an idea.'

Roz flicked through the other articles in her pile. 'Do I get the impression that you think there's something fishy going on with the Gordens' land deal, Graham? It's a bit far-fetched, isn't it?'

Graham looked up from where he was kneeling. 'Not when you see this it isn't.' He held up his pile of papers and read, "Designated green belt countryside areas in East and West Sussex." An article dated spring last year on stringent building regulations on green belt sites. December last year: "Local town planning rejects scheme for redevelopment of rural area." And so it goes on. Up until February this year there are seven references I found on the net to planning and they all reject the sort of development proposed for the Gordens' land. So I went to the town hall yesterday in Hersley to look up some things on building regulations and I found these . . .' He held up a clear plastic folder filled with photocopies. 'These are the regulations for building in the region. We are considered a green belt countryside area, the whole village is. Building here is almost impossible. The land can't be built on.'

Roz was losing patience. 'So?'

'So how come the Gordens got an offer on their land if building here is so impossible?'

'I don't know, Graham. Perhaps there's a get-out clause in the rules that the developers know about. There could be any number of reasons. Whatever they are you can be sure that we won't know about them.'

'Exactly!' Graham stood, and looked at her smugly. 'Because you can bet your life that they're not above-board and legal. There's something going down at that office, Roz, and I'm going to find out what.'

Roz had lost her patience. For once in her life she had done something successful; she had stopped farting about and got on with it and she now had £2,000 to show for it. Yet here Graham was, head in the sky, making ridiculous suggestions about corruption in local government and she was supposed to be impressed. 'This is nonsense,' she said cuttingly. 'You're wasting your time.'

'No, I'm not. There's something going on, Roz, I'm convinced of it. In fact I'm going to see a private investigator on Monday morning. I want him to sniff around for me.'

Roz started to laugh. 'Is it really worth it, Graham? Wouldn't you, we, be better off focusing on rallying support and getting up petitions?'

'We'll do that as well,' he replied. 'We've got to do everything and anything that we can, Roz, if we want to save Chadwick Farm. Don't ridicule me for making an effort.'

Roz looked down. 'I'm not ridiculing you,' she said, 'I'm simply questioning the viability of your idea.'

'It's worth a try,' Graham said finally, and Roz, even though it was against her judgment, had to agree with that. She crossed the room and reached up to hug him. 'All right,' she said. He held her close and kissed her hair.

'Did you come up here for a reason?' he asked.

Roz held her breath. She hadn't planned it, she hadn't even known she would do it until that moment when she said, 'Just to see if you wanted a coffee.' She didn't tell him. The success of the investment club was her secret.

Janie was at the PC in the upstairs study when Andrew came home. He was so rarely in for lunch that it felt quite illicit opening the front door to a silent house, and a couple of stolen hours with his wife.

'Janie?'

Janie came to the top of the stairs in her gardening sweater, socks and knickers.

'Is that an invitation?' he asked, looking up.

Janie frowned. 'No, I had to take my gardening trousers off because they were muddy and I couldn't be bothered to change.'

'I'll come up, shall I?' Andrew started for the stairs, but Janie said quickly, 'No, Andrew, don't. I mean, I've, erm, I've got to finish this list.

I've just spoken to Marcus and he's given me a list of stocks to look at.'

'Oh.' Andrew was used to this kind of rejection; their sex life had long since stopped being spontaneous. 'How about a pub lunch then? I've got a couple of hours off from the surgery.'

Janie's frown deepened. Why couldn't he take her seriously? When she said she had work to do, that's what she meant. 'I really do want to get this list finished before I go off to school this afternoon,' she said, 'then I can give it to the others to look at over the weekend.'

Andrew looked at her for a moment, then said, 'OK, I'll go on my own.' He moved towards the front door and Janie called, 'You're not cross, are you, Andrew? I mean, you do understand, don't you?'

Andrew turned. 'I understand, Janie,' he replied. 'You've seemed much happier lately and I thought that perhaps you'd changed for the better. But now I realise that I was mistaken. You've swapped one obsession for another.'

Lucie was in the bathroom applying her make-up when Marcus came in, dressed for work. She watched him in the mirror as he came to stand behind her and gently laid his hands on her shoulders. It was the first time he had touched her in weeks.

'You feel tense,' he said.

'Hardly surprising.' Lucie had worked most of the weekend. 'I don't feel as if I've done anything but work for the last ten days.'

Marcus said, 'You haven't.' He began to massage her neck.

'Hmmm, that's nice.'

His fingers were strong and he had a knack with massage. It was something they used to do a lot.

'Have you got much on today?'

'No, thank God. The document should go off this morning and after that I plan to take it easy for the rest of the day. I don't think I can slope off home, but I think I'll go to the gym at lunchtime or maybe even sit in Finsbury Park with a sandwich and a magazine.'

'The *Investor's Chronicle*, I hope.'

Lucie smiled. 'Definitely not the *Investor's Chronicle*.' She looked at his reflection. 'What about you? Have you got much on?' She thought, this is ridiculous, this impersonal chit-chat, but it was at least free of acrimony.

'Not a lot.'

'Maybe we could have a sandwich together?' As soon as she'd said it she knew she was going to be rejected and wished that she'd kept quiet.

'I don't think so,' Marcus said. He gave no reason and despite the silences, the lack of affection, the moods, all of which she had got used to, his reply still cut her to the quick.

He dropped his hands away and said, 'I've been thinking of taking a holiday. In a month or so. What do you think?'

Lucie hesitated. She wasn't sure for a moment if he was asking her if she'd like to go or if she minded him going without her.

'It's a good idea,' she said, 'a break would be good.' That gave him an indication that she would like to go without inviting another rejection.

'That's what I thought.' Marcus combed his hair, then re-aligned his shirt cuffs with his jacket sleeves and said, 'I'll book my holiday then.' And, glancing at Lucie, he said a brief goodbye and left the house.

'Dodi? Door please,' Jack called and she went out onto the landing and pressed the buzzer for the door downstairs. She stepped forward to look down over the banister.

'Mr and Mrs Betts?'

'Yes, hello?'

'Hi, I'm Dodi, Jack Lowe's gofer. Come on up.'

Dodi smiled at Roz and Graham when they reached the top of the stairs and took them through to Jack.

'Would ya like coffee? I've got it all ready?'

Roz said, 'Yes, please, we both would; thanks.' She glanced round the shabby, dim office and wondered what on earth they were doing there . . . She tuned into Jack's conversation with Graham.

'I made a few photocopies for your information,' Jack was saying, 'Have a look through those and you'll see what I mean.'

Roz looked quizzically at Graham, who began to explain.

'Jack was just saying that after we spoke the other day he went along to the planning department to check on plans for buildings in our area and found that the regulations for West Waltham are incredibly stringent, not only because it is a green belt countryside area but because it is also a flood plain area.'

'I just wanted to check for myself that there was some kind of case to answer. I didn't want to take it on and waste your money,' Jack said. 'A flood plain area is regulated by all sorts of restrictions from the environment agency, who basically want no building on it at all. Planning is not, shouldn't be, an option.'

'So they won't be able to build?'

'Not in theory, no. That doesn't mean they won't though. Look, at the planning department I copied two house plans for houses that have been built in the last six months and you'll be able to see how strict the regulations are. Any houses that have been approved have a minimum garden size of fifteen metres' depth and a front drive area of six metres before the garage. You can't have window to window interlooking, the minimum distance for back-to-back gardens is twenty metres. You'll be able to see from that house there what I'm talking about.'

'Yes, I do see . . .' Graham opened out the plan so that Roz could look.

'And here I have some other plans. These are for a development by Glover Homes that was built last year. It was in a green belt countryside area and the houses don't comply at all with regulations. See? Here, look. Houses that size should have parking for at least three cars and the drive area is tiny.' Jack handed the plans across.

'Do you think I am right—is something going on?' Graham asked.

Jack went round the desk and sat down opposite them. Dodi brought coffee in, handed it round, then she too pulled up a chair.

'Dodi has been making a list of all planning applications over the last two years for the whole Hersley area. Already she's found three instances where Glover Homes has been successful when others have failed. Now that may just be because they're a good building company with very skilled land buyers, or it may be something else.'

'So, how do we find out which one it is?'

'Well, the first thing to do is to find out which developer has made the offer on the land adjacent to your property. If it is this particular builder, we need to track their planning application. There should be objections because of it being a green belt area, and if they want to put six or seven big homes on to the site then it won't fit with regulations. I would guess that their application is being reviewed at this moment. If they've put in an offer, they must be pretty confident of getting planning. So . . .' Jack took a slug of coffee, swallowed, then went on. 'Firstly, I'd want to track the land buyer for the developer and find out if he's spending time with anyone from planning. Secondly, I'd want to track the planning application officer or officers at Hersley planning department, and thirdly, I'd need to check on each member of the council committee that pass the applications. I'd look at things like who has a new car, who's spending time with who or who's been on an exotic holiday, that kind of thing. I might even do some credit checks; there's lots of things I can access if I need to.'

Roz was taken aback. 'Is it all legal?'

Jack smiled. 'Yes. I work well within data protection laws and privacy laws. The thing is that anything of this nature—fraud, corruption and so on—is very difficult to prove. People cover their tracks, they are careful, but they do make mistakes and it would be my job to keep watch for those mistakes.'

Roz glanced at Graham and he said, 'You didn't answer my question earlier. Do you think there's something going on?'

'At the moment, I don't know. There *is* something that needs to be looked at, but that's as much of an answer as I can give you, I'm afraid. You don't have to make up your mind now you know,' Jack said. 'Take some time to think about whether you want to go ahead.'

'How much are we talking about here?' Roz asked.

'I've done a quote for you, Mrs Betts.' Jack took out an invoice and handed it across to Roz.

Roz looked at it and handed it across to Graham.

'And what if you find out that the planning office is corrupt?' Roz asked.

'You blow the whistle on them. I'll have put together enough of a case to be convincing, hopefully with photos, witness statements, financial evidence, that sort of thing, so there should be enough corroborative evidence to report them. It will certainly put an end to the land deal with your neighbours at least.'

Graham looked at Roz but he didn't have to say anything. He could tell just by the look in her eyes that they were in agreement on this one. He said, 'We'd like to accept the quote, Jack. How soon can you start?'

Jack smiled. 'This morning.'

'That was good work, Jack,' Dodi said after they had gone. From his performance this morning no one would ever have known that less than a week ago he could hardly drag himself up the stairs to work. 'I don't know what that lady did to you on your date the other night, Jack, but you've—'

'She did nothing,' Jack cut in. 'She didn't show up. I got as pissed as a fart and drowned my sorrows in seven pints and three shorts.'

Dodi's expression was hard to read. Jack thought it was a mixture of distaste and pity. But it was in fact shock and hurt on his behalf. He didn't deserve that.

'I'm sorry,' was all she could manage to say.

He shrugged, suddenly embarrassed. 'Well, I'm not. It made me realise what a pathetic figure I must be.' He switched on his PC, ready to continue work. 'Not any more though. It's about time I pulled my finger out and stopped being such a failure.'

Alex was waiting for Lucie at Joe Allen's. He stood up as she came to the table and kissed her. Lucie let him kiss her cheek, but made no effort to return his affection. She hadn't wanted to come, had in fact only done so because he had rung her that morning and almost insisted that she join him for lunch.

'What would you like to drink? Wine, beer?'

'I'll have a glass of wine please; white, dry.'

Alex ordered for her and passed her across a menu. 'They have good salads,' he said. 'You like salad, don't you?'

Lucie put her menu down and looked at him. 'What's this all about, Alex? I thought you understood that things were over between us.'

'Are they? I understood that you wanted some cooling-off time but I didn't think it, we, had finished.' He reached across the table for her hand and she couldn't be bothered to resist. He wove his fingers between hers. 'It's not, is it?'

Lucie shrugged. She knew what she was doing was wrong for her, that betrayal left her weak with guilt. She didn't want to lose her marriage, but what sort of a marriage did she have? She co-habited with Marcus, but they had separate lives. She couldn't remember the last time he had held her hand across a table. She loved him, but where was all that love going? Nowhere. It needed an outlet, and her need for affection—the basic human need—had to be satisfied.

'I don't know what I want, Alex,' she said. He kissed her hand and it felt good.

'Do any of us know what we want, Lucie? I don't really know what I want, so I take what's there and enjoy it. I love to lie with you, Lucie, you make me feel good. That's enough for now, isn't it?'

Lucie shook her head. 'I don't know,' she said again and Alex continued, 'You're unhappy and stressed and lonely and I can ease all that. You like being with me, don't you?' He smiled and kissed her hand again.

Grudgingly Lucie smiled back.

'You like sex with me, don't you?' He was still smiling. 'Come on, admit it? And you like salads, which is why I've brought you here for lunch . . .' He moved his fingers up her hand and stroked the soft, smooth skin on the inside of her wrist. 'You do like salads, don't you?'

'Yes!' Lucie replied. Suddenly she laughed. 'God, Alex, you're such a salesman.' She pulled her hand away. 'Why are you so persistent with me when you could have a nice, uncomplicated single girl in your bed?'

'Who wants nice and uncomplicated? I like complex. I like the way that you meet me in a suit, holding your briefcase, and ten minutes later you're lying underneath me, naked, all sense abandoned. I like the way you moan and move your hips and then dress and leave as if nothing had ever happened between us. And I like the secrecy and the intimacy of knowing that no one else knows . . .'

'You're a thrill-seeker,' Lucie said. 'You get off on risk, don't you?'

Alex placed his hand on her thigh under her skirt. He moved it up between her legs and looked at her. 'I don't know what you mean,' he said.

Lucie smiled, then gently moved his hand away.

'Come back to my flat after work tonight?' he asked.

She sighed. 'I don't think so, I . . .'

'Please?'

She thought, he really wants me. She looked at her hands on the white tablecloth, hands that needed to touch, that needed to be held and kissed, and she said, 'OK.'

Marcus finished on the phone and looked at his watch. It was twelve thirty. He called the Pavilion in Finsbury Square and booked a table for one o'clock, then he dialled Lucie's office. He wasn't sure what he was going to say to her. He'd hurt Lucie, he knew that much, but he wasn't very good at saying sorry. How to get on to a secure footing with her again, he had no idea. Things recently had begun to go very wrong. He had somehow become closed off from her, from life itself really, and he didn't seem able to open himself up again.

Lucie's secretary answered and told him Lucie was out. Did he want to leave a message? Marcus gave a curt no and rang off. He pulled his jacket on, took his car keys out of his desk drawer and left the office.

In the street, Marcus stepped into his open-topped car. He had parked on a meter, then offered one of the boys from the settlements twenty quid in cash to pop down every hour and feed the meter for him. He put on his sunglasses, put a CD in the player and pulled out of the space. Lucie would be at the gym. He would go there and take her out for lunch. He turned down Threadneedle Street and accelerated. He attracted attention—a good-looking, well-dressed man in an expensive car—and he enjoyed it.

At the gym, Marcus parked outside and went into reception. He asked the girl if Lucie had signed in and she checked on the computer.

'No,' she said, 'there's no card gone through for Lucie Croft.'

Instantly irritated, Marcus said, 'Are you sure? Could you just tannoy her, to make quite sure?'

'She couldn't have got past me. There's no way she could have—'

'Could you just tannoy her, please?' Marcus asked, as calmly as he could.

The girl rolled her eyes, switched on the tannoy and called out Lucie's name. Marcus walked across to the seating area, picked up a copy of the *FT* and flicked through it.

'Excuse me?' the girl from the desk called. 'I wouldn't bother to wait,' she called across to him, 'she's not here.'

Marcus said nothing. He dropped the *FT* back onto the coffee table, turned on his heel and walked out.

Back in his car, he felt irritated and disappointed. He had no desire to go back to the office. It had been a shitty morning anyway and he was owed weeks of holiday. He might as well call it a day. He would drive down to Sussex, go and see Janie. She would be glad to see him and might even cook him dinner. He could have a pint in the local with Andrew. Cheered by this idea, Marcus pulled out into the traffic. Perhaps not a pint with Andrew, it wasn't that kind of relationship, and maybe not dinner there, it would be too much, but the drive would be good. He was closing himself off again, shutting himself down and leaving not even half an inch for anyone to get anywhere near him.

Janie was in the kitchen when Marcus rang the doorbell at Bank Cottage. She was making a cake in a direct refutation of Andrew's comment on Friday about her exchanging obsessions. They hadn't spoken about it at all over the weekend, but she had made damn sure that the house and the social activities had been run with clockwork precision.

'Marcus! My God!' She was momentarily lost for words. What the hell was he doing here? 'Gosh, erm, what a nice surprise!'

Marcus had bought a huge bunch of expensive flowers and he handed them over saying, 'Is it? You don't mind me crashing in like this, do you?'

'Of course not, it's . . .' Janie held the flowers, embarrassed by their extravagance. 'It's wonderful. Come on in, please.'

Marcus stepped inside and smelt cake. He instantly thought that that was a smell his and Lucie's house would never possess. 'Are you baking?'

'Yes, to prove to Andrew that I *can* do two things at once.' She laughed and led the way through to the kitchen. 'These flowers are beautiful.' She went to the sink, ran the tap and said over her shoulder, 'I'll pop them in some water and then I've got to go and get Katie. Will you come with me? She'd be delighted to see you at school.'

'Does she know who I am?'

Janie turned, but saw that Marcus was smiling and smiled with him. 'It's been a long time, Marcus,' she remarked.

'I know. Sorry. Shall we go in my car? Katie could just about squeeze in the back of the Porsche. It's a convertible.'

Janie took her apron off. 'That would be lovely,' she said, as she thought, where will it end? Will he ever spend enough?

Sarah was waiting in the playground at school when the Porsche pulled up. She was stunned to see Janie climb out. She waved and Janie brought Marcus across.

'Hello, Marcus.'

'Sarah. Nice to see you. How are you?' He leaned forward and kissed Sarah's cheek. 'Have you been playing tennis?'

'Oh no, nothing nearly so civilised. It's my warm weather kit-shorts, T-shirt and trainers. Scruffy and comfy.'

'Sarah, I'll leave Marcus with you if that's OK? I just want to pop in and have a chat with Miss Meaney,' Janie said.

'Yes, that's fine.'

'So? How's it all going?' Marcus said. 'I heard about the coup with Rightbuy dot com. Well done. What's next on the hit list?'

'We're meeting tonight to discuss it.'

'Did you see the article in the *FT* at the weekend about media groups?'

Sarah shook her head.

'It was very interesting. Small media companies constantly falling prey to the giants. As soon as they go public they're snapped up. There's only a few left apparently. I'll fax it to you if you like?'

'No fax.'

'Oh well.' He shrugged.

Sarah said, 'Is it worth looking at small media groups, d'you think?'

'Probably. Anything connected to cable or satellite communications is a good bet. Don't be fooled by the press though, journalists aren't always right and the biggest diamonds aren't always the easiest to spot.'

'So is that a yes?'

'You might think it is, but I couldn't possibly comment.'

Sarah laughed. Marcus looked at her. 'You have a wonderful laugh, Sarah, it's very . . .' He searched for the right word. 'Spontaneous.'

'Spontaneous is a very kind way of putting it, Marcus. Others have described it as neighing, erm, loud and raucous.'

Marcus chuckled. 'Well, I like it.'

Sarah smiled. 'So, do you think it's worth looking at small media groups?' she asked.

Marcus narrowed his eyes. 'Ah, haven't given up then? Why don't I give you that article? I've got to see a client down this way. I could drop it in to you, along with some other stuff on the market, if you like.'

'Oh no, I wouldn't want to put you out.'

'Not at all. In fact, I'd enjoy it. Maybe we could have a sandwich at the pub and discuss it?'

Sarah hesitated for a moment, then thought, why not? 'I'd like that,' she said. 'It'd be nice.' It would be too; something to look forward to. Sarah liked Marcus. He was up front and easy to talk to; uncomplicated.

Sarah saw Janie coming towards them with Rory and Katie. 'When did you have in mind?' she asked. 'I work every day until one but I might be able to get off early.'

'Friday? I think it's Friday I'm due down here. Is that OK?'

'Yes, that sounds fine. Good.'

'What's good?' asked Janie.

'This whole investment thing,' Marcus replied before Sarah had a chance to explain. 'It seems to be going very well.'

'Well thank you, Marcus, nice of you to say so.' She turned to Sarah. 'He is quite nice sometimes,' she said. Sarah smiled. Then she saw Rory. The sight of her son, alone and forlorn, walking across to her trailing the bag with his microphone aid in it behind him made her heart sink. Everything else simply went out of her mind.

The meeting at Sarah's that night started at eight thirty. Each of the women had made a list of what they wanted to look at. Sarah had phoned Roz, and she had got Graham to print out of all the articles in the financial press on small media groups over the past six months.

'Preferred stocks,' Janie said, to kick off. 'Who wants to go first?'

Roz got out her notes. 'Small media groups,' she said. 'I think Marcus could be right, there's one or two that look very interesting. Actually, I narrowed it down to one—Prestwick Communications. There's lots of stuff in the press about them. Quite a bit of speculation about a bid from the Searson Group, the media giant. Here, I copied the articles for you both.' She handed over a couple of photocopies.

'Was there anything else?' Sarah asked.

'There was Sarasota, an advertising and marketing group, but they're not very well reviewed. No one has ever tipped them.'

'What do they do?'

'Advertising, obviously; they've got a big public relations arm, PRP, and they run a couple of TV shopping channels.'

Sarah looked at her. 'Where? What network?'

'Sky.' She looked at Sarah as it began to make sense. 'They're very cheap at the moment, undervalued as far as I can see . . .'

In her head Sarah kept going over what Marcus had said about the best companies not necessarily being the ones that were favoured in the press. 'If they're cheap and undervalued, wouldn't they make a better bid proposition for Searson Group than Prestwick?'

Janie, who had been reading through the news print-outs, said, 'Are you two saying that you want to take a risk on a company that might be subject to a take-over bid?'

Roz and Sarah looked at each other. The thought that they might be in with a chance of repeating the success of Rightbuy was tempting.

'I don't know,' Sarah said honestly.

'Well, I do,' Roz said, 'and the answer is yes, Janie. Marcus has told us to watch small media groups and I'm happy to go with that tip.'

'But was it a tip?' Janie asked. 'Did Marcus make a recommendation?'

Sarah, more cautious than Roz, shook her head. 'No, it wasn't a recommendation as such, it was more like a subtle hint.'

'How much would you want to invest?' Janie said.

Roz took a breath. 'All the money.'

Sarah stared at her. 'Are you sure, Roz?'

'If we can pinpoint the right stock then, yes, I'm sure. The way I see it is that the market is moving up, so, we put our money into something that isn't as volatile as IT stocks but will more than likely grow with the market at worst and might be subject to a take-over at best. According to what I've read, Searson Group are anxious to make a bid for something. If they do and it's not for whatever we've invested in, then it'll still have a positive effect on the share price of our stock. Activity in the sector always does.'

Sarah stared at Roz. 'You're wasted on pigs and sheep, Roz. I think that sounds really impressive. Janie? What d'you think?'

What Janie actually thought was, Terrific! It's all my idea, I do the legwork, get it all organised and then Roz comes along and starts taking the whole thing over with her bigger and better ideas. But she didn't voice any of this. She wanted to add her bit. So she said, 'Was there any other company, Roz, that might be subject to a bid?'

'Only the two that I mentioned.'

'Well,' Janie ventured, 'maybe we should have a closer look at the market over the next few days and then invest. There's no immediate hurry, is there?'

Both Sarah and Roz agreed that there wasn't. 'You are always so sensible, Janie,' Roz remarked. She saw the look on Janie's face and added quickly, 'I mean that as a compliment.'

'Yes, well . . .'

'So, we're all agreed,' said Sarah. 'If after a more careful look Sarasota seems like a good bet, then we want to invest in it. Yes?'

'For a two-month period,' Janie added. 'Then we think again.'

'Yes,' Roz said.

Sarah looked at them. 'How much?'

Janie shrugged. 'In for a penny, in for a pound,' she said. 'All of it.'

'Roz?'

Roz smiled. 'If we're into metaphors, then we've got to speculate to accumulate . . .'

Sarah rolled her eyes. 'And let's just hope that the early birds catch the worm.'

Roz and Janie groaned and then they all burst out laughing.

CHAPTER SIX

THE HOUSEWIFE TRUST bought 16,949 shares in Sarasota plc on April 25 for fifty-nine pence a share. On May 19 the Searson Group put out an offer for Sarasota plc and the share price leapt to one pound seventy pence a share. The trust sold their shares at one pound sixty-nine pence a share and then had a working capital of over £27,000.

In the course of the next few weeks they watched the market and made several quick deals, raising their capital to £50,000. Then they started to track the dot com companies, which were now rocketing out of all proportion. The trust began to double its money on certain deals. They had a run of luck in buying shares in two more companies just before a take-over announcement was made, and although Sarah spoke to Marcus on a regular basis the women put their success down to precision research and pure and simple luck.

By the end of June they had amassed a staggering £110,000. It was time, they all decided, to spend a little of it.

Marcus looked across at Lucie. She was curled up comfortably on the sofa, her glasses on, watching the television.

'You look tired,' he remarked. 'Why don't you get off to bed?'

Lucie didn't answer; she barely even heard him. It had been the usual Friday night for them. She had come in late with an M&S ready meal in a carrier, which she then stuffed in the oven while she poured herself a large glass of wine, and seethed with resentment that Marcus did not ask where she had been. She had begun to drink half a bottle of wine before dinner at weekends. It was the only way she could unwind.

'Lucie? I said you ought to get to bed,' Marcus repeated. 'You look exhausted.'

Bleary-eyed, Lucie heaved herself into a sitting position and stretched. 'I am exhausted,' she said. She yawned and got to her feet. 'Where are you sleeping?' she asked. Marcus had taken to using the spare room on occasions recently, telling her that she needed the rest and didn't want him snoring and turning beside her. She knew in her heart it was an excuse not to have to lie beside her.

'In the spare room,' Marcus replied.

Lucie nodded and made her way to the bedroom. 'Good night,' she said. She didn't make any gesture or even turn to look at him. Doing so only invited more rejection.

There was a time when every night she would shower before bed so that she would be clean and scented for Marcus. Now she flopped into bed with the grime of the day still on her body and having barely removed her make-up and brushed her teeth.

She climbed into bed, switched off the lamp and passed out within seconds. She didn't hear Marcus come in to gaze at her in the semidarkness while she slept. He did so for at least ten minutes, not touching her, then he turned and walked away.

Back in the living area Marcus looked through the papers that Lucie had left on the table, then checked her diary. It was exactly as he had expected it to be. He went to his own briefcase and took out the travel brochures he had picked up from the agent that afternoon. He wanted to be out of the country in a few days' time. The destination wasn't really that important. He looked at a few places, marked the pages and determined to ring the agent first thing in the morning.

Janie woke up early on Saturday morning. It was only just light outside and the birdsong was loud and vibrant. She stretched in the warmth next to Andrew and rolled over carefully so as not to disturb him, to peer at the alarm clock. It was five thirty.

'Why are you awake?' Andrew murmured.

Janie rolled back and looked at him. 'Sorry, did I wake you?'

'No. It's those perishing birds.' He put his arm out. 'Come here and give me a hug,' he said. Janie moved towards him and snuggled down into his embrace. His body was warm and familiar and she relaxed under the gentle pressure of his fingers.

'It's been too long,' Andrew whispered, moving above her, 'you've been a bit preoccupied.'

Janie returned his kiss. 'I'll have to reward you for your patience,' she murmured, reaching down to caress him. Andrew moaned softly. As the light broke across the sky Janie and Andrew took pleasure in each other.

At eight, having both fallen asleep again, they woke when Katie came in and asked to go down to watch television.

Andrew sat up and reached for his dressing gown. 'Come on, Kate, I'll take you down and get you some hot chocolate. Tea, Janie?'

'Please.' Andrew left the bedroom and Janie put some pillows up against the headboard and settled down to read a magazine. Andrew came up a few minutes later with a tray of tea. 'Not *PC World* again,' he remarked.

'There's an ad here for a mail-order company and they're including a scanner and a colour printer with the *PC*, all for a thousand pounds.' She looked up. 'Not bad, eh?'

Andrew had poured the tea and was adding milk. He didn't answer. 'Andrew? Haven't you got any interest at all in updating our system?'

He came across with her tea. 'Actually, Janie, no I haven't. This is going to be your system, not ours. This is for your business. We already have a perfectly good PC for our family needs.'

Janie took her tea. 'Do you mind me spending money on a PC?'

'No, I don't mind.' Actually he did mind, he found the whole thing about Janie's investment club infuriating. These last few weeks all she had talked about was share prices and the market and how much everything was worth. They seemed to have disconnected as a couple. They had two separate worlds, and whereas Janie used to long to hear about Andrew's day, almost as stimulation for her own life, now she could hardly be bothered to ask him what he did. He got into bed next to her and took a sip of his tea. 'You've always talked of this investment club as a short-term thing,' he said, 'so I just question whether buying a new computer will really be value for money.'

'I used to think of it as short term, but now I'm not so sure. I mean, we've been bloody successful, Andrew.'

'You've been lucky,' Andrew said. He climbed out of bed and went into the bathroom. 'It's been a very good market,' he said, 'and you've had tips from one of the city's top analysts.'

He disappeared again and Janie heard him filling the basin. Why couldn't he, just for once, recognise what she had achieved and say well done? She followed him into the bathroom. 'If you don't want me to do this, then you've only got to say,' she challenged.

'Of course I want you to do it,' he replied. It was true, he did want her to have an interest, he liked her happy and successful. 'I just . . .' He broke off. He could see that there had been a void in her life and he could see that she had occupied a space that had needed to be filled. He just hoped that the space wasn't a gap in their marriage, wasn't something lacking in their life together. He said, 'I just hope it doesn't take us over.'

Janie stood behind him with her hands on his back. 'It won't,' she said. But as she said it she was already thinking about something she had read in the *FT* yesterday.

Alex had owned a brand-new BMW with a soft top for less than twenty-four hours and he was delighted. He had taken the afternoon off work on Friday and as soon as it had arrived he'd put the roof down, got in it and taken to the road. He had driven all round town, cruised down

King's Road with his stereo blaring and had gone round to five of his closest friends to show off.

All his life Alex had wanted a fast car. He had wanted to be looked at and admired and thought to have wad loads of cash and now he was. He was where he wanted to be and it felt good.

He was up at eight the next morning for an early game of tennis and was still high on excitement. He arrived at the Riverside Club in new Ellesse kit with a Prince racket worth £120 slung over his shoulder. He had revved the engine of his BMW in the car park and noticed that a young women getting into her car was staring across at him. He couldn't keep the smile off his face as he walked into the club.

'Hello, Alex!' He turned from reception to see Aiden Thornton, a colleague from work. 'Aiden! Good to see you. What are you doing over in this neck of the woods? I thought you lived in W1.'

'The girlfriend. She's got a place in Barnes. Nice car,' Aiden said. 'I saw you coming in. How long have you had it?'

'Some time,' Alex lied.

'I bet your girlfriend likes it. All women love fast cars.'

'Girlfriend?' Alex was confused.

Aiden suddenly flushed. 'Oh, sorry, the person you were with the other night? Sophie and I saw you with her in the Rat and Ferret off Sloane Square. I, erm, thought it was your girlfriend.'

'No,' Alex said. That must have been Lucie. Shit, he thought, shit, shit, shit. 'She was an old flame,' he went on. 'We met up by chance and had a drink together. Where were you hiding?'

'Oh, we didn't stop. We came in, I spotted you and was about to come over when Sophie dragged me out saying it was too crowded. Ah, Sophie.' Aiden looked relieved to see his girlfriend. He was embarrassed. He had obviously stumbled on to something indiscreet and couldn't wait to get away. 'You ready to go then?' Sophie looked puzzled. 'Alex, this is Sophie, my girlfriend. We're off to have breakfast. Sophie, this is Alex Stanton. He's a fellow broker.'

Sophie nodded. She got the hint about breakfast. Whoever this smug person in the flash tennis kit with the flash car outside was, Aiden didn't want to spend any more time with him.

'We'd better go,' she said. 'Nice to meet you, Alex.'

'Yup. Have a good weekend.' Alex watched them go, then turned with relief towards the tennis courts. He'd managed to get away with a bit of quick thinking and a clever lie. He had no idea that when they got outside Aiden said to his girlfriend, 'He's bonking someone he shouldn't. That's who he was with the other night. He got dead cagey when I asked if it was his girlfriend.'

'Looks like he's earning something he shouldn't as well,' Sophie replied, nodding towards the BMW. 'And don't try telling me that's his company car.' They walked over to Aiden's Golf GTi and climbed in. 'Because if it is, then why haven't you got one as well?'

Aiden couldn't think of an answer.

Sarah was in her track suit when Lindsay arrived on Saturday morning, but Rory was dressed and ready to go. He had his swimming bag and his packed lunch by the front door and was watching TV.

Sarah opened the door and Lindsay came in. 'Hi.' She popped her head into the sitting room. 'Morning, Rory.'

'Hello.' Rory managed to wave, smile and say hello without taking his eyes off the television.

Back in the hall Sarah said, 'Thanks, Lin, for today.'

Lindsay smiled. 'It'll do you the world of good, a day out with your friends. You were lucky to get tickets.'

Sarah led the way into the kitchen and put the kettle on. 'It's a corporate day for entertaining clients, but apparently Marcus's guests dropped out so he's asked me and Janie instead. I think his wife's coming too,' she went on. 'Coffee, Lin?'

'Please, I'd love one.' Lindsay picked up a glossy brochure on hearing aids from the kitchen table. 'What's this? New hearing aids?'

Sarah turned from the cupboard. 'Microlink. It's a miniature attachment to Rory's hearing aids that can pick up a microphone.'

Lindsay flicked through the brochure. 'They look amazing,' she said.

'Hmmm.' Sarah brought the coffees over. 'They get a lot of interference, apparently, but they might be better than the box.'

'How much?'

Sarah smiled. 'Expensive, very expensive. We've all agreed to take some money out of the investment club and I thought I might spend mine on these. If they work properly, that is.' She took a sip of her coffee. 'So, what's in store?'

'*A Bug's Life* this morning, at the Port Solent Megaplex, then sandwiches watching the boats and an afternoon on the beach at Wittering.'

'Lindsay, that's fantastic! I didn't expect you to do all that with him.'

'Any excuse for an old bird to act like a young one,' Lindsay said. 'Actually, I'm looking forward to it.' Sarah smiled and they went through to round up Rory for his day of fun.

When Lindsay and Rory had gone, Sarah went upstairs. She had been planning this time alone ever since Marcus had rung on Thursday night, and the first thing she did was to run herself a long bath, sprinkling some rosemary and sandalwood oils into it. While the bath was filling, she laid the outfit she had just bought on the bed and smiled. It was cheap, a snip in fact, and she was thrilled with it. Sarah didn't often shop and when she did it was nearly always for new jeans because her old ones had worn through the knee, or for new boots because the heel had fallen off the ones she'd used to death. But this outfit was a knee-length pink silk dress with shoe-string straps and cut on the bias. She would probably never have the opportunity to wear it again, but she couldn't resist. To go with it she had bought a pink rib-knit cardigan and pink high-heeled strappy sandals.

Sarah put on a face mask and climbed into the bath. She closed her eyes, slipped two pieces of cucumber over them and lay back to relax. A couple of minutes later she dropped the cucumber into the bath and reached for the soap. After nearly seven years of sprint showering, lying around with salad on her eyes just wasn't her thing. She was all pampered out. She gave herself a good scrub, washed the face mask off and climbed out of the bath. Pulling on her dressing gown, Sarah blow-dried her hair and painted her toe nails. She went downstairs to get on with the ironing and had whizzed through two baskets by eleven. She got ready with maximum speed and minimum of fuss, and she was ready by eleven fifteen, just as Marcus pulled up in a bright red Porsche.

As he climbed out alone, she felt a moment of panic. Where was his wife Lucie, and Janie?

Marcus was wearing a navy linen suit with brown suede brogues and carrying an enormous bunch of pink lilies, wrapped in hot pink tissue. Sarah went out to meet him and he said, 'I knew you'd be wearing pink. Here, these are for you.'

She took them, blinking nervously, and said, 'Where're the others?'

Marcus frowned. 'Others?' There was a short silence, then he said, 'Oh God, didn't I tell you? Lucie had to work and I didn't ask Janie in the end. It's just us, I'm afraid.' He looked at her. 'You don't mind, do you?'

It was a bit of a surprise, Sarah had to admit, but no, she didn't really mind. Besides, she thought, I suppose I should really think of Marcus as a friend now; I've seen enough of him these past couple of months. 'No, of course I don't mind,' she said.

'Good.' He glanced at his watch. 'If we get going straight away we can have a drink at the hotel.'

'Hotel?'

'Yes, I booked a table at the Goodwood Park Hotel for one o'clock.' He laughed momentarily. 'You look startled, Sarah. Everyone who goes to Goodwood racing has lunch or dinner at the Goodwood Park Hotel.'

Sarah felt foolish. 'Do they? Great, well, I'll put these in water and grab my bag and a scarf,' she said. She led the way inside. In the hall Sarah tied a pink paisley headscarf in front of the mirror, Audrey Hepburn style. She slipped on a pair of sunglasses, sleek and black, then turned.

'You look amazing,' Marcus said, and he meant it.

'Thank you . . .' Sarah faltered. She was so rarely complimented that it quite took her by surprise; she couldn't deny that she was flattered. 'Erm, shall we go?' she said hurriedly.

Marcus followed her out of the house and as she locked up he took her hand. 'This is for the neighbours,' he said. 'I just saw the curtain twitch to our left so we might as well give them a good show.' He led her to the car, opened the passenger door for her and she slid inside, her face burning. He jumped over the driver's door in one athletic stride and into his seat.

'Oh my God . . .' Sarah clasped her hand to her mouth and Marcus laughed. 'Come on, Sarah, today will be fun, even without the others, I promise. I rarely go out on a jolly, so we might as well enjoy it,' Marcus added.

Sarah thought, nor do I. He's right. She settled back in her seat, glanced up at the blue sky, then finally smiled. She was going to enjoy herself and why not? She had earned a bit of fun.

The entire Betts family was waiting for the lorry that chugged up the drive of Chadwick Farm at noon that Saturday. The vehicle stopped with a hiss just short of the front door and the driver climbed down.

'Mrs Betts?'

Roz stepped forward. 'That's me.'

'Delivery of one prize Jersey cow. Where d'you want her?'

'We've got the stable ready. It's round the side,' Roz replied. The driver went round to the back of the lorry and unlocked it. The whole back panel came down and Roz saw the cow, heavily in calf, shuffling and straining against her rope.

'All right, Damson,' the driver called in. He jumped up to untie her. He held onto her rope and eased her backwards. 'She's coming down,' he shouted.

Graham went to one side of the ramp, Roz to the other, and they gently steered the cow down the centre of the ramp. 'There's a good girl,' Roz said. 'Come on, we'll show you to your new home.'

Graham took the rope, the children walked alongside him and Roz followed behind. The driver walked beside Graham. They led Damson into the stable yard and he took her rope, tying her to the gatepost.

'She'll be fine in the field,' he said, 'but bring her in at night and make her comfortable.' He stroked the cow's neck and patted it. 'I'll leave you to it then,' he said finally. 'Bye, Damson.' He looked at Graham. 'Give us a hand to turn the truck round could you, mate?'

'Yup, sure.' Graham followed the driver to his lorry and guided him down the drive.

Back at the house, Roz was in the kitchen when Graham came in. 'I've put her out in the field,' she said.

'Good. How much did she cost?' Graham asked. Roz had been waiting for this. 'A thousand pounds.' She was standing behind the table, avoiding his eye. Now, looking up, she said, 'Graham, there's something I need to tell you.'

He sat and looked straight at her. 'I thought there might be.'

Roz took a breath. Up to now she hadn't said much about the investment club. It had been her secret, her own precious piece of success and she hadn't wanted to share it. It was selfish, she knew that, but after so much failure with Chadwick, she just wanted a bit of private glory before she opened up what she had done for criticism. She said, 'This investment club, it's, well . . . we've made quite a bit of profit.'

'That's good to hear.' Graham folded his arms across his chest. 'At least we've got our capital intact.'

'Yes, we've got that, and a bit more.'

'How much more?' Suddenly curious, Graham unfolded his arms and leaned forward. 'Five grand?'

'More.'

He narrowed his eyes. 'Come on, spit it out. How much.'

Roz took a deep breath. 'Over a hundred thousand pounds.'

Graham was stunned into silence. He sat for a few minutes staring into space, then he shook his head. 'You're not joking, are you?'

'No.'

Graham was still shaking his head. 'I can hardly believe it. So Damson's cheque came from your profit?'

'Yes. We all decided to take out two thousand pounds to spend.' Roz twisted her hands together. 'I had some work done on the stable; new door, replaced a bit of the roof, replaced some rotted timber and the plumber came and has put in a new boiler . . .' She looked at him and they were silent for a few moments. 'I'm sorry I didn't tell you.'

'Why didn't you?'

'I wanted to keep it to myself for a while and I . . . I didn't know what you'd say.'

'Great is what I say!' Graham stood and came round the table to her. 'Come here and give us a cuddle. Why would I say anything other than well done, love?'

Roz relaxed against his chest. 'Because you don't approve?'

He pulled back to look at her. 'No, you're right, I don't entirely approve, but you wanted to do it and you've made a success of it. How could I not be pleased for you?'

Jack Lowe had booked a table for one person at midday in the restaurant at the Goodwood Park Hotel. Not that this sort of place was usually his style, but after weeks of listening in to conversations in the pub, and the café frequented by various junior staff at the planning department, he'd finally heard something more interesting than the ins and outs of a twenty-something's love life. Two junior members of the planning department had been invited to Goodwood Races on a corporate day out. Who it was with and why Jack had yet to find out, but his guess was that it was something to do with Glover Homes.

He sat in his car at five to twelve and opened his briefcase, quickly transferring the equipment he'd brought with him into his pocket. He had a powerful tiny microphone, the size of a small button, with its own miniature recording system, in his top blazer pocket. The stuff wasn't exactly legal, but the tape he took was purely for his own private consumption. It would give him a foothold on the case—a foothold he badly needed on this job; he wasn't really getting anywhere. There was something really dodgy going down here, but how he was going to prove it he still didn't know.

Jack walked into the restaurant and checked in with the maître d'.

'A table for one,' he said. 'The name is Lowe.'

'Ah yes, sir, table four. If you'd like to follow me?'

'Lovely, but could I ask you to check something in the kitchen for me before I sit down? I've got an allergy to garlic and I wondered if there was any dish that the chef could prepare for me that would be completely free of it?'

'Of course, sir. I'll check with the chef now.'

The maître d' hurried off and Jack glanced down at the lunchtime bookings. Table eleven was booked for eight in the name of Redfern. Walking across the restaurant, Jack found table eleven and picked up the large floral display from the centre. He hooked the miniature microphone onto the stem of some foliage. He turned as the maître d' came back into the restaurant. 'These flowers are spectacular,' Jack said, holding the vase up. 'Are they the Goodwood colours?'

'No, sir, we have them done locally to match the restaurant deçor.'

'Very nice indeed.' Jack replaced the vase and looked at the maître d'. 'Table four you said?'

'Yes, sir. It's this way. The chef has said that he has an excellent fillet of wild Scottish salmon which he can grill for you, or there's a rack of lamb which, without the sauce, is garlic-free.'

'Wonderful.' Jack took his seat at table four, directly across the restaurant from table eleven; he had a good view.

He was handed a menu and a wine list and left alone. A party of eight came into the restaurant. The three women went first. Jack knew the type; all highlights and high-lift bra. He watched the group sit down, recognising Bill Redfern, the land buyer for Glover Homes, and Stan Gamley, chief planning officer for the local council. There were three others with them: the chairman of the council—nice one, Jack thought—and two junior members of the planning department, one of whom had discussed this event in the pub—thanks very much. All eight were dressed for a day at the races and it was clear as they sat down that Redfern was their host. Jack reached into his pocket of his blazer for the recording system to switch on the tape. He settled back with the menu strategically placed so that he could keep his eye on the party.

Sarah climbed out of the Porsche and wondered, as she heaved herself up with her legs sprawled apart, if that place for young ladies that taught them how to get gracefully out of sports cars was still in existence. If so, a few lessons might be a good idea. Marcus, thankfully, was looking towards the hotel and so missed the main part of the spectacle, but as they walked towards the hotel he said, 'Nice knickers, Sarah,' and she determined to stick to trousers in future.

Inside the hotel, Sarah excused herself and went to the Ladies'. She rarely bothered much with her appearance, but today she didn't feel like Sarah Greg; she felt altogether more glamorous and exciting than the woman who was a single mum and who worked in Duffields. She smiled at herself in the mirror and, opening her bag, slipped the scarf away, ran a comb through her hair and then reapplied her pink lipstick. Marcus was waiting for her in reception and stood up as she reappeared. 'Is everything pink today?' he asked, smiling at her.

She blushed, but fired back, 'No, not everything is pink. The veins on my legs are blue.'

Marcus burst out laughing and, in the restaurant, Jack Lowe turned to see who was having such a good time. He recognised Sarah immediately, took in the dress and the make-up and the wonderful high-heeled strappy shoes and thought, shit, shit, shit.

Sarah and Marcus were shown to their table, just two away from Jack.

Jack didn't know what to do. His first feeling was panic. His hands began to sweat and his face felt hot, but then he took several deep breaths and managed to calm himself. But he couldn't stop the sick, sinking feeling of embarrassment that swamped him. He tried to focus on the menu and signalled to the waiter that he wanted to order.

'Yes, hello, erm, I'd like to order the salmon please. No starter, just the grilled salmon for my main course.' Jack said all this with the menu lowered only sufficiently enough to see the waiter.

'Vegetables, sir?'

'Sorry? Oh yes, erm, peas and carrots and chips please.'

'Right, sir.' The waiter reached for the menu, but Jack held firmly on to it. There was a moment's tussle, then the waiter realised that Jack wasn't going to relinquish it and backed off. Jack cringed, then lifted the menu once again to cover his face, but just as he did so he noticed Sarah glance in his direction. From the corner of his eye he could see her look at him for a moment, then she said something to her lunch partner and Jack heard him laugh. It was too much for him. He stood and retreated into the Gents', where he leaned against the wall and put his head in his hands. 'Shit,' he said aloud. 'Why now when I'm working, and appear a sad, lonely bastard who can't find anyone to lunch with!' He banged his head against the wall. 'Shit, shit, shit.'

The door opened and he stood up straight. In the mirror he saw two men enter—Gamley was one of them—and go to the urinals. Jack headed for the cubicle, went in and locked the door.

'Jesus, 'Redfern can't half put it away.' Jack put his ear to the door. That wasn't Gamley, that was his companion. 'He's had three pints and at least half a bottle of champagne.'

'Watch yourself, son; don't get so pissed that you don't know what you're saying, all right? This is business.'

Jack sat on the toilet seat and listened.

'No chance, Stan. That Deb's been giving me the come-on all day. I don't want to waste an opportunity like that . . .'

'You listen to me, son,' Gamley said, 'Redfern pays these girls to keep the likes of you and me sweet. You make sure that you watch your back, right? Don't get yourself in over your head because Redfern'll have you if you do. Understand?'

Gamley flushed the urinal. 'Come on, let's get back. We've got what Redfern wants, but remember that he's not getting it for free.'

The men crossed to the basin to wash their hands. They left the room a minute or so later.

'Thank you, thank you, thank you,' Jack murmured. He had finally struck gold.

All he had to do now was retrieve the microphone, by saying he had dropped his tie pin on their table when he'd been looking at the flowers. Not bad for a day's work. Despite Sarah, not bad at all.

It was after five when Marcus pulled into the car park of the Wayfold Inn. He climbed out and went round to help Sarah who said, 'Thanks, but one showing of my underwear is enough. I'll get myself out.' He smiled and turned towards the garden.

'It's my round,' Sarah said from behind him. 'I'll share my winnings.'

'OK. I'll have a coke please,' Marcus said, and went through the back door of the pub into the garden and found a bench looking out at the view over the downs. A few minutes later Sarah came out carrying two glasses of coke and sat down next to him. 'Cheers!' she said. Marcus said, 'You seem to be on a bit of a winning streak. The investment club and now the races.'

'I do, don't I?' Sarah smiled. 'I must say it makes a nice change.'

'You know, while you've got it you should make the most of it.'

Sarah looked at him. 'What?'

'Your luck.' He turned to her. 'You know I think I've got a bit of a tip, picked up from Alex. It concerns a small organic food company that produces dairy products and has expanded into ready-prepared meals. They're doing incredibly well, they're undervalued and I'm pretty sure that any minute now, literally, they're going to be snapped up by one of the big food giants.'

Sarah put her drink down on the grass, hesitating before she answered. 'Pretty sure?'

Marcus smiled. 'You know what my pretty sure means by now, don't you, Sarah? I don't mention anything unless I've done my homework.'

'So you think we should invest?'

Marcus paused. 'I think,' he said, 'that you should try to raise as much money as you can and buy heavily into this stock. It's a really good opportunity and I don't often say that.'

Sarah was mentally calculating in her head how much stock they could buy with their current fund when Marcus continued, 'If you could raise seventy-five thousand pounds each then you could make enough money to retire on, Sarah.'

She looked at him. 'There's no way I could raise seventy-five thousand pounds. No way.'

Marcus shrugged. 'No, perhaps not.'

'Anyway, who said I want to retire? I like Duffields.'

Marcus suddenly laughed as Sarah had meant him to. 'Of course you do. So you could send Rory to a really good school, a small prep school say, with small classes, the sort of quality teaching that he needs . . .'

Sarah held up her hands. 'Stop! I can't raise the money, Marcus, so there's no point in talking like this.'

'No, of course you can't.'

Sarah stared out at the view but didn't really see it. Marcus had put the germ of an idea in her head and it was multiplying by the second as they sat there.

She sat in silence, then she said, 'I've got a couple of insurance policies. Can I cash them in, d'you know?'

'I think it depends on the policies. Have you got an endowment on your mortgage? You could cash that I'd have thought.' Marcus finished his drink. 'D'you want another?'

Sarah shook her head. He had hit a raw nerve and all she could think of, all she could see, was the possibility of some sort of future opening up for Rory. School was such a struggle: the big classes, the noise, the lack of scope in his learning, the microphone aid, the teasing. He wasn't unhappy, but he was hardly happy either. She didn't think he was achieving all that he could.

'Are you all right, Sarah?'

She turned, keeping her eyes averted. 'I was just thinking,' she replied, 'how wonderful it would be if Rory could go to Ledworth House. It's a small, boys' prep school with wonderful sports facilities and classes only half the size of Wynchcombe Primary. We looked at it, Nick and I, but after Nick left there was never any possibility of . . .' She broke off. There had not been any possibility of much really, after Nick left. She bit her lip and looked up at Marcus again. 'If we could raise the money,' she asked, 'when would be the best time to invest?'

'As soon as possible, while the share price is low.'

'I must ring Janie,' Sarah said, suddenly excited. 'I'm sure she'll . . .'

Marcus had placed his hand on her arm and she looked down at it.

'Janie doesn't know about us, does she?'

Sarah was wary. 'What about us? What is there to know?'

'That we meet up quite a bit, enjoy each other's company . . .' He took his hand away. 'No, you're right, what is there to know?'

'No, I've never told her anything, not that I think there's anything to hide . . .' Sarah felt it was important to say that. 'It's more that I'm not sure how she'd feel about it, knowing Lucie as she does.'

'No, you're right. Thanks.' There was another silence, then he glanced at his watch and said, 'It's nearly six you know, we ought to get going.'

'My God, is it?' Sarah picked up her glass and finished the coke. 'I will have to talk to Janie,' she said, as they made their way back to the car.

'Of course. But it's your idea, OK?'

She smiled. Everything he had ever mentioned to her was 'her idea'. She supposed it was just his modesty.

'OK,' she said, and they drove home in silence, Sarah with her dream and Marcus with the net to catch it in.

As soon as she finished work on Monday, Sarah hurried home and dialled Alex's mobile number. She got the message service. She asked Alex to send her everything he had on Wye Valley Organic Foods and call her. Then she got on with the daily chores and went to school to collect Rory. In the playground she saw Roz, who handed over a clear plastic folder filled with print-outs from the computer. Sarah had asked her to look at the organic food company on the internet. 'Looks interesting,' she remarked. 'Can't wait to hear what it's all about.'

'It is and you will,' Sarah replied. As she was leaving, she ran into Janie and said, 'I've had an idea, a hunch about an organic food company. I think it's a good one but we need to talk it through tomorrow.'

'Great. What time d'you want us?'

'Eight? Eight thirty?'

'See you then.' Janie went on to collect Katie, who had invited another little girl for tea, and Sarah watched her for a moment, feeling envious. She rarely did teas; what with homework and extra lessons and just keeping Rory's head above water, there didn't seem to be any time left for enjoying themselves. She sighed and took hold of Rory's hand. What she wouldn't have given for a normal night at home, with Rory playing outside with a friend and her cooking chicken nuggets and chips.

On Monday evening, Alex left work early. He slipped the photocopies of all the latest reports on Wye Valley Organic Foods, of which there were only two, into an envelope and sent it first class, along with a copy of his notes. He was tired, still drained from a rather extravagant and wild weekend. The last thing he wanted to do was see Lucie, but she had requested the meeting. She was, he felt, getting steadily more depressed by the state of her marriage.

At the wine bar she was already waiting. When she saw him she waved and hurriedly stuffed her papers into her briefcase. 'Hi.'

He went across and smiled at her.

'I'll get a bottle of wine, shall I?'

Lucie glanced at her watch. 'Not for me. I'll only have one glass, I've got to work tonight.'

Alex felt thwarted; he had expected Lucie to want to come back to his flat as she so often did now. 'Two glasses then,' he said and went across to the bar.

Bringing them back, he sat down and took a gulp of his wine.

'What's up?' he asked, 'You sounded a bit low earlier.'

'Work. I'm just up to my eyes in it.'

'Lucie, you are always up to your eyes in it. I don't know how many times I've heard that refrain.'

'You're right, of course I am, but recently I've started to feel, oh, I don't know, sort of isolated by it. As if I'm just on my own struggling with it.' She sighed.

'D'you want to talk about it?'

'Can't,' she said, 'it's a bid situation, or it will be shortly.'

'So what do you want me to do about it?' Alex asked. He tried to keep the irritation he felt out of his voice, but there was something so annoying about someone who was down when he was on the up.

'I suppose I just wanted a bit of company,' Lucie said.

'And a whinge,' Alex added.

She looked at him. 'Does that bother you?' She took a sip of wine. 'I thought that was all part of the relationship thing—sharing problems, bemoaning one's lot, someone to rely on for comfort.'

Alex said, 'This is an affair, Lucie, not a full-blown relationship.'

Lucie took a sharp intake of breath and looked away. Stupid, stupid, stupid, she thought, of course it's only an affair, you never wanted more.

Alex continued to wrestle with his conscience. He wasn't unkind by nature, but irritation had got the better of him and Lucie's sorrow was more irksome than distressing. He felt very little sympathy.

'Don't take it all so seriously,' he said at last.

'No, you're right. I should lighten up.' She stood. 'I must go to the loo and then I've got to get going, I'm afraid.'

Alex winced. He'd been too harsh on her, but there was no way of retracting his words so he promptly dismissed his fleeting regret. As Lucie moved off he took a ten-pound note out of his wallet to pay for the drinks and went to stand up. As he did so he dropped the note and bent to pick it up again. He saw Lucie's open briefcase, and, simply unable to resist the temptation, pulled several files out of her case. He opened the top file, saw the title and felt the blood rush to his face. Glancing up to check he was out of sight, he flicked through the rest of it. He read the various headings, then dropped the file back into Lucie's case. He picked up the briefcase, and then crossed to the bar to pay for the drinks. Lucie appeared while he was waiting for his change and said, 'I'll be off then.'

'OK.' Alex reached for her hand and gave it a squeeze. As a general rule they never kissed in public, it was too risky. 'I'll see you?'

She nodded. 'Ring me,' she replied. Then she picked up her briefcase, smiled, and disappeared out of the wine bar. Alex stood where he was. The blood was pulsing round his body to his brain and he was thinking more clearly than he had done all day. He ordered himself another drink and went to sit down in the corner. He took out his Filofax and started to work through some figures. He sat there alone for over an hour, absorbed in his work. Then he stood up, put some money for the wine on the table and left the bar. Outside, he took out his phone, brought Sarah's number up on to the screen and pressed dial.

On the way to the tube station, Lucie dialled home. Marcus answered straight away.

'Hi, it's me. I've got to work late, I'm afraid, might be very late. It looks like this deal's going through in the next week.'

Marcus flipped the top off his beer on the edge of the granite work top in the kitchen area. 'The Wye Valley Foods one?'

'Marcus!' Lucie still occasionally confided some of her work problems to Marcus, but only in the security of their own home.

'Sorry. What time will you be in then?' he asked. Not that he was interested, he would be in bed when she got home.

'I've no idea. We might be going into a bid situation, so who knows?'

'I won't wait up.'

'No, of course not. See you in the morning then.'

Lucie rang off and carried on walking to the tube. How could a woman with two men in her life feel so very alone, she wondered, as she passed the barrier and headed down to the trains.

In the house in Notting Hill, Marcus drank his beer, then dialled the travel agent. He gave his booking reference for a three-week holiday in Capri and changed the travel date. He would leave on Wednesday night. He was on top of things at work—a couple of extra days' holiday wouldn't make any difference. He hung up, having given his credit card details in order to pay extra for the flights, and went into the bedroom to pack.

Alex Stanton was late on Tuesday night, half an hour late, but Sarah didn't want to start the meeting before he arrived. So she served wine, the women chatted and the sense of expectation escalated.

When he had arrived—offering no excuse for his lateness—they got straight down to business. Sarah talked about Wye Valley Organic Foods, outlined the facts and the figures, and Alex added certain things that he'd gleaned over the past twenty-four hours. He had been working hard and he'd found every scrap of information there was to be had about them and had analysed the entire operation. He was certain, after hours spent working on the Wye Valley project, that the whole proposal stood up.

'So why invest such a large sum of money?' Roz eventually asked, after an hour of discussion. 'I mean, I get the point that it looks like a very good opportunity, but the words "looks like" still prefix the "good opportunity", don't they? I mean, why not stick with a percentage of what we've already made and see what happens?'

Janie nodded. 'We've done incredibly well so far, why take unnecessary risks?'

'Because I don't think this is an unnecessary risk. I think this is as sure as it can get,' replied Alex, a little impatiently.

Roz narrowed her eyes. 'Do you know something that you're not supposed to, Alex?'

'What on earth do you mean?'

Roz shrugged. 'Well, insider trading or whatever that phrase is.'

'Good Lord, no!' Alex was aghast. 'I'm staggered that you could even suggest it. I'm a broker, I have no connection with the company whatsoever.' He was affronted and let his offence show.

'I'm sorry,' Roz said, 'but you never know . . .'

'As far as I'm concerned,' Sarah said, digging the corkscrew in another bottle of wine and twisting, 'Wye Valley is virtually out on its own in the market in terms of value and product line, not to mention management strength, and it's sitting there just saying "buy me". There's been at least three articles about how Grand Met and Unilever are both vying for top position in the food market and neither have a good organic outlet on board, and so we do as we've always done.' She poured the wine. 'We make a decision based on what we know.'

'But this isn't three thousand pounds, Sarah, this is . . .' Janie looked at her. 'How much did you say you want to invest?'

'We each need to put in seventy-five thousand pounds,' Sarah said, 'and Alex wants to put in a hundred and fifty thousand. That way we'll have roughly up to two and a half per cent of the company, and then our vote is worth having.'

'A small percentage of the company in one shareholder's hands can definitely have an effect on the price in a bid situation. It can only work to our advantage, plus when the company is sold, the bigger the investment the bigger the return.' Alex looked round the group. 'It's the chance to make some serious money.'

Everyone was silent, each locked in their own thoughts. After several minutes, Alex said, 'I don't think there's anything else I can tell you to convince you except that I intend to invest as much money as I've got in this stock, whether you decide to go ahead or not.' He shrugged, then stood up, 'I'd better go, Sarah. I'll leave everything with you and if you have any questions call me.'

Sarah saw him out and waved as he drove off. Then she went back to Roz and Janie.

'What d'you think?' she asked, sitting down.

'It's a hell of a lot of money,' Roz said. 'We can net thirty-one thousand pounds each from what we've made so far, but how are you going to get the extra forty-four thousand?'

'I'm going to cash in my endowment policy,' Sarah replied. Both Janie and Roz stared at her. 'I'll get about two-thirds of its value back, which is roughly forty-eight thousand. I'm going to invest the lot in Wye Valley.' Roz and Janie continued to stare at her, but neither of them said a word.

'You think I'm mad, don't you? Well, I probably am mad, but I've seen a way forward for Rory and me; I've seen a chance to change Rory's life. Not just new hearing aids but a small private school where he can flourish, not simply survive. This for me is about changing our life. It's an opportunity to realise a dream, and I'm not going to let it pass me by. I've calculated the risk and I'm prepared to take it.'

Janie glanced round at Sarah's house, at the worn-out throw over the sofa, the threadbare carpet. She looked at the microphone aid on the coffee table, on top of a book about speech therapy. Finally she looked at Sarah, at the face that had never really shown the signs of distress or loneliness or struggle that she must have felt, and Janie thought, of course you'll take the risk and so would I in your shoes. She said, 'If I can raise the money, Sarah, I'll back you.' She had her own reasons, her own dream, not as noble as Sarah's but valid to her none the less. She wanted to prove to herself, to Andrew, that she could do it, that she could make money and really achieve something. She wanted to refill that empty space that had begun to open up again in her life, despite the investment club. Looking across, she asked, 'What about you, Roz?'

Roz shook her head. 'I don't know,' she answered. What could she do with the sort of money Sarah was sure they would make? What couldn't she do? It would mean finally getting the farm on its feet; it would mean comfort and no worry. It could even mean buying the Gordens' land. She said, 'I think it sounds amazing, but I can't see where I'm going to get my hands on that sort of cash. I mean, we've got investments, Graham and I, but they're for our retirement . . .' Her voice trailed away as she thought it through. 'I could ask the bank I suppose . . .' She bit on her lip. 'Please,' she said, then, 'would it be all right if we went over the whole Wye Valley thing again? It's just that I want to be absolutely clear on it all before I go home and talk to Graham.'

Sarah smiled. Her talking to Graham meant she was interested. Talking to Graham meant there was a chance that it might happen.

The following morning Sarah went to her bank. She spoke to their financial adviser, a young man in a sharp suit who looked as if he was earning too much commission. He advised her not to cash her endowment policy in; he suggested that if she offered the policy as security to the bank then they would lend her seventy-five per cent of the policy's value. That way she would keep the policy going, and she would also have her money.

'And how long will it take?' Sarah asked, 'I was hoping for the money by the end of the week.'

'It should only take a couple of days,' the young man answered.

This, Sarah considered, was good advice. The young man in the sharp suit obviously earned his commission. She left the bank excited and optimistic. After so many years of disappointment, could things really make a turn for the better, just like that? She walked on to Duffields.

'Mrs Greg, you are late,' the supervisor said. Sarah apologised and explained that she had asked permission yesterday to come in half an hour late this morning.

'Well, you can stay half an hour extra this afternoon,' the supervisor remarked, 'to make up the time.'

'Of course,' Sarah murmured. No, perhaps things couldn't really change just like that. Perhaps that was asking a bit too much.

Janie had been in touch with Lloyds Bank in Chichester. Andrew and Janie shared a savings account there. Made up primarily of a lump sum that Janie's aunt had left her in her will, and some money that Andrew had been given by his father. It was untouchable except in an emergency; it was there as a safety net and in an account with an instant withdrawal facility, enabling Janie to take money out without Andrew's signature.

This she arranged to do. She asked for a banker's draft for the sum of £45,0000, to be made up in the name of the broking house that Alex Stanton worked for, and told them she would pick it up the next morning.

The process of securing funds for Roz was not quite as easy. Every penny of profit that Graham had scraped out of his antiques business went into their personal equity plans. They were by way of a pension for them and it was the only money they had saved up. Not an easy decision then to cash them in.

'I don't agree with it,' Graham had told her. 'You know my views, Roz, it's tantamount to gambling and I don't like it.'

Roz had outlined all the points that Sarah had put to her but still Graham wouldn't budge. It was, he felt, taking things too far. Roz had made some money, now it was time to call it quits. He wasn't wooed by large sums of promised profit. This was money that he had slogged for, driving up and down the country in the van. The PEPs were Graham's only insurance against having to rely on the pathetic state pension.

'It's the principle,' Graham told her at three in the morning, when the argument had been round the block and back again. 'I am not a gambling man.' But Roz was an expert at turning the tide of opinion and he felt himself being swept away by the undercurrent.

'You took a chance on Chadwick Farm though,' Roz countered, the force of her want and need lifting him up and towards her. It was, he supposed, part of loving her. He wasn't a weak man; quite the contrary, he'd stood his ground on many, many occasions in the past. Finally he sighed and said, 'Life is all about striving to achieve what we want to, Roz. More often than not we don't achieve even half of what we'd hoped to and what we do achieve turns out to be nowhere as easy as we thought it would be. That's the case with Chadwick Farm; it's not lived up to expectations at all, it's been bloody hard work but it was what we wanted to achieve and we've done it.'

Roz turned to him. 'I don't get your point,' she said sharply.

'My point,' he said wearily, 'is that if you really want to do this investment thing then go ahead, if you really think that's the way to go, but don't expect it to be a doddle. It might not—in fact probably won't—live up to your hopes for it.'

Roz stared at him. 'Are you saying that I have your blessing?'

He shook his head. 'No, I'm saying that it's up to you. Use the money from the PEPs if you really have to. I'll leave the decision to you.'

'That's not fair.'

He shrugged and turned round to remove one of the pillows and plump up the one underneath ready for sleep.

Roz reached over and turned off the lamp. She lay in the dark and watched the shapes in the room come into focus as the light from a full moon shone through the gap in the curtains. And as the clock crept towards the dawn of a new day, she knew that she would phone the bank and sell the PEPs and buy into Wye Valley Foods. Because life was arbitrary, she knew that she would take any opportunity offered to her, that she would take the risk.

The investment club met in the school playground, while the children ran around, and collectively decided to make the purchase of shares in Wye Valley Organic Foods. They had all raised the money, a feat in itself and a good omen. Sarah would ring Alex and ask him to purchase the stock. The deed was done.

They all shook hands and went their separate ways, but they were all headed, metaphorically speaking, forward and upward. They were chasing the dream and the catcher was just a phone call away.

Marcus called Lucie at the office. He left a message for her as she was in a meeting and five minutes later she called back.

'You told my secretary it was urgent,' she said. 'Is anything wrong?'

'No, but I'm leaving in a few minutes for the airport.'

'Airport?' Lucie's mind went blank. 'Why?'

'I'm taking a break, Lucie. I need some time away.'

There was a silence and Lucie sat still in her chair. She couldn't even utter a word.

'I've left everything on in the house, I suppose you'll be going home?'

'Where else would I be going?' Lucie managed to say.

Marcus glanced at his watch. 'I'd better go,' he said, 'my taxi will be here in a few minutes.'

Lucie tried to swallow down months of sadness and loneliness, months of mistakes and deception and words that should have been said and never had been, but the lump in her throat was impossible to budge and her eyes filled.

'I'll see you when I get back,' Marcus said.

'Yes.' That was all she could answer. She put the phone down, walked down to the Ladies'. Once there, she locked herself in a cubicle and began to cry.

Marcus, on the other side of the City, climbed into his taxi for Heathrow. The deed was done. The dream catcher had a job to do; he didn't need any more help from Marcus.

Chapter Seven

JACK LOWE SAT READING the paper in his car, which was parked outside the district council offices in Hersley. Frequent glances in the direction of the building made sure that no one drove out without him noticing. From the taped conversation he'd picked up at the lunch table at Goodwood he knew that Gamley was off for the weekend. He was waiting to find out where to.

Another thing that Jack was conscious of was a bloke with a newspaper standing across the road outside the station, supposedly reading. A bloke who hadn't taken his eyes off Jack since he'd arrived. Not that he looked particularly suspicious, more that he didn't really fit.

Jack had a nose for things that didn't really fit; like Gamley's relationship with Redfern—nothing obvious but odd nevertheless. He'd picked up on that one through watching and listening, staking out the pub they all used, and making the connection between the number of times Gamley was the planning officer for Glover Homes. But despite feeling absolutely sure there was something going on, Jack just couldn't pin it down. There was nothing else to connect the two men together; no showy gifts, no conspicuous spending from Gamley or from anyone else in planning.

So here he was, hoping that Gamley's weekend away might offer up some kind of clue, and wondering why the hell the bloke in the beige mac kept looking over at his car. Jack checked the rearview mirror. Yup, he thought, still there, still watching me.

Across the road, Gamley came out of the main entrance of the building and walked across to his car. Jack turned on his engine, shifted into gear and waited. As Gamley drove out of the car park, Jack pulled out. He was three cars behind Gamley and heading on the A264 towards Crawley. Gatwick, Jack thought.

At the North Terminal, Jack followed Gamley into the short-term car park. They went up to level three where Gamley parked. Jack, turning three rows away, did the same. He waited, watched Gamley get out, take a small case from the boot and walk towards the lifts for departures. Jack climbed out and ran for the stairs. He got to the top after a short, sharp sprint, just as the lift doors opened. Gamley went towards the BA desk for the Channel Islands. Jack hovered, just out of sight.

Gamley checked in. He greeted the ground staff, who obviously knew him, handed over his suitcase and took his boarding pass. The flight was for Guernsey and, by the look of the chat going on at the desk, it was a flight that Gamley took regularly.

'Halfway there,' Jack murmured under his breath, and as he turned he walked smack into someone. 'Shit!' he exploded. He stared up at the bloke in the beige mac, who took one look at him and turned on his heel, running across the concourse.

'Hey!' Jack called after him. 'Oi! You!' He sprinted after him. The bloke headed for the car park. Jack sprinted up to level three and saw the bloke climbing into a 2CV. He ran across and threw himself onto the bonnet of the car. The bloke inside, instead of shifting gear and accelerating off as Jack had expected him to, threw his hands up over his face and shouted, 'All right, all right . . . don't hurt me, please.'

Jack climbed off the car, opened the car door and said, 'What the hell is going on? Why are you following me?'

The bloke climbed out and stood with his head hung. He couldn't have been more than twenty, twenty-two at the most.

'Who are you?' Jack demanded. 'And why are you following me?'

The bloke lifted his eyes, but not his head. He had a nasty bout of acne on his forehead, Jack noticed. 'My name's Rupert Sayer, I work for the *West Sussex Gazette*, freelance. I'm an undercover journalist.'

'A journalist?' Jack's mouth fell open. He stared at him. 'Undercover? What the hell do you mean, undercover? What's going on?'

Lifting his head, Rupert dug his hands in his pockets. Now he knew that he wasn't going to be punched, his natural confidence—arrogance the editor called it—expanded to its normal proportions. 'I'm onto a story, something big, and I reckoned you might be involved.'

'What story?' Jack asked.

Rupert eyed Jack, then said, 'Why are you following Gamley? Is he a mate of yours?'

'I'm a private investigator,' Jack answered. 'I'm on a case.'

Rupert was impressed, as Jack had meant him to be.

'Bloody hell,' he murmured. 'What sort of case?'

'I'm not at liberty to say,' Jack replied.

Rupert looked at him. 'Dodgy town planning?' he said. 'Carving up green belt land for no reason I can see other than greasing Gamley's palm?' He narrowed his eyes. 'You're onto him, aren't you?'

Jack didn't answer. Rupert Sayer could be anybody. He shook his head. 'I've got no idea what you're on about,' he said. 'Sorry, mate, but you're way off the mark.'

Rupert stood straight. He might have been young and naive but he wasn't stupid. 'Whatever you say,' he remarked. He took out a business card. 'Give us a ring some time. I've got a wad of stuff on Gamley.'

Jack took the card. He noticed that it didn't have any mention of the paper on it. 'Are you working independently or with the paper on this one?' he asked.

'Independently, actually. I don't want to be tied in to a local rag when this one hits the fan.' The truth was he didn't have enough of a story to take it to the paper. It was mostly a hunch and a few coincidences.

'Well, you watch your back, Rupert Sayer,' Jack said and walked off towards his car.

Jack pulled into the long drive of Chadwick Farm and stopped in front of the house. He was here for two reasons: to finish a gardening job he'd started several evenings ago and to update Roz and Graham on the Gamley case. He climbed out of the car and went through the gate into the courtyard at the side of the house, formerly the bit of paving where the bins were kept. He stamped his foot down hard on the brick terrace he'd laid two days ago to check it was solid, and called out to Roz.

Minutes later Roz appeared, drying her hands on a towel.

'Hello, Jack! I'll put the kettle on, shall I?'

Jack smiled. Every situation in this house seemed to demand that someone put the kettle on. 'Thanks, Roz, but I'll get on if you don't mind. What time's Graham back?'

'Depending on the traffic, I'd say about six-ish, hopefully.'

'Good, that gives me plenty of time.' He began rolling his sleeves up as he headed back out to the car.

Inside the boot he had more plants than he'd been paid for, but then that was his birthday present to Graham. He was creating a courtyard garden for Graham during the three days he was away on a buying trip to Newcastle. It was his way of saying thanks, not only for the case—something decent to work on at last—but also for the numerous pints down the pub, the kitchen suppers, the first overtures of friendship that he'd had since he moved down almost a year ago. Jack heaved out six bags of compost, then the plants, and went to work.

Sarah received the call from Alex mid-morning at Duffields. He had bought 459,000 shares in Wye Valley Organic Foods, just as the price slipped from fifty-one pence a share to forty-nine. He had invested the total sum of £375,000 which was big enough for a private client broker to feel slightly uneasy about. It was all legit, though, the Housewife Trust and his own involvement in it. All he had to do now was wait. But as easy as it sounded, that was actually the most difficult thing to do.

Sarah had been excited and filled with optimism until Alex had rung, then the full reality of her decision hit her and she had to sit down. She was almost paralysed with anxiety. She had taken out a £40,000 loan from the bank and invested it in the stock market on a tip, a whim. Was she completely mad? What if the stock dropped? What if she lost the whole lot? It would ruin her life and Rory's. She dropped her head in her hands and closed her eyes.

'Oh God,' she murmured, 'oh God.' A customer appeared and she immediately stood up. 'Can I help you?' she asked. She smiled at the woman returning a bunch of tulips with three of the heads broken, and took the attitude she had always taken. It's bloody done, she thought, and taking the flowers she just got on with it.

Sarah decided to go and see Roz on the way to school to pick up Rory. She had to pass Chadwick Farm anyway, so she stopped and called into tell her that the deal was done.

Pulling up outside the house, Sarah parked next to the estate car already there and went round by the bins to the back door. Only it wasn't the bins any more; it was a small brick terrace filled with flowering terracotta pots and a beautiful old bench. She wondered for a moment if she was in the wrong house—knowing Roz's usual clutter and mess—and called out, 'Roz? Hello, Roz? Is anyone in?'

'Hello!' Roz appeared with a teapot in her hands and beamed. 'Sarah! What a nice surprise. Come on in. We're going to have tea in our new courtyard.'

Sarah said, 'Roz, it is absolutely beautiful. Where on earth did you find the time to do all this?'

'I didn't,' Roz answered, leading the way into the kitchen, 'Jack did it.' Jack stood up. Roz continued, 'Jack Lowe, this is Sarah Greg; Sarah, Jack.'

Sarah's smile froze on her face and there was a short, tense silence, then Jack said, 'Sarah and I have met actually, Roz, once or twice in Duffields.'

'Have you?' Roz smiled. 'You never told me, Sarah! She's a bit of a dark horse you know, Jack, she's difficult to pin down is our Sarah . . .'

'I know,' Jack said. The painful memory of that night waiting alone in the pub came back to him.

Sarah forced herself to smile. You never rang, she thought, you never rang to see if I was all right and find out why I hadn't turned up. I could have had an accident. She eyed him. I bet you weren't even there!

'You'll have tea, won't you, Sarah?' Roz asked.

'I can't stop,' Sarah said, 'really I can't. I just called in to tell you that Alex bought the stock this morning.'

'Blimey,' Roz said. She held the teapot full of boiling water in her hands and didn't even notice the heat. She stared at Sarah, then suddenly said, 'Ouch! That's hot!' and plonked the teapot down on the worktop.

'Shall I pour the tea?' Jack interrupted. He took the teapot over to the table. Then he turned to Sarah and, briefly meeting her eye, said, 'Stay for tea, we have to christen the courtyard.'

'I can't, really, I've got to get to school to collect Rory.' She didn't want to have tea with this man—it was as much as she could do to be civil to him—although why she was so angry she didn't quite know.

'Please stay,' Roz went on. 'I'll give Janie a quick buzz and ask her to collect Rory as well as Justin and Katie.' She didn't want Sarah to go, she didn't want to be left alone to think about the enormous risk she had just taken. The reality of it was just too daunting. 'Come on, Sarah, I've made a cake. Please stay.'

Sarah was caught. 'OK. I mean, thanks, I'd love to.'

'I'll ring Janie then,' Roz said. She disappeared out of the kitchen and Sarah was left alone with Jack. 'Tea?' he asked.

'Yes, thanks.'

He poured Sarah a mug of tea and added milk. 'I didn't know you knew Roz and Graham,' Jack said, to fill the silence.

'Yes,' Sarah replied, 'Rory is in Justin's class.'

'School, of course.' Jack picked up his own tea and took a sip. Both he and Sarah made a conscious effort not to look at each other. This can't continue, they both thought separately, it's painful.

Jack looked up at her suddenly. 'That night at the pub,' he blurted. He had to clear the air. He couldn't leave it, he was too honest, too open for that. 'The night we were supposed to meet.'

He's going to apologise for not turning up, Sarah thought with panic. He thinks I'm pathetic, he imagines that I was sitting alone in the pub waiting for him to arrive. Oh God. She said, 'Forget it, it should never have happened.'

Jack blinked. He stared at her and she said again, 'Forget it. I have.'

Roz reappeared and said, 'I caught Janie just as she got to school. Shall we go outside?'

Sarah made to move but Jack stood stunned for a few seconds. Is she for real? he thought. Not a word of regret, not a hint of remorse. Hell, she couldn't give a stuff. He decided he just had to get out of there.

'Roz,' he said, walking outside, 'sorry, but I've got to go. I've just realised the time and I've got to get back to the office.'

'But Jack, I—' He headed towards the gate before she could finish.

'Thanks for the tea. Wish Graham happy birthday for me.'

As he drove off, Roz frowned. 'What on earth was all that about?' Sarah shrugged and studiously avoided her eye. 'Oh well.' She picked up her tea. 'Just us then,' she said.

Alex was talking to a client on the phone when the announcement flashed up on the screen. Wye Valley Organic Foods were subject to a take-over bid from Unilever. He stopped listening and stared at it. His client sensed that he wasn't being listened to and stopped talking. Alex watched the share price of Wye Valley rise six pence and then the client said, 'Hello? Alex? Are you still there?'

Alex shook himself. 'Oh God, yes, sorry, David, I was watching some movement in the market.' With great difficulty he listened to the rest of what his client had to say then made his suggestions. To his relief the client said he'd think it over and call back. Alex hung up, then rang Sarah. She was out. He tried Janie; she too was out, but her answer phone gave out her mobile number so he rang that.

In the courtyard at Chadwick Farm, no one took much notice of Janie's mobile going off in her handbag. She answered it, walking round to the front of the house to get a better signal, then returned to the tea party. Roz and Sarah were talking, Kitty and Oliver were washing up in a big plastic bucket, the older children were screeching and yelling with delight, and into all this walked Janie, her face white.

Roz looked up. 'What's up?'

'That was Alex,' Janie said. She stared at them. 'Unilever just made a bid for Wye Valley. The share price is on the up.'

Roz let out a yell. 'I don't believe it! It's happened, it's bloody happened, Sarah!' Sarah put her hands up to her face. The relief, coupled with excitement, overwhelmed her. She wiped her face on the back of her hands. She smiled, then she caught Roz's eye and the smile widened.

Janie stood straight. 'A drink,' she said, 'we need a drink.'

Sarah looked at her watch. 'It's four thirty, Janie.'

'Then we're only an hour and a half off six o'clock. Roz? What have you got in your fridge?'

'Some rather tired-looking vegetables, butter, cheese, left-over baked beans. She smiled. 'But I've got a bottle of red in the cupboard.'

'Then fetch it,' Janie said, 'at once.'

Sarah looked at Janie. 'Do you really think it's going to work?'

Janie nodded. 'I do,' she said. 'Yes, I do.'

At four forty-five that afternoon, in the surveillance unit at the Stock Exchange, a young woman called Janice Stimpson picked up an alert signal on her screen. Janice had been pensioned out of the Metropolitan Police three years ago with a back injury sustained whilst on duty. She had an ample income and was able to devote her time to gardening and cooking, or looking after her elderly mother. But Janice wanted to work. She had looked hard for the right sort of job, nothing too physical but something that would be an outlet for the strong sense of justice she had. A friend had mentioned that the Stock Exchange were recruiting people to train for their computer surveillance system, IMAS, for sniffing out financial fraud. Janice went for an interview and knew she had found her mission.

In the past two years she had been assigned to twenty special cases, one of which had made it to prosecution—a rare occurrence. Once she got her hands on a case she couldn't rest until she had done her all. She was punctual, diligent and meticulous. She was also not very well liked. She was too good, and being too good did nothing to inspire friendship. So Janice worked long and hard. She spent hours in front of the screen and her particular speciality was insider trading.

She and a large team of people were trained to watch the sophisticated monitors that built up a profile on every company traded on the Stock Exchange. Any unusual share dealings came up as an alert. That afternoon, Janice had been watching the monitor for Wye Valley Organic Foods when the alert sounded. Someone had bought just under three per cent of the shares only hours before the announcement of a take-over bid. It may have been a lucky coincidence, or it may have been planned. Whatever it was, Janice Stimpson would find out.

She looked up the purchaser, a nominee company called the Housewife Trust, and went immediately to see her supervisor.

Knocking lightly on his open door, she put her head round it and said, 'I think I've got something on Wye Valley Organic Foods.'

The supervisor stopped what he was doing. He didn't like Janice any more than the rest of the team did, but since she'd joined them they had won three awards for best performance and now he gave her his attention whenever she needed it.

She placed a print-out on the desk and he looked at it. 'Two point eight per cent of the shares,' she said, 'bought this morning. Either someone likes organic yoghurts a lot and they were born lucky or there's something odd about this one.'

The supervisor smiled. 'Look into it then, Janice,' he said.

'Thanks,' she said, flashing a rare smile back at him. 'I will.'

CHAPTER EIGHT

JACK WALKED INTO THE OFFICE early on Saturday morning and sat down at his desk. They sometimes worked a half-day at the weekend to catch up with the paperwork. He'd hardly slept, drunk too much wine, and the net result was a crummy hangover and a nagging feeling of failure. Sarah Greg, he thought. Nice smile, pretty, warm and soft, but not a pushover. A woman who gets on with life, a woman he had been immediately attracted to. And he'd made a complete asshole of himself. In fact, she held him in such low regard that she wanted to forget ever having made an arrangement with him. Jack put his head in his hands and closed his eyes.

'All right, Jack?'

He lifted his head. 'Oh, yeah, sorry, Dodi, I didn't hear you come in.' He busied himself by shuffling papers. Dodi crossed the room and sat on the edge of his desk. 'D'you mind?' he said, tugging an invoice out from under her bottom.

'What's up?' she asked, ignoring his pique. 'What did you get on Gamley? Any leads?'

'Ah.' Jack sat back. 'Possible leads, I think. He was off to Guernsey for the weekend and, by the look of it, it's a trip he does pretty regularly.'

Dodi chewed the end of a pen. 'Guernsey. Tax-free, right? So you think he's got accounts there and is stuffing money away?'

'Maybe.'

'How do we find out?'

'I don't know at the moment, but I'll get onto it.' He looked at her. 'There's got to be something, Dodi. There's got to be some financial connection with Redfern, money under the table, I'm convinced of it.'

'But that's not the problem, right?' Dodi narrowed her eyes and looked at him. 'There's more. Come on, spit it out.'

'If only I could.'

'Whoever she is, Jack, she isn't worth it.'

'No, perhaps you're right.' He had tried telling himself as much last night. A night in front of the footy, nice bottle of plonk, a take-away pizza waiting to be eaten. What more could a man want? Why spoil all that for a woman? But there was something about Sarah, something that he connected with. 'I'll forget her,' he said. 'Delete her file from the great computer that is my brain and move on.'

Dodi suddenly laughed. 'Now I know you're joking. Your brain a computer? Ha!' She headed over to her own desk still chuckling.

Janice Stimpson was also working on a Saturday morning but she had no plans to take a half-day. She didn't intend to move from the screen. She was onto something here and she was going to find out what.

The first thing she did was to look up all the trades in the name of the Housewife Trust. That took nearly five hours because once she had the name of the stock, she then had to build up a profile of it to see if there was anything unusual about the dealings. For the five dot com companies that the trust had invested in there was a good deal of shrewd purchase and luck involved. All five stocks had performed outstandingly well. All five were absolutely normal in their profiles and there was nothing that pointed to fraud. Then, after a sandwich and a walk around the park, Janice uncovered her first small irregularity. The Housewife Trust had bought 16,000 shares in Sarasota plc back in April, just before the announcement that it was subject to a take-over bid. The shares were purchased and sold within a couple of weeks. The share price during that time had risen rapidly.

Janice sat back and stared at the screen. Twice then, twice the company had invested in a stock that was subject to a bid, twice they had made a substantial profit. Janice decided to look through all the bid announcements on the Stock Exchange over the past three months. It took half an hour and by the end of it she had matched up two other incidences of the trust dealing in shares before an announcement.

The pattern of dealing was well-spaced and the rise in IT stocks had camouflaged things very nicely. But Janice was certain there was something going on here. Insider trading, the penalty for which, if convicted, was seven years inside. She went back to her desk and began to pack her things away. She would find out who and how and why.

Stan Gamley was on his knees with his pelvis rammed up against the large, white, naked bottom of a lady he had met at dinner; a forty-something divorcee who was on her own for a weekend break in Guernsey who had insisted on coming up to his room to see the view. The moment she'd sat on the edge of the bed and unfastened her blouse, he'd known she was up for it. 'Oh, it's hot up here, Stan,' she'd said, reclining on the pillows and opening her blouse to let the air get to her chest. 'I think you should take some of those clothes off and get yourself more comfortable.'

Of course he'd had to perform, it would have been rude not to. Stan had stripped down to his socks and joined Brenda on the bed.

Brenda moaned and Stan speeded up the rhythm—as much as he could physically manage—but he was having trouble keeping it up. He had the faint burn of indigestion in his chest and could feel a trickle of sweat running down the side of his face. He concentrated hard, and began to pick up momentum again. He started to grunt, Brenda set up a high-pitched sort of growling noise and it was all nicely coming together when the phone rang.

'Oh shit!' Stan exploded. He tried to bring his breathing under control. The phone rang on. 'Sorry, love,' he muttered and reached for the receiver. 'Hello?'

On the other end of the line, Derek, a junior member of the planning department, said, 'Hello, Stan? It's Del, from planning.'

'How did you get my number?'

'I called your wife. I'm sorry but I thought I'd better ring you. It's about this bloke I met in the pub last night.'

Stan Gamley was having trouble keeping his temper. 'What bloke?' he snapped.

'A young bloke, Mr Gamley. He was asking questions about you, like did I know exactly where you'd gone for the weekend and did you have a house in the Channel Islands. He seemed to know quite a bit about you. He was . . . I dunno, suspicious, I guess.'

'What did you tell him?'

'Nothing. I kept me mouth shut.'

'Right, Del, you did well to call me, son, well done.' Brenda was dressed now and Gamley mouthed the words, 'Please stay.' She was no spring chicken but she wasn't bad looking. 'Just don't talk to anyone about where I am, all right?'

'Yes, Stan. Of course. See you Monday then.'

Gamley hung up. Brenda had slipped out of the room and he had to admit he was relieved that she had gone. He was too old for this kind of malarkey. He reached for his jockeys and, pulling them on, walked across to the mini-bar. He took out a miniature gin and a can of tonic, poured them both into a tooth mug, then went out onto the balcony to drink it. He had a problem and he was going to have to sort it.

Bill and Sheila Redfern were entertaining. They had invited Bill's director for dinner, along with a few friends from the golf club. Most of the guests had just arrived and Bill was serving jugs of Pimms in the garden. Sheila was in chiffon: a long skirt and matching top which tied at the waist and showed how much tennis she played. Bill was in an open-necked shirt and a pair of immaculate chinos. They were both perfectly dressed for a casual but smart summer evening dinner party. They were a couple without children who liked to focus very much on themselves, and tonight was a testament to how much they had achieved.

Sheila was just handing round a large Portuguese plate layered with the best selection of nibbles that M&S could provide when the phone rang. They didn't get calls on a Saturday night, and Sheila and Bill exchanged a look. He said, 'You pour the Pimms, darling, and I'll get it.'

Once inside the house, he picked up the receiver and said, 'Bill Redfern.'

'Bill? It's Stan. I think we've got a problem.'

Bill bristled. '*We* don't have anything, Stan,' he replied coolly. 'If there is a problem then I'm afraid that it has nothing to do with me.'

Gamley, who had downed all three miniature gins from the mini-bar, was clearly drunk and not taking any nonsense. 'If it's my problem, Bill, then it's your problem. There's a bloke, he's been asking about me. Knows I'm in the Channel Islands . . .'

'Stan, of course people ask questions about you. You're an important man,' Redfern cut in. 'You've got a high profile, you're head of town planning.' Redfern wanted Gamley off the phone; if there was a problem now wasn't the time to talk about it. 'Everything is fine, Stan,' he continued. 'Calm down. We're careful and we know what we're doing. Now, why don't you just forget all about this until Monday and we'll discuss it then. OK?'

Gamley slumped back against the bedhead. He'd phoned on a drunken impulse and now regretted it. 'You're right, Bill,' he said.

Back out on the patio, Redfern took his glass of Pimms and raised it. 'Cheers everyone,' he said, taking a large gulp.

'Here's to the land buyer with the magic touch,' his director proposed, smiling and raising his glass. 'Long may it continue.'

At nine fifteen on Monday morning, Sarah was shown into the headmaster's office at Ledworth House and asked if she would like a coffee while she waited. She said yes, coffee with milk and sugar, and the secretary disappeared to get the headmaster, leaving Sarah to look at the book-lined study and wonder what she was doing here. She had made the appointment on Saturday morning on an impulse after a row with Rory. A stupid, pointless row because he couldn't say the word 'think'. A basic word, she'd told him, that he should be able to say. What was she spending all her hard-earned money on if he wasn't paying any attention to what he was being taught?

'Think,' Sarah had said loudly to him as they chatted over breakfast.

'Th, Th, Th . . . Think. Say the "th", Rory. It's the "th" sound, not the "f" sound and it ends in a kicking k . . .'

Rory had turned away and ignored her. 'I don't fing that I want to.'

She cut in. 'Rory, it's the "th" sound. Come on, please.'

But Rory had stood up abruptly and slammed out of the kitchen. That had done it for Sarah, she'd well and truly lost her temper. She had stormed out after him and shouted up the stairs. He had shouted back that he wasn't ever going to be normal, no matter how much she tried, and that he was sick of her pretending that he would be, and the whole thing had escalated into an angry slanging match. In the end she had fled out into the garden, tearful and angry, and dug the flower beds until she had a blister on her right hand and her face was wet with tears. Then she had phoned Ledworth House. It was a premature, rash gesture, but she felt she had to do something.

'Ah, Mrs Greg.'

The man who had just entered the room was tall and slim, dressed soberly in a grey suit, and was relaxed and smiling. So used was she to harassed headteachers who could spare just a few minutes, Sarah blinked in surprise, then smiled back and shook the hand offered to her.

'Thank you for seeing me at such short notice,' she said.

'It's my pleasure,' he replied. 'You wanted to talk about your son, Rory, who is seven, nearly eight, and partially deaf. Is that right?'

'Yes, that's right. He's doing well at school, but I think he could do much, much better. He needs a smaller class and more individual attention and that's really what I'm here for.'

The headmaster, Mr Tully, smiled again. 'Then let's discuss it,' he said. 'Please, Mrs Greg, take a seat.'

And Sarah sat. It was the first time she had ever been asked to sit and discuss the needs and wants of her son, and it felt good.

First thing the same Monday morning, Janice Stimpson had a sizable print-out of the share dealings of Alex Stanton at White Lowen over the past year. Nothing looked unusual until April of that year. In April he had started trading for the Housewife Trust and from that moment on things began to look odd. It was almost certainly a case of insider trading. Janice had her hypothesis, now she had to prove it.

Leaving the office mid-morning, she went along to White Lowen and met the human resources director. She had made an appointment to discuss Mr Stanton, telling her that it was a matter of the utmost confidentiality. She asked the standard questions and checked Alex Stanton's CV. There had been no earlier offences, and there seemed to be no tangible connection with any source of inside information. Janice made a note of a couple of colleagues that Stanton spent his lunch hours with and took their numbers from the switchboard list, but there was nothing more to go on. If he was insider trading then he had to be obtaining insider information from somewhere. The question was where?

Aiden Thornton sat anxiously outside the meeting room on the third floor of the Stock Exchange building. To be called in by the surveillance team was serious. He'd never done anything even remotely wrong, but he was still as nervous as hell.

Janice Stimpson appeared clutching a file. 'Mr Thornton?'

'Yes?' Aiden stood up.

'Hello, my name is Janice Stimpson. I'm investigating one of the brokers that you work with and I'd like to ask you some questions. Is that all right?'

Aiden blinked; it wasn't him. The relief flooded his face and he smiled. 'Yes, yes, that's fine.'

Janice led the way into the meeting room. 'Please, take a seat,' she said and pulled out a chair.

'This is an informal interview, Mr Thornton, to try to find out a bit more about the broker involved. His name is Alex Stanton and we are concerned about some of his dealings on the Stock Exchange of late.'

Aiden wasn't surprised and that too showed on his face.

'You're friends with Mr Stanton, is that right?'

'Not friends exactly. We don't socialise away from work but we do have the odd beer at lunchtime and after work.'

'Has he got a girlfriend?'

Aiden hesitated. Alex obviously had a girlfriend, the woman he'd seen him with several weeks ago, but he'd flatly denied it. 'Not that he's ever told me about,' he replied. He glanced away. It wasn't a lie but then it wasn't the whole truth either.

'Has he talked about anything he's recently bought? Like a new car, a property? Has he mentioned any holidays?'

'No, he . . .' Aiden hated the idea of snitching on his mates.

'I should remind you, Mr Thornton, that withholding information won't do you or Mr Stanton any good at all.'

Aiden swallowed. He wasn't under any oath. Besides, Alex expressly said the car wasn't new.

'No, he hasn't said anything to me about any of that.' That wasn't a lie.

'So there's nothing out of the ordinary about Mr Stanton's behaviour as far as you can tell?'

'No. He seems completely normal to me.' That wasn't the truth either. The last time he'd seen Alex he'd been distinctly odd, dead cagey about the girl he had been with, but also kind of smug.

'I see.' Janice made a note on her pad. It read: Not admitting all he knows. Find out more. 'Well,' she said, 'to sum up, then, you are absolutely sure that Mr Stanton has not mentioned anything to you that might be construed as out of the ordinary. Is that right?'

'I'm not "absolutely sure". No, I think, "to the best of my knowledge" is a better phrase. I'm not absolutely sure about anything to be honest with you, Ms Stimpson.'

Janice made another note. It read: Will buckle under pressure.

'OK, then. Thank you for your time, Mr Thornton. And if there's anything at all that you think might be relevant to our enquiry, then please . . .' Janice held out her business card and Aiden took it. 'Do give me a call, won't you?'

'Yes, thanks, I will.' Aiden headed for the door, but before opening it he turned and said, 'What exactly are you investigating Alex for?'

Janice looked directly at him. 'Insider trading,' she said.

Aiden took a breath. 'Right, I see.' He left the room and made his way outside. He took out his phone and immediately called Sophie. He had the awful feeling that he saw only too well.

Bill Redfern swung his silver Mercedes into a space at the opposite end of the car park to Stan Gamley's Rover, and climbed out. Stan was waiting by the café, drinking tea from a polystyrene cup.

'Stan.'

Gamley stood up and chucked the last of his tea onto the ground.

'I'll just get myself a drink and then we can go for a little wander,' Redfern said. He went to the café and bought a carton of orange juice. He dug the straw into the carton and took a sip. 'Come on,' he said, 'let's walk.' The two men headed up the path towards the woodland.

'I took a trip to the pub this morning,' Redfern said. 'The young girl behind the bar told me quite a bit about your young man.'

They were walking uphill now and Gamley was short of breath. He didn't answer.

'His name's Sayer, Rupert Sayer, and apparently he's a freelance journalist. He's working on a story about local council planning.'

Gamley stopped and looked at Redfern. 'What the fuck's going on? Jesus! If any of those little bastards in my office have been shooting their mouths off, then I'll . . .'

'Calm down!' Redfern snapped. 'No one's said a word. OK. It's all speculation at the moment, hence the snooping around. He's got nothing on you, Stan, and nothing on me. He's just been cataloguing development over the past year and he thinks he's made some kind of connection. He knows fuck all!'

Redfern started walking again. Gamley hurried to catch up.

'What if he does find something? What if he gets lucky?'

'What is there to find out, Stan? Who the hell knows about this whole thing? You, me, and Derek. There's a couple of people on the council who I deal with but they're too well paid to blow their own cover. So how can there be a problem, Stan? Everything is under control.'

Gamley went quiet for a moment. 'So what do we do?' he asked, as they reached the path on the other side of the patch of woods and started back for the car park.

'*We* don't do anything,' Redfern replied. 'You just wait. If things start to get out of control then I'll handle it.'

Gamley had always sensed that Redfern had a ruthless streak. He let very little get in his way. He said, 'What's that supposed to mean, Bill?'

Redfern shrugged. They were back in sight of the car park now and he cut across the grass towards his car.

Gamley stopped, watched him for a moment and wondered about running after him, demanding an answer. He dismissed the idea as ridiculous and turned away. Whatever it meant, perhaps it was better not to know.

Janie was in the kitchen when Andrew came home. It was early, six thirty, but Katie was in bed reading and the house was quiet. She was cooking. She'd been cooking all day.

'Hello.' He came in and across to her, without kissing her cheek. 'What's all this?'

'I'm filling the freezer,' she said. And filling my life, she thought.

'Ah.' Andrew took his jacket off and hung it over the back of a chair. He seemed tense, upset even, but Janie didn't ask why; she wasn't sure she wanted to know. He poured some wine and left a glass on the side for her. Janie washed the pastry off her hands and took the glass. She sipped, waiting for Andrew to speak.

'I had a call from the bank this afternoon,' he said. Janie started. He'd said it so casually that it almost sounded like a normal comment. 'What on earth do you need forty-five thousand pounds for?' His voice was calm, restrained, and it unnerved Janie. Andrew wasn't angry, he had gone past that. He had a contained, deep-seated fury that had hardened into something much worse than anger.

'That is, or was, our emergency money in case we ever had to bail ourselves out of serious trouble. You took it away, you took our security away, Janie. I presume it was for investment into the stock market?'

She nodded.

'I thought so.' Andrew finished his glass of wine and walked over to the sink where he rinsed the glass. He walked out of the kitchen. Janie went after him. In the bedroom he had put a sailing bag onto the bed and was filling it carefully with his clothes.

'Andrew? Andrew, what are you doing?' Janie tugged at his arm. 'Andrew?' He shrugged her away and carried on. 'Andrew, stop it! Please, can't we talk about it?'

He faced her. 'Janie, that is exactly what I have wanted for a long time, for over a year. But you wouldn't; you wanted to do your own thing. Well, you've done your own thing, you've gone ahead without any regard for anyone else. It's been all about you.' He took his toiletries bag off the bathroom shelf and put it into the holdall. 'I need some space. I need to think.' He picked the bag up and headed for the door, but Katie stood out on the landing in her nightie, blocking his way. She said, 'What's the matter, Daddy? Where are you going?'

Andrew dropped his bag and took both her hands in his. 'I've got to go away for a little while, for work. I'll ring you, though, tomorrow night, and I'll see you maybe at the weekend . . .' He broke off as his voice cracked and Janie had to turn away. She said, 'Jump into bed, poppet, and I'll come and tuck you up in a few minutes, OK?' Katie stood where she was. She could sense that there was something horribly wrong, but she didn't understand it. She stood her ground for a few moments longer, then she went back to her room. Janie's heart ached.

'Andrew, please . . .' Andrew headed down the stairs. In the hallway Janie held on to his arm. 'Andrew, please don't be rash . . .' But he pulled himself away and walked out of the house. Minutes later he had driven off and Janie stood, still in the open doorway, staring at the empty drive.

Aiden met Sophie for a drink after work. He told her all about his meeting with Janice Stimpson and all the time he was talking he turned her business card over and over between his thumb and forefinger.

'Will you ring her?' Sophie asked.

'And tell her what? That I think Alex might be up to something or that he might be having an affair with someone? It's all "might be's" and hearsay, Soph. It's not enough to snitch on your friends for.'

'Sorry, I didn't realise he was a friend,' Sophie said. 'I didn't realise that he'll be helping you out if you get done for withholding information in the course of an investigation.'

'They can't do that, can they?'

She nodded. Actually she didn't know, but she wasn't going to have Aiden take a chance for that arrogant, smug bastard. 'Look, Aiden,' she said, 'you know that Alex Stanton is seeing someone but he flatly denied it, and secondly that he's making an awful lot more money than you, either legitimately or not. That's all you have to tell this woman. Both of those things are not hearsay. Let her decide what they mean.'

Aiden shook his head. He really didn't know what to do.

'Aiden! I really don't see your problem. It's him or you. Do you really want to get done for perverting the course of justice?'

Aiden stood up. Sophie was right, of course she was right, but he was sick of hearing she was right. 'I'm off home,' he said.

'But you haven't finished your beer.'

He shrugged. 'You have it,' he said, and he walked out of the pub.

Half an hour later, when he got home, Aiden Thornton rang Janice Stimpson. He told her what he knew, nothing more, but he hated himself for doing so.

Janice Stimpson was in work early; after the phone call from Aiden Thornton last night she was eager to get started. The first thing she did was to re-work her way through the list of phone calls that Alex Stanton had received from February through to the present day. She was looking for clues as to who Stanton might be involved with. By lunchtime she knew that if Stanton did have a girlfriend, it certainly wasn't a relationship he was admitting to. He'd had a fair number of personal calls, but none intimate as far as she could tell. Why not if he was seeing someone? He was obviously as careful with his personal life as he was with his professional life, and that begged questioning.

Janice went to see her supervisor. 'I'd like to request some time off for surveillance,' she said.

'It's not customary, Janice,' he replied. 'Surveillance work is not something that we recognise.'

'I realise that, but there are some answers that I'm not going to find unless I get out there and start searching. In the past I've . . .'

Her supervisor looked at her. 'Janice, in the past you have requested time off to work at home on the case.'

She looked at him. 'I see. So I need to request some time off to work on this case at home, right?'

'In writing please, Janice. If you can put a note on my desk within the next hour or so, I can grant you time off with immediate effect.'

Janice smiled. 'Thank you,' she said. 'I'll do it right away.'

It was just before lunch, and so far that morning Alex had watched the screen for nearly three hours. The price of Wye Valley Organic Foods had shot up from fifty-five pence on Friday night to one pound eighty pence. He was mesmerised by the screen; every phone call he'd taken he had cut short so as to be able to get back to the ever-changing, ever-increasing numbers.

But Alex didn't feel excited or triumphant, he just felt nervous. To take a big position in a stock almost immediately prior to the announcement of a bid situation was always cause for speculation and sometimes even investigation by the Stock Exchange. That was the last thing he needed. The atmosphere in the office this morning was certainly tense, and, ridiculous as he knew it was, he couldn't help feeling that everyone knew that he'd taken a massive position on Wye Valley. It made him uneasy. Perhaps he should just call it a day and sell at one eighty. Hell, it was a phenomenal profit with that amount of stock. He jotted a few figures down on a piece of paper. They looked good. He'd ring Sarah, that's what he'd do. He'd call her and see what she wanted to do.

Sarah had come in from Duffields with four bags of shopping, all sopping wet from the sudden torrential downpour of rain that had hit just as she'd climbed out of the car. She heard the phone, dropped the shopping just inside the front door and ran to pick up the receiver.

'Sarah, it's Alex Stanton. I'm just ringing with the latest on Wye Valley. It's up to one eighty and I was thinking that perhaps, if you agree, we should get out sooner rather than later.'

Sarah sat down. 'How soon?' she asked.

'Possibly by the close of play.'

'Why?'

Alex thought, because I'm stretched to breaking point on this one and I don't know if I can take the stress. I just want out and done with it. But he said, 'Because we've done bloody well and I don't want to take the risk any further.'

Sarah said, 'I'd better ring round, Alex.' They had a hell of a lot at stake and he was edgy, but then they'd bought all that stock in order to be able to use it to their advantage and they hadn't even got close. What was the point in taking such a big position if they weren't even going to use it? 'Let me ring you back. OK?'

Alex wanted to say, no, it's not OK. I'm the broker, take my advice. But he had always been deferential to clients.

Janie was in bed when the phone rang. Organised, diligent Janie had left the house in a mess, last night's supper remains still on the plates in the kitchen, the chaos of breakfast things untouched, no curtains drawn, beds unmade, nothing done. She rolled over and tried to ignore the bleeping, then when it carried on she answered it.

'Hello?' Her stomach turned. Her head was thumping.

'Janie? It's Sarah. Are you all right? You sound terrible.'

Tears welled up in her eyes. She blew her nose. 'I'm fine,' she said, but Sarah knew she wasn't. 'I just feel a bit . . .' but she couldn't finish. 'A bit weepy . . .' she said finally. Sarah looked at her watch and thought that she could probably get over there for an hour before she had to pick Rory up from school.

'I'll come over,' she said.

'No,' Janie answered, 'no don't, please, I'm fine.' Janie couldn't bear to think of anyone seeing her. 'What did you want, Sarah? Was it anything important?'

'Alex Stanton wants to sell today. The price is one eighty and for some reason he wants to get out. What d'you think?'

Janie sighed. What did she think? She thought that she had been stupid, that she had risked everything for nothing. She thought that she had been trying to fill a void in her life that she would never be able to fill. It was there, whatever she did, a big gaping hole waiting to swallow her up. She said, 'I think we should do what Alex says.'

Sarah rang Roz, but caught her at a bad moment. Kids screaming and the cow with some sort of infection that threatened the calf. She listened to what Sarah had to say, then made her decision. She didn't want to take any more risk than they had done already. She had enough on her plate; if the deal was ready to be closed, then close it, don't piss about.

Sarah rang off, not offended, but uncertain that anyone was thinking straight. She wondered what to do. Then she had an idea. She had Marcus's mobile phone number. It was a bit of an imposition, to interrupt his holiday; he hadn't said he'd call her while he was abroad, but this was important. It would be crazy to make the wrong decision just because Alex said so. She dialled.

'Marcus, hello. It's Sarah.'

'Sarah?'

Sarah blushed. 'Sarah Greg,' she said, 'from the investment club.'

'Oh, of course.'

Sarah waited for something else, some sort of warm and friendly greeting, but nothing was forthcoming so she said, 'Sorry to bother you, Marcus, on your holiday, but I've got a bit of a problem with this Wye Valley Organic Foods investment, the one you recommended?'

There was silence, then Marcus said, 'I don't remember recommending anything to you, Sarah. I might have mentioned something in passing, but I certainly never make recommendations outside of my job.'

Sarah's first reaction was surprise, her second was embarrassment.

'No, no, of course not, it's just that I, erm, I just thought, wondered, if you might know whether it would be right to sell them now or . . .'

'I am afraid that I really have no idea.'

'No, no, of course not,' she murmured.

'Was there anything else?'

'No, nothing else.'

'Goodbye, Sarah.'

That, Sarah thought, had to be one of the most painful phone calls she'd made in a long time. She took a long deep breath to calm herself, then picked up the phone again to call Alex.

Alex sold the shares in Wye Valley for a total of one pound ninety-five pence a share at two o'clock that afternoon. Immediately afterwards he called Lucie and arranged to meet her after work. He needed some company and was hoping for a little physical comfort. They usually went up to the West End to drink, but tonight Lucie didn't have time. Desperate to see her, Alex arranged to meet her at a wine bar in St Paul's. After that he called Sarah to let her know that he had sold the shares.

In the Stock Exchange surveillance room, IMAS picked the transaction up and Janice Stimpson, just going off for the day, knew that she was on to something substantial.

Sarah called Janie and said, 'Alex sold the shares at one pound ninety-five pence a share. That means we've each made roughly two hundred and twenty-three thousand pounds.' She was hardly able to contain her excitement. 'Janie, it's amazing and it's all down to you! You were the one who started all this. I can't believe it, I . . .' Sarah stopped. 'Janie? Janie, are you still there?' But Janie wasn't. The line was dead and when Sarah tried to ring straight back all she got was the engaged tone. She tried several times more, then she called Roz.

Roz put the phone down in the kitchen and stood looking out at the small courtyard garden where Graham was sweeping away the rain debris. But she didn't see Graham, the brickwork or the pots or the rain. Roz saw the fields at the back of her land and she knew that they could be hers. The relief made her want to cry. She went outside and stood in the shelter of the doorway for a moment.

'Don't just stand there, woman,' Graham muttered, bending with a piece of card to scoop the debris into the wheelbarrow.

'Why not? You do it so beautifully it seems a shame to interrupt you.'

Graham smiled. 'White, one sugar, please, love.'

'You'll be lucky.'

He finished the job in hand, then looked up at her. 'Can I help you?'

'The shares,' Roz said, 'in Wye Valley Organic Foods. Alex sold them this afternoon. We made a profit of one pound fifty-five pence per share.'

Graham came across to her, taking her into his embrace. He said nothing and neither did she. They stood like that, hugging tightly, then she said, 'Shall we buy the Gordens' land?'

Graham stroked her cheek. 'Not at developers' prices, no. We'll wait until Jack's done his bit and then we'll offer them what it's really worth.'

Janice sat in the foyer of the Chartered Municipal opposite White Lowen and waited for Alex Stanton to leave the building. It was six fifteen, and as she glanced down at her watch, then up at the building again, she saw someone she thought might be him come down the steps. She checked the photo the bank had given her and saw it was definitely Stanton. 'Bingo!' she muttered. She kept her distance and followed Stanton towards St Paul's. She saw him enter a wine bar on the corner of Paternoster Row and bought herself an *Evening Standard* before following him inside. She took a seat at the other end of the bar, ordered herself a glass of wine and took out the paper to wait.

Lucie was feeling frail. She had been working long hours, she was tired and lonely, and she needed this time with Alex. Coming into the bar, she saw him just inside the door and smiled. He smiled back; a warm, charming grin that made her heart melt. Lucie had always been tough and given as good as she got, but she had also always had a fatally romantic side. Without thinking, she went across and kissed him.

He kissed her back. He was feeling euphoric and for a moment he didn't give a shit about being careful. He just wanted to feel the warmth of her lips and breathe in that wonderful, sharp scent that she wore.

'Hello. Drink?'

'Wine, please. No, stay there, I'll get it.'

Lucie went to the bar. She ordered a bottle of Meursault and took out her credit card to pay for it. Normally they had the house white, but tonight she wanted to treat them both.

She took it back to the table with two glasses and Alex poured.

'You look tired,' she said to Alex.

'Not really, just a bit stressed.' He wanted to tell her about Wye Valley, but he couldn't. The investment was a subject they simply didn't discuss. 'And you,' he went on, 'look wonderful. It's good to see you, Lucie.'

She smiled again, enjoying the moment. She didn't know what was going on in her life, what Alex wanted from her or indeed what she wanted from him, but she did want this moment. They tapped glasses and drank to each other, then Alex said, 'Move a bit closer.'

Lucie shuffled her chair in towards him and under the table he gently stroked her leg. Why not, he thought? No one can see us..

Across the bar, Janice didn't miss a trick. Watching Alex and Lucie, she took in every movement made, every intimacy shared. She observed them for the hour they spent in each other's company. She watched them leave the bar, saw the goodbye kiss. Then she went up to the bar.

'Can I have a word with the manager? No complaint, I'd just like to ask him something.'

'Oh, sure.' The young woman disappeared and a man returned in her place; mid-thirties, Janice thought, public school.

'Can I help you?'

'Yes, I hope so. My name is Janice Stimpson.' Janice held up her card. 'I work for the Stock Exchange surveillance team. There was a young woman in here a few minutes ago who paid for a bottle of wine on her Visa card. It was a bottle of . . .' Janice glanced down at the note she had made on the back of the *Evening Standard*. 'A bottle of Meursault. Could I possibly have a look at the credit card slip?'

The manager raised an eyebrow. 'I'm not sure,' he replied. 'This is a very peculiar request.'

'Not at all, it is simply part of an enquiry.'

The manager stared hard at her ID, then, after hesitating for a few moments, agreed. He opened the till, found the slip. He handed it over.

Janice looked at the slip. Lucie Croft. She took her notebook out and began to write down the number, but the manager stopped her. 'I'm terribly sorry,' he said, 'but I really can't let you take down the number. You could be anyone. The name's as much as I'm prepared to give you. If you'd like to come back with the police, then . . .'

Janice smiled. Uptight bastard, she thought, definitely public school. She said, 'Of course. Thanks anyway.'

The office was empty when Janice got back there at eight that evening. Any normal person would have dealt with it in the morning, but then Janice wasn't normal, not when it came to work anyway. She had a kind of evangelistic zeal for justice.

So she set about finding out who Lucie Croft was. Everyone who worked in the City could be traced, one way or another, through the Stock Exchange or the Financial Services Authority. There were lists from the banks and finance houses, there were lists of analysts and accountants. It was a mammoth task but it was not insurmountable. If Lucie Croft worked in the City—and Janice was convinced she did—then Janice would find out who she was.

Then she would nail her. Just like she'd nailed every other thieving bastard she'd uncovered in her work at the Stock Exchange.

CHAPTER NINE

BILL REDFERN STOOD at the front door of his executive home—built by Glover Homes, with four bedrooms and a luxury kitchen—and waved to Sheila as she reversed out of the drive. He glanced down at his trousers—Hugo Boss—and shifted his belt—Giorgio Armani—so that it sat perfectly in the centre of his waistband. Things, the image they and the label they carried, mattered to Bill. He was under the impression that a designer label meant he had made it. And all Bill Redfern cared about was the fact that after years and years of struggle he had arrived.

Bill Redfern was a well-groomed forty-one, with all his hair intact and a still reasonably firm six-pack in his abdominal region. He was happily married to Sheila, a woman who shared his drive for materialism. Bill was ambitious. He had worked for Glover Homes for twenty-one years. Twenty-one years of hard graft, of clever manoeuvring. He was the land buyer now; he earned a high five-figure salary, had an excellent pension plan and looked forward to a good eight to ten per cent bonus every year. He was a clever operator was Bill Redfern. He wasn't an honest man, but then who was in business? He got the job done and that's all that mattered to Bill. With his careful land buying, Glover Homes had made some insightful decisions over the past ten years, decisions that had taken them up into the top league of builders.

Yes, Bill Redfern had made it. Only recently, in the midst of all this success, there had developed the tiniest irritation in Bill Redfern's life, like a small mosquito bite on his arm.

He waved once more to Sheila, then went inside to the study and switched on his PC. He was working from home today; he had something to sort out that he didn't want to do at the office. So he replied to his emails then began making his calls. He started with the Glover office in Lewes, East Sussex.

'Hello, planning and development please,' he said when the line connected. The switchboard put him through.

'Hello. Pat Belling, please.'

'I'm sorry but he's in a meeting. I'm the office secretary, can I help?'

Bill already knew this; he had all the planning meetings in his diary and Sharon was the one he really needed to speak to. 'Oh, yes, hello, Sharon, I wonder if you can. It's Bill Redfern here, from head office.'

'Hello, Mr Redfern, what can I do for you?'

'Sharon, I've had a couple of calls from some of my people saying that there's been some journalist bloke ringing round asking questions and I just wondered if he'd got through to you at all?'

'Yes, Mr Redfern, he called on Monday. He wanted to know who dealt with our land buying for this area so I gave him Mr Belling's name and number. I told him as well that most of the decisions were made by yourself and Mr Ashby, the director.'

Shit, Bill thought. 'You told him, did you, Sharon, that we have a strict land-buying policy and that it is always adhered to?'

'Yes, Mr Redfern.' Actually she hadn't said that at all, she'd had quite a nice chat with Rupert Sayer. He'd been so easy to talk to and they'd arranged to meet for a drink a week on Wednesday.

'Well done, Sharon. Did he want to know anything in particular?'

'No, not really, Mr Redfern, just general stuff.' That wasn't true either. He'd asked quite a bit about the decision-making process for land buying and whether she knew of any connections Mr Redfern had with the district council. He'd said he was doing a feature on local development and the benefits for the community, so she'd told him about the funding for the leisure centre and the proposal for a small, covered shopping area, which she wasn't supposed to know about, but then when you typed things you couldn't help reading them, could you?

'Good, glad to hear it. Now, if he rings again could you possibly give me a call, Sharon?'

'Of course, Mr Redfern.'

'Thanks, Sharon. Take care now.'

Bill hung up. Sharon couldn't tell a lie to save her life. Rupert Sayer had been chatting her up, that much was obvious, and she had fallen for it. He probably had a good idea by now that there were many things that influenced a decision to buy land, not just price, location and availability. Redfern reached for the phone to make his next call. As he did so it rang and startled him. He picked the receiver up.

'Hello, Bill Redfern speaking.'

'Bill, it's Peter Ashby.'

'Hello, Peter, how are you?' Peter was his director.

'Fine.' Ashby was short and abrupt. 'Bill, there have been a couple of calls, to various offices, from some journalist chappie.'

'I know, I'm on to it.'

'Good.' There was a brief silence, then Peter said, 'Make sure you are, Bill, because Glover Homes has a reputation and we can't afford for any members of our team to be caught doing something that they shouldn't.'

Bill got the message. All the senior management knew how land buying went. Quality land had to be worked for, bargained for and it involved risk. Bill looked at his screen. There was an email from the MD; another warning. So the risk's all mine, he thought; whatever's been done in the full knowledge of the senior management is now something I have to take sole responsibility for. He cleared his throat and said, 'I've got it completely under control, Peter.'

'Thank you,' Ashby said. And he hung up.

Bill thought about what he'd done for Glover Homes, about what he'd achieved, and where he wanted to be. He wouldn't finish the calls, there was no point. He had other things to do now, important things.

Rupert Sayer stood in the lounge of his small terraced cottage and surveyed the papers strewn across the floor; maps, flow charts and brochures for housing developments. He had everything worked out and he was extremely pleased with himself. Now he had to find the hard evidence and he needed help with that. So far it was all circumstantial.

Stepping over his filing system to the phone, he picked up the receiver and dialled. The line answered and he said, 'Hello, Jack Lowe? This is Rupert Sayer. You probably don't remember me, but we met at the airport. I'm doing a story on Glover Homes.'

In his office, Jack said, 'Of course I remember you. You run like a bloody whippet. How are you doing?'

'I'm doing pretty well, actually, Jack. I've made good progress with this story. I think I'm onto something.'

Jack was wary. 'Really?' If Rupert was onto something he hoped to God he was keeping quiet about it.

'Yes! you wouldn't believe what I've managed to wangle out of the secretaries over the phone. I've called every single Glover regional office and I've got some ace stuff out of it. I've . . .'

'Hang on a minute, Rupert,' Jack interrupted. 'Are you saying that you've been ringing the Glover offices personally?'

'Yes! I spoke to the secretary of each planning department . . .'

'Shit!'

'What's the matter?'

'Nothing! Only the fact that you've probably blown my whole bloody case!' Jack was really angry. 'Do you really think that all these calls won't get back to Redfern and then Gamley? They'll be onto you by now and running shit-scared. They'll tighten up every tiny little crack in the operation. God, Rupert, the chances are that you've gone and ruined everything I've done so far!'

'Yeah? So you already know about Redfern's involvement in four other counties, do you? You already know that all land-buying decisions have to go through Redfern, despite the fact that there are separate offices for Kent, East Sussex, West Sussex and Surrey. I suppose you know that in East Sussex Glover Homes funded the building of a new leisure centre and there are plans underway to fund a new shopping area, although nothing has ever been released for public knowledge on the subject.'

Jack was silent. He was thinking, Shit, this boy really has done his stuff. He said, 'Rupert, I didn't know any of this. I'm impressed. But you've put yourself in a difficult position, Rupert. This was hardly covert, was it?'

'I told them I was from the *Telegraph*.'

Jack rubbed his hands wearily over his face. Naïve was a word that sprang to mind; it was kinder than stupid.

'Look, Rupert. . .' Jack took a breath. 'I don't think that will have fooled anyone. We are dealing with a big corporation that has a good reputation it will want to protect. Whatever is going on, it will go to extraordinary lengths to cover it up. Believe me. You should drop it,

Rupert, at least for now. Take a break and let things settle down.'

Jack's words didn't frighten Rupert, they just added fuel to his already burning ambition. This was his passport into the world of investigative journalism and he wasn't about to relinquish it.

'I rang you for some help,' Rupert said. 'I thought you'd be only too happy to take advantage of my knowledge in return for nailing Redfern and Gamley.'

'I'm sorry,' Jack said, 'I can't give you any help, not with the situation as it is.'

'That's a shame,' Rupert said. 'I'll have to do it on my own then.'

Jack wanted to warn Rupert, to offer advice, to try to talk him down, but he reckoned it was pointless so kept his mouth shut. The boy was too young to listen, too impetuous, too arrogant. He did say, 'Rupert, be careful. Whatever you do, please, be careful.'

'Yeah,' Rupert said, 'thanks.' And he hung up. If Jack wasn't interested in helping then he'd have to go it alone. He was halfway there and, despite what Jack said, he wasn't going to give up now just because someone might be onto him.

It was 11.00am and time for a coffee. As Janice Stimpson made her way past the fax machine, she saw the fax coming through with her name on it and smiled.

Janice knew who Lucie Croft was. She had found out last night from one of her lists. She had rung the human resources manager of World Bank where Lucie worked in corporate finance, and had requested, under Stock Exchange jurisdiction, a list of all the deals that Lucie had been involved in over the past year. The fax had the details and Janice would have bet her last pound on what was on that list.

Janice took a cappuccino from the vending machine and sat down at her desk. She sorted the sheets into order and took a sip of coffee. Then, and only then, did she look at the list. She smiled again. There it was, just near the bottom: Wye Valley Organic Foods.

'Done it,' she said aloud.

Janice's supervisor was in a meeting when Janice knocked on the door. He looked up, saw her and said to his associate, 'I'm afraid I'm going to have to postpone our meeting until later.' He could see the brown file under her arm and he knew what was coming. In one way it filled him with awe that someone could be so diligent, and in another it annoyed the hell out of him. He wished that Janice would get a life.

Janice came in, smiling. 'I've got a case for primary insider dealing and very probably for secondary insider dealing as well.'

The supervisor nodded. 'Well done,' he said, without returning her smile. 'Sit down, Janice, and let's see what you've got.'

Janice sat down and opened the bulging brown file.

'I have here a list of trades for Alex Stanton, a broker with White Lowen, done for a nominee company called the Housewife Trust as well as in his own name. These trades, I believe, were made when he was party to price-sensitive information on each company. This information, I believe, was given to him by Lucie Croft, a corporate finance manager for World Bank, who was part of a team working on the take-over bid for each company. Stanton has been having an affair with Ms Croft.'

The supervisor raised an eyebrow. 'And the secondary insider dealing?' he asked.

'The Housewife Trust.' Janice sat forward a little in her seat. 'The Housewife Trust is made up of three names: Sarah Greg, Roz Betts and Janie Leighton. Janie Leighton is the clue. Her maiden name is Todd. I found that out when I was checking her bank details. Anyway, Todd is also the name of Lucie Croft's husband—Marcus Todd—and it's my betting, although I haven't been able to find this out yet, that Marcus Todd is the brother of Janie Leighton. That's the connection.' She sat back triumphant, waiting for praise.

'Well,' he began, 'Janice, you have surpassed yourself. That really is a remarkable piece of work.' He wasn't exaggerating either, he was amazed. 'I think that the next stage is a foregone conclusion, Janice, don't you?'

She tried not to look eager. 'Sir?'

'Let's hand it over to the DTI for a prosecution.'

Janice nodded. 'Quite right,' she replied.

He finally smiled, albeit wearily. He had to, it would have been rude not to. 'Congratulations, Janice,' he said. 'Let's prosecute.'

On his way back from Chichester, Rupert Sayer took the road to Storrington with the intention of calling in at the Boatman just outside Amberly for a drink. It had rained overnight, and the roads were wet and slippery. Rupert drove fast as he sang along to Travis on his stereo, with a cigarette in his right hand.

Behind him a silver Mercedes came up close. It had its lights on and he couldn't clearly see the driver. The Mercedes came up so close that it touched his rear bumper and Rupert momentarily lost control of his car. He swerved. He was coming into a sharp bend and he straightened rapidly, oversteering and hitting the grass verge. The wheels went out of control and the car swerved across to the other side of the road as Rupert tried desperately to steer, but he couldn't do it. In a reflex action his foot jammed down on the accelerator and, just before a spot where people stopped to take photographs of the stunning views over the River Arun, his car left the road and plummeted over the edge. It was a sheer drop. The car bounced twice at the bottom, crumpling on impact. It fell a total of 150 feet, then stopped. There was a moment of silence, then Rupert's head fell forward onto the horn and its shrill sound split the air. The silver Mercedes didn't even stop.

It was August 1, and it was miserable. Arctic winds blew in from the North Atlantic and, as Lucie made her way along from the tube, it began to rain. She didn't have an umbrella and her pale, fawn linen suit took on a pattern of small, dark stains.

She reached the bank and went inside, shaking the water out of her hair and greeting the reception staff. The two girls smiled back, but by now it was all round the bank and Lucie knew what they were thinking. Stupid prat, they thought; as if earning a quarter of a million pounds and a one hundred per cent bonus wasn't enough.

She made her way to the lifts, and went up to the third-floor meeting room. She knocked on the door. She was told to come in. Her director was there, James Colley, along with the MD of the corporate finance division and a board director.

'Lucie, come in and sit down, please,' her director said. Lucie sat down and waited. She was outwardly composed, but her mind was blank and her hands shook.

'Lucie, you know Michael Steadman, of course, and I think you've met Henry Trotten a few times, haven't you?'

'Yes, yes, of course.' She tried to smile, but it didn't really work.

'Good. Lucie, as you are obviously aware, the Department of Trade and Industry has decided to go ahead with its investigation into this alleged illegal trade in Wye Valley Organic Foods and Sarasota plc.'

She was aware, but the sound of it still chilled her to the core. She nodded.

'Of course, we've listened to what you have to say about your own involvement in the case, but I'm afraid, Lucie, that although we are all very much on your side, we have to think of the bank's reputation and our clients. Any doubt on your integrity, no matter how misguided, will reflect on the bank. I'm sure you understand that.'

Again Lucie nodded, but she couldn't speak. Ten years, she thought, ten years I've worked for you and you don't believe me.

'We have decided, Lucie, that it would be best if you took an extended period of leave on a full salary, until the matter is resolved.'

Lucie swallowed and willed herself not to cry. She had never, not once in the last ten years, shown her emotions at work. She was a professional. But even as she told herself all this, a small tear fell and splashed onto her skirt. She bent, took a handkerchief out of her handbag and blew her nose.

'Is there anything that you would like to ask me, Henry or Michael?'

'No . . .' Lucie coughed to clear her throat. 'No thanks, James.'

James said, 'Thank you for coming in, Lucie. If you'd like to clear your desk now it'll save you having to make another journey. I've asked Molly, the group secretary to book you a cab home when you're ready.'

Lucie glanced up, shocked. 'Oh, I see.' She picked up her bag. This was as good as a dismissal. The bank couldn't fire her, so they were letting her go on extended leave, and when everyone had forgotten about her, when this whole thing had been cleared up and she was found not to have been involved at all, then they would terminate her contract and pay her off. She turned and held out her hand. 'Goodbye,' she said, shaking each man's hand. 'And thank you.' Though what she was thanking them for she had no idea. She had made them a great deal of money in the last decade. She had been shown no loyalty, no trust. What did D.H. Lawrence call it? 'The bitch-goddess Success'. How right he was.

Sarah stared out at the rain that hammered onto the brick courtyard outside Roz's kitchen, knocking the heads off the red geraniums. It was dismal, but it was somehow fitting for the mood of anxious depression that had engulfed Sarah and Roz.

Roz came in and went straight across to switch on the kettle. She lit a cigarette, taking a long, deep drag.

Sarah turned. She wanted to say, Oh, Roz, that is such a shame, but she didn't. 'Seven years,' Roz said angrily, 'seven years I've not smoked. And because of all this fucking mess I've started again. I tell you, if I ever get my hands on that Alex Stanton, I'll bloody kill him.'

'Ditto.' Sarah came over to the dresser and took two mugs down.

'I'll be better when Graham gets here,' Roz said. Graham was on his way back from a buying trip in Ireland.

'What time did Andrew say he'd come over?' Sarah asked.

'Ten-ish. Apparently he's taken the morning off.'

'Bully for him,' Sarah retorted and Roz looked at her. 'I'm sorry, Roz,' she went on. 'But he walks out on Janie, for God knows what reason, and then when all this blows up two days ago, he doesn't even right her.'

Roz took the hissing kettle off the Aga and said, 'I think your anger might be a bit misguided, Sarah.' She spooned coffee into the mugs and poured on the scalding water. 'Milk?'

'Thanks.' Sarah helped herself to milk as a car drove up.

'He's here,' Roz said. 'I'll go and let him in.'

Sarah was making a third coffee as Andrew walked in.

'Hello, Sarah.' Andrew hung his waxed jacket over the back of the chair and sat down. 'So,' he said, 'what's this all about?'

Sarah and Roz exchanged glances. Janie hadn't told him.

'Have you spoken to Janie in the last forty-eight hours, Andrew?'

'No. I collected Katie on Saturday night and returned her yesterday, but we barely spoke. Why? What's up?'

Roz took a drag of her cigarette and came to sit opposite Andrew. 'The broker who has been dealing for us has been suspended pending an enquiry by the DTI into an allegation of primary insider trading.'

Andrew narrowed his eyes. 'I don't understand.'

'It appears that Alex Stanton was having an affair with Janie's sister-in-law, Lucie Croft, who is also being investigated by the DTI on the same charges. Lucie works for a bank and apparently had access to price-sensitive information on two of the stocks that we invested in. It is alleged that Alex Stanton dealt in the shares knowing that they were about to be the target of a take-over bid, a primary insider offence. It is also alleged that because of our connection with Lucie Croft we knowingly allowed Alex Stanton to do so, a secondary insider offence. We too will be investigated by the DTI.'

Andrew's face had clouded. 'Let me get this right, Roz. Are you saying that the broker has been insider trading? And that this in turn means you could be liable for charges of the same offence?'

'Correct.'

'Oh Christ!'

'I can't believe that Janie didn't tell you,' Sarah remarked.

Andrew put his head in his hands for a few moments, then he looked up. 'Janie doesn't tell me anything important, Sarah.' He stood up. 'I'd better get over there and talk to her. She must be in one hell of a state.' He reached for his jacket. 'The first thing you need to do is contact a lawyer. I'll get home and on the phone. Katie's godfather, Ed, is a lawyer, he'll be able to root around for the right person to help you. I'll come over again later with Janie and we can talk it all through. OK?'

Sarah nodded. 'OK.'

'I'll see you later,' Andrew said.

Lucie opened the front door of her house and walked in, wet and cold and numb. She took her jacket and skirt off, both soaked, opened the fridge and took out the half-empty bottle of wine she hadn't finished last night.

'It's a bit early for the booze, isn't it?'

Lucie jumped. 'My God, Marcus! You gave me a bloody fright! You're supposed to be on holiday somewhere, aren't you?'

He smiled, but his eyes were cold. 'That's a nice welcome. Janie rang me last night. I got on the next plane home.'

'I see.'

Marcus walked into the kitchen. 'Are you all right?'

Lucie shrugged. 'What do *you* think, Marcus? I'm being investigated by the DTI for primary insider trading, something I am certainly not guilty of, and I've lost my job. Apart from that, yes, I'm fine.'

Marcus held her gaze. 'And Alex? How is he?'

Suddenly Lucie's face flooded with colour. She dropped her eyes away and stared hard at the ground.

'Janie told me everything. I presume it's true?'

Lucie couldn't answer. In the end she simply said, 'I'm sorry, Marcus,' and Marcus said nothing. They stood like that for some time until Lucie began to shiver and Marcus told her to go and have a warm bath.

Some time later, when she was dressed and lying on the bed, Marcus brought her a cup of tea. He put it on the bedside table and sat down beside her. 'Thanks,' she murmured.

'So,' Marcus began, 'it looks like you've all been used by Alex Stanton.'

Lucie closed her eyes. That's what she'd been telling herself for the last forty-eight hours. But somehow it hadn't sunk in yet, somehow she just couldn't see it. Not Alex, he didn't have the drive.

'How did he do it, d'you think? He must have had access to your briefcase and looked at files, that's the only way I can think . . .'

'I am extremely careful with price-sensitive information, Marcus. I don't go leaving my briefcase open for all and sundry to look into.'

'I know, but there must have been times, I mean during your affair, when he had the opportunity to . . .'

Lucie stared at him. Was he doing this on purpose to humiliate her?

'I don't want to talk about it,' she said. 'I'm surprised that you do.'

Marcus shrugged. 'If you get convicted you could get seven years, Lucie, I think we should talk about it, don't you?'

What the hell was wrong with him? Where was his passion, his anger? 'OK,' she snapped, 'yes, I did carry documents to and from the office to work on at home, and very probably had them in my case when I met him on more than one occasion. I can't think of any other way he did it. I never talked about my work, the only person who ever knew anything about my job was you. So, yes, he must have been snooping in my briefcase. You're right, OK? Does that make you feel better?'

'It's not a question of feeling better about it, Lucie, it's a question of getting you off this charge. I can help you, Lucie, if you'll let me. We can work through this together.'

She couldn't answer him; she was too humbled in the light of such forgiveness. Marcus left the room and Lucie began to cry.

Janie saw Andrew's car from the bedroom window. She had been having a lie-down while Katie watched a video, and as she opened the curtains he pulled into the drive. She went into the bathroom to splash some cold water onto her face and was bent over the basin when he came to the door.

'Are you all right?'

She straightened and reached for the towel. 'I'm fine,' she said. She walked past him into the bedroom and began to find some clothes to put on. Andrew watched her. Her hair was dirty, something that was unthinkable for Janie.

'Why didn't you tell me about the DTI investigation?' he asked.

Janie began to dress—yesterday's underwear, tracksuit bottoms, a grubby T-shirt.

'Janie?' Andrew caught her arm. She shrugged him off. 'Janie, please,' he said, placing his hands gently on her shoulders, 'please talk to me.'

Janie looked at him. 'What's the point?' she asked. 'I've tried talking to you, Andrew, over the years I've tried, but you don't listen. You think you've heard but you haven't, you walk away, both emotionally and physically. So, what's the point?'

Andrew let her go. She was right and he knew it. He spent his life listening to other people's problems, and when Janie spoke he only listened to what he wanted to. He made decisions for her too, did what he thought was best. Occupational hazard he had always called it, but to Janie had it meant something else altogether? Arrogance, control?

'Janie, we have to sort this thing.'

'Of course,' she said, 'whatever you say.'

'What the hell is it, Janie?' he suddenly snapped. He grabbed her arms and forced her to look at him.

Her face set and her eyes hardened. 'You really can't see it, can you?'

'No! No, I bloody well can't!'

'There's a gap in my life, Andrew,' Janie said, 'a gaping chasm that is threatening to swallow me up. I look at the next twenty years of this, of losing Katie as she grows up, of fiddling around the periphery of your life as a country GP, of mindless gardening and cooking and cleaning, and I can't bear it, I just want to kill myself.'

Andrew felt like he'd been slapped. He looked at her for a few moments, then he said, 'Do you care so little for me and Katie?'

'It's myself I don't care for, Andrew. I'm valueless, unfulfilled.'

Andrew touched her cheek. 'What do you want, Janie? Tell me what it is that you want and I'll try to give it to you.'

'I want what I can't have,' she said slowly. 'I want a baby.'

Andrew was silent for a while, then he said, 'Is that what all this investment thing has been about? Having a baby?'

'Yes! No, I . . .' Confused, Janie shook her head. 'I don't know. Maybe underneath it has. All I could think of was filling the gap. It obsessed me. I thought that making money would do it, or taking a risk, doing something radical, but I was wrong. After I'd invested the money, I felt nothing. It was the same as before. I was empty.'

'Oh, Janie . . .' Andrew released her and moved away to look out of the window at the endless rain.

'And even now you don't listen,' she said. 'You are turning away from me because you don't want to hear what I have to say.'

'No, no, that's not true, Janie. I am turning away because your pain overwhelms me and I don't know how to deal with it. I never knew. I thought after the last miscarriage that you had . . .' he shrugged, 'I don't know, come to terms with it.'

'So did I.' Janie looked at him and wondered, was it that he hadn't listened or was it that she had stopped talking?

He took her hand. 'Janie, we've got to put this on hold, you know.' She nodded. 'We've got to sort this investigation thing out first, you understand that, don't you? And I need to get onto Ed and see if he knows a lawyer who could help us. But I am listening to you, I have heard what you've been saying and we will deal with it, I promise.'

She nodded a second time, but she thought, no baby. Then she thought, so how? How, Andrew, will you do that?

'Right,' Andrew said. 'So we're agreed on priorities then?'

Roz, Graham, Janie and Sarah all nodded. They were sitting round Roz's kitchen table, with a couple of empty wine bottles in front of them and the remains of a take-away curry. Five children were asleep in various bedrooms over the house, it was late and they were all worn out.

'First, you need to get records of the phone calls that Alex Stanton made to you, both on the BT line and on your mobiles. Second, you need to think hard about what went on between you three and Alex. That meeting you had when you decided on Wye Valley; did you make any notes? Can you remember exactly what was said? What reasons did he give you for investing in Wye Valley? Go through the same procedure for Sarasota plc. The key to all this, I think, is going to be cataloguing in detail exactly what was said and when. If you can categorically state that no mention of inside information was ever made to you, it has to be a strong point in your favour.'

'And there's the whole Lucie thing as well,' Roz said. 'I mean, we never saw her, we had nothing to do with her. Hell, none of us had any idea that she was having an affair with Alex. You didn't, did you, Janie?'

Janie shook her head. 'Nor did Marcus.'

'Do you think that Lucie is involved, Janie?' Graham asked. 'You know her better than any of us do.'

Janie shrugged. 'I have no idea,' she replied. 'I keep asking myself why would someone with such a dazzling career, such a huge income, risk it? And why would she involve me? In my heart I don't believe it, but everything points to her. She was the one with the information.'

There was a murmur of assent, then Graham said, 'It doesn't add up, does it? I think we should get Jack Lowe involved on this, you know.'

Roz groaned. 'What good would a private investigator be?'

'He'd get to the bottom of it.' Graham liked Jack; they had made the sort of connection that men rarely do. 'He's bloody good at what he does and he's fond of us. I bet he'd do it if we asked him.'

Sarah looked at Roz. 'Graham's got a point, Roz. How can we get off this thing unless we find out what really happened? If, by some chance, Lucie isn't involved, then presumably we can't be involved either.'

'Good thinking, Sarah!' Andrew turned to Roz. 'Who is this Jack chap?'

'He's someone who's been helping with the Glover Homes land thing,' Roz replied. 'He's been investigating the whole business for us.'

'Is he good?'

'Yes, he's good. He hasn't got a result yet, but he's certainly uncovered some incredible stuff about corruption in town planning.'

'I think you should talk to him,' Andrew said, 'and get his angle on things at least. I'll put that down as your priority then, Graham. As for me,' Andrew went on, 'I'll get back to Ed tomorrow morning about the lawyer. I'll also call the DTI and find out exactly what an investigation involves. Then at least we'll have some idea of what to expect.' He looked round the table. 'For the moment,' he said, 'I think that's it.'

It was well after midnight and Jack Lowe was working in the dark. There was a full moon and he had been digging for hours. He was sweating and his T-shirt clung to his body. He was oblivious, though, to the time or the energy it was costing him to do such a task and to the fact that it was the middle of the night. His mind was blank save for just a few words that went round and round in his head.

And in the kitchen was the weekly local paper. On the third page it carried the tragic story of the fatal accident of one of its freelance journalists,

Rupert Sayer. Aged just twenty, he had been killed when he lost control of his car on the bend up at the Hersley beauty spot. It wasn't enough, Jack told himself as he dug; what I said to him the other day simply wasn't enough.

CHAPTER TEN

LUCIE WATCHED MARCUS with wary unease as he made her some toast. For the past twenty-four hours he had been almost unrecognisable from the Marcus she had got used to, and it unnerved her. He should have been upset, distressed, angry and humiliated; anything but this cloying concern, this forgiveness. Did he care so little for her that her affair didn't even matter? Or was he really capable of such largesse? Lucie didn't know. But she did know that Marcus operated a strict code of justice in his head. He scored people on their misdemeanours and punished them accordingly. Some friends she knew had been banished entirely for doing the wrong thing. So this, this didn't make sense at all.

Marcus caught her staring and asked, 'Jam or marmalade?'

Lucie blushed. How could she harbour such unkind thoughts?

'Marmalade please.'

He passed her the plate, filled the kettle, and put it on for tea. Tea, she thought, from the man who could previously hardly be bothered to turn on the tap.

'I thought I might go to the gym for an hour or so,' she said. 'What time are you off to work?'

'I don't think I'll go in actually, I think I'll stay here and keep you company. I've got a couple more days of my holiday left anyway.'

'I see.' A month ago she would have been pleased, would have taken it as a sign that things were improving between them, but now, now she wondered if things hadn't gone too far to ever recover properly. She stood up and left her toast uneaten. 'I think I'll get going,' she said.

She went into the bedroom—which they now shared again—and sat to pull on some trainers. What the hell is going on, she thought.

Alex had been waiting across the road from Lucie's house since eight that morning. Finally at nine thirty Lucie came out carrying her sports bag and Alex set off after her. He'd been calling for the past three days but she just wasn't answering her phone. He had to speak to her, to make her understand. He had to convince her to help him.

He crossed the road several yards in front of her and stopped by a low wall. As Lucie came into view he stepped out directly into her path. She jumped back, startled, and he took hold of her arms.

'My God, Alex! What the hell are you doing here? You gave me a fright, you stupid bastard!' She yanked her arms away from his grip.

'Lucie, sorry, I didn't mean to scare you, Lucie . . .' She set off and he walked after her. 'Look, Lucie, we've got to talk, please?' Something in his voice made her stop.

'Alex, you used me,' she said. 'I don't know how you did it and I'm still trying to come to terms with it, but you abused my trust.'

'I didn't use you, Lucie, I swear I never did anything wrong, never. I don't know what the hell has happened. I had no idea that you were working on Sarasota or Wye Valley, how could I have done? You never once told me anything about your work.'

'No, I didn't, but you had countless opportunities to look in my briefcase, Alex, and you took them.'

'I never looked in your briefcase,' he cried.

'You swear, Alex?'

Alex stared at her. He stared and then dropped his eyes.

'I thought so,' she said and turned to walk away.

But he grabbed her and swung her round. 'All right, I did look in your briefcase once, the night we met for a drink in Red's wine bar. It was open and it was too much of a temptation. I looked and I saw a document on a merger between Rightson Electronic plc and the KEC group. I glanced at it and I thought shit, I could do something with that. Christ, I even worked out some figures! But I didn't do it, Lucie, because you trusted me and because I'm not fucking stupid. Besides, I was making money legitimately, or so I thought, with this investment club!' He held her arm so tightly that it hurt. 'I have never dealt shares using inside information, Lucie, never.'

Lucie pulled her arm away. 'Get off me,' she cried, and started to walk away.

'I'm honest!' he shouted after her. 'I've been fucking set up!' She increased her pace, hurrying away from him. 'I didn't do it, Lucie,' he shouted. 'Check your files, see what you had in your bag that night. I didn't do it . . .'

She ran across the road and jumped onto a bus. She had no idea where it was going but she didn't care. As the bus drove off the words 'I didn't do it' reverberated in her ears.

Jack Lowe's office was open and Graham walked in, calling out from the bottom of the stairs. There was no reply so he carried on up.

'Hello? Jack? Hello?'

Dodi and Jack stood by Jack's desk, a huge plastic crate between them which Jack was maniacally filling.

Jack looked up. 'Oh, hi, Graham.'

'What's going on, Jack? Moving offices?'

'No, he's shutting offices,' Dodi said, her face like thunder. 'He's giving up, bottling out . . .' She looked at him. 'Coward. We're making money for the first time and you want to throw it all away!'

Jack stopped packing. 'I am not a coward, Dodi, quite the contrary. I'm looking after our interests. Besides, this is my office and I'll do want I want with it.'

'What's going on?' Graham asked again.

'I'm closing down for a while,' Jack said. 'I was going to tell you that I'll have to end your investigation and will refund half my fee.'

'You'll do nothing of the sort,' Graham said strongly. 'You earned that fee. Why are you closing, Jack?'

Jack turned to him. 'A young man, Rupert Sayer, a freelance journalist, came to me with a story on corruption in local town planning. I ignored him. I didn't want his interference in my own investigation to make things difficult for me. Result? He's dead. Seems a bit odd, don't you think? He rings Glover Homes, manages to wangle God knows what out of the secretarial staff, and then ends up in a fatal car accident. Sorry, but it's too much of a coincidence for me, I'm out of here.'

'Hang on, are you saying that someone connected with Glover Homes murdered this young man?'

Jack thought for a moment. 'Yes, I suppose that is what I am saying, but how I'd ever prove it I don't know.'

'That is a bloody serious accusation,' Graham said.

'If I'm right and Glover finds out that I'm on to something, how do I know that I'm not next, or Dodi, or you or Roz, or one of the kids?'

'Jack, you are totally over-reacting. How do you know it wasn't a simple case of an RTA?' Graham asked. 'Is there really any need to go to these sorts of lengths?'

'I think so,' Jack replied sharply. 'And before you say anything else, you won't change my mind. I'm giving up. And as for you, Dodi, you'll get another job. You're a bright lass. And you've got a couple of months' money so there's a bit of time.' He bent to unplug the phone. 'Anyway, what did you want, Graham?'

'I wanted to get you on another job, but I see there's no point now.'

'Nope, none at all. Sorry, mate.' Jack fought the temptation to ask what the job was about and Graham said, 'I won't keep you then, Jack. Give me a ring when you've got organised and we can have a beer.'

Jack looked up. 'Yeah, I'll do that, thanks, Graham.'

Sarah was loading shopping into the boot of her car when Graham caught sight of her in the car park behind Duffields. She had taken leave from her job for a couple of weeks with the original intention of taking Rory away on holiday, but that wasn't going to happen now.

'Hi, how are you?'

'All right. Shopping as per usual.'

'Where's Rory?'

'I got him in at a football course at the leisure centre. He loves it.'

'Good.' Graham dug his hands in his pockets. 'Jack Lowe said he can't help us, I'm afraid. Apparently he blames himself for the death of some young journalist and he's decided to close up shop for a while.'

Sarah frowned. 'Really? I saw that in the paper. What on earth could Jack have to do with that?'

'He thinks it's connected with the investigation he's been doing into Glover Homes. He thinks . . .' Graham stopped. 'Oh, it doesn't really matter what he thinks, the point is that he's giving up.'

Sarah slammed the boot shut and looked at Graham. She was disappointed but she didn't want to show it. She said, 'Oh well,' and shrugged. 'What next?'

Graham shook his head. 'To be honest, Sarah, I really don't know.'

Sarah drove home, made herself a coffee and sat down at the kitchen table to open a letter from BT. It was an itemised list of the phone calls that she had made and received over the past three months, as requested. She looked down. At least eleven to or from Alex Stanton. She started to make notes. She wrote the time of each call and tried to remember what they were about, but for some reason, she couldn't. She put her head in her hands. For the past three days she had been stunned by all this, dazed by the sheer unreality of the whole thing, but now the full terror of it hit her. She could go to prison. The nausea rose in her chest to she took several deep breaths to try to control it. Prison.

Suddenly she jumped up and grabbed her car keys off the table. What did he mean he was giving up? Bloody Jack Lowe, giving up when he could do something positive to help.

Jack was about to lock up when Sarah banged on the downstairs door. 'Who the hell's that?' he demanded. He went down the stairs and unbolted the door.

'I've got something to say to you, Jack Lowe!' Sarah snapped, barging past him and going up the stairs. She was up and into the office before he could stop her.

'OK,' Jack said, when he reached her. 'Say it.' He stood opposite her with his hands on his hips and she glared at him.

'You are a weakling,' she spat, 'a pathetic weakling. You give up at the first sign of adversity and it makes me sick! You've no guts. You throw in Graham and Roz's investigation because you can't handle it, with absolutely no regard for how much they could lose. You ask me out for a drink and you never even turn up without any explanation at all, and now you won't even consider helping us, at a time when we need all the help we can get. You're a . . .' She could feel the tears welling up as she searched for the right word. 'You're a wet!' she finally cried.

'Now just wait a minute!' Jack shouted. 'I did turn up for that drink. I waited until closing time and you never came. You didn't ring to let me know and you never even apologised.'

'I rang the pub and you weren't there. They looked for you and you weren't there. So don't try and bluff me! Of course I didn't apologise because there was nothing to apologise about.'

Dodi, standing in the kitchen, held her breath. Either Sarah would hit him or kiss him.

'I was there and I never got a call. You never rang.'

'You weren't.'

'Oh, for God's sake!' Dodi suddenly burst out. She stamped into the room. 'Why don't you just agree that you called and even though he was there he didn't get the message? He might have been in the karsey, or just didn't hear his name. He *was* there, all right? End of row.'

Sarah's face had dropped into an expression of shock and Dodi thought, I've overstepped the mark here, but now I've done it I might as well finish. She had nothing to lose; she didn't work here any more after all. Dodi turned to Jack. 'She's right, you know, you shouldn't be giving up. If this Rupert bloke was murdered, then it's up to you to make sure some justice is done . . .'

'Justice!' Jack burst out. 'What the fucking hell has justice got to do with it? When was anything ever just?'

'Oh take the chip off, for God's sake!' Sarah snapped.

Jack turned to her. 'And what's that supposed to mean?'

Sarah, who had listened to Dodi firstly with shock, then with growing admiration, thought, if she can do it, so can I.

'It means, stop moaning and get on with it, that's what the rest of us have to do.' She took a breath. 'I was given a damaged baby, Jack, not his fault, not mine, and I did the only thing I could, I got on with it. He's still damaged, but he's also a confident, strong, intelligent, healthy child. I could have given up, but I didn't.' She looked at him and, in a moment of stark realisation, knew that it wasn't him she was angry with, it was everything. She'd been angry for years and had never been able to say it. She stared down at her hands, suddenly acutely embarrassed. 'I'd better go,' she said, 'I think I've said far too much.' She looked at Jack again. He was watching her with an expression she couldn't fathom. 'Sorry,' she murmured, moving past him to the door. She walked out and down the stairs, wondering what the hell she had been thinking, but feeling—and this was the odd part—mildly euphoric.

'Wow,' said Dodi, when the door downstairs had slammed shut and Sarah had gone, 'that is some girl.' She turned and went to pick up her jacket and handbag.

'Where are you going?' Jack asked.

'Home,' she said, 'to look through the situations vacant pages.'

'No, you're not,' Jack said.

'I'm not?' Dodi wanted to smile, but couldn't quite let herself.

'No, you're going to give me a hand with unpacking this crate, then we'll phone Graham and Sarah Greg to see what the hell is going on.'

Marcus was out when Lucie got in from the gym and she was relieved. She made herself a coffee and then she went to the box she had brought home from the office yesterday. She took out her desk diary, and went back to the time she had met Alex.

For every meeting that they had had she hadn't put any names or times or places, but she had marked the date with red ink so that she didn't forget. Then she tried to match up the dates she had met Alex with the meetings that she'd had on that day or the following day, with a view to seeing what she might have had in her briefcase. It was a laborious job, but by the middle of the afternoon she had a list. There was a bit of confusion around the Wye Valley deal; she had met Alex, but she didn't have a Wye Valley meeting penned in on that day or for the day after. But she remembered working on the bid, because she had told Alex that she was working on something that would soon be announced.

She sighed. Certainly no meeting with Alex had ever coincided with a meeting at work for Sarasota plc and also, interestingly, he had been telling the truth about Rightson Electronics. She had been working on that merger the night they'd met at Red's. What if Alex was telling the truth? She picked up the phone and dialled her secretary at work.

'Hello, Molly, it's Lucie Croft here. Molly, could you do me a favour? Could you check on the PC for my chargeable hours for the following dates and let me know what they were and for whom?' Lucie read out the dates. 'Great, thanks.' She hung up. Molly was thorough and quick. She waited five minutes, then Molly rang back.

'Oh,' Lucie said, when the reply came. 'Right, I see.' She had been working on the Wye Valley deal on the day she met Alex. 'Thanks,' she added. She hung up again. 'Bugger,' she said aloud. That put the ball firmly back in Alex's court. The trouble was that now she just wasn't convinced.

'Right,' Jack said, 'let me get this absolutely straight.' He was sitting on his desk facing Sarah and Graham, while Dodi sat at the desk and made notes. 'The big question mark is over Lucie Croft's involvement, right? It seems unlikely to all of you that she would have taken such a risk. That's our first line of investigation I'd have thought. Is that OK?'

'Fine,' Graham said.

'Good. The other thing I think we need to find out is exactly what Alex Stanton has to say for himself. For now I think that's all we can do. I'd like to speak to your lawyer once you get hold of one. How's it going, d'you know?'

'Andrew is apparently having a bit of trouble finding someone. This is a very specific case and no one seems to know that much about it.'

'Oh.' Jack jumped off the desk. 'OK, well, if Dodi's got all the details, then I won't keep you.' Graham and Sarah stood up and Jack saw them downstairs to the main door.

'Right, well, I must dash,' Graham said. 'Thanks, Jack, and good luck.' He kissed Sarah. 'We'll speak soon, love.'

Sarah stood for a few moments and watched him disappear up the street, then she turned to Jack. She had something to say but she had nowhere near the courage she'd had that morning.

'Jack, I . . .' She broke off, very uncertain of herself, looked away, then something suddenly struck her. 'You know, Jack, if you really are worried about this Rupert Sayer thing then you can always check the cars of the people you think might be involved, see if any of them have paint on them from Rupert's car?'

'It'd be like looking for a needle in a haystack.' He shrugged. 'Nice try though. If you need a job any time . . .'

Sarah smiled back. 'Actually, that wasn't what I was about to say. I was about to apologise.'

'What for?' Jack tried to act cool but the truth was that he thought Sarah was amazing and just standing next to her threw him off-balance.

'For being rude this morning. I was out of order. And also for not turning up that night we'd arranged a drink.'

Jack took her hand and held it gently between his own long, thin fingers. Sarah watched him and held her breath. 'It's forgotten,' he said, looking up at her. 'But, thanks.'

She nodded and he released her hand. 'I'll let you know how I'm getting on,' he said. 'Try not to worry, I'm sure we can work this thing out.'

'Yes, OK. Bye, Jack,' she said, moving off.

'Goodbye, Sarah,' he replied.

She walked away, tucking the hand that he had held into her pocket, and thinking that she would have liked Jack to go on holding her fingers in his for a lot, lot longer.

Lucie woke early, but Marcus was still asleep beside her as she slipped from the bed. She brushed her teeth and had a quick wash in the dark. She didn't want to turn the light on or shower because she didn't want to wake him. She gathered the clothes up that she had left on the chair and in the living area she dressed, collected up the sports bag she had packed the previous night, and left the house. It was six fifteen.

At six forty-five her taxi pulled up outside the bank and she climbed out. Going in, she asked the security men if Molly Kirk had come in yet and they checked on the list. She hadn't.

Lucie walked down the road to the café that Molly used and ordered herself a coffee, taking a seat in the corner. At seven thirty Molly came in and queued for her daily take-out cappuccino and round of toast.

'Hello, Molly.' Lucie stood behind her and Molly turned.

'Oh, Lucie . . .' She stopped, momentarily embarrassed, then said, 'Hi, how are you?'

'I'm fine, Molly. Can we talk?'

Molly looked uncomfortable and glanced at her watch, but Lucie touched her arm and said, 'Please, Molly, it's important.'

Molly shrugged. 'OK.'

Molly ordered her breakfast and sat down.

'So,' she said. 'What's up?'

'I need a bit of help,' Lucie said. 'I need to find out if I've been set up in this thing.'

'Help?' Molly looked decidedly uneasy. 'What d'you mean by help?'

'I need to find out if I had the documents for the Wye Valley Organic Foods deal in my briefcase on a certain night in July. The only way that I can think of doing that is to check the files in the computer. If, for example, they were still being transcribed, then I couldn't have had them in my bag, which means that Alex Stanton, the broker, couldn't have looked into my case and got the information, which is what is being alleged.'

'So how did he do it?'

Lucie shook her head. This was something that she had been putting to the back of her mind for the past twenty-four hours. She swallowed hard and looked at Molly. 'He didn't,' she said, 'someone else did.'

Molly looked away. She had always liked Lucie Croft, had been shocked when all this had come out. Lucie didn't seem the type. But then she was having an affair, and Molly had been shocked by that too.

'It would put me in a very difficult situation,' she said at last.

Lucie said, 'All I'm asking is that you check the computer, Molly, and give me a ring. I'm not asking you to do anything illegal, I promise. It would . . .' She broke off. It would what? It would raise questions that Lucie didn't know that she wanted to answer. It would, perhaps, be the end of her marriage. 'It would make things much clearer for me, Molly.'

Molly took a deep breath, then stood up. 'I'll do it now,' she said, 'before anyone comes in. Give me your mobile number.'

Lucie wrote her number down on a slip of paper and handed it over. 'Thanks, Molly. I'll wait here,' she said.

In the office, Molly switched on her PC and went straight into the system. She looked up the file for Wye Valley Organic Foods and went into file management. She wrote down the dates and times that the document had been worked on and noticed that the file hadn't been created until the July 12. It had been a rush job, she remembered that now, a deal done at the last minute.

Lucie listened carefully to what Molly had to say and made a note of the dates and times that she read out. She should have felt excited, this was the answer that she needed, but she didn't. She felt more angry and distressed than she had ever felt before in her life .

Alex wasn't sleeping well. He went to sleep all right but then he would wake, any time between two and four in the morning, and he'd be wide awake, lying in the dark and worrying, wondering how his life could have taken such a turn.

He had just got up when the buzzer went for the front door. It was nine o'clock, and this morning he had drifted off to sleep at about seven and slept for a couple of hours. He felt reasonably refreshed, better than he had done all week. He pressed the buzzer, heard Lucie's voice and opened the door for her.

'Hi,' she said. She didn't smile, in fact her face looked worse than he had ever seen it, ashen and tear-stained. He followed her into the flat. 'What's up?' he asked.

She turned. 'I've checked all my meetings and the documents at work. You couldn't have looked in my briefcase at price-sensitive documents. On all the occasions we met I didn't have the documents on me, except for the Rightson document, which you openly admit you looked at but did nothing about.'

Alex felt the immediate pulse of excitement, then Lucie began to cry. He crossed to her, put his arms round her and attempted to comfort her.

She blew her nose and took control of herself. 'We had a drink on the 9th of July, and the Wye Valley documents weren't typed up until the 12th. You dealt on Friday the 13th and we had no other meeting between the 9th and you dealing. I never spoke to you about that deal, I never even took the documents out of the office. You had no access to the files so there's no way you dealt on price-sensitive information. No way at all . . .' Her voice wavered and she stopped to get a grip of her emotions. She blew her nose and looked at him. 'So, I know you didn't do it and you know you didn't do it, but what do we do now?'

Alex felt the life flow back into him again and his brain begin to clear. 'You've got proof that you didn't have the documents on you?'

'They're dated, on the system, I couldn't have taken them home.'

'Right . . .' He walked away from her to the window. He looked out and his excitement suddenly dropped. 'But this only proves my innocence to you, doesn't it?'

She swallowed, there was a silence, then finally she said, 'Yes. As far as the DTI is concerned I could have told you about the deals.'

Alex stared out of the window.

'Alex? Can I have a drink?'

He turned. 'Shit, oh God, of course, sorry . . .' He went over to her and led her to a seat. She was so pale that she looked suddenly fragile.

'I'll get you some tea.' He disappeared and she could hear him putting the kettle on and opening cupboards in the small kitchen. How long would it take him, she wondered, to come to the same awful conclusion that she had?

Alex appeared with her tea.

'Lucie,' he began, 'I don't know how to say this, but . . .' He stopped and stared at his hands for a moment. 'The thing is . . .'

She put her hand on his arm. 'If it wasn't you, then there is only one person I have ever talked to about what goes on in my office and . . .' Again her voice wavered as her emotion got the better of her.

'Marcus?' Alex asked.

She nodded again and her eyes filled with tears. 'I'm sorry, I . . .' She fumbled for her bag and Alex bent for it, passing it to her. She took out her last tissue and wiped her face.

Alex was thinking, what the fuck is going on? 'But why?'

Lucie shrugged. 'I keep asking myself the same question. It is too awful, too terrible to think that Marcus could want to do this to me, or to you. But then I think he's the only one who knows anything about my job. He talked to you, to the investment club, to me; he's the link. He's the one that set it all up, he's the only one it could possibly be and . . .' She put her hands up to her face. 'And I don't know why.'

Alex took a deep breath. 'Unless he knew about us.'

Lucie shook her head. 'No, that's ridiculous. How would he have found out?'

'Did he guess? Did you unknowingly give something away? I don't know, Lucie, but it seems more likely than anything else.' Alex perched on the arm of the sofa. 'Look, let's try and work this thing out carefully, shall we? Now, I first met Marcus in March. He was at a cocktail party at Heaton Alliance, and he came over and introduced himself.'

'Did he? That's very unlike Marcus, he never usually chats to anyone unless he's forced to. Whose party did you say it was?'

'It was Heaton Alliance, the big insurance company, a party to launch their new European fund.'

'Marcus never goes to things like that, never. He doesn't need to, he doesn't waste his time. Why did he introduce himself to you?'

Alex shrugged. 'I think he said we had someone in common. I can't honestly remember. Maybe I let something slip then . . . What about bills? Could he have seen my number on an itemised bill?'

'I don't think so. I honestly can't remember if my bills are itemised, I usually get them at the office because it's a work phone. He might have listened to one of your messages on the mobile, though when is the question. I nearly always have it on me.' She stopped. 'You know, I've been wondering the last two days, thinking that his reaction to this whole thing wasn't right . . I don't know, he was so unemotional about it, so calm. Christ, what if he'd planned it all along? What if . . .' She wasn't able to finish. This was her husband she was talking about, a man she had loved; no, did love, didn't she? 'Oh God, Alex, I just can't believe it, I just can't.'

Alex stood up. 'Right, let's find out if he knew and then we can move on from there. You need to check that you don't get an itemised bill that he could have found and I'll call the hotel we used and check that no one has asked any questions about us.' He went across to the phone, while Lucie took her mobile out of her bag and called the phone company. A few minutes later she pressed end and looked at Alex.

'The hotel gave absolutely nothing away,' he said. 'You?'

Lucie's face had drained of all colour again. 'My husband requested an itemised phone bill earlier this year, in February. He was sent it.' Alex came across to her and held her. She laid her face against his chest, but wasn't comforted; she had gone beyond comfort. 'I have to ring Janie,' she said, pulling back.

'No, don't ring her, go down and see her.'

She looked up at him. 'D'you think so?'

'Yes, I do. It's always better to see people in person. Borrow my car and drive down today.' She nodded but he could see that she wasn't listening. 'Why?' she asked, looking at him.

Alex shook his head once again. 'I really don't know, Lucie,' he said gently, but he did know. It was the oldest, most raw, basic and powerful of human emotions. It was jealousy. It was love, twisted and thwarted and gone bad. It was revenge.

Jack had addresses for all of the people he considered part of his investigation; and the registration numbers of their cars. He had decided that Sarah's idea was worth a shot, even if it was a long one.

He started with Stan Gamley. He went to the council offices, parked and, checking up at the windows of the building, looked first at Gamley's car, then at the cars of the three people who worked for him. He looked all round the cars, under the front of each one, along the wings and particularly around the bumpers. There was nothing on any of them; just as he'd expected.

He then drove the thirty miles or so to the main West Sussex office of Glover Homes. He drove round the car park looking for Redfern's car and, seeing it wasn't there stopped to look at the map. Redfern lived fifteen miles from Burgess Hill and Jack headed off to find the house.

It proved easy to locate. Jack parked halfway down the cul-de-sac of executive homes and looked across at Redfern's house. The car was in the drive which meant Redfern was very probably in. Was it worth the risk? Yes, he decided, it was. Three minutes maximum; he could easily check the car in that time. He walked to Redfern's house and bent to look under the front of the bumper. Along the right-hand side there had obviously been some kind of collision. There was a small graze along the plastic and the tiniest scrape of white paint. Jack hurried to his car. He took his digital camera out, went back to the silver Mercedes and took ten photographs, from all angles, very quickly, and then walked away. Back in his own car, as he started the engine, he realised that his hands were shaking. 'Shit,' he said, then, 'Got you, you bastard.'

It was lunchtime and Marcus had had no word from Lucie. He sat in the living area on the sofa and kicked at the leg of it. He could see that she'd been through her box from work and taken her diary. Files had been looked at too, things rifled through; it unnerved him. He needed to protect himself. He reached for the phone and dialled a number he had come to know well. It was answered after five or six rings and he said, 'Hello, Sarah. It's Marcus. I just rang to see if you're all right.'

Sarah had run in from the garden where she was mowing the grass. She was tired and out of breath. She hated mowing the lawn, but at the moment she would do anything other than sit and think.

'Hello, Marcus.' She was cool; she remembered their previous phone conversation and almost couldn't equate this charming, smooth voice with the one she had last spoken to.

'I am so sorry, Sarah, about all this trouble,' he said. 'I just wanted to ring and let you know that.'

'Yes . . .' Why did it sound insincere? Sarah shook herself. 'Well, erm, thanks,' she replied, 'it must be awful for you too.'

'Yes, yes it is. Look, Sarah, I want you to know that I'm here if you need anything, any advice, or want to talk things through with me . . .'

'Right, erm, thank you.' She softened. She'd caught him at a bad time on holiday, she knew that. 'I appreciate it, Marcus.'

'And how's it going? Do you know exactly what happened?'

'Well, we're not sure that Lucie—' The doorbell rang. 'Sorry, could you hang on a minute, Marcus?'

She went to the door, opened it and Jack stood there. She smiled. 'Come in, Jack, I'm just on the phone.' Going back to the receiver, she said, 'Sorry, Marcus, someone has just arrived. Can I call you back?'

'Yes, yes, of course. You didn't think Lucie what?'

'Oh nothing. I'll talk to you about it later.'

'Sure. Bye, Sarah.'

Sarah hung up and turned towards Jack.

'Hi.' Jack stood uneasily. He was tall and looked out of place in Sarah's small, pink hallway.

'Come in and I'll make some tea,' she said.

He followed her into the kitchen and looked beyond it at the garden. 'Been busy then?'

'Oh yes, the grass. I hate it, but it takes my mind off things.'

'I'll do it for you if you like. Once a week after work.'

'Oh no, I couldn't possibly let you . . .'

'It would only take ten minutes. I bet it takes you over an hour.'

Sarah smiled. 'Yes, it does!' She switched the kettle on and waited. He was obviously here for a reason

'I came to thank you. I went to see a car this afternoon. A car belonging to someone I thought might be involved in Rupert Sayer's accident.'

'And?'

'It was.'

Sarah swung round. 'Bloody hell. Have you been to the police?'

'Not yet. I wanted to ask you something first.' He dug his hands in his pockets. 'I wanted to ask you if you'd help me with something tomorrow morning.'

Sarah frowned. 'What?'

'There's a bloke called Gamley. He works in town planning. Bill Redfern, the land buyer for Glover Homes, pays him off on a regular basis. I know it and Rupert knew it, but I need proof and there isn't any. I reckon he's taking the money to Guernsey in a suitcase. I need you to act the part of a researcher at Gatwick short-term car park tomorrow and intercept Gamley so that I can have a look in the boot at his case. If I can find out that he's got cash in his case then I'll shop him to Customs.'

'Why not just shop him anyway and let them look?'

'Because if he's not taking anything with him this time then he'll get scared and change his routine and then I'll never get him.'

Sarah made a pot of tea. 'Is that why you've offered to cut my grass?'

Jack shrugged. He decided not to lie. 'Yes,' he replied.

Sarah poured the tea. 'Oh, why did I open my big mouth yesterday?' She glanced up at Jack and smiled. 'I'll give it a go.'

'Great, I . . .' He stopped, interrupted by the phone. Sarah headed into the hall to answer it. 'Help yourself to tea,' she called. Jack heard her say a few words, then hang up again. She came to the kitchen door. 'Actually, don't help yourself to tea,' she said. 'That was Janie. Lucie Croft has just turned up and she says she thinks that Marcus set her up.'

CHAPTER ELEVEN

LUCIE WAS SITTING in Janie's kitchen when Sarah and Jack arrived. Everyone else was there—Roz, Graham and the three children and even Andrew, who had somehow wangled cover for his afternoon surgery. The house was noisy; Justin and Katie ran in and out of the garden chased by Kitty and Oliver, and everyone was talking.

'I don't think you've met Lucie, have you, Sarah?' Janie said.

'We met once,' Lucie said, 'at a barbecue here, a couple of years ago.'

'Yes, we did,' Sarah replied, but this frail, worn-out figure in jeans and a sweater bore no resemblance at all to the sleek, linen-draped power woman she'd met, a woman who had exuded confidence and control.

'I'm sorry,' Lucie said, 'for all this awful mess.' She couldn't meet Sarah's eye and Sarah shrugged; she had no reply.

'Coffee?' Janie asked Sarah.

'Please.' She pulled out a chair and sat at the table next to Lucie.

Janie poured the coffee and brought the mugs over to the table. Jack sat next to Sarah and she glanced at him, catching his eye. There was something about him that she liked, something easy and unassuming. He smiled at her and she smiled back.

'Thank you all for coming over,' Andrew said, as Janie finally sat down. 'Lucie wanted us all to be here so that she could explain things in her own words.' He glanced at Lucie.

'Thanks, Andrew.' She took a deep breath. 'I, erm, I suppose that I need to say sorry, I . . .' Her voice broke. She took another deep breath and then went on. 'I don't know how all this happened, I really don't. One minute my life was ordinary, unhappy, yes, but very ordinary, and the next it is extraordinary. I didn't do anything to change that, except . . .' Once again she had to stop and Sarah winced. It was terrible listening to someone else's pain. 'Except that I had an affair and that's where I think that things went very wrong. Janie, I know that this is as hard for you as it is for me, but I am beginning to think that this whole thing has been engineered by Marcus.'

Janie's face creased into a frown. 'I just don't understand it. How could it have had anything to do with Marcus? He told me that. . .'

Andrew touched Janie's arm to stop her. 'Let Lucie speak, Janie, and then we'll talk.' He squeezed her arm.

'I took no interest in this investment club thing because I didn't agree with Alex being involved. I know I have never given him any details of projects I've worked on or let him have access to information that was price-sensitive. I even checked on the computer and have proof that I've never carried files on my person that contained price-sensitive information on the occasions that I met him . . .' She paused. 'No, that's a lie. I did carry some documents home one night that outlined a deal for Rightson Electronics with another company and Alex admitted to me that he looked at them, but he didn't do anything about them because it was too risky and he isn't that stupid.' She sighed. 'I believe him, I've checked and his story is true. So we started to think about who might possibly have had access to the inside information that Alex so naïvely dealt on . . .' She shook her head. 'Marcus is the only person I have ever talked to about my work, he knew about every deal. He also, we think, knew about our affair.'

'No,' Janie said. 'No, he didn't, Lucie. I told him about your affair when I rang to tell him what had happened and he was shocked.'

'He had requested an itemised phone bill for my mobile, Janie, back in February; it had Alex's number listed several times.'

Sarah said, 'I just don't see it, Lucie. I've had quite a lot to do with Marcus over the past few months—he's given me a lot of help with this investment club. He didn't want any of you to know it was him. He wanted to help us and every tip he passed on to me, to us, has been from Alex.'

'Who told you they were tips from Alex?' Lucie asked.

'Marcus, of course . . . He's been really kind, he . . .'

'Have you been seeing Marcus on a regular basis?' Roz asked.

Sarah blushed. 'Yes, I mean no, not seeing him like that, it's been just friendship.'

'Why didn't he want any of us to know he was involved?' Roz asked.

'He was worried it would be misconstrued.' Sarah stared at Roz. 'And from the looks on your faces he was right!' She stood up.

'Perhaps he wanted to make sure that no one questioned his motives, Sarah,' Jack said. Sarah looked at him and her heart sank. She had never questioned the information Marcus had given her. It had never occurred to her that he was anything other than completely honest. He was her best friend's brother, why should she think he would ever lie to her?

'Did Marcus tell you about Wye Valley Foods, Sarah?' Lucie asked.

Sarah nodded. 'He said that he had had a tip from Alex.'

'Alex couldn't have had any tips about Wye Valley, I never told him about it and he had no access to documents in my case or anywhere else,' Lucie said. 'I told Marcus about Wye Valley.' She looked again at Sarah. 'Did he tell you about Sarasota plc?'

'Yes.'

'Passing on a tip from Alex?'

'That's what he said.'

'I'm sorry, but I'm convinced he was lying.'

Janie put her head in her hands. 'I can't believe it,' she murmured, 'I can't believe he'd do it to us, to me . . .' There was a shocked silence around the table.

'He was the one who mentioned the idea of an investment club in the first place,' Lucie said quietly. 'He knew then that I was having an affair and he needed to be able to set the whole thing up . . .'

'No!' Janie said. 'I just can't believe it, Lucie, I know him and I know that he couldn't do something like this.'

Jack had been thinking hard. He said, 'What if, and this is only a guess, what if Marcus knew that you weren't going to get prosecuted?'

'What?' Andrew looked at Jack. 'The woman from the Stock Exchange, Janice Stimpson, told Janie that they were handing the file over to the DTI for investigation with a view to prosecution. Prosecution means criminal charges.'

Jack frowned. 'Yeah, but what if Marcus knew that they wouldn't have a case. I rang the DTI this morning and I found out that they get thirty cases of insider trading a year to investigate and they bring probably one to trial, if they're lucky.'

'Bloody hell.' Andrew looked at Janie.

'That's the best news I've had all year,' Roz said. 'Are you sure, Jack?'

'That's what the chap said. That's maybe why you're having a bit of trouble finding a lawyer to take the case on. It seems to me that to prosecute there would have to be some kind of concrete proof, like phone tapes or video footage or witnesses. In this case there's nothing except connections and someone in corporate finance who denies having passed on insider information. I don't see how it can wash. Unless they can prove that Lucie passed on price-sensitive information to Alex, by way of taped phone conversations, then I don't see how they can prosecute.'

'Are you saying that you think it might all have been a ruse? What? To scare me?' Lucie couldn't keep the shock out of her voice.

Jack stood. 'Mind if I make more coffee, Janie?'

'No.' Janie's voice came out as a whisper and Andrew thought, This is harder for her than for anyone. Marcus betraying Lucie I can just about understand, but betraying his sister I can't. He reached for her hand under the table and she clutched it.

They sat in silence, waiting for Jack to come back. He brought the cafetière back to the table and silently poured coffee. Then he sat down and said, 'If we find out whether or not Marcus did know about the affair, will that make things clearer for everyone?'

'It would at least give him a reason,' Andrew said.

'I don't think it was him,' Janie said stubbornly.

'That means you think it was me,' Lucie said. 'It's my word against his. You have to decide who you believe.'

'I don't think it was you,' Janie protested. She looked away. 'I don't know who I think it was,' she murmured.

'Lucie, was there a café or restaurant or somewhere that you went on a regular basis with Alex, somewhere Marcus might have seen you?'

Lucie flushed. 'We used a small hotel in the West End, but Alex rang them and they said they'd never had any enquiries about us.'

'I'll check it out,' Jack said.

'Would you?' Lucie was eager; she wanted an end to the speculation.

Jack looked at his watch. 'It's three thirty now, I could be up there by five thirty.'

'You sure, Jack? D'you want me to come with you?' Graham asked.

'No. I'll get off,' he said. He glanced at Sarah. 'Sarah, I couldn't have a word, could I?'

She stood, puzzled, and followed him out into the hall. He smiled at her and she knew then for certain that she liked him. 'Sarah, I've made a mistake. I realised it as soon as I said it but I can't go back on it, so I need help.'

'OK.'

'My ex-wife, Sandra, is dropping Jamie off tonight at six and, well . . .' He shrugged. 'I'm going to be in London.'

'You want me to go round and wait for Jamie?'

'Would you mind?'

Actually she'd quite like a glimpse of Sandra. 'I don't mind at all. I'll take Rory, I have to collect him from football at four thirty, and then we might go out for pizza or something. Will he mind? He doesn't know me.'

Jack coughed. 'I've, erm . . . I've mentioned your name a few times and of course he'll recognise Rory from school.' Jack handed her his house keys and dug in his pocket for his business card. 'Home address is right under the office address. It's dead easy to find.'

She smiled. 'OK.'

'Thanks, Sarah.'

He leaned forward and kissed her on the mouth. She pulled back, caught her breath and blinked. 'See you later,' he said.

Sarah pulled into the drive of Jack's home and stopped. The brick and flint cottage was covered in wisteria, all in bloom, and there were terracotta pots and huge urns in the front that spilt a profusion of wonderful things Sarah had never seen before. She said, 'Come on, Rory, let's have a look at the garden. Jamie's dad is a bit of an expert at growing things.'

And he was too. Around the back of the house the garden had been divided into several areas. The first was a traditional cottage garden, the perfect fit for the house, but through a gap in a yew hedge there was another pocket of garden that was neatly laid out into squares and planted with lines of box hedges and lavender. In the centre of each square was a shaped box hedge. A small path ran on into the next pocket of garden; a long rectangle of still water filled with water lilies and reeds, backed by a glass wall that had water cascading down it. The water and the glass combined to create an image of dazzling light as they caught the rays of the late afternoon sun.

'Wow,' said Rory. He went across to the water. 'There are lights at the bottom, Mum, it must be lit up at night.'

Sarah was stunned. 'It's beautiful,' she said quietly, 'really beautiful.' They wandered slowly back through it all to the cottage.

'Can I open the door, Mum?'

Sarah gave Rory the keys. 'Go ahead.' But she didn't want to go in yet, she wanted to stay and take in the garden. When he said gardening, Sarah thought, I didn't realise he meant this.

'Mum,' Rory called, 'Jamie's got the Pokemon official handbook!'

Sarah smiled and went inside.

Jack was surprised how quickly he'd made it up to London. He'd driven to Gatwick, got on the express to Victoria and jumped in a cab. He climbed out now and paid the cab driver and had a look at the building. Not very glamorous but then, in his experience, people who had affairs rarely had them with any style. It was obviously aimed at middle-bracket American tourists: nice and clean and comfortable with the smart mock-Victorian look that most of them liked. He looked for the back entrance. He found the door to the kitchens, opened it and called out. One of the kitchen staff came up and Jack said, 'Where would I find laundry? I've got a package for one of the chambermaids.'

'Carry on round the back and it's through the main door, along the corridor and second on the right.'

'Thanks, mate.' Jack found the main door, opened it and went into the hotel, where the smell of laundry was overpowering. 'Hello?' He opened a door, and looked in. Two girls were in there smoking, despite a No Smoking sign on the wall.

'Can I help you?' one of them asked.

'I don't know, maybe. I need to know if either of you can remember or know of a bloke who came round earlier in the year asking questions about a couple who used the hotel regularly?' Both girls were staring blankly at him. 'No? Don't remember anything at all?'

'Nah, sorry. Nothing.'

Jack nodded and left the room. He decided to try reception.

There was a young woman on the desk. Jack went over to her.

'Hello, can I help you?'

Jack read her name badge and said, 'Hi, Lorna, I wonder if you can. I'm trying to find out if anyone has been seen in your hotel earlier in the year making enquiries about a couple who stayed here regularly.'

She was immediately wary. 'I'm afraid it is hotel policy not to give out any information on our guests whatsoever.'

'OK, thanks.' Jack turned and headed out of the hotel.

He was on his way down the steps when someone touched his arm. He turned.

'There was a bloke, he was here in February.'

Jack faced a young man, about eighteen, in full bellboy livery.

'Really?' Unlikely, Jack thought, he's jumping on the bandwagon.

'Yeah, he talked to my girlfriend, she's one of the maids here. He offered about fifty quid as far as I can remember.'

Jack took his wallet out.

'Not here,' the young man said. He edged Jack forward and round the side of the steps, out of sight of the main doors.

Jack took a note from his wallet and held it. 'Make it worth my while.'

'This bloke came and asked Dilly if she'd check on a room, to see if there was a couple in there. They'd just checked in so she went up and knocked and opened the door. They were, you know, at it, so she apologised and ran down again. He gave her fifty quid, or it might have been a hundred . . .'

'Don't push it,' Jack warned. 'Did she describe the bloke who was asking these questions, or the couple?'

'She said the bloke was posh, didn't look like a journalist, more like a bank manager. And he drove a snazzy car.'

'What sort of car?' Jack asked.

'A red Porsche.'

Marcus, Jack thought. He said, 'And the couple? Names? Did he ask Dilly to check the register?'

The young man nodded. 'He hung around and when they'd gone Dilly checked the payment on the computer.'

'Any idea at all of the names?'

'Nah, don't remember.'

Jack handed over twenty pounds. 'Thanks,' he said.

Sarah glanced at her watch as she heard a car come up the drive. It was a black Mercedes soft-top, it had a CD blasting out of the stereo and the roof was down. It stopped, the music cut off and Sarah waited, suddenly nervous. The doorbell went and she crossed the hall to answer it.

'Hello.'

Sandra stood with her arm round an embarrassed Jamie. She was nut brown, bottle blonde and wafer thin. She stared at Sarah, looked her up and down, then smiled, but not at all warmly. Sarah said, 'Hi, I'm Sarah Greg, a friend of Jack's. I'm sorry but he's been held up in London on a job and I said I'd get over here to meet Jamie. He won't be long, he should be back after supper.' Sarah looked at Jamie. He was staring at the ground.

Rory appeared behind Sarah and said, 'Hi, Jamie. How come you've got two Machokes? I could swop you Machoke for Haunter if you like. You've got Gastly but you haven't got Haunter. It's got sixty hit points.'

Jamie looked up. 'OK. Have you got two Haunters then?'

Sarah stood aside as he went into the house after Rory and Sandra called, 'Jamie darling, aren't you going to say goodbye to Mummy?'

'Bye!' he shouted from upstairs and Sandra smiled tightly.

'Would you like to come in?' Sarah asked.

'Oh, no, no thank you, I must get going. Tell Jack I'll be back on Friday to collect Jamie.'

She turned and headed for the car. Sandra waved, the engine started, the music blared and Sarah went inside. She glanced down at her pink dress and high-heeled sandals and smiled. They may only have been on for fifty seconds but it was more than worth it.

Roz took the call from Jack and told Lucie, who was staying at Chadwick Farm, exactly what he'd said. Lucie looked wretched and Roz didn't know what to say.

'Andrew's talking to a lawyer this evening,' she offered. 'You never know, what Jack said could be right. The investigation by the DTI might not come to anything . . .' But Lucie didn't even seem to hear her. She stared blankly at the wall and Roz left her to it.

Jack got the seven forty-five train to Gatwick and was home by nine. When he got to the cottage he found Sarah in the kitchen, all dressed up, with her notes, her diary and her phone bill out on the kitchen table. The boys were in bed, sharing Jamie's room.

'Hi. You look nice.'

'What? This old thing?' Even as she said it Sarah knew it didn't wash. She blushed and, meeting Jack's eye, said, 'OK, I got dressed up to meet Sandra. I couldn't let her see me in scruffy shorts and a T-shirt.'

Jack pulled out a chair. 'I bet she was pea-green by the time she left.'

'I'm not sure. She's tough competition.'

'Not for you, Sarah.' He said it so casually that she almost missed it; almost. He reached for her phone bill. 'What's this?'

'I've been doing some thinking,' Sarah said, 'and some checking. I'm not sure, but look at this. Marcus always phoned me on his mobile, but when I was checking my phone bill for any clues, I found a number I didn't recognise, here. It's Marcus's office. I rang it to check. I obviously phoned him once. I then had a look through my notebook and saw that the date I called him was around the time of the Sarasota deal. I'm pretty sure that it'll be on his office line.'

'And taped,' Jack said. 'This might be useful, Sarah.'

'How?'

Jack stood up. 'Let me go and see the boys, you open some wine and then we'll sit down and talk about it.' He headed for the door, then turned. He took two paces back to the table and kissed her mouth for the second time that day.

'Oh, I . . .'

He pulled back. 'Yes?'

She blushed. 'Nothing,' she murmured.

Jack stood straight. 'No, it's not nothing, Sarah,' he said. 'It's something, it's definitely something.' Then he turned and left the room.

Lucie pulled into a parking space directly outside her house. She had left Chadwick Farm on impulse, creeping away without telling anyone. It had taken her two hours to get home from Sussex but she was too strung-out to be tired. She looked up at her house. She hated it, it was chic, glossy and expensive, and empty of any warmth or comfort. It wasn't a home, it was a place she slept in, a place she was unhappy in. She would put it on the market as soon as she could.

She went inside. She took the extension lead out of the cupboard in the kitchen and took it into the bedroom. Marcus was at work; she knew that because his briefcase had gone. He must have gone in to check what was going on in the office, to see if the DTI had contacted him.

Lucie plugged the extension lead into the socket next to her bed and then took her hair dryer out of the drawer and plugged it into the extension lead. She stood and checked she could throw it into the bath from outside the bathroom. She could; she was ready. She rolled the extension lead up and carefully placed the hair dryer behind her bedside table. When Marcus got home after a day in the City he always took a bath. He would be home soon and then she would be free of him. She went upstairs to the guest suite and sat in the dark waiting for him to come in.

Sarah put her spoon and fork down neatly in the centre of her plate and said, 'That was the best spaghetti and tomato sauce I have ever had.'

Jack smiled, 'It was linguini and the sauce was supposed to have had mushrooms and bacon in it. Never mind, you obviously enjoyed it.'

'Gosh, did it show? Was I that greedy?'

'No, but you've got it on your chin.' Jack leaned forward. 'Come here.' She tilted her chin upwards and gently he touched it with the tip of his napkin. 'There.'

'Thanks.'

He didn't move back but stayed close to her, their faces almost touching. 'Sarah?'

Sarah held her breath, her stomach did a back flip and, without thinking, she reached forward and eased his mouth onto her own.

'Sarah, I . . .' She pressed her finger to his lips and stood up, moving back a pace to lean against the work surface. One of the straps of her dress had fallen down and as Jack stood in front of her he kissed her bare shoulder and licked the skin. 'Spaghetti sauce,' he murmured, 'how did it get there?'

Sarah smiled and closed her eyes. Jack moved his lips across from her shoulder to her neck. She slipped the other strap down and gently eased the dress to her waist. 'My God,' Jack whispered, 'you are so lovely.' He moved his hands up her thighs under her dress and put his mouth on to her breast. Sarah gasped. Then the phone rang.

'Shit . . .' Jack stopped and looked up. 'Don't move, I'll answer it and be right back.'

Jack hurried to answer the phone. Sarah stood where she was and pulled her dress up. A few minutes more and he came back into the kitchen. 'That was Graham. Apparently Lucie has gone off, just left without telling anyone.'

'So?'

Jack frowned. 'She left a note for Janie. It says . . . "I know you loved him; sorry, sorry, sorry."' Jack looked at Sarah.

'Oh shit,' she said.

It was late when Marcus got in; he had been for a drink with a colleague. He didn't know where Lucie was but he wasn't worried. Personnel had confirmed this afternoon that the DTI had looked at him and passed him over as not involved in Lucie's case.

He went straight into the bedroom and undressed. Then he ran a bath. He went into the living area naked, and slipped a CD into the player—they had speakers in the bathroom; it was Elgar, slow and soothing.

Back in the bathroom Marcus had a shave and sprinkled some lavender oil into the bath water. It was a ritual he had most nights—a ritual Lucie knew only too well.

When Marcus slipped into the bath, Lucie headed quietly towards the bedroom. She saw his suit and shirt discarded on the floor, just as she had been discarded without any care or consideration, and she hated him. She heard him humming to the music and she hated him with every living fibre in her body. She pulled the extension lead to the door of the bathroom and switched the hair dryer on. Her heart was beating fast. Just one throw into the water and the current would electrocute him. One step forward, one lunge through the door and one throw. She took a pace forward.

The phone rang. Springing back, Lucie held her breath but the phone went immediately on to answerphone. She switched off the dryer and heard Janie's voice.

'Lucie, please call me now. Lucie, don't do anything silly, please, just pick up the phone if you're there or call me . . . please . . .' The line went dead and Lucie closed her eyes. Oh God, oh dear God, what was she doing? How had she come to this? She dropped to her knees and hugged her arms round her body. 'I could have killed him,' she whispered to herself. The tears came uncontrollably and she had to bite back the sobs that rose in her chest. Trembling, she got to her feet and made her way out of the house. In the street she finally let herself cry. She stumbled to Alex's car, climbed in and bent double with the pain in her heart. She had lost everything, but much, much worse than that was the fact that she had almost lost herself.

Janie looked at Sarah and said, 'I don't know if I can do it, Sarah.'

Roz lit a cigarette. 'If we don't do it then the bastard gets off scot-free—doesn't he? Are you happy with that? Because I'm not.'

Janie rubbed her hands wearily over her face. 'Sarah? Are you sure you want to go through with it? Do you honestly think it will work?'

As soon as they had heard from Lucie, Sarah had called a meeting. It was after midnight, but none of them seemed to realise the time. They were at a point where nothing mattered except getting it straight.

'Jack seems to think it'll work and I trust him.'

'And if you don't call his bluff?' Janie asked. 'Will you go through with the threat?'

Sarah shrugged. 'Maybe.'

Janie shook her head. 'No,' she said, 'there must be another way. Perhaps if we talk to him, reason with him?'

'I want revenge and I'm sure Sarah does too.' Roz yawned and stretched. 'I've got to get home, Sarah; I'm sorry but I'm shattered. I'm with you on this one. Do it, Sarah love, and do it tomorrow.' Sarah looked at Janie.

Janie closed her eyes for a moment. She didn't know about revenge, she just knew about pain and people getting hurt.

'No one will get hurt,' Sarah said, as if reading her mind.

Janie opened her eyes and returned Sarah's gaze. 'OK,' she said.

Sarah let out a breath. 'Good.' But she didn't smile at all, her face was set in grim determination.

CHAPTER TWELVE

JACK WOKE SARAH UP with a cup of tea. She had slept in his spare room—she hadn't wanted to, but she hadn't had the courage to say so. She sat up and rubbed her eyes and he said, 'We need to go over everything one last time, Sarah. Is that OK? Are you up to it?'

'Yes, that's fine. How're Jamie and Rory?'

'They're watching CBBC. They seem to be the best of friends.'

Sarah smiled. 'Right,' she said, 'I'll get up then.'

'There's a clean towel in the bathroom for you.' He hovered by the door. 'After today, Sarah,' he began.

'Yes?'

He coughed. 'I mean, once we get through it all, would you, erm, I mean, can we . . .'

She looked at him. 'Go to bed? Yes, we can, Jack.'

He took a pace back and stared, then suddenly smiled. 'Oh, gosh, I was going to ask you if we could have dinner, but going to bed is fine.'

Sarah screamed and dived under the duvet. 'Oh God, oh God, this is so embarrassing, this is so awful . . . I can't believe I said that, I . . .'

Jack came across and lifted a corner of the duvet, looking under it at her. 'Just joking,' he said. 'Actually, I was going to say "cement our relationship", but going to bed is what I meant.'

Janie arrived with Katie at eight thirty sharp to look after Rory and Jamie. Sarah and Jack were ready, the equipment was packed. Jack spoke quietly to Janie while Sarah got the kids some drinks.

'As soon as you get my call, drive to the nearest phone box, ring the police and ask to be put through to CID. Tell them you saw a silver Mercedes—give the registration number, I've written it down there for you—purposely drive into a 2CV. Give the time and date, and say you don't wish to be identified. OK? They'll trace the call but it'll be a public phone so you should be safe. Then get back here and be ready to go when we arrive.'

Janie looked at him. 'You really think this is the right thing to do?'

Jack touched her arm. 'Yes, I do, but you don't have to come if you don't want to, Janie. I'm sure the others will understand.'

Janie shook her head. 'I do have to come,' she answered, 'they need my support. And besides, I started this so I should finish it, right?'

Jack nodded. 'Right.' He turned as Sarah came into the hall. 'OK, Sarah, let's go!'

Stan Gamley parked his car in the short-term car park at Gatwick airport. An attractive woman with a clipboard came across to him as he did so and said, 'Excuse me, sir, but I'm from the airport authority and I wonder if you could spare me a short amount of your time?'

Gamley shook his head. 'Sorry, love, I've got a plane to catch.'

'It's just five minutes and we're giving away free parking for up to five days in this car park as a reward. It's five minutes at the most, really.'

Gamley sighed. 'All right, go on then.'

The woman smiled. 'Great! Thank you. If you wouldn't mind stepping towards the lifts, sir, the light's better there.'

Gamley went with the woman to the lift area and Jack crouched down at the back of Gamley's car and picked the lock on the boot. He raised it and saw the combination lock on Gamley's case.

'Shit,' he muttered. He tried the catch anyway. It opened; Gamley hadn't locked it yet. Gently, Jack prised the lid off the suitcase. Clothes. He dug his hands in and came across something smooth. He pulled. A wadge of money—fifty-pound notes—came out.

He smiled. 'Gotcha.' He pushed the case shut, clicked the boot down and crawled five cars along. Then he stood up and went towards the lifts.

'You can take this to the airport authority desk inside the terminal and get your free parking,' the woman said. 'Have a nice flight.'

Gamley took the voucher and walked off. He collected his case from his car and headed towards Departures. Jack, already inside the terminal, had just made his call to Customs and Excise. He watched as Gamley went to check in. Two Customs officials appeared and asked him to accompany them. Jack smiled. He took out his phone and called Janie.

Back at his car, the woman with the clipboard was waiting for him. 'Bloody nice work, Sarah,' he said. 'Gamley is history.' He took her hand. 'Janie is calling the police, so hopefully that's Redfern taken care of. Now, let's give that little Marcus what he deserves.'

Bill Redfern was in a meeting when one of the secretaries knocked and put her head round the door. He was just about to present his brief on future development in West Sussex to the chairman and chief executive.

'Mr Redfern?' she said. 'I'm sorry to interrupt, but we've got someone from Crawley CID here and he'd like to talk to you.'

Redfern frowned. 'Can't it wait? I'm just about to start my—'

'I think you should see to it, Bill,' the chief executive said. Redfern nodded and left the meeting room and outside in the corridor met two uniformed officers along with two men from CID.

'Mr William Redfern?'

'Yes.'

'I wonder if you'd be good enough to accompany us down to the station, sir. We are making enquiries into a road traffic accident on the 17th of July and we believe you might be able to help us.'

He glanced at the cold face of the CID officer. Beyond him, through the plate-glass window, he saw a swarm of officers closing in on his car. He closed his eyes for a moment, then he said, 'I'll just get my jacket.'

Marcus was more than surprised when he was told that Sarah Greg, Roz Betts and Janie Leighton were in reception. He hurried down, hoping that they weren't there to make a scene.

'Ladies, good morning.'

'Hello, Marcus,' Janie said coolly. 'We need to talk, is there somewhere we can go?'

He looked momentarily confused. 'Oh, yes, erm . . .' He looked behind him at the girl on reception. 'Is there a meeting room free?'

She checked her book, then said, 'Meeting room three.'

'This way please . . .' Marcus led the way up to the first floor. Once inside, he said, 'I'm sorry for all this mess, I really am. If there's anything I can do to help, then please, let me know.'

'You could start by telling the truth,' Roz said.

'I'm sorry?' Marcus frowned. 'I don't understand, I . . .'

'Oh, for God's sake, Marcus!' Janie snapped. 'Stop it, will you? This is me, Janie, your sister, remember? I know what happened. We all know what happened, that it was you . . .' And despite her steely determination not to get upset, Janie had to stop and bite back the tears.

'Janie, this is ludicrous! What are you saying? Why on earth would I do something like that?'

Sarah interrupted him and said, 'You were the one that set this up. You used Janie, Roz and me to further your own ends. You pretended friendship, fed me information that you gleaned from Lucie, illegal knowledge . . .'

Marcus stood shaking his head. 'I simply can't believe this!' He looked at Janie. 'Who told you this? Was it Lucie?'

Janie looked away.

'I thought so! You would rather believe a woman who deceived me, a woman who was sleeping with someone else in her lunch hour, lying, cheating . . .' He spat the last two words out so vehemently that Janie jerked round to look at him. "You would rather believe that slut than me, your own brother. How could you, Janie?'

Janie took a sharp breath in and Sarah stepped forward. 'You've known about Lucie's affair for months and this was your revenge, wasn't it, Marcus? Well, it didn't work. We know what you've been doing and we're going to talk to the DTI about it.'

Marcus suddenly laughed. 'And how will you talk to the DTI? You have proof, do you?'

Sarah clenched her fist. The temptation to hit him was strong. 'Yes, I have proof, Marcus. On my phone bill I have a call that I made to your office. I made a few notes before I called, look . . .' Sarah opened her notebook. 'I rang to ask you what the chances were of Sarasota being taken over. You said, and I've written it down, you said, "a very strong chance, upwards of ninety per cent". There's no way you'd make that sort of comment if you didn't actually know that the company was going to be taken over. All I have to do is ring Ms Stimpson, she's the woman at the Stock Exchange who started the investigation, and ask her to check your calls.'

Marcus snatched the phone bill that Sarah held out to him, screwed it up into a ball and stuffed it into his pocket. 'This is rubbish. I never said that, I wouldn't be that stupid. The DTI will have checked my tapes. You're making it all up.'

Sarah smiled and said, 'I might be, but are you prepared to take the risk? If you're completely innocent, let's ring Janice Stimpson and check.'

Marcus took a pace back and gripped the table behind him. Sarah could see that his knuckles were white. He turned to Janie.

'Give me a minute with Sarah,' he said. 'Please?'

Janie glanced at Roz and they moved towards the door. 'We'll be right outside, Sarah,' Roz said. 'Shout if you need anything.'

Marcus looked at Sarah. 'What d'you want, Sarah?' he asked. 'Money? How much do you want?'

'I want you to tell me the truth to start with and then we'll negotiate. I want your time and your expertise and then I want you to do something that isn't for you, but something that's for someone else.'

Janie and Roz were waiting for Sarah out in the corridor and when she left the meeting room they turned to look at her.

Roz raised an eyebrow and Sarah shrugged. They stood in silence for a few moments then walked towards the lifts.

'Is it over?' Janie asked.

'Yes, in one way,' Sarah answered. She took a deep breath and let it out slowly. 'And in another,' she said, 'it's only just beginning.'

CHAPTER THIRTEEN

SARAH PUT THE PHONE DOWN and shouted up the stairs. Jack appeared at the top of the stairs tying his tie and Rory was right behind him.

'Come on,' Sarah said, 'we'll be late if you don't get a move on.'

Jack came down, two stairs at a time. 'Who was on the phone?' he asked.

'It was an order for six Christmas terracotta urns. I said you'd suggest the plants and that they started at sixty-five pounds each.' Rory came down and Sarah said, 'You look great, Rory. Have you got your microphone aid?'

He smiled and patted the belt round his waist under his sweater.

Jack kissed Sarah on the forehead. 'Thanks, SG.' He then looked at Rory. 'All wired up?'

'Yup.'

Jack ruffled his hair. 'Top man. Let's go then.'

Sarah led them out and glanced behind her at the house that was now her home. She smiled. She had an awful lot to smile about.

Roz was driving, Graham was combing his hair in the passenger seat, Kitty was fighting with Oliver in the back and Justin was singing loudly as they pulled out of the drive of Chadwick Farm.

'Stop a minute, love,' Graham said. 'The Gordens are up the road.'

Roz ground her teeth. 'Graham, we haven't got time.'

'Just slow down and I'll wind the window down.' He looked at her. 'Come on, love, all's well that ends well.'

Roz slowed and Graham wound the window down. When the deal with Glover Homes had fallen through, Graham had made the Gordens a good offer for their land but they wouldn't sell. It had enraged Roz, She'd thought it was petty and mean. But after buying the Major a drink in the pub, Graham had secured the promise of first refusal should the Gordens ever want to move.

'Good morning,' Graham called to the Major as they passed by.

Cecil Gorden turned. 'Hello there, family Betts. Yes, it's a glorious morning. How about coming over for a drink later, just before lunch?'

Surprised by the invitation, Roz turned and Daphne Gorden waved.

'We'd love to,' Graham said. 'What about midday?'

'Perfect,' the Major declared and finally Roz smiled.

As Graham wound the window up, Roz said, 'Wonders will never cease.' And Graham smiled.

'If you'll let them,' he replied.

'Tell Mummy we're going to be late if she doesn't hurry up,' Andrew said to Katie, but just as she was climbing out of the car the post van pulled up and Janie slammed the front door shut, taking the mail from the postman as she passed him.

She climbed into the car, looked through the letters and found the one she had been waiting for. She glanced at Andrew. 'Open it,' he said. She nodded but still held the envelope, too frightened of what it might or might not contain to open it.

Andrew took it from her. 'Shall I do it?'

'Yes.'

He ripped it open and pulled out the letter. He read, '"Dear Janie and Andrew, it is with great pleasure that I am writing to inform you that you have been accepted onto our foster programme and I will be in contact soon to arrange an initial meeting with our foster team."' He stopped, then reached over to hug Janie.

'What's the matter, Mummy?' Katie asked. 'Why are you crying?'

Janie pulled away from Andrew, and blew her nose. 'I'm crying because I'm happy, darling,' she said.

The church was packed for the Ledworth House Christmas service. It was an annual occasion; the choir sang, the boys did readings and the headmaster spoke about the year for the school. Sarah sat in the front pew next to Jack and Jamie, Roz and all the Betts family and Janie, Andrew and Katie. Rory sat with the rest of the boys further down at the front, ready to sing and nervously awaiting his reading.

They sang the first carol and then the headmaster stood up to speak.

'It is with great pleasure that I welcome you all here this morning for our Christmas service,' he began. 'But it is with particular warmth that I welcome our guests, the Betts family and the Leighton family, all of whom have been instrumental in setting up a trust fund. . .'

'Half of his bonus,' Sarah whispered to Jack.

'Donated by Mr Marcus Todd, one of the City's top analysts, and invested in the stock market under his own expert management. The interest from this fund will pay for two assisted places in the school for the coming academic year.' There was a round of applause and Sarah caught Roz's eye. She winked.

Later, outside the church, Sarah, Roz and Janie stood together, as they had stood many months earlier outside school.

'There'll be no trips to London to catch up on the latest fashions,' Roz warned. 'No turning up to school looking as if you've had your hair done.'

Sarah threw a look at Roz that warned her she was going too far.

'I mean,' Roz said, 'that life with toddlers is very different.'

'Good,' Janie replied. 'Different I can handle.'

Sarah squeezed her arm. 'Well, I think it's great. Good on you, Janie.'

Jack joined the women and took Sarah's hand. 'Heard from Lucie?' he asked Janie as they walked off towards the cars. Janie nodded. 'Lucie is in Africa, working for Oxfam. She sent me a letter the other day. She's . . .' What could Janie say? Lucie was bitter and angry and full of recriminations. It wasn't a letter, more a diatribe on Marcus, but she didn't say any of that; pride wouldn't let her. 'She's fine,' Janie finished. There are some things, she thought, that you never get past, some things that almost destroy you and she knew that she was thinking about herself as much as Lucie. But she had got past it—in a way—and she had not been destroyed. She was lucky. They had all been lucky. The dream catcher, she realised, wasn't about catching dreams but making sense of them.

MARIA BARRETT

Maria Barrett left university in the mid-eighties with ambitions to make a splash in the money markets. Indeed, she was absolutely thrilled when she was offered a fantasic job as a broker in an investment bank. However, it did not take her long to realise that she was in the wrong job and make a lateral move into financial PR. This time she felt that the job was right—but not very satisfying, so she started to write a novel, which her secretary typed for her. 'It was fun, but at that time I had no thoughts that it would lead to a new career,' Maria told me. 'Then a friend recommended that I send my novel to someone they knew who was having a break from the publishing industry.' This turned out to be Philippa Harrison, now Chairman of Little, Brown, who gave Maria a great deal of encouragement and guided her through a number of rewrites. Spurred on by this encouragement, Maria decided to give up her PR job and, to earn some money while writing, she started teaching fitness classes. Her first novel, *Elle*, was finally published in 1993 and now, nine successful novels later, Maria Barrett is delighted with her career as a novelist.

'If you are dedicated, writing is something that you can combine with motherhood,' says Maria, and she should know, for she has three children all

under the age of seven: William, Lily and Edward. 'In fact, the idea for *The Dream Catcher* came about because of the children. I was listening to a radio programme on investment clubs in the school car park and it started the novel rolling.' Maria goes on to reveal that *The Dream Catcher* is the most personal novel she has written so far. 'One of my sons is deaf,' she told me, 'so writing about a deaf child in the novel came very much from my heart. We found out that our son needed a receiver aid in the classroom last year and that, for me personally, although he had been aided for years, was a very visual statement. I found being able to write about it was a very cathartic experience '

When I met Maria Barrett she had just been to the Victoria and Albert Museum to do some research for her next novel, which has some scenes set in Victorian times. She told me that 'writing a novel is very much a marinating process, you just keep adding in little bits you hear or read, but sometimes you have to do in-depth research as well.'

Maria starts her working day with a four-mile run, after which, she admits, 'I sit for ages over breakfast, reading the paper, doing the crossword, procrastinating over when to go to my study and start writing. It's not that I don't enjoy writing—I love it—but it can sometimes become a job just like any other. And who wouldn't prefer to relax rather than work!'

Jane Eastgate

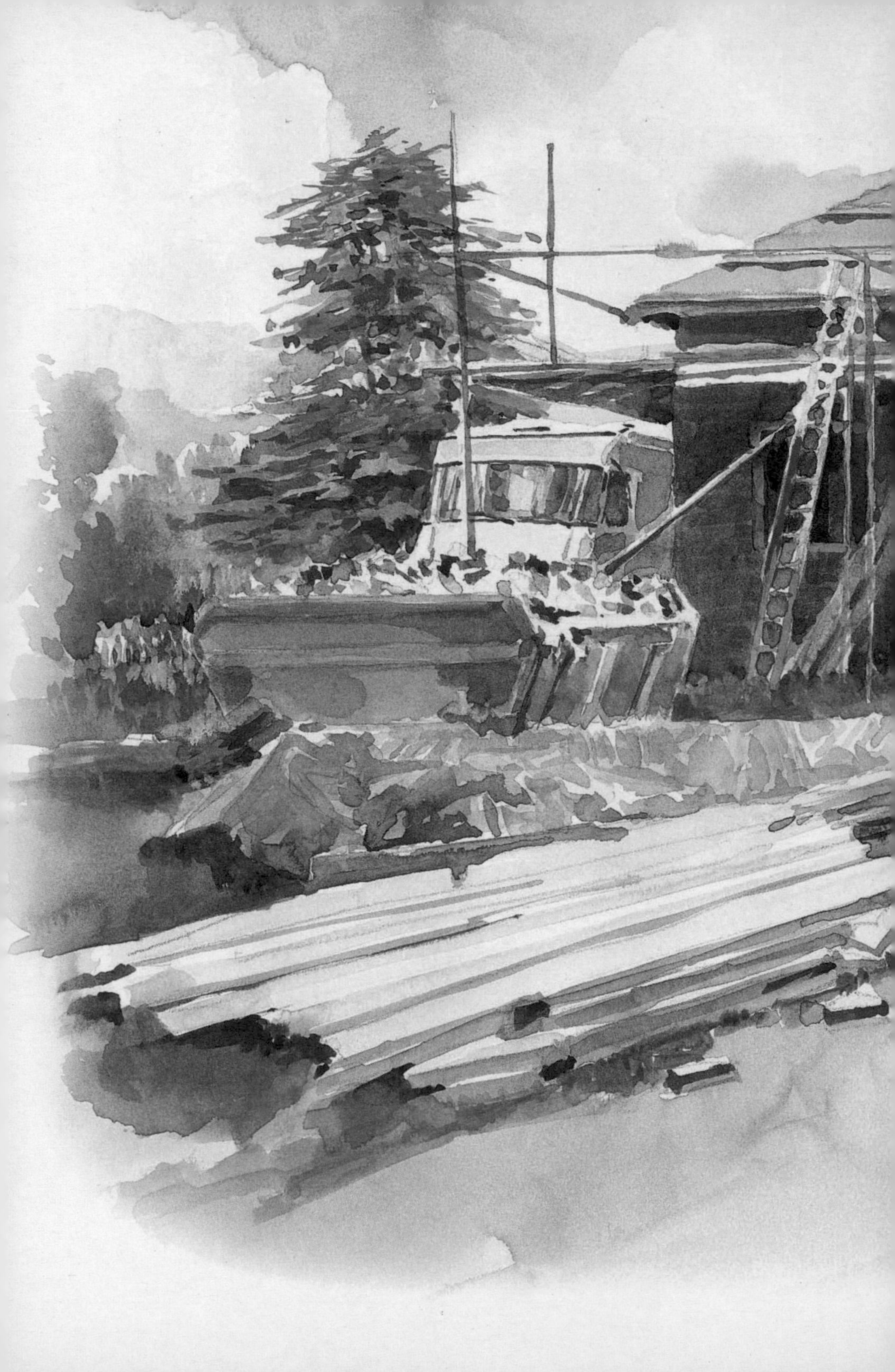

OLIVIA'S
LUCK
Catherine Alliott

When Olivia inherits her dream house in St Albans, she sees it as a forever place where she and her husband Johnny can raise their daughter Claudia. Yes, it needs major renovation, but the builders can sort that out. Then, one day, as Olivia is debating what colour to paint the hall, Johnny announces that he is leaving. As Olivia tries to come to terms with why he has gone and how she is going to carry on alone, she finds herself caught up in a tide of events that will sweep her into new, unchartered waters.

Chapter One

ALF REGARDED ME with his one good eye. It was brown and troubled and beginning to look as glassy as the other one. He frowned as he tried to make sense of it all. 'What—you mean he's left you, like?'

'That's it, Alf.'

'For good? Scarpered?'

'So it appears.'

'And—and so what, ain't he never coming back then?'

I caught my breath at the brutality of my husband's plan laid bare. 'No, Alf, apparently not. Total desertion seems to be his game plan.'

Alf continued to look mystified. He scratched his head, and then the penny—slow to drop at the best of times—began its gradual descent.

'Well, bugger me,' he gaped, stunned.

I licked my lips. 'Quite.'

Leaving him to his astonishment, I turned briskly to my other two builders, who, thus far, had been silent throughout this exchange.

Alf's brother, Mac, the foreman, and the brains of the team, was watching me closely, his blue eyes assessing this dramatic shift, while Spiro, the emotional young Greek in my incongruous masonry trio, was having trouble keeping his jaw from wobbling. His black, mournful moustache drooped low and his dark eyes were filling ominously.

'Your husband *leave* you?' he spluttered incredulously. 'Alone, here, with a young child and a falling-down house and bad drains and—' his eyes grew wide as he regarded me with horror—'looking so *terrible*?'

'The house, I hope, not me, Spiro,' I quipped nervously.

He frowned. '*Ti?*'

'Um, no, never mind. Yes, well, of course, you're right, the house *is* in a terrible state but then it's bound to look worse before it looks better, but once it's gutted—'

'*You're* gutted!' he roared. '*I'm* gutted! I cannot believe what sort of a man *do* this to you!' With that he snatched his tea-cosy hat from his head and, with a great wail, buried his face in it. I had a sudden urge to snatch it from him and do exactly the same. Instead I patted his shoulder.

'So you'll be giving all this up then, will you, luv?' asked Mac.

I straightened up to my working foreman, ever the pragmatist, and met his bright blue eyes defiantly. 'How d'you mean, Mac?'

'Well, now that it's all gone pear-shaped you're not gonna want to carry on wiv all this malarkey just for yourself and Claudes, are you?'

He jerked his head dismissively at the building site around us: the excuse for the kitchen where we were standing, with its open rafters covered by a flapping blue tarpaulin; the soggy concrete at our feet; the rotten sash windows with their broken cords; the sixties-style Formica units. Yes, this 'malarkey' that was my home.

I cleared my throat. 'Actually, Mac, that's exactly why I've asked you all to down tools for a minute. You see, the thing is, I fully intend to go on.' I drew myself up to my full five foot three and tucked my short dark hair behind my ears, struggling to look braver than I felt. 'The fact that my husband has seen fit to abscond is neither here nor there, because we're going on as planned. I took on this tip of a house with the sole intention of restoring it to its former glory, and that's still my dream. As far as I'm concerned this is still a forever house and I want—' I broke off as, to my horror, my voice wobbled.

Around me, there was embarrassed scuffing of toes in the dirt and faces turned to the floor. A moment later I'd regained my composure.

'Listen, boys, I'll level with you,' I said quietly. 'I wanted to put you in the picture because I know you've all been wondering where the hell "the guv'nor" is. Well, frankly, I'm fresh out of ideas. I'm right out of courses he might be on, or weekend golf tournaments that seem to go on all week, and—oh God, I'm just sick to the back teeth of having to lie. Constantly. To you, to my friends, to everyone at Claudia's school.'

There was a short and sympathetic silence. Then Mac spoke. 'What about the moolah then, luv?'

I blinked. 'Sorry?'

'The dough, the money. I hate to seem heartless, but if he's done a runner and we're gonna go on wiv the work as planned, we need to be clear that at the end of the day, we're gonna get paid.' He raised his eyebrows and gave me a wry, quizzical smile. 'Know what I mean?'

'I understand your concerns, but believe me, you've got no worries on that score. My husband might have seen fit to remove himself physically, but financially, I'm OK. You will be paid in the usual, mutually acceptable manner of folding readies in a big brown envelope.'

Mac pursed his lips thoughtfully. Then he smiled. 'We'll get on wiv it then, shall we, luv?' said Mac kindly. 'Get back to work, like?'

'Please, Mac.' I smiled gratefully, but I also knew that this was my cue to leave. Now that the delicate little matter of the money had been 'sorted', the interview was over as far as Mac was concerned. No worries, just so long as they all got paid.

I'd been testing some Crown Matchpots in the front hall when Johnny had announced his intentions.

There I was, behind the front door, painting away merrily, when I heard the garden gate go, heard his familiar footsteps up the gravel path. Knowing instinctively that hotfoot from his evening commute he'd be tired, bad-tempered and in need of a drink, I sat back on my heels and arranged my expression into one of amused contemplation. As his head came round the door, I looked up with a wry smile.

'You know, anyone would think they aim these paints at the dirty-mac brigade,' I said, holding up my two little pots. 'You have a choice here, my darling,' I waggled them at him, 'Beaver or Muff!'

I grinned, enjoying my little joke and waiting for him to laugh, but as he stared back I noticed his face was very pale, his lips tight.

'I don't care what colour you paint the sodding hall,' he muttered. 'I'm leaving.'

And so saying, he pushed past me and on up the stairs, at which point I do recall that I at least managed to say, 'Beaver it is then!'

Yes, that was how my husband left me. Those were the very special words with which he chose to end our marriage.

Functioning on automatic, I dipped my brush conscientiously into the turps to stop it drying out, then, somehow, I eased myself up and stumbled blindly towards our tiny makeshift kitchen. In the middle was a small pine table. I sat down shakily, resting my elbows and clasping my hands together, almost in an attitude of prayer. I listened. Upstairs, drawers were shooting in and out, coat hangers were clanking and the wardrobe slammed shut. Then it grew quieter and I could tell he'd moved to the bathroom, getting his shaving things together, his toothbrush. I fumbled for my cigarette packet and lit one, blowing the smoke out in a long straight line to the fridge. I stared. On it was an ancient photograph of me and Johnny. It was one Claudia had found at the bottom of a drawer, pounced on in delight, and screaming with laughter at our impossible eighties clothes and hairstyles, had stuck up with a magnet. I narrowed my eyes at it now. I was about, ooh, seventeen, I suppose, and in someone's garden, Johnny's perhaps. There I was, small, skinny, awkward-looking, with wide-apart grey eyes and a slightly too large nose. And there was Johnny beside me, who to my mind hadn't changed. Tall, broad-shouldered, laughing merrily, those bright blue eyes staring challengingly at the camera, and a flop of blond hair falling permanently in his eyes, as it still did. In the background I could see Imogen and Molly . . . it must have been about seventeen years ago. Half my life, when I'd first met Johnny.

I'd been with Molly and Imogen at the time, of course. Everything I did in those days was with them and, to a large extent, still is.

It was Molly who saw him first, at the fair on the village green. He was standing with a couple of friends in the queue for the big wheel; tall, tousled, blond, with wicked blue eyes, and roaring with laughter. He oozed glamour but also, at a glance, that automatic social ease that comes from an expensive education. Our plan had been to head back to the ghost train, but without a word of discussion, the three of us turned as one, and made our way to the big wheel. Molly, vivacious, curly-haired, with dark, dancing eyes, pranced up, and deliberately queue-barged her way in front of him, with Imogen and me giggling in her wake.

'Hey, what's your game?' he rounded on her.

'Sorry, we didn't realise you were queuing,' she smiled sweetly.

'Oh right, so what did you think we were doing then—standing in a line behind total strangers just for the hell of it?'

Molly's dark eyes widened. 'Well, it's a possibility.'

Nudging and giggling we then piled into the next empty cart and Johnny and his friends had to make do indignantly with the one behind. As we soared up into the night sky they hooted and catcalled after us, pelting us with peanuts, and we dutifully squeaked and ducked, pretending to be outraged, but loving every minute of it.

Of course, we trailed around after the boys for the rest of the evening then, as they, in turn, went through the adolescent ritual of groaning and trying to lose us. Inevitably, though, all six of us ended up together outside the only pub on the green, equipped with far too many goldfish, candy floss in our hair, cigarettes glowing competitively, and all eyes bright with possibility. Johnny, aged eighteen, went in for the drinks and we sat on the grass outside. We gleaned from the other two boys that they were all at Harrow, but they'd been allowed out for the evening. 'So long as we're back by—ooh—' one of them coolly flashed his Rolex—'about midnight, I suppose.' Suitably impressed by their bravado but just about managing not to show it, we'd sipped our lager-and-limes; Molly, flirting like billyo, Imogen, blonde and beautiful and not needing to, and me, certainly needing to but not having the confidence.

After that first meeting, it somehow seemed only natural for the six of us to hang around together. During this time we more or less lived at Johnny's parents' house, which was something of an eye-opener. I'd never seen anything quite like the McFarllens' estate, and probably never will. It was huge, it was Jacobean, it was turreted—it was even *moated*, for God's sake. The lifeblood of the place was the stables, which were adjacent to the house and run like a slick, well-oiled machine—just like the thoroughbred racing machines they housed.

Inside, the house was full of colour and drama. There was a blood-red dining room, a pale blue morning room, vibrant chintz in the sitting room, murals in the bathrooms and each bed had a huge crucifix hanging over it. This, it transpired, was down to Oliver, Johnny's father, who, born a Protestant, made a dramatic conversion to Catholicism and had filled the place with the trappings of his new-found religion. But for all Oliver's religious fervour, one didn't have to look far to find signs of a hedonistic lifestyle. There were shotgun cartridges in the bath, empty whisky bottles behind the loo, and betting slips in every overflowing ashtray, all of which, I thought, gave the place a thrilling air of debauchery.

It spoke to me, released something pent up and suburban in my soul. Never in my life had I come across such warmth, such unbridled fun for the sheer hell of it, such a house that rocked, almost literally, with laughter, and in the middle of it all, of course, the golden boy, Johnny. You see, there wasn't a great deal of joy in the house I grew up in. My father had left home when I was four, but before he'd flown off to Canberra with Mum's best friend, Yvonne, he'd thoughtfully provided for my education by leaving the wherewithal for me to stay at The Sacred Heart Convent School until I was eighteen.

Whether Mum's religious fervour was as strong before Dad's departure as it was after, I'm not sure, but I do know that once deserted, alone and grief-stricken, she'd transferred any passion she had left in her soul to God, and Jean Muir, and not necessarily in that order.

The bizarre Jean Muir fixation had come about because she'd worked as a fitter in Miss Muir's couture house, and, from the day Dad left, she dressed solely in navy-blue shift dresses, with only a string of pearls and earrings, her hair styled neatly in a bob, all very chic, all very à la Jean.

Looks were everything to Mum, who was half French, and she hoodwinked the world quite successfully, so that it always came as a surprise to people to realise we were poor. After all, I went to an expensive private school and Mum looked like she'd fallen out of *Vogue*, so it was only when people came to the house—a tiny, Victorian terraced villa with threadbare carpets and cheap furniture—that the dawn came up.

But the summer of fun didn't last for ever, and that October, after a final, wild goodbye party at the McFarllens', Johnny and the boys went off to university. Molly and I still had another year together at school, but Imogen, being bright as well as beautiful, went up to Oxford a year early to read Fine Art. Coincidentally, Johnny also went up to Oxford, to read Classics, and funnily enough, within a week or two of term beginning, he'd asked Imogen out.

Imogen and Johnny went out for three years, all their time together at Oxford, while Molly and I kept watch from less traditional, more red-brick, seats of learning. And they were surely the golden couple: Imogen, tall, slim, with her sheet of blonde hair slipping silkily down her back, slanting blue eyes and high forehead—cruising for a First with an icy cool nerve—while Johnny scraped a Two-two—'A gentleman's degree,' he told us with a broad grin, 'means I've had a good time'—and always with the serene, unflappable Imogen on his arm. Deliriously happy, yes, but when they came out of university together, still very young, still only twenty-one, no one had given a thought to marriage.

As I sat in my tiny, makeshift scullery kitchen, I blew a stream of smoke at the faded old photo on the fridge. Yes, it was funny really, I reflected. Molly had found him, Imogen had loved him, but at the end of the day, it had been me who'd married him.

One of the McFarllen parties that sticks particularly in my mind was for Johnny's youngest sister, Tara's, seventeenth birthday. Johnny had rigged the barn up in a parody of a seventies disco, with flashing strobe lights and a jukebox belting out Abba in the corner, and Tara and her friends were giggling in flares and headbands. Entering into the spirit of the thing, Molly, Imogen and I pranced about around our handbags, while the boys played imaginary guitars, shutting their eyes and banging their heads together in mock ecstasy. While we danced, I remember looking out through the open barn doors to the house beyond. Through the dining-room window a dinner party was in full swing, and as I watched, I saw Johnny's father, Oliver, get up, take the decanter around the table, and pause to kiss his wife, Angie, on the back of her neck.

Later, after we'd all piled out of the barn and into the swimming pool, hot and exhausted from dancing, they'd joined us; Angie, ostensibly leading her guests out through the French windows for a drink by the pool, but secretly anxious lest one of Tara's friends had had too much to drink and sank to the bottom. They were all pretty tanked up too, and as they watched us swim relay races, one particularly loud, portly individual peeled off his dinner jacket and prepared to join us. As he jumped in, suddenly a shout went up from Johnny, and he and his sisters rushed to ambush him, intent on debagging. Amid the inevitable splashing and shrieking, I crawled out of the other end, laughing and enjoying it all but, as ever, not wanting to get too involved. Oliver was beside me. He handed me a towel and I wrapped it around me, giggling as fat man got his comeuppance.

'Perfect, aren't they?' he murmured.

I glanced back and followed Oliver's gaze to where Johnny and his three sisters were still streaking through the pool, their tanned, lithe bodies glistening in the moonlight.

I smiled. 'Perfect.'

I mention this party because I remember it well, but also because it was the last one, you see. A couple of weeks later, something happened that was to change all our lives. On an equally balmy, hot August evening, Oliver McFarllen put a gun to his head and shot himself.

The party line was that it had been an accident. That he'd been climbing over a fence and had fallen on top of his gun which he'd propped up carefully on the other side, and that it had simply gone off. But Oliver McFarllen had been handling a shotgun since he was twelve; accidental death didn't hold much water, so suppositions abounded. The fact was, however, no one knew why on earth he'd done it, least of all his wife.

The grief almost swallowed her whole. She clung to her family, but their world had gone black too, especially for Johnny. His beloved father, whom he believed himself to be so like, only not so magnificent—to have ended it all in this terrible way.

Imogen came back immediately, of course. She'd just started a post-grad fine arts course in Florence, but she put down her paintbrush and was by Johnny's side for the funeral and for a couple of days after, too. But then, of course, she had to go back. Life goes on, and all the other usual clichés, and she couldn't just abandon her course.

Johnny understood. Weeks went by, and he had to struggle on as normal, making his daily trudge to the City where he'd started in the corporate finance department of a large investment bank. But more than six weeks later, with plenty of weekends in between, still Imogen didn't return. Johnny, baffled, flew out to Florence, and took a taxi straight round to her flat. Hot and dishevelled from his journey, he was greeted at the door by a swarthy young Latin called Paolo, who, wearing nothing but a towel and a cynical smile, had informed him that Imogen was busy. Johnny, furious, didn't stop to find out more and flew straight home, whereupon Imogen, distraught, phoned every hour, begging him to believe that Paolo was just a friend—a neighbour, actually—who was just using her shower until his was fixed. But Johnny was like prosecuting council, pushing her to admit that she was having an affair. Finally, she broke down and admitted she was.

Johnny was not a man to take infidelity lying down, as it were, and against a backdrop of his father's death, there was no mitigation, no room for forgiveness. A wall of silence went up between them, made worse by the fact that Imogen continued to see Paolo. Molly and I were appalled, but she was adamant that she was the victim.

'He cast me aside, don't you see? If he'd loved me he'd have forgiven me one small indiscretion.'

'Yes, but you're still seeing Paolo! You're making it a huge indiscretion now—what's he supposed to think?'

'Well, he can think what he bloody well likes!'

And Johnny did, indeed, think a great deal. When I met him for our customary lunchtime drink in the City, where I was doing a poxy secretarial course, he was erudite on the subject.

'She's a tart,' he said simply.

'Oh, Johnny, that's unfair,' I murmured loyally.

'It's true, Livvy. Has she told you she loves him?'

'Well, no, but—'

'So what's she doing with him then?'

I sighed. This was typical of Johnny. If you weren't whole-hearted, what was the point? Whole-heartedness had been part of his father's make-up, and therefore part of Johnny's.

'How's Angie?' I asked, changing the subject.

Johnny reached for the bottle of Chardonnay and refilled our glasses.

'Sad,' he said simply. 'Sad and quiet. Come and dig with her this weekend, Livvy. You know how she loves that. Come and stay.'

I smiled. It had been a long-standing joke from way back, this eccentric—at my age apparently—love of gardening. Like his mother, I liked nothing more than to be down among the slugs and the earthworms, sowing and separating and potting on, and this secretarial course was really only to mark time until I got up the nerve to tell Mum that I'd applied for a course in garden design at Cirencester.

'I don't know where you get this earthy streak,' she used to say, as she watched me trowelling away in our back garden. 'Must be your father's side. There's nothing remotely agricultural about the DuBrays.'

Yes, well, there was nothing remotely human about the DuBrays either. My maternal grandmother had fallen out with my mother years ago, and although she lived only a matter of miles from us, in the centre of St Albans, as a child I was forbidden to see her. I did try to make contact once, when I was about sixteen, but had been told very sternly by the elderly woman on the other end of the phone in a heavy French accent that 'your grandmother ees not at home', although it was quite clear it was she I was talking to. As I'd put the phone down I'd had a sneaking sense of regret for Mum. With a mother like that, was it any surprise she'd ended up as she had?

'OK,' I said now to Johnny, putting down my glass, 'I'll come this weekend. I need to sort out your herb garden, anyway.'

To tell you the truth, I'm not entirely sure how one weekend's gardening turned into another, and then another, which in turn led to pub suppers alone with Johnny, then trips home on his motorbike under the stars, and finally, of course, trips to bed. To me it seemed entirely natural—after all, I'd been dreaming about it for years, but I suppose if it took anyone by surprise, it was Johnny.

Imogen had to be told, of course, and Johnny certainly wasn't going to do it, so I wrote a long and guilty letter about how it had just sort of happened and how I hoped she didn't mind.

'Go for it!' came back her instant missive on the back of Michelangelo's *David*.

Meanwhile, the motorbike rides, the pub suppers, the larks, and the bedroom romps continued apace, until, that is, one Saturday, when I received a letter. I didn't say anything, but later on that day, as Johnny was helping me scythe down some nettles in Angie's wild flower meadow behind the barn, he stopped suddenly.

'What's up?'

I rested on my scythe for a moment, panting. 'Nothing's up, why?'

'Well, you've been totally silent all morning. In fact you've hardly said a word since you got here. What's occurring?'

'Oh. Have I? Oh, well, nothing really.' I shrugged. 'It's just . . . well, it's just, I've got into Cirencester. I'll start there in September.'

He gazed at me for a long moment. 'But that's great,' he said slowly.

I swallowed. 'Yes. Isn't it?'

We picked up our scythes again and worked away in silence for a bit. Then he put his down.

'Marry me, Livvy.'

I straightened up, gawped. 'You don't mean that!'

'Yes, I do. Don't go to Cirencester, marry me. I don't want to lose you, Livvy, and I know that if you go up there, the chances are some beefy farmer will snap you up and take you off to his piggery in Shropshire. You and I were made for each other. We want the same things!'

'We do? Like what?'

'Like—all this!' He swung his arm around and I knew instantly what he meant. Not the house exactly, but more the metaphorical hearth: the family, the unit, something I'd never had, and something he'd lost and desperately wanted to recapture.

'And?' I challenged, meeting his eye.

'And I love you.'

'You've never said.'

'I'm saying it now.' He walked forward and took my filthy hands in his. 'I love you, Olivia Faber, with all my heart. Don't give up on me, Livvy, don't go away, please. Stay, stay with me, and do me the honour of becoming my wife.'

Well, what could I say? It was an undeniable truth that I loved him completely and uncritically and always had done, so I was on a hiding to nothing. I didn't even pause for breath, didn't waver for one moment. I just looked into his bright blue gaze and said—yes.

In my heart I think I knew Angie wasn't entirely happy, and I certainly knew Mum wasn't. As she helped me get ready on the morning of my wedding, I turned in delight at the reflection of my ivory gown in her bedroom mirror, and suddenly thought how small and fragile she looked beside me, standing watching me in her dark blue coat. I swooped to hug her but, to my dismay, tears poured down her cheeks.

Johnny and I were ecstatic, though, and not even Mum's distress could dampen our spirits. We couldn't take our eyes off each other, and as I swept out of that little Catholic church on the village green with Molly, Imogen and Johnny's three sisters in shocking pink behind me, I thought I must be the happiest girl alive. We'll prove them all wrong, I thought as I smiled confidently into the camera. We'll show them!

And so we did. We moved into a tiny basement flat in Hammersmith and were blissfully, ridiculously happy. Johnny began to enjoy his trudge to the City more. As for me, Cirencester forgotten, I got a job at a very smart nursery in Chelsea, which amused my mother no end.

'A garden centre! You've got an English degree and you end up as a shop girl!'

I gritted my teeth and swore I'd own the bloody place before long, set up a flipping chain of them just to show her. But before I could embark on my horticultural empire, all of a sudden I was throwing up in the loo and having trouble with the zip of my jeans. Johnny was delighted.

'But this is what we wanted!' he declared, leaping up onto our terrible old sofa and bouncing about like a child. 'This is marvellous!'

'You don't think it's a bit soon?' I said doubtfully, peering at the wholly conclusive Predictor blue line.

'Of course not!' He jumped off and hugged me delightedly. 'The sooner the better! A family, Livvy!'

Claudia was born that Christmas. Six weeks premature; tiny, delicate, sickly, unable to sleep, unable to feed from me, and perhaps, not quite what Johnny had in mind.

'Is she always going to scream like that? I mean, all night?'

'Of course not,' I said, hauling myself out of bed, numb with tiredness. 'She'll settle down. It's just these first few weeks.'

But it wasn't the first few weeks, it was eighteen months before Claudia settled into anything like a routine, and even then she was always fragile; an asthmatic, sickly child, susceptible to any bug going, allergic to milk, totally distraught if left with anyone other than me—an exhausting child. We adored her unreservedly, of course, but longed for a bright, bouncy boy to save her from being quite so precious.

Nine years later we were still longing. I suppose it's fair to say we were disappointed, but we weren't obsessive about it. And, while I wouldn't say our marriage floundered, it's true to say it went into remission.

It was as if we were going through the motions, and if, at times, Johnny became more distant at home, I learned to cast around to provide some distraction to take his mind off the present, and possibly even the past.

Strangely enough, it was my mother who provided the necessary diversion. She rang one Sunday afternoon as the three of us were slumped in front of an old black and white movie.

'Good news, darling! Your grandmother's dead!'

'Mum!' I was deeply shocked.

'Oh, you won't be so pi when I tell you the really good news. She left you the house.'

'What—her house? To me? But why?'

'Well, she wasn't going to leave it to me; she hated me.'

'But she didn't even know me.'

'Which is precisely why she didn't hate you too!'

'Thanks, Mum.'

There was something disarming about her lack of hypocrisy, though, and I have to say, Johnny and I were secretly thrilled. We'd sell it, of course, and then we'd sell our own poky flat, and with the proceeds, move to somewhere central and spacious. It was just the boost we needed; it would be a turning point in our lives.

Full of plans we leapt into Johnny's old Bristol—in fact Oliver's old Bristol—and went off to see it. Amazed that it took us only half an hour to get to this old Roman city of St Albans, we then spent another half-hour trying to find the wretched house. Finally, when we'd marvelled at the ancient, towering Abbey, we found a lane, tucked away behind some cloisters, which led to a crescent of beautiful Georgian town houses. Just as the crescent ended, almost tacked on as an afterthought, was a high brick wall, with green, double barn doors slap bang in the middle.

'This must be it,' I said doubtfully, consulting my instructions and map. 'Orchard House, The Crescent.'

'Aptly named for a house in a city,' said Johnny sardonically.

'Oh, I don't know,' I said, lifting the latch on one of the doors and pushing on through. 'It might be—Oh crikey, look at this!'

There, before us, was the most exquisite little Queen Anne house surrounded by about an acre of tangled, unkempt garden. Down at the back, the lawn, dominated by a huge old cedar tree, swept down to a stream that flowed across and along the back of The Crescent. All was walled, all was totally private, and all was a million miles from what either of us had been expecting.

'Oh, Johnny, it's heaven!' I breathed.

'Hardly. It's completely dilapidated and that's just the outside. Don't get excited, Livvy.'

'I won't,' I promised, but I already was. That garden—oh that garden!

Obediently I followed him inside. It was, of course, just as an old lady had left it, with a general air of death and decay, but I saw a doll's house, four, perfectly square and symmetrical rooms downstairs and four above, all with working fireplaces, floor-to-ceiling sash windows, cornices and picture rails, and all, what's more, with views of the garden.

'There's no central heating,' warned Johnny, gazing around upstairs. 'It'll need gutting, rewiring, replumbing, a new bathroom and a totally new kitchen. We're talking big-time building works here, Liv.'

'So we'll sell the flat in London and use the money to renovate it.'

'Lots of money. Lots of time too.'

'Fine!' I laughed. 'We've got plenty of both now! Oh gosh, you can see the cathedral from here! Look, Johnny, there and—oh! Look!'

I had my head well out of the window now, marvelling at the view, but suddenly I popped it back in. I grabbed his hand and ran downstairs, pulling him out through the French windows, across the terrace to the lawn. As we slid down the bank on the other side together, we came to a halt at the bottom, panting. Johnny stared. There, tucked away behind a tall holly hedge, was a small, brick-and-timbered barn.

'I could keep the Bristol in here, maybe get Dad's old Lagonda in too!' he said excitedly. He walked in and peered up at the beams.

'Quite!' I squeaked. 'And you'd never get a double garage in London.'

He bit his lip thoughtfully, then he turned to me. 'We'll see, Livvy. Let's go home and think about it, OK?'

'OK!'

We did, but I knew then he was as smitten as I was. The idea of being half an hour from central London and living in a pretty period house with an acre of garden for me and plenty of garaging for classic cars for him, was not to be sniffed at. We did our sums and jumped in with both feet.

That autumn, Orchard House became our home and we were blissfully, ridiculously happy. So what if the eccentric East End builders we'd employed, together with their Greek sidekick, had practically moved in with us? Johnny surprised me by being very enthusiastic in the DIY department, I was ecstatic in the garden, and Claudia was happy at her new school, not needing her inhaler nearly as much. So all was fine. All was peachy. For a while, anyway.

Until . . . something happened, something I couldn't put my finger on, but I reckon it happened about five months ago. And now, as I sat here, staring at an old photograph, I realised I was about to find out why.

I glanced up at the clock: seven forty-five. It seemed to me he'd been upstairs for ever, but it must only have been a few minutes. He'd come back on his usual train, after all. Suddenly I jumped. Yes, now I could hear movement on the landing. He was coming down. I quickly lit another cigarette and was just exhaling the smoke as he came past the kitchen door, jacket on, a case in each hand. He saw me sitting there, and stopped, framed in the doorway. His blue eyes were full of remorse.

'Sorry, Livvy.'

I nodded. Swallowed hard. 'Johnn—' I tried again; my voice wouldn't work. 'Johnny,' I managed, 'is there someone else?'

He held my eyes for a moment, then slid them down to his shoes. 'If you mean am I having an affair, then yes, I am.'

'And do you—' Couldn't say the love word. 'Is it serious?'

He took a deep breath. 'It wasn't . . . was never meant to be . . . but now . . . . Yes, it's serious.' His eyes came back to me. 'I'm sorry, Livvy.'

He hesitated a moment longer, picked up his cases, opened the front door, closed it softly behind him, and set off down the path.

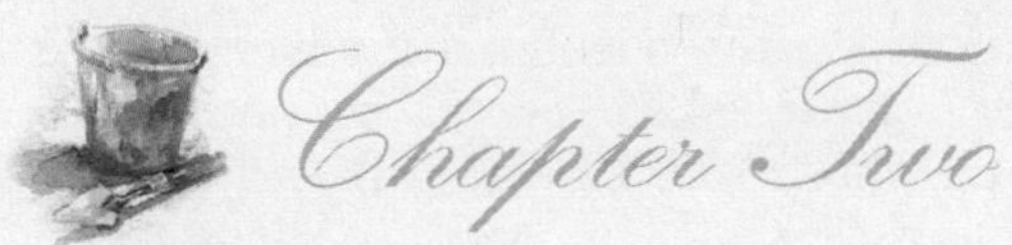

Chapter Two

'LIVVY, YOU ARE KIDDING?'

'I'm not kidding. Would I kid about something like that? Molly, do me a favour, don't quiz me on the phone. Just get over here, OK?'

There was a stunned silence. 'But I'm shocked. *Johnny!* Of all people!'

'*Molly!*'

'Yes! Right. Right, I'm coming. And Imogen?'

I swallowed. 'Please. But, listen, could you tell her?'

She paused then. 'Course I will, darling. I'll see you soon.'

Half an hour later Molly was ringing my bell. I opened the door to find her clinging to the door frame, hugely pregnant, one arm holding her bump and the other just about holding Henry, who at eleven months wanted to be set free.

'Jesus Christ,' she gasped, 'don't let anyone talk you into unprotected sex in October. I tell you, lugging three extra stone around in a heat wave as well as this little bugger is no joke.'

'I think sex, protected or otherwise, is rather off the agenda for me at the moment.'

'Oh, Livvy!' She dropped Henry, put her arm round my neck and hugged hard.

'Fine, I'm fine,' I muttered finally. 'Come on in.'

She followed me into the chaos of my tiny kitchen.

'So when did he go?' she gasped, collapsing into a chair.

'About two weeks ago.'

'Two weeks ago!' She sat up. 'My God, why didn't you tell me?'

'Couldn't. Couldn't speak to anyone for about a week, Molly; couldn't even get out of bed. I finally broke it to Claudia, who I'd been fobbing off with a Daddy's-got-a-conference-in-New-York-again line, and then when she'd gone off to school, collapsed in a heap again.'

'How did she take it?'

'She said she knew. Suspected, anyway—had done for a while.'

'And is she OK?'

I sighed. 'Seems to be, but you know how Claudes is. Never lets much show, but you can never really tell with children, can you?'

'Listen, she'll be fine. It's *you* I'm worried about. Has he phoned?'

'Oh yes. He rang last week to speak to Claudia, and when I picked up the phone he very sweetly gave me his telephone number in case I should care to call him. Or Her? I asked. Sorry? he said. Well, I explained, surely it was Her telephone too? Oh, he said hurriedly, he'd just meant in case of an emergency.'

'Ah. So there is a her?'

'Oh yes, didn't I mention that? That's why he's gone.'

'But you don't know who she is?'

'No idea.' I gazed beyond Molly, out of the window. 'No idea at all.'

'And you didn't see any of this coming, Liv? I mean—is this a complete and utter bolt from the blue?'

'Total. Well, the girl and the moving out bit is, but . . .' I hesitated, 'if I'm honest, Mol, I knew something was up. *Have* known something was up for ages really. I just stupidly never thought it would be this.' I reached up to a shelf for a wineglass, but as I tried to pour Molly a drink, I realised my hand was shaking violently.

She got up, took the glass and reached into the fridge for the bottle.

'He'll be back,' she said, pouring out a large one and handing it to me.

'Of course he will,' I said quickly, wanting her to say that.

'After all, this is what men do, isn't it? But—*Henry, no!*'

She lunged as Henry, left to his own devices, was helping himself to the delights of a toolbox left open by the builders and about to insert a six-inch nail down his oesophagus. Molly grabbed it, but then a struggle ensued with Henry prepared to sink his brand-new teeth into his mother's hand to keep it.

'Ouch! You little—' She bared her teeth viciously at him and snarled back. Miraculously, he dropped the nail.

'Well, that certainly worked!'

'Oh, yes,' she panted. 'He bit me the other day, you see, and I bit him back—in Tesco's, actually. Caused quite a stir in the checkout queue. Someone even ventured to ask if I was fit to have another baby, to which I replied, "No, I'm not, so give me your address and I'll let you have it."'

I smiled. Within weeks of giving birth, Molly had fallen for that fatal old wives' tale which tells you you can't get pregnant while you're breastfeeding. Now, on the point of having two children under thirteen months, she was living proof that you can. Married to a lovely, penniless actor called Hugh, who was always *just* on the brink of making that big break, but meanwhile doing adverts to tide them over, she lived from hand to mouth in a tiny rented cottage not far from here. But Molly had Hugh, she had Henry, she had her bump, and she was bright enough to know that was more than most—which reminded me.

'Did you get hold of Imogen?'

'Yes. She said she was just locking up the gallery, but she'd come straight down, be here about nine.'

I grabbed one of Molly's cigarettes and gazed out of the window. The light from the caravan just across the stream at the bottom of the garden shone out like a beacon in the fading evening light. Mac and the boys, sick of crawling in from Billericay every day, had asked if they could stay during the week, and since it was in my interests to have them start at eight o'clock rather than ten, I'd said yes. The next thing I knew their truck had arrived dragging a socking great caravan.

I turned back to Molly. 'I haven't seen Imogen for ages.'

Molly was on her knees, changing a nappy. 'No, neither have I, really. Not since she split up with Dominic anyway.'

I swung round. 'She split up with Dominic?'

'Yes, didn't you know?'

'No! When?'

'Oh God, I don't know, four or five months ago?'

'Four or fi—but she didn't tell me!'

'Oh, well, heavens,' she looked up, awkward suddenly, 'you've been so busy with this house, Livvy, and she's been frantic at the gallery. Anyway, she was never really serious about him.'

'She's never been really serious about anyone except—' I shook my head. 'And I've spoken to her loads of times, Molly. She never even mentioned it.'

'Molly shrugged and snapped the new nappy on. 'Perhaps she wanted to see you to tell you. You know what Imo's like.'

'Four or five months, Molly. Don't you see? That's exactly when it started, four or five months ago.'

'Livvy, how could you? Molly said, horrified. Of *course* it's not Imo!'

'Why not?'

'Because she's your best friend!'

'Doesn't count, Mol.' I shook my head violently. 'Love cancels out everything like that. Friendship, loyalty—it all goes out of the window and, God, they were *so* in love all those years ago and—'

'Livvy, you have got to stop being so insecure about that! Just because he went out with her, for God's sake.'

'It was more than that and you know it. She broke his heart with Paolo, and then through her own stupid pride broke her own heart too. Imo's never found anyone else, Mol, and look at her now, chucking in the towel with one guy after another.'

I was ranting now, pacing the floor. 'Don't you see, Molly, it would *have* to be someone as serious as Imo. Johnny would never leave me just for a fling. It's not his style.'

I froze as I heard tyres on the gravel drive.

'Don't you dare,' breathed Molly, staring at me.

I held her gaze for a moment, then went to the door. I stood for a moment, regarding the paintwork. The doorbell went, I waited a moment longer, then finally opened it.

She was looking as beautiful as ever in a grey, sleeveless Ghost dress, her blonde hair slipping silkily over her shoulders, her pale blue eyes wide. They filled up with tears when they saw me.

'Oh, Livvy. You poor darling.'

I was so glad she hugged me. So glad I could hide my shame in her hair. I was wrong. So wrong. I knew that instantly. But this was what he'd done to me, you see. This was what the love of my life, the ache in my gut, had done. Made me see treachery in childhood friends.

'How are you?' She held me at arm's length and scanned my face.

'Terrible,' I grinned. 'Despicable too, and nasty with it, but all the better for seeing you. Come in before Molly and I finish all the wine.'

'Molly's drinking?' she enquired doubtfully.

'Er, well, just a thimble or two.'

'And smoking!' she said, catching Molly stubbing out a cigarette.

'My doctor says it's fine,' she said defiantly. 'He says that one or two is not going to hurt, *plus* a little glass of wine and *plus*, Imo, if *you* were seven months pregnant, flatulent, exhausted, incontinent, and with a one-year-old with a charming habit of projectile vomiting, *you'd* have the odd ciggy too!' Molly got up to kiss her friend. 'How are you anyway, you old bag?' She plonked Henry's bottle in the microwave.

'Well, sorry I spoke. But—blimey, it can't be all that bad, surely? I mean, let's face it, millions of women do it every day, don't they? Have babies?' She gave a bright smile, perfectly designed to wind Molly up, and sat down on the only available seat, which was an upturned milk crate. After crossing her elegant legs and flicking back her long, blonde hair, she cleared her throat.

'Livvy darling, I'm afraid I've got something to tell you.'

My heart stopped. Ah, so this was it, then; my hunch had been right.

'What?' I whispered.

'He's seeing someone else.'

I nodded. 'I know. He told me.'

'Ah.' She paused for what felt like an eternity. 'And did he tell you who?'

I shook my head. Couldn't speak.

She gave a brief confirmatory nod. 'Her name's Nina Harrison.'

My jaw dropped. 'Nina . . . what? Who the hell's Nina Harrison?'

She shrugged. 'Search me, but I saw them in a restaurant about a month ago, having supper together.'

'No!' I gaped. 'Why didn't you tell me?'

'Oh sure, come on, Livvy. How was I to know it wasn't a colleague from work or something, or even just a brief fling that would be much better you didn't know about?'

'Better I didn't . . .' I was speechless for a moment. 'Well, God,' I blustered finally, 'I think I might have told *you*!'

'Oh, me, maybe, but I'm single with no kids. Think about it, Livvy. Would you have told Molly? Pregnant? With a small baby?'

'Oh, I'd have been delighted,' said Molly as she took the bottle from the microwave and handed it to a grabbing Henry. 'I dream of Hugh having a concubine. I'd be very happy with light scullery duties, just so long as she took over in the bedroom and breeding department.' She gave a bright smile and I knew she was trying to lighten the atmosphere.

'So how come you know her name?' I persisted, stunned.

'Looked at her credit card. She paid the bill—which was why I thought it could have been a client or something—and then when the waiter took the saucer away to the counter, I crept to the loo with my pashmina over my face. Saw it as I went past.'

'Did you see her?'

'Not clearly.'

'But?'

She shrugged. 'Small, fairish—not blonde—and pretty, I suppose, but in a very mousy, nondescript sort of way. Nothing special at all.'

She was being protective. Dear, sweet Imo, who twice in the space of five minutes I'd cast as a she-devil in my husband's bed.

I got up and cleared away some glasses. I knew my eyes were filling up, so I ran the taps at the sink and dithered ineffectually with a dish-cloth to hide my face.

'*Christ!*' Imo shrieked suddenly. I spun round to see her clutching her head, as a stream of yellow liquid splattered on the wall behind her.

'What was that!' she yelled, frozen to her milk crate.

'Projectile vomiting,' muttered Molly, grabbing a dishcloth and hastening past her to mop it up. 'I believe I mentioned it earlier. So sorry, Livvy, your wall. I'll—Oh, Imo, did it get in your hair? Here, I'll—'

'*Not with that!*' screeched Imo, leaping to her feet as Molly brandished a vomit-soaked rag. 'No, really, Mol, he missed,' she breathed. 'I'm fine, truly.' She sat down again shakily. 'Jesus, does he always do that?'

'Periodically,' admitted Molly, scrubbing away, 'although he's supposed to have grown out of it. Most babies do at about three months, but not my Henry. He doesn't know when the joke's over.'

'Evidently,' said Imogen weakly. 'God, remind me to avoid this child-bearing lark. I'll have one in a test tube, or adopt. Yes, that's it, I'll send out for one, like a pizza—except, hang on, now here's one I *would* take home with me. Hello, darling, how's tricks?'

Claudia had appeared in the doorway in her nightie.

'Claudes!' I moved to the door. 'It's ten o'clock! What's the matter?'

'Couldn't sleep,' she said. 'But tricks is fine, thanks, Imo. I do like your dress.'

She kissed her godmother, fingering the grey, silky dress covetously—very much a DuBray in the clothes department was Claudia—before going to kiss her other godmother and pick up the baby.

'How come Henry isn't in bed and I am?' she said, crouching down.

'Henry doesn't sleep, darling,' said Molly, ruffling her hair fondly. 'He's a changeling. He doesn't behave like other, normal babies. He's only been put on this earth to vex his mother. He's from the planet Thwart.'

Claudia giggled, then suddenly looked serious. She straightened up, folded her arms. 'She's told you then, has she? About Daddy?'

There was a silence. I hastened across to her anxiously. 'I did actually, darling. Do you mind?'

'Course not,' she said, pushing her dark fringe back impatiently. 'I said you should share it more, not bottle it up.'

'Well, quite.' My daughter was ten, going on twenty-four.

'And how do *you* feel about it, my love?' asked Molly gently.

'Oh, I'm OK. Daddy says he'll see me on Sundays and I know from books that he'll feel guilty about making me a product of a broken home, so I'll get loads of treats and things. I won't get spoilt, though. Susan, in *The Chalet School* adventures hasn't got a father, but she's not spoilt 'cos her mother's strict but fair, so I expect I'll be the same.'

'Good, good,' said Molly faintly.

'And, anyway, something good will come out of it, I'll be bound.'

'I'll be—' Molly turned wide eyes on me.

'Angela Brazil,' I muttered. 'She found all my old books.'

'Ah.'

'And Mummy should get out more,' Claudia said firmly. 'Maybe go to the pub with the builders.'

I gulped at this child of mine.

'Why not?' she insisted. 'They go out every single night to the Fox and Ferret before picking up their curries. Well, you could go with them, Mum, get a curry too. You like curries.'

'And some tinnies too, perhaps?' murmured Imo.

'Good idea. And then when Dad comes over to pick me up, you could be down in the caravan, watching telly with them. It's tactics, Mum. I saw it on *EastEnders*. Bianca did it to Ricky. You've got to get Dad to wake up a bit, make him jealous!'

'Right, darling.' I nodded. Tactics. From a ten-year-old girl, drawing on fifties boarding-school books and contemporary soaps.

'It's just a case of getting out and about. I mean, Nanette's *always* asking you over.'

'Oh God, not Nanette, Claudes.'

'Who's Nanette?' pounced Molly.

'She lives in The Crescent,' said Claudia. 'She's always having things called fork suppers with men in blazers called Clive, and Mum never goes.'

'I think you get the picture,' I muttered drily.

'Sounds rather fun,' grinned Molly maliciously. 'Where exactly does this Nanette hail from?' She got up and peered out of the window.

'There, over there on the end.' Claudia joined her, pointing eagerly at a lighted window with frilly Austrian blinds. As I joined them, to my horror we saw a hand wave back.

'Oh God, she's *seen* you, Claudes. She thinks you're *waving*!'

'Well, that's OK.'

'And now she's disappeared! She's probably coming over!'

'Well, fine, that's fine. She can have a drink. I like her, Mum.'

'And I do too, darling. She's very kind, but—' I spotted her garden gate opening. 'Oh no, she *is* coming over—hide!' I dived down under the table. 'Tell her I'm out,' I muttered.

'Mummy, that's silly. She'll *know* you're here; your friends are here, for heaven's sake. Of *course* you can't hide.'

'I think Claudia has a point, Livvy,' said Imogen.

There was a familiar crunch of gravel, then 'Coo-ee!'—and a rap of jewelled knuckles at the door. Claudia flew to open it, and two seconds later in came Nanette, just as I was crawling out.

'Nanette, it's lovely to see you,' I lied as I scrambled up. 'Um, come in and sit down. We were just having a drink. This is Molly Piper, by the way, and Imogen Mitchell, my best friends.'

'Oh, *rea*lly?' Nanette looked enchanted, and extended a suntanned hand. Fortyish, she was resplendent in a tight cerise sweater, white pedal pushers and high, pink mules. 'Gosh, I'd *love* a little drinky but I can't stop, I'm afraid. I'm on my way to my sexual awareness and crochet group tonight, but I'm thrilled to meet you both!'

'You too,' murmured Molly and Imogen, totally agog at this vision.

'But what I *have* brought,' Nanette went on, brandishing a leather-bound book, 'is my diary, and I intend to pin you down once and for all, Olivia! *So* sad about all this ghastly business,' she murmured *sotto voce*, turning to Imogen and Molly, for all the world as if I wasn't there. 'Of course she's told you . . .? Well, of course she has and, actually, I'm afraid everyone knows. But don't you think she should get out more? Show that randy old so-and-so just who's boss around here?'

'I'll get Mummy's diary!' chirruped Claudia happily, as my friends nodded mutely. 'Here!' She grabbed it off the dresser and handed it to Nanette. Two heads then bent low together, as my daughter and my neighbour compared, conspired and pencilled in, with Molly and Imogen exchanging mouth-twitching, eyebrow-raised glances.

Nanette snapped her diary shut, satisfied. 'Friday next week. Nothing too formal, six or maybe eight of us in all, and I'll make sure the guest list is suitably yummy. Eight for eight fifteen, be there or be square! Toodle-oo!' And with that she bustled out with a dinky little wave.

'Toodle-*oo*!' chorused my friends and daughter joyfully.

The moment the front door closed behind Nanette I strode to the counter, seized the breadknife, raised it high above my head, and with a bloodcurdling screech plunged it straight into the heart of a granary loaf.

'Traitors!' I bellowed. 'The lot of you!'

'Oh, Mum, it'll be fun!' insisted Claudia, giggling.

'Of course it will,' gasped Imogen, wiping her eyes. 'It'll be brimming over with gorgeous Clives, and possibly a few Nigels too. You'll love it!'

Molly caught Imogen's eye and they both dissolved into giggles, until abruptly Molly froze. Her eyes bulged.

'Oh *God*!' she squeaked, snapping her legs together. 'Help!'

'Serves you right,' I said callously as I reached into Henry's changing bag and chucked her a nappy. 'Here, try this on for size.'

A few days later I was lying in bed mulling it over. Nina. *Nina*, for God's sake. Who on earth was called Nina these days? It sounded so prewar, like she wore a cardy and slippers, or even—yes, that's it—maybe she was foreign? Nina Mouskouri—no, no that was Nana—or, OK, Nina Simone? No, far better she was the cardy type. I sighed and turned over, bunching up the pillow—then stared. Claudia was beside me, feigning sleep, eyelids flickering. I groaned.

'Oh darling, you said you'd try not to *do* this any more.'

'I know, but I couldn't sleep. And anyway, Daddy's not here, so there's plenty of room.'

Well, there was no arguing with that. The sun was also streaming persistently through the curtains now, so I turned back and seized the clock, peering myopically at it. Twenty to eight.

'Claudia! It's twenty to eight!' I shot up like a rocket.

'I know.'

'Well, don't say "I know", flaming well get a move on! You'll be late for school—again!'

She rolled out of bed, and dragged herself to her bedroom. 'That, Mother dear, was precisely the idea,' she muttered sardonically.

I flew around the room looking for clothes, desperate for a shower but knowing there wasn't time, listening to Claudia slowly opening drawers and dragging her feet. Hardly the sounds of frenzied activity.

'Claudia, come *on*!'

'I *am*!'

I sighed and went to the window.

At the far end of the garden I could see movement in the caravan on the other side of the stream. The door opened and Alf came out. I watched his listing movement across the rickety bridge and onto the grass, large and lumbering in his blue overalls, bound, no doubt, for the Portaloo, and a few quiet moments with the *Sun*.

Alf was soon followed by Mac, coming down the caravan steps and looking critically up at the sky. Far too blue for his liking—what they needed was some rain to curdle the cement, to make bricklaying out of the question, to ensure that they could huddle under the blue tarpaulin and smoke and drink tea for a bit. Finally, came Spiro, woolly-hatted even in a heatwave, dark eyes peering into the sun, and naturally, clutching his Wotsits. Despite a monumental fry-up in the caravan every morning, Wotsits were essential to get these boys through the next half-hour, together, of course, with their mobile phones. These wonders of modern technology were never out of their hands, and they could quite easily plaster a chimney breast with one hand and talk to her indoors with the other: Spiro to her in Greece, Mac to his third wife, and Alf to his first, with whom he'd notched up twenty years' hard labour. Her name was Vi and she was a legend in her own front room, according to Mac; a shrew of the first order, who nagged Alf something rotten.

As Alf came out of the loo now, his phone went. Vi, of course. My bedroom window was open and I could hear him as he approached the kitchen. 'Orright, luv, the lean-to, yeah, I'll sort it. I know, it's a mess . . . OK, it's a buggerin' mess . . . Yeah, I will, I'll do it on Sunday . . . Orright, Saturday, yeah . . . As soon as I get home, yeah. Love you. Bye.'

Harangued but devoted, you see. Perhaps that's where I'd gone wrong? I'd noticed recently, as I analysed marriages, that women who harangued and nagged on a permanent basis generally had very well-behaved husbands. I looked at mine as he grinned out at me now from our wedding photo on my dressing table. Bloody photos were everywhere, I thought, glaring at it. Then my eyes caught the clock.

'*Claudia!*'

I raced across the landing to her bedroom. 'Claudia, will you hurry up. We're going to be—Oh, for God's sake!'

Claudia was tucked up in bed again, sleeping like a baby.

We finally swung into the school gates three-quarters of an hour late, with Claudia insisting she was going to claim a doctor's appointment and that I should write a note to that effect.

'But that's a barefaced lie, Claudia. I'm not doing that!'

'Oh Mummy, you're such a goody-goody. Everyone else does.'

'I don't care what everyone else does, we are not "everyone else".' My God, did I sound like my mother or what? 'No, we will simply say that we got held up by the builders.'

'But that's a lie.'

I screeched to a halt in the car park.

'Claudia,' I snarled, 'would you kindly stop splitting hairs and remember that I am the mother and you are the ten-year-old girl!'

I got out and slammed the door behind me, then raced round the back to the boot where, puffing and blowing, I lugged out her games bag, her lacrosse stick, her flute, her gym kit, her swimming bag, and all the other energetic paraphernalia that she regarded with such cynical detachment and refused to use. As Claudia yawned and leaned against the car, I threw it all onto my back and, like a trusty old packhorse, made off, puffing away across the playing field, with my daughter, shuffling along behind me, hands deep in her pockets. Through a chink in the hall curtains I could see that assembly was still in full swing and, yes, with any luck she could sneak in at the back.

'Go on,' I whispered, giving her a little push. 'I'll put your stuff in your locker and you creep in. If anyone asks, say you've been here for ages, went to the loo or something.'

Claudia opened her eyes wide. 'Mum—*another* barefaced lie!'

I ground my teeth. 'Claudia McFarllen, one of these days—'

'OK, OK, I'm going!' She reached up, gave me a quick, disarming peck on the cheek then, grinning widely, sauntered off.

As I trudged off to the locker room to dump her stuff, I went past the nursery school. Outside the window I saw a mother I knew, Sarah Parker, struggling with a screaming baby. She had him hoisted up on her hip and was trying to quieten him as she peered through the nursery window at her four-year-old.

'Is he OK?' I asked, coming up beside her.

'Oh, hi, Olivia. No, he's not—look.' She jabbed her finger at a screaming four-year-old on the other side of the glass.

'They've got a new teacher this term. Miss Pinter's retired, and the new one's really sweet, but it takes Ned ages to settle with anyone new.'

'Plus he knows you're out here,' I pointed out.

'Yes, but if I just leave him I'll feel terrible.'

'I'll tell you what. I've still got to dump Claudia's stuff. Why don't you sit in the car and when I come back past, I'll tell you if he's OK? I bet you anything he's calmed down.'

'Oh, would you? Only this one's dying for a feed so I could give him a bottle in the car.'

'I'll see you there in a minute.'

She scurried off gratefully and I wandered off to find Claudia's locker in the changing rooms. As I came back out, I went down the internal corridor to get a better look at young Ned Parker through the double glass doors. Sure enough, there he was, dry-eyed, not a care in the world. I smiled, and was about to move on, when the sign on the classroom door caught my eye. I stared. Miss Harrison. I stared some more. I went hot, and then very cold.

I turned and ran, panting, gasping, all the way down to the car park. Sarah, sitting in her car, saw me through her windscreen. She saw my face and, clutching her baby, shot out of the front seat, hand to mouth.

'Oh my God—what's happened! Is he all right?'

'He's fine, Ned's fine,' I gasped, clutching the top of her open door. 'Sarah—the new teacher in there. Miss Harrison, is it? Have you any idea what her first name is?'

'Her first name?' She screwed up her face and thought for a moment. 'Oh God, yes I do know, because one of the other mothers told me . . . something old-fashioned and . . . Nina! That's it, Nina Harrison.'

'She's a bloody teacher at Claudia's bloody *school*!'

'Terrible, terrible. Here, have an aspirin.'

'I mean, what am I supposed to do, walk past her classroom every morning and say, "Good morning, Miss Harrison, and how was my husband's performance last night?" It's out*rageous*!' I bellowed.

'Course it is. Here, have a nice cup of tea.'

Mac handed me the cup while Alf stirred some sugar in. Spiro was bustling around my feet with a stool. I succumbed to having it positioned just so under my feet, then leaned my head back and gazed around in a dazed fashion. I appeared to have collapsed in the sitting room and I stared bleakly at it now with its half-stripped walls, ripped-up floorboards, and, in the foreground, a slightly blurred vision of my work force, faces full of concern. I groaned.

I stared blankly at them. 'She'll have to be sacked!' I snapped.

'Of course she will,' soothed Mac.

'The head won't stand for that. What, having an affair with one of the pupil's fathers? *Hah!* No, no, she'll have to go!' I clutched my mouth. 'Oh, my poor Claudia! My little girl! Imagine the shame, the humiliation!'

'I go,' said Spiro, turning. 'I go now and keel the beetch!'

'No, no, Spiro.' I put a restraining hand on his arm. 'You're sweet but, actually, we can't kill her. We can just render her unemployed.'

Mac sucked his teeth dubiously. 'Yeah, well, if you *can*, like, luv. Give her the tea now, Spiro,' Mac ordered.

Spiro obediently put it to my lips like a baby, not letting me hold the handle. 'I do it,' he muttered fiercely. 'I do it for you. Now, more aspirin.' He took one from Alf's hand and popped it in my mouth like a Smartie.

This is surreal, I thought as I crunched away maniacally. Here I am, in this chaos of a building site, collapsing in a pathetic heap in front of the builders. I've lost it, I've totally lost it. I shut my eyes tight. A bloody *teacher*! My eyes snapped open suddenly. So how the hell had he met her then? At a parents' evening? But Sarah had said she was new . . . so he must have met her just after we moved here—about six months ago—that way the timing made sense. But, good grief, a nursery school teacher? That didn't make sense at all! I shut my eyes and groaned.

I was vaguely aware that not a lot of work was being done around here, but I was unable to take command. After a bit, Mac spoke.

'I bin meaning to talk to you about that kitchen.'

'Oh yes,' I mumbled. Kitchen. Good. We could call this a site meeting.

'Yeah, it's about them cupboards.'

'Mmm, yes,' I muttered. 'There does seem to be a curious lack of cupboards, Mac, and you did say—'

'I know, I said I'd make them for you, nice and farmhousey, like, stressed pine.'

'Distressed, I believe, but give them ten minutes in this house and they'll be stressed too.'

'Whatever. Anyway, the fing is there's a lot of them buggers to make, more than I originally fought, and I'm gonna need more labour.'

'Oh?'

'Yeah,' he sighed. 'I mean what wiv Spiro on bricklayin' and Alf on concrete, I can't do all the joinery meself, so I was thinking of bringing in my Lance—he's my eldest. He's a chippy by trade, like me.'

'Ah.' Yes, well that cleared something up. I'd been wondering what Mac was.

'He'll be down here by the end of the week and then we'll get cracking on them cabinets straight away, orright?'

I gulped nervously. 'Yes, but heavens, Mac—four labourers!'

'Now don't you go worrying your head about the money, luv,' he soothed. 'I'm doin' you a nice little package deal here, bein' as how you're in straitened circumstances an' that. There, that's settled then and if you don't mind my sayin', what I suggest you do is get down to that school double quick and give them merry hell. If you look sharp and get your skates on you could bend that headmaster's ear in his lunch hour.'

I sat up and glanced at the clock. Gosh. Yes. He was right. If I went now I might just catch old Michael Harty before afternoon lessons started. I got unsteadily to my feet—I wondered if that really was aspirin Spiro had been slipping me, or valium perhaps. I staggered a bit and then lunged for my handbag. My audience watched my performance politely and I noticed that nobody seemed to be getting up to do any work, but then again, they had been very sweet.

'See you later then, boys.' I tottered unsteadily out to the car.

I put my foot down, roared off down the high street, reaching for my mobile phone. Molly was out, but I managed to track Imogen down in the dealing room of Sotheby's pursuing some fine art. I'm not sure it was entirely convenient, but she listened loyally to my tirade and was suitably outraged, albeit in hushed tones.

'They'll have to sack her,' she hissed firmly. 'She's completely compromised you—be with you in a minute, Damien—the school will have to let her go, they've got no other option.'

Sadly, the headmaster seemed to think they had quite a few. 'Well, this is, of course, a very delicate situation, Mrs McFarllen, and I can see how difficult it must be for you, but the problem is, she's an awfully good teacher and that's so important in the nursery, you see—so crucial in the formative years. The parents will be up in arms if I let her go.'

'And I'll be up in arms if you let her stay, Mr Harty!' I hissed, getting to my feet and resting my palms on his desk. 'Miss Harrison's position here is totally untenable. You must see that. She has to go!'

I was shaking with rage now, glaring at him over his oak desk. I wanted her head on a plate and I wanted it now. Mr Harty squirmed in his swivel chair, fiddled with his wedding ring, his *second* wedding ring, if I remembered rightly, because . . . oh God, it was all coming back to me now. He'd left his first wife, hadn't he? For the biology teacher. There'd been a hell of a furore about it at the time, but Mr Harty, being *such* a good headmaster, and being *so* well thought of, had stayed on and married Miss Quigly. I groaned, and picked up my bag from the floor.

'Well, Mr Harty, I can quite see how this is a tricky one for you, bearing in mind your own personal history. Miss Harrison is hardly a trailblazer, is she?' I eyed him beadily. 'It's a well-worn path, isn't it, and of course, one wouldn't want to appear hypocritical, would one?'

With that I swept out of his office, head high, cheeks burning. I strode to the car park and roared home at top speed, finally screeching dramatically to a halt outside my house. I sat for a moment, feeling the anger thickening inside my head—clotting actually. Finally I got out and slammed the door. And if they're not working in my bloody kitchen, I seethed to myself as I strode up the path, if they're still in *my* sitting room, swigging *my* PG Tips . . . I flounced in, ready for action.

'*Mac!*' I yelled. Nothing. I strode down the hall. '*Mac!* Oh!' I stopped; stepped back as I went stomping past the kitchen. 'Hello, Mum.'

My mother raised herself from the dusty Lloyd Loom chair she'd perched herself on in the scullery and brushed the back of her skirt.

'Mr Turner is working in your new kitchen,' she informed me. 'I presume that's what you employ these people to do?'

'Oh, yes. Right. How are you, Mum?'

'I'm well, which is more than I hear can be said of you.'

'Yes, well, things aren't too great around here at the moment,' I admitted, dumping my bag and reaching for the kettle.

'And I have to be the last to know?'

I spun round. 'I'm sorry, Mum. I would have rung only—'

'Mrs Hinton, the greengrocer, told me when I went in for some Granny Smiths. Said she was so sorry to hear about my little Olivia, being left on her own with a kiddie like that.' She shuddered. 'Yes, that's how I heard that my daughter had separated.'

'Well, I'm sorry, Mum, but I was a bit distraught, OK?' I slammed the kettle down angrily on the counter. 'And I didn't want to break down in front of you because I knew I'd just get a lot of I-told-you-sos. I thought I'd wait until I was a bit stronger before I tackled you, all right?'

She regarded me for a moment, then sniffed and sat down again, folding her hands in her lap and crossing her ankles.

'There's a cup of tea in the pot. It'll still be hot.'

'Oh. Right.' I turned and found the pot covered with a tea cosy she'd given me and I never used. I filled up the cup she passed me and one for me too. Cups and saucers. Never mugs. I turned and leaned against the counter, sipping tea.

'When did he go?'

'Three weeks ago.'

'Is there someone else?'

'Oh yes.' I laughed hollowly. 'And I don't know what's worse. To be left for someone else, or to be left because he simply couldn't stand me any longer.'

'The former, I think,' she said quietly.

I looked up quickly. God, how stupid of me to miss the parallel. Of course. This had happened before.

'It was . . . the comparison that I couldn't bear,' she said softly.

I nodded, and a chill went down my spine. Never, never, had I thought I'd be in the same boat as my mother.

'Do you know who she is?'

'Yes, she's a teacher at Claudia's school.' I didn't recognise my own voice. Flat, toneless. 'I'm going to get her sacked.'

'I see.' There was a silence. 'Do you think that's wise?'

I paused, my cup midway to my lips. My eyes darted to hers. 'What?'

'I said, d'you think that's wise?'

'Yes, I heard you, I just couldn't quite believe it. She's at Claudia's *school*, Mum.'

'Do you want him back?'

'Yes, of course I want him back.'

'And so d'you think that getting his popsy sacked is going to further your cause? Do you think that he's going to look favourably on you, think: dear little Livvy, how well she's behaving, how controlled, how dignified? Or d'you think he'll think: poor, sad, vindictive little bitch?'

I opened my mouth dumbly. She put down her cup, leaned across and, for the first time in years, held my hand.

'I've been here, Olivia,' she said softly. 'And I did all the things you're about to do. I ranted, I raved, I threw plates, I slashed clothes, I wrote terrible letters. And do you know what? I found out later that it had only been a whim, your father and Yvonne. A drunken nonsense after a party. He would have come back, apparently, and she would have gone back to Derek, but I drove them relentlessly together, Olivia. I drove them out of the country. They emigrated to Australia, I made their lives such a misery. I did it all terribly wrong. Don't follow my example.'

I gazed at her. 'I never knew that.'

'I never told you. Too much pride. Have some now, Olivia. Walk tall and hold your head high. If you see her, smile, be polite. He'll be back. Give him six months and he'll wonder what he ever saw in her. But you get her sacked and you'll never see him again.'

Chapter Three

DAYS PASSED AND NANETTE'S dinner party loomed. On the day of the actual event, I tried to get out of it a few hours beforehand by coughing wretchedly into a bloodstained hanky, but Claudia wasn't impressed.

'Alf saw you do that in the kitchen with the tomato ketchup bottle,' she informed me sternly riffling through my hangers. She threw a short red dress at me.

'Oh, don't be ridiculous, Claudia. I haven't worn that in years! If I'm going out at all I'm wearing my black, and that's final—*if* I'm going out.'

'Oh, Mummy, not your black *again*,' she wailed. 'You always wear that; you look like Batman.'

'Rubbish. I look thin and mysterious,' I said, wiggling into black trousers and a velvet shirt.

'And old and tired.'

'Thank you *so* much, my angel.'

'Well, you could at least wear chunky jewellery or that pashy thing.'

'My pashmina—' I reached for it.

'No, not the grey one, the red one, and look, you tie it like this . . .'

'Yes, I know how to tie it.' I snatched it from her hands and sat at the dressing table to arrange it. Then I dropped it. Groaned. 'Oh God, what am I *doing* here? Dressing up to go to some godawful party of Nanette's to talk to some ghastly greasy Herbert she's lined up for me?'

'How d'you know he's going to be greasy? How d'you know he won't be absolutely gorgeous?'

I gazed at her in the dressing-table mirror; turned. 'Claudia, what's the *matter* with you? Don't you want Daddy to come back?'

'I've told you, Mum, this is tactics. I know you think I'm the only one in my class from a broken home but I'm not. Chloe Chandler's dad went off with a floozy, and d'you know what Mrs Chandler did? She went straight down to B&Q, where lots of men hang about, followed a few around and, when she found one she liked, she brought him back home and—guess what—Mr Chandler came back!'

'Claudia—'

'And it doesn't have to be a Homebase-type thing. Chloe says you can do it anywhere. For instance, you could go to a garden centre! There's bound to be some there. They're everywhere!'

I shut my eyes. 'Claudia, I am not creeping round garden centres looking for a like-minded soil tiller, and neither, my love, is your father going out with a floozy.'

'Teacher then.'

I swung round aghast. 'How did you know that?'

'He told me last Sunday. Said in case I found out from someone else.'

'And how do you feel about it, my darling?'

She shrugged. 'OK, I suppose. I'm glad she doesn't teach me, though.' I clutched my mouth at this horrific thought. She screwed up her nose. 'She's pretty average, too. I had a look at her in the playground. Not vampy and black-knickerish like I expected.'

I shut my eyes again. I didn't want to think about the colour of her knickers. I sighed. It never ceased to amaze me how much straight talking children could take, and come back with too. Or was it just my child? My one and only, mature beyond her years. 'Claudia, I want you in bed by nine o'clock tonight,' I said as I swept out to the landing.

'Who's baby-sitting?' She snatched up her crisps and followed.

'Mac. He's downstairs in the kitchen, I think.'

'Not Spiro?'

I turned halfway down the stairs. 'No, Claudia. Not Spiro. Spiro is in the Fox and Ferret having a pie and a pint. He's twenty-four years old, married with a child, and you, my darling, are ten.'

'I know!' She coloured dramatically. 'Just asking, OK?'

'OK. Just telling.'

'Oh!'

Her exclamation came as we both came barging through the kitchen door together, sniping at each other, before the extraordinary vision before us stopped us in our tracks. A devastatingly attractive man, tanned, blond, with eyes nearly as blue as Johnny's and wearing black jeans and a white T-shirt, was sitting at the little scullery table eating a bowl of Frosties.

'Blimey!' Claudia added, just for good measure. 'A*don*is!'

He got to his feet in confusion. 'God, I'm so sorry. My father said you were out and that he was going to baby-sit or something. I had no idea—you must think I'm appalling, sitting here eating your food.' He smiled an apologetic but faintly winning smile.

'Good gracious, you must be Lance then,' I said, recovering.

'That's it. I'm really sorry if I surprised you, but my father said you wouldn't mind.' He gestured to the bowl.

'No! No, not at all.' Heavens. My father? Not Dad? Pop? The old man? And when had any of my other workers ever got up when I'd come into a room? Most of them promptly sat down.

'Right! Well, I must be off. I take it you're joining your da—father while he baby-sits, so if you could just tell him I'll be back at about—'

'Right here, luv,' said Mac, coming in through the kitchen door behind me. 'You've met my boy then?' He nodded at Lance.

'Yes! Yes, indeed.' I smiled brightly. 'Now, run along, Claudes, there's a good girl. Half an hour of television and then bed, OK?' I turned to Mac. 'You know where I am, don't you?'

'Number 32, The sequinned busybody.' He looked at me approvingly. 'You look smashing, by the way, luv, don't she, Lance?'

'I think that's something of an understatement,' grinned Lance. 'Have a good time.'

'Will do,' I managed as I scuttled to the door.

I shut it gratefully behind me. Phew. Feeling a bit hot in there, for some reason. I tripped thankfully down the steps. Suddenly I stopped, wrapped my shawl dramatically around my shoulders, lifted one eyebrow and growled, 'I think that's something of an understatement.' I giggled. Still, I reflected as I reached Nanette's steps, the vast old Abbey towering right above me, Lance might be more interesting than most labourers to have around. He was certainly more decorative.

Moments later Nanette opened the front door and my high spirits took a dive.

'Darling!' She stepped back for me to admire. She was dressed in an extraordinary sort of embroidered silk pyjama ensemble; her neck weighed down with heavy silver beads; her feet skippy in floppy gold sandals; her toenails bright red and dazzling. Rude not to comment.

'Nanette, you look . . . amazing.'

'Isn't it divine? Roger had the whole lot sent across from Hong Kong and I simply *had* to wear it. Poor bunny, he's still stuck out there, I'm afraid. I can't *wait* to get him back and kiss him to bits!'

'Ah, so he's not here?' That was a bonus, anyway. Roger was her current amour, a computer salesman: smooth, dark, and softly spoken.

'No, but I have got some *super* people for you to meet, Olivia. Come on, come on through!'

I followed her jangling beads and floppy sandals down her shiny parquet hall and into her ornate, swagged, dragged, beribboned and bowed drawing room. Four people stood in a silent, awkward circle around a glass coffee table, each clutching a glass of pinkish wine. Nanette clapped her hands prettily, as if to break up the bustling chatter.

'Everyone! Oo-oo! This is Olivia, my very good friend from just along The Crescent, and, Olivia, these dear people are Cliff and Yolanda Blair, who are desperately old friends of mine—'

'No relation!' piped up Yolanda, 'but I'm a big fan of Cherie's!' It was clearly her habitual opening gambit so I smiled politely.

'—and Sebastian, who, actually, you *might* know because he lives in The Crescent. And Malcolm here, who if I was a single girl I'd want to keep *all* to myself because he's a complete and utter cutie-pie and makes an absolute *fortune* at the BMW concession in Luton!'

I wanted to turn and run right now, but we all smiled and I shook hands; first with Yolanda, a broad-beamed lady, who managed to prise her hand from Cliff's arm for literally two seconds before firmly replacing it, then with Cliff who was tiny and frail and failed to meet my eye, then Malcolm who was very golf-club tie and belted grey slacks, and finally with Sebastian, tall, pale, with slanting, watchful eyes and rather too long dark hair, and who, now you come to mention it, I did recognise.

When I'd first moved in here, Nanette had made it her business to bustle straight over with a kettle and a fruit-cake. She'd introduced herself as 'a very merry widow' and had sunk down into my Lloyd Loom chair and proceeded to give me the lowdown on the entire neighbourhood. This one, Sebastian, was apparently, 'decidedly odd'. Not only, she'd hissed to me over the Nescafé and the fruit-cake, did he sometimes pace up and down at his window, waving his arms about and shaking his head like a mad dog, but he'd also been seen squeezing the grapefruit in Waitrose, still wearing his pyjamas. At thirty-six, he still lived at home with his mother. Apparently, he taught at the boys' school in town, but Nanette reckoned it was just a way of integrating him back into the community. And now here he was, at my left elbow, staring distractedly at a spot somewhere above the top of my head.

'Now, you'll have a little drinky, Olivia?' Nanette fluttered her hand bossily in Malcolm's direction. 'Do the honours, Malc, there's a love. It's kir, Olivia—I don't know if you've had that before? And then if you'll excuse me for just two secs, I'm going to put the finishing touches to the canapés in the kitchen. Don't fight over her now, will you, boys!'

Well, that surely put the kiss of death on any intelligent conversation. We stood about a bit more in the awkward circle, and somehow, Malcolm and I managed to exchange a few, polite words about the traffic congestion in the city, while Sebastian continued to stare above my head. After several minutes of torture I made my excuses and escaped, on the pretext of helping in the kitchen.

'Nanette!' I hissed as she squirted some squiggles of pâté out of a tube and onto some tired-looking Ritz biscuits. 'Isn't that the arm-waver in there? Are you trying to set me up with a nutter?'

'Ah!' She put the tube down. 'Yes, Olivia, it is, but listen, he's fine, honestly. I had a chat to him in the street the other day and he was wearing perfectly ordinary clothes and I really think he's absolutely normal!'

'Oh, come on, you've changed your tune! You told me that he was certifiable!'

'Well I know, but I really think that was just a phase or something. After all, we all get depressed, don't we? And anyway,' she went on hurriedly, 'Gerald cancelled at the last moment so I just sort of asked him, otherwise you'd have been the odd girl. He just needs bringing out.'

'Well, not by me!' I hissed. 'I might bring out a lunatic!'

'Ssh, he'll hear you. Well, OK, Malcolm then? Christ, I gave you a choice! Malcolm's lovely. He's a complete catch, you know.'

'Nanette, I do not want to "catch" anyone!'

'Oh, don't be ridiculous, Olivia. You can't hunker down like a hermit for ever. You've got to live a little. Johnny has to be shown that you're a very desirable woman!' And with that she picked up her plate of canapés and marched past me into the drawing room.

If drinks were torturous, supper was worse. Malcolm, beside me, of BMW fame, told me in confidential tones exactly why the sixteen-valve fuel-injected 318IS was a superior machine to the 1SE. He even hinted that if I played my cards right, he might take me for a test drive.

'What car do you drive?' he asked.

'Hmm?' I raised my eyes from the psychedelic pattern I'd created on my plate, and suddenly remembered Johnny's garage. My tired eyes flashed in their brave old sockets.

'I've got a Bristol and a Lagonda three-litre drop-head coupé.'

As he spat his mousse across the table, I turned coolly to Sebastian.

'I gather you're a teacher,' I said gently. After Malcolm I could be kind. I could bring him out, just an inch or two.

'Well, yes, occasionally. Just a couple of days a month really.'

Ah, so it was like day release. 'That's good. You must enjoy that?'

'Yes, I do.'

'And what is it you teach, exactly?' Even more softly.

He paused, perhaps trying to remember. 'Music,' he intoned eventually.

'Music! Lovely! Songs, and things?'

'Um, some . . . songs, yes.'

'Super!'

A silence ensued.

'And do you play?'

'Sorry?'

'An instrument, you know, the violin or—' oh God, no—'the recorder? I used to play the recorder!'

'Really.' Rather drily perhaps.

'Yes, at school. Not any more. If people ask "What do you play?" I just say, "Oh, the fool!" '

Suddenly I cringed. Oh God, you idiot, Olivia—the fool! He'll think you're taking the mickey! I cast around desperately.

'I—um, and—how is your mother?'

He turned almost 180 degrees to look at me. Really rather closely. 'She's well, thank you. How's yours?'

'Oh! Oh, fine.'

He stared at me with his slanting, dark eyes, as if I had two heads, but happily Yolanda was causing a diversion on the other side of the table.

'I'm *so* sorry, Nanette, it's such a bore, but they do say no liver, no blue cheese, no unpasteurised products and absolutely nothing that's been in the microwave. I take it the mousse had raw egg in? Ah yes, well, that's why I left it, and I'm afraid this hollandaise sauce is out, but if you scrape if off I can eat the salmon.'

She patted what I now realised was a burgeoning stomach and smiled smugly at Cliff, the father, it transpired, of her five children. For these weren't newlyweds, who couldn't keep their hands off each other as I'd originally imagined, but a fabulously fecund couple who were about to inflict their sixth child on the world.

'I'll take the sauce off,' muttered Nanette, removing the plate.

'Oh dear, what a shame, but one really can't be too careful and I'd never forgive myself if anything happened. Has anyone else got little ones here? Nanette, yours are all grown up now, aren't they?'

'Er, well. Not so grown up.'

'But teenagers, surely? At university?'

'Just.' Nanette ground her teeth.

Malcolm held up his hands and was quick to claim no offspring whatsoever. Sebastian failed to answer, and I was forced to admit I had one.

'Just one? A baby then, is it? The first?'

'No, she's ten.'

'Oh gosh. Nanette did say, but I forgot.' She puckered her brow in consternation. 'You've had a sadness, haven't you?'

'Well, no one's died,' I muttered.

'No, but didn't your husband—'

'Through into the lounge for coffee?' warbled Nanette gaily, coming to my rescue.

Cliff was the first up from the table saying, 'The baby sitter will be waiting, my love. We must be off.'

At the mention of babies Yolanda was instantly galvanised, fussing about midnight feeds and bed-wetting and getting up at six to make breakfast, as Cliff helped her into her coat.

They left, and the evening limped on. Sebastian stood at the window, staring fixedly at a tassel on the curtains, Nanette snuggled up to Malcolm and I threw the hottest coffee imaginable down my throat.

'Finished,' I gasped. 'Must be off, Nanette. Mac will be waiting.'

She followed me to the door, where I promised her that I'd had the most fantastic evening, that of course I'd come again, and agreed that Malcolm was indeed a complete honey.

'He really liked you,' she hissed, glancing back over her shoulder. 'In fact I think he might ring you!'

'Excellent,' I said, too tired to argue. 'Couldn't be more pleased.'

As I walked back up the street, it occurred to me to wonder whether it was my knickers he was trying to get into, or my Lagonda.

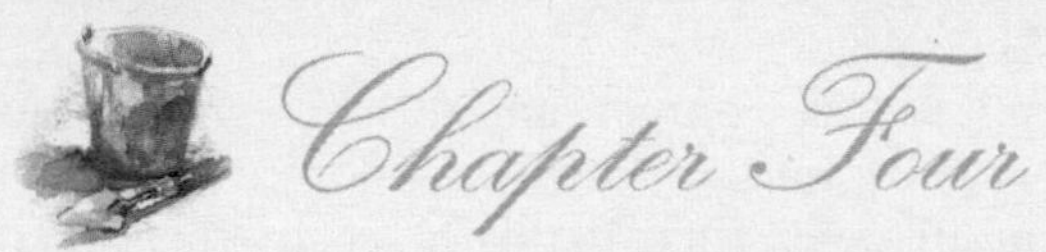

Chapter Four

THE FOLLOWING WEDNESDAY, after I'd dropped Claudia off at school, I returned home to find a car in my usual parking place. I knew this blue BMW. Well, it had to happen some time. I drew up behind it.

After a moment, I got out and walked past it, noticing a huge dent in the front wing. I trailed round to the back door to give myself a moment to compose myself before I went to the sitting room where I was sure she'd be but, as I turned the corner, I realised my mistake. It was a beautiful day and, of course, the party was taking place in the garden. Down by the stream, under the spreading cedar tree, draped in various positions about my white, wrought-iron garden furniture, my builders were At Home.

Alf was standing pouring tea from a china pot, Spiro sat cross-legged on the grass, Mac relaxed in a deck chair and Lance was mixing what appeared to be a large gin and tonic. Sitting centre stage, looking radiant in a crisp white shirt and brown linen trousers, her copper-coloured hair shining in the sun, was Angie. I smiled in spite of myself. Wherever Angie went, people flocked around. Not that my builders needed much excuse to flock.

'Livvy!' she called to me, raising her hand in a wave, just as if nothing had happened. As if her son hadn't left me. As if she'd seen me since. I walked towards her, down the gravel path edged with lavender bushes, under the rose arbour, stooping, as I reached her, to kiss her cheek.

'Angie, it's lovely to see you.' I suddenly meant it; felt almost choked at the sight of her.

'Darling, forgive me for not getting up but look what I've done to my stupid foot! Too maddening.'

I glanced down and noticed her shoe was off and that her foot was badly swollen. Spiro—whom I seemed to remember attending to my own feet very recently—was wrapping a wet towel round it.

'Some lunatic pranged into me just as I was coming round your corner—didn't even stop!'

'Oh Angie, how awful.' I dropped down beside her. 'Are you OK?'

'No, she not,' growled Spiro.

'I'm absolutely fine, and this dear boy is doing wonders. I just banged my foot on the pedals, that's all. In fact *all* these boys have been sweethearts. Thank you, Lance.' She looked up and took her gin with a smile.

Heavens, it had certainly all been very matey here, hadn't it? First-name terms and buckets of gin.

'Oh—and Lance has been showing me all his bits and pieces!'

I boggled. 'Has he?'

'Yes, didn't you know? He makes coffee tables, chessboards—all kinds of things, and all with the most marvellous inlay and marquetry—terribly talented. Has he not shown you his portfolio?'

'I only arrived the other day,' explained Lance quickly, looking slightly embarrassed, as well he might. Yes, he'd only arrived the other day and so far I'd seen him do little more than eat my Frosties, drink my tea and mix my gin.

'There hasn't really been time, has there, Lance?' I said smoothly, but Angie caught my tone. She looked around.

'Well, boys, now that Mrs McFarllen's back, I'm sure I'm going to be fine,' she said, beaming. 'Thank you all, *so* much.' Despite her charm, there was no disputing that this was a directive for them to leave. Mac got to his feet, yawning. 'Come on, lads, back to work,' he muttered.

'Nice boy,' murmured Angie, to Lance's departing backside. 'And very talented. More of a cabinet-maker than a chippy.'

Angie stretched out and squeezed my hand as I sank into Mac's vacated chair.

'How are you, my dear?'

'Pretty good.'

'The garden looks lovely,' she said conversationally, sipping her gin. 'You've made a super job of those borders. I love the way you've contrasted those mauve campanulas with the Boule de Neige.'

'It's my refuge,' I said quietly. 'I've lost interest in the house, but this is where I get rid of all my angst. Blow out my passion.'

She nodded. 'I remember when Oliver died, I had this strange compulsion to have my hands in the soil at all times—remember? It made me feel closer to him, somehow.'

A silence broke over us. Suddenly I could bear it no longer.

'Have you seen him?' I blurted out.

'I have.'

'So—he's told you?'

'He has. A couple of weeks ago.'

A couple of weeks ago. But she hadn't come to see me.

'I didn't want to intrude,' she said gently. 'Hoped you'd come to me.'

'Well, I—just wanted to be on my own for a bit. You know.'

'I understand.' She patted my hand.

'Did you . . . meet her?' I managed.

'Yes. Johnny and I met for lunch. She just came for a drink first.'

'And so . . . what did you think?' Vocalising it was awful.

She turned to face me fully for the first time. 'Well, if I was being kind I'd say she was a sweet little thing, but as you and I both know—since it appears that by some horrific coincidence she teaches at Claudia's school—that's generous. She's *très ordinaire*. What the devil's he up to, Livvy? I expected Claudia Schiffer at the very least, but, good heavens, that bosomy little nobody! To leave you for her!'

I sighed. 'I know. Defies belief, doesn't it? And there was I thinking you might be able to shed some light on it.'

'The only light I can shed is the little I gleaned when she left the restaurant—which she tactfully did when she'd had the drink.'

'And?'

'Well, it seems . . .' she hesitated, 'it seems he'd been rather unhappy.'

I jumped. 'Here? Did he say *I'd* made him unhappy?'

She looked uncomfortable. 'Not in so many words, my darling, but he said it bothered him that you had no life of your own. That everything you did revolved around him.'

'But—but I thought he liked that!'

'What I am saying is that you're too considerate, Livvy, that's your problem,' she went on. 'I think he needs a bit of a shock. I think he needs to see that you're not just sitting about waiting for him to come back.'

'Too bloody *right* I'm not!'

'That you're still a very attractive woman—'

'You *bet* I'm attractive! God, I'm—I'm gorgeous!'

'Still highly desirable—'

'Yes!' I shrieked, banging the back of the chair with my fist.

'And I think he needs to see—'

'A man!' I interrupted, eyes wide.

'That's the spirit, but make sure it's what *you* want,' she said anxiously.

'But I just want my husband back. Is that totally sad, as Claudes would say?'

'No, it's totally understandable,' she said slowly. 'All I'm saying is . . . enjoy the process. Enjoy the means to the end. Because, believe it or not, you may enjoy the means, even more than the end.'

I thought about this. 'Unlikely, but I take your point. I also agree that it's got to be more fun than sitting around waiting for him.'

'Of course it has!' she squeaked. She raised her glass. 'You, Olivia McFarllen, are about to have some fun!'

The following morning, I rang Imogen. 'D'you know any nice men?'

She paused, taken aback. 'What sort of men?'

'Attractive, sexy, single men, of course!'

I felt her switch the phone to her other ear, give a little cough and shuffle her chair around. Perhaps the gallery was busy. 'What d'you want one for?' she muttered.

'I want to make Johnny jealous, of course. What d'you think!'

'Ah, right. That old chestnut. I wondered when you'd come round to that way of thinking. Hang on, I'll get my address book.' She broke off for a second. 'Right, now, let's see . . .' I heard her flipping through the pages. 'Well, there's Giles, of course, who would have been perfect . . .'

'Yes?'

'But sadly he's come out. Such a waste . . .' more page flipping, 'Ah—hang on, Rollo! Yes, now Rollo's lovely. Works for the Foreign Office, frightfully rich, terribly intelligent, fabulous flat in South Kensington—'

'Sold,' I purred. 'Perfect, Imo. He sounds totally perfect. Invite me to dinner tomorrow. Then I'll invite him back here this weekend.'

'Tomorrow? God, you must be kidding! I couldn't possibly suggest anything for his diary without a couple of weeks' notice.'

'A couple of weeks!' I shrieked. 'I need him on Sunday, when Johnny comes to take Claudia out.'

'Sunday. Gosh no, I'm sorry, I don't think I'd be able to deliver the goods by then, Livvy,' she said doubtfully.

'Never mind,' I said quickly. 'Forget it, Imo. Thanks, anyway.'

'Sorry, but, listen, I'll tell you what. I was going to take the parents to that big concert they're doing in the Abbey next week on the 15th. Dad really wants to go and Rollo's a real music buff. Why don't you come with us? It's something to have in reserve if nothing else.'

'What big concert?' I said dully.

'You *know*. God, it's on your doorstep, for heaven's sake. Faulkner's new orchestral piece. It's going to be absolutely packed.'

'Is it? Oh, OK, fix it up. Speak to you soon, Imo.'

I put the phone down and gritted my teeth. Malcolm. It would have to be Malcolm. Oh God, could I really bring myself to? Yes. Yes, I could. This was an emergency. Before I could change my mind I hastened round to Nanette's for his number.

Nanette answered the door with Roger, beaming away behind her. Both were in matching kimonos and both looking very postcoital. She was nearly sick with excitement when I told her my mission.

'Oooh, I just *knew* you two would hit it off! Didn't I say so, Rog? I'm *so* glad you liked him, Olivia!'

'The old dog!' hooted Roger. 'Getting his feet under your table in double-quick time, eh? I must say, I thought it was more the form for the boy to ring the girl, but then I don't know many emancipated women, do I, pumpkin?'

'To be honest, Roger, I'm not that emancipated myself, but this is a bit of an emergency,' I said grimly. 'Thanks, Nanette.' I took the piece of paper she'd scribbled the number on, hurried down the steps and back home to my telephone, fingers itching to dial. Time was of the essence.

Malcolm seemed delighted, if astonished, to hear from me.

'Sunday? Er, yes, sure. What sort of time—eight thirtyish?'

'Eleven o'clock in the morning,' I said firmly. Johnny would be arriving at eleven thirty to take Claudia out.

'Oh! Right. At your place?'

'That's it.'

'And then lunch?'

'Er, no. No, I've got to go out to lunch, I'm afraid.' God, I couldn't cope with him for any longer than was absolutely necessary.

'Ah. Right. So—what time are you going out?'

'Oh, about twelve . . . thirty,' I added charitably.

'So . . . you want me to pop round for about an hour and a half. On Sunday morning. Is that it?'

'That's it,' I agreed brightly.

'OK . . . fine. And then we'll take it from there, shall we?'

'Yes, why not?' I agreed blithely.

'Right,' he said faintly. 'See you then, then.'

'Excellent, Malcolm, see you then.'

The following day I raced into London and took Knightsbridge by storm. I flew around Harvey Nichols as if my life depended on it, wriggling into far tighter and sexier outfits than I would normally entertain, finally rejecting them all and settling on a very elegant cream linen dress and a pair of kitten-heeled, navy mules.

That was Friday, but the complicated bit of the plan revolved around Saturday. It dawned and, as I sat at the scullery table, I grew thoughtful. The thing was, I didn't particularly want Claudia around, a) to see Malcolm and double up with mirth, b) to witness any potential shit hitting the fan depending on whether Johnny, i) hit the roof, ii) hit the road, or iii) hit Malcolm. She was due to go to her best friend Lucy's house for the day, and had originally been asked for the night, too, but I'd refused on the grounds that Johnny would be coming to collect her on Sunday morning. However, a quick call to Lucy's mother could change all that . . .

I was just replacing the receiver, when Claudia sat down for her cereal. She hurriedly shook out a bowl of Frosties, sloshing milk on top.

'Can you drop me at Lucy's in about ten minutes? We're going to make a Ouija board.'

'Sure. Is anyone else going?'

'Lottie and Saskia. *They're* both staying the night.' She glared at me as she munched away.

'Are they? Well, darling, I've been thinking—seeing as it's become a bit of a party, why don't you stay too? You could see Daddy next Sunday. I'm sure he wouldn't mind.'

She nearly dropped her spoon. 'Really? Oh, cool, Mum! Oh, that is totally cool! They're going to see a film on Sunday morning, and have lunch in Café Rouge. Can I do that too?'

'Of course.'

'Of *course*? Good grief, what's happened to you? This is brilliant! I'll just go and pack a bag.' She jumped up.

'I've done it, darling. There.' I pointed to her rucksack at the bottom of the stairs. She stared.

'But—hadn't we better ring Lucy's mum?'

'I've done that too,' I smiled.

'Oh, Mum, you are awesome this morning!' She ran to pick up her rucksack, then stopped. Turned. 'Oh—but will Daddy mind?'

'Of course not, my darling, and I'll explain that it was a very special sleepover, planned ages ago. He'll be fine.'

'OK,' she said doubtfully. 'And give him lots of love. Oh—I know, why don't I ring him and tell him? Would he like that?'

'No, no,' I said quickly, 'I'll do that. I've got to ring him anyway.'

'Thanks, Mum. Hey,' she looked at me suspiciously as we got to the front door, 'you're not by any chance seeing anyone tonight, are you?'

I flushed. 'Of course not. Why?'

She grinned. 'Just wondered. You seem awfully keen to get me out of the house, that's all.'

'Don't be ridiculous!' I spluttered. 'The very idea! Now get in that car, young lady, before I change my mind!'

Sunday dawned even brighter and sunnier than the previous few days. As I came in from the garden and went up to the bathroom to have a shower, I paused at my bedroom window to gaze out at my handiwork. I smiled. Under the cedar tree, down by the stream, I'd put a small round table, covered it with a red gingham cloth, and placed two French café chairs either side. A posy of white roses was set just so already, but in an hour or so, when Malcolm got here, I'd add a basket of warm croissants, a jug of orange juice, fresh coffee, and a pot of raspberry jam. When Johnny arrived for Claudia, rang the bell, got no answer because, of course, I could pretend I hadn't heard it from the garden, and walked round the back, he'd be presented with an arresting tableau: his wife and a strange man, sharing what could only be construed as a very late breakfast. A lovers' breakfast.

I was just about to move away from the window and hop into the shower, when something stopped me. I stared. To my horror, I saw the caravan door open. Good grief, hadn't they all gone home for the weekend? It was Sunday, after all. I watched in fury as Lance came down the steps, dressed in shorts and a T-shirt, his tool bag under his arm. Suddenly I remembered he'd said he was going to work this weekend because Mac wanted to get the Aga in next week and the cabinets had to go in first. Damn. I didn't particularly want him sniggering behind his hand at me and Malcolm, but at least, I reasoned, if he was ensconced in the new kitchen with his lathes and drills going, he probably wouldn't be any trouble. Relieved, I hopped in the shower.

As I lifted my face up to the warm water I felt nervous, but strangely excited too. Gosh, perhaps Angie was right. This 'taking control' lark was rather stimulating, and if Johnny took the bait, heavens knows what sort of passions and jealousies could be aroused. I wondered if—Damn. I paused mid-scrub as the telephone rang from my bedroom. Swearing and dripping I grabbed a towel and ran to get it.

'Hello?'

'Hello, Olivia? It's Malcolm.'

'Malcolm! Hi!' Gosh, I was almost delighted to hear from him, almost as if he really were my lover. I could quite get into this role-playing.

'Olivia, I'm awfully sorry, but I've just realised I'm supposed to be somewhere else this morning. I do apologise, but I'm afraid I'm not going to be able to make it.'

I stared, dumbstruck, into the mouthpiece. What did he mean, he had to be somewhere else? I sat down heavily on my bed, aghast.

'Malcolm, I don't believe it. Where have you got to be?'

He cleared his throat. 'Olivia, am I right in thinking you're separated?'

'Yes.'

'And you have a young daughter?'

'Yes.'

'Who, presumably, your husband has visiting rights to on a Sunday?'

I licked my lips. Couldn't speak.

He sighed. 'Olivia, when you've been single as long as I have, you get to know the ropes. The Sunday morning routine is an old one. I don't particularly want my lights punched out by your estranged husband.'

I was speechless. All my plans, my schemes, dripped off me, evaporated into the duvet. But a small part of me felt awful too.

'Malcolm, I'm so sorry. I feel dreadful now, and I really did like you.' I crossed my fingers hard here. 'I didn't ask you over just to—well to—'

'Use me?'

I gulped. 'Um, look. Maybe—maybe we could get together some other time?' I said generously.

'I don't think so, do you?'

'Er, right. No, no, maybe not.'

'Goodbye, Olivia.'

'Goodbye.'

I replaced the receiver. Stared at it. Bugger. Bugger, bugger, bugger! Now what the hell was I supposed to do? God, Johnny would be here in—I glanced at the clock—less than an hour.

I paced about the room wrapped in a towel, racking my brains madly. What on earth was I going to do?

I wrung my hands wretchedly, gazing out of the window at my

perfect table, my flowers, when suddenly, right underneath my window, from out of the kitchen door came Lance. I stared down at him. I blinked. Of course! Why didn't I think of it before? Lance! Hell, in anyone's book he was completely bloody gorgeous, far more gorgeous than Malcolm. Yes, yes, Lance was perfect! But how on earth could I set it up without him thinking I fancied the pants off him? Suddenly I remembered something. Quick as a flash I got dressed in the cream dress, the navy shoes, brushed my hair, tucked it neatly behind my ears, added lipstick and mascara, and went downstairs.

Out in the garden, Lance had set up a workbench outside the back door, and was planing away, his broad back bent low over his work bench, blond curls curling at the nape of his neck.

'Hi!'

He turned. I gave a breezy smile. A dinky little wave.

'Oh, hi there.' He looked me up and down. 'You going out?'

'Um, no, just sort of, felt like a change from jeans, really.'

'Oh, right.' He turned and went back to his planing.

I walked round the bench so that I was facing him. 'Um, Lance?'

'Yes?' He paused, looked up.

'I was having a look at that portfolio you showed Angie the other day, with all your tables and chairs and things in it?'

'Oh right,' he brightened.

'Yes, and I was just wondering, would you have time to make Claudia a bedside table?'

'Sure, I can do that. Which one caught your eye?'

'Well, I was wondering if we could discuss it later. You know, have a sort of meeting. At about eleven thirty?'

He shrugged. 'OK, but I can talk you through it now if you want.'

'Er, no, that's all right. I've got to—do the washing-up. But I thought, if we could catch up later, ooh, let's see, say under the cedar tree? Over there where the table is?'

He turned and followed my gaze. Slowly he took in the two chairs, the checked tablecloth, the flowers, the jam, the coffee cups. He looked startled for a moment, then his face cleared. As he turned back, his eyes glinted, as though he'd just had a brush with possibility. He grinned.

'Under the cedar tree it is. Shall I have a rose in my teeth?'

'Don't be ridiculous,' I spluttered. 'Now if you'll excuse me I've got jobs to do.'

I turned and stalked off, hopefully with dignity, towards the back of the house. But his voice stopped me in my tracks.

'What time's Johnny coming?'

I turned. Flushed. 'What?'

'I said, what time is your husband coming?'

'I—don't know what you mean!'

'Oh, I think you do, Olivia.' His voice was gentle now. Less flippant.

He gazed at me, blue eyes very intense. I took a deep breath. Raised my chin. After a long moment, I spoke.

'Eleven thirty. And yes, Lance, you've seen right through my little plan. I did want to make him jealous, wanted a reaction from him, but, unfortunately, the candidate I originally picked for the job also smelt a rat and cried off ten minutes ago, so I asked you instead, satisfied?' I turned and started to go towards the house, tears already pricking my eyelids. Just short of the French windows, he caught up with me.

'Hey, hang on. Don't go off in a huff. I just think you could do it better.'

I stopped. Turned to face him. 'What?'

'You want to make him jealous, right?'

'Well, yes, I—'

'What time did you say he was coming?' he interrupted.

'Half eleven.'

He glanced at his watch. 'He'll be here in ten minutes. Right. We have to get a wiggle on. Now, what we need are a couple of these,' he walked across to the washing line, reached up and grabbed a couple of towels and laid them on the grass.

'Now,' he frowned, 'let's see . . . I'll take off this—' he whipped his T-shirt over his head—'and these—'

'No!' I squeaked as his hand went for his flies.

He grinned. 'Only teasing. No, I'll just lie down like this, I think.' He settled back on the towels, arms locked behind his head, legs stretched out, brown chest, with its smattering of golden hair, bared. His blue eyes squinted up at me, into the sun. He shaded them with his hand.

'You look ridiculous, if you don't mind me saying so. You look like you're going to the Tory Party Conference and, apart from anything else, it's eighty-five degrees. Go on, go and get your kit off and put your cossy on. Oh, and grab some suntan lotion while you're at it.'

I gazed down at him incredulously. Get my kit off? Suntan lotion?

'He'll hit the roof. Seeing us laid out out here, all sort of—'

'All sort of . . . naked? And isn't hitting the roof the general idea?'

I gulped, hovered tremulously for a moment, but didn't make the mistake of hesitating again. He might change his mind. I ran inside, up the stairs, across the landing and into my bedroom, pulling out drawer after drawer, riffling around for my costume. My costume—oh God, could I do this? My hand stayed abruptly. I shut my eyes tight. Thought of Johnny. How I wanted him. Yes, I bloody could.

What I actually came down in—rather sheepishly—was something of a compromise: a bikini top and shorts. Lance was still supine, hands locked behind his head and eyes, thankfully, shut. I was grateful for that small amount of tact as I slunk down beside him.

'Got the Ambre Solaire?'

'Yes,' I whispered.

'Good. To be applied later. With vigour.'

He was grinning across at me, seeing me for the first time with not a lot on, when the doorbell rang.

'Shit!' I squeaked. 'He's here! Oh God, Lance, I'm not sure I can do this.'

'Don't be ridiculous, of course you can. Here'—he passed me the Ambre Solaire—'Now, sit up and rub it into my shoulders. Firmly.' I hesitated. 'And don't forget, Olivia,' he murmured, 'I'll bet he's just given that Nina of his a right good seeing to.'

That did it. I knelt up, emptied half a bottle onto Lance's chest, and got stuck in. His skin was soft and velvety and I could feel my heart pounding for various reasons as I kneaded the lotion in. A silence prevailed. Then the bell rang again. Then all went quiet. For ages.

'Oh God, he's not coming round!' I hissed, panicking.

Lance raised himself up on his elbows. 'Quite normal,' he whispered. 'He feels he doesn't live here any more, so he wouldn't presume to come round the back. I'll go and see him.' He jumped nimbly to his feet.

'Lance! No, you can't! What are you going to say?' I gasped.

'Oh, I'll say you're in the bath, soaking, and that in all the excitement you forgot to ring and tell him Claudia was away. I might yawn a bit too, scratch my sleepy head, and then as he goes, I'll turn and walk back upstairs to the bedroom.'

'Lance!' I shrieked, but it was no good. He'd gone.

I flung myself down on the towel and stuffed the corner in my mouth. *Omigod omigod!* He'd freak! He'd go insane, he'd—he'd hit him! Would he hit him? I took the towel out of my mouth. I had a feeling Lance was just a little bit bigger, and Johnny wasn't a fisticuffs sort of man but, oh Lord, the fur would most certainly fly. I shut my eyes tight and just as I was thinking I might actually faint from a combination of frayed nerves and heat, Lance reappeared, hands in his shorts pockets.

'Well?' I breathed, sitting up.

'He's gone,' he smiled.

'And?'

'And, he seemed most put out. Astonished. Stunned even.'

'What did he say?' I squeaked, kneeling up.

'Oh, well he spluttered fairly incoherently for a bit—particularly when I explained how exhausted you were—but then he finally said something about ringing you later.' He grinned.

'Oh!' I squealed, clutching my mouth. Blimey, what would Johnny think? Well, he'd think naked massaging, that's what. I felt a bit queasy now, but then abruptly my blood boiled. After all, that was probably what *he* got up to, wasn't it? If not worse! Why should I feel guilty? Serves him bloody well right, I thought fiercely.

Lance lay down beside me and I shut my eyes, feeling the sun on my eyelids, my skin soaking up the heat. The sun was making me drowsy. I mustn't drop off, though, I thought sleepily. My skin would absolutely scorch out here. Just two minutes, then I'd get up.

Some time later, I was woken by the doorbell. It was ringing and ringing. I opened my eyes and sat up, startled. Lance was kipping beside me. It rang again, then again, sharp, and insistent.

'OK, OK!' I muttered, staggering to my feet. I weaved sleepily up the garden, through the French windows. When I reached the hall, I caught sight of myself in the mirror. My face and chest were a livid red, and my hair, wet and sweaty, plastered to my head. I groaned. The bell went again.

'I'm bloody *coming*!' I shrieked, as I reached for the doorknob.

There, on my doorstep, stood Johnny.

'Johnny!' I gasped, taking a step back. I wrapped my arms protectively around my bare midriff.

'Hi, Livvy.'

'Sorry, I'm a bit late, but the traffic was appalling.'

'Late for what?'

'Well, I've come to collect Claudia, of course.'

I stared at him, aghast. 'But—you came earlier!'

'What?'

'Didn't you come earlier?'

'What d'you mean?'

'Well—someone came!'

'To collect her?'

'I don't know, I didn't speak to him!'

'So who did?'

'Lance! He's my . . . my cabinet-maker.'

'Your cabinet-maker?' He blinked. 'Blimey, exactly how rarefied are these builders getting, Livvy? OK, so where's Claudia?'

'Oh! She's not here!'

Johnny paled. 'You mean . . . you let her go? With this person who spoke to your cabinet-maker and—and handed over my *child*?'

'No! God, no.' I pushed my hands desperately through my sweaty hair. 'She's at Lucy's, you see. She stayed the night there, and I meant to ring you and tell you, Johnny, but—well, I forgot.'

'Ah.' He nodded. 'Right. So . . . I've just sat on the M1 for two hours, when you could have made a quick phone call, is that it?'

'Well, I *meant* to ring, of course, but I've been so busy, you see!'

'Clearly,' he said drily. He glanced behind me, through the French windows to the garden, where Lance was spread-eagled on a towel.

'I take it that's the master craftsman?'

'Yes,' I hesitated, 'that's—Lancelot.'

He snorted. 'Lancelot! So—let me guess—you're Guinevere?'

I regarded him for a moment, then folded my arms and raised my chin at him.

'Johnny, do I poke fun at your relationship? Do I make derogatory remarks about your fluffy, winsome, bosomy little teacher?'

He looked suitably chastened. Nodded. 'No, no, you're right. Sorry, Livvy. You're behaving very well. Much better than I am.'

A lump came to my throat and, as his blue eyes apologised, I wanted to throw myself on him, hug him to bits. But I didn't.

'So,' he scuffed his shoes on the doorstep, 'it is a relationship, then?'

Ah, so he'd picked up on that. Good. I gave a dismissive little shrug.

'I'm not sure yet. It's still early days.' Play it cool, Livvy, dead cool.

He nodded. 'Right. Well, anyway, it's none of my business,' he said hurriedly. 'I'll be away.'

'You don't want to—' I stood aside to let him in—'get a drink or anything? I mean, if you've been in the car for ages . . .'

'No, no,' he said quickly, glancing at Lance. 'No, thanks.' As he turned to go, he glanced back. 'Incidentally, I should put something on that chest. You're going to be as raw as hell in the morning. And tell Claudes I'll see her next week.'

I nodded. Couldn't speak now. He walked to his car and raised his hand in a final salute as he got in. I waved back, watched as he drove off, then sat down on the bottom step of the stairs and burst into tears.

After a while I wiped my eyes and blew my nose violently. Get a grip, Olivia. I peered in the mirror again. God, I couldn't have looked more awful. Bright red skin, sweaty hair—I hardly presented a seductive spectacle, and actually, I felt a bit shivery now. I grabbed a cardigan from the banisters, threw it on and went out into the garden. Lance wasn't exactly looking his best either. Shame Johnny had had to see him like that, but then again, if he'd met him at the door—oh God! Who *had* met Lance at the door? I hastened across the lawn to wake him.

'Lance! Lance!' I crouched down and shook him hard. '*Lance!*'

He came round sleepily. 'Hmm? What?' He raised himself up on one elbow and peered blearily at me. 'Christ,' he muttered, 'what time is it?'

'Almost twelve. We fell asleep. Listen, Lance, you know the guy who came to the door?'

He sat up and yawned widely, scratching his head. 'Johnny?'

'No, it wasn't Johnny! Johnny's just been. He got stuck on the M1!'

'Oh. Really?' He frowned, looked bewildered.

'Yes, really, so what the hell did the other guy look like?'

'Oh.' He peered into the distance, trying to remember. 'Well—quite tall, I suppose, longish dark hair, and sort of . . . yes, slanty eyes.'

I stared. Sat back on my heels. 'Oh God!' I clutched my mouth. 'I think it was Sebastian, from down the road! And there you were, telling him I was recovering from a monumental seeing-to. Now I'll have to go and bloody explain, apologise, do *something*, otherwise it'll be all round the flaming neighbourhood—how the abandoned wife at Orchard House spends her Sunday mornings.'

He shrugged, locked his hands behind his head and lay back. 'Could do, but what does it matter if he thinks you're a goer? It's no bad thing.'

'Oh, what would you know?' I snapped as I marched off round the side of the house, out onto the road. I strode off along the cobbles, practising my apology, then climbed the steps to Sebastian's tall, elegant town house, rang the bell and gazed at the red front door. I was just about to go away when his mother opened it. Just a fraction. I'd never seen her close up before, and I nearly gasped. She was sensationally ugly: her upper teeth protruded and were slightly pointed, making her look like a small, anxious rodent, and her steely grey hair was tied back in a bun, giving her a startled-ferret expression.

'Yes?' she whispered.

'Oh! Um, hello!' I smiled brightly. 'I'm Olivia McFarllen, from down the road. I came to see Sebastian. Is he in?'

'No, he's not.'

'Ah, right. Will he be long? D'you think?'

'I've no idea. He's out delivering leaflets.'

'Oh, leaflets! Lovely!' I enthused. 'Getting out and about then?'

She narrowed her eyes at me suspiciously, declined to answer. No, quite right. Probably fiercely protective.

'Well,' I hastened on, 'when he comes back, perhaps you could just say—that I'd love to have a chat? When he's around?'

'I'll give him the message.'

She shut the door and left me staring at the paintwork again. God, what an old harridan, I thought as I turned and went slowly down the steps. Poor old Sebastian. Heavens, it was no wonder he was like he was with a mother like that.

I slowed my pace as I approached my gates and stopped. Hesitated. It was funny, but now that I was out, I didn't much feel like going back. I'd go into town, get the papers, wander around for a bit—why not?

Being Sunday, the town was fairly empty—just a few tourists, sitting around in cafés and wine bars, studying guidebooks. I bought the Sunday papers and suddenly realised I hadn't eaten since breakfast, so I stopped off in one of the sunnier watering holes and sat down outside, under a shady umbrella. As I shook out the review section of the newspaper, I felt a delicious sense of freedom. No Sunday lunch to cook, no Johnny to worry about. Just me, a glass of chilled white wine—I studied the menu, and—yes, a Caesar salad. I smiled up at the attractive Italian waiter and gave him my order. This really wasn't so terrible, was it? A beautiful day, with no one to please but myself.

When I'd finished my lunch and read most of the papers, I paid the bill and strolled back home, smiling as I rounded the bend into my road, admiring the roses that cascaded over my garden wall. I was also pleased to see the back of Lucy's mother's car parked outside. Ah good, Claudes was back then.

Lucy's mother, Amanda, was sitting in the front seat. When she saw me in her rearview mirror, she shot out of the car. I saw her face and stopped short, as if I'd hit a barrier.

'Is she with you?' she called. I'll never forget the sound of her voice.

Her face was pale, strained. I made myself go on, broke into a run.

'What?' I called stupidly, knowing.

'Claudia, is she with you?'

'Of course not! She's with you, isn't she?'

Amanda's face crumpled as I reached her, her hand clutched her mouth. 'Oh God, Olivia, this is all so awful and it's all my fault! Claudia's gone missing!'

'What d'you mean, gone missing?' I said trembling. 'Slowly. Tell me exactly what happened.'

She wiped mascara from under her eyes with the tips of shaky fingers. Nodded. 'Sorry.' She took a deep breath. 'Well, this morning, Claudia seemed rather quiet. I asked her if she was OK and she said she was fine. I dropped them all off at a ten o'clock matinée of *Titanic*. When I picked them up outside, the other two were larking about as usual, but Claudia was still withdrawn, so I took her aside and asked her what was wrong. Her eyes filled with tears. She said she normally saw her daddy on a Sunday, but she'd chosen to come here instead, and now she felt awful because she thought he might think that she didn't want to see him.'

'Oh, Claudes!' My hand flew to my mouth.

'So I said, well, OK, what time did Daddy normally come round? And she said, oh, about lunchtime, I think, so I said—well, look, Mummy's probably put him off, but d'you want to go home and check, and maybe ring him to see if there's still time to see him? Well, her face lit up at that, and she said she did.' Amanda paused for breath, took a huge gulp of air. 'Anyway, we all piled in the car and drove straight over, but you weren't here. There was a note on the door from someone called Lance who said he was in the Fighting Cocks if you wanted to join him, but otherwise the place was deserted.' She gave a tremulous sob. 'Except that the back door was open, and Claudia said that if you'd left it open like that you wouldn't be long.' Amanda raised her chin to hold back tears. 'Anyway, the other two were going on and on about how I'd promised them Café Rouge and how they were starving, and Claudia was insisting that she didn't want to come, and then the baby started screaming and—oh God, Olivia, in the end I just left her here!' She turned guilty eyes on me.

I nodded. 'It's OK, Amanda. I might well have done the same.'

'So off we all went for lunch and, of course, sitting there in the restaurant, I worried, so I rang to make sure you were back but there was no answer. Then I really panicked. I hurried the girls through their pudding and then I dropped them all off with my neighbour before dashing back over here. The back door was still open and I looked all over the house and the garden and she just wasn't here. Oh God, Olivia, what are we going to do!'

I swallowed. Right. So she'd searched everywhere and Claudia wasn't here. My head told me that she was very sensible for her age and that she wouldn't be far, but my heart told me that she was ten years old and she was on her own somewhere, and I didn't know where.

'Should we ring the police?' trembled Amanda.

'Not yet. You go and ask next door. I'm going to check out a few places near the river.'

I flew round the back of the house and down the garden. Most people assumed the stream was our boundary, but our land—such as it was—carried on over the other side. Amanda wouldn't have been down here. I ran over the bridge and into the little thicket where Claudia had her tree house. Oh, please let her be sulking up here, I begged as I climbed the rope ladder. *Please!* I reached the top and peered in. Empty. I clattered back down again and ran across to the caravan. I flung open the door. Nothing. I felt panic rising, but made myself stop and rack my brains. As I shut the door I had a thought: the note on the door from Lance. If she'd read it, and thought—oh, Mum's gone to join him in the pub—then she'd surely come and find me there! Of course!

I ran breathlessly back across the bridge, then veered off left to Amanda in the drive.

'She wasn't next door!' she shouted.

'OK, stay here in case she appears, but I think I know where she is.'

'Oh, thank God!' She clasped her hands. 'Where d'you—'

But I didn't wait to explain, I was gone. The Fighting Cocks was only a couple of hundred yards from our house, at the end of The Crescent. The garden was heaving when I arrived. I spun around, squinting against the sun to spot her. There were children everywhere—but no Claudia. Then I spotted Lance, sitting at the end of a long table he was having to share with a multitude of others. My hand shot up.

'Lance!'

I dashed across. 'Lance—is Claudia with you?'

'Ah! You made it at last.' He smiled. 'D'you want a drink?'

'No!' I shrieked. 'Is Claudia with you!'

Lance got up. 'No, she's not, why?'

'Oh, Lance, she's missing!' I gasped, rapidly losing control. He came round the table, took my arm and led me away.

'When was she last seen?' he muttered gently.

'Lucy's mother brought her home—I think about an hour and a half ago. We must both have just left the house!'

'You mean, she left her there?'

'Yes, because she thought I'd be back in a minute!'

'Now don't panic. She's a sensible girl, and it's not as if she's a baby, for heaven's sake. She's probably just popped round to see a friend.'

'No.' I shook my head. 'It's not like that, Lance. She doesn't go to the local school, none of her friends live round here, she gets ferried everywhere by car. Oh God, where is she!'

I started to run up the road, heart pounding.

'Why did she come home?' he said, walking fast to keep up with me. 'I thought she was staying for lunch?'

'She was, but she wanted to see Johnny. She felt bad about going to Lucy's when she usually saw him on a Sunday.'

'OK, so then wouldn't she have rung him? Possibly gone to find him?'

'What—in London!' I shrieked, stopping dead in my tracks.

'Steady—*steady*,' he insisted nervously. 'No, I doubt if she'd actually *go* to London—she's not silly—but she might try to contact him, surely?'

'Yes! Yes, you're right, she might!' Hope flooded back for a second. 'I'll ring him.' I hurried on.

Amanda came running down the road to meet us. 'Well?'

I shook my head.

'Oh God, this is awful!' She was sobbing now, and Lance was trying to calm her, knowing she was doing me no good at all. She was nodding as he cajoled her into the front seat of her car, and I saw her reach, sniffing, for the ignition key. As I watched her drive off, Lance came back to me.

'I gave her a job. She's going to ring all the girls in Lucy and Claudia's class, just to make sure she hasn't tried to get hold of one of them.'

I was in the hallway now, front door open, looking desperately for Johnny's number on the hall table. I felt incredibly dizzy.

'I can't find the bloody number!' I sifted through papers, lifting them up and letting them drop with hopeless hands.

'Well, what's it written on?'

'The back of a milk bill, I think—ah! Here!' My trembling fingers pounced on the scrap I'd jotted it down on, not wanting the number in my address book. Too permanent somehow. I dialled. Nina answered.

'Is Johnny there?' I barked. She knew it was me. Yet I'd never rung there before, he always rang here. He came on.

'Livvy?'

'Johnny, is Claudia with you?'

'Of course not. I've just this minute got back from you, why?'

I explained in a quavering voice.

'Oh Christ, this is all my fault,' he said quietly.

I was stunned, but I rallied. 'Of course it's not your fault, Johnny, but we must find her. Ask Nina, has she tried to ring while you were out?'

He turned and I heard him talk to her. I had to clench my teeth, so painful did I find the sound of their murmuring voices. He came back.

'No, she hasn't. Livvy, ring the police and I'll come down.'

'No, Johnny, she may be coming to see you!'

'Nina will be here in case she arrives. I have to be with you on this one, Livvy.'

He had to be with me. But he'd qualified it. *On this one, Livvy.*

'OK.' I put down the phone, swung round to Lance. 'She's not there. Now I'll ring the police.'

'In a minute. Just check first—has she taken any money?'

'Oh!' I dropped the receiver. 'I don't know . . . Wait!'

I raced upstairs two at a time, dashed into her room and seized her china pig. I pulled out the plug. I knew she had about thirty pounds, enough to get her to London and back. It was still there.

'No!' I screamed as I crashed back down the stairs. 'It's still there—that's good, isn't it?'

'I think it is,' he said slowly. 'I think it means she isn't far away. Nanette?'

'Oh God, of course! Nanette!'

I jumped the last few steps and lunged again for the phone. Roger was in, Nanette was at her mother's, and no, he hadn't seen Claudia.

'Who else?' demanded Lance. 'Your mother?'

'Yes—brilliant, my mother! But she'd need money to—'

'Ring her anyway.'

I did. She was out. Her answering machine was on. Lance paced up and down the hall, biting his lip, eyes narrowed. I watched helplessly.

'What would she do,' he muttered, 'on a normal Sunday morning?'

'Read, maybe play on the playstation.'

'OK, but if she was outside?' he urged. 'If she was out in the garden?'

'Well, her bike, I suppose, or—Her bike!'

I ran out of the front door and round the side passage to the shed. Lance followed.

'It's gone!' I yelled. 'Her bike's gone!'

'Right,' he breathed. 'Now we're getting somewhere.'

'Oh, Lance, she's just gone for a bike ride! That's all, isn't it?'

'Hopefully. Where does she ride it?'

'In the park,' I said quickly. 'And also along the towpath by the stream; it runs along the back of The Crescent.'

'Right. I'll take the park, you take the towpath. If we meet back here with no joy in ten minutes, we'll call the police.'

Off I raced, back down the garden, but this time, with a lighter heart. She wasn't in London, she was just pootling about on her bike, waiting for Mummy to come home. I crossed the bridge and turned right along the towpath. As I hurried round a bend, I nearly mowed down an old lady walking her pug.

'Oh—sorry!' I steadied myself, holding her shoulders. 'Have you seen a girl?' I panted. 'Of about ten, riding her bike?'

'I haven't, dear,' she said, startled. She adjusted her cardigan where I'd held her. As I broke into a run again, she called me back.

'There is a bike, though. Further along, in the hedgerow.'

I stared at her. Couldn't speak. A bike. In the hedgerow. Full of fear and foreboding I raced round the corner—and there it was. Claudia's bike. Pink, too young for her she'd insisted recently, with a basket on the front, and in her basket, an apple and a book. No Claudia.

My eyes shot about. '*Claudia!*' I screamed. Silence.

'*Claudia!!!*' I felt bile rush to my mouth. My eyes darted back to the bike, abandoned on its side, front wheel at an acute angle, like a silent distress signal. Oh God, she must have been dragged off the path, into the bushes! Through the bracken I crashed, sobbing now.

'*Claudia! Claudi-aa!*'

Low branches tore at my clothes and face as I plunged off in all directions, going round in circles, always coming back to the same spot, glancing helplessly at the bike before tearing off again.

'Oh God, oh God,' I sobbed, stumbling further down along the towpath. A couple of amorous teenagers, arms and tongues entwined as they walked blindly towards me, eyes shut, were suddenly confronted by a madwoman, face scratched and bleeding, sobbing wildly.

'Have you seen a girl!' I cried.

'What?' The spotty youth unstuck his lips and blinked.

'A girl! Look, there's her bike back there—about ten, in red shorts probably—have you seen her?'

'Nah, sorry, luv.' He made to move on.

'Oh yeah, hang abou'.' His girlfriend held his arm. 'Yeah, we did, remember? Wiv that man, Gary? You know, the one back there?'

'What man!' I roared, voice hoarse but nearly fainting with fear.

'She was wearin' red shorts an' all, and he 'ad her by the arm.'

Oh God. Oh dear Jesus and God. 'Which way?' I choked.

'Over there.' She pointed behind me. I swung about. She was pointing back to The Crescent, to the row of back gardens.

'She was cryin' an' that, too, weren't she, Gary?'

'Dunno.'

'Yeah, she was, an' I watched them go, 'cos I fought it was funny, wasn't sure if he was her dad, an' he took 'er up that parf, into that house there.'

'Which one?' I breathed.

'There, that one wiv the green back door, over there.'

She jabbed her finger. I followed it. Stared—then froze with horror. Oh God. Oh dear God Almighty. Sebastian. It was Sebastian's house.

I flew across the footbridge and down the path that led along the back of The Crescent gardens. Sebastian's house was in the middle, tall, and red brick at the back, in contrast to its white stucco façade, and with a strip of immaculate lawn stretching down to wrought-iron railings and a gate. With a pounding heart I ran along the path to the gate. He'd forced her through here, sobbing, the bastard. The gate was still open. I ran through, then, realising the French windows at the back of the house were also wide open, veered left and shot behind a shed. I flattened myself against it for a moment, panting hard. I had to get her out of there, but I had to be careful. If I charged in, he might put a kitchen knife to her throat, hold her hostage. Oh yes, I thought, my mind racing, it was all becoming very clear now. He was obviously taking some sort of warped revenge for having my sexual exploits thrust in his face by Lance.

Peering cautiously round the shed, I made an angled dash across the lawn, leaping an immaculate flowerbed and making it to the relative safety of the wall. I flattened myself against it, heart going like a bongo drum. Slowly, I inched my way along to the door frame and peeped round. I could hear noises, voices, and for a moment I thought there were a few people in the room, until I realised the television was on. I couldn't see anyone, except—yes. Suddenly I realised that that was Claudia, sitting hunched in an armchair at the back of the room. Except I hardly recognised her. Her hair looked lank and too dark, and she was wearing a dressing gown. A man's dressing gown. *His* dressing gown. A little yelp escaped my lips and I could bear it no longer. A garden rake was propped up against the wall beside me. I seized it and charged in.

'*Claudia, get behind me!*' I shrieked, spreading out my arms and brandishing the rake. Claudia looked up from the television in astonishment.

'Mum!'

'*Get behind me!*' I yelled.

'But—'

'*Just do it!*'

Claudia, never having seen me in totally-lost-it mode, waving a rake, leapt up and scuttled behind me.

'Where is he?' I barked.

'Who?'

'Sebastian!'

'Oh well, around, I think.'

Around. I swung about, pushing her behind me, still shielding her with my body.

'Now, back,' I hissed. 'Out of the French windows!'

Catching the madness and urgency in my voice, Claudia obeyed.

'Did he touch you, my love?' I whispered brokenly.

'What d'you mean?'

'Well, did he—' I choked back a strangled sob—'hurt you in any way?'

'Of course not!'

'But he took your clothes?'

'Yes, but—'

'The bastard!' I spat. 'The dirty, filthy bastard. How *dare* he—*aha!*'

A figure materialised from the shadows. A figure coming through the far door, bearing a tray of tea and biscuits. Sebastian, in a white shirt and faded brown cords, blinked in surprise as he confronted a scratched and bleeding woman in his sitting room, hands gripping either end of a horizontal garden rake, kung fu style.

Sebastian stopped, astonished. 'Good Lord, what on earth—'

'Don't you Good Lord me,' I hissed, 'you dirty, scummy degenerate—*Keep backing away, Claudia!*'

Claudia, who for a moment had popped her startled head out, hastily obeyed and began making her way out to the garden.

'Now run!' I yelled over my shoulder. 'Run home and I'll cover you. I'll follow later. Now! *Go!*'

Claudia didn't wait to argue with a mother in this mood. She took to her heels and scampered off, scared witless, no doubt.

'Mrs McFarllen, are you taking drugs?' enquired Sebastian calmly.

'How *dare* you?' I breathed as I slowly followed my daughter, backing out, but keeping my rake rigid at chest level. 'How dare you abduct a poor defenceless child? You're not just a harmless half-wit like everyone says, you're a bloody pervert! The lowest of the low!'

'Good God,' he muttered. 'You need help.'

'Help!' I barked derisively. 'Ha! You're the one who needs help, you little creep. You were seen,' I hissed, curling my lip, 'by a decent, upright young couple out walking, seen dragging an innocent child, screaming, *sobbing*, on her knees practically, into *your house*!'

'This is outrageous!' His face clouded and he came towards me.

'*No closer!*' I bellowed, swinging the rake so it pointed straight at him. I brandished it at his chest. 'No closer or I'll—'

Thwack! As he took another step I jerked the rake up, slamming it under the tray and sending it flying. It performed a neat somersault, and steaming Lapsang Souchong and garibaldis leapt high in the air—then splashed straight down in his face.

'Christ!' he clutched his eyes.

Temporarily blinded, he staggered about a bit, and I took advantage. I flung down the rake, shot one last look at the stumbling, gasping figure with his face in his hands—then fled. Across the immaculate lawn I tore, leaping the flowerbed, through the gate, down the towpath, through our own wrought-iron gate, then back down the garden, through the French windows—and home. I slammed the glass doors shut behind me, shooting bolts across with quivering hands. I spun round.

'Claudia!'

'In here,' came a flat, dead-pan voice.

I flew off in its general direction and found her, sitting with Lance, at the kitchen table. She was still huddled in the dressing gown and drinking orange juice. I dropped to my knees beside her.

'Darling, oh, my poor darling,' I sobbed, hugging her knees. 'Are you all right? Shall I call the police?'

'Don't be ridiculous, Mum. You've made a complete and utter pill of yourself,' snapped Claudia, shaking me off. 'I'm so embarrassed. He didn't hurt me at all, he just hauled me out of the river.'

My mouth fell open. I stood up. 'Wh-what?'

'My bike hit a rut and I went in headfirst, bumped my head on a rock. He was at an upstairs window and saw what happened. He came out to help me. I was absolutely soaking, so he lent me a dressing gown and put my clothes in the tumble drier.'

'But—they said you were crying,' I gasped. 'And being held by him!'

'I *was* crying. I cut my knee, look.' She lifted the dressing gown to show a newly bandaged knee with blood still seeping through. 'It hurt like anything, and he wasn't holding me, he was just helping me 'cos I could hardly walk. He was so kind and put a bandage on, and made tea and everything, and then you appear like bloody Boadicea, looking totally insane, screaming and hollering, with blood all over your face and a *rake*, for God's sake. You looked like such a spasmo.'

'Oh God.' I sank down onto a chair. 'You mean he didn't—'

'No, of course he didn't, and I'm really disgusted by your mind sometimes, Mum. You thought he was showing me his privates, didn't you?'

'Well I—'

'I'm going up to change.' She got up and stalked out.

I sat, staring after her for a minute. Then slowly, I pushed my hands into my hair, clutched my head and groaned.

'Oh Lord!' I whispered. 'Oh Lord, Lance, I went berserk. She's right. I was like a madwoman in there! Called him names, all kinds of terrible, *ghastly* names and—oh God—' my eyes bulged with horror as I remembered—'I knocked hot tea all over him! Scalded him, gave him third-degree burns! He'll probably have me up for assault!'

'Probably,' Lance agreed calmly, pouring me a cup from the pot he'd just made. 'Anyway, the main thing is, Claudia's back.'

'Yes,' I breathed, leaning back in my chair with relief. 'Yes, you're right, thank God. Helped out of a river by Sebastian.' I raked my hands desperately through my hair again, punishing it. 'Oh, Lance, I must go straight back—yet again—and apologise, sort things out. Poor, simple, decent, innocent man! I've probably scarred him for life!'

'What, with the tea or the insults?—' He broke off suddenly, glancing out of the window. 'Oh-oh. I think you'll have to go and make your neighbourly peace some other time. Right now you have a visitor.'

I glanced out of the window.

'Johnny!' I breathed. 'Oh God, I'd forgotten about him. I should have rung him on his mobile, told him she was OK!'

'I'll make myself scarce,' muttered Lance, making for the back door.

Johnny's face when he got out of the car was very pale, his mouth set in a taut line. I jumped up and raced out to meet him. I knew that every moment of thinking she was missing was torture, and that if I ran, I could spare him one or two.

'It's OK!' I cried as I flung open the front door. 'She's back! She went for a bike ride and fell in the stream, but she's fine!'

He stopped still at the gate. His face cleared. 'Thank God. Oh, Livvy, thank God.' He broke into a run, and as I raced out to meet him, he swept me up in his arms and caught me to him. As he held me tight, my face pressed into his chest, my arms round his warm shoulders, I shut my eyes. It was like a drop of water to a parched soul.

'Where is she?' he said, releasing me, holding me at arm's length.

'Upstairs, changing. I'll tell her you're here. Oh, Johnny, I'm sorry, I should have rung you on your mobile. You've had to come all this way again on a wild-goose chase!'

'Wild-goose chase?' He stared. 'Don't be silly, I'd have wanted to be here anyway. She's my daughter, Livvy.'

'Yes. Yes, of course,' I nodded meekly, humbled. 'Sorry.'

We turned to go in, just as, clattering downstairs, in leggings and a pink T-shirt, came Claudia. She yelped with delight when she saw Johnny. He ran, and she leapt the last few steps into his arms.

'Hello, pixie,' he muttered into her hair. 'I hear you've been having huge adventures. Lone bike rides and falling into rapids, very Enid Blyton. You'll have to let me come with you next time.'

'Daddy,' she pulled back from him, 'I'm—I'm sorry about this morning, about not seeing you.' Her voice cracked and it broke my heart. I don't imagine it did much for Johnny's, either.

'Don't be silly, Claudes. That wasn't your fault, it was mine. Why should you have to choose between me and your friends? You should be able to have both—see me when you get up in the morning and then go out to play with your friends. I've done this to you, I made you choose.'

I found myself nodding boisterously behind him and had to arrest my neck muscles. Steady. All the same, it sounded encouraging, didn't it? Sounded like he'd seen a degree of light. Perhaps this misadventure of Claudia's was going to have a little morality tale at the end of it? Be a bit of a catalyst for a happy ending? Encouraged, I followed them inside, but as they made to go into the kitchen, Johnny turned.

'Livvy, d'you mind if I have a quick word with Claudes? I just want to get one or two things straight in her mind.'

I blinked. 'Sure! No, gosh, good heavens, you go ahead. You, um, go in there and I'll—well, I'll wait in the garden.'

I went to the end of the garden and buried myself in the herbaceous border, savaging a piece of ground elder that had seeded itself around the delphiniums. Some time later, I heard the back door open.

'I'll be off then, Livvy,' said Johnny from a short distance.

I gave a little jump, just to show I'd been totally absorbed. As I turned, though, his blue eyes held me. Squeezed my heart. He shaded them with his hand against the sun. I wiped my perspiring face with my hand and realised it was covered in mud. Yes, yet again, I thought bitterly, I'd dressed up for Johnny. Scratched and battered by brambles, and now covered in earth, I'd made myself utterly desirable. I thought longingly of the cream linen dress and my kitten-heeled shoes upstairs.

'Bye, then,' I said with a cheery grin. 'See you in a couple of weeks.' I went to go back to my border.

'Look,' he took a step closer, 'I'm just going to pop in and thank that chap down the road. It seems he did Claudia a really good turn.'

I swung back. 'Oh! Hang on, no, don't do that, Johnny!'

'Why not?'

Claudia strolled up beside him. I shot her a glance. Had she . . .? No, bless her, she clearly hadn't told him about the harridan episode.

'Oh, well,' I faltered, 'because—'

'Because Mum wants to. Don't you, Mum?' She eyed me beadily. 'We thought we'd go together.'

'Yes, that's it,' I breathed. 'Take some flowers, do it properly, you know.'

He shrugged. 'OK. But be sure you do, won't you?'

'Of course I will,' I bristled. God, anyone would think I was a child.

'Bye, then.'

'Bye.'

I watched him go, picked up my trug and walked slowly back to the house. Whatever happened, I thought, I mustn't ask Claudia what Johnny had said in the kitchen. That would be an intrusion into her privacy and into her relationship with her father. I put the trug by the back door, breezed in, humming a little tune, and put the kettle on. She was reading an old *Beano* annual at the kitchen table.

My hand went for the tea caddy. I paused. Turned. 'Um, Claudes?'

'Hmm?'

'What did Daddy say?'

She glanced up from her book. 'What?'

'You know, your, um—little chat.'

'Oh. Oh, just stuff about wishing it didn't have to be this way. Hoping I'd understand when I was a bit older. The usual bollocks.'

'Claudia!'

'Sorry. Just a bit fed up with it all at the moment.'

'Claudia, I'm sorry. I've said I'm sorry. I was worried about you, that's all.'

She got up. 'I'm going upstairs. I've got some homework to do.'

Later that evening I rang Molly and confided the details of my hideous day, graphically depicting the ghastly Sebastian episode.

'I was like a madwoman in there, Molly. I reckon if I'd had a knife in my hand instead of a rake, I'd have stabbed him with it.'

'Well, he was lucky, then. Just the tea and biscuits. And I'm not so sure you weren't right,' she said slowly. 'I mean, why did he take her back to his house? Why not your house? It's just as close. And I don't like the idea of her handing over her clothes to him, either. I really don't know what you're worrying about, Livvy. In fact, I wouldn't even bother to apologise in person. Just pop a little note round saying you're sorry if you got the wrong end of the stick. But make sure you keep that "if" in there. Because if ever I heard an iffy story, it's this one.'

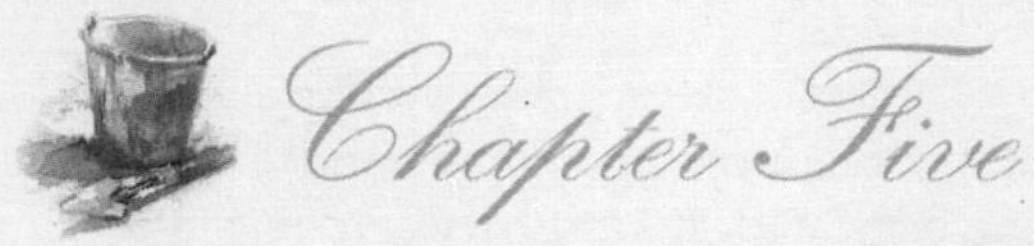

Chapter Five

THE BUILDERS WERE BACK the following morning, and with them an uncharacteristic air of doom and gloom.

'What's up?' I whispered to Mac as I staggered in with a steaming tray of tea, the first of many morning cuppas.

Mac glanced round to make sure we were alone. 'Alf's wife's left him,' he confided soberly. 'He got back on Friday night to find a note on the kitchen table. Said she'd had enough of him, and don't try to find her 'cos she ain't never coming back.'

'No!' I set the tray down, aghast. 'Vi? But they're on the phone night and day. I thought they adored each other!'

'Oh, he adored her orright—couldn't please her enough—but she bossed him around somefing chronic and now she's up and left him, ungrateful bitch. Gone to Spain.'

'Spain! Gosh, poor Alf.'

Spiro sidled up beside us with a piece of skirting board on his shoulder. 'He say his life is over. He say—oooooh!' Emotion overwhelmed him, the woolly hat came off and he dabbed at his streaming eyes.

'Get a grip, boy,' growled Mac. 'We've got a lot to do today. So get mixing, Zorba, my son.'

Spiro hastily replaced his hat and shuffled over to the mixer.

Lance appeared from the caravan and fell in seamlessly, greeting me with a low 'Have you heard?'—to which I nodded back my sympathies, and then the three of them scurried around under Mac's direction, hammering, mitring and plastering like whirling dervishes. Presumably Mac thought that if he got them working flat out it would take their minds off their troubles.

Work had been occupying my mind lately, too, now that I couldn't even include 'getting my husband's supper and ironing his shirts' in the domestic equation, as Claudia had so succinctly pointed out to me on the way to school this morning.

'Even Mrs Chandler's got a job now,' she'd informed me sternly, 'and Mr Chandler said it was more than his expensive strumpet had.'

I cast my mind back, at the same time trying not to go up a lorry's backside. 'Mrs Chandler? Chloe's mother?'

'That's it.'

'Whose husband left her?'

'Yep.'

'But . . . wasn't she the one that went off with some youth from B&Q, whereupon Mr Chandler came back with his tail between his legs?'

'Ah yes, he did,' she twisted excitedly in her seat to face me, 'but it's all changed now. Mr Chandler *did* come back, but then his strumpet—'

'Must you say that word, Claudia?'

'Yes, I like it—his strrrr-umpet' she trilled, 'mounted a huge campaign, cycled past his factory gates with her shirt undone and no pants on, that sort of thing—and he went back to her.'

'Right,' I'd said weakly, negotiating a roundabout. 'So, then Mrs Chandler got herself a job, in—don't tell me—'

'B&Q.'

'Naturally.'

I pulled up in the car park. 'Well, three cheers for Mrs Chandler.'

She got out. 'Oh—it's OK, Mum,' she said quickly as I went to get out my side, 'I'm a bit late so I'll just run in. By the way, that letter's for Sebastian. Can you put it through his door? Plus the one from you, too,' she added meaningfully.

I glanced down at the note she'd left on her seat, turned it over and wondered what she'd written. '*Sorry about my barking mother? She really should get out more, sell a few rotary saws and cycle round St Albans with no pants on?*' I sighed, put it down. No, she was right. I must pop it through his door, and add sincere apologies of my own, too. I riffled around in the glove compartment for a bit of paper. I'd write a note in the car right now, pop it in, and then that would be the end of it.

I finally found an old shopping list on the floor under my seat, scribbled out *Domestos, butter, Immac*, and wrote on the back:

Dear Sebastian. I'm so sorry. What must you think of me? I got totally the wrong end of the stick yesterday, made a complete fool of myself and couldn't be more ashamed.

Best wishes, Olivia McFarllen

There. Short, gushing, and to the point. Perfect.

On the way home, I stopped outside his house and ran up the steps. I slipped Claudia's note through the letterbox, and was about to add mine to the doormat when I suddenly realised I was being watched. I glanced down and saw the mother, her toothy, ferrety face pale and watchful, staring up at me from the basement window below. I hesitated. My note wasn't actually in an envelope, and she'd most certainly read it, and then what on earth would she think? No, no, I thought hastily, I'd go home, write it out again, do it properly and then drop it by later.

I tucked it in my pocket and hurried back down the steps, feeling those sharp grey eyes in my back all the way to my car. I shot off down the road, scurried up the drive to my house, ran in, and shut the door fast behind me. Home.

The day limped on, and by midafternoon, the temperature had hit the nineties. Claudia was dropped home by a friend, and lay in a cool bath for half an hour before taking to her bedroom. I, meanwhile, wilted restlessly on the terrace, listening to the sounds of banging and crashing as the boys ploughed on, unceasingly, through the heat, with no radio blaring, no chatting, no whistling, no breaks for tea—on they toiled. I was astonished, but deeply impressed. Later, when they'd finally drooped back to the caravan to collapse, before heading off to the pub, I crept in to inspect their handiwork. I was even more impressed. Golly, I thought as I gazed around in wonder, all this in one day.

The flapping blue tarpaulin had gone, and in its place, the ceiling and walls were pink and plastered. The soggy concrete floor had also been replaced, by a gleaming, reclaimed wooden one. At the far end of the room, the huge, concrete plinth was *in situ*, ready for the Aga to be enthroned, and around the perimeter of the room, some of Lance's carefully sculpted oak cupboards were already in place. I scurried across the shiny floor and pulled out a drawer. Smooth as silk. I spun round, a delighted smile slowly spreading across my face. My goodness, yes, it was really taking shape, and it was perfect! Just perfect.

Imogen rang the following morning.

'Right, I take it you're still on for tonight?' she said briskly.

'What's happening tonight?'

'The concert, remember? In the Abbey?'

'Oh. Right.' Well, yes. OK, somewhere, dimly, at the back of my mind, it rang a bell.

'Rollo's coming especially for you!'

'Rollo?' I blinked.

'Honestly, you won't be disappointed, Liv. He's totally gorgeous, and so excited about meeting you.'

'If he's so gorgeous,' I said, 'why aren't you going out with him?'

'Oh, I know him far too well,' she said airily. 'Shared a house with him at Oxford. He's like a brother to me really. Come on, Livvy. You've got to come. Mum and Dad are dying to see you too.'

'Oh, all right,' I caved in pathetically.

'Great. Parents' place first, for drinks at seven o'clock.'

Imogen's parents lived some distance from the city. Twenty minutes to the west, in fact, in a glorious Elizabethan farmhouse complete with beams and gables and tiny leaded lights glinting in the evening sun.

As I walked up the path to the front door, Ursula Mitchell, a tall, elegant, faded blonde with a rather hawklike nose, and wearing a bright red shot-silk ensemble, was outside greeting her guests and directing them round to the terrace, where I realised drinks were being served.

'Olivia!' She took both my hands in hers. 'I'm *so* glad you came!'

'I'm glad too,' I smiled up at her, and I was.

'Come and meet everyone,' she insisted, linking my arm in hers. 'I'm bored with standing sentry at the door so I'm going to show you off. You look simply marvellous, my dear, and I must say, your Rollo seems quite a dish too.' She winked. 'So isn't that perfect?'

As she beamed conspiratorially at me I nervously smoothed down the cream linen dress which had finally got an outing. My Rollo, eh?

'And Imo?' I asked, as I followed her through a wrought-iron gate. 'Does she have a dish of the day?'

'Oh, my dear, haven't you heard?' She stopped, turned, and for extra emphasis, touched my arm confidentially with cold fingertips. 'The conductor, Hugo Simmonds! He's been here for dinner a couple of times. He's on the podium tonight and he's absolutely mad about her!'

'I think quite a lot of men have that problem,' I remarked.

'Well, quite, but does she give them a chance? No! Hugo *is* rather special. Have a word if you can, would you? Tell her how scrummy he is?'

I laughed. 'I'll try,' I promised. 'Is he here?' I looked around.

'No, no. He's limbering up with his baton at the Abbey. You'll see him later. Ah, now here we are—Imo! Imogen, darling!'

She called to her daughter, who was talking to a tall, slim man on the other side of the terrace. Imo turned. Her pale, golden hair was piled up on her head with tendrils escaping and curling at the base of her neck, Grecian style. She wore a simple, black shift dress, pearls, was lightly tanned, and looked amazing.

'Livvy!' She came over, simultaneously catching the tall man's sleeve and dragging him with her. 'God, *fin*ally! You look terrific.'

'Thanks,' I grinned, 'so do you.'

'Oh, Livvy, this is Rollo. Rollo, Olivia McFarllen, who together with Molly Piper, who is predictably late, is my dearest friend.'

I shook hands with him. 'Molly's coming?' I said delightedly. 'I didn't think this would be her sort of thing?'

'Of course it isn't, I bullied her into it. Told her a bit of culture would do her good instead of gormlessly watching *Friends* and *Frasier*. Anyway, I've got to go off and relieve Mum at the door, so I'm going to stop wittering on, dear hearts, and leave you both in peace. Toodle-oo!'

I gazed after her. Blimey, don't make it too obvious, will you, Imo?

'Imogen's tact is legendary, of course,' said Rollo, smiling down. 'She once had the hots for a friend of mine in the diplomatic service, but I told her she'd make a disastrous diplomat's wife. You can't just plonk John Prescott next to the King of Tonga, tell them they've got a weight problem in common and then swan off hoping for the best.'

I laughed. But first, I had to wipe my face. Because good-looking though Rollo undoubtedly was—with his toffee-coloured hair, which rather cunningly matched his toffee-coloured eyes—he had a problem. He spat. I took a discreet step backwards, lobbed up a social 'And what do you do?' and studied him closer.

Yes, it was the front teeth, I decided as he prattled away happily about the Foreign Office. Too big, and too far apart. Way too far, as Claudia would say. I reached for a canapé and made a mental note that Claudia must have as much orthodontic treatment as she needed, whatever the cost. Bugger. He was gazing expectantly at me.

'Um, sorry?'

'I said, what do you do?'

'Oh! Oh nothing much. I used to garden, you know, pre-children. Professionally, I mean. I used to do garden design.'

'Terrific!' he brayed. 'Did you ever do Chelsea?'

'Er, not as such.' I reached nervously for more food and munched away. Suddenly my hand shot up.

'Molly!' Oh, the relief. 'You made it!'

'Finally,' she hissed, coming over and kissing me rather damply as she reached into her shirt to hitch up her bra strap. 'Bloody baby sitter was late and then Henry sodding well threw up over me as I kissed him good night—do I stink?' she asked anxiously.

'No,' I promised, then realised she did. 'Here,' I handed her my bag. 'There's some Chanel No. 19 at the bottom.'

'Thanks,' she muttered, grabbing the bag, and was about to scuttle off when she spotted Rollo, hovering territorially.

'Oh! Sorry, Molly Piper, Rollo . . .?'

'Somerset,' he offered toothily, complete with ocean spray. Molly flinched but, quick as a flash, I'd turned to kiss Hugh, her husband. All yours, Moll.

Hugh, small, clever, and very theatrical, was gazing about him at the crowd, blinking with mock wonder. 'People,' he muttered dreamily. 'People talking . . . socialising . . . yes, yes, I remember now, it's all coming back.' He sniffed his drink. 'Alcohol too.'

I giggled. 'You're not about to tell me you don't have a life any more, are you, Hugh?'

'Oh, but I don't, my love, I don't,' he said, putting an arm round my shoulders and leading me away. 'Just a pukey little toddler and a soon-to-be-podding wife, and wait till that one pops out: you won't see us for years.' He knocked back his glass in one go and smiled abruptly. 'You, on the other hand, dear heart,' he said, 'seem to have it all worked out. You manage to make this whole childcare business look graceful and effortless, and all on your tod now, too, I gather. Tell me,' he added gently, 'is it a midlife crisis, or has he just gone blind? You've never looked lovelier.'

I smiled. 'He's a bit young for a crisis, isn't he, Hugh?'

'Lord, no, everyone's doing things so much earlier these days. Sexually speaking one's finished at forty. Johnny's obviously doing a spot of panic-buying and making a total dick of himself in the process.' He grinned. 'His loss, not yours. Oh, excuse me, young man.' He grabbed a passing waiter. 'That was so delicious, I believe I'll have another.' He put his empty champagne glass on the tray, plucked another full one, and emptied it in one, smacking his lips. 'Yum yum.'

I giggled. 'Hugh, I'm not convinced this is quite the place to get plastered.' I glanced around at Ursula's cronies.

'Oh, but it is, my love, it is. Not only have we got all these stiffs to talk to here, but we've got the wretched concert to get through yet. If I drink myself to a standstill, with any luck I'll sleep through it.'

I giggled as Molly came charging up. 'He spits!' she said, horrified.

'Doesn't he just?' I agreed.

'Bloody hell, don't I get enough bodily fluids at home without being subjected to more at a party?' She wiped her cheek. 'Outrageous! Is he supposed to be yours? What is Imo thinking of? Send him back!'

'Shh, he'll hear. Oh Christ—look out, we're being hounded.'

We smiled sociably as Ursula Mitchell bore down on us. She swooped, encircled our shoulders with bony arms, then confided in hushed tones, 'The seats *are* numbered, my dears, but it's better to get there early. If you youngsters wouldn't mind making a move to the cars then I think the others will take the hint and follow.'

Dutifully I followed Molly and Hugh to the loo, to the coats, to the door, to the cars, and thence, to the Abbey.

The Abbey looked fabulous, lit up and glowing in the clear night sky, and the chattering, excited crowd that jostled politely to get through the huge oak doors couldn't have been more appreciative.

In the area just within the doors, people milled about talking loudly, waving programmes above their heads to friends they'd spotted in the crowd. As I nudged through, I stopped suddenly. The back of a woman's head, a few feet away to my right, looked terribly familiar somehow, but I just couldn't place her. I peeled off from Rollo for a minute, took a quick peek around the side—and gasped. It was my mother. Except that I hardly recognised her. Her face was lightly made up and shining as she smiled and chatted. She was wearing a peach linen coat dress with peach lipstick to match, and her hair, which had been lightened and subtly streaked, was swept off her face in waves, curling softly at the edges. At her throat was a turquoise necklace which matched the bracelet on her wrist, and, I noticed, the sparkling gems in her ears.

'Mum!' My mouth, literally, hung open.

She turned. Saw me. 'Oh, hello, darling. I wondered if you'd be here.' She kissed my cheek. I stared. For a moment I simply couldn't utter.

'M-Mum—what are you doing here!'

'Hmm?' She looked surprised. 'Oh well, I was invited, of course!'

'Really?' I looked around. The women's group? Or the church, perhaps. 'But, Mum, this isn't our church, so—'

'Oh no,' she laughed, 'no, not the church, darling. Howard asked me.'

'Howard?'

It was then that I realised there was someone standing right beside her, right by her arm. I just hadn't connected them. He was mid-fiftyish, tall, with a hint of a paunch, silver-grey hair and a moustache to match, and he was smiling proprietorially down at my mother.

'Howard, this is my daughter, Olivia.'

'Oh!' I gazed, shook his extended hand, but couldn't speak.

'At last,' he grinned. 'I've heard so much about you.'

'Oh!' I said it again, aware that my mouth was still open.

'Howard's a doctor,' offered Mum, helpfully. 'We met when I took my usual stack of old magazines into the hospital.'

He grinned. 'The nurses kept telling me about this glamorous lady who was keeping them, not only in English *Vogues*, but in French and Italian ones too. I'm ashamed to say they plotted our meeting in an orthopaedic waiting room and I was an entirely willing participant!'

I gazed. Don't say 'Oh' again, you moron, just don't. 'S-so you're a doctor then?' I stammered.

'Well, actually, I'm a urologist.'

I racked my brains. 'Ears?'

He laughed. 'Not even close. If I said that renal canals were a speciality, would that help?'

'Oh! Yes, it would!'

We laughed. *Mum* laughed. Mum, who couldn't even mention a front bottom without pinched lips, was laughing at renal canals? I gaped at her. And the *peach* number! I just couldn't help it.

'Mum—the clothes!' I blurted out. 'I mean—I've never seen you in anything remotely like that, ever!'

She laughed. 'I know, isn't it strange? But Howard said he couldn't be doing with all that navy blue. He bullied me out of it, said it reminded him of the sisters on his ward.'

I loved him. Oh God, I loved him already.

'So what d'you think?' Mum glanced at me shyly.

'Gorgeous!' I enthused. 'I love it, Mum. You look fab!'

She laughed, blushed a little too. 'Go on, darling, catch up with your party. I saw Imogen go past ages ago.'

I turned, realising that the rest had gone on, but that Rollo was still hovering, not exactly beside me, but close. I hesitated. No, I couldn't introduce him, not after Howard. It would be such an anticlimax.

'See you later, Mum.' I kissed her warmly and beamed at Howard. 'Goodbye, *so* good to meet you.'

'You too,' he smiled, and I'd swear he winked too.

'Sorry, Rollo,' I muttered, as I fell in beside him, 'got—caught up.'

'That's OK,' he smiled.

We walked on in silence. Maybe I should have explained that that was my mother, only I hadn't recognised her because she'd changed beyond all recognition and I'd been too astonished to introduce him. My God. For years now my mother had been pained, irritable and bitter. Could it be that one man was changing all that? Could it be that one, single, beating heart had caused her to transform herself, to come alive again? What power! And wherein lay the moral for me? Was it that I'd better move fast? Seize the disastrous dental arrangement beside me, or maybe the blond Adonis back in the caravan, pick one of them up and run with it? Make the best of it? God Almighty! I shuddered.

I wandered on, lost in thought.

'Olivia!'

It was Angie, plucking my sleeve.

'Oh—hi!' I peeled off from Rollo once again.

She was looking stunning in a pale, silver-grey suit, and as I went to greet her I realised two of her daughters, plus husbands, were with her as well. I glanced around fearfully.

'Johnny isn't here, is he?' I murmured anxiously to Angie.

'I'm afraid he is, my dear.'

'But they're not with us,' put in Serena quickly.

'They?' My mouth dried.

She nodded, hugged me hard. 'Bastard,' she muttered in my ear. In an instant Imogen was beside me. I held her arm, felt genuinely giddy.

'He's here,' I whispered.

'I know, I've just seen him. Came to find you.'

'Imo, I'm not sure I can do this. I'm going to slip out.'

'Don't be ridiculous,' she hissed. 'Stick that head up high and walk with me. I've seen her, and she looks like a dog's dinner and you, my darling, have never looked better. Come on.'

I took a deep breath and walked down the aisle with her. When we got to about four rows from the front, she bundled me in, sandwiching me between her and Rollo, who'd already taken his seat.

'Where is he?' I gasped, as I sat down.

'Other side of aisle, about two rows ahead of us to the left.'

I shot my eyes across and saw Johnny, in a dark suit, blue shirt, spotty tie, tanned and very handsome, of course, his blond head bent with hers over a programme. She, Nina, had her hair pushed back in a velvet hair-band, very average blue shirt, grey skirt too short for her legs, twenty denier tights. All of this I took in in a nanosecond, then looked away. Their heads. Touching like that. I felt sick, physically sick.

I watched in a daze as the orchestra, high up on a specially constructed platform in the nave, tuned up. Tears threatened. I raised my eyes to the heavens and concentrated hard on the intricate painted panels of the choir ceiling, and gradually I felt the tears subside. I swallowed hard, slowly lowered my head. Happily, Rollo was engrossed in his programme.

'But this is very exciting, Imogen,' he was muttering as he leaned across to her. 'It says that this is the first time this piece of Faulkner's has been performed.'

'Yes, apparently he wrote it some time ago but recently changed it, and has only now allowed it to be performed.'

Despite my turmoil I was dimly fascinated to observe that Imo wiped her wet face without even appearing to notice.

'Gosh, this is such a treat!' said Rollo.

A treat? Really? Particularly for me, of course, to be closeted here with my husband and his floozy, for all the world to see—maybe even my mother, I thought with a sudden pang—and with my consolation prize of Spitty Dicky beside me. I caught Molly's eye further down the row and she grimaced sympathetically in Johnny's direction. I nodded and raised my eyebrows indicating that yes, I too had clocked them.

Suddenly there was a hush, and then a roar, as Hugo Simmonds took the podium to tremendous applause. He greeted his orchestra, then turned to the audience and smiled. He had quite a presence, if you liked narrow, pale faces with high foreheads, swept-back fair hair, and slightly hollow cheeks. His sharp grey eyes darted about the audience, quickly searching the rows until he'd found what he was looking for. His gaze fell on Imo, beside me. Cool as a cat, Imo acknowledged him with a slight inclination of her blonde head and a Grace Kelly smile.

Satisfied, if not satiated, Hugo turned his back on us, and faced his orchestra. His raised arms paused briefly in midair, then came down with a flourish, and the music began. I sank back in my chair and let it wash over me. Modern, explosive occasionally, but at the same time strangely melodic, and I was thankful for its blanketing effect, for being able to hide behind it, but the urge to look to my left, across the aisle, was becoming overpowering, and as the music went on I found I did—continually, compulsively, couldn't help it—until eventually the inevitable happened. She looked too. I caught her eye, looked away, and realised she'd tell Johnny I was here. In that split second, knowing he'd glance across, I dived my head playfully into Rollo's shoulder, gazing up at his face. He glanced down, surprised but pleased, and as I turned back, I was just in time to see Johnny turn away, a slight flush on his cheek. Good, I thought viciously. I hope that hurt.

Rollo, on the other hand, was far from hurt. Hugely encouraged, he nestled in close, an alarming look in his eye. I groaned inwardly. Oh hell, I didn't want him thinking I was sitting here in an agony of erotic anticipation. I shook my head in disbelief and listened on.

On and on. Interminably. No interval, of course, I discovered gloomily from my programme, so held in thrall were we all supposed to be by this sodding symphony. Just the two hours of purgatory then, looking rapt and cultured with an aching heart and an aching bottom, waiting for the agony to end.

Finally, of course, it did, and to my astonishment, the applause was deafening. There was a sudden roar of approval, tremendous clapping, and then the audience got to its feet as one. Dropping my handbag and programme I hastily followed suit, catching Molly's eye as she nudged Hugh awake and he too got up.

Hugo Simmonds, flushed, elated and dripping with sweat, raised his hands and gave us his orchestra. They stood and bowed, as Hugo, with elaborate gestures, singled out the stars: his leader, his flautist, his brass section, his percussion, before finally, turning himself to bow to thunderous applause. He soaked it up for a moment, stood, waved, then turned and disappeared off-stage, only to reappear a moment later and receive the same treatment. But still the applause went on. Louder now, and more insistent, as if something was missing, some need waiting to be gratified. Hugo Simmonds smiled and nodded knowingly. Then he simply gestured to someone near the front of the audience to come up. As people craned their necks to see, murmuring, 'There he is!' I realised it must be Faulkner himself. When he got to the top step and turned to the audience, there was a deafening roar of approval, and for the first time I saw his face. My hand shot to my mouth.

'Bloody hell!'

I gaped in horror, unable to take in what I was seeing. For up there on the podium, smiling shyly but delightedly, bowing, and waving occasionally to acknowledge the tremendous applause, was Sebastian. Sebastian. Sebastian was . . . Faulkner? How on earth could that be? Sebastian . . . Faulkner. God, yes, of course, even I, with my modicum of classical music knowledge, had just about heard of him.

'Christ,' I murmured.

'What's up?' yelled Imo into my ear, above the applause.

'I know him,' I muttered.

'No!' she squeaked, swinging around to face me. 'How come?'

I opened my mouth to speak, but, happily, didn't have time to elucidate, as in a matter of moments, Ursula was upon us, bustling importantly along the row, sending programmes flying, eyes shining.

'My dears, *such* a thrill,' she breathed ecstatically. 'Hugo Simmonds has conveyed to us, by means of a sweet note, that he'd be delighted to have us all join him backstage for a small celebration. Imagine, Imo, we'll meet Faulkner too!'

'Oh, but Olivia already knows him,' said Imo excitedly.

'Er, well,' I gulped, 'sort of . . . ish.'

'No!' Ursula gasped. 'My dear, why didn't you say?' Her eyes shone alarmingly. 'Is he *totally* enchanting?'

'D'you know I'm—not sure, Ursula, because to be honest I don't know him terribly well, and—and actually, what with the baby sitter waiting I really must be getting—'

'Nonsense,' she insisted, seizing my wrist urgently, the possibility of a personal introduction gleaming in her eyes. 'Imogen was telling me how wonderful your builders are, always stepping in to help you out. They won't mind another hour. Come!' She called me to heel, dragging me through the crowds as she made for the back of the Abbey in a frenzy of excitement. 'Come along, my party!' Ursula threw back imperiously over her shoulder as she marched me, lamblike to the slaughter.

'Here we are!' Ursula gave a sharp tap at the refectory door. It was instantly opened and, to my relief, the room was packed with the orchestra, their friends and relatives, and various hangers-on. Happily, Hugo Simmonds was close to the door. He spotted Ursula instantly and, raising his glass above the crush, came squeezing across to greet her.

'Ursula!'

'Hugo! Many congratulations! Imo . . . say hello to Hugo!'

'Heavens,' he said, flicking his hair back nervously, as Imogen obeyed orders and kissed him on the cheek.

'It's l-lovely to see you, Imogen. D-did you enjoy it?' he stammered. I was stunned. Was this the same commanding man of moments ago?

'It was wonderful,' Imo enthused warmly, 'really wonderful, Hugo.'

'Thank you,' he gasped. 'I-I must say, Imogen,' he gulped, 'you look absolutely marvellous.'

'He wants to give her one right now,' muttered Hugh in my ear.

I giggled, but I was simultaneously scanning the room nervously for Sebastian. Ah, there he was, right over the other side, thank God, with his back to me. If I stayed right here by the door, had a quick drink and slipped away in two minutes flat, I'd be fine. I took a glass of champagne from a tray as it passed by, and sipped from it, shielding my face with a programme. I simply couldn't believe who he was. He'd never said, had he? Never mentioned it, and he'd had ample opportunity, surely?

I raised my eyes nervously above the programme, only to see Sebastian Faulkner, pale-faced, stony-eyed, making determined strides in my direction, pushing fixedly through the madding throng, his dark eyes as hard as a couple of flints. And it was at that moment that I remembered I had never sent him a note. *I had never apologised.*

'Help!' I squealed, as I pushed for freedom, but I was three deep from the door now, and it was impossible to shove through the crowd. I felt like a fox being hunted, the hounds right on my tail, but as I glanced back, panic-stricken, I suddenly saw Ursula Mitchell step out right in front of him, blocking his path.

'Mr Faulkner, *might* I say how absolutely marvellous I thought that was!' she gushed. 'Truly magnificent, maestro!'

He gave a small bow. 'Thank you,' he muttered, and made to sidestep her, his eyes still fixed and predatory, but dear old Ursula hadn't finished. She blocked his way—bless her—and tried desperately to catch Sebastian's eyes, which were not on her at all. 'Mr Faulkner, I was saying to—' she gave up and followed his gaze. 'Olivia! I was saying to Olivia, who, of course, you know!'

In one bony swoop of her arm, like a python snatching its prey, she lunged out, plucked my arm, and pulled hard, sweeping me into her inner circle. I felt like a child being hauled before the head. My knees began to knock, and my eyes, when I finally dared to raise them, found his: cold, dark and forbidding. He gave me a look that froze my spine.

'You *do* know each other, don't you, Olivia?' insisted Ursula, in case I'd made it up.

'Yes, we, um, do,' I faltered.

'Unhappily,' he barked sharply.

I wouldn't say you could hear a pin drop, but certainly everyone fell silent.

'Mrs McFarllen,' he continued in a low voice, 'are you so deprived of social engagements that you seek out even those where you are unwelcome?' His voice was soft, but bitter and scathing.

I cleared my throat and plucked up all my courage. 'I owe you a belated apology,' I said, looking up into his stony face. 'I made a very foolish mistake the other day, and accused you,' I made myself meet his cold brown eyes, 'of a dreadful thing.'

'What? What dreadful thing?' urged Ursula, just a little too agog.

'She accused me of being a child molester,' said Sebastian.

A horrified gasp went round the room.

'No!' someone breathed, then, 'Good God!' and, 'Slanderous!'

'Olivia, how could you!' gasped Ursula.

I felt incredibly light-headed, but I managed to meet his eyes.

'How could I?' I said. 'Because I was frightened. Terrified, actually. I don't know if you have children, Mr Faulkner, but let me tell you, the most frightening thing in the world is losing them. I lost my child,' I said, forcing myself to look round the room, to catch anyone's eye who was interested, 'last Sunday. My ten-year-old. She slipped off on her own on her bike, and when I followed the route I imagined she'd taken, through the woods, down by the river, I found something that confirmed my worst fears. Her bike, dragged into the bushes and abandoned. When I asked a passer-by—no, screamed at a passer-by—if she'd seen a little girl in red shorts, she said yes, going into a nearby house, sobbing, and being taken by a tall man. This tall man.'

Even Ursula looked slightly askance at this. She shot a look at Sebastian, who was still staring at me.

'So without stopping to think, I stormed into that house, all guns blazing, to find my little girl, sitting in this same man's house, and wearing nothing at all, but his dressing gown.' I paused. 'Now, Ursula, what would you have thought?' I turned demanding eyes on her.

'Well I—I . . .' she floundered, turning bewildered eyes on Sebastian.

'Exactly. You'd have thought the same as me. But you'd be wrong, as it happens, and that's why I apologise, Mr Faulkner.'

There was a stunned silence.

'S-so what did happen?' stammered Ursula.

'Claudia fell in the river,' I said. 'She hit a rut on her bike and went headfirst into the stream, banged her head on a rock. Mr Faulkner saw from an upstairs window and rushed out to help her. He dried her clothes, gave her a dressing gown, and made her some tea. I have a lot to be thankful for. She had a pretty bad bump and had he not seen her, it could have been a different story. I might even have lost her. As it was,' I turned back to Sebastian, 'I called you every foul and vile name under the sun. In my defence I might say that I had no idea who you were, although I doubt that would have made any difference. To an enraged mother a famous composer is just as culpable as a man in a dirty mac. But I was wrong.' I was aware my voice was beginning to wobble so I speeded it up. 'Very wrong. I'm deeply sorry and ashamed. I'd like to thank you for being so quick-witted and helping Claudia, and—and I deeply regret,' I rushed on, 'any pain I've caused you. I'm sorry.'

With that I turned, and without waiting to hear his, or Ursula's views on the subject, pushed my way out of the room. I went back through the Abbey, and out into the night, whereupon I burst into tears.

Chapter Six

THAT NIGHT I SLEPT FITFULLY. I dreamed I was up on the Abbey stage, a key member of Sebastian's orchestra, performing his masterpiece with a vast, outsized cello clamped between my legs. As I screeched and scraped away hopelessly, making a terrible din and ruining the symphony, the front row of the audience became mutinous.

'Off! Get her off!' they yelled.

I glanced up from my bow, sweat pouring off me, to see Angie, Howard, my mother, my builders, Imogen, Ursula, Johnny and Nina, their faces all contorted with rage, baying for my blood.

'She never could play!' yelled Johnny, on his feet now. 'She's a fraud!'

Finally Sebastian stalked on from the wings, enraged.

'I can't play!' I wept. 'I never said I could, I—'

'Mummy, Mummy!' I was being bounced up and down now, my head nearly coming off my shoulders as it rocked back and forth.

'Aaggh! Don't! I'll learn, I swear to God I'll learn, I'll—Claudes!'

I'd opened my eyes to see Claudia, astride me, dressed in her stripy summer school uniform, bouncing me up and down on the bed.

'Learn what?' She frowned down at me.

'Oh my God,' I breathed, blinking sweaty eyelids and pushing back my hair. 'What a terrible nightmare. What time is it?'

'Twenty to eight, and I've got my ballet exam today.' She yanked the duvet off me.

I sat up and looked at the clock.

'Your ballet exam! You're supposed to be there in twenty minutes!'

'I know.'

'All tutu'd up with a hairnet on!'

'I know.'

I stared. 'And you deliberately didn't wake me earlier because you don't want to do it! Claudia, you are a devious, mendacious little—'

'Don't say the F word.'

'I wasn't about to say the F word!'

'It shows lack of character. And, anyway, what's the problem? I'm waking you now, aren't I?'

'Claudia, I'll give you lack of character!' I seethed, leaping out of bed and grabbing my jeans. I plunged my legs into them. 'Just get your tail downstairs *now*, grab your tutu and get in that car and I'll join you there in two minutes! *And don't forget the bloody hairnet!*'

Three minutes later, unwashed, dying for a cup of tea, mouth like the bottom of a budgie's cage and armpits decidedly pongy, I was nevertheless reversing at high speed out of the drive.

'You'll make it,' I snarled as she sulked beside me.

'Yeah, I know,' she sighed, resignedly.

Ten minutes later I stopped the car in the car park.

'Bye, my love, have a good day. I'm shooting off now.'

'Because you haven't got your make-up on and you don't want to bump into Nina.' She grinned.

I pulled her straw boater down over her eyes. 'You're too sharp for your own good, young lady.'

'I know, just call me Razors.'

I smiled. 'Well, here's something I'll bet you don't know, Razors.'

'What?'

'Granny's got a boyfriend.'

'No!' Her eyes widened with disbelief. '*Granny!* Brilliant! Since when?'

'Since I don't know, but I met him last night, at the concert.'

'Cool! A boyfriend! What's he like?'

'Well, he's about her age,' I said. 'Tubbyish and grey, but kind-looking. Stares at her a lot, you know, into her eyes.'

'Oh yum!' She was excited by that. 'Can I meet him?'

'Of course. I thought we'd ask them for tea on Sunday, and listen,' I added quickly, 'whatever we think, Claudes, it's lovely for her, don't you think?' I asked anxiously.

'Oh *yes*. And I think if Dad doesn't come back it would be lovely for you too, Mum, even someone tubby and grey. Think how you've worried about Granny all these years, wished she hadn't been so lonely. Well, that's going to be *me* worrying, if you're not careful!'

I ground my teeth. 'Claudia, shall we discuss this when you're twenty-five and have been worrying for fifteen years, and not, perchance, when you're ten and have been worrying for all of two months? Anyway, you're a child, you don't need to worry about me!'

'Children feel things very keenly,' she informed me soberly, getting out of the car. 'Don't keep me talking, Mum, I've got a ballet exam to get to.'

'Oh Christ, your exam!' I yelped, clutching my head in horror. 'I'd forgotten again—go—*go!*' I pushed her. 'Why aren't you *running*?'

'I'm going, I'm going,' she said, as she turned and trudged wearily across the car park. I watched her go, aghast. Her exam! That's why we'd been rushing! I shook my head hopelessly. There was no doubt about it, I was really, really losing it.

When I got back home, I made some tea and took it into the new kitchen where the boys were beavering away.

'I'd say we'll be out of your hair in a couple of weeks, luv,' said Mac.

'Really?' I was startled. 'What, finished?'

'Yep, now that the Aga's in and the cupboards are nearly there, we've only got the new bathroom suite to plumb in upstairs.'

'Yes, you're right, that'll be it then,' I said, cranking up a smile. I walked across and stroked the top of the shiny, navy-blue Aga which had finally gone in yesterday. Its concrete plinth built, it had been ceremoniously set, then plumbed in upon it, and was now heating up nicely.

'You'll be glad to see the back of us,' said Mac.

'Yes!' I laughed, but it had a hollow ring to it. 'I expect everyone's glad to see the back of you, aren't they?'

'Too right they are!'

'Still,' I said softly, 'it'll be quiet without you.'

I caught Mac's eye. He looked away quickly. Well, of course he would. An embarrassingly sad housewife who was admitting to a flicker of regret at seeing her builders go? Crikey. Most people hung out the flags! I wandered through to the front hall, biting my lower lip. And not just regret, I realised in horror, also—yes, I felt a wee bit panicky, too. Alone then, in this house—apart from Claudes—for the first time since . . . well, you know. And you see, because of the boys, I hadn't actually been alone, yet. I stopped and picked up the mail from the mat, marvelling at myself. Good grief, I *was* sad, wasn't I? Genuinely pathetic.

I turned briskly to the letters I'd picked up, and opened a bill from Barclaycard—before dropping it hurriedly on the mat again. Heavens!

Really? As much as that? I peered down, kicking it around so I could see the print. Oh, OK. Wretched linen dress and kitten-heeled shoes. I hated them already. I leaned back against the front door and flicked through the rest of the post . . . Hello, what's this? I stopped flicking and turned over a rather smart cream envelope, addressed to Mrs Olivia McFarllen, and penned with something of a flourish. No address or stamp, so hand delivered. I ripped it open.

Dear Olivia,
That was a brave thing you did last night. Come for drinks tonight at seven, if you can.
Yours, Sebastian.

I stared. Read it again. Brave thing. Me. Drinks. Tonight. Me brave. Him Sebastian. Thing. I did. Blimey!

I lowered it for a moment, and stared. How very, very sweet, and how—well, forgiving. And, gosh, yes, of course I'd go, but . . . I gulped, golly. Talk about going back into the lion's den. But then again, he didn't sound very lionlike, did he? I raised the paper and read it again. No, more dovelike. More dove with olive branch in beak, in fact. I turned and walked slowly upstairs, one hand trailing thoughtfully on the banister rail, one still clutching the note, then sat, my heart hammering slightly, on the edge of my bed.

So . . . off to Sebastian's, eh. What on earth did one wear for a bevvy with a famous composer, for heaven's sake? And was it just me, or would there be others? And anyway, why are you so excited, Olivia? I'm not excited, I reasoned, just—flattered. That's all. And relieved. That he's no longer angry. But I'm not *excited*. Why, only the other day I was thinking of him as Sad Sebastian, for goodness' sake; he was still the same person now, wasn't he? Why should I be any more interested? Quite.

When I finally ran out of the house at seven that evening and beetled across the cobbles, I wondered if I looked too frivolous in peacock-blue pedal pushers, and tried desperately to look intelligent. Oh, and musical. I hummed a little tune. Abba. Hopeless, Olivia, just shut up. As I ran up the steps to the front door and rang the bell, it occurred to me to wonder if mother would be in. I hoped not.

Two seconds later, the door was thrown back to reveal—not mother, but Sebastian. Such was my relief, I beamed.

'Hi!'

His face, which I realised had been on the point of holding on to some reserve, relaxed at my smile.

He grinned. 'Hi, come in.'

He stood aside to let me into a huge, smoky-blue hallway, covered in prints and drawings, with a vast iron and stone staircase which swept up and up, curling finally to an enormous round glass lantern in the roof, storeys high.

'Gosh!' I stared. 'I had no idea these houses were so big!'

'Deceptive, aren't they?' he agreed, following my gaze. 'That's what I liked about it when I saw it. Very understated on the outside and full of surprises within.'

He turned back to me, and I suddenly realised that I was exactly the reverse. Very overstated on the outside in these ridiculous peacock-blue trousers, and no surprises at all within. Sebastian himself was wearing ancient cords and a blue shirt. We stood there smiling at each other.

'I just wanted—'

'Olivia, I—'

We laughed. 'Go ahead,' he said, 'you go first.'

I felt my meagre supply of words dwindling but ploughed on regardless. 'Well, I—I just wanted to say how sorry I was. You know, about all that ghastly business with Claudia and then at your party last night when I should have known better. I've—well, I've been a total imbecile and I'm sorry.'

He smiled. 'Forget it. Come on, let's go through and sit in the garden. It's too stuffy in here.' He guided me through the house and onto an elegant terrace, spilling over with urns of ivy and dusty white geraniums. I sat down on the French café chair he held out. Thankfully, it was just the two of us.

'You know,' he continued, as he sat beside me, a tiny iron table between us, 'I'd forgotten about that tigress instinct mothers have, but looking back I seem to remember mine was just the same.'

I took the beautifully chilled glass of Pouilly Fumé he offered me. 'Is your mother here now?' I glanced nervously around.

He put down his glass, sat back and regarded me curiously. 'The first time I met you, Olivia, you showed an inordinate amount of interest in my mother. She lives in Dorset, with my father. Why on earth would she be here?'

'In Dorset! Oh! So—so who's that—that woman then?' I jerked my head back housewards. 'With the hair,' I scraped mine back to demonstrate, 'and the teeth.' I stuck mine out rattily.

'Maureen? She's my housekeeper. She's got a flat in the basement. Why on earth did you think she was my mother?'

'Because Nanette said—' I stopped, flushing, as I remembered what Nanette had said. She clearly hadn't a clue, but wanting to appear informed, had creatively filled in the gaps.

He folded his arms, mouth twitching slightly. 'Yes, what exactly *did* Nanette say? I'm keen to learn, if only to discover why, at that godawful dinner party of hers, you addressed me in words of only one syllable. At first I thought it might be because you were brain dead, but then it occurred to me that you might imagine I was, am I right?'

'Oh God, Sebastian, this is all so embarrassing,' I mumbled. 'You see—well, the thing is, Nanette told me you were a bit . . . unhinged.'

'Unhinged.' He mulled the word over. 'Right. Why so, exactly?'

'Oh, such silly reasons, too stupid to even—'

'No, no,' he interrupted, 'I insist on being enlightened. It might happen again you see, and I need to know how to curb my derangement in public.'

I giggled. 'Well, OK. She said'—I gazed at my trousers—'she said you stood in front of your window waving your arms about.' I glanced up. 'Oh, and she also said you went shopping in your pyjamas. But, listen, Nanette's hopeless; she gets everything wrong and—'

'No, no, not at all. As a matter of fact, our Nanette is very observant, and I might have to plead guilty on both counts, but would you first hear my defence, before you send for the men in white coats? The arm waving is perfectly legit, and stems from me conducting as I compose in my head. Does that make sense?'

'Perfectly,' I beamed.

'But the pyjamas . . .' He scratched his head. 'I can only assume it was that time I ran into her in Waitrose when I was probably wearing some comfortable old stripy trousers I picked up in a market in Afghanistan. I tend to work in them—oh, and a crumpled T-shirt that probably looked—to our manicured Nanette—like I'd slept in it. And of course I always look appalling when I'm working and haven't had a haircut for months. Mad, probably. Will that do? Or do you need further particulars?'

'No, no,' I laughed, 'that will do.' His brown eyes were merry and far from steely now as they met mine over the white wine.

'And the teacher bit?' I blurted quickly, realising I was staring shamelessly. 'Nanette had some crazy idea that you were let loose on small boys as a means of integrating you into the community!' I laughed, then stopped abruptly. 'Oh—well, in fact *you* told me that you teach, too.'

He nodded. 'Well, it's true, although teaching's probably overstating it. I go to the High School about once a month to talk to the boys.'

'Oh, right. What about?'

'Music, Olivia,' he said patiently. 'Composition and theory.'

'Oh! Of course!' I laughed nervously, but flushed dramatically. God, you moron, Olivia, you must stop sounding so inane. I tried to think of something intelligent to say.

'I loved your music last night,' I lied.

He smiled. 'Thank you. Was it your sort of thing? I mean, is that what you like to listen to, as a rule?'

I hesitated, sensing a sure-fire way to ingratiate myself, but could I then bluff my musical way for an entire evening? I licked my lips.

'Um, listen, Sebastian, could I retract that last remark? Only, the thing is, I was so preoccupied last night I didn't actually listen to a note.'

His eyes widened. 'Oh. Right.'

'I'm quite sure it would have been my thing,' I hastened on. 'The reason I wasn't listening was because my husband turned up with his girlfriend, and I had trouble concentrating on anything other than the pair of them.'

'Dear me,' he stammered, scratching his head. 'Yes, that must have been very—difficult.' He reached for the bottle and looked awkward.

Ah, well done, Olivia. You're embarrassing the socks off him now, airing all your dirty linen in public. But something told me to plough on. That in order to establish any sort of rapport, all small talk had to be banned, even if it meant making a monumental fool of myself in the process.

'He left me several weeks ago, you know.'

'Yes, I had heard. Nanette . . .' He hastily refilled his glass.

'Went off with a teacher at Claudia's school. That was pretty hard to take, but I guess I'm getting over it.' I nodded across at him bravely.

He smiled, put the bottle down. 'From my experience, Olivia, it takes a lot longer than a few weeks to get over something like that.'

'Your experience?' I pounced. Ah, now we were getting somewhere.

'Oh, very limited,' he said hastily. 'We weren't married, like you are, and no children, so . . .' he shrugged dismissively.

'But it was serious?'

He paused. 'Very.' There was another long pause, but I kept quiet, knowing that was the only way. That he'd go on only if he wanted to.

'We met five years ago. Quite late to fall in love, I suppose—I mean, properly, for the first time. I'd got to the ripe old age of thirty-one thinking it would never happen. It was madness when I think about it. We were both too set in our ways, too attached to our customs, our countries—'

'Our countries?'

'Lara's Russian. She plays in the Russian National Orchestra and we met when one of my symphonies was being performed over there. I went across to oversee rehearsals; she was a first violinist.'

'How romantic. Didn't you try to make it work?'

'Oh, sure. I spent two years in Russia and she spent a couple over here, but I hated the place and couldn't compose there and England had pretty much the same effect on Lara.'

'Gosh, how sad! So she went back?'

'Fourteen months ago. Precisely. Which is why I say to you, Olivia, don't expect the scars to fade so quickly.'

'I know,' I said in a small voice. 'I was being flippant when I said I was used to it. Of course I'm not. It's like getting used to having your arm chopped off. I don't think I'll ever be whole again.' I took a big shaky breath. 'I miss him so much.'

'I know,' he said quietly. 'I know how you feel. And some days are better than others, aren't they? Some days you can kid yourself you're all right, that you're actually staggering from the depths towards dry land, and then just as you reach the beach, a bloody great tidal wave crashes over your head and drags you back in again.'

'That's it,' I wobbled, 'that's exactly how it is. It's like I'll never reach that bloody beach.' To my horror and eternal shame, a great tear ran down my nose and plopped into my lap. I brushed it away furiously, not sure if he saw, but if he did, to his credit, he tactfully pretended not.

'Right,' he said suddenly, standing up, 'enough of all that. Since you missed out on so much music last night, let me play you something wonderful tonight. Bach is my big passion at the moment, but I'm open to Schubert on a beautiful evening like this.'

'Oh!' I smiled. 'Well, that would be great, but couldn't we listen to something of yours?'

'Of mine?'

'Yes, since that's what I missed last night. Has that Abbey thing been recorded yet?'

He grinned. 'That "Abbey thing" hasn't, as yet. It'll have to be something else, but then again they're all pretty similar.' He turned and went inside through the French windows, crossing the drawing room to the CD player. 'I churn out the same old rubbish, as a rule.'

'What rot,' I said warmly, picking up my glass and following him in. 'Everyone says how marvellous you are!'

'Anyway,' he slipped a CD in and sat down in a wing-back chair on one side of the marble fireplace, 'here goes. Oh, by the way, I'm assuming you'll stay for supper? Maureen put some sort of casserole in the oven. She's a disastrous cook, but she's been with me for years now and I haven't the heart to tell her. Would you care to join me in picking the gristle out of her goat's bladder stew?'

I giggled and sat in an identical chair opposite Sebastian. 'That's the most attractive offer I've had in a long time. I'd love to.'

'Good.' His hand went to flick the switch, then abruptly—paused. He frowned. 'I say, this is awfully pretentious of me, isn't it? Asking you round then foisting my music upon you?'

'Don't be ridiculous. You didn't foist anything on me, I asked!'

'Righto.' He gave a mock salute and obliged with a grin. 'Well, this particular piece is called *The Rigorous Judgement*.'

Blimey, *The Rigorous Judgement*. I braced myself and waited.

The Rigorous Judgement, however, began sublimely. Breezy flutes and other pleasant windy things piped softly and wistfully and I imagined we were somewhere—oh goodness, somewhere pastoral and sylvan, with a bird perhaps—a piccolo was it?—lifting the melody. I gazed contentedly into the empty grate, letting myself be lulled along, until, abruptly, the mood changed. The bird seemed to cry out in alarm, and suddenly, it seemed the woods were upon us. Dark, base notes sounded ominously, coming like footsteps, and simultaneously terrified piping noises whirled overhead, swooping and crying as the strings gathered momentum. The intensity built, and as drums and cymbals joined the violins, there was a sudden sprawling change of key, as horns and trumpets heralded some sort of procession. I sat up a bit. More and more triumphant waves unfolded until there was a great orchestral wall of sound, and then suddenly—it stopped. A single flute piped on, to a clearing, perhaps, where the strings started up again, softly. They played quietly for a while until, finally, they too faded away, as the picture faded too, leaving nothing behind, but a tantalising afterglow.

I stared at Sebastian in silence for a moment, realising I was on the edge of my seat. I was speechless. I felt my cheeks flush red.

'Good heavens, that was beautiful!' I finally managed.

'Really?'

'God, *really*!' I gasped. 'I mean, well, I've never sat down and listened properly to that sort of music before so I'm not the best person to ask—a complete philistine, in fact—but I could *see* it, Sebastian, and *feel* it too! I had no idea you got pictures with music!'

He laughed. Stood up. 'Good.' He rubbed his hands together briskly. 'Well, come on, let's go down and get some supper, before you start reminding me of some of the more pseudy music critics I know.'

He caught my eye and I laughed, but I could tell he was pleased, and as I got up and followed him down the steps to the basement kitchen, it was with a considerably lighter heart. That music, dark and forbidding though it had been in parts, had changed the mood of the evening.

I sat down, as he manoeuvred a heavy Le Creuset casserole out of the stove to the table, and then lifted the lid. We stared into it for a moment in silence, then at each other. His mouth twitched.

'Bloody hell,' muttered Sebastian under his breath, and on an impulse, turned and tipped the whole lot in the bin.

He then had a surge of guilt about Maureen's hurt feelings, and, giggling wildly, we had to lift out the steaming bin liner and wrap it in three more. While Sebastian was getting rid of the evidence in the dustbin outside, I managed to rustle up a mushroom omelette, find some rather good Brie lurking in the fridge, and Sebastian came back and opened another bottle of wine, and then, finally, we sat down. The wine and the conversation flowed, barriers were lowered—I knew his past, or the important bits anyway, and he knew mine—and it seemed that we could now get on with the business of discussing friends, family, work, children, this single life—anything, in fact, of great, little, or no importance that sprung to mind. It was easy, it was relaxed, and later, as I toyed with the cheese, laughing as he recounted some anecdote, I even forgot to answer him.

'What?' he demanded.

I looked up. 'Sorry?'

'What were you thinking?'

I grinned. 'I was just thinking how different you are from that night when I first met you at Nanette's. I don't think you said more than two words to anyone, but just stared fixedly at the curtains.'

He wiped his mouth on his napkin. 'Ah yes, the dinner party from hell, with the used-car salesman, the couple who wanted to talk us through all eighteen of their home births, and the strange woman beside me, keen to hear about my recorder classes.' He grinned and I smiled back at him over the table. The kitchen clock ticked on in the silence. I glanced up it.

'Sebastian, I must go. It's way past twelve!'

'Is it?' He looked up. 'God, and I've got to do some work tomorrow. Come on, let's get you out of here otherwise I'll be too wide awake to sleep and I'll start tinkering with that wretched piano.'

I laughed. 'Is that what you're like?'

'Oh, totally. It's compulsive, this music lark, I'm afraid.'

We got up and he walked me to the door, opening it onto the warm, dark night, at which point, the first awkward moment of the evening arose. I turned, smiled.

'Good night then, and thanks, Sebastian.'

'Night, Olivia.'

We hesitated, and then I sort of lunged cheekwards, while he, unfortunately, lunged the other way. We laughed as we crashed noses, tried again, and finally accomplished a dignified social peck on the cheek.

'I should walk you back,' he called as I tripped down the steps.

'Don't be ridiculous, you can *see* me back from there.'

He laughed. 'True.'

As I walked across the cobbles in the warm air, a crescent moon was rising over the tower of the Abbey, and I was aware and pleased that he was indeed watching me. I got to my gate, turned and waved, smiling. He raised his hand back in salute, and then the door closed as he went in. My smile faded and I stared into the darkness for a moment. Swallowed. Yes, that's what I miss, I reflected. Having a laugh. A giggle. Having—well, the companionship of a man. I sighed. It wasn't the same as being with Johnny, of course. I realised, sadly, this evening had been something of a poisoned chalice. It made me realise what I missed. No one could ever be Johnny. And up to now, that had never been so glaringly apparent, because up to now, I'd met pretty second-rate men. But Sebastian was first rate, and, nice as he was, he couldn't match up to Johnny.

Days passed. The weather, if it was possible, grew even warmer and Claudia's school term began to draw to a close. It occurred to me, as I took her in one baking hot Monday morning, that I only had three more days of avoiding Miss Harrison before eight weeks of summer holidays, followed by Claudia passing on into the senior school in September, which, although in the same grounds, was in a separate building.

On the afternoon that Claudia broke up, my mother and Howard came for tea. Claudia and I had gone to town; making scones, biscuits, a chocolate fudge cake, piling bowls high with strawberries and cream, and setting it all out on a table under the cedar tree. Deeply giggly about 'Gran and the Man' as Claudia called them, we sat and waited.

Half an hour later they breezed in, arm in arm, and held court, recounting stories of how they'd met, teasing each other like children, as Claudia and I sat and stared, our heads going back and forth from one to the other, like the Centre Court crowd at Wimbledon.

'I finally plucked up the courage to ask your mother to a hospital dinner dance, you see. Well, you should have seen the assembled company's faces when "Poor Old Howard" turned up, glamorously accompanied!' He squeezed her hand and grinned.

'Poor Old Howard, my eye! You were the life and soul of the party!'

'Nonsense, I was brought out of my shell that night.'

'Well, I didn't exactly need a tin-opener, did I?'

Claudia's mouth simply wouldn't shut, and as I followed her into the kitchen with a pile of empty plates I had to tell her to stop staring.

'I don't see why. They don't notice. It's as if we're not even there! Mum, it's so extraordinary, it's like she's a totally different person. It's like—someone's cast a spell! Jesus, I just can't *believe* it!'

'Shh, they'll hear you, and don't swear.'

She stared at me, eyes still wide. Then she gave herself a little shake.

'Well, I think it's brilliant,' she said soberly. 'In fact, I think it's more than brilliant, I think it's wicked. But just think, Mum, she could have been like this all along, all sort of fun and larky! Isn't that awful? That it was all lurking inside her and we didn't know?'

I smiled sadly, began wiping up. 'I know. That's exactly what I thought when I saw her the other day.'

Later, when Claudia took Howard off to see her guinea pigs and Mum and I were alone—side by side in deck chairs and straw hats, mopping our brows periodically—I shaded my eyes into the distance, to where Claudia and Howard were, down at the hutches.

'Mum, d'you think Claudia's had enough of that school? If she goes on into the seniors she's got seven more years of it.'

'Oh, she's talked to you then?'

I stared. 'No, why, has she talked to you?'

'Oh yes, she rang the other night. We had a nice long chat. Yes, she's bored there now. She'd be happy to go.'

I sat forward, gaped at her open-mouthed. 'Well, why the hell doesn't she tell *me* that!'

'I don't know, darling.'

'And where does she want to go? To the High School?'

'No. She wants to go to boarding school.'

I stared at her, aghast. '*Boarding* school! No! Why?'

'Because she thinks it would be great fun, as I'm sure it would.'

I felt very sick suddenly. 'She wants to get away,' I breathed shakily. 'She's had enough of living in a broken home with a distraught, neurotic mother and—oh God—she wants to get out of here!'

Mum laid a hand firmly on my arm. 'Which is precisely why she didn't tell you. She knew that was how you'd react, so she wanted to sound me out first, and that is absolutely *not* why she wants to go. She's an only child, Olivia; she needs the company. She's read all the books—*Mallory Towers*, Angela Brazil—she thinks it would be a hoot.'

'I never meant her to be an only child. I still think . . . maybe . . .'

'I know you do, I know.'

Of course. Like she had, too. Hoping against hope that my father would come back, and me, knowing full well I was destined to be an only child, as Claudia surely did too. I remembered reading all those books, dreaming of midnight feasts in the dorm, pillow fights, shrieks of laughter, a world away from the sourness that pervaded my childhood. It gave me a physical pain in my gut to realise Claudia felt the same way

'Think about it,' Mum said, as Claudia and Howard walked back.

'But—I'd miss her so much. I'd miss her!'

'Of course you would, but promise me you won't talk to her about it until you've calmed down, OK?' muttered Mum urgently.

'OK,' I whispered, for they were back, bearing guinea pigs.

'Howard likes Edward best,' announced Claudia, holding a speckled one aloft. 'But the only thing is, he says he's not Edward at all, he's Edwina, which might explain why, cooped up with Pandora all day, they've never had babies!'

'I knew my medical training would come in handy one day,' laughed Howard. 'If only for sexing guinea pigs!'

Later, when they'd gone, I gave Claudia a big squeeze as she went off for her bath, burying my face in her hair, suddenly ambushed by tears.

'Mum!' she cried in alarm. I sat on the bottom step of the stairs and she sat beside me, hugging my neck hard.

'Is it Dad?'

'Yes!' I sobbed, grateful for that. 'Yes, yes, it's Dad.'

She hugged me some more, but then abruptly, her arm froze.

She sat back. 'It's not Dad, is it? Gran told you, didn't she!' She wriggled free and moved along the stair so she could see my face properly.

Damn, I rooted in my pocket for a hanky, this was so awful! So like I'd sworn I'd never be, loading guilt onto children, so like my mother.

'Don't be silly. This has nothing whatever to do with that. I'm just a bit tired and overwrought, that's all.'

'I'm not going,' she said vehemently, shaking her head violently. 'No way. I'm not going. I *knew* you'd think I want to get away!' she wailed.

My tears dried up the moment hers started. 'Now, Claudia, listen. We certainly mustn't rule it out.' I blew my nose determinedly. 'In fact the more I think about it, the more I think it's a very good idea. You're on your own so much here, and now that Daddy's gone—'

'*No!*' She sobbed wretchedly. 'You think I don't love you! You do, you think I don't love you, and it's just not true!'

Well, that set us both off. Tears streamed in torrents down our faces as we hugged, kissed, wailed, reassured each other, said how incredibly special we both were, then wailed some more, until finally, totally spent, we sank back on the stairs. Then we got to our feet, and arm in arm, went as one to the fridge for the chocolate fudge cake. Setting it between us on the table we dragged up stools, and armed with a spoon apiece, dug straight into the middle, sniffing loudly. Naturally, in time, our equilibrium recovered, as naturally, in time, our blood sugar levels were raised.

'We'll see,' I said sternly, between dripping chocolaty mouthfuls, back in mother mode again. 'We'll have a look at one or two, and we'll see, OK?'

'But not too far away,' she warned, waving a spoon bossily at me. 'It's got to be close, and back at weekends.'

'Agreed.' I nodded.

The following day, Molly came round. As we basked, beached whale-like on sun loungers on the terrace—Molly, considerably more whale-like than me—I told her about Claudia. Henry was splashing happily in an ancient paddling pool I'd found, as Claudia dashed inside to find some boats for him to play with.

'It'll be good for her,' pronounced Molly roundly. 'She's incredibly sociable and she'll have a terrific time.'

'I know,' I said sadly.

'Of course, the only one who'll lose out here is you,' said Molly.

'Precisely.'

'On your own.'

'Thank you, Molly, it had crossed my mind.'

She narrowed her eyes thoughtfully. Was silent for a moment.

I cleared my throat. 'Molly, I do hope you're not about to say, "Perhaps you could get a dog"?'

'No, I wasn't, but—well, how's Sebastian?'

'Oh, thanks!'

'No, seriously, didn't you say you'd seen him again recently?'

I sighed. I had. More than once, actually. Twice, to be precise. After our supper I'd phoned him to say thank you, and he'd asked if I'd like to see a film with him later on in the week. Naturally that had led to supper in a little bistro afterwards, and then walking home, we'd spotted a poster advertising an open-air concert in the park, which naturally we'd gone to too, a few days later. 'Yes, I've seen him.'

'And?'

'And . . . well, he's very nice,' I said lamely.

'Thought so,' she retorted smugly. She sat up and pursed her lips. 'Right, tell you what, why not bring him round for supper? On Friday?'

I turned to look at her properly. She was being suspiciously determined about all this. 'Sure, I could bring him,' I said slowly. 'But what's the rush? Why the indecent haste?'

She was quiet for a moment. Put her sunglasses on, sat back and gazed out at the view, which, with the sun glancing off a stream full of floating water lilies, was carrying on like an Impressionist painting.

'They're going away together,' she said quietly.

I swallowed hard. 'I . . . suspected,' I muttered. Johnny had indeed telephoned to say he was going away for a while and couldn't see Claudia for a bit.

'Where are they going?' I said in a small voice. Molly was friendly with a few of the nursery mothers, so I knew she'd know.

'St-Jean-de-Luz.'

'St-Jean-de-Luz! That's where we went for our honeymoon!'

'I know.'

I breathed deeply, bit the inside of my cheek hard.

'I'm just telling you what I've heard, that's all. Because I think you should be prepared.'

'For what?' my heart stopped.

'For . . . any serious developments.'

I stared at her. A long silence prevailed. Eventually, I took a deep breath. 'Molly, we'd love to come.'

She frowned, miles away now. 'Hmm?'

'To dinner, Sebastian and I.'

'Oh good!' She brightened. 'Friday then?'

'Perfect.'

Chapter Seven

SUPPER ON FRIDAY began somewhat inauspiciously, as we stood for what seemed like an eternity on the doorstep of the Pipers' little flint cottage, getting absolutely no answer at all from their cranky old bell. Finally we tried the door, pushed tentatively through, and happened upon a sitting room that looked for all the world as if it had been burgled. We glanced at each other, startled. There was an astonishing lack of sofas, chairs, tables—or indeed any sort of furniture at all—and all that remained on the rather grubby carpet were piles of books and magazines. Neither Molly nor Hugh was anywhere to be seen.

'Looks like they've moved out,' muttered Sebastian, gazing around. 'The thought of me coming for supper was clearly too much for them, they've done a runner.'

'Either that or the bailiffs have been,' I said nervously. 'They've clearly forgotten we're coming, anyway. Come on, let's go.' We turned hastily back to the door.

'Well, bugger off, then, Oh ye of little faith!' cried a voice behind us and we swung round to see Molly, sweeping through the French windows in a billowing maternity smock.

'We're out here in the garden and we've got no garden furniture, so we dragged all our stuff outside.' She threw her arms around her barren sitting room. 'Makes a refreshing change, don't you think? We thought we'd have a barbecue so Hugh can do macho things with tongs.' She grinned and kissed me on both cheeks, then beamed up at her guest.

'Sebastian, welcome. Now,' she linked both our arms with a squeeze and turned us gardenwards, 'come and meet the man responsible for my condition. You can't miss him, he's the one in the vest and the shorts who thinks he looks like Bruce Willis in *Die Hard*.'

We strolled outside with her where, sure enough, scattered about the long, unmown grass and the daisies, was the sitting-room furniture. And in the middle of this alfresco furniture was Hugh, in what looked like his underwear, fighting desperately with a furious, flaming, spitting cauldron that was more reminiscent of Sputnik than a barbecue.

'Remember these, Moll?' he cried, waving a huge pair of barbecue tongs. 'I borrowed them from the maternity ward. They'll be needing them back when you go in!'

'*Au contraire*, my darling,' she sang, 'they'll be needing them back for your vasectomy, for when I have your balls off. Sebastian, this is my husband, Hugh. He's an out-of-work actor, and as the evening wears on, you'll appreciate why.'

Sebastian smiled, shaking Hugh's hand.

'Good God, Molly, call yourself a hostess? These good people haven't even got a bevvy!' grinned Hugh.

A jug of Pimm's was discovered lurking under a table. Hugh poured four huge, lethal tumblers, and the evening slipped happily along. And as we sat, laughing and chatting, slumped in their comfortable old chairs, in their tiny, magical cottage garden, surrounded—more by accident than Molly's design—by hollyhocks, phlox and lupins, we gazed onto a veritable Constable scene of traditional English haystacks in the fields beyond. When Hugh waved his tongs in a final triumphant flourish we ate our traditional English barbecue: charred spare ribs, sausages that were black on the outside and raw in the middle, and vast baked potatoes that were as hard as bullets, but no one seemed to mind. And all the while, the drink and the conversation flowed.

'So what sort of thing do you do yourself then, Hugh?' asked Sebastian finally, picking the charcoal from his teeth.

'Oh, quite a lot of telly, you know, that type of thing,' Hugh said airily.

'He does sanitary towel ads,' said Molly grimly. 'If we're lucky.'

'Sanitary—but surely . . .?' Sebastian looked perplexed.

'Wrong gender?' Hugh offered brightly. 'No problem. I change sex; after all, I am an actor! No, seriously, dear boy, I don't wear them myself. No, no, I'm the gorgeous young buck she bounds confidently up to in her skimpy white shorts—for thanks to Panty Pads, our lass *can* wear skimpy white shorts—and whose shoulders she playfully straddles—for our lass *can* straddle shoulders with no embarrassing repercussions—and whose hair she playfully ruffles. Recognise me?'

'It's all coming back to me,' grinned Sebastian. 'And, um, when you're not doing important feminine hygiene ads? Dare I ask?'

'He lolls about at home, getting in my way,' said Molly.

'What my dear wife means,' said Hugh, 'is that when I'm not making passionate love to her on a sultry afternoon among the buttercups, I am in fact, rehearsing for my play.'

'Ah, and that is?' Sebastian brightened.

'Oh, dear boy, sweet of you to ask, but it's very much a fringe thing, at a modest venue just off the Hammersmith Broadway.'

'The Lyric? D'you mean the new Simon Gallway play? The Roman one, um—*Death of a Conqueror's Son*?'

Hugh nearly fell off his chair he was so excited. 'Yes!' he rasped, nearly choking on a rib bone. 'Fuck me, yes! Have you seen it?'

'Certainly I have. It was excellent.'

Hugh's chest expanded until it was fit to explode. 'Well then, surely you recognise me!' he squeaked. 'I'm the corpse!'

'Oh!'

'Front of stage the whole time,' he said proudly, 'lying doggo and deceased. Remember?' Hugh collapsed flat on his back in the daisies to demonstrate, eyes shut.

'Oh, er, well, yes. You were . . . unforgettable.'

'Wasn't I just?' beamed Hugh, sitting up. 'If I say so myself I was *bloody* unforgettable. Yep, I really got into that part.'

'He made me see it four times,' muttered Molly. 'And he does nothing! He just lies there, for God's sake!'

'Ah, but I *feel* dead, Molly,' he urged. 'I actually feel it, and I convey my deceased state to the audience. Seb here will back me up, won't you, Seb? Oh—and I'll tell you someone else who will, Imo and Hugo whatsisname, the conductor!'

'Imo came?' said Molly. 'You didn't tell me that.'

'So they're still together,' I mused. 'Have you spoken to her recently, Moll? I haven't seen her since the concert.'

'I asked her to come tonight,' said Molly, sucking the orange from her Pimm's, 'but she had a work thing to go to. I did ask how things were going, though, and she said she was besotted.'

'Really! With him?'

'Well, presumably. She didn't say, but I imagine so.'

'I saw the pair of them the other night, actually,' said Sebastian. 'The Mitchells asked me to dinner.'

'And was Hugo there too?' demanded Molly. 'Playing footsie next to

Imo and shooting her hot looks over the vichyssoise?'

'He was, although not next to her. I suspect even Ursula's not that obvious. I sat next to Imogen, actually. I thought she was charming. Very easy on the eye and much less intense than her mother.'

'But scary,' warned Hugh, wagging his finger.

'Imo? No, why?' I said, but I knew what he meant.

'Oh, come on, Livvy, Ursula's overeducated her. Any fool can see that. All those violin lessons at four and cuboid maths at five—you feel you can't open your mouth without her thinking—Christ, what a berk!'

'Valid in your case,' said Molly, getting up. 'More booze, anyone?'

We drank on and on, and I had far more than I should have done, first because I wasn't driving, but also because I felt I might need it. I'd shaved my legs, you see. And my armpits. And as Molly doled out the strawberries and cream, I gazed at Sebastian as he chatted animatedly with her and wondered just how reckless I was being here. Not very, I decided, taking another swig of Pimm's, and studying him carefully, roaring with laughter at something Hugh had said, head thrown back. He caught my eye as he shook his head in bemused wonder at Hugh, and I grinned back happily, holding his gaze for just a little longer than was strictly necessary. As I finally looked away it struck me, rather gloriously, that some time later this evening, I was indeed, going to live again. I wondered, with a jolt, if I could remember how to do it.

I followed Molly into the kitchen, and as she wiped her eyes on a tea towel at the sink, still hooting and dissolving with laughter at something Hugh had said, I stared at her.

'How are you managing this, Molly?'

'What?' she gasped.

'All this hilarity. You haven't laughed like this for weeks!'

'Oh!' She pulled up her dress. 'Plastic pants! Huge ones, absolutely marvellous, and padded out with stacks of those wingy ST things Hugh brought back from the shoot. I was so bloody sick of sitting around po-faced, I thought—damn it, I'm going to have a laugh tonight. Honestly, I've practically got a nappy on here, Liv, and I can skip—' she demonstrated across the kitchen—'And I'm sure I could straddle some gorgeous hunk's shoulders if I really—Shit!' she squeaked, suddenly clutching herself.

'What!' I leapt forward.

She peered down. 'I'm leaking!'

We gazed in frozen horror as torrents of liquid poured down her legs.

'God, that's more than a leak, Moll!'

'My waters! Quick—I've got to keep some! My midwife told me to, so they can test the amniotic fluid. Get a plastic bag!'

'Where?' I flew wildly round the kitchen.

'Top drawer—there,' she pointed. 'Hurry!'

'They're huge!' I wailed as I pulled out a John Lewis carrier bag.

'Never mind!' she squeaked. 'Just get some of this ruddy stuff!'

'Oh, for God's sake, Molly,' I yelped, 'you should be at the hospital, not worrying about your amniotic fluid—*Hugh!*'

'What?' drifted laconically up from the garden.

'*Get in here—Now!!*'

I reached down deep into my lungs for this, and it did the trick. Hugh and Sebastian arrived at the double, just as Molly, tottering across the floor towards her husband, collapsed stiffly on his neck.

'It's coming,' she moaned. 'Finally, Hugh! Ten bloody days late, but it's actually, finally coming!'

Sebastian, childless, and probably having only ever seen births on episodes of *Casualty*, where it all tends to happen in ten seconds flat on the floor of a phone box, looked horrified. 'What, here? Now?'

'No, no,' I said hurriedly, seeing Sebastian's aghast face. 'She's got a while to go yet. Come on, Moll, let's get you into the car.'

'We're off, we're off!' chortled Hugh joyfully, hopping about from foot to foot. 'Come on, my sweet.' He helped his huge wife, who seemed to have gone completely rigid now, out of the kitchen.

'Your case?' I asked anxiously, following them out of the front door.

'Boot of the car,' she gasped, 'packed and ready. I knew this would be a bloody emergency. Oh, bye, everyone!'

'Bye!' Sebastian and I yelled back enthusiastically.

Moments later they were away, roaring off in Hugh's ancient MG, roof down, waving frantically, when suddenly—my hand shot up in the air.

'*Stop!*'

Hugh obediently squealed to an emergency halt in the middle of the lane. His head swung back. 'What!'

'You've forgotten Henry!'

Molly and Hugh exchanged horrified looks then—'Shit!' in unison.

Hugh performed an immaculate three-point turn in the middle of the lane and came roaring back.

'So we have,' he muttered as he raced past me and on up the stairs. Two seconds later he was racing back down with a sleeping bundle, wrapped in a duvet, in his arms.

'Hugh, why don't I stay? Or take him back to my house?' I urged.

'No, no,' he insisted, dashing past me, 'family occasion.'

We watched as he ran off down the path, bundled Henry in the car—and then with a throaty old roar of the engine they were away.

Sebastian and I stood and waved until they were out of sight. All was quiet for a moment. Then Sebastian voiced what I was thinking.

'I envy them,' he sighed.

I nodded. 'Me too.'

There was a pause. 'Come on, let's clear up and get out of here.'

Much of the drive home was spent in companionable silence, both of us exhausted. At length though, Sebastian chuckled.

'What?' I turned, smiling.

He shook his head. 'Just—that pair. What a riot.'

'I know,' I smiled, pleased to have introduced him to a riot.

After a bit, he pulled up in front of my house. 'Here we are, then.'

I turned. Took a deep breath. This was my moment. 'Um, would you like to come in?'

His dark eyes widened with surprise. 'What, with Maureen there?' Maureen had offered to baby-sit, as the builders had a pub night planned.

'Well, she could go home,' I said, somewhat brazenly.

He scraped back his hair nervously. 'A little, um, awkward, don't you think? Bye-bye, Maureen, see you later, nudge-nudge?'

I licked my lips. 'Well, why don't we go to your house then, have a coffee there?' I offered brightly.

He regarded me for a long moment. Smiled gently. 'Let's leave it, Livvy, eh? Not tonight.'

I stared. It took me a moment to realise I'd been rejected. Not tonight, Olivia. I felt for the door handle, struggled with it, flushing to my toes.

'You're right,' I said, rustling up a bright smile.

Suddenly he lunged towards me—yes, he couldn't help himself—and I pitched forward too, kissed his ear as he—opened my door for me.

'It does stick a bit,' he confessed as I retrieved my lips from his hair.

'Oh, right!' I gasped. God, did I get away with that? Did he know I'd tried to snog him? I got out, covered in confusion.

'See you soon then,' I warbled.

He smiled up at me. 'Definitely. 'Night, Livvy.'

'Good night.' I turned, not waiting to see him drive off the few yards down the road, and walked dazedly up my drive.

Well. What d'you make of that then? Had I really misread the signs so badly? Had we not, after all, been swimming in a sea of mutual attraction for the best part of the evening? What was wrong with the man? Had I said the wrong thing? I didn't have time to ponder further, however, as Maureen opened the front door.

'Ah, you're back,' she said caustically. 'I thought I heard a car.'

'Yes, we're—I'm back.' I sighed. 'Hi, Maureen. All well?'

'Fine. Claudia's been asleep for hours. I sent her up at nine, she was so tired, but . . .' she paused.

'Yes?'

'Well, there's a man here.'

'A man? Where?' I peered past her, through the open front door.

'He's sitting out in the garden, on the terrace. Been here for a while, actually. He says he's your husband!' she hissed.

I stepped back. Stared. 'My . . . Johnny?'

She nodded, wide-eyed, and stood aside to let me in.

'Um, thank you, Maureen,' I muttered. 'How much do I owe you?'

'Oh, well, now let me see. I arrived at seven so—'

'Here.' I pressed far too much into her hand, not having time for the mental arithmetic.

'I'll see myself out,' she said diplomatically, but with a tinge of regret.

I nodded, didn't answer, but all the same waited until the door had shut firmly behind her. Johnny? Here? What on earth for?

I walked slowly out onto the terrace, tucking my hair carefully behind my ears. My heart was pounding. As I emerged through the French windows, I saw him sitting on the terrace wall, his long, elegant legs dangling. He stood up.

'Hi, Livvy.' His face was strange, taut and pale in the moonlight, yet I knew he had a tan, and he was smoking, for God's sake. Johnny almost never smoked. Then in a blinding flash, I knew. Knew what this was. Why he'd come. This was what Molly had hinted at.

'Sorry to crash in on you like this.' He cranked up a smile.

'That's OK,' I said carefully.

He took a nervous drag of his cigarette and I moved past him and sat just a bit further along the wall from where he'd been sitting.

'I thought you were in France,' I said lightly.

'I was, we were, but . . .' He bit his lip. 'Well, I needed to talk to you. It wouldn't keep any longer, so I flew back this afternoon.'

I nodded. This afternoon, eh? I gripped the balustrade behind me firmly. 'I see. Well, here you are then.' I raised my chin. 'Fire away.'

He took a quick nervous drag of his cigarette, dropped it and stubbed it out. His eyes came up to meet mine. Clear as a summer's sky.

'I can't bear it, Liv. I miss you too much. In fact I miss both of you too much. This has been the biggest mistake of my life. I thought I could do it, but I can't. I love you so much, Livvy. I want to come back.'

I stared at him incredulously. My mouth fell open with shock.

'You . . . want to come back?'

'Look, I know it's a hideous cheek and I should have rung or written—prepared you in some way—but I—I just needed to see you.'

I stared into his wide blue eyes, speechless. He wanted to come back?

'But—you left *me*!'

'I know.'

'For her!'

'I know!' He shook his head despairingly. 'And God knows why. Well, no, I *do* know why, exactly why, but that's not important right now.'

'It's important to *me*!' I spluttered. 'Why *did* you leave me, Johnny?'

'Sex,' he blurted out, holding my gaze. 'Pure and simple.'

I nodded. Stared back unflinchingly. 'Better than with me?'

'No, different.' He shrugged. 'The thrill of the unknown, that kind of thing. Pathetic.' He shook his head remorsefully.

I nodded, trying to keep calm. 'Well, it's not exactly trailblazing, is it, Johnny? You're not the first, and you certainly won't be the last, but—God—all this heartache, just for sex? Couldn't you have gone off and had an affair? Seen her in your lunch hour, maybe even had a few dirty weekends, got it all out of your system that way, so no one knew?'

He stared at me, aghast. 'You mean—you'd have *liked* that?'

'Oh, I'd have *loved* it! *No*, Johnny!' I cried. 'I'd have liked it about as much as having a cup of cold sick poured over my head, but I'd have preferred it to the ghastly public humiliation, to the mockery you made of my life, of my marriage, and to the grief and the agony my child went through! It would have been tacky but preferable!'

'And deceitful.'

'Oh, Johnny!' I cried, exasperated, banging the palms of my hands on my forehead. 'You and your bloody honour! It's so misplaced, so misguided! You really think you're doing the decent thing by coming clean and walking out on your wife and child and not sneaking around? *Well, I disagree!* The only thing that assuages is your conscience!' My fists were clenched with anger, and for a moment I couldn't speak. My voice, when it finally came back, was low, shaky, quivering with rage. 'You destroyed me, Johnny, and you've destroyed our marriage. And now, as I'm beginning to come to terms with the grief, you stroll back in here, and declare you'd like to be part of this family again. Lie in your old half of the bed, wash the car, dig the garden, do the washing-up, poke the boring old wife for the rest of your life—well, I'm just not having it, Johnny! I'm just not convinced!' With that I burst into tears. Great racking sobs rent my body and tears poured down my face. He rushed to put his arms around me.

'*Piss off!*' I shrieked, pushing him away. 'Just piss off!'

He backed off and I sobbed on. I couldn't stop. It was as if he'd taken a brick out of the dam and it had just burst all over the place, exploded everywhere. Eventually my sobs subsided and I gazed blankly up into the night. I simply couldn't believe this was happening.

'You have every right to be furious.'

'Of course I have,' I muttered.

'And every right not to have me back.'

'That goes without saying.'

'But, think about it, Liv,' he urged. 'Think about what we had, what we'd be throwing away.'

'How *dare* you! God, these past few months—what we'd be throwing away—how *dare* you . . . what *you've* thrown away, you bastard!' Suddenly I was on my feet, fists raining down on him, pummelling him. He caught my wrists, held them tight, and to my horror, as we struggled I was sobbing again. This time he pulled me close. My strength failed me and I collapsed onto him, wept into his cotton T-shirt. It smelt of fresh air, hay. Of Johnny. He stroked my hair, kissed the top of my head, his arms tight but shaky around me. And it was lovely. Normal. Like coming home. Johnny, the love of my life, the soul mate I'd had beside me since I was a teenager, my only family, back where he belonged. Who wouldn't be tempted?

I drew my head back from his chest. 'And her?'

He sighed. Loosened his grip on me. Looked away. 'It just didn't work, Livvy. She's so—possessive, so jealous. I couldn't move, couldn't breathe, it was suffocating, stifling.'

I thought back to when I'd seen them together, two blond heads bent over the concert programme. 'You didn't look very stifled at the Abbey.'

'God, that was so awful. Seeing you there, with that guy.'

I frowned. Rollo? Of course Johnny wasn't to know he spat.

'And then tonight, waiting for you, knowing you were out with someone.' He gazed, hurt clouding his eyes. 'Some guy?'

'It's none of your business, Johnny,' I said quietly.

He nodded, head down. 'No, you're right.'

My God, his penance would be huge, though, wouldn't it? I thought, looking at his blond head, bent low, sorrowful, remorseful. He'd have to toe the line for the rest of his life. I'd have the upper hand entirely. But would that be healthy? Would that, at the end of the day, help either of us? Surely if this was to work, it had to be with a clean slate. It had to be even handed, facing the world together. But how realistic was that? Then again—what was the alternative? To say: no, Johnny, sod off, I'm making my own way now, having a great time? Was I? I thought about that one carefully. No, a better time, I decided, but not a great time. And how come I was even weighing it up? I thought, suddenly startled. *Seriously* weighing it up too, genuinely thinking of telling him to get lost, and yet this was what I'd longed for, yearned for, all these months!

'Do you still love me, Livvy?' Quietly, it stole out of the night. I took a deep breath. Ah. The trump card.

'Yes.' Of course I did. How could I not?

'And can you imagine us . . .' he took a deep breath to steady himself, 'not growing old together?'

Sorry, no, *this* was the trump card. The other one was just the knave. 'No,' I whispered. 'No, I can't imagine not doing that.'

'And if not for all that'—he took me in his arms and squeezed me tight. I could feel his heart racing—'if not for me, for us, then'—his voice cracked—'for Claudes? And . . . and, who knows, Liv?' he said, his heart thumping away now. 'Maybe another child?'

For the third time that evening I burst into tears. You wouldn't think there'd be any left, would you? But there were.

We sat on that wall for a long while on that warm, still, July night, talking softly, until eventually, it seemed as natural as anything to take one another by the hand, to walk through the house, and to mount the stairs to bed. Oh yes, by rights, I should have made it much, much harder, but actually, I wanted him very badly.

We made love with a frenzy and a passion that I don't think, in all our years of lovemaking, had ever possessed us before. Finally we fell apart, satiated, replete, relieved. We stared up at the ceiling, panting, the duvet in a heap on the floor, the warm night air stealing in across our naked bodies.

At length I reached down and pulled the duvet back. We curled up and lay together like spoons.

'Where is she now?' I asked quietly, as reality came seeping stealthily back. So many questions. So many answers I needed.

'She's back at her flat.'

'Oh. Not in France?'

'No. France was a disaster. It was a last-ditch attempt of hers to bring us together. She booked a hotel in St-Jean-de-Luz as a surprise. She wasn't to know we'd spent our honeymoon there, of course, but it couldn't have been more fatal. We spent a ghastly few days in a stifling, hundred-degree heatwave, she, in dark glasses in our room to hide her red eyes and me, walking the streets. I came back only for silent meals, picking at food in happy, bustling restaurants, with her, still in dark glasses, sitting opposite me. Awful.'

I stayed silent.

'After three days of what should have been a three-week holiday, we checked out.'

'She wanted to go too?'

He hesitated. 'Yes. It was a mutual decision.'

I spotted a lie. The first one. I swam towards it—then let it go.

'And now?'

'Now?'

'Well, either she's accepted the fact that the affair's run its course, or she's distraught and in a heap.'

He swallowed. 'Distraught and in a heap.'

For a brief moment I felt a pang of pity for her.

'Oh well,' I said, 'I don't suppose it'll take her long to find another married man to play with.'

He didn't answer. Ah, I thought. He wasn't prepared to rubbish her, then. I wasn't sure if I liked that or not. 'Isn't that her game?' I demanded.

'She—got caught up in something,' he said, picking his words carefully. 'I take the blame. For everything. But now, because she's desperate to cling on, she's changed.'

This was better. I took a deep breath. 'In what way?'

He propped himself on one elbow and struggled to explain. 'It all started when Claudes went missing, remember? God, I was upset—thought it was all my fault, and I'm sure that's when she felt me slipping away. She invented aches and pains, even made me drive her to the hospital. All spurious, of course, but I remembered thinking then that in some warped kind of way it was a cry for help. I had—' he hesitated—'been passionate about her, helplessly so, and I think she was trying to rekindle that passion. Trying to say—look, imagine life without me. Does that make any sense?'

I blinked. 'Blimey. Bit extreme.'

'She is,' he insisted. 'She's nutty. She'd do anything.'

Naturally that frightened me for a second. I thought of Claudes, of *Fatal Attraction*, of boiling bunnies. 'She'd bloody better *not* do anything,' I said hotly. I shuddered.

He turned from his side onto his back and I gazed at his profile. Gazed at this husband of mine, lying beside me in the moonlight, as his eyes shut and Morpheus welcomed him down the dark lanes of sleep. And as I stared and stared, I thought—how weird. How strange. Four hours ago I'd been in Molly's garden flirting with another man. Two hours ago, I'd been in aforementioned man's car, as near as damn it propositioning him. And now, here I was, in bed with Johnny. If your probing, investigative, fly-on-the-wall reporter had slunk through my bedroom door right now, and hissed urgently, 'So how d'you feel, Mrs McFarllen?' I'd have had to have answered, in the words of the tabloid press—gobsmacked. If he'd persisted, pursued his tack with, 'But happy? Happy, surely, Mrs McFarllen?' I'd have replied—yes. Very. But, I decided, turning over to face the wall, I'd qualify that with 'unsettled'. Happy, but unsettled. Those, I decided as I too, finally shut my eyes, were definitely my overriding emotions of the moment.

The following morning, feeling I really should pinch myself extremely hard, I took in the surreal scene around me. Johnny was still asleep beside me, his brown arm flung over me in its habitual fashion, his eyelids just beginning to flicker. They opened, and as he saw me, a huge smile spread instantly across his face. It was so instinctive, so very much the moment he'd opened his eyes, so free of any ghastly doubt, that I beamed back, delighted. And it was at that, highly seminal moment, that the door opened and Claudia appeared in her nightie. She stopped dead in her tracks, her hand frozen on the handle. Her jaw dropped.

'Daddy!'

He turned quickly towards her. She stared in astonishment, her grey eyes huge, first focused on him, then on me.

'It's Daddy!' She gaped incredulously at me, as if perhaps I didn't know. I smiled, waiting.

Johnny sat up and stretched out an arm to draw her close. She came, but slowly, looking to me first for reassurance. I nodded, still smiling.

'Daddy, what are you *doing* here!' she squealed suddenly, leaping forward excitedly, jumping high in the air, and coming crashing down on top of him with her knees bent, catching him neatly in the groin.

'Oooomph . . .!' he groaned, in pain. 'Aaarrgh! What am I doing? I'm being beaten up by a ten-year-old,' he gasped, 'and on the day of my homecoming too.'

'Home . . .?' Again, wide grey eyes shot across to me.

'Daddy's coming back, darling.'

'Really?' Her mouth dropped.

'Really,' said Johnny firmly.

There was a silence. She didn't whoop, didn't shriek, and for a moment, I was nervous. But then a slow smile spread over her face.

'Well, about time too,' she said, giving him a clip round the ear.

He laughed, and then they rolled about on the bed, wrestling and fighting amid shrieks of giggles.

I watched them for a moment, tussling away beside me. Just like old times. Extraordinary. Like he'd never been away. How could that be then? Because he had been away. I blinked, shook my head in wonder, then grabbed my dressing gown, rolled neatly out of bed and slipped into it. Then I realised, in a sudden rush, the enormity of what I'd done. Realised what a huge leap of faith I'd taken. I also realised, with something approaching panic, that having taken that leap, it simply had to work. It had to. If not for me, then for Claudia. We couldn't do this to her only for Johnny to disappear again, could we? But of course that wasn't going to happen, was it? I thought hastily. He was back for good now and we were a family again. I gave myself a little inward shake.

'Right, you lot!' I said with a bright smile. 'Scrambled eggs and bacon in the kitchen in ten minutes.'

It was a beautiful morning. I threw open the back door and humming happily, gathered some eggs from the fridge. Yes, breakfast in our new kitchen, cooked on my shiny blue Aga, with the sun streaming in on the pale yellow walls, hung now with blue and white plates, casting shadows on the smooth, mellow wooden floor, and all of us here, together, back where we belonged.

As I fried the bacon at the stove, simultaneously laying the table with orange juice, toast, cereal, quickly flicking on the radio, Johnny and Claudia came bounding in. They flopped happily down at the table, still chattering away, and occasionally, Johnny would catch my eye as in, 'Isn't it great? She's delighted!' And I'd respond with a smile which agreed.

Meanwhile, the laughter and the jokes continued apace. But it seemed to me, as I listened, my hand pausing for a moment as I went to break an egg in the pan, that somehow, he was hiding behind Claudia . . . *No.* I cracked the egg. No, you're wrong, Olivia. It's just that he's bound to be slightly nervous.

That day, and the next few, proceeded in much the same pattern. I seemed to vacillate between strange extremes of emotions. One moment I'd be almost incandescent with happiness, hugging him to bits, showering him with kisses, and the next, tears of doubt and rage would spring and I'd be stomping round the house in fury. Johnny did his best to ride the waves. He also indulged my rather erratic desire for information, as one minute I decided I wanted to know everything about Nina, and the next, nothing. Sometimes, the minute Claudia had gone out to play, I'd sit him down, and demand, 'Where? How did you meet her?'

And he'd light a cigarette and patiently explain, yet again, that the day we'd been to look around Claudia's new school, a year or so ago, on the open day, Nina had been there too. As a new teacher, available to meet new parents.

'You picked her up at an open day!'

'No, I just talked to her, but for quite a while because you wanted to see the new science block, remember? The headmaster took you, and while you were gone, we chatted, that's all.'

'And then?' I demanded. 'How the hell did you progress from there?

'It happened quite by chance, actually. A couple of months later the gears were playing up on the Lagonda, so I took it into the Classic Car garage in Finchley—you know, the one Dad used to go to, and the one I still use. Well, it was quite extraordinary, because there she was, just coming out of the front door to the flat next door. She recognised me and smiled, and at first I couldn't think who the hell she was, but then I remembered. We got chatting and it turned out that her father owns the garage, which is extraordinary really because I've known Bob Harrison for years, and—well, I suppose we laughed about the coincidence, talked for a bit.' He shrugged. 'It just went from there.'

'How?' I yelled. 'How did it "just go from there"!'

He sighed, frowned. 'I suppose . . . I asked her if she fancied a drink.'

'What—just like that? Oh golly, Nina, what a coincidence, your dad mends my cars, fancy a lager and lime?'

'Well, it was a hot day, the pub was opposite . . . I don't know. It seemed natural at the time, somehow.'

'Natural?' I sneered. 'But you're married, Johnny. A married man.'

'I know.'

'And then?'

'Well,' he shifted uncomfortably, 'then I suppose we arranged to meet again, only this time it was for dinner, and then—'

'*Stop, Stop!*' I cried, clapping my hands over my ears. 'Stop this minute! I don't want to hear another word!'

And so it went on, with me oscillating wildly between a greed to be informed and a revulsion at the details. I seemed to veer from an insatiable desire to run down the street shouting, 'He's back! My husband's back!' to not wanting to answer the telephone in case it was Someone Who Should Know. My mother, for instance, or Angie, maybe Molly, or Imogen. Of course we did tell these people, but gradually, letting it leak out over a period of days. Looking back, their reactions fell neatly into two camps: modified rapture from my mother, Molly and Hugh, and unmitigated delight from Angie and Imogen.

My mother's subdued reaction—'Well, darling, I'm pleased for you, of course I'm pleased, it's what you wanted, isn't it?'—was somewhat predictable. But Molly surprised me.

'And you've taken him back?' she demanded from her hospital bed, newly delivered of a nine-pound baby girl named Flora, after the cottage garden she was very nearly born into.

'Well—yes. I have.'

'No questions asked?'

'Of course, Molly, many.'

'Good. Well, I just hope he's got some answers.' A pause. 'Sorry, Livvy, I'm delighted for you, of course I'm delighted. God, ignore me, I'm just hormone soup at the moment. Hugh's here and he's thrilled for you, aren't you, Hugh?' She held the phone out to Hugh for confirmation.

'Am I?'

There was some muffled confusion as her hand clamped over the mouthpiece, a fair amount of hissing, then—'Thrilled!' came back a chipper male voice. 'But tell her I thought she was doing pretty well under her own steam, too.'

Angie cried on the phone, so relieved was she, and promised to come round soon.

Imogen, though, surprised me most. I left a message on her answering machine at work—she was out at Sotheby's—and that evening she appeared on my doorstep, loaded with flowers, hugging us through her tears and her orchids, hugely overcome and emotional.

'Oh God, guys,' she gasped, 'this is so much what I'd hoped for! It's just the answer to everyone's prayers! I'm so, so happy for you!'

She sat in the garden with us a while, shared a bottle of wine with us, but when she left, I closed the front door thoughtfully and went, biting my thumbnail, back to Johnny on the terrace.

'I can't believe she came all that way just to give us some flowers,' I said in astonishment. I had no idea she'd felt my loss so keenly.

Claudia was skippy and happy most of the time, but cautious too, I noticed. And then of course there was Sebastian.

We'd never been lovers, but I was pretty sure we'd been more than friends, and I couldn't exactly have him popping round wondering if I fancied dinner; couldn't just leave it hanging in the air like that, could I? And so I went one afternoon without warning, simply because I saw his car outside and I knew he'd be in. Maureen opened the door.

'He's in the study,' she said with a brisk jerk of her head upstairs.

And so I crept up the millions of stone stairs, knocked gently on the study door, and on hearing a curt 'Come!' entered.

Sebastian was standing at the tall, floor-to-ceiling Georgian window, facing the street, fingertips pressed to temples, eyes shut.

'You old poser,' I muttered brightly as I went in. He opened his eyes and swung round, and for a moment, my heart stopped. I instantly wished I hadn't said it. His eyes were distant and preoccupied, about to be annoyed, but then remarkably, his face cleared, in the way I remembered, but had recently forgotten.

'Olivia!' He was across the room in seconds. 'How extraordinary, sixteen more bars of this wretched piece and I was coming over to see you! Did you get my postcard?'

I nodded and sat down quickly on a button-backed chair. 'From Paris, I did. How did it go?'

'Marvellous,' he beamed, dragging up a chair, eyes shining. 'To my utter relief they absolutely loved it, and let me tell you those Parisians are harsh taskmasters. They even got to their feet, for God's sake!'

'Oh, Sebastian, I'm so pleased. You were so nervous about Paris. And Hugo conducted?'

'Quite magnificently. Best yet, actually.'

I smiled. 'Imo's memory must have stirred him to passion.'

'Oh no, not the memory, no, no, she came out.'

'To Paris? Did she!'

'Oh yes, for four or five days. God, we had some fun, though, the three of us—lots of laughs, lots of gastronomic delights and a huge amount of drinking—too much, actually, bearing in mind that at least two of us were supposed to be working.' He glanced down. 'Oh Christ, Olivia, excuse my clothes. I'm in my nutter outfit.'

'But how odd,' I mused, gazing past him, ignoring this. 'I mean—I saw Imogen the other day, and she never even mentioned it.' I glanced back and felt his eyes upon me. Abruptly I remembered why I was here. I took a deep breath. 'Look, Sebastian, what I came to tell you was—' I went on in a rush—'well, Johnny's home.'

There was just a flicker of surprise, as if he'd momentarily forgotten who Johnny was, then his eyes widened in recognition. Slowly, a lovely, warm smile spread across his face.

'But this is wonderful news, Olivia, and just exactly what you'd been hoping for, isn't it?'

'Yes, yes it is.'

'How amazing! And a complete surprise?'

'Complete,' I breathed, relieved he was taking it like this.

'I'm delighted,' he beamed. 'You're back together again, a family, and it's how it should be. Claudia must be thrilled!'

'She . . . is,' I said, confused. Confused about how I felt, as much as how he felt. I studied his face, lean and elegant with those high cheekbones and dark brown eyes, which gave no clues, but which regarded me kindly now, rather as one would a small child.

The phone rang and he got up and went to the piano to pick it up. His back was to me. I gazed. I'd forgotten how tall he was. How dark his hair was. He half turned and his face clouded as he listened.

'Yes, yes, I know,' he said, scratching his forehead, 'but, God, Louis, their timing is absolutely lousy. I can't just churn these things out at a drop of a hat . . . Yes, yes I know . . . Yes, I said I would so I will, of course I will, but . . . they'll get it. Relax . . . You too . . . Bye.'

He replaced the receiver and grimaced. 'My agent, Louis. Apparently some film director is screaming for this score I'm supposed to be writing, although why I ever agreed to do it in the first place, I'll never know.' He glanced surreptitiously at his watch and moved towards the door. Suddenly I realised I was being shown out. I got up hurriedly. Perhaps I shouldn't have come at all? Perhaps we hadn't even remotely been 'an item' as Claudes would put it, but surely . . .

'There's still your London premiere, isn't there?' I said nervously as he held the door open for me.

'At the Wigmore Hall, that's right.'

'Well, good luck,' I faltered.

He smiled. 'Thanks, I'll need it. I'll be a nervous wreck that night.'

I went past him and out towards the stairs. 'Oh, you don't have to come down—' I glanced back as he made to follow.

'It's OK,' he said easily, 'I need another pot of coffee and I feel horribly guilty if Maureen has to puff all the way up here. By the time she arrives at the door she has steam coming out of practically every orifice, except the coffeepot, of course, which is stone cold.'

I smiled, but couldn't think of anything to say in reply. I was drained of all wit and words suddenly, and talking to him had always been so easy. Finally we were at the bottom.

'Well, goodbye,' I said hesitantly.

'Goodbye, Olivia.'

He smiled, held the front door open for me, lightly touched my shoulder and kissed me warmly on both cheeks. Out I went.

The red front door shut fast behind me, and the sultry, heavy, mid-afternoon air wrapped itself around me like an electric blanket, hot and oppressive. I walked down the steps and wiped my forehead. God, why the hell did it have to be so hot all the time? This was supposed to be England, for crying out loud, not Madagascar. And talking of crying, I realised with alarm, there seemed to be a bit of a lump in my throat. As I walked up the cobbled street, I appeared to be gulping down a fresh supply of tears. God Almighty, I was so overemotional at the moment, and—well, I was supposed to be the happiest girl alive! What the hell was the matter with me?

Chapter Eight

VARIOUS FACTORS COMBINED to convince me to pay Nina Harrison a visit. Outright curiosity, for a start, together with a desire to tie up all the loose ends and to see that all the stories did indeed tally, but I could have resisted both of these impulses, were it not for the fact that Johnny's mood swings were beginning to rival mine. Now, I was allowed to be volatile—I was the wronged wife, for heaven's sake—but over the last few days, Johnny, from a standing start, was whipping up a performance that was positively Wagnerian in style. I began to wish he'd go back to work, just to give myself time to think, to regroup, to consolidate, but as far as the office was concerned, he was still ostensibly in St-Jean-de-Luz and had time on his hands.

But it was Mac and the boys who really took the full force of his boomerang style. Since Johnny had been back he'd been wont, at the end of a very warm day, to take a six-pack from the fridge and wander upstairs to the bathroom, where they'd all be sweltering away among the archaic plumbing. There he'd open a can or two with them, take a debrief on the day's work, and perching on the side of the bath, recall his own days as a student, when he too had worked on a building site, joking laddishly with them the while. Now, suddenly, puce in the face with rage, he was telling them their work was shoddy, and that they had to redo the entire bathroom.

My builders were subdued. Johnny's return had been greeted with polite congratulations and a searching look from Lance which I'd ignored, followed by studied concentration and a deep desire to finish the job and get the hell out as soon as possible. Any hopes of finishing that imminently, though, were dispelled by Johnny, who made it quite clear that much of the work done in his absence had been second rate.

As Claudia and I sat at breakfast one morning, listening to him berating them upstairs, I felt sad. On the whole I believed their work to be good and professional, but aside from this, I'd been close to these people. They were my friends. They'd helped me when Johnny hadn't been there and had seen me through some very dark days. I felt a sense of betrayal as Johnny's irate voice resounded through the rafters.

'It's just incompetent!' he was saying. 'Just downright incompetent!'

Claudia was wide-eyed over her Coco Pops. 'Why is Daddy so cross?'

'I don't know,' I replied. I pushed my chair back and got up. 'But I intend to find out.'

Clarendon Road wasn't hard to find and I drew up slowly, right opposite number 32. I checked my scrap of paper. Yes, 32, next door to a garage, Johnny had said. I gazed out of the window. And yes, there it was, with a couple of classy vintage cars parked outside.

A silver-haired, narrow-faced man looked up from polishing a hubcap as I got out of my car. As I locked my door I felt his eyes on me and I wondered if he was just a mechanic or indeed the father. Either way I ignored him as I walked across the street, glancing up at a rather dear little mews house. I reached the green door and stared nervously at the bell: 32A or 32B. Oh help, which one was she? I couldn't remember.

Suddenly I realised that the silver-haired man was behind me.

'Can I help?'

I turned. I knew at once it was her father. I managed a smile. 'Oh, well, I was looking for Nina actually.'

'Ah, you want the top flat then. We're down below in the servants' quarters where we belong.' He chuckled. 'Hang about, I'll see if she's around. Sheila?' He rapped his oily knuckles on a downstairs window.

A net curtain parted and a middle-aged woman, attractive in a faded blonde sort of way, appeared.

'What?'

'Is Nina about?' he yelled.

She shook her head and smiled, indicating that she couldn't hear a thing. 'Hang on,' she called. 'I'll come out.'

I groaned inwardly. Oh God, did we have to get the whole family involved here?

The green door opened and the woman peered round. I spotted a wheelchair behind her in the hall.

'This lass has come to see Nina,' explained the silver-haired man.

'Oh, has she now?' she said, coming more squarely into the doorway. 'Well, she should be up there, luv. Have you tried the bell?'

'No, I—' haven't had a chance, I wanted to say through gritted teeth, but stopped short of saying anything at all as I heard a clattering down the stairs behind her. Pink, fluffy slippers appeared, then nylon encased legs, a floral skirt, and then Nina was beside her mother in the communal hall. She looked tired, dishevelled and without make-up. Her face was very pale. As she stared at me, her right hand slowly reached out and gripped the banister rail tight.

'What d'you want?'

Her parents caught the tone of her voice and turned quickly. They glanced at her, then back at me. As they did, I could see the penny making its slippery way down and, as it dropped, so did their smiles.

'Well, I—I wanted to talk to you,' I faltered nervously. I flushed, from nerves, sure, but actually, from anger too. Jesus, who was the wronged party around here? Nina's eyes dropped to the lino floor, almost, I thought, in recognition of this. She nodded.

'You'd better come up.'

'Nina, d'you want me to—' her mother shot out an anxious hand.

'No, Mum, I'll be fine.'

They both watched as I followed their daughter upstairs, and as I turned at the top, I saw the man put an arm round his wife's shoulders.

A separate front door opened onto a tiny hallway with a night-storage heater and not much else, which in turn issued onto a light, airy sitting room. I followed Nina through and realised it stretched the length of the flat—which wasn't large—with two sash windows onto the street. Coir matting covered the floor and a pair of identical white sofas stood either side of a wooden fireplace. I tried to imagine Johnny here, full length on one of those creamy sofas, reading the Sunday papers, swigging a beer. Suddenly, I realised I could. Yes, why not? Fury rose and it strengthened my resolve.

'So this is it,' I sneered. 'The love nest.'

'Would you like a cup of coffee?' she asked, wrong-footing me.

I stared. 'Um, yes, all right,' I muttered.

I followed her into a little white galley kitchen, and watched as she fiddled about making real percolated coffee, something we never bothered with at home. I didn't think Johnny liked it.

'I don't know why I'm surprised,' she said suddenly. 'I half expected you to come every day.'

'Really? Why?'

'To fit the jigsaw together, I suppose. Find out about the other side of the story, eh?'

It was said gently, but I found the 'eh?' patronising. Nonetheless I nodded, followed her back into the sitting room and perched on the edge of a sofa as she bustled about getting mats for the mugs. I took a deep breath.

'Johnny says—well, he says he left you because he missed me too much. He says he made a mistake, that it was a madness that should never have happened. He's adamant he loves me more than ever now, but I need to know that for sure.'

The pain this gave her made her catch her breath, but I didn't care. She gripped her cup, glanced down at the carpet. Presently she nodded.

'Yes, he left me because he missed you.' She raised her eyes. 'And I dare say he loves you above me. There now.' She smiled. 'Is that what you wanted to hear?'

She gazed at me with her steady baby blues, and it seemed to me she was mocking me. I hesitated. Somehow I'd expected her to deny it, say that he'd only returned to me through feelings of guilt, of marital duty.

'Well, obviously I came to get the truth.'

'The truth.' She smiled again, eyes still on mine. She shook her head slowly. 'Well, I'll answer any questions you care to ask truthfully, but what about the ones you don't know how to ask? What about them?'

I stared. 'I . . . don't know what you mean.'

'No. You don't. How could you? And actually, it doesn't matter. You're right, all that matters is that he left me to go back to you. Nothing else matters now.' Her eyes flitted, involuntarily almost, to a large black and white portrait photograph in a silver frame. I realised with a start that it was a picture of Johnny as a baby, dressed in a sailor suit. It was very similar to one that Angie had given me. I reached across.

'Where on earth did you . . .?' I studied it. 'It's Johnny, isn't it?'

'No, it's not Johnny. Everyone says that, but it's not.'

As I stared I felt the blood drain from my face. Suddenly I dropped it. It clattered down onto the carpet, still face up. I gazed down. No, it wasn't Johnny. It was too modern a pose. It was very like him, but—it was his son. I put my hand to my eyes. Covered them so as not to see.

'Oh God.' I had a moment of complete light-headed nausea. They had a son. Johnny had a son.

'How—how old is he?' I whispered.

'Nine months.'

'Nine—' My eyes shot back to her. 'But he's only been with you for—'

'Six years.'

My mouth dried. 'Six years!'

She nodded. 'But I've known him a lot longer than that.'

'But how! How can you have!' I blurted out, clenching my fists.

'Because every Saturday for years, he used to come here with his father, tinkering with cars with Dad. I've known him since I was about twelve, when Oliver gave him his first car, in fact. He must have been—oh, about seventeen.'

'Seventeen!' I gasped. 'But—but Johnny told me he met you at an open day. At the school, he said—'

'Yes, well, he would, wouldn't he?' she interrupted without a hint of irony. 'Of course he would. He didn't want you to discover he'd been living a secret life for years, had a mistress. What husband would? You might have been a mite upset had you known he came here most Wednesdays, had a chat with Dad and a cup of tea with Mum, before nipping up here and making love to me. I dare say he also didn't mention the fact that last year I gave birth to a son. Of course he didn't!'

'Where is he?' I whispered, glancing nervously about, half expecting a small blond head to pop up behind a sofa.

'Peter? He's downstairs with Mum. She has him every morning. Usually I'm teaching, but she still has him for me in the holidays. It gives me a bit of a break.'

'Convenient,' I muttered drily.

'Well, yes, I suppose so, but it's also fairly essential. We all need a break from him now and again. Peter's got cerebral palsy.'

I stared, shocked. 'Oh! God, isn't that—serious?'

'Very. Although some kids are not too badly affected. But Peter's very ill. Very—severe.' She swallowed and her eyes filled.

I gazed. 'I'm . . . sorry.' I was. Confused and angry and shocked as I was, I could still feel sorrow for a handicapped child.

'My God—Johnny!' My hand clutched my mouth. 'How did he—'

She nodded. 'Totally devastated. We only found out when Peter was six months old. That's when he moved in with me.'

I gazed at her incredulously. 'You mean—that's when he decided to leave me? When he heard the child was sick?'

'Yes, he said he couldn't leave me alone with him then. We'd never intended to live together, you see. I'd always known I was just a mistress. I thought I was lucky to have him as a lover, but I never thought long term. But then Peter came along.'

'But couldn't you have had an abortion?'

'I could, but I didn't want one. Johnny wanted me to, of course. He was horrified when I told him I was pregnant, but I assured him I'd be no bother. I wasn't trying to trap him or anything. I didn't want any money either, said I'd never intrude on his life in any way, that once the baby was born he wouldn't see me for dust.' She sipped her coffee, two hands cradling the mug. They were trembling.

'Well,' she whispered, gazing at the carpet, 'Peter was born, and Johnny sent some flowers to the hospital. He didn't come to see us, but that was fine, I didn't expect him to. Then a few months later I had this awful shock. Peter had been having all sorts of tests, routine they said, but then the paediatrician at the hospital called me in and gave me this terrible diagnosis. Mum was with me, and when we got home, sobbing our eyes out, she persuaded me to tell Johnny, said it was unfair to keep it from him. So I rang him at work.' She gulped. Brought her eyes up from the carpet to meet mine. 'I couldn't believe it. Twenty minutes later a black cab drew up and he was on my doorstep, his face as white as a sheet, and when Dad let him in, he cried. I'll never forget it. I came downstairs and he just stood there in the hall, leaning against the wall, the tears streaming down his face. We all cried then. We came up here, Mum, Dad, Johnny and me, and we sobbed. Then after a bit Johnny got all forceful and said he wanted to live with me, said he couldn't possibly leave me with a disabled child, that he wanted to share the responsibility. We were all astounded, of course, but Johnny was adamant. Said he wanted to be fully involved, and swore he'd devote his life to Peter and me. We were staggered, but all so grief-stricken and confused, especially coming on top of Martin.'

'Hang on,' I said, bewildered. 'Who's Martin?'

'My brother. He's fourteen now, but he's been in a wheelchair all his life, so it seemed like history repeating itself. Anyway, we let Johnny have his say and thought that in the cold light of day he'd probably change his mind, but later that night he arrived, with all his bags, ready to move in, but still as white as a sheet, as if he'd seen a ghost.'

In a flash that night came back to me. The night he'd left me. Is it serious? I'd asked. 'It wasn't,' he'd replied, ashen-faced and sweeping past me with his suitcase, 'was never meant to be . . . but now . . . yes.'

'Anyway,' Nina went on, 'when he moved in—well, I told myself not to fall in love with him. Told myself it wouldn't last, that he'd be gone, but how could I help myself?' Her eyes appealed to me. 'But then, as the weeks went by, and living together in this cramped flat with Peter screaming all hours of the night, needing constant attention and massaging, and my parents running up and down the stairs to help—well.' She grimaced. 'You can imagine. He'd sacrificed himself at the altar of "care" and hadn't realised he wasn't sacrificial material. He couldn't do it. And if anything,' she said sadly, 'he'd made it worse. His fine gesture had worsened the situation.'

'Why?'

'Because I became infatuated with him, and previously I'd never allowed myself to do that. But he was with me every moment of the day now, you see, every night. I couldn't help it. He could see it too—my obsession. I couldn't hide it.' She gulped and picked at some ancient pink nail varnish on her fingernail. 'About a month ago, after Claudia went missing, and after he'd seen you at the concert with someone else, I felt him slipping away. I panicked. And the more I tried not to, the worse it became. I've always had a nervous, respiratory thing, a bit like asthma, and when I'm worked up I can hardly breathe. It's all psychosomatic, of course—panic attacks they're sometimes called—but I had to admit myself to hospital to be put on breathing apparatus. Johnny thought it was a ruse, thought I was attention-seeking.' She shook her head sadly. 'Now do you understand why I needed Johnny so badly? Do you see that I wasn't just some scheming opportunist who'd briefly got her claws into someone else's man, some ghastly husband-snatcher.'

I regarded her for a moment clutching her mug, in her pink slippers, with her round blue eyes. I cleared my throat.

'But you are, Nina. That's exactly what you are. Because in the beginning that's precisely how it was. Just a bit of fun, a roll in the sack, with someone else's husband. Oh, you'd never met her, the wife, but who cares? You'd known *him* all your life, hankered after him for years, so somehow, it seemed all right. Somehow, it seemed justifiable. But when the shit began to hit the fan, when the "fun" had some terrible repercussions and you gave birth to a disabled child, you began to think you were entitled to some dignity. Well, I don't think so. You're still the same person, Nina, all that's changed is your situation. You've gone from being a fun-loving mistress to a single mother, only your task as a mother is harder than most. I do pity you, Nina, if pity's what you're after, but funnily enough,' I gave a shaky little smile and reached down for my bag, 'I pity me and my daughter more.' I stood up, turned, and made my way to the door.

'Are you going to tell him we've had this conversation?'

I paused, leaned against the door frame for a moment. For support. 'I don't know,' I replied without turning round. 'To be honest, Nina, I don't know what I'm going to do.'

I drove home in turmoil, my mind racing. The heavy, oppressive weather had finally broken while I'd been in the flat, and a fierce storm had erupted overhead. The windscreen wipers danced at top speed in a manic fashion as my brain cells, at an equally accelerated rate, attempted to clear the chaos in my mind. As I tore perilously around the Finchley backstreets, heading blindly for the M1, my insides heaved with revulsion. A love child. A six-year relationship. Not a quick fling with a local girl he'd picked up on a whim since we'd moved house, but a long-running affair with someone he'd known since he was a child. A mistress—yes, that was the word, that was her job description—who'd had a role in his life, almost as large as mine, for God's sake.

Gripping the wheel tightly and totally ambushed by tears, I careered onto the motorway. But how much did this really change things? How much did it actually matter? A lot, my head suggested grimly, but my heart was set on damage limitation. Not necessarily all that much, it declared, defiantly.

With thoughts still jostling furiously for position in my mind, I pulled up in my drive and instantly realised my mistake. Why on earth had I raced, instinctively, back home when what I really needed was time to think, hours—days in fact—to let this sink in? Now I literally had minutes before I had to confront Johnny.

Feeling panicky I quickly started the car again, and was about to plunge it into reverse—when I realised it was too late. I'd been seen. Johnny was, even now, walking towards my car at the same time as yelling something furiously over his shoulder to Claudia, who was running after him in floods of tears. As I turned off the ignition and slowly opened my door, I spotted my mother and Howard in the porch, looking distinctly shaken.

I got out. 'What's going on?'

Howard and Mum came scuttling towards me.

'Oh darling, this is all my fault,' she breathed, putting an anxious hand on my arm. 'We just popped round, you see, on an impulse, and we had a lovely cup of tea in the new kitchen with Johnny and Claudia, but then stupidly I put my foot in it, just as we were leaving.'

'What d'you mean?'

'Well, I brought up the business of the schools,' she hissed, wide-eyed. 'You know, the boarding business. I gather Johnny didn't know.'

'No, it's out of the question!' Johnny was saying, as he strode towards me. 'God, this is ridiculous, Livvy. There's no question of her going away, especially now I'm back!'

'Why, especially now you're back?' I asked calmly.

'Well, I can see that the two of you here on your own might have seemed a bit quiet, but now that I'm back, well, we're a family again!'

'Ah. So you make all the difference?'

'I didn't mean it to sound as arrogant as that,' he spluttered, 'but I certainly make *some* difference to home life, surely?'

'It's got nothing to do with that!' sobbed Claudia. 'I wanted to go away before you went! And Mum said I could, didn't you, Mum?'

'I said we'd discuss it,' I said quietly. 'And that's what we will do, but not in the middle of the drive in front of Granny and Howard.'

I turned to Howard, who was looking distinctly embarrassed. I managed a smile. 'Howard, what must you think of us?'

'I think you have a mighty characterful daughter who knows her own mind,' he said, scratching his chin. 'But I also think it's not our place to get involved. Come now, Sylvia, we'll be on our way.' He held out his arm to Mum, who took it hastily. I walked them to their car.

'Absolutely right,' muttered Johnny in a low voice, coming up behind me. 'Mind your own bloody business.'

Mum and Howard were very definitely in their seats at this point, so didn't hear, but I did. I waved them off, then turned slowly. My hands were clenched by my sides.

'Johnny, he might have heard you.'

He shrugged. 'So what? It isn't any of his bloody business, just as it isn't any of his bloody business how "characterful" my daughter is, either. Jesus! And your mother! Honestly, Liv, what a joke!'

'What?'

'Well, I mean those clothes! Mutton dressed as lamb, or what?'

'I think she looks lovely!' blurted Claudia, her voice cracking, her pale face stained with tears. 'And we like Howard too, don't we, Mum?'

I turned to her and took her shoulders. 'Darling, go upstairs, wash your face and have a lie-down on your bed. I'll be up in a minute.'

'But—'

'Now, Claudia.' I gazed down at her and she caught my eye and the tone of my voice. With a last defiant glare at her father she brushed past us, marched in, and slammed the front door behind her.

'You must admit, my love,' laughed Johnny, moving to put an arm round my shoulders, 'it's hardly love's young dream, is it? Christ, I found the whole thing positively embarrassing, cooing and holding hands at the kitchen table, I didn't know where to look!' He chuckled and made to lead me back to the house.

I shook his arm off and backed away.

'Johnny, why didn't you tell me you had a son?'

He turned, stared at me. I watched him visibly pale. 'You know?'

'Yes, I went to see Nina. She told me.'

His arms came up from his sides, then flopped down limply in a gesture of defeat. His knees apparently wouldn't hold him any longer, because he slumped back on the bonnet of my car.

'Livvy, I'd have done anything to have spared you this.'

'So it appears. Like lying through your teeth for years.' I knew I was trembling, but I felt a terrible clenched calmness too.

'Look, it's not that I was never going to tell you,' he said desperately. 'I knew if I came back you had to know, and I was going to tell you—this week, in fact. That's why I've been so upset these past few days, but it's so hard—*so* hard!'

'Not as hard as it is for me, though, surely, Johnny? Please don't ask me to pity you too. As I told your girlfriend earlier, I'm afraid I'm claiming the monopoly in that department, because nobody, Johnny, not you, not your mistress, not anyone, has taken quite as much shit as I have.'

'Except . . . perhaps my sick son.'

'That's out of my jurisdiction. And Godlike and all-controlling though you most surely think you are, for once, it's out of yours too.'

'Divine retribution,' he muttered, 'for all my mistakes.'

'I doubt if He's that interested in you. No, Peter's affliction was caused by the law of averages governing the amount of oxygen reaching babies at birth.'

His face contorted with pain at this. He clenched his fists, rapped his knuckles on his forehead. 'I've tried so hard to make it up to him, to do the honourable thing! I was prepared to sacrifice everything, and it was only for the child! I—'

'Oh, don't give me all that honour-and-duty crap, Johnny,' I snapped furiously. 'Was it honourable to poke the garage owner's daughter in the first place? Was it honourable to get her up the duff when you had a wife and child of your own at home? Hmm?'

He gazed at the gravel, couldn't look at me. I stared at that troubled blond head that I'd loved so much. Finally he looked up piteously.

'I'll never see her again, never see either of them again.'

'That seems a little harsh, particularly in Peter's case. It's all or nothing with you, isn't it, Johnny?'

His blue eyes widened, and the first truth for a long while fell from his lips. 'I don't know how else to be.'

I nodded. 'I know.' I regarded him silently. 'Pack a bag, Johnny.'

'What?' he said, startled.

'You heard me. Pack a bag. I really don't think I can live with you any more.' With that I turned on my heel, and left him standing, staring after me as I walked into the house.

I went on through the hall, up the stairs and across the landing to Claudia's bedroom. I peeped round the door. She was lying on her side on her bed, fast asleep. I closed the door softly and went downstairs, turning smartly right at the bottom and going out of the back door so as not to encounter Johnny, then on down to the potting shed.

As I let myself into the cool, dark space, shutting the door behind me, I let out a long shaky, breath. My God. What had I done? Well, I'd sent him packing, that's what I'd done. I'd known instinctively, as I stood there facing him, that I simply couldn't take any more. Didn't want to either. Didn't want him in my life. My eyes widened in the darkness, boggling at this revelation. God, had I really admitted that? Surely in the car just now, I'd been so convinced I could overcome it all, could overlook everything . . . But I couldn't.

After a moment I sat down shakily at the potting bench. Peered into my seed trays. Yes, those antirrhinums were getting a bit leggy. Could do with pricking out. I noticed my hands were trembling as I went about my business, but I also knew that I was quite clear about what I'd done.

When I emerged, a while later, he had gone. To her? I wondered, as I crept around the house. Who cares? At that moment I really didn't; I just wanted to be on my own. Alone with Claudia. As I went upstairs to find her, it occurred to me that I might sell this house. Oh, I'd loved it in the beginning, we'd both loved it, thought of it as a forever place, but he'd been living a lie in it even then. That soured everything, and I wasn't sure I wanted it any more. On a practical level, as well, it was too big for us. We'd need something smaller now, the two of us. A cottage maybe, near that school that I knew Claudia was really keen on, but hadn't mentioned because she thought it was too far away. The one on the cliffs in Dorset, with the sea beating against the rocks below, and the ponies in the paddocks above. I'd found the prospectus hidden under her bed, well thumbed and with 'Cool!' scrawled all over it. She'd thrive there, of course, in a place like that, and I could be close by in—yes, I thought wildly—a little whitewashed cottage, with a fabulous cottage garden full of poppies and lupins that she and her friends could come back to at weekends. I sighed and trudged on up the stairs.

Claudia was still fast asleep, spread-eagled on her back now. I took off her shoes and brushed the hair back from her face. Her forehead was hot and damp and I moved to the window to open it, to let a breeze in. As I flung it open, I hung out for a moment, feeling the wind on my own face. Gazing into the hazy sunshine, marvelling at the turn my life was taking, I suddenly spotted Imogen's car coming round the corner. Yes, that was surely her distinctive red Mercedes, indicating right now, and cruising slowly down our road.

I raised my hand in welcome and was about to call out, rush downstairs, throw open the door and drag her in for a much-needed gin and tonic on the lawn, when abruptly, she stopped short. Not outside my house, but Sebastian's. Oh, of course, I realised, she was probably with Hugo. Sebastian's concert was about to be premiered at the Wigmore Hall and he was no doubt having last-minute consultations with his conductor. I watched, disappointed, as she got out, looking stunning in a sleeveless cream dress, her blonde hair swinging and shining like a girl in a shampoo advert, and waited for Hugo to get out the other side. But Imogen was on her own. As I watched Maureen let her in, I thought what fun they must have all had in Paris. Imo and Hugo, happy and in love; Sebastian, carefree, delighted his piece had been such a hit, high on success. God, if only I'd played my cards right I might have been there with them, instead of which I'd welcomed my errant husband back with open arms. Fool.

As I made my way slowly downstairs, lost in thought, I suddenly spotted Spiro, hovering on the front step. He was twisting his hat in his hands and peering through the glass, clearly looking for me. I stopped, sighed. And so life goes on, I thought wryly. I might, just this minute, have discovered my husband's love child lurking in a north London bedsit, I might, tomorrow morning, have to tell my sensitive ten-year-old that her family unit had once more collapsed, but no matter. Come what may, one still had to deal with the builders.

'Spiro, come in,' I said, throwing back the door. 'Do just walk in and yell if you can't find me. What can I do for you?'

'Mac, he say to me—can I please bring Meesis McFarllen the latest bill and ask her, very, very kindly, for an advance on the readies?'

'Oh, he did, did he?' I took the bill he proffered and looked at it. Looked again. Blinked. 'Bit steep, isn't it, Spiro? How many weeks in advance is this for?'

'Only one, but he say we need so many building supplies, breeks, copper piping, cement, and so he order it, but he no pay for it yet. It all here, see?' He pointed to a shopping list of masonic items in Mac's hand.

I sighed and tucked it in my pocket. 'Yes, I see. Well, I'll certainly give him some of it, but I'm not sure I can ante up the whole lot right now.'

Spiro looked anxious. 'But he say to be sure to bring it back and—'

'Look, I'll talk to him, Spiro, OK? Now don't you worry, no one's going to shoot the messenger.' I smiled, and was still smiling as I went to the safe to get some money out for Mac. As I punched in the combination number, I looked at the scrappy piece of paper Spiro had given me. I'd give Mac half, I decided, slowly opening the safe door. Two thousand pounds really was too much all in one go. I counted out the cash, popped it in an envelope, and then shut the safe again.

I put the envelope in my skirt pocket and wandered down the garden to the caravan. I knocked on the door and Alf answered.

'Oh, Alf, look, Spiro gave me this bill, but I have to say it's rather hefty and I'm minded to give you only half at the moment. I'll speak to Mac about having the rest later. Is he about?'

'E's in the karzy, luv, d'you wanna wait? He won't be long.'

'Er, well, no I won't, if you don't mind,' I said nervously, eyeing the Portaloo door, not convinced I wanted to encounter Mac before he'd washed his hands. 'Just ask him to pop up and see me, would you?'

'Yeah, orright.' He looked anxious. He glanced at the envelope in my hand. 'I'll take that little lot then, shall I? Just for the minute?'

'Oh—sure.' I handed it over, then I made my way slowly back to the house. As I wandered through the French windows I closed them behind me, shooting the bolts up firmly. Now that the weather had broken there was a chill in the air and the wind was getting up. In fact, it occurred to me that the reason it was gushing through here like a raging monsoon was because the front door was wide open. God, no wonder there was such a gale. As I crossed the room to the hall and went to shut it, a small, bald-headed man in a beige, belted raincoat stepped out from the shadows, a middle-aged, peroxide-blonde woman in a well-worn, shiny C&A suit beside him.

'Mithith McFarllen?' the man enquired softly. He had a lisp.

'Yes?'

'I believe a gentleman named Mithter Alfred Turner ith currently in your employ. May we thpeak with him, pleathe?'

'Oh! Well, yes I—'

'Police,' the woman informed me helpfully, flicking out her ID card.

'Oh!' I gasped. 'Good heavens, well do come in. In fact—no, no, don't come in, there's no point. We'll go round the back. They're down in a caravan, you see, in the garden.' I began to lead the way.

What did the police want with Alf? I thought, my head spinning as I led them down the garden. I banged on the caravan door.

'Mac! Alf!'

Spiro answered. 'Yes, Meeses McFarllen?' with studied politeness.

'Oh, Spiro, are the others in?'

'No, Meeses McFarllen, they have just gone out. They have gone to the public house.'

'Do you happen to know which public houthe?' whispered the man in the raincoat.

Spiro smiled ruefully. 'I am so very sorry. I am so very afraid that I do not know wheech public house.'

Raincoat turned to me. 'What'th the neareth local then, Mithith McFarllen, the Fighting Cockth?' He paused. 'Mithith McFarllen?'

'Oh, I'm sorry.' Just behind Raincoat, I'd suddenly caught sight of Mac, hiding in the rhododendron bushes. I'd also spotted Lance, tucked away behind him. Lance put a finger to his lips. I turned wide eyes on Raincoat. 'What . . . did you say?'

'I thaid, ith the Fighting Cockth the nearetht?'

'Yes, yes, that's it.'

'But they go on a creep, I theenk,' added Spiro, imaginatively.

The policeman stared.

'A pub crawl, he means,' I put in quickly.

'Ah.' Raincoat pursed his lips. 'Well, how very inconvenient, but I don't believe I shall trouble to "creep" around the local hothtelrieth after them. Would you thimply inform Mr Turner that I would like a word with him on a matter of great importanth, and will return tomorrow morning, Mithith McFarllen?'

'Of course!'

'And meanwhile, thank you for your time.' He inclined his head slightly, then with a sharp 'Come!' to his colleague, they turned to go.

Spiro and I watched as they made their way up the garden, not quite goose-stepping but almost. My eyes darted briefly to the rhododendron bushes, but then suddenly, on an impulse, I ran after them.

'Um, excuse me,' I called breathlessly, catching them up, 'since Alf Turner is staying on my premises—can I just ask what this is all about?'

Raincoat turned. 'Yeth of courthe. It'th about hith wife.'

'Whose wife—Alf's?'

'Yeth. She appearth to be mithing.'

'Missing! Oh, oh no, officer,' I said eagerly. 'If you mean Vi, she's gone to Spain!'

He gazed witheringly at me. 'No, Mithith McFarllen, she hathn't gone to Thpain. For one thing she hath never in her life pothethed a path-port. She'th mithing, believe me. In fact we're very much afraid she may be dead.'

I stared. 'Dead!' My hand shot to my mouth. 'Oh!' I gasped.

'Exactly. Oh,' he repeated quietly. 'Bear that in mind, Mithith MacFarllen, when you anther any more of my quethtionth, hmm?'

And with that he turned and left.

Chapter Nine

'DEAD!' I STARED after his retreating back. Spiro came up behind me.

'Spiro, she's dead!' I gasped.

'Who dead?'

'Vi, Alf's wife!'

He gazed at me, open-mouthed. Slowly it dawned. 'Oh! Oh no, so poor Alf! He be so sad, Meeses McFarllen! He—'

Mac and Lance materialised from the bushes and came over the bridge, just as Spiro was filling up and reaching for his hat. Mac jerked his head. 'Vamoose, Spiro.'

'*Ti?*'

'You heard, Zorba, beat it,' he snarled. 'Go on, get out of here.'

Spiro's eyes widened. 'Ah yes, yes.' He backed away.

'Excellent. Now.' Mac's steely-blue eyes met mine. 'We need to talk.'

'We certainly do,' I muttered.

'Over here.'

He led the way back across the bridge, pausing only at the caravan to reach in and grab a six-pack from inside the door. Then the three of us sat down on the grassy bank. Lance was silent.

'She's dead, Mac,' I breathed, staring into the water.

'I know.'

'Does Alf know?'

He turned his head, looked at me for a long moment.

'He killed her?' I gasped.

'It was an accident.'

'Jesus!' I got to my feet, knocking his Pils over.

'Sit down,' hissed Mac, reaching up and taking my arm roughly, dragging me down. 'Now listen,' he breathed hoarsely in my ear, 'it was a terrible, tragic accident. It happened that weekend, a while back, when we went home, and Lance stayed here, remember? Real scorcher?'

I thought back desperately. My mind whirled for a moment, then memories of slapping the Ambre Solaire all over Lance in the garden and Claudia going missing jostled for position so—yes, that weekend, it must have been . . . 'Yes, yes, I remember,' I muttered.

'Well, previous to that, she'd bin ringing and ringing, all week, and always givin' him earache—remember that?'

'Oh yes, yes, I do remember.'

'Well, what she was on about, was some kitchen cupboard she wanted puttin' up. So anyway, he went home that Friday night and said—yeah yeah, orright, luv, stop givin' me grief, I'll put it up. Tomorrow morning, like.'

'"No, I want it tonight," she says. "You never do sod all round this place for me, Alfred Turner."'

Mac took a deep breath. 'So anyways, old Alf, he hauls himself out of his chair, even though he's knackered and he ain't even had his tea or anyfing, and goes to the shed and gets this cupboard, right? He's made it already, see, made it the weekend previous—and then he gets the step ladder out too, an' he starts fixin' it up, an' all the time she's standin' there givin' him earache below. Well, finally, right, he gets this cupboard up on the wall, hammers it home, and he's wobblin' about on top of the ladder and he calls down, "About there orright, luv?"

'And she stands back and says—"Bleedin' heck! It's not even bleedin' straight, you useless lump of shit!"

'Well, Alf, he loses it then. He's tired and he's hungry and he slams his hammer down on the floor—chucks it away in disgust. Only what he don't realise is, she's moved forward, hasn't she, and she's standin' right underneath him now. Well, it gets her—WALLOP!—right on the side of the head, right on the temple, and she falls to the floor in a heap. Well, the next thing Alf knows, he's crouched down beside her in a pool of blood, feeling for her pulse, which she ain't got.'

'Oh God,' I breathed.

'So anyways, tremblin' and sobbin' like, he gets straight on the blower to me. Really cryin' he is, and I can hardly make out a word he's sayin', but I get the gist orright when I hear him say, "I've killed her, I've bloody killed her, Mac!" So I get round there sharpish and when I burst through the door, there he is. Sat there, poor sod, sobbin' his eyes out on the kitchen floor, covered in blood 'cos he's tried to revive her, and the poor bitch is in his arms, cradled like a baby.'

'Oh Christ.' My hand flew to my mouth.

'Well, I'm in a right state now, aren't I? On the one hand I'm all for ringin' the police and tellin' it straight, but on the other, I've got Alf, see, moanin' about how he didn't mean to do nofing, and in that split second

I fought—well, who the hell are they goin' to believe? Not my little brother, that's for sure. He'd be useless in the dock. He'd be in that slammer before you can say hot porridge, and we all know he don't deserve that, not life imprisonment. No, he don't deserve that.' He reached for his Pils, sucking on his can with a vengeance.

'So . . . what did you do?' I asked tentatively.

Mac swallowed hard and I realised he was in trouble. He shook his head to indicate he couldn't speak. Lance cleared his throat.

'He got her out of his arms—prised her, apparently. Alf was clinging on to her for dear life. Stripped off all of Alf's clothes and burnt them, then he gave him a shower. Then of course he had to scrub the kitchen, and the shower, and then . . .' Lance swallowed.

'Then I realised there was no goin' back,' Mac continued gruffly. 'I'd done it, then, see? Burnt the clothes, scrubbed away the blood, got rid of the evidence. All in a matter of minutes. It dawned on me then that there was no way I could go to the police. I had to carry on.'

'And the body?'

Lance shook his head. 'Dad won't tell me.'

'Alf and I dealt wiv that,' said Mac gruffly. 'It's not for the lad to know, an' it's not for you to know neiver.'

'No! No absolutely not, don't tell me, Mac!' I knew far too much already. 'But—but surely, Mac, now that the police have got a whiff of this, now that they think she might be dead, surely you could both tell them what you've just told me! I believe you, so why shouldn't they?'

'Don't be soft,' he scoffed. 'The only reason you believe us is 'cos you know us, and trust us. They'd take one look at us, root around in our backgrounds—which are tidy, but not immaculate—see how we've tampered with the evidence, and then they'd be rubbing their hands wiv glee! Nah, Alf's gone, anyway, see. Gone to a safe place.' He checked his watch. 'In a couple of hours he'll be out of the country, heading for the Spanish—'

'*Oh, Mac, don't tell me!*' I shrieked. 'I—I don't want to know!' I groaned, clutching my head. Oh God, he also had a thousand pounds in folding readies stashed in his pocket kindly donated by yours truly. No wonder he'd wanted more.

'And you? You and Lance? They'll be back to question you in the morning, surely?'

Mac lit a cigarette and sucked hard. 'I'm sure they will, and we know nofing. All we know is what Alf told us, that Vi left him, went to Spain. And as far as we know, that's where she still is. Right, Lance?'

'Right,' Lance muttered bleakly.

'And Alf? Where's Alf, they'll ask.'

Mac shrugged, expressionless, just as he no doubt would in the police station. 'Alf? Dunno. Really, dunno, guv. Christ, I'm not my brother's keeper, am I?' His blue eyes widened innocently at me.

Oh, but he was, he most definitely was, and always had been.

'I'm counting on you to stay shtumm, luv,' said Mac quietly. 'Not to lie or anyfing, but just to say nofing. Say you don't know, orright?'

'You need to know, Mac, that I can't do that,' I said quietly. 'I won't go to the police, but if they come here asking me questions, I won't stay "shtumm", either, as you call it. I have to tell them all I know.'

I held his eye firmly as he looked at me. Finally he nodded.

'Yeah, well, I rather thought you'd say that. Two different walks of life, eh? Somefing to do with morals and duty—rules, too, I expect.'

'Something like that.'

'Yeah, well,' he said thoughtfully, scratching his chin, 'but what it does mean, though, is I might have to make tracks sooner than I thought. Might have to—'

'Mac, enough!' I gasped, jumping up. 'Just do what you have to do, but don't tell *me* about it, all right? Keep it to yourself, OK?'

He gazed up at me for a moment, pursed his lips, then sprang athletically to his feet. 'Yeah, yer right,' he agreed. 'The less you know the better.' He jerked his head. 'Come on, Lance, we've got work to do.'

Lance got miserably to his feet and then they both made to go, but suddenly Mac turned back, regarded me squarely. 'Lance and Spiro will finish up here, luv, orright?'

'Orright,' I growled. 'I—mean, right.'

He held out his hand. 'Goodbye then, Olivia. Nice doin' business wiv you. Only do us a favour, eh? Give us a day's grace before you go an' spill the beans?'

I stared at him. 'Well now, how on earth am I supposed to do that,' I said slowly, looking at his outstretched hand. 'They'll be back here tomorrow morning, Mac, first thing. You heard him say so yourself.'

'Ah, but not to speak to you, luv, to us. You could make yourself scarce for the day, couldn't you?'

I could feel Lance's eyes on me too now. I licked my lips. Could feel myself wavering for a moment. 'Well, I suppose . . . I could try, but—'

'Good girl,' he beamed. 'You're orright, Olivia. You're straight and you mean what you say. I like that. *Arrivederci*,' he said briskly, giving a mock tug of his forelock and turning smartly on his heels. Lance fell in quickly behind him.

I watched, somewhat slack-jawed, as they went back to the caravan and disappeared inside. Then I saw the door slam behind them. I walked slowly over the bridge and on up to the house.

Dusk was falling fast now, and the fireflies were doing a last frantic dance in the low, flickering light. My own head was dancing fairly frantically too, and, I realised, with a start of horror, that Mac had very subtly turned the tables on me there. With his steely blue eyes upon me I'd promised . . . What exactly had I promised? I stopped still. To disappear for twelve hours so as not to blow their cover while Mac slipped the country? Oh Lord, Olivia, that's—that's tantamount to harbouring criminals, isn't it? Or at least aiding and abetting them? I walked quickly inside, hastened to the kitchen calendar. Blank. Damn. Except, what was this at the bottom, in pencil? I peered. *Claudia to Lucy's for night.*

Ah, yes, of course, I remembered now. Amanda, Lucy's mother, of the disappearing-child episode, was desperate to have Claudes back and prove her worth as a competent mother, so if Claudia was away all day and all night, I reasoned rationally, what would I normally do? Well, I'd go to London, of course, that's what! Yes, I thought with a surge of joy.

I quickly lunged for the telephone and rang Amanda, who instantly thought I was cancelling.

'Oh God, Livvy, I'll look after her,' she wailed.

'Don't be silly, Amanda,' I scolded. 'I'm simply ringing to say could you possibly have her slightly earlier than we said? Like—ooh, I don't know, sort of, breakfast time?'

'Of course,' she agreed happily. 'Really, *any* time, Livvy.'

'Don't tempt me,' I said grimly.

I put the receiver down and noticed my hand was trembling. I stared. Well, it would, wouldn't it? I thought, regarding it with interest. After all, here I was, an ordinary housewife, coolly, coldly and calculatingly working out the perfect strategy to give the police the slip.

The following morning the alarm went off at ten to six. I sat bolt upright, felt a bit sick, couldn't think why—then remembered. I showered quickly, got dressed, and went to wake Claudia.

'Claudia. Claudes, wake up!' I shook her shoulder.

She turned bleary eyes on her clock. 'But it's only six o'clock!'

'Yes, but you're going to Lucy's, and I have to go to London today, remember? Remember I told you I was going, darling?'

'No,' she muttered, stumbling out to the loo. 'I don't.'

I left her to it and dashed downstairs to the kitchen. Seizing the calendar I wrote in bold felt pen *Shopping in London!*

Twenty minutes later, I was banging on Amanda Harper's mock-Georgian, twin-pillared front door. Claudia beside me, yawning and looking like a bag lady as she clutched her possessions in a Tesco's carrier she'd had to grab hastily as I'd hustled her out. Finally Amanda appeared in her dressing gown, hair on end, mascara down her cheeks.

'Oh! Livvy. Gosh, I didn't realise you meant sparrow's fart.'

'Amanda, I'm so sorry. I know it's terribly early,' I breathed, 'but I'm off to London today, been looking forward to it for ages. Shopping trip, you know.'

She rubbed her eyes. 'Blimey, at this hour? God, you'll be there in half an hour, there'll be so little traffic. I'm not sure the shops open at seven thirty, do they?'

'Ah, but I'll get a good parking place,' I beamed. 'I've been—'

'Looking forward to it for months,' said Claudia wearily, pushing past me with her arms full. 'She's lost it,' she informed Amanda as she went on past her and trudged upstairs to find Lucy.

Oh God, was I overdoing it? I wondered, as I fled back down the path. Making too much of a meal of it? That would look even more peculiar. I must calm down. Nevertheless, as I roared up the M1, an image of Alf, kneeling, and holding a blood-soaked Vi in his arms, would spring to mind and make me put my foot down in an attempt to distance myself.

As a result, I found myself in central London by seven forty-five along with all the early bird commuters. I parked in a Knightsbridge NCP, bought a paper, then had tea and toast in the Brompton Arcade. The minutes ticked by. I looked at my watch. Eight fifteen. Good grief, only eight fifteen!

I read the *Daily Mail* more minutely—from cover to cover, in fact—until I noticed that, according to the horoscope, Saturn was dominating my sphere and would undoubtedly be my downfall today. 'Don't expect to come up smelling of roses if you've deliberately deceived someone' it warned grimly. I put the paper down with quivering hands and, in an effort to calm down, I emptied the entire contents of my handbag onto the table and sorted it out methodically. This, in the event, was just as well, because it was during this little operation that a plan was hatched. You see, as I sorted around among the parking tickets, the sweetie wrappers and a very tired-looking tampon, there, nestling at the bottom of my handbag, I spotted two tickets to a concert at the Wigmore Hall.

I sat back and stared at them. Of course, Sebastian had sent them to Johnny and me and I must have stuffed them in my bag. I took a sip of tea, turning them over in my hand. Yes, why not? Why not, in fact, spend the entire day preparing for this very event? Why not go to the hairdresser's, buy a new dress to wear and then, looking drop-dead gorgeous swan off to the concert in the evening? Imogen would be there, of course, and naturally Sebastian would be there too . . .

I took another sip of tea. I hadn't allowed myself to think about

Sebastian yet, you see. Since Johnny had gone, I realised I'd mentally put Sebastian up on a high shelf so I couldn't reach him. Not out of my mind, because that was impossible, but out of reach, because that was where I knew him to be. But I missed the easy friendship we'd had and his downright niceness but, more than that, something in my heart ached for him too. If I allowed it. Mostly I didn't, but just occasionally I'd let it out of its cage, give myself a glimpse of him, at Hugh and Molly's maybe, his face creasing up with sudden mirth, or hauling a dripping Claudia out of the river, or just the two of us together, giggling as we threw Maureen's casserole in the bin . . .

I traced the gingham pattern on the café tablecloth sadly. I knew I'd blown it, you see. I realised that. I knew I'd always thought of Sebastian as a first reserve, a sort of—well, if Johnny doesn't come back then who knows? And I'd more or less said as much, hadn't I? Said, sorry, Seb, old boy, Johnny's back now, I'm afraid, so it's bye-bye and on yer bike, OK? Well, I could hardly turn round now and say—hey, guess what, great news! He's gone, so you're on again! Except that Johnny hadn't gone. I'd thrown him out. Surely that changed the whole complexion of the situation somewhat? And maybe if I explained that to Sebastian, maybe if I didn't ask for too much, no more than our familiar old friendship back, then perhaps—perhaps something deeper could develop.

Packing up my bag again, I felt relieved to have a plan. Something to cling to. Resolving to stick to it, I tottered to the counter to pay for four cups of tea and the toast, then embarked on my exhausting day.

As I trailed between Harrods and Harvey Nichols, filling in cancelled manicures here, and leg wax appointments there, it occurred to me to wonder how on earth French women managed it? All this beautifying? On a weekly basis? How very tiring, and how on earth did they find time to prick out their dahlias?

I finally ended up at the hairdresser's, with Marco, a drop-dead gorgeous blond, standing behind me. He gave a little sigh.

'So what are we doing today then?' he enquired in a bored little voice.

'We're doing sex and glamour,' I informed him firmly.

'Ambitious,' he murmured doubtfully, plucking sniffily at my split ends. 'But then again,' he murmured, 'I always like a challenge.' Pausing only to shriek imperiously, 'Cindy, a coffee for my lady, please!' he flexed his scissors and went to work with alacrity.

Well, I have to say that half an hour later, albeit with a frightening amount of hair on the floor and an exhausted Marco behind me, the end result wasn't half bad. He'd cut it short, shorter than I'd normally have it, but had given me a long and sexy fringe which flopped right down over one eye, and which I had to flick back if I wanted to see daylight.

'What am I supposed to do with this then?' I said, lifting it doubtfully.

He sighed. 'You're supposed to smoulder through it, darling.'

'Oh!' I dropped it. 'That's not a problem at all, watch.' I pouted kittenishly at him in the mirror.

'Scary,' he muttered drily.

I sailed out, feeling really rather sassy and pleased with myself. I kept catching glimpses of myself in the mirrors as I rode the Harvey Nicks escalators, and the effect was so gratifying, it gave me the confidence to sail straight into the hushed portals of the Donna Karan franchise and try on the first little black dress I came across. Yes, OK, it was a bit tight across the bottom and perhaps a bit short—sleeveless and backless too—but, boy, did it look terrific.

'I'll take it,' I said.

Outside, I hailed a taxi to take me to the other end of the Kings Road, where I was pretty sure the latest Hugh Grant film was showing, and where I was also pretty sure I could hole up for a couple of hours.

The first time I watched it I laughed, the second time I slept through it, and then when I awoke, some time later, it was five thirty. I looked at my watch and blinked. Perfect. I'd had a nice relaxing snooze, felt totally refreshed, and now I had precisely half an hour in which to go back to Harvey Nichols, monopolise the Ladies', put on my dress, fiddle with my fringe, apply make-up, and dump my clothes and shopping bags in the boot of the car.

I arrived at the concert early. There was no one else going in and I didn't want to be the first, so I pretended I was studying the programme, which was stuck up in a glass case like a restaurant menu.

'*Night of the Spirits* by Sebastian Faulkner; performed by the London Symphony Orchestra.'

I swallowed. Quite something, really, one way and another, to have one's work performed here. People appeared to be arriving in dribs and drabs now, and even going inside, so I crept in behind a hugely sartorial group, pulling my dress down a bit at the back.

I bought a programme on the basis that I could at least put it across my knees to hide some thigh, and then went into the hall, wondering nervously if Sebastian would be in the auditorium. I realised, with a little leap of pleasure, how excited I was about seeing him. I glanced around. He didn't appear to be about just yet, though, so I found my seat and perched on the edge, peering at the now gathering throng and looking for Imo.

It soon became clear that this was a very sophisticated London audience: they were all very much in the Ursula Mitchell mould, until I realised that one of them actually *was* Ursula Mitchell, and that a few paces behind her was her daughter, Imo. She looked stunning, in an ankle-length blue slip of a dress.

I kept my eyes trained on the group, watching closely as they made their way to the very front, then, seeing them cluster around some seats, murmuring excitedly, I left my chair and hastened down.

Ursula was holding forth in hushed tones to anyone who cared to listen, when she saw me appear. 'Olivia!' She turned in surprise.

Imo swung round. 'Good heavens—Livvy! What on earth are you doing here? How lovely!'

'I was in London, so I thought—why not?' I said, kissing them both.

'Why not indeed?' agreed Ursula, generously. 'And what fun! Tell me, is Johnny with you? You can't *imagine* how delighted I was when Imogen told me you were back together again. Oh, Simon! Lovely to see you!' She turned as someone approached.

'Well no, it's not good news, actually,' I grimaced to Imo. 'You see, we're apart again now.'

'No!' Imo clutched my arm in horror. 'Oh God, I don't believe it! Don't tell me the bastard did it to you again?'

'Noo,' I said slowly, 'actually, Imo, I did it to the bastard this time.' I smiled wryly. 'I just realised how appallingly badly I'd been treated by him, you see. It was almost as if I had to have him back to realise it. In the end I realised—well—I just realised I didn't love him enough to swallow it all, I suppose.'

'Really?' Imo looked startled. Bewildered even. 'Gosh. B-but, Livvy, surely now that you've got the upper hand—well, you can call the shots for a change, can't you? Be in the driving seat for once?'

'No,' I shook my head firmly, 'still wouldn't work, because you see I was in love with a dream. A fantasy Johnny, who just didn't exist. The *real* Johnny McFarllen was a weak, selfish, vain, manipulative man who—Oh, but don't get me on all that now, Imo,' I grinned. 'I'll tell you another time. What's more important now,' I lowered my voice excitedly, 'is that for the first time in years, I find myself seriously attracted to someone else. Someone who up to now—well, I've just been so blind to!'

She gazed into my bright, excited eyes. 'Who?'

I grinned. 'Sebastian.'

'Sebastian?'

'Yes, Sebastian. Oh, Imo, I *knew* he liked me and I was so stupid, I simply couldn't do anything about it until I'd got Johnny out of my—'

'Imogen—' Ursula suddenly put a hand on her daughter's arm.

'So sorry to interrupt, Livvy, my dear, but I'd just love Imo to meet Simon Allsop, the impresario, and this is absolutely her last chance. Hector!' She called loudly to her husband. 'Hector, darling, introduce

Imo to—' She pointed wildly to a man in a flamboyant red coat, then turned her daughter round and gave her a little push in their direction.

'Now.' Ursula turned back to me, smiling broadly. 'Olivia, did you say Sebastian, my dear?'

'Sorry?'

'Just now to Imo. About someone you were fond of?'

'Oh! Oh yes, that's right!'

'Well, good heavens, I must warn you, I really must.'

'What?'

'Well, Imogen is seeing Sebastian.'

I stared. 'Imogen's . . . what?'

'She's seeing Sebastian. They've been together for some time now, quite some time, and terribly in love. They're off to Vienna tomorrow, in fact. Sebastian has a performance out there.'

'But . . . she was seeing Hugo!' I felt panic fly through every vein.

'Oh, Hugo,' she interrupted impatiently. 'Heavens, he followed her everywhere, hung on her every word. No, no, Sebastian is eminently more suitable for Imo.' She smiled, raised her eyebrows confidentially. 'D'you know, I think I can confidently say that This Is It, Olivia.'

I gazed into the grey eyes beaming down at me. But what about me? I wanted to say. Surely I found him first?

She put a hand on my arm as if reading my thoughts. 'Olivia, I've known you for many years, since you were a little girl, in fact. I'd hate to see you make a fool of yourself.'

'I have no intention of doing that.'

'Good, because I feel I must warn you that this time you'd be out of your depth. This time you're in an entirely different league.'

'What d'you mean, *this time*?'

Her sharp grey eyes went cold. 'I mean this time, as opposed to last time. When you crept in and took Johnny right from under her nose.'

I stared at her, aghast. 'I did *not*!' I managed to gasp. 'God—how can you *say* that? Imogen finished with Johnny, she—'

'Oh, she cooled it with him, all right,' she said impatiently, 'but she was just testing him. She wanted to marry Johnny, you see, and we all knew that. Frankly I'm surprised you didn't, or perhaps you chose not to, hmm?' She pursed her lips as I gazed, horrified at her. 'For a long time, too, I'd felt that Johnny had had the upper hand in the relationship, so I suggested she make him jealous, make him see that there were other men besides him who were attracted to her, see what his reaction would be. And he reacted pretty well, I must say. He even trekked all the way out to Italy to get her back, and I was impressed. I thought that she'd have him begging to marry her.' Her eyes hardened. 'But I hadn't reckoned on you, Olivia. Hadn't reckoned on your part in the tale. Because then you appeared on the scene, didn't you? You, with your green fingers and your broken home, winding yourself like bindweed around a brokenhearted Johnny.'

'Mrs Mitchell!' I gasped. 'You're rewriting history! He was devastated about Imo, sure, but he was equally adamant he wouldn't have her back, not after what she'd done!'

She smiled. 'Oh no. *You* persuaded him he was adamant he wouldn't have her back. You played on a vulnerable young man, Olivia, a man whose girlfriend was conveniently studying abroad and whose father had just died. It was calculated, and very, very shrewd, I'll give you that.'

I gazed at her, aghast. My God. All these years she'd harboured this bitterness, considered me the fly in the ointment. And Imo too? But I'd asked Imo, I'd cleared it with her when Johnny and I had first—

'I *asked* Imo. I wrote to her in Florence, got a letter back saying—'

'Oh yes, and that was clever of you too, wasn't it?' she sneered. 'You knew she'd give you the all clear. She even came back from Italy to be your bridesmaid, and I'll never forgive you for that because the following day the poor child nearly had a breakdown.'

I caught my breath in horror. Her face was taut with pent-up loathing. 'My precious girl,' she breathed, 'you did that to her. And she never found anyone like Johnny.' She raised her chin high. 'But she has now, you see. She's all right now. She can be whole again—Sebastian's seen to that. They're in love, Olivia, very much in love, and I'm not going to ask you not to interfere, because this time, you can't. No one could possibly come between them now.'

I stared at her jutting jaw and her hawklike nose which seemed to be almost quivering with rage, just as Imogen came rushing up.

'Mummy! Are you all right? You . . . you look so upset!'

Ursula raised a brave chin. 'I'm fine,' she whispered. 'I was just explaining something very fundamental to Olivia here.'

She held my eyes a moment longer, then turned and walked away.

The orchestra were ready on the stage now, tuning up, anticipating the appearance of their conductor. Imo stared after Ursula, then shot me a confused, anxious glance, before hastening to her mother. I watched them go, transfixed, literally welded to the spot by the ferocity of Ursula's words. A moment later, I saw Sebastian materialise from a side door. He glanced about at the audience, then, seeing Imo at the front, quickly walked across to join her as she stood, comforting her mother. I watched as he lightly touched Imo's back and kissed her cheek.

What is it, what's wrong? I saw Imo ask her mother. Ursula began to speak but I couldn't hear what she was saying, could only watch

Sebastian's face grow darker, more concerned, more—angry. Imo's eyes widened, her jaw dropped, then they both turned and stared in my direction. There was a brief moment when we all locked eyes. Then they turned away, back to Ursula. I saw Sebastian put a hand under her elbow for support, and as she gravely nodded to them both that she was fine, fine now, they helped her into her seat.

The orchestra had gone very quiet and the audience were hushed with anticipation, with only the odd muffled cough punctuating the silence. Imo sat down next to her mother with Sebastian beside her. Realising suddenly that I was the only person in the hall left standing, I turned and made my way shakily back to my place at the rear of the auditorium. A moment later, Hugo Simmonds took the podium to an enormous roar from the crowd. I sat, dazed and bewildered, watching blankly as he acknowledged the audience, then turning his back on them, he raised his arms, brought them down with a flourish, and with a blast of trumpets and horns, the symphony began. I looked down and realised my programme was shaking on my knees. I must have listened to three, maybe four bars of the symphony, before getting up, gathering my bag and my programme, and leaving the hall.

I don't remember hailing a taxi, or even arriving at the car park, and somehow, dazedly, finding my car. I do remember the drive home, though. I remember how I had to keep a really firm grip on the wheel to stop my hands from shaking and the car from veering into another lane. But if my body was having problems reacting properly, my mind was compensating by going into overdrive. Imo and Sebastian—of course. God, what a fool I'd been! It was him she'd been angling for all along, not Hugo. Cosy dinner parties at her parents' house, all no doubt arranged by her Svengali, Ursula, and then yesterday—why, I even *saw* Imo, alone, going into his house. Why hadn't I clicked? And of course, she'd been so thrilled when Johnny and I got back together, coming round with flowers, hugging us, tears of relief in her eyes: 'Oh God, guys, this is what we've all been hoping for!' Well, of course it was.

So—how long had it been going on? While he'd been seeing me? If indeed he *had* been seeing me, I thought with a jolt, because actually, in *his* eyes he probably hadn't, which would explain his reluctance to comply when I offered him my body on a plate after Molly and Hugh's barbecue, and his bemused expression when I popped round later to inform him that our tempestuous affair was over. No wonder he'd looked surprised. As far as he was concerned I was Mrs Friendly Neighbour with whom he had the occasional matey drink when he wasn't canoodling with his main squeeze, Imogen Mitchell! 'Don't make a fool of yourself,' Ursula had said. Well, it was too late for that. I'd been doing it for thirteen years.

Yes, thirteen years ago, I thought with a wave of misery, when Imo had apparently decided she wanted to marry Johnny, but unlike me, had known she had to bring a man like Johnny to his knees, at which point she'd have tossed her blonde head, and had him right where she wanted him. Except that she hadn't reckoned on me.

I gritted my teeth and breathed hard. And I'd never been enough for him, never—I saw that now. He'd always wanted more, needed more, and so he'd turned to Nina. It wouldn't have happened if he'd married Imo—she was more than enough for any man—and now, because of me, because of my pathetic eagerness to have him at any cost, there was carnage all around. Broken marriages, mistresses, thwarted love affairs and at the heart of it all, a small, fatherless, disabled boy. My heart lurched. My fault. All of my making.

When I finally pulled up in my drive, I turned off the engine and sat for a moment reliving Sebastian's face as he'd turned to look at me. Shock and disbelief seemed to be the overriding emotion in those dark eyes. So what had Ursula said? I rested my head back wearily on the headrest, and it was at that moment that I realised I wasn't alone.

Just round the corner of the house, in the little carport that no one ever used, was a blue Escort, I think, and it occurred to me that I didn't know anyone who drove a car as middle-aged as that. Why yes, of course, I realised with a start, it belonged to the protagonists in the *other* disastrous chapter in my life, the chapter which had clearly been unfolding relentlessly in my absence. The jolly old police. Oh good. More music to face, and why not? Might as well get it all over in one day; might as well face a symphony as a string quartet.

I got out and slammed the door hard, rehearsing, slightly defiantly in my head: Why, yes, officer, I'm well aware that one of my work force recently knocked off his wife, but seeing as it was a complete and utter accident I decided to give him a day's grace to get away. You see I—

'*Ahhh!*'

I leapt inches in the air as someone stepped out of the shadow of the hedge and caught my arm from behind. Terrified, I swung round.

'Lance!'

'Shhhh!' He put his hand gently over my mouth, glancing quickly about to check I hadn't been heard.

Wide-eyed I stared at him, then nodded to let him know I wasn't going to shriek again. Slowly, he took his hand away.

'What's going on?' I gasped. 'What's happened?'

'I'm waiting for Spiro,' he whispered. 'The police should be back with him any minute. I don't want them to know I'm still here.'

'Spiro?'

'Yes, poor bastard, he's down at the station. They took him there this morning. He's been there all day, being questioned.'

'Oh God! And you too?'

'Most of the day, but they let me out a couple of hours ago.'

'Did they want to speak to me?' I whispered fearfully.

'Yes, but only as a formality, so they said, and certainly not as desperately as they wanted to speak to us,' he added drily.

'But,' I glanced back at the house, confused, 'why is Spiro down there? I mean, if they're up here—'

'Who?'

I jerked my head. 'Isn't that their car?'

He stared, then clicked. 'Oh no, that's your mother-in-law. I let her in.'

'My—'

'Livvy? Is that you, darling?'

The front door opened and Angie stood there framed, shading her eyes in the gathering gloom.

'Good God, does *she* know anything about all this?' I hissed, appalled.

'Of course not,' he hissed back. 'What d'you take me for? No, by all accounts she just came round to discuss the state of your marriage.'

'Oh terrific,' I groaned.

'Livvy, is that you?' she called again.

'Go on.' Lance gave me a little shove. 'Go in and act naturally, for heaven's sake. I'll let you know when Spiro gets back.'

He slunk back to his position behind the hedge. I raked a despairing hand through my hair. God, Angie. She was all I needed right now, but then again she was preferable to the police. I trudged dismally up the path and kissed her on the doorstep.

'Angie, I didn't recognise your car.'

'It's a hire car, darling. I pranged the last one. And the bloody door leaks like a sieve so I have to put it under some shelter when I park. Good gracious, you look all in! Come in and I'll make you a stiff gin and tonic. Are you feeling all right?'

'Period pains,' I said weakly, and not untruthfully. 'But I'll take you up on that gin,' I said following her in and collapsing into the nearest armchair. 'It's the best offer I've had all day.'

She bustled off to the kitchen and I rested my head back and gazed blankly at the ceiling. So, Spiro was, at this very moment, being grilled rotten in some cold grey interview room, was he? I wondered when they'd be back for me. I shut my eyes and rubbed my forehead wearily, Angie reappeared with two large gins. She handed me one and I took a large gulp as she settled herself opposite. Her face wore an anxious look.

'Livvy darling, I know what you're up to,' she said, finally.

'Oh?' I blinked. Crikey, I wish I did.

'With Johnny. I know the game you're playing.'

'I'm not playing any game.'

'Yes, you are, and you've played it brilliantly, quite brilliantly. But listen, darling—he's desperate. You've brought him comprehensively to heel now, brought him right back into line, so don't make him suffer any more, eh? He so badly needs to come home.'

I frowned. 'So—he's with you?'

'Of course he's with me, where did you think he'd be?'

'Well, funnily enough, Angie,' I said slowly, 'I had a sneaking suspicion he might be with another woman. The woman who, actually, was the initial *cause* of my throwing him out.'

'Oh her,' she said dismissively. 'No, no, that's all finished. He's over her now, and that's all thanks to you, my dear. Golly, you've really brought him to his senses, my love, and it was absolutely what he needed. But . . . I'm worried now.' Her well-preserved forehead puckered with anxiety and she clasped her hands tight. 'I'm worried that if you leave him in the wilderness any longer your plan might backfire, that he may find some other distraction.'

I swirled my drink thoughtfully in my glass. Frowned into it. 'But . . . I just told you, Angie. It's not a game. I don't want him back. Ever.'

I looked up and met her hazel eyes. Saw a wave of hurt pass over them. I steeled myself.

'D'you have any idea what he's done?'

She nodded quickly, swept her hair back nervously. 'I—I know about the child,' she admitted quickly.

'And *you'd* forgive him?'

'Yes,' she nodded. 'Yes, I know I'd find it in my heart.'

'Would you? Really, Angie?'

'Oh, for God's sake, Livvy, grow up!' she snapped. 'Women have put up with infidelity for centuries! Johnny's not exactly the first oversexed man who went off to relieve himself elsewhere!'

I stared into her eyes. Slowly it dawned. 'You mean . . .?'

'Oh, yes.' She smiled thinly. 'Yes, for years.'

I stared, incredulous. 'But . . . you and Oliver. You were so happy!'

'Exactly.'

'But—'

'Happiness doesn't necessarily conform to the storybooks, Olivia,' she said impatiently. 'We *were* happy, genuinely happy, but we'd ironed out our own *modus vivendi*, not one decreed to us, laid down by society.'

'But didn't you care? About the affairs?'

'Of course! Desperately, at first. But, in time, I also began to realise that actually, his affairs had no bearing on me, were no reflection on our marriage at all. He loved me, you see, adored me, probably even more so at the height of each adulterous liaison than at any other time. Physically, too, that side of our marriage never died.'

'So, then why did he need them? Why did he need those women!'

She shrugged. 'Different, I suppose, so therefore exciting. Different women—different sort of sex too, if you know what I mean.'

'But how could he face you? Wasn't he mortified? Ashamed?'

'Oh, totally, but that was his problem. He was riddled with guilt.'

'And . . . is that why . . .?' I asked softly.

She swallowed. Shook her head. 'No. Well, yes. Yes and no, really. It wasn't *why* he did it, but shooting himself was a direct result of his infidelity. There was a baby, you see.'

'Oh!'

'Only one. When I found out that this particular woman was pregnant, suddenly it all made sense. I realised why Oliver was walking endlessly round his paddocks in the early hours, why I'd find him weeping on the bathroom floor, why, on one occasion, he even tried to tell me.' She took a large swig of gin; stared into space.

'So,' I cleared my throat, 'so when the child was born, is that what pushed him over the edge?'

'No. When the child was born,' she said carefully, 'Oliver was all right. It was as if the inevitable had finally happened and the pressure was off. He didn't know I knew, of course, but I watched him carefully as the days went by, very carefully, and I was relieved. But then the terrible news came that all was not well. That the baby was severely disabled. Blind as well as crippled. That evening Oliver went out into the field and blew his brains out. He blamed himself, you see, thought that his sins had been singled out for retribution, and been manifested in his son. My God, you've gone so pale, Livvy. I've shocked you.'

I was on my feet now. 'No, no . . .' I crossed to the window, my hand clutching the sill, trembling. Disabled. Like Johnny's child. I swallowed.

'Have you seen Johnny's baby?' I whispered, staring at the lawn.

'Of course not, and neither shall I,' she said staunchly.

'And—' I cleared my throat—'and, Angie, does Johnny know all this? About his father? About how the baby was?' I turned.

She shook her head. 'No one knows. I prided myself on that.' Suddenly Oliver's words came back to me, that night, that last party at the McFarllens', Tara's birthday party, as he and I stood by the pool, watching Johnny and his sisters swim. 'Perfect, aren't they?' he'd said. I shivered. I cleared my throat. 'I wouldn't tell Johnny about his father, Angie, wouldn't disillusion him. To him, Oliver was a god. Let him at least hang on to that memory unscathed.'

If anything could completely destroy Johnny, I thought, this surely would. Like dysfunctional father, like dysfunctional son. And I didn't hate him enough to want him to know himself and his father for what they really were.

We were silent for a while, Angie and I. I thought of little Peter and his struggle through life. Perhaps Johnny would go back to them? How odd that I didn't care; quite wished he would.

'What happened to Oliver's child, what became of him?'

'Oh, he lived, but other than that, I don't know. His mother was one of the few of his women I ever actually met though.'

'She was a friend?'

'No, no, not a friend.' She gave a wry smile. 'Oliver was not susceptible to our own class. Only the lower orders brought out the beast in him. No, her husband mended Oliver's cars. They had a vintage car place in Finchley, and I had to take one of Oliver's Lagondas in for him once. I saw her there.' She frowned. 'Livvy, what is it?'

I'd crossed to the French windows, shot back the bolts and flung them wide despite the rain. I stood there, letting the cool breeze gust into my face, blowing back my hair. 'Nothing.' I shook my head. 'Nothing, Angie.'

Oh God. Oh *God*. I remembered the faded blonde prettiness of Nina's mother. The kindly, no doubt unsuspecting father who'd believed he'd fathered the crippled, unseeing lad whose chair I'd seen. Nina's brother. Martin. Oliver's child. Feeling quite faint now, I gulped down great gusts of air. Angie was behind me, her hand on my shoulder.

'What is it, darling, what's wrong?'

'Nothing,' I murmured, 'nothing at all. It's all in the past.'

And if it remained Angie's intention to have nothing to do with Johnny's child, then that's where it would stay, I thought as I shut the doors again and bolted them.

At length, I found my voice. 'Angie, please tell Johnny from me, that I'll be serving him with divorce papers just as soon as I've contacted my solicitor. Tell him that access to Claudia will of course be amicably arranged, and that I also intend to sell the house and move further away into the country. You can also tell him that—'

'Olivia, you don't mean this! You're upset, I've upset you with all this talk of Oliver! Think it over, please. You'll regret acting hastily, I swear it! This is *Johnny* we're talking about. He's worth more that that, he's—Oh!'

At that moment there was a loud bang, as the front door flew open on its hinges. A great gust of wind billowed through the house, and then a moment later, two bodies lurched through, like a couple of desperate souls reaching their journey's end. Staggering down the hallway came Lance, looking wet and bedraggled, and supporting someone I almost didn't recognise. With his black hair mussed all over his face, eyes wild and staring, one arm slung round Lance's shoulder and dragging his feet like a dead man—was Spiro.

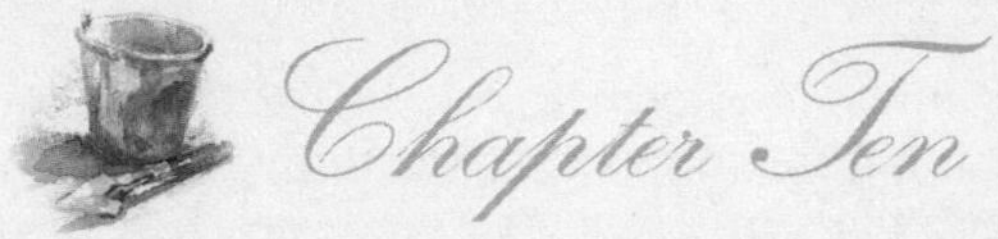

Chapter Ten

'SPIRO!' I RAN TO THEM.

Lance, panting, dragged Spiro to the nearest chair and deposited him heavily, whereupon Spiro put his head in his hands and wept.

'Good heavens, what on earth's happened to the poor boy? Livvy, what's wrong with him!' Angie wrung her hands.

'Nothing, he's fine,' said Lance shortly. 'He's just upset, that's all.'

'Lance is right,' I said quickly as Lance shot me a meaningful glance and jerked his head towards the door. I picked up Angie's handbag and took her by the arm, propelling her doorwards. 'He's absolutely fine, Angie,' I said firmly, 'really he is, but sadly—well, sadly he's had some bad news. From home.'

As I hustled her out and down the drive I had one ear on Lance behind me, listening as he placated a distraught Spiro.

Angie shook her head sadly, groping about in her bag for her keys. 'That poor boy,' she sighed, shaking her head and suddenly looking very old. 'There just seems to be so much sadness about at the moment, doesn't there?' She hesitated. Glanced up hopefully. 'Will I—will I say anything else to Johnny? Give him a few words?'

'Yes,' I said grimly, 'you can give him a few words. Give him—' I stopped, ashamed, as her eyes grew round and fearful. 'Just—give him my best,' I finished lamely.

She nodded, and I saw her eyes fill. 'You know, Livvy, sad as I am about this whole wretched situation, about losing you, I admire you for what you've done. Truly I do. I couldn't have done it.' We regarded each other for a long moment.

'You haven't lost me,' I whispered.

She gave a grateful smile, nodded again, turned, and got in the car. I watched as she reversed out of the carport, turned out of the gateway, and waved as she purred off slowly down the road. Then I stood for a moment, remembering. Remembering happier times, long ago, when we'd gardened together up to our knees in brambles and—

'*Livvy—get in here!*' Lance's voice came roaring through my memories, and abruptly I came to. Oh Christ—Spiro!

I dashed back into the house. Slamming the door behind me, I hurtled to the sitting room where I found Spiro, being violently sick into a potted plant.

'Oh, help—hang on. I'll get him some water.' I took the pot, hustled it to the loo, couldn't face chucking it in, so just shut the door on it, then ran back via the kitchen to get a glass of water. As I flew back in, Spiro reached out and took it with a shaky hand. I dropped to my knees beside him and took his hand, appalled.

'Spiro, what did they *do* to you in there!' I gasped.

'They didn't *do* anything to him,' said Lance drily, lighting a cigarette and perching on the arm of the chair. 'This isn't Occupied France, you know, Livvy; we're not living with the Gestapo. They just questioned him, that's all, frightened the life out of him, I expect. I don't know what they said to him actually, he hasn't uttered a word yet.'

I squeezed Spiro's hand. 'Spiro, it's me, Livvy. What happened?'

Suddenly he sat up bolt upright, his dark eyes wide and strange. His head turned slowly—and his gaze fell on Lance.

'I so sorry!' he blurted out, staring at him.

Lance frowned, shook his head. 'Why, Spiro? Why are you sorry?'

'Because—because they go on and on, questions, questions, and I know nothing of what they speak, but then—then I theenk of something, and—' He broke off, gave a strangled sob, hid his face in his hat.

'What?' Lance insisted. 'What, Spiro?'

Spiro lowered his hat. 'I theenk I let the rabbit out of the bag!'

'Cat.'

'*Ti?*'

'Never mind. What rabbit, Spiro, what did you say?'

He glanced about furtively. 'They want the body!' he hissed.

I jumped back. 'The body!' I yelped.

'I know,' said Lance calmly, 'that's what they kept asking me. Where was she, where was she buried, what have they done with Vi? But we don't know that, do we, Spiro? I don't, so you certainly don't.'

'No, I don't, but they keep saying—theenk, Spiro, where could she be? Where you theenk they could have put her? What were Mac and Alf doing at the time, in those few days of her death?'

'Well, they were working here,' I said staunchly, 'that's what!'

Spiro turned to me and nodded, wide eyes full of portent.

I stared at him. 'Shit!' I squeaked suddenly, leaping to my feet.

'And the bald man, he say *th-e-e-nk*, Spiro, *th-e-e-nk*. Was there not a day when you sent elsewheres? And I theenk, and slowly, *very* slowly, I say, yes, yes there *was* such a day, because I remember Lance, that day when we have so much to do, so very busy, and we both surprised, because Mac—he send us both to builders' merchant for bricks, remember, Lance? Remember what Mac and Alf have to do all alone here on that day?'

Lance had gone very pale. 'I do.'

'And I hadn't theenk of it before, but the police, they griddle me, griddle me something rotten, and I say it without even theenking and—'

'What!' I gasped. 'What did you say? What were Alf and Mac doing?'

Spiro went quiet. Glanced down at his hands.

'It's all right, Spiro,' said Lance softly. 'I thought of it too. Not before, but when they were questioning me, down at the station. It suddenly occurred to me, too. I could just as easily have said it.'

'*What?*' I shrieked. 'What could you just as easily have said? Tell me, you bastards, or I'll—Christ!'

I broke off as a terrible banging came on the door. We all swung around—then stared back at each other. I froze.

'They're here,' I breathed. 'It's them.'

Spiro whimpered, got up from his chair and backed away into a corner. Lance didn't move.

'Open it, Livvy.'

I nodded and went to the door, holding my side now where the stomach cramps and the shock were searing through me, making me feel light-headed as my hand went up to the latch. I swung it back. Sure enough, the bald-headed man in his raincoat and his blonde accomplice, in her shiny suit, were neatly ranged on my doorstep. But this time, they weren't alone. Behind them stood two much larger men, wearing blue overalls and carrying tool bags, and behind them stood a couple of uniformed policemen, too. Six, in all.

'Yes?' I breathed.

'Mithith McFarllen,' Raincoat lisped, 'tho thorry to bother you, but we have here a warrant to thearch your houthe and garden.' He quickly flashed a piece of plastic at me, eyes pale and watchful.

I felt both hot and faint. 'A-any . . . particular reason?' I faltered.

'Oh, yeth. For the very particular reathon that we believe the body of Mithith Violet Turner to be buried here.' He kept his eyes on me.

'I see,' I gulped. 'And did you have a particular corner of my beloved, much-treasured home or garden in mind for excavation, officer?'

'Yeth,' he said softly, slowly making his way past me in the direction of the kitchen, 'yeth, we do have a particular corner in mind.' He stopped, just beyond me, in the doorway. 'You thee we believe, Mithith McFarllen, that she'th embedded in concrete.'

'*Concrete!*'

'Yeth, or to be more prethithe, in a concrete plinth commonly built to thupport a heavy, free-thtanding, catht-iron, range.' He turned to face me in the doorway. 'In fact it'th our belief, Mithith McFarllen, that Violet Turner ith buried underneath your thtove.'

I gaped. 'My . . . thtove?'

'Your Aga, Mithith McFarllen.'

I jumped, then stared incredulously past Raincoat to my new kitchen. To my shiny pride and joy at the far end of the room, surrounded as it was by Portuguese tiles, with its pine shelf above brimming with pretty plates, antique jugs and Mary Berry cookbooks; where I stood every day, frying the bacon, prodding Claudia's fish fingers, contentedly cradling a mug of coffee, chatting on the phone . . . and all the time . . . yes, all the time, stretched out beneath it, face-up perhaps, hands clasped across her bosom, or maybe in a black bin liner, eyes shut, or possibly even wide and staring . . .

As the dawn came up, I gasped in horror as a stab of pain seared straight through my abdomen. My hand clutched at my stomach, and I had white lights flashing before my eyes. My ears roared, my brain sizzled, as with a gasp of 'Shit!' I collapsed insensible at Raincoat's feet.

'Best thing you could have done,' said Hugh, dunking a soldier into his son Henry's boiled egg.

'What?' I raised my head feebly from their breakfast table.

'Faint like that, last night. Makes it so convincing, so much more obvious that you had nothing to do with it.'

'She didn't have anything to do with it,' snapped Molly, opening her dressing gown and clamping Flora firmly onto her left bosom.

'No, all I'm saying is that when the police rang and asked us to come and get her, it looked pretty good,' said Hugh. 'You were still out for the count, Livvy, flat out on a sofa, whereas poor old Lance and Spiro were shifting about pretty nervously, I can tell you.'

'I still don't quite understand how they came to ring you,' I said.

'Apparently Lance suggested us when the police said they wanted you out of there,' said Hugh. 'Presumably they couldn't cope with you doing the dying swan all over the place when they had a house to excavate and a body to exhume.'

'Macabre,' shuddered Molly. 'And to think you'd been *cooking* there, Livvy, and all that time she was—'

'Oooh, stop it!' I moaned. 'I really don't know how Alf and Mac could have *done* that to me!'

'Well, to be fair, Liv, they never meant for you to find out,' said Hugh, reasonably. 'Rather an apt ending, I feel, for a harridan of a housewife. Back to her roots, as it were?' His eyes gleamed. 'And it gives a whole new dimension to the old Aga saga, eh?'

Molly gave an exasperated little cry and put Flora over her shoulder to wind her. 'And what about those two bastards who dropped you in all this? Mac the knife and Alf the half-wit? Where are they while all this drama unfolds? On the Marrakesh Express or something?'

'I don't know,' I sighed, 'and, Molly, I know it sounds crazy, but they weren't really bastards. Just a couple of hard-working guys who got caught up in a horrific domestic drama and then—well, then did the wrong thing. Ran, instead of facing up to it.'

'All the best murders happen like that,' observed Hugh, sagely, wiping Henry's eggy mouth. 'Ninety per cent are committed within the family, which makes a copper's job something of a doddle really.'

'So why do they still want to speak to me then?' I said, suddenly fearful. 'If it all hinges on the family, why ring me here, at the crack of dawn this morning, and ask me to present myself down at the station!'

'Just routine they said, remember?' soothed Molly. 'Nothing to worry about. What time did they say they wanted to see you?'

'Ten o'clock,' I said, glancing at the clock.

'D'you want me to come with you?' She squeezed my hand.

I shook my head. Gulped. 'No, I'll—be fine. You've got Flora to see to.'

'Well, Hugh's not doing anything today. He could easily take you.'

'No, no really, I'm sure you're right,' I said quickly. 'I'm sure it's nothing to worry about.' I wasn't sure I could cope with Hugh wisecracking his way to the police station, because suddenly I felt very scared. I wished I could just hole up here in Molly and Hugh's chaotic kitchen.

'So what happens next?' said Molly softly, as if reading my thoughts.

I grimaced. 'You mean, what am I going to do?'

She nodded.

'Well, sell the house, of course.'

'Of course,' she agreed.

'And move, I suppose, but God knows where. I'll have to decide soon, though, because Claudia's term starts in September.' I hauled myself out of the cosy Windsor chair. 'Right now, though, I have to gird my loins for my chat with Shiny Suit and Raincoat. Perhaps it'll be Pentonville for me, with Claudia on visiting rights.'

'Don't be silly. It's quite obvious you were just an innocent bystander,' Molly protested. Nevertheless, I noticed, rather nervously, that they both followed me to the door and that Molly had her arm round my shoulders when we got there.

'You're both welcome to stay here as long as you like, you know that, don't you?' Molly gave me a squeeze. 'Whatever it takes.'

'Thanks.' I forced a smile. 'But it'll only be a few days. We wouldn't want to cramp your style.'

'We don't have a style,' announced Hugh loftily, sticking his chest out. 'Makes life so much simpler.'

'Speak for yourself,' muttered Molly. 'I wouldn't mind a bit of style.'

'Nonsense, my dear, you're totally à la mode as you are, modelling for us this morning this season's must-have basic, the cheesy dressing gown with baby puke down one shoulder and—Oops! There she goes again!' He caught Flora's sickly projection and grabbed Molly's muslin to mop it up as the baby proceeded to do another mouthful.

'She keeps doing this,' said Molly anxiously. 'I keep waiting for her to take aim and get my mother in the face, like Henry used to.'

'Well, I can't see this little angel doing anything as gross as that,' I said fondly, stroking her daughter's cheek.

'She's going to be a stunner,' Hugh said.

'And talking of stunners,' Molly rearranged Flora and looked me in the eye, 'I heard about Imo.'

'Ah.' I scuffed my toe on the doormat. 'That.'

'Flaming cheek!' she said hotly. 'You were well in there first!'

Hugh cringed. 'Well In There? Is that how you speak of us men?'

I sighed. 'Yes, but while I was making up my mind, Moll, Imo saw a gap and went for it. And who can blame her?' I added ruefully.

'Saw a gap and . . .? Good heavens,' gasped Hugh faintly, clutching the door frame for support. 'We're just a mere line of traffic now, are we? With gaps! Whatever happened to romance?'

'What indeed?' I agreed ruefully. Suddenly I felt like Flora: I wanted to be sick all over someone's shoulder.

'Livvy?' Molly was watching me anxiously. I forced a bright smile.

'Bye then. Wish me luck in the cells.' I made towards my car, which Molly had driven back last night when I'd been in Hugh's.

'Good luck!' they chorused. 'As if you're going to need it,' added Molly scornfully.

In the event, they were right, I didn't. Down at the city police station Raincoat was conspicuous by his absence, and since I'd clocked him as being the more dynamic of the duo, I relaxed when I discovered that Shiny Suit was going to interview me alone. As I followed her into a little grey room, sat down and regurgitated all I knew, I could tell by her demeanour that she was only going through the motions.

'So why on earth didn't you come straight in and report to us the moment you knew she was dead!'

'I was scared,' I admitted, with more than an element of truth. 'I knew I should have done, but I'd never been involved in anything like this before. What Mac and Alf told me terrified me. I shot off to London like a bat out of hell, but while I was there I realised I'd done completely the wrong thing,' I added quickly.

'Did you indeed?' she snorted doubtfully. 'You know, of course, that I could throw the book at you for sheltering known criminals and withholding crucial evidence?'

I nodded dumbly.

She sighed wearily. Closed her file. 'But under the circumstances,' she said, 'I think it's fair to say you've probably been through the mill enough. It's not every day you find a corpse under your cooker.'

I gulped. Too true. 'Thank you,' I whispered gratefully.

'We will, of course, get them, though,' she added, fixing me beadily. 'Your chums, Mac and Alf. There's no question of that.'

'Of course,' I agreed, wishing she hadn't called them 'my chums'.

'So.' She folded her arms and gave me a thin, professional smile. 'I imagine you're free to go.'

I sprang to my feet. 'Thank you!'

'Provided,' she warned, 'that you don't wander too far afield. We will need you later on to give evidence and I don't want to find you've skipped the country or anything dramatic.' She got up and opened the door for me. 'Your house has been put back pretty much in apple-pie order, you'll be pleased to hear. Forensics have been in and out already. She frowned. 'I'm not sure the cooker is fully operational, though, but other than that,' she flashed me a wintry smile, 'you wouldn't even know we'd been there!'

I managed a tremulous smile in return and even muttered a thank you before scurrying away. Wouldn't even know they'd been there? I thought, bug-eyed with horror as I sped down the corridor in the direction of the free world. Excuse me, but I think I would. Oh, I'd know all right. I'd know every time I lifted the hob to put the kettle on, every time I bent down to take the roast chicken out of the oven. Bloody hell! I wouldn't stay in that house now if you *paid* me, I thought, barging through some swing doors.

Once in the car park, though, all thoughts of anything other than the fact that I was a free woman paled into insignificance as I threw myself with relief into my familiar old, boiling-hot sauna of a car. Free. Thank

God. I gave myself a little shake and started the engine, then realised, with a jolt, that I didn't know where the hell I was going. I turned it off again. Frowned. Right. So, Livvy. Here you are on your own again. I bit my lip. And what now? Where to? Long term I had absolutely no idea, but more immediately . . . I narrowed my eyes, frowned into the middle distance, then started the engine again. Yes, yes, I *did* know, actually. Knew exactly where I was going. It had to be Orchard House. Let's face it, at some point I had to go back because Claudia and I had no clothes at all at Molly's—as it was I was wearing a skirt of Molly's to avoid climbing into the disastrous Donna Karan number—so I may as well go and get it over with. I was due to pick Claudes up from Lucy's this afternoon and if the poor child had neither a father, nor a home to come back to now, she should at least have a clean pair of knickers.

With a gathering sense of dread I turned left into The Crescent and I couldn't help driving very, very slowly and peering up at Sebastian's house. His car wasn't outside so I knew he wasn't in, and for some reason all the shutters were closed. It looked shut up, as if he'd gone away for some length of time, too. Was he in London? I wondered. Living at Imogen's, maybe? I gritted my teeth and pulled up outside Orchard House.

I sat for a moment, drumming my fingers on the wheel, steeling myself, and not relishing this little visit one iota. Finally, telling myself not to be stupid—it wasn't as if she was *there* any more, was it?—I got out, opened the barn doors, and marched up to the front door. Studiously avoiding the kitchen, from which I reasoned I needed precisely nothing, I nipped upstairs, humming maniacally to calm my nerves. Once there, I dragged a large suitcase out from under a bed and, working quickly, emptied all of Claudia's drawers into it, not forgetting a few books, her jewellery case, her schoolwork, and a much-loved blue rabbit. Then I ran across the landing into my own room, did exactly the same, lugged the almost exploding suitcase heavily back downstairs, dragged it across the gravel, through the barn doors, and heaved it up into the boot of the car. I slammed it shut. There. I brushed off my hands and stared back at the house. Now. Anything else? I paused. And as I did, a lump came to my throat. My garden. My precious, beloved, glorious garden. I could quite happily leave the house, but the garden—oh, I had to say goodbye.

I went back inside the house, walked into the sitting room and opened the French windows. Flinging them wide, I wandered sadly outside. Around the terrace, stone urns tumbled with white pelargoniums, hostas and variegated ivy, and in the surrounding beds, day lilies and Michaelmas daisies jostled for position while lamb's-lettuce crawled towards my feet over the mellow York stones. The lavender path ahead was humming with bees and above it, arches of heavy, tumbling climbers—Albertine, Madame Alfred Carrière and my lovely, lusty Rambling Rector—nodded invitingly to me in the breeze. Dredging up a great sigh from the soles of my feet, I ducked under it for the last time. It brought a lump to my throat to think there'd be no one out here with the hose at seven o'clock as usual tonight, seeing them through this dry spell, giving them just a few more days of precious growth.

Down the yellowing lawn I wandered, my skirt brushing the fragrant brooms, shading my eyes to the stream, to the glorious cedar tree, spreading its branches to give a cool blanket of shade beneath. I gazed across the stream to the caravan. Still there, of course, I thought wryly, except that—blimey—hang on, no—it was off! The bloody thing was moving! There was a car attached to it. I ran down towards the water's edge to watch, but just then the car stopped. Somebody got out, slammed the door, and walked round to peer down at the caravan's wheels, checking to see if they were stuck. I stopped. Lance.

'Lance!' My hand shot up in delight.

He turned, shaded his eyes, then waved. 'Livvy!'

I grinned and ran, picking my way across the rickety bridge.

'Are you all right? I tried to ring you at Molly's but she said you'd gone,' Lance asked.

I nodded. 'I'm fine now, absolutely fine, it was just—well, it was just such a shock, Lance.'

'Well, quite. It's not every day you discover a dead body lurking in your kitchen. I tell you, Livvy, I felt like passing out myself.' He regarded me earnestly with clear blue eyes. 'And I really didn't know anything about it, Livvy, you must believe that.'

I nodded. 'I do know that, of course I do. It's not your fault. I just wish they'd gone for the more conventional East End burial ground.'

He smiled ruefully. 'They shouldn't have done that either. They should have gone straight to the police, right from the start.'

'Bit late now,' I said grimly.

Lance scratched his head. 'You'd think so, wouldn't you, but you know, perversely, apparently not. The police say there's a good chance they'll get off with manslaughter if they return to face the music. Apart from anything else their story is perfectly true, and everybody will back them up—oh, and apparently there's some left-wing brief who's prepared to take Alf's case on, and all on legal aid too—he stands a really good chance of getting off. I just have to persuade them to come back, that's all, and that might be tricky.' He grinned. 'Spiro reckons the ouzo will agree with Dad and I can just see Alf—'

'Ouzo?' I interrupted.

'Oh,' he flushed suddenly. 'Oh, no, nothing.' He bent down quickly, attending to the wheel.

Ouzo, I thought, astonished, and Spiro knew about it, so—so not Spain at all. Greece, or to be more precise, I thought rapidly, a little island off the tip of Greece, called Mexatonia. An island, where a certain Gullopidus family pretty much ruled the roost, ran the show, owned the boats, the goats, the bars, and where a couple of Englishmen—friends of young Spiro, who'd been looked after so magnificently during his stay in England—could quite easily be found shelter, houses, jobs. God, I could just see Alf, mending boats on the beach, and Mac—yes, Mac behind the bar in town, measuring out the Metaxa, becoming part of the community . . . I smiled. Well actually, in spite of myself, I grinned. What a life! They'd never come back!

'Forget I said that,' muttered Lance, straightening up for a moment.

I smiled. 'Forget you said what?'

He grinned, but I glanced away, point made, but not wanting to prolong that conversation, thank you very much.

'Well, bye then, Livvy. Best of luck.' He kissed my cheek.

'Bye, Lance,' I said with a smile, then I turned to go, making my way across the bridge and back up the parched lawn. A few steps on, though, his voice halted me.

'Oh, by the way, that musician chappie called round.'

I swung back. 'Oh?'

'Yes, he's gone to Vienna.'

'Oh. Right.' My heart thudded on again. Of course. Ursula had said. With Imo. Hence the shuttered house.

'But he popped in to say goodbye. Left a note, I think.'

'Really? Where?'

He shrugged. 'Kitchen table?'

Kitchen. Bloody kitchen. I hurried on up the garden, heart racing again, through the French windows, then steeled myself to—Yes, yes I could . . . I went in. I avoided looking at the Aga and glanced quickly at the table. Nothing. Totally bare apart from the fruit bowl. In the fruit bowl perhaps? No. Notice board? No. Counters, surfaces, pinned to the larder door? No, no note, nothing. I glanced all about now, even casting a desperate eye at the Aga. All was neat and tidy, and there wasn't a fluttering piece of paper to be seen. He must have changed his mind. Dejected, I turned to go, but just as I was leaving, noticed that the rubbish bin was practically overflowing. Damn, I'd have to empty that or it would stink to high heaven in this weather. Irritated, I pulled out the plastic sack, but as I did, realised there were some balls of screwed-up paper on the top. They were from my telephone pad. I opened one.

Dear Livvy,

I popped round to say goodbye, but I also wanted to say

I opened another.

Dear Livvy,

I'm off to Vienna today, but I just wanted to write to

And another.

Dear Livvy,

I dropped them back in. One by one, slowly. Stared at the wall. What? What had he wanted to say? And why start a letter three times? I moved towards the front door, just as the telephone rang. I picked it up.

'Hello?'

'Livvy, it's Imo.'

I gazed into the hall mirror, saw my eyes widen. 'Imo, hi.'

'Darling, I'm so sorry.'

'What about?'

'My bitch of a mother.' Her voice wobbled.

I lowered myself very slowly onto the hall chair. 'How did you know?' I whispered. 'I mean—did she tell you what she'd—'

'No, no, of course not,' she sniffed. 'When she came across to us in tears at the concert she just said you'd insulted her, accused her of being a culture vulture or something, but Daddy overheard the whole thing, he was just too terrified to interfere. We're all too terrified. Have been for years.' Her voice sounded small and sad.

'So you know—'

'Not quite everything, but I'm keen to learn because, believe me, it'll all be bollocks,' she rallied defiantly. 'It always is with Mum, and there's no way she's coming between you and me, Livvy, no way on earth. So go on, darling, spill the beans. What's the old cow been up to now?'

I licked my lips. 'Well, she said . . . well, first of all she told me about Johnny. Imo, I had no idea. I never knew you were so besotted back then. If I'd thought for one moment you were still in love with him—'

'You'd never have married him?'

There was a silence. I swallowed hard.

'Don't be silly, Livvy,' she went on quietly, 'you'd have followed your heart, and quite right too.'

'So—you were in love with him then?'

'Oh, back then, yes, I was, but the balls-up on that front was nothing to do with you, it was my own private tragedy, and my own stupid fault, too. You weren't to know what was going on, but yes, there was a plan afoot, instigated by Mum, of course.'

'So that was true? She did intervene?'

'Of course! You know Mum. She knew that I was deadly serious about Johnny and was adamant that if he was going to take me to the altar so young he had to deserve me, or some such crap. Not coming back for weeks on end after Oliver died was her idea. It was all her idea.'

'And Paolo?'

'The son of a gallery owner she knew. He just arrived at my apartment one evening, asking if I'd like to have supper. Oh, I didn't *have* to sleep with him, of course, but in those days I did most things Mum suggested, and look where it's got me. I've gone from man to man to please her. Oh, she thought Hugo was marvellous in the beginning, but then Sebastian came along and he was even *more* marvellous. It's been the story of my life. I don't even know what I think any more,' she said unhappily.

I licked my lips. 'She said—Ursula said—that you were in love with him. With Sebastian.'

'Ah. Yes. That much, at least, is true. But then again, it's not the whole story. You see, sadly, he's not in love with me. And no point forcing a square peg into a round hole, eh?' She gave a hollow laugh.

'But you're going to Vienna with him! Your mother said—'

'Well, of course she bloody did. I'm surprised she didn't book the bloody ticket, drive me to the airport, shove me on the plane and strap me into the seat next to him, taking absolutely no notice of his horrified face!'

There was a silence.

'It's you he wants, Livvy,' she said softly. 'You must know that.'

'Wh-why should I know that?'

'Because . . .' she struggled. 'Oh, I don't know, don't know for sure, but—listen, darling, I spoke to him this morning, before he left for Vienna. I wanted to set the record straight—*my* record straight, at least. Oh, but that doesn't matter right now, the important thing is that he was asking about you. I think he might try and get in touch with you, Liv, write to you perhaps, or even—'

'Oh!' I nearly dropped the phone.

'What?'

I couldn't speak for a moment. I went hot, then finally pulled myself together and dragged my eyes away from the window by the door. In the mirror I could see the colour rising rapidly up my neck.

'Imo, it's—it's all right,' I breathed. 'He's here.'

'You're kidding!' Imo's voice was still in my ear even though I wasn't with her. I was glued back to Sebastian's eyes again as he looked at me through the hall window. 'Gosh, I thought he'd gone. Well, good luck then, Livvy. You deserve it.'

Her subdued tone made me glance into the receiver. 'Imo?'

'Hmm?' She sounded distant.

'Lots of love.'

She paused. 'You too, darling. You too.'

I slowly put the receiver down and stood up to open the door, my heart hammering around somewhere up by my oesophagus. Sebastian was there on my doorstep, leaning against the door frame with his hands in his pockets. He was in khaki trousers and a pale blue shirt—quite smart for him, not his usual battered composing kit—but his eyes were the same as ever, dark and glittering, and he was wearing that devastating smile, the one that transformed his face.

'Hi.'

'Hi.'

With these modest monosyllables, I felt my whole body begin to glow and every nerve tingled.

'Can I come in?'

'Hmm?' I gazed, wantonly.

'Inside?'

I jumped. 'Inside? Oh—no!' I hurried distinctly *out*side, and joined him on the step, slamming the front door firmly behind me. He looked surprised.

'Ah. I see. A doorstep conversation then.'

'Well, it's just that—I'm rather off my house at the moment,' I explained hastily. 'It's—the wallpaper.'

'The wallpaper?'

'So depressing.' Or did that sound neurotic? 'Er—no, OK, it's not the wallpaper, but it's a long story, Sebastian, and a rather tortuous one at that, so I won't go into it right now, but . . .' I glanced about desperately, no, not out the back because Lance might still be there so, 'tell you what, let's go and sit over there.'

I hastened down to the front wall, excitement mounting. It was a bit high and covered in creeper, but somehow, with a superhuman spring, I managed to jump up, and then contrived to look comfortable even though I had ivy up my bottom. He glanced at the filthy wall and in his smart clothes, clearly decided to stand. Suddenly it occurred to me he was spruced up for travelling.

'Imo said you were off to Vienna.'

'Imo?'

I flushed. God, why did I have to mention Imo? Right at this moment? 'Yes, that was her on the phone just now.'

'Oh, right.' He coloured too, then recovered. 'Yes, well, she's right, I am, but the plane's been delayed. I'm leaving any minute actually.' He glanced at his watch. 'The taxi will be here soon. I just came round to say goodbye. The symphony's going to be played in the Musikverein tomorrow evening,' he explained, 'so I'm flying out tonight to listen to the rehearsal. I'm leaving the house, too, hence all the activity.' He jerked his head down the street. I looked, and realised that his front door was wide open and that two men were busy heaving a heavy desk down the steps to a lorry. 'My desk and my piano are the only things I actually brought with me to the house, so they're going down to the country. The rest stays.' He grinned. 'I thought you might think it a bit odd if I disappeared from the neighbourhood overnight without saying goodbye!'

My throat felt curiously dry all of a sudden. 'Oh . . . right. Yes, I'd forgotten you . . . only rent it.'

'Oh yes, I'd never bu it. Renting was ideal. I needed to be here to write the music for the Abbey, because, somehow, being close to the old building got the inspiration going, but now that it's finished, I don't need to be here any more. I'm keen to get away, actually.' He smiled, his eyes creasing up at the corners.

For some reason his words chilled me. 'Of course,' I heard myself saying. 'That part of your life is over. Time to move on.'

'Quite. And my parents have been dying to move out of their house to a cottage in a village nearby. It's far too big for them now, so I'm taking it over. It's an old rectory with a lovely garden, and I'm not really a city person. It'll be good to work in the country again.'

'I see,' I said quietly. I met his gaze. 'You're all set up then, aren't you? I'm moving on too, you know.'

'So I gather.' He grinned.

'Who told you?'

'Your builder, the chap round the back.'

'Ah. Yes, well, I'm sure he didn't tell you exactly why, but believe me, it's out of necessity. I don't have your luxury of choice.'

'To Dorset?' He grinned again.

'Sorry?' Why was he grinning at me like that.

'Aren't you going to Dorset?'

'No, no, to Chiswick, that's where Claudia's school is.'

'Chiswick!' He looked appalled.

'Yes, she's got into St Paul's Girls' School. It's a hell of an opportunity and it would be crazy of us not to take it up, so I'm pretty sure we're going to be moving up there, although I have to say,' I grimaced, 'I haven't squared it with Claudes yet. Might go down rather badly.'

He stared at me. 'Livvy, is this because . . . is it because of Imogen?'

I frowned. 'What?'

He licked his lips. 'You know, we were never an item.' He ran his hands through his hair. 'I mean I know it *looked* as if we were, and if I'm honest, that's the way I *wanted* it to look. I wanted you to think that I was going out with her, I was so bloody furious.'

I gazed at him, completely lost. What did Imo have to do with me moving to London?

'And I didn't seek her out deliberately, either, didn't make a beeline for her at all, but when she kept asking me to supper at her parents' house, practically zooming into position beside me at the dinner table—with her mother doing most of the shoving incidentally—well, I was so bloody cross, I thought—why not?'

'But—why?'

'Why?' he spluttered. 'Because I was feeling very firmly rejected and pissed off, since you ask!'

'Rejected?'

'Yes, Livvy,' he said patiently. 'By you.'

'*Me!*' I gaped. Eventually I found my voice. 'God—how can you say such a thing? Good grief, that—that is so not true!' I slipped into Claudia-speak in my outrage. 'I mean, that night after dinner at Hugh and Molly's I practically *threw* myself at you in the car! Asked you in for coffee, fluttered the old eyelashes seductively, the whole damn bit, and you sat there beside me like a frigging ice man, before politely showing me the car door! Oh, no, no,' I said vehemently, 'I think you'll find that if there was any rejecting going on it was instigated by *you*, Sebastian! God—and what about that day I came round to see you, to explain about Johnny coming back—you couldn't have cared less! In fact, if I remember rightly, you sat down next to me with a big cheesy grin on your face and said how *pleased* you were for me, yes—gosh, how *nice*, Livvy, your husband's back—and then you couldn't hustle me away quick enough, so desperate were you to get back to your composing! Oh no, I think you'll find the cold-shouldering was all yours!'

He lifted his chin and folded his arms, regarding me, pink and indignant as I was, perched up on the wall.

'Fine, Livvy,' he said quietly. 'OK. Let's take this step by step, shall we? The night you "threw yourself at me", as you put it, after Molly and Hugh's, you were drunk.'

'Oh, excuse me,' I blustered, 'I most certainly was *not* dru—'

'Oh yes you were, and you'd intentionally got plastered too. I watched you knocking it back, glug after glug of Pimm's. I watched the way your mind was going too, you were so bloody desperate to forget Johnny and you kept glancing at me in that garden with "he'll do" written all over your forehead. Oh, your body might have been with me that night, had I taken you up on your oh-so-generous offer, but your heart most certainly wouldn't have been. It was with that bastard Johnny, as you so neatly proved by opening your arms and your bed to him again that very evening.'

I gazed at him in horror for a moment. Then my mouth shut. 'I had to do that,' I muttered defiantly. 'Couldn't help myself. I had to have him back in order to exorcise him. I had to get him out of my system.'

'The other occasion you refer to,' he swept on, ignoring me, 'was when you so sweetly popped round a few days later to inform me of Johnny's return. And believe me, that was equally galling. Livvy, I do have eyes in my head. I do live in your street. I do stand at the window every day waving my arms like a lunatic, composing my stupid tunes. I did *see* him, believe it or not, in his *car*, going in and out of the *house*, playing with Claudia in the back garden, helping you in with your shopping, and how d'you think that made me feel? Bloody wretched, actually, and very smartly kicked in the teeth, but I damn well wasn't going to show it! Oh, I'm absolutely de*ligh*ted you found me so cool and distant when you tripped merrily into my study that day, because believe me, I'd had a few days to think about it, and that's precisely how I'd planned it. That's how I fully intended to be!'

'But—'

'And now,' he went on, with a sort of clenched fury, 'you have the gall to sit up there, grinning like a pixie and telling me you're *not* moving to the country after all, you're going up to London! Jesus Christ, what is it with you, Livvy? Can't you make up your bloody mind just once!'

My jaw dropped as I stared uncomprehending at him. Finally I shook my head. 'Sebastian,' I said at last. 'I'm really sorry, but you've completely lost me now. I have absolutely no idea what you're talking about. What on earth has us moving to Chiswick got to do with anything?'

'I thought Claudia wanted to board,' he said patiently.

'She does.'

'At a school near Frampton.'

I blinked. 'Well, yes, that was her first choice, why?'

'My parents live near Frampton. Or should I say—' he thumped his chest—'*I* now live near Frampton.'

I gaped. 'You do? Good heavens, what a coincidence!'

'Not really.'

'Why not?'

'Because I suggested the school to Claudia.'

'You . . .?' I boggled. 'When?'

'Oh, ages ago, when she was chatting about where to go. My niece went there and loved it. It's got an excellent reputation, and I showed her a prospectus. Ponies, swimming, all that sort of thing.'

Suddenly I remembered the much-treasured prospectus under her bed, well thumbed and scrawled over. He'd given it to her. My head swam. 'But—why?'

'Because I wanted you close by.'

A huge wave crashed over my head. I gazed at him, but actually, didn't seem to see him. My world was starting to spin. Those sweet, precious words: 'I wanted you close by.' He gazed back at me and suddenly the spinning abated, and everything fell into place. Everything went very still. Very quiet. And it seemed to me that, in that silence, his eyes gazed into my very soul.

'Mr Faulkner?' A cab drew up beside us.

'Yes,' muttered Sebastian, not turning.

'I called at the 'ouse, like, but they said you were over 'ere. 'Op in, mate, if you're coming, 'cos we're gonna have to shift if you're gonna catch that plane. The traffic's diabolical.'

'Your taxi,' I muttered, not taking my gaze from those dark, shining eyes.

'I know.'

The sound of running feet didn't distract us either, when towards us, down the street, came Maureen, dragging a case on wheels.

'Well, thank heavens for that,' she gasped, panting. 'I had a feeling you'd be here but you might have said! You'll catch it if you hurry.' She grabbed his arm and hustled him to the waiting taxi. I watched as Maureen thrust some tickets in his hand. 'Get in or you'll miss it!'

She bundled him in, together with his case, then slammed the door shut behind him and passed his passport through the window. I swung my legs round to the other side of the wall. Jumped down. Despite all that activity, we'd hardly taken our eyes off each other. I'd followed him all the way round. The driver shifted into gear.

'Hang on,' I heard Sebastian say. He leaned out of the window, past Maureen.

'I wanted to give you time, Livvy,' he called, 'that's what you need. I didn't want to rush things. I did that before and it didn't work out, that's why it's good that I'm going away. You *need* that time, Livvy, to recover, to get over Johnny.'

I nodded, greedy with longing. Johnny, bloody Johnny.

'I'll ring you from Vienna and we'll meet when I get back, take it from there.'

I nodded again, tears of joy and relief and all sorts of other scrambled emotions making my eyes swim.

'And while I'm gone, go to Frampton,' he called. 'Go to the school, see if Claudia likes it. She may not!' He grinned.

I opened my mouth to find my voice, but the taxi had moved off. All

I could do was wave, eyes flooding now, and with a bemused Maureen beside me. I waved until he was out of sight.

'Well then, dear,' said Maureen eventually, when we were left alone in silence. 'What a to-do, eh? Still, must get on.' She gave me a sly, secret smile, squeezed my arm, and then bustled off down the road, leaving me there on that hot, empty pavement.

I stood for a while, then moved on myself. Away from my house, and away from Sebastian's house. I needed to go somewhere quiet and green, like the park. Yes, the park would do, to think, to hug my joy. My feet tripped lightly along the hot pavements. Yes, I'd wait, I thought, dizzy with longing. I mustn't be greedy, mustn't be impulsive. He was right: we both needed time. And then when he got back, we'd see. Nothing was certain. But I could ring the school, plan a visit. I could even find a cottage, maybe, go and see some estate agents. There was a lot to do and—

'Livvy!' I stopped. Didn't turn. I must have imagined it. Then: 'LIVVY!' again, only louder. His voice—no doubt about it—and running footsteps too. I swung about. Down the old cobblestones of George Street, worn smooth with the traffic of time, and under the gaze of the ancient towering nave of the Abbey, came Sebastian. At the double. I stood still, could hardly breathe, and waited, until he arrived in front of me, panting hard.

'Come to Vienna,' he gasped. 'Bugger restraint, bugger giving you time—come to Vienna!'

My head swam. 'Wh-what now? I can't, I—'

'Tomorrow, we'll both go tomorrow.' His voice was taut with emotion. 'I can miss the first rehearsal tonight. It always sounds lousy with an unfamiliar orchestra and I wonder how I ever wrote the wretched thing. Come tomorrow!'

I stared. 'Sebastian, I can't, Claudia—'

'Oh, God, kiss me first, and then say you can't.' He took me in his arms and kissed me very thoroughly on the mouth. I could hear his heart pounding against mine, and when I came up for air, his eyes were glittering intently into mine, searching my face.

'God, you're lovely, Livvy,' he breathed, 'and what really flips my heart over is that you don't know that. No one's ever told you, have they? That bastard Johnny never breathed a word, did he, kept it to himself, and you've lived most of your life thinking that people like Imogen Mitchell are better than you.' He traced my mouth with his fingertip. 'It's criminal, actually. You're special, Livvy. When I saw you I confess I simply lusted after you, but when lust turned to love I was lost. Come with me, Livvy. Come and love me in Vienna.'

I gazed up at him. 'Yes,' I breathed, 'I'll come. I love you too, I know that now. I've known it for ages, actually, and couldn't believe I'd been so stupid. Mum can have Claudia and—'

'Bring her,' he commanded. 'Don't leave her behind. Bring her, we'll all go.'

My head swam. Lovers together in Vienna, holding hands over café tables, walking arm in arm down boulevards, drowning in each other's eyes . . . with a small, agog, ten-year-old girl in tow.

'No,' I said firmly, 'no, she can stay with my mother, she'll be fine there and—*oh!*' Suddenly my hand shot to my mouth. 'Oh God, no, I *can't* go!'

The taxi, with a bemused driver behind the wheel, still full of luggage, had trailed Sebastian back and was trundling up behind us.

'Why not?' demanded Sebastian.

'Because I can't leave the country! I'm sort of on bail!'

'Bail!' He stepped back in horror.

'Yes, well, I was this morning, anyway. You see there was this murder and—'

'Good God!'

'No—no, manslaughter, actually,' I added hastily, 'but the body ended up in my home—'

'Jesus!' He tore at his hair.

'I know, dreadful, under my cooker of all places, and the thing is, I promised the police I'd stay around, but—well, Vienna isn't far away and they won't need me for ages yet. There won't be a trial for some time, I'm sure, so—so maybe if I asked—maybe I could come next week!'

He stared at me in astonishment. 'Right,' he said eventually, looking totally bewildered.

'You coming, mate, or what?' from behind us.

'He's coming!' I called. 'Go,' I insisted softly, pushing him gently. 'Go. It's enough for me to know you *wanted* me to come. I don't *need* to go to Vienna now, but I'll join you when I can, I promise.'

He gazed at me, still with a degree of astonishment, then stepped forward and gently took my hands.

'Livvy, it seems to me you lead a very unusual and complicated life. You see nutters and weirdos at every corner, you rant and rave and wave rakes in defence of your child, you consort with murderers, you stow dead bodies in your house and you're on intimate terms with the local police. Heaven only knows what I've been doing with my life apart from writing the odd symphony, but I want you to know that I'm keen to be a part of this rich and varied tapestry of yours. If being with you means sitting in damp cellars forging passports, laundering money and stowing spare bodies away, then I'm your man. I'll follow your lead blindly, be Clyde to your Bonnie, if that's what you want.'

I giggled. 'Idiot. I'm not in any sort of real trouble, it's just—well, strange things have happened recently.'

He smiled. 'You're telling me.'

'There's twenty quid on the meter, mate!'

'Go.' I bundled him in, and this time he went. I shut the door, and he held my hand through the window until the taxi trundled away.

I watched Sebastian's face in the back window, and as the cab turned into the main road, I raised my hand in salute, as he did too. I stood on that hot pavement, and knew I had yet more tears in my eyes. But this time, I knew why. I never thought I'd say that to a living soul again, not after Johnny. Those three little words. Not a living soul. Never believed I'd have that sort of luck. But I had. I'd said it, and what's more—I sailed joyfully off along the hot pavements, my shoes feeling as if they'd got wings on—what's more, I meant it.

CATHERINE ALLIOTT

Catherine Alliott met me on a warm and sunny day at a hotel in the middle of St Albans, which is not only the city at the heart of *Olivia's Luck*, but also only twenty minutes from where she lives. As we sat having a drink on the hotel terrace, overlooking a sparkling lake, with a spreading cedar tree in front of us, Catherine told me how she became a writer. 'I was working as a copywriter in an advertising agency, but spent most of my time writing my first novel, *The Old-Girl Network*, surreptitiously under the desk. Unfortunately, before the novel was finished, the agency somehow divined that my heart was not in advertising and therefore they decided to "let me go".' The only problem was that Catherine and her barrister husband, George, had just bought a large, ramshackle house and needed every penny of their joint income to renovate it. '"Well then," said George, "you will just have to make money from your writing now."' And that is just what Catherine Alliott has done with her five best-selling novels to date.

With three children and a house to renovate, it is easy to see where Catherine got her material from for *Olivia's Luck*. 'We had builders in for over two years,' Catherine says with a wry smile. 'Luckily, they did not camp out in the garden—or bury anyone under the Aga!—but we did become friends and I did feel very responsible for them. It was like having extra children about. But I have to say that I would never do it again.'

Catherine Alliott writes most weekdays for a couple of hours every morning and will often return to her writing after the children have gone to bed. 'I

write longhand into exercise books, so I can write anywhere. In the winter I sit by the fire, and in the summer, especially when the children are home from school, I take a Thermos flask, a floppy hat and a deckchair and go and sit in the field.' Catherine writes a novel every two years. 'Writing,' she says, 'has its own momentum and, if you let it write itself, it usually works. But if you get in a paddy about it and think: I've got to fix this chapter to make that chapter work, you end up in a stew.' As she writes, Catherine lets her characters develop to such an extent that they dictate how the plot evolves. 'In *Olivia's Luck* I didn't know if Johnny would come back to Olivia for good, or whether he would have to go again. I think originally I thought he *would* come back and it would be a happy ending. But then I realised that actually he had been just too naughty, especially with the twist with the child later on. Then I knew he would have to go because I knew that I couldn't respect Olivia if she had him back.'

Catherine Alliott refused to be drawn on the subject of her next book. 'Once I've talked about it, that kills it for me,' she explained with a laugh. 'I don't even tell my husband what it's about. Part of the excitement of writing is not knowing what is going to happen next. I need that element of surprise and suspense to keep me going.'

So I'm afraid that I and her many other fans are just going to have to be kept in suspense as well.

Jane Eastgate

Redemption Blues

Tim Griggs

Sam Cobb, a policeman struggling with demons from his past, is reluctant to become involved in any new relationship. Then, one night, he is called to the scene of a ghastly tragedy—a car accident involving rock star Matt Silver. During the police investigation that follows, Sam encounters the overwhelming grief of Matt's wife and daughter and finds himself increasingly caught up in their lives. And, slowly, it seems possible that the healing power of love may save them all . . .

Chapter One

BEFORE DAWN, on the second anniversary of her death, Cobb left the farm and climbed towards daybreak. Above and around him the rim of the black hills stood against the stars. He breathed hard and, though his breath plumed from him in the bitter air, it was too dark for him to see it. He moved mostly by instinct and memory: he had climbed this path many times before and he knew it well.

At length he felt for the field's top gate and found its timber, furred with frost. He opened it and stepped through. He stumped the last few yards, feeling with his boots for the low turf ridge which marked the wall of the ancient churchyard. He trod over it and took up his dawn station, seated with his back to the trunk of the oak which stood there.

He liked to think that the oak might have been growing here when the lost village was populated by the living as well as the dead. That was in 1665. Twelve generations ago; not so very long.

Cobb heard Baskerville blundering in the gorse near him, panting hard. He rubbed the mongrel's ears and felt the dog shudder with delight and slap at his face with his tongue. The dog lay down on the frosted grass of the gravemound at Cobb's feet.

Cobb felt his own heartbeat slow after the effort of the climb. His spirit took joy in the warm presence of the dog and in the salmon wash of light that spread from the east. He took comfort too in the company of the dead beneath his feet. Against such casual extinction his own loss, if not comprehensible, seemed at least part of a shared grief. Clea was as completely at rest as these long-dead villagers. Their peace was her peace and in their company he was in hers. He felt less alone. He was not bitter. He had been bitter once but not any more. It was less of a life now. He accepted that, and accepting it he was very nearly content.

Silver could not see beyond the blast of the lights but he could feel it there, the many-mouthed beast he had to feed. He closed his eyes, trying to shut it out. But the glare burned red into his brain just the same. The last shrill chord of his treble run hung there, ringing through the vast stadium, and the audience clung to it, invisibly, silently begging him to go on. At the last moment he did so, his left hand flicking down the frets—a barré at the eighth, a long glissade, the guitar howling in pain, and at the exact moment the crash of drums and bass smashing the cage of the music, releasing him from the song.

Silver bounded out of the light, the bellowing of the crowd breaking over him like a following surf. The band came after him, blowing like horses as they ran, their sweat flying in the lights. Silver saw the familiar bulk of Tommy Hudson in the wings, clapping the musicians on the back, mouthing ritual congratulations over the din.

Silver backed into the shadow behind the scaffolding which framed the stage, his heart bouncing from the adrenalin. He noticed for the first time that a fine rain was falling over the unprotected crowds in the stadium. The huge audience didn't care about the rain. They whooped and whistled and drummed the damp turf with their heels, baying for more, chanting, a hungry pitiless chant. More of him. And more. And then more. They were lighting candles now. In a few seconds the small yellow flames were flickering all over the dark acres, a swarm of bright pinpoints, swaying to the chant.

'Look at the bastards,' Tommy Hudson hissed in Silver's ear.

'Tommy, listen—'

Hudson cut him off. 'We're too old for this, Mattie.' After a moment, the big man added, more gently: 'Give them what they want.'

Silver snatched the Gibson from the stagehand and bounded on to the stage. The audience erupted. Silver stood motionless in the lights, waiting until the torrent of noise withered away. When the silence was complete, he struck the first chord and the audience bellowed their approval.

You people climbing on that Narrow Way,
Can climb from cradle to the Judgment Day
You want to win, but first you gotta lose
That's what they call
That's what they call
Redemption Blues

Silver sent the aching chords across the stadium. The sound system picked up the buzz of his fingertips against the binding of the bass strings. Then the last line, hurled high in Silver's diamond-hard voice—and he was finished, flinging his arms wide, the guitar in one fist flashing like an unbuckled breastplate, his black hair swinging. And then he was running out of the dazzle of lights and into the wings.

Suddenly spent, Silver hung against Hudson's rough coat until his breathing steadied and the din engulfed them once more. Hudson took charge, standing Silver upright, tossing the guitar to an aide, slinging a jacket across Silver's back. 'OK, my son. We're gone.'

He gripped Silver's upper arm, steering him quickly out into the sweet cold night behind the stand, where a stretch limousine stood with its back doors open.

Silver pulled his arm free. 'You go ahead, Tommy. I'll meet you later.'

Hudson glanced up at him. 'Don't be a prick. Get in.'

Silver backed away. 'Need some space, Tommy. No big deal.'

'Mattie, we've got a meeting—'

'Catchya, Tommy.'

Silver backed out of Hudson's range and into the darkness, smiling. Hudson knew it was pointless to argue. He got in the limousine himself, banging the door behind him. He lowered the window and shouted: 'It's Berlin tomorrow, you tosser. Don't you forget it. You hear me?'

Silver did hear but gave no sign of it. He was already lost in the chaos of trucks and generators and trailers behind the stadium. The drizzle was heavier now, turning to rain, gathering in pools on the tarmac.

He found himself coming down. The anonymity helped. He caught the smell of fried onions on the night air and found a hamburger stand and bought a coffee as thick as tar. He leaned against a trailer to drink it. Something, perhaps the foreign accents around him, flung him back thirty years to Dr Gottschalk's basement studio at the Conservatorium. He saw himself again, a truculent boy of sixteen, hunched over his guitar, staring rudely out of the window.

'You are a very bad classical student, young Mr Matthew Silver,' Dr Gottschalk told him in his clockwork English. 'But you haff something very big to say. Get out from my sight and say it.'

Something to say. But what story was so important that this vast weight of manpower and equipment and transport and technology was needed to tell it? There had been a time when Silver had said whatever he had to say with an old acoustic guitar. He was not a romantic. He did not believe in the good old days. They had been hard days, hard and squalid. But he also knew he had lost touch in some way, somewhere between there and here. At some point his own voice had been drowned out by the grinding of this great machine designed to project it.

Twenty thousand in the crowd tonight. He should have been incandescent with the power they sent him, these unknown young people. Two years ago—less—he would have been airborne with it. But now it left him drained, confused. What did these young French people see? What could Redemption Blues mean to them?

The song had come to him as he huddled in a bus shelter on the outskirts of Hull on a bleak November evening a hundred years ago. Their Dormobile had finally packed up on the ring road and Tommy was off scaring up new transport. From the grim council estate across the road came the jagged sound of a shouting match. Lauren, feverish and ill, slept curled in a sleeping bag on the concrete of the shelter. A solitary bus prowled past. It did not trouble to stop and Silver remembered the desolate whine of its gears as it pulled away. He did not know why it depressed him so.

At his feet Lauren moaned softly in her sleep. He knelt down and stroked her hair, murmuring to her. Then, unbidden, the refrain was in his mind. He let it play, finding its form, until it was clear enough for him to hum it aloud. When the girl was sleeping again, he moved away and found the cardboard lid of a takeaway container in the gutter and scribbled on it in fitful blue Biro. It took him perhaps twenty minutes to get the verses down. When he had finished he looked up to find Lauren watching him, propped up against the seats. She looked like death under the yellow streetlight, sick and shivering. But she smiled at him, a smile of such confidence and courage that he felt his heart lift and he knew it would be all right. It had been her song from that moment.

Silver pushed himself upright. As he did so the children's Christmas letter crinkled in his breast pocket. He dragged out his mobile and punched the keys. Engaged. He swore, tried again. And again. And again. Hunched in the wet night while this toiling army of strangers deconstructed the world around him, he dialled and redialled endlessly.

Lauren Silver paused by the door of the rumpus room and watched her daughter reading. Serious little Freya, after nine years on the planet, was as grave and quiet as a medieval bishop behind her big glasses. Gudrun, naturally, was not quiet at all. She was singing snatches from the school musical in which she had starred just the week before. It gave Lauren a pang. There would be no more musicals for Gudrun. Not in that school, anyway. She wondered if her bright, talented, irrepressible daughter would ever forgive her. But she knew, even as the thought formed in her mind, that she would. Gudrun did not hold grudges. She was too busy living—living with a spirit which Lauren recognised only too well because it had once been her own.

Freya would be a different story. You could never tell with Freya. Gudrun was so much easier to decode than her sister that it was sometimes hard to believe the two girls were twins.

As she stood watching, both her daughters glanced up and saw her. Gudrun smiled her careless smile, as open as a sunflower. Freya gazed solemnly at her, her eyes owlish behind her glasses. Lauren wondered if they suspected anything. She waggled her fingers at them, made a funny face, closed the door gently and crossed to the room she called her study. In reality it was the room she came to when she wanted to drink and smoke in peace. To call it a study was pretentious, like so much else in her life. Lauren had to admit she had never truly studied anything. She had barely started her first year at Leeds University before she heard Matt Silver play at the Union, and that had been it, more or less. Within a few hours she found her way into his tobacco-smelling sleeping bag in a chill tenement overlooking the University. She remembered standing at the window the next morning with the concrete campus spread out at her feet. That was the last time she ever saw the place. Later that day she climbed aboard Matt Silver's camper van and smoked dope with the keyboard player all the way to their next gig in Newcastle.

At the time she thought that dropping out of university in this dramatic way had been her big break, her bid for freedom. Freedom from the awful suburban primness of her mother. But looking back she could see that her flight with Matt Silver had been the opposite of escape. He had snapped his fingers and she had followed.

There had been good times in the early days. She could not bring herself to pretend it had all been bad from day one, even though that might make tonight easier to bear. For tonight marked their final failure, hers as well as his. God knows, she had fought hard enough to avoid it. If he had only fought with a tenth of the same tenacity, maybe she wouldn't have to do this. But she could not carry their relationship alone. It was so dreadfully heavy. If she did not put it down now, it would crush her.

The thought of Matt made her glance at the phone on the desk. She had thought that perhaps this Christmas he might at least call. She glanced at her watch. It was exactly eleven. Midnight in Paris. He had been off-stage for an hour or so. Lauren felt a spurt of anger, not with him but with herself. Why should she care? And yet she did care and this made her angry. She crossed to the desk and flicked the handset off its rest, so that it lay rocking on the leather.

She walked to the sideboard, poured herself a vodka, lit a cigarette and pulled hard at it. She caught a glimpse of her reflection in the window and saw a strained woman of forty with dry blonde hair, screwing up her eyes against the smoke.

'Mummy, are we going out?'

Lauren spun on her heel so quickly that vodka slopped from her glass. 'God, Freya! You scared me to death! Creeping in like that.'

The girl watched her gravely through her big round glasses. Lauren found the child's composure unsettling. She took a deep breath. 'Going out, sweetheart? What gave you that idea?'

'You left the car out. You always leave it out if we're going somewhere.'

'We'll start calling you Sherlock Holmes, huh?' Lauren pinched Freya's nose gently, but the child was not to be charmed so easily.

'Where are we going?'

'Never you mind.'

'When's Daddy coming home?'

Lauren stiffened. 'Daddy's touring. In France. You know that.'

'When's he coming home?'

'Freya, for Chrissake, don't interrogate me!' She saw the girl flinch and in a second was across the room and sweeping her daughter into her arms and hugging her hard. 'Frey. I'm sorry. I don't mean to shout. But you mustn't question me like this. I'm doing my best. For all of us.' She felt the child's arms creep hesitantly round her neck.

Lauren rocked back on her heels. The child's eyes were full of suspicion. She turned away from her mother's arms and walked towards the door. With her back still to Lauren she said: 'I don't want to go anywhere. It's nearly Christmas.'

Lauren splashed another inch of vodka into her glass. She was drinking too much, she knew, not just tonight but for months past. A couple of years, perhaps. But—what the hell? If she couldn't make it a little easier on herself tonight, when could she?

She ran through the preparations again. Her single case standing in the corner. A bundle of money—her escape fund—in the drawer. She opened the drawer and put the money on the desktop. A couple of big stretch bags for the twins' toys and clothes. And a box of sandwiches and drinks in the fridge. Matthew's tour finished in Berlin tomorrow. That was her deadline. She wanted to know exactly where he was when she made her move, and that meant she had to go tonight.

Silver abandoned the cab near the Gare du Nord and walked the rest of the way, cursing the Christmas traffic and the rain. He stopped in a doorway and tried Lauren's number again. When that didn't work he checked the street, crumbled a little of the white powder onto the back of his hand and snorted it clumsily, licking away the residue.

Silver reached the hotel wild-eyed, stoked with synthetic energy. He rode the VIP lift up to the executive level, rubbing rain out of his hair, and hammered on the door of Hudson's suite. When it opened, he strode into the room, his shoulder banging the door back against its hinges.

Silver threw himself down onto the grey leather sofa, pushing his hands through his long wet hair.

'You're soaked, you silly bastard,' Hudson said. 'Where you been?'

Silver did not reply and Hudson went into the bedroom and found a fresh shirt and a towel and tossed them onto the sofa. Silver stripped off and scoured himself with the towel and stood to pull on the dry shirt. As he did so he glanced through the half-open door into the next room. Three young women sat at the glass-topped table, chatting and sipping drinks. He said: 'Who the hell are they?'

Hudson crossed to his desk, sat down and settled a pair of surprisingly dainty half-moon glasses onto his nose. 'You been so bloody miserable lately. Think of it as a Christmas bonus.'

'Get them out of here, for Chrissake.'

'It's not like you to be particular, Matt.'

Silver crossed to the dresser, opened a drawer and banged it shut again, returned to his seat. He drew two neat lines of powder on the glass coffee table, patting them into exactly parallel tracks with the edge of a platinum American Express card. He snuffed up the first line. 'I need to talk, Tommy,' he said, his head tilted back. 'So get them out.'

'Mattie—'

Silver swept a crystal bowl from the table and exploded it against the wall. Fruit thudded and rolled and one of the women squealed. Silver quietly resumed his ritual while Hudson ushered them out.

Hudson crossed to the bar and took a couple of miniature brandies and broke some ice out of the freezer. He brought glasses and bottles over to the table. He slid one drink across to Silver.

Hudson put his big fists on the table. 'Mattie, is there any danger of you telling me what the fuck's going on?'

Silver opened his eyes. 'I'm going home, Tommy.'

Hudson straightened up slowly, all his senses straining to see where this was leading. 'It's the end of a hard tour, Matt. We're all knackered.'

'It's not the tour.' Silver swept his hand in a gesture which took in the tiny casket of cocaine, the sterile opulence of the hotel room, the very hour of the night. 'It's all this.'

'You should get some better grade angel dust,' Hudson said. 'Go sleep it off. We'll talk tomorrow.' He flipped his hand at Silver in dismissal.

Silver didn't move. After a while he said: 'I've been having some trouble with Lauren.' He frowned at the sound of this and rephrased it. 'I mean, we've been having trouble with one another.'

'Oh?' Hudson moved his head cautiously. 'And that's news?'

'I'm going back, Tommy. Now. Tonight. Fix it for me, will you?'

Hudson sipped his drink. 'You'll be home in time for Boxing Day. Kiss and make up then. Laurie'll forgive you. She always does.'

'That's not good enough.' When Hudson didn't speak, Silver tapped on the table with his forefinger. 'By tomorrow.'

'Don't be fucking silly, Matt. It's just a spat, like every other time.'

'I'm serious, Tommy.'

'You're not serious. This is serious, what we're doing here.'

'I haven't had a Christmas at home with my kids for five years, Tommy. They're nearly ten. And I'm forty-five. *That's* serious.'

'OK, Mattie,' Hudson said. 'Let's think this through, before we get all aerated about it. First off, we're going to call Laurie up, right now.'

'It's off the hook.'

'You've tried ringing her?' Hudson was astonished that Silver had made the attempt. He reassessed rapidly. 'Well, OK. I'll send one of the lads round to check she's all right—'

'Tommy, listen.' Silver leaned forward urgently. 'Get this straight. I'm going. Tonight. Are you going to fix it or am I?'

Hudson straightened in his seat and his face hardened. 'Matt, get real. We've got Berlin tomorrow night. You know that.'

'Cancel it, Tommy. I mean it.'

'Don't talk like that.' Hudson moved forward and grabbed Silver's arm. 'Look, Mattie, you know what I feel about Laurie and the girls. Nearest thing to family I'll ever have. Goodie's my goddaughter, for Chrissake. Now, I promise you we're going to find a way—'

'It was those bloody candles.'

Hudson blinked. 'Candles?'

'Christmas. And twenty thousand French kids light candles for me.' Silver looked up at the big man frankly. 'I do something for those kids, Tommy. It's time I did something for my own.'

'This is a joke, right, Mattie? You treat them like shit for years on end, and now you want to put things right in five minutes flat?'

'Tommy, they're still my kids. And I'm still their father.'

'You, Matt?' Hudson gave a bark of contempt. 'You're not their father. You just fucked their mother.'

Silver stood up slowly. Already anguish and guilt were spreading across Hudson's heavy face. Silver picked up his wet jacket.

'Mattie . . .' Hudson was on his feet too. 'That came out all wrong. You know I didn't mean—'

'It's all right, Tommy.' Silver walked quietly to the door, leaving

Hudson standing in the middle of the room. Silver took pity and said again more softly: 'It's all right.'

But it was not, and never would be again, and they both knew it.

Lauren jolted awake to the thud and bounce of the empty glass on the carpet. She felt sick and confused. The furred green numerals of the digital desk clock told her it was 4.37 in the morning.

'Oh, Christ.' She fumbled for the vodka bottle. It was empty.

Maybe she could leave it until tomorrow, until after Christmas, until the New Year. But a voice in her head told her: Go now. Walk through to the rumpus room, bundle the twins in the car. Go *now*. She turned, the bottle still in her hand, and headed for the door.

'Hello, Silvergirl,' he said, 'am I too late to join the party?' He lounged against the door frame, unshaven, unkempt, smiling that smile, car keys dangling from his hand. She stood in silence, her reactions locked. He tilted his head quizzically at her. 'I've come back, Laurie.'

'Back?'

'Back for Christmas. Back home.'

'Home?' she repeated stupidly.

He seemed to hesitate for a moment, and then took two strides across the room towards her. As he touched her she felt herself flinch, and she knew with absolute clarity that this was going to go horribly wrong.

'No,' she said. She pushed him away. 'You can't just bounce back in here like a pantomime genie. Change everything.'

'Sure I can, Laurie.' He smiled that smile at her again. 'I just did.'

For the first time she noticed his eyes. 'You're flying, Matthew. Did you drive in that state?'

'I got nervous before my big entrance.' He laughed. 'Me! So I did half a line in the street outside. It's no big deal.'

She shook her head. 'I don't understand. How did you get here?'

'I cancelled the tour.'

'You did *what*?'

'Cancelled it. *Finito*. All over.' Then in a different voice he said: 'It's all going to change, Laurie, I promise you that.'

She groped behind her for a chair and sat down. He sat in the leather swivel chair by the desk. She felt hollow and sick. Even now a part of her wanted to forget it all, to give up. But his confidence goaded her. Her life was in ruins and his very optimism was an insult.

'You've rehearsed all this, haven't you?' she said. 'You've gone through this scene so many times that you really think it ends the way you want.'

'Laurie, it doesn't matter. All that stuff that went before. Believe me. All that matters is that it's all over.'

'Just like that?'

'That's right. That's how I do things, Laurie. Just like that.'

'And what about the way I do things?'

'Laurie. Let's not argue. Not now.'

'Why not now? We can't argue any other time. You're never here.'

'Laurie, you don't understand. That's all over. Gone. Behind us.'

'No, Matthew. This is what's all over and behind us. This. Us.'

He suddenly looked tired. 'Don't say anything you'll regret, Laurie. I don't expect this to be easy. But don't let's be hasty.'

'Hasty?' she heard herself laugh, a short ugly sound. 'This isn't hasty, Matthew. This has taken a lifetime.'

'OK, OK.' He began to lose patience. 'Look, Laurie, I've given up a lot for this. All I want—'

'You?' she cried. 'You haven't given up a damn thing, Matthew! In six months you'll be bigger than ever. The only thing you've given up is me.' Silver looked at her with weary disappointment. He shifted in his seat and the back of his hand brushed against the bundle of money she had left on the desktop. He picked it up, frowning.

'I'm leaving, Matthew,' she said. 'I've had enough. I'm leaving and I'm taking the girls. I put everything into making this work, and it isn't enough. I should have realised it a long time ago, but I realise it now.'

She stood up, collected her bag, smoothed down her skirt. When finally she looked at him, she saw that a small tic was working in the corner of his mouth.

'No, Laurie, listen.' He seemed confused, and there was a note of alarm in his voice. 'This is crazy. This isn't what either of us wants.'

'It's what I want, Matthew.' She drew herself up, fully in control at last. 'I'm taking them, Matthew. Give me my money.'

He looked at her outstretched hand. He seemed unable to believe that this was happening. He said: 'Laurie—wait. We can work it out.'

'Good line,' she said. 'Why don't you write a song about it?'

Perhaps this was what triggered it. His head came up quickly and he looked directly into her and then through her, and to Lauren it was as if something slipped out of place behind his eyes. He dropped the money into the pocket of his jacket. He seemed disorientated, as if he had just come to and was puzzled to find himself here. It frightened her.

Across a gulf she called to him: 'Matthew!'

He looked distant. 'Do you know, Laurie, I chartered a jet to get back? So keen to get home.' He frowned at her: 'Did I do something wrong?'

'Matthew, you must know I'm not doing this just for me.'

'I would honestly have tried, Laurie,' he said. 'Just for once, I really meant it. Ironic, huh?' He smiled at her, a rueful smile. Then he left the study and walked into the room where his daughters lay sleeping.

She flailed at him with her fists but her blows had the weakness of blows in a dream. He brushed past her, swept up the sleeping Gudrun and marched straight down the hall and through the open front door. She followed him out on to the gravel, trying to shriek, trying to beg. His car was slewed across the drive, engine running. She was overwhelmed by the realisation that he would win, as he had always won, and the last of her strength trickled out of her. She sat down on the frosted stones and sobbed.

Silver laid the sleeping child in the front seat of the car and strode back into the house. In a second he returned with Freya. Lauren, weeping on the gravel, could see the silent girl's white and wakeful face against the black of her father's jacket. Lauren reached out her arms as Silver placed the child in the back of the car. He closed the passenger door and walked over to where Lauren lay crumpled on the driveway.

'Matthew . . .' She fought for breath. He hunkered down in front of her. She swallowed hard and won some control.

'For God's sake, Matthew. You don't need to do this. You've got everything you ever wanted.'

'But they're my kids, you see, Laurie.' He spoke softly but there was a strange wild light in his eyes.

'I'm their mother, Matthew,' she moaned. 'I'm their mother.'

He turned away from her and she lunged at him and gripped the cloth of his jeans and he slapped back at her as if swatting a wasp. The edge of his hand caught her across the mouth and she felt a tooth crack and fell back on to the stones tasting blood. A second later the car roared past her, flinging gravel into her face. She caught a glimpse of Freya's grave and ancient eyes searching for her through the passenger window. Then the tail lights were ruby streaks in the darkness and the rumble of the car's engine shrank away to nothing.

He would soar away, far away from the accusations and the reproaches, and he would find peace. The car swept down the black tunnel of the highway that would take him to the city—his city—and to freedom.

'Daddy?' Freya's voice quavered from the back seat. 'Why was Mummy crying?'

He shut his mind to it. He must shut his mind to it. The lights of the suburbs rushed towards them and he swung the car on to a two-lane highway sharply enough to make the back wheels tramp. The road was lit by sickly yellow streetlamps, the houses dark behind tall hedges. He accelerated and the wan lights stretched into golden rails.

'She fell over. I saw—Mummy fell over and you didn't stop.'

Somehow, everything had gone wrong. But he could make it all right again. Life would be different. His life would change. All their lives would change. He would make amends. If they would just all leave him alone long enough to get it straight in his head.

'Where are we going, Daddy?' There was a rising note of fear in Freya's voice but he closed his mind to her.

Chapter Two

SERGEANT DENNIS MCBEAN stopped the patrol car in a pool of shadow a few yards short of Clapham High Street. That was merely habit. With its Day-Glo markings the car was obvious to anyone who looked, shadow or no shadow. Not that anyone would be looking now. It was too late—or too early, whichever way you looked at it. He and Hayward might get the odd call to a break-in or a fire, or just possibly a domestic, but otherwise McBean expected the shift to end quietly.

The Jaguar rocketed through the junction a few yards ahead of them in a blur of light and noise. It left a small whirlwind of litter in its wake and seemed to rock the police car with the power of its passing.

'Fuck me,' said Hayward simply. He grabbed for the radio. McBean was already gunning the engine. They swerved away from the kerb, lights and siren springing on together, and fishtailed into a turn that took them in hopeless pursuit.

Silver saw the blue lights flashing in his wake. There were lights everywhere now, streaking past in bands of blurred neon. Why would they not leave him alone? A bus pulled out and Silver swerved past it on the wrong side of the bollards and a black cab bounced up the kerb to avoid him. He swung right and the great river was spread out beside him, polished ebony daubed with colour from the high crystals of the city spires. There were more blue beacons now, one ahead which he closed upon and left spinning in his wake, another jumping out of a street just abreast of him, two, three, more behind. There was a wailing too which he associated with the blue lights and yet which was plaited together in some way with a child's terrified screaming, very close to him.

It came to him all at once. Aim for the dark. Fly into the dark where they would never find him. There was a gap to his left up ahead and he trod on the throttle so that the car sank down on its haunches then leapt as he spun the wheel. There was a splintering impact and debris spun past him. And then the thin shriek of the child: 'Daddy!'

And at last her terror broke through to him. In the fraction of a second left to him he saw the gap in the railings ahead and saw the black water smirking below and he wrenched the wheel to save them all and felt it spin loose under his hands and knew that it was too late.

A moment of sweet silence. And in that silence for the first time that night he spoke to her. 'It's all right, Freya. Daddy's with you.'

A monstrous concussion and something like a great white flower bloomed in his face and he was stunned and in terror and the world was turning over and something was ripping at his face and a torrent of icy cold was crashing against him, hosing his body, stinking like a tomb, utterly black, and he knew he was not a god after all.

McBean pulled up just short of the bridge and he and Hayward left the car with its lights still flashing and ran to the parapet. McBean saw the Jaguar at once, wheels up but afloat in the current of the Thames.

'Jesus!' Hayward said, his voice breaking. 'What a fucking *jump*—He must be forty feet out.'

McBean watched, peering at the sinking wreck for any sign of life. The current nudged the Jaguar around and pushed it towards them, towards the piers of the bridge. Hayward, nearly weeping with frustration, was fighting his way out of his anorak.

McBean put a hand on his arm. 'What d'you think you're going to do?'

'They might still be in there!'

'Don't be a prick. Water like that? You'd last about a minute.'

'But we've got to—'

'See if you can make out the plates. Do something useful.'

'Right.' Hayward pulled himself together. 'Right, Sergeant.'

A small crowd was at the parapet now, shouting questions, gabbling to one another. McBean and Hayward ignored them as the Jaguar, now directly beneath them, began a slow dive.

'Did you see the plates?' McBean asked. 'I couldn't make them out.'

'MKS or maybe MBS 001,' Hayward said. 'Personalised plate.'

'Call it in.'

The Thames closed over the Jaguar, and now all they could see was the pinprick rubies of its rear lights and the eerie white spokes of its headlamps. The beams lurched and circled, still falling, and abruptly died. The crowd fell silent. McBean made to turn away but Hayward hung back, craning over the wall.

'Wait.' He gripped McBean's arm and pointed. There was a small flurry of movement in the depths and a second later a trickle of bubbles boiled up through the water, then a fat belch of air which rocked the river's surface.

'Hayward!'

But he was already across the road, shedding jacket and cap as he ran, and in a moment he was clattering down the steps and McBean heard him crash into the black water.

It was before seven in the morning and still dark, but London was vibrantly awake by the time Cobb drove on to Cromwell Road.

He glanced at his watch. It had taken him an hour and ten minutes from the farm, which wasn't bad in this old heap. The call had come through at five-thirty while he was trying to milk his father's one cow, a Guernsey called Mrs Buckets. It was an irritation but Cobb didn't mind much. The truth was that he liked to be summoned, and he was especially glad of it today. No, the main problem with being called back into the city at this hour was that he had not had time to change from his farm clothes. Kapok was hanging out of the sleeve of his jacket and his boots were balled with mud from Mrs Buckets's stall. The boots worried him. He could change in the office—he kept a spare suit there—but he had a nagging suspicion he had forgotten to throw a decent pair of shoes in the back of the Land Rover.

Cobb crossed the Thames southwards at Vauxhall Bridge, turned left and followed the southern bank. Ahead of him at the end of Lambeth Bridge he saw a knot of ambulances and police cars. There were barriers of striped tape across the road and men in luminous jackets were setting up signs and directing traffic. A heavy crane, up on its jacks, squatted on the crown of the bridge with its jib jutting into space. Cobb parked, climbed out and ducked under the tape. A dozen police and paramedics on the bridge were leaning over the parapet and nobody seemed to notice him. A tall black Sergeant was standing back a little from the others. Cobb walked across to him.

'McBean?'

'Yeah. And you?'

'I'm Detective Inspector Sam Cobb.'

'Sorry, sir. It's just that we're nervous about the media. It'll be a circus when they get hold of this. Mr Liston is in charge. He's down there on the pontoon.'

Cobb glanced out over the river. It was a bleak enough stage for the great Matt Silver's last performance, he thought. 'Who else was in the car?'

'His two little girls, sir. Twins, they were.'

'Out with Daddy at that time of night?'

'They've got this massive place in Virginia Water. Silver turns up in the middle of the night and just bundles the kiddies into his Jag and away he goes. Mr Liston got the local station to send a couple of their people over to break the news to the mother.'

Cobb grunted. He tried to guess what kind of a job two young constables would make of telling Lauren Silver that her husband and one of her daughters were dead. He did not envy them. It crossed his mind that, judging by her celebrity bitch reputation, Lauren Silver would not make it any easier for them. At once he felt guilty for thinking so.

'Silver's not in the car, sir,' McBean said after a moment. 'One of the divers went down. The driver's door's busted open, but no body.'

'It'll turn up. The tide running like this, it'll be at Battersea Bridge by now. A nice surprise for the Christmas shoppers, if they're looking.'

Cobb, not a tall man, pushed himself up on his hands to see over the parapet. The cable from the crane was taut and straining. It passed directly down into the water on the outside of one of the bridge piers. Two blue and grey Thames Division launches hung in the current and the cable lanced down between them. Three divers in drysuits floated mask-down in the water, the rods of their torch beams probing beneath them, following the angle of the cable. Cobb pitied the divers.

Cobb jerked his thumb back towards the road. 'He went through there, did he?'

Where the main road turned on to the bridge the granite parapet gave way to wrought-iron railings. Several sections of railing were missing. Inside the police tapes lay a scatter of lamps and traffic cones and broken chunks of timber.

'They were fixing the railings last night, sir. They were supposed to be finished by midnight.'

'Did you see him go over?'

'We were well behind, so we couldn't see much. But he must've just sailed through the gap. It was like he thought the road carried on through.'

'Speed?'

'Hayward and me, we both guessed at about a hundred and twenty. He just flew off into space. He missed the ferry pier by a mile.'

Cobb pushed himself up on the parapet again and took another look over. The rear bumper of the Jaguar was just breaking surface. Black water spouted from a shattered rear window. Someone raised a hand to the crane operator and winching stopped again and the divers swam in close and wrenched at the passenger door.

'You always hope, I s'pose,' McBean said. 'For the kiddie, I mean.'

Cobb glanced at the man's face and McBean saw his look. In answer to the unspoken question he said: 'We've only got one, sir. A daughter.'

The arc-lit scene below them fell silent and a diver emerged from half inside the hanging car with a broken doll in his arms. Several of the men on the police launches looked away, and one of the divers crossed himself in a quick and furtive motion out of sight of the others.

Cobb and McBean turned away from the parapet and leaned against it. Cobb said: 'The mother can be thankful for your partner, at least.'

'Hayward? He did well, sir,' McBean said hotly. 'Really well.'

'I'll remember it.'

'Did you hear how she was, sir? The kiddie he pulled out?'

'They say she'll be all right. Physically, I suppose they mean.'

'Christ.' McBean's voice was awe-struck. He knew how close he and Hayward had come to missing the tiny figure face down in the water.

Cobb moved quietly along the bridge through the gathering crowd. He ducked under the tape, flashing his warrant card when a Constable challenged him.

Splinters of striped wood and nuggets of glass lay scattered over the tarmac. Down at the water's edge below him Cobb could see a couple of automatic warning beacons. Cobb checked the road behind him. Even in the wan light of the winter morning he could see no skidmarks on the tarmac. The Accident Investigation people would check that but it looked clear to him. Silver had not braked, which meant that he had not seen the hazard. Or that was presumably what it meant.

They were winching the wrecked car towards the road now, clearing a space for it. Cobb caught sight of the uniformed Inspector Liston trotting up the stone steps from the water's edge. He knew the man slightly, a dull but solid officer nearing retirement. Cobb positioned himself to one side so that the car would swing past within a few feet of him.

At first sight the vehicle looked only slightly damaged. The windscreen, driver's window and sunroof were gone and the driver's door hung open. The bonnet and the driver's side were scratched and dented. Perhaps that was from the crash barrier. Through the open door Cobb could see the white collapsed balloons of airbags, upholstery smeared with filth, and nothing much else. He decided he could leave Inspector Liston to it, and walked towards his Land Rover. A solitary ambulance was parked at the roadside, with a knot of paramedics clustered around it. As he walked past, the back doors of the ambulance opened. A man in white police coveralls stepped out and almost collided with him.

'Sam?'

Cobb looked up in surprise.

'It's me. Phil Latimer.'

Cobb took the doctor's hand and shook it. 'Sorry, Phil. Miles away.'

'Have they put you back on accidents these days, Sam?'

Cobb laughed, but it suddenly struck him that this was literally true and he found himself stuck for an answer. Finally he said: 'Someone at Area's leaned on Horrie Nelson. He just wanted me to take a look.'

He knew this sounded apologetic, but it was the best he could do. Perhaps tactfully, Latimer didn't pursue it. Instead, he nudged Cobb and stepped back into the rear of the ambulance, beckoning.

'Get in here out of the cold. I've got something to put some fire in your belly.'

Cobb, unable to escape without rudeness, followed him. 'I'm pretty filthy. I just came in from the farm.'

'Won't make any difference in here now,' Latimer said. He rummaged in his bag, found a leather-clad flask and handed it to Cobb. 'Sit down, Sam. Wherever you can find room.'

Cobb took the flask and perched himself on the red-blanketed bunk.

'Not on that one,' Latimer said. 'That one's occupied.' He flicked down the red blanket and the dead child stared into Cobb's eyes. Black hair lay daubed in shocking streaks across her blue-white face. Cobb stood up slowly until his head touched the roof. Her eyes followed him.

Latimer was talking, his attention elsewhere. 'Get that down you, pal, that'll fuel you up.' Then Latimer looked up and saw him and stopped. He quickly folded the red blanket over her, embarrassed. 'Sorry. I should've thought. Not the pleasantest way to start the day.'

Cobb pulled himself together. It was only that the dead child looked a little like Clea. He sat on the opposite bunk. 'It's OK. She just reminded me of someone for a second.' He took a nip of the flask. It was more brandy than coffee and he was grateful.

'We get a bit blasé,' Latimer said awkwardly.

'Don't worry about it,' Cobb said.

'It gets to people, when it's children,' Latimer said. Some of his bounce seemed to have gone out of him. 'But you haven't got . . .?'

'No kids,' Cobb said. 'It wasn't that. Forget it.'

'She didn't feel much,' Latimer said. 'Her neck's broken. She'd been in the water for an hour, but we tried everything anyway.'

'Of course you did, Phil.'

To Cobb's surprise Latimer uncovered the dead face again and stood staring at it. After a moment's hesitation Cobb looked too, and when he did her eyes were still fixed on him.

Cobb drove to the office and edged the Land Rover under the roof of the underground car park. He bundled the torn anorak under the driver's seat and took the fire stairs up to the third floor.

He dodged quickly past the CID office. It was after eight now, and the place was thoroughly awake, and he was anxious to avoid meeting any of his team before he had a chance to clean up. He tapped on Horrie Nelson's door, walked in as soon as Nelson answered, and closed the door behind him. Nelson surveyed him from behind his desk.

'Well, if it isn't the gentleman bloody farmer.'

'Morning, Horrie.' Cobb pointed at the wardrobe, already shrugging out of his sweater and shirt. 'Is it OK?'

'You carry on, lad.' Nelson affected a martyred voice. 'Don't mind me.'

Horrie Nelson looked more like a great tragedian than a Superintendent. His magnificent head of silver hair was legendary and he had the kind of patrician profile associated with leading men in black-and-white movies. He was the only one of Cobb's colleagues who had a wardrobe in his office with a full-length mirror inside the door. Nelson had grown accustomed to Cobb using his office as a changing room whenever he was called in at short notice from the farm. Since Cobb had first talked about resignation these visits to Nelson's office normally attracted a lecture, but Cobb liked the big Yorkshireman and he thought that access to the mirror was just worth the lecture.

'This wasn't your idea, was it, Horrie?'

'My idea?'

'Turning me into some sort of an accident investigator.'

Nelson regarded him innocently. 'Well, now, Sam. I suppose you'll have to be like the rest of us and take the assignments you're given.'

'This isn't an assignment. It's a car crash. Liston could do it all right. He'd enjoy it.'

'It wasn't my idea. Mr Sykes called me as soon as he heard, and told me he wanted you to handle it. He thinks it'll be another Princess Di. This chap Silver was so big, apparently.'

'What does he mean, "handle it"?'

'Well, go to the scene. Take a look.'

'I took a look. It's a car smash.'

'Mr Sykes also tells me the wife is saying Silver isn't really dead.'

'He's dead all right.'

'Well, you have it your own way, Sam. You usually do. But you'll still have to handle it.' They were silent for a minute, and Nelson said: 'I suppose you'll be going over to the hospital now?'

'I suppose.' Cobb checked himself in the mirror. After a shave he'd look pretty good. Down to the ankles, anyway. Nelson seemed to decide something, got up, walked round his desk and leaned against it.

'Sam, you can call me a superannuated old fart if you like . . . but I think you're a bloody fool.'

'I know you do, Horrie. But I'm leaving, and that's it.' Cobb turned to face him. 'Horrie, we both know why Stan Sykes leaned on you to give me a shit job like this.'

Nelson stiffened. Despite his affection for Cobb, Nelson was a formal man who believed in discipline, and this was very plain speaking. 'The Detective Chief Superintendent is an excellent police officer,' he said.

'I didn't say he wasn't, Horrie. But he doesn't like me. Stan Sykes is an old-fashioned thieftaker. He hasn't got any time for failed fast-trackers who spend half their lives in the country when they're not telling him how to run the police force.'

Nelson took a deep breath. 'I can't imagine why that is,' he said.

'And while he's there I'll never go any further.'

Nelson pursed his lips. 'Sam, are you sure that Stan Sykes is the problem?' He waited for a moment. 'It's been two years, you know.'

'So it has.' Cobb straightened his lapels. 'Horrie, can I ask you something personal?'

'Of course, lad.'

'What size shoes do you take?'

'Ten.'

'Bugger it.'

The Staff Nurse led Cobb along a bright corridor hung with Christmas decorations of tinsel and coloured paper.

'I don't know how much you'll get out of any of them,' she was saying. 'The doctor's in with the little girl right now and the mother's not really with us, if you take my meaning.'

Cobb liked the Staff Nurse at once, liked her practical busyness and her Midlands accent.

'How is the child?'

'She's a bit knocked about, poor lamb. Cuts and bruises. I think she'll turn out to have a greenstick fracture. But you know, Mr Cobb, people get worse taking a tumble down the stairs. I don't think she'll even need stitches. It's a miracle, really, considering.'

Cobb thought of the crushed car and the cold black river. 'Yes, it is.'

'But of course she's in shock. She hasn't said a word since they brought her in. Not a word. That's her, by the way, poor little pet.'

She pointed to a double door and through the porthole window Cobb had a glimpse of a doctor and a nurse, bending over a small figure. Cobb could not see the girl's face behind the doctor's shoulder. The Staff Nurse had marched on and he had to hurry to catch up.

'And the mother?'

'Can't get much of a fix on her. But that great hunk of a minder is a pain in the backside.' They stopped outside a set of double doors. The nurse said, 'Here,' and made to open them. She paused, her nose wrinkling. 'Can you smell something? Like cowpats maybe?'

'Not a thing.' Cobb quickly pushed open the door and walked in.

A big man in a loud check jacket was standing by the window. He turned as they entered. A woman sat perched on the edge of a green plastic sofa, smoking in defiance of hospital regulations.

The Staff Nurse ignored that, walked across the room and bent over the woman solicitously, touching her arm. 'Mrs Silver, Mr Cobb's here from the police. It's just one of those routine things.'

Lauren Silver looked up vaguely, frowned, and gave a small couldn't-care-less shrug. She looked crushed and exhausted. Her clothes were crumpled and her hand quivered as it held the cigarette. As she parted her lips to smoke, Cobb saw that one of her front teeth was broken off at an angle, and he noticed too that her lip was cut.

'The doctor will be finished in there soon and you can go back in,' the nurse was saying. 'But your little girl seems to be fine, thank the Lord. Do you need anything? No?'

As the nurse clucked over her, Cobb found himself feeling sorry for the way the Silver woman looked. As he watched her she glanced up at him with a flicker of interest, but before he could speak the big man stepped across from the window and bulked between them.

'What do we want the p'lice here for anyway?' The voice was East End, addressed to the room at large. 'No one's done a crime, have they?'

Cobb ignored him and turned to thank the Staff Nurse, who lifted an eyebrow in sympathy as she marched away through the swing doors. Then he turned back. 'And you are?'

'Matt Silver's manager.' The man stared rudely over Cobb's head.

'Have you got a name?' Cobb said. 'Sir?'

The big man faltered. 'Hudson. Tommy Hudson.'

'Well, Mr Hudson, in answer to your question, two people are dead. That's why the police are involved.'

Distress sat almost comically on Hudson's battered face. He took a deep breath and started again, his tone conciliatory. 'I'm sorry—Mr Cobb, was it? We're all really upset, see.'

Hudson's pain was so obviously real that Cobb relented. 'I understand that, of course, Mr Hudson.'

'But what I meant was, it's not like someone's done a crime, exactly.'

'There was a crime.' Her voice was very clear and much stronger than Cobb had expected. 'Matthew stole my two babies—'

'I don't think you ought to say anything just now, Laurie—'

'He stole them from me and he murdered my Gudrun.' She looked up suddenly at Cobb. 'He murdered Gudrun, Mr Cobb. That's a crime, isn't it? Murder is still a crime in this country?'

'It certainly is, Mrs Silver. Tell me what happened.'

'She's not up to this.' Hudson's voice was anguished. 'Can't we do this later, Mr Cobb?'

'Let me just get a few basic facts while they're still fresh in everyone's mind,' Cobb said, 'then I'll leave you in peace.'

The woman tossed back her dry hair and reached for cigarettes and lighter again. 'You haven't found him yet, have you?'

Cobb waited while she fumbled with the gold lighter, holding it the wrong way up at first and taking too long to discover her mistake. The woman was drunk. He didn't blame her. But it was nine in the morning. He filed the fact away.

'I said, you haven't found him yet. Right?' Her voice was slurred.

'Mrs Silver, it's true we haven't found your husband's body yet—'

'Not his *body*, Mr Cobb,' she said with heavy emphasis. '*Him*.'

'This is probably hard for you, Mrs Silver, but I think you should start to accept that your husband is almost certainly dead.'

'You don't know him.' She looked at him directly for the first time.

Cobb went on: 'Let me just say these things, Mrs Silver, and then you can work on them in your own time, OK? Your husband's car is badly damaged. In my opinion the driver could not have survived. At this time of year the water temperature in the Thames is about five degrees. Very few people survive in those conditions for more than a few minutes, especially if they're injured or shocked.'

She tossed her head defiantly. 'Freya got out. So did he.'

'All right, Mrs Silver.' Cobb got to his feet. 'We'll talk later.'

As he turned to the door it opened and a white-coated doctor leaned in. 'Mrs Silver, would you like to come through?'

She marched quickly past Cobb and through the door and down the corridor with the doctor following. Cobb watched her until she found the door of her daughter's room and pushed through it. He followed her out of the door and began to walk away down the corridor.

'Mr Cobb? Hang on a minute.' Hudson caught up with him. 'I just wanted a word, Mr Cobb, without Laurie—Mrs Silver—around.'

'Sure.'

'You're not just preparing her for the worst, like? You really don't think there's any hope?'

'None at all, Mr Hudson. That's my opinion.'

'I guess it will be easier when you find him. His body.'

'They turn up sooner or later. It's usually better when they do. I'm not trying to play psychiatrists here, Mr Hudson, but I've got a feeling she won't come to terms with one death until she's accepted the other.'

'Right.' Hudson looked away. 'You're right, I expect.'

'Were you close friends with Matt Silver, Mr Hudson?'

'Brothers. We was brothers.' Cobb saw the big man's eyes fill with tears. 'And that little kiddie was my goddaughter. Might as well've been my real daughter, I loved her that much. If you'd known her, Mr Cobb. So full of life . . .' Hudson's voice caught in disbelief.

'At least her sister's alive,' Cobb said. He was unreasonably nettled. Perhaps because a young policeman had risked his life to save this girl, he felt somehow that Hudson was being ungrateful.

Hudson glanced at him. 'Frey? You're right, of course. Absolutely right.' But then his voice faded away. 'Still, you should've seen Goodie, Mr Cobb. You should've seen Goodie.'

The exchange troubled Cobb, but there seemed no point in pursuing it. Then Hudson was holding out his hand, thanking him for sparing the time to talk, and Cobb took the warm paw and shook it. Hudson turned and pushed open the door into the child's room. On impulse Cobb stepped forward and blocked the door with his shoulder before it closed. For a moment Hudson's back obscured the child from him, but he could see Lauren Silver seated on a straight chair on the far side of the bed. Her face was carved in marble and the child's small hand lay limp and untouched in her lap. Cobb tried not to be judgmental but it saddened him that she had not taken her daughter's hand in her own.

After a moment Hudson moved around the bed and put his big hand on Lauren's shoulder and Cobb could see the child's face clearly for the first time. A plain little girl with mousy hair, eyes downcast and staring at the coverlet. He felt strangely relieved; she might be Gudrun's twin but she looked nothing like her dead sister. And then something else. As he stood propping the door open with his shoulder she lifted her head and stared directly at him. Her eyes focused and he knew that she had seen him. He looked back at her and smiled and said clearly: 'Hello, Freya.'

Her mouth opened a little and for an instant he thought she might actually answer him. But then Hudson, glancing up with surprise, broke the spell. 'You've got a way with kids, Mr Cobb.'

'No,' Cobb answered. 'No. Not at all. Excuse me.' As he turned to leave he glimpsed her face again, eyes vacant once more.

It was strange how calm she felt. Lauren did not fool herself that this was healthy, nor that it would last for ever. But it was useful. In a cold and practical sense it allowed her to function. At least, she supposed that was what she was doing. Functioning.

She could see everything very clearly. Far too clearly. She could see, for example, how much she resented the love she was supposed to lavish on this child when she had none to give. It wasn't Freya's fault. It was just the way it was. Lauren looked down at the girl's soft hand in her lap. She wasn't sure how it had got there. Maybe the nurse had placed it there. She knew she should take it in her own hands, chafe it, murmur to her baby. But she simply did not have the energy. Lauren glanced at the child and saw that she was sleeping, curled into her big pillows. There was a nurse in the room, she noticed for the first time, a pretty Asian girl, and for a moment Lauren watched her work.

'Give me a drink, Tommy,' she said abruptly, and held out her hand. Hudson was speaking, protesting. She ignored his voice and clicked her fingers impatiently until she felt the weight of the flask in her palm. She drank from it. 'I want to see my daughter,' she said.

'Your daughter's right here, Mrs Silver,' the Asian nurse said gently, thinking perhaps that she did not know what she was saying.

'I want to see my daughter,' Lauren repeated and stood up.

'You shouldn't be doing this, Laurie.' Hudson had to hurry to keep up with her brisk stride. 'There'll be time for this tomorrow.'

'Tomorrow?' she said scornfully. 'And what's she supposed to do until tomorrow?'

Hudson, unhappy and afraid, said no more. She couldn't see what was wrong with him but she didn't much care and strode on, gathering a retinue as she moved quickly down the corridors. There were whispered consultations around her, snatched conversations on the run.

Rubber doors, a chill bright cavern, metal tables glimpsed through a porthole window, a reek of chemicals. She waited, tapping her feet on the brilliant tiles, as green-clad attendants hurried to make unscheduled preparations around her. Someone drew curtains around a cubicle and she was ushered in by an indignant fat man in glasses and coveralls.

A trolley trundling on rubber wheels. The curtains moving aside. Hudson's arm clutching around her waist, locking there.

The blanket was folded back over the china white face with its bell of black hair, washed and combed now. Hudson gasped audibly beside her and Lauren felt his shock. But she was not shocked. That was no longer possible. She turned the blanket down further, revealing the birdbones of the child's shoulders.

'For God's sake, Laurie,' Hudson begged. 'Leave her be.'

So small. Too small, in fact. Gudrun took up so much more space in the world than this cold doll. Lauren touched the silken hair, ran her knuckle down the white cheek. Lauren stared hard at the pinched little face. She felt nothing. Disappointed, perhaps. Irritated at this pointless deception (did they think she would fall for *this?*). She felt nothing for this snow carving. She flipped the blanket back into place.

'Laurie, this isn't doing you any good. Let's go now.'

'Don't be silly, Tommy,' she said. 'I can't *go*. Not until I find her.'

'She's gone, Laurie.' His voice cracked. 'We've seen. Let's go home.'

'But where is she?' She was unable to comprehend his stupidity when the matter was so clear to her. 'You don't imagine this is Goodie, do you?'

'Come on now, love.' He steered her away a couple of steps.

'You're not going to let them get away with this, Tommy?' They were back in the glaring anteroom now, Hudson's powerful arm locked around her, half carrying her. Others came to help him. Someone opened the door for them. Twisting her head around in panic, she caught sight of the fat man with glasses standing near the far wall. 'You!' she screamed at him. 'What have you done with my daughter, you bastard?'

The fat man looked sadly at the floor as they dragged her away along the echoing corridors, shrieking like an animal in a trap.

Chapter Three

COBB TOOK THE LIFT to the third floor and used his security pass to open the double doors. The CID room was the usual wasps' nest of activity, a clatter and buzz of keyboards, phones, raised voices. Cobb moved through the melee towards his own desk. Before he got there Nelson appeared in the doorway of his office, gesturing to him.

'Sam?' Nelson had to shout over the noise. 'A minute, lad.'

Cobb followed him into the office and pulled the door half-closed behind him, shutting out some of the machine-room jangle.

'What's up, Horrie?'

Nelson waved him to a seat and paced in front of his desk. He seemed restless. 'Mr Sykes wants us to set up a task force.'

'A task force? For a car smash?' Cobb was incredulous. He failed to register Nelson's warning glance so that Sykes was through the door and standing behind him before he knew it.

'We're looking for another corpse, Cobby,' Sykes said, with his usual mix of aggression and jocularity. 'We've only got one of those so far.'

Cobb stood up. 'Sir.'

Sykes gestured for him to sit down again and himself took the chair opposite. 'Did you meet the grieving widow?' He was a hard man in his mid-fifties who grinned a lot, baring small teeth.

'Yes, sir. I talked to her at the hospital.'

'She doesn't think hubby's dead. She keeps calling to remind us about that. Keeps asking for you, as a matter of fact.'

Cobb wondered where this was going, but he already had a fair idea. 'Silver's body will turn up in a few days,' he said. 'Maybe sooner. Sir.'

'Well, that's fine. Because you're in charge of looking for it.' Cobb stared at him and Sykes continued: 'There you go, Cobby. The Matt Silver Task Force. What you always wanted. Your very own team.'

Cobb swallowed. 'Sir, I've been working with DI Peters on the Beulah Road break-ins. And I'm on the West London Car Crime programme—'

'Put them on hold. Hand over your notes.'

Cobb said, 'Sir.'

Sykes turned to Nelson with a look of mock surprise. 'I don't think he likes it much, Horrie.'

Nelson frowned. Cobb said: 'With respect, Mr Sykes—'

'Listen, Cobby,' Sykes cut across him, 'I know it's a pisser, and you probably think I've done it to shaft you, but I need it done. There's a feeding frenzy out there and I don't want anyone saying we haven't done every last fucking thing to find this bloke.'

'Silver's dead, sir,' Cobb said. 'It was an accident.'

'Of course it was, Cobby. This isn't about reality. This is about public bloody relations. You look all right, Cobby. You can give an interview without saying fucking too often, unlike me. And you're not doing anything important. So you deal with it.'

It was Hudson's voice that woke her. He was giving an instruction to the driver, telling him to pull up. Lauren opened her eyes. The windows of the car were plates of ebony. So it was night again. But then, between the backs of the seats, she saw the green numerals of the dashboard clock and it told her that it was only six in the evening.

She was wrapped in a coat or a blanket, warm and comfortable, curled in the back seat of the car. She didn't remember getting there. She was sleepy and dull and knew that she must have been sedated. She didn't blame them. She knew how she had been.

'Laurie? Are you awake?'

'Yes, Tommy.' The concern in his voice was so palpable that she stretched out her hand and squeezed his arm. 'It's OK now.'

'Jesus, Laurie. I been so worried.'

'I'm all right, Tommy.' She shuffled herself into a sitting position, discovering that her body was raw and bruised.

'What they done to you . . . I had to help them, Laurie. I hope I never . . .' He shook his head. 'How are you now?'

'OK. I'm OK.'

She glanced out of the window. Home, or very nearly home. She could not decide whether this was good or bad.

Hudson had punched numbers into a mobile and was murmuring into it. The voice that squawked back was clearly audible to Lauren.

'It's pretty crazy here, Tommy. We'll have all the overseas media here by midnight, too, and the local law aren't much help.' The voice paused. 'You might think about giving this a miss. Stay away for a day or two.'

Hudson covered the phone. 'Laurie, we ought to go somewhere else. We can come back here in a couple of days maybe.'

'I'm going home, Tommy.' She stretched across in the darkness and patted his arm again. 'You'll take care of everything.'

'You there, Tommy?' the phone bleated again.

'Yes. We're coming through. Right now. OK?'

'Just as you say, Tommy.'

Hudson leaned forward to slide open the driver's partition. 'Give it a bit of welly as you go through, Col, but try not to kill anyone.'

'Right.'

'Tommy—' Lauren stirred beside him.

'You stay down for the next minute and it will all be OK.'

She moved her hand down his sleeve and gripped his thick wrist briefly. 'Couldn't have got through today without you, Tommy. Thanks.'

She gave him a pallid smile. Then they were sweeping towards the lights and lenses. He told her to duck down, but she was too dazed to care and, as they drove through the popping flashguns, her lost white face against the glass was an offering to the cameras.

The car bounced to a stop on the drive and the security men ran up and Hudson helped them bundle her towards the house. The dark garden leapt into stark negative behind them as TV lights sprang on and a riot of scuffling and shouting broke out beyond the security cordon. Then the front door was open and Hudson pushed her through and slammed the door behind them and locked it and leaned against it.

She could feel him watching her as she moved away from him down the hall. She felt hollow, nearly weightless.

'I'll call someone for you,' he said. 'A friend or someone.'

'A friend?' She made a sad face at him. 'Not many of those any more. All Matthew's. Everything was Matthew's.'

'That's not true, Laurie. You'll see.'

'I'm going to take a shower, Tommy. Freshen up. You're a sweetheart for bringing me back here but you don't need to wait.'

'I'll wait, Laurie.' He stood at the end of the hallway. 'I'll wait.'

She walked back up the hall to him with unfaltering steps and kissed him quickly on the cheek. 'Dear Tommy. Always there.'

When she had gone upstairs, Hudson poured himself a Scotch at Silver's dining-room bar. He sipped the drink, set it down and then moved around the room ripping down the Christmas decorations. He fetched a rubbish sack from the kitchen and bundled up the bright tinsel, the smiling Santas and reindeer, and crushed them all into the sack. Only when he had finished did Freya cross his mind. Should he have left something for her? The truth was that he didn't much care. He had tried to be good to both children but Freya had always held back. It was her nature, he supposed, but the result was that now he really had no room for her. It was a pity but there it was.

Hudson stuffed the bag of decorations out of sight behind the sofa and then stood and nursed his Scotch, gazing mournfully around the room. The house had been home to Silver's family—and a second home to Hudson himself—for twelve years. He had come here as often as he could, bringing presents, staying over. He was Matt Silver's friend, sometimes his confidant, sometimes Lauren's, Goodie's godfather. Yes, Lauren and Matt might have troubles, but who didn't? But whatever their problems the Silvers were family, and to Hudson this was home.

All over now. All over for Silver, and for little Gudrun. The image of the child's face appeared to him again and Hudson sat down on the brocade sofa with a bump. He had never expected grief to be like this; every time he thought about Goodie the memory knocked him sideways. His vision blurred and he squeezed the bridge of his nose hard. Laurie didn't need any of that nonsense right now.

Lauren walked through the bedroom to the en suite bathroom, turned the shower on full and left it that way. With the rush of water masking all other sounds, she returned to the bedroom door and locked it from the inside and then walked across to the dressing table and sat down. A photograph on the dressing table showed her and Matthew with the two girls at the Eiffel Tower. She remembered that it had been taken two years before on the last of their reconciliation trips. She wasn't sure why she had kept that photo particularly. His recommitment to her had not outlasted the Paris trip by more than a week. Yet now it was his image that she gazed at, this unreasonably beautiful man, his head tossed back, laughing as if to challenge the whole world.

'Matthew,' she told the picture quietly, 'you've killed us all.'

Lauren went through the drawers of folded clothing until she found what she wanted and when she did she drank from the bottle. She rose to her feet and walked into the bathroom. She found surgical scissors and half-a-dozen bottles of pills. She emptied some of the pills onto the coverlet and sat on the bed and tossed the scissors onto the blanket beside her. How good it would be if they did find him. Perhaps then, the threat removed, she could let go. How she longed for that. And it would be so simple. Extinction, the end of all her failures. She found a loose coin on the bedside table and played at tossing for it: heads the bottle, tails the blade. After a while she stopped, for of course she could not be that easy on herself. She picked up the photograph. She opened her blouse and cradled the picture there, the glass cold against her bare breast, and rocked it against her like a baby.

Tommy Hudson realised he had finished his drink and that made him aware that time had passed. He set down his glass and walked quickly through into the hallway. He peered upstairs and could see the line of light under her bedroom door and could hear the hiss of the water.

'Laurie? You OK up there?' Probably she couldn't hear him, but the silence worried him anyway. He trotted up the stairs and knocked hard on her door. 'Laurie?'

He tried the handle. The door was locked. He put his big shoulder against it and popped the oak inwards like plywood. The shower was rushing in the bathroom and steam billowed through into the bedroom. Lauren sat cross-legged on the bed, nursing the picture. An empty vodka bottle stood on the bedside table. The coverlet was scattered with small bottles and loose multicoloured tablets. He saw the glint of the scissors against the blanket. He marched through to the bathroom. He turned the water off and came back and stood over her. He gripped her shoulders and shook her so that her head snapped back.

'Did you take any?'

'Tommy—'

'Did you?'

'No. I didn't take any.' He let her go.

He turned away, breath coming fast, then he swung back on the ball of his foot. 'You got a little girl to take care of!' he shouted suddenly.

She stared at him, motionless. 'I know that, Tommy.'

'A little girl!' His fists were opening and closing. When he spoke again his voice was tight. 'Laurie, you know I always . . .'

'Tommy,' she said, 'none of that matters now.'

He seemed about to say more but stopped himself and straightened slowly to his full height. He stood there silent for a long while, then he scooped up a wastebin and moved slowly around the bedroom gathering up her litter. He stopped distractedly and shook the bin at her as if she were a naughty schoolgirl. 'I won't stand for all this, you know,' he said. 'I won't stand for it.'

She rocked the framed photograph in her arms, watching him. 'Just take care of everything for us, Tommy.'

'The cops again? Why don't you let a chap get some peace?'

'Open up, old man,' Cobb commanded. 'It's bloody cold out here.'

When the low front door opened a crack, Cobb shouldered through it into the hall. He noticed that Fred was wearing purple pyjamas with a smiling pig motif on them.

'Are you ever going to leave me alone?' the old man muttered.

Cobb closed the front door and followed him. The house was dark and Fred snapped on a light and waved Cobb through into a pleasant firelit lounge. 'What are the neighbours going to think, eh?'

'Give it a rest, Dad,' Cobb told him. 'Long day.'

'It's not natural, hanging around your father day and night.'

Cobb smiled to himself as the old man grumbled on. They both knew, but neither could admit, that Fred lived for his visits. Cobb followed him into the kitchen, fetched a beer from the fridge and then went back into the lounge and put the TV on low volume. He sat in the leather armchair next to the banked fire and poured out the beer. Baskerville lay slumped across the rug in front of the fire. In the low room the old mongrel looked the size of a small pit pony.

Silver's disappearance was top of the late news. A girl with copper hair and a low, urgent voice traced Matt Silver's career. There was old footage of Silver on stage, his long black hair flying as he sang. There was no doubt the man had charisma, Cobb had to admit. Unlike most rock stars Silver was genuinely handsome and evidently knew it. Footage from interviews projected an image of an articulate, intelligent, sardonic personality, one who handled fame easily, who always looked in control.

The report cut to the steps of St Thomas's Hospital where the camera caught Lauren Silver through a cordon of security men, hurrying across a rainswept pavement to a black BMW. As the group reached the car Tommy Hudson materialised in front of the camera and spoke to the journalists, distracting them as the car pulled away behind him.

Then the TV flashed up a picture of two little girls. Gudrun, at once radiant and coquettish, beamed like a searchlight. Beside her, Freya might have been sketched in sepia.

'Little Gudrun Silver,' the voiceover intoned. 'Dead tonight at the age of nine. Meanwhile, the search goes on for her famous father.'

Sipping his beer, Cobb found himself hoping that they soon found Silver dead, for his own sake. It was impossible that anyone could live with himself after bringing about the death of his child and the destruction of what was left of his family.

He shook himself and realised he was hungry. 'Hey, old man,' he called into the kitchen. 'Are you ever coming out of there?'

Fred emerged almost at once with sandwiches on a tray. Cobb always let him do this: cooking for his son had been one of Fred's great joys for as long as either of them could remember, even while Cobb's mother had still lived with them. Cobb flicked channels while he ate, running into the Silver story again almost at once.

'Pity about this chap,' Fred remarked, nodding at the screen. 'I rather like his stuff.'

'You do?'

'And what's so surprising about that?'

'Dad, you're seventy-eight. He's a rock star.'

'I'm sorry? I fail to see the connection.'

Cobb knew better than to rise to that. 'Then you'll be pleased to hear that Matt Silver's my new case. You're looking at the head of the Matt Silver Task Force.'

Fred watched his son carefully. 'That's rather good, isn't it?'

Cobb sighed and set the plate of sandwiches aside and snapped the TV off with the remote. 'I'm resigning from the Met.'

Fred blinked. 'I see.'

'Dad, I knew you'd be disappointed.'

'You're not a child, Samuel. You must know your own mind.' Fred stood up, ramrod straight. 'Am I allowed to know what your plans are?'

'I don't really have any. I'm all right for money. I just thought I'd—'

'Don't think for one moment, that you're going to hang around here. I too have plans for the rest of my life, however long or short that may be. And watching my own son mooning around in some sort of endless mourning is not included in them.'

'That's not fair.'

But Fred was not to be stopped now. 'There's life, you know, Samuel. There's life out there. It goes on despite you. You can't turn your back on it for ever.' Then he swung on his heel and marched to the door. Cobb heard him slam his bedroom door hard enough to make the crockery rattle in the dresser.

Gloomily, Cobb munched the rest of his sandwich in silence. When he had finished he roused Baskerville and ordered him out into the yard, waiting while he shambled around on the cold cobbles and found somewhere to pee. Then he let the dog back in and walked down the short passage into the garden room.

He turned on the desklight and closed the door behind him and patted the bed in which Clea had died. It was a small ritual which said hello to her. Cobb was not superstitious. He simply felt better in here. Calmer. And the ritual was part of that.

He sat at the desk and swung round in the swivel chair. He had left a few of her books on the shelves, ones that seemed too personal to throw out. There were also three framed photographs of her on the dressing table and a few of her tennis trophies. The room was reminiscent of her but Cobb was satisfied it hardly qualified as mawkish indulgence. The only truly personal memento of her was a pink stuffed toy which now sat grinning on the mantelpiece. It had cost him nearly £20 to win it for her at the St Giles Fair in Oxford the October before she died. He went over, picked the thing up and dusted its nylon fur. Clea had taken such an uncharacteristically sentimental liking to it that after she had gone it seemed a betrayal to throw it out. He turned it over in his hand. It beamed at him with idiot glee.

Fred's tapping on the door did not startle him: he had been half expecting it, hoping for it. He opened the door.

'Room for an old 'un?' his father said. He carried a small wooden tray with the Laphroaig and two shot glasses.

'That'd get you in anywhere,' Cobb said, taking the tray and setting it on the end of the bed and turning a chair for his father. He poured the smoky spirit and handed one to Fred.

'You know, Samuel . . .'

'I know, Dad.' Cobb lifted his glass and touched his father's with it. 'Cheers.'

'Flew off the handle a bit . . .'

'I know.'

'Will you stop telling me you know?' Fred said testily. 'I want to tell you that if you really must go ahead with this resignation nonsense, of course you can spend as long here as you need. It's your home. Always has been.' He looked away awkwardly, sipped his drink. 'Cheers.'

'I won't say I know. But I do.'

They were silent for a while, drinking. Then Fred looked around the room. 'Nice room, this,' he remarked. 'Always liked it.'

Cobb smiled. 'Too nice for a shrine, eh, Dad?'

'Good Lord, Samuel. You tread heavily.'

'Perhaps I do. It comes of being a flatfoot.'

'I just meant—'

'You're right, Dad. I'll clear it out after Christmas. Redecorate it maybe. I'll have the time then, I suppose.'

'Samuel, you must know that all I want . . .' Fred's voice trailed off.

'Yes, I think I do.'

'You can't . . . close down. Not at your age.'

'I understand.'

'I mean, leave the force if you must. It's not treated you especially well in my view.' Fred was sniffy about his son's lack of promotion. 'But start something new. Don't retreat. Don't ever retreat.'

'Dad, I hear you.'

'My boy, if you heard me, I wouldn't have to say it.' Fred sighed. 'And maybe you wouldn't be standing there cuddling a stuffed dinosaur.'

Six hours later Cobb stood at the kitchen window, sipping coffee, and stared out at the night which people called morning at this time of year. It was raining gently—he could hear it trickling in the gutters. Despite the black rain and the hour, Cobb felt good. He had told Fred: that meant he had crossed the Rubicon. The old man might not like it but he had come up with no argument Cobb himself had not already considered. It was time for a big step. Resignation was no retreat. Cobb would spend a couple of months at the farm, get some peace and quiet. Then he would work out what else to do with his life.

He locked the back door and crossed the yard to the barn. He threw his parcel into the back seat with his briefcase, slid in a Bach CD and then backed the Saab out and drove up the rutted track to the main road. He turned the car onto the M40 and joined the twin tracks of light heading east. On impulse he decided to go to the hospital first.

It was still only seven thirty when he stepped out of the lift at St Thomas's. There was a sense of offstage bustle, jingling trays, a rattle of crockery and the smell of food. A uniformed policeman dozed in a hardback chair against the wall. The Staff Nurse from the day before was leaning against the desk in the reception area, chatting to an orderly behind the counter. Both wore red felt Christmas hats. She looked up as he approached. 'What brings you here so early, Inspector?'

'I've come to leave something for the child,' he said.

'Oh, I see.' She crossed her arms. 'I'll find out if she's awake.'

'That's not necessary. I just wanted to leave her something.'

'Oh, no, Inspector,' she said firmly. 'That won't do at all. Little Freya would love a visit. Just you come along with me.' She set off at the brisk pace he remembered from yesterday and he hurried to catch up.

'I really can't visit her. There should be people present—'

'Why? What are you going to do? Use thumbscrews?'

'It's a regulation—'

She strode on. 'I won't tell if you won't.'

They stopped outside the door.

'The point is it's Christmas Eve tomorrow and she's not going to see her mum any time soon. So you just pop in and say hello, all right?'

'Look, I don't really want to get into this. I shouldn't be hanging around here before the kid's mother even arrives. It doesn't look right.'

'The mother threw a fit yesterday.'

'She did?' Cobb told himself he didn't want to know.

'Insisted on seeing the body, then wouldn't believe it. She threw a real wobbly. Restraint, sedatives, the lot. She wouldn't let us admit her. That big ape took charge. I must say, he was useful when it came to it.'

She swept him into the room. The child was sitting up, lost in the bed. There were dark rings under her eyes and she did not look as if she had slept. They had found her some glasses. They were evidently not her own, for they had severe black frames and were too big for her. Through them she stared owlishly at Cobb over the Staff Nurse's shoulder as she fussed around her, plumping the pillows.

'This is Mr Cobb come to see you again, sweetheart. Do you remember him from yesterday?' She ruffled the child's mousy hair. 'Mr Cobb's come to see how you are, that's all. Breakfast soon, pet.' She kissed the girl lightly on the forehead and bustled out of the room. The door swung to behind her.

'Hello, Freya,' Cobb said. 'I just wanted—' Then he stopped. She was not looking at him but at his shoes, craning over the side of the bed to see them. 'You do remember,' he said quietly, and could hear the wonder in his own voice. 'You really do remember.' He laughed aloud. 'They were pretty filthy, Princess, weren't they? Do you think anyone else noticed? But look—they're clean this time.' He lifted one polished black shoe and then the other, hopping around, clowning for her. She gazed steadily at him. 'Hey, I've got a little present for you. It's a bit early for Christmas and it's not much.' He put the parcel on the bed. 'But open it anyway. Go on—rip it. It's always more fun if you rip it.'

Rather to his surprise she did. Within a few seconds the neat bed was littered with Christmas paper and the pink dinosaur was bestowing its beatific grin on her. She looked at it thoughtfully for a moment then gathered the dinosaur up in her arms and rocked it hard against her.

'There you go, Princess,' he said. 'From one lovely lady to another.'

Abruptly he felt his throat tighten and turned quickly away to stare out of the window. He was suddenly flooded with loneliness and loss.

'She's called Bronty, Princess,' he said, turning back to face the child. 'We have lots of them on the farm. Great big ones. Much bigger than Bronty. She's only a baby. Cows and chickens and horses and things too, of course, but our speciaity is pink dinosaurs. You don't believe me?' The girl stared at him, rocking the toy against her face. 'Well, I'll tell you what. If you don't believe me, you can come down and see them for yourself, as soon as you're out of here. How's that? And that's a promise.'

The door swung open sharply and the Staff Nurse bounced back into the room. 'Well, sweetheart,' she said, 'is that what the Inspector brought you? That's lovely, that is. Who'd've thought he was a softy?'

Cobb looked away.

'But I have to take the nice Inspector outside for a minute, love. So say goodbye now.'

'Goodbye, Freya.' Cobb leaned forward to pat the child's hand. 'You take care of her. And yourself.'

He followed the Staff Nurse out into the corridor.

'Sorry to drag you away just when you're playing Santa,' she said, 'but Mrs Silver is about to make a liar of me.' She gestured to the reception desk at the end of the corridor. It was bustling with people. Among them he saw the tall, square figure of Hudson.

'I'd better sort this out.' The Staff Nurse strode towards the melee.

Cobb moved off in the opposite direction. He had barely rounded the corner when he almost collided with Lauren Silver. She was alone. They both stopped. She looked, Cobb thought, as fragile as cut glass.

'Mrs Silver, I'm Sam Cobb. Perhaps you remember?'

'I know who you are. Have you found him?'

'No. I just came by to drop in a present for Freya.'

She looked through him without interest. 'She doesn't need presents.'

'I don't suppose she does, Mrs Silver. I just felt like giving her one.'

Her eyes focused on him for the first time. 'I know how to look after my own child, Mr Cobb. I know my duty as well as you know yours.'

'Your duty?'

'Perhaps you had better get on with your job, which is finding my child's killer, Mr Cobb. And I'll get on with mine.'

'Your *duty*, Mrs Silver?' He stared at her in disbelief as she brushed past him. It stunned him that she could say such a thing, and stunned him still more to discover how it outraged him. He got a grip on himself and for reassurance crinkled the resignation letter in his pocket. This was definitely the right decision. Definitely.

There were four male and two female officers in the incident room and Cobb could sense their resentment. It did not surprise him. They were hardly the pick of the bunch. They knew it, and obscurely they blamed him for it. Two of them he recognised—a solid Welshman called Owens who was under investigation for assault, and a female Constable called Carlow who was sleeping with a Drugs Squad DI.

'Settle down, people,' he said, and leaned over to the notice board. He flicked the glossy enlarged print with his nail. 'Matthew Kelso Silver. He is a missing person and we are going to find him.' He looked belligerently around. 'You have a problem with that, Constable Owens?'

'No, sir. Not exactly, like.' The Welshman pulled a face. 'But we know where he is, sir, don't we? He's in the river. He'll float up in a day or two.'

'Where?'

'Well, how would I know that, sir?' He looked around for support.

'Get on to the Thames Division as soon as we finish here and find out. The ten most likely places, given the tide.' Cobb looked around. 'Any more comments before we get on with this?'

He dismissed the briefing half-an-hour later. Cobb was grimly amused by the whole charade. But once the meeting was over a pressure began to build in him, a pressure that demanded release. He felt like a terrorist with dynamite strapped around him. He longed to place himself in front of Detective Chief Superintendent Sykes and then detonate.

But it was not so easy to find Sykes. By five thirty his moment still had not presented itself. Cobb logged off his work station and stretched back in his chair. He swept a couple of loose paper clips off the desk and returned them to their packet in the top drawer, straightened the phone, arranged a scatter of photos into a neat stack.

'This the Jag?' said Horrie Nelson from behind him. He took the pictures and dealt through them like a deck of cards, clicking his tongue at each new image of twisted metal. He said, too casually: 'Still no sign?'

Cobb took the photos back and put them away in the top drawer. 'Horrie, you know and I know that Matt Silver is either stuck under a barge, in which case he'll bloat and float in a week or so, or he's past the Thames Barrier by now. Not that anyone will convince his wife of that.'

Nelson nodded. 'Good psychiatric care is what she needs.'

'Yes.'

'Got to come to terms with it sooner or later.'

'Horrie, is there any danger at all of you letting me go home?'

Nelson looked guiltily at him and blurted: 'Come to the club for a drink.' He saw Cobb's expression and added, a little plaintively: 'It's Christmas, Sam.'

'You know I never go to the club. *You* never go to the club.'

'Mr Sykes would like you to go to the club, Sam.' Nelson looked away. 'And don't argue for once. Just bloody do it.'

It reminded him of all the things he had hated about the Union Bar at university twenty-five years ago: a cavern full of smoke, loud heartiness, shouted laughter and the click of snooker balls.

'Cobby! We got you here at last.' Sykes was leaning against the bar. 'What'll you have, Cobby? Wine? Scotch?'

'Prefer bitter, sir.'

'Bitter, is it?' Sykes made big eyes as if this were a daring request. He called the barman and ordered the drink.

Sykes said: 'Horrie Nelson tells me you're thinking of leaving.'

Cobb moved his hand towards his breast pocket.

Sykes grinned. 'Don't give it to me now, Cobby,' he said. 'Swear to God, if you do, I'll burn it in that ashtray without opening it.'

Cobb collected himself. 'With respect to Mr Nelson, sir, he shouldn't have told you any such thing. I could then have told you myself.'

'Yes. But I wanted to deny you that pleasure, see, Cobby. So I wheedled it out of the old bugger.' Sykes handed Cobb his beer. 'Look, I know what you think. You think I've got it in for you and that's why you don't get moved up. Well, it's true I don't much like you, Cobb. But the reason you haven't moved on is because you're no more than an all right copper. It's as simple as that. You'd be better, but you spend too much time inside your own head.'

'It's more interesting in there, sir.'

Sykes watched him steadily. 'I heard about your wife, Cobb. I didn't know. Me being a newcomer.'

'It's no secret, sir.'

'I might have thought twice about this Silver business if I'd known.' He pushed himself away from the bar. 'I don't suppose we'll ever be mates, Cobb, but even I know you need all types in a job like this. Not just beer swilling old warhorses like me.'

'Sir.'

Sykes paused. 'Think about it over Christmas, Cobby. Maybe this is a bad time for you to make decisions. If you still want to resign after the break, I'll accept it.'

They had settled Freya on the couch in a nest of cushions. If her injured leg pained her she gave no sign of it. It lay stretched out in front of her, strapped with flesh-coloured tape. She lay in her soft nest, brushing her toy's pink fur against the nap then smoothing it down again. But she did not smile and she did not speak. Lauren knew that if she had fired a gun in the room the child would not have looked up at her.

Merilda, the Portuguese maid, bustled in with a tray, filling the room with noisy sympathy, fussing around the child, pushing her tear-stained face close to Freya's. Lauren watched for a while longer, but something about the scene set her teeth on edge.

Lauren got up and walked to her study. Tommy Hudson was sitting in the leather chair by the desk, his elbows on it, staring out of the black square of the window. He looked up as she came in.

'Sorry,' he said. 'Did I startle you?'

'I don't think anything will ever startle me ever again, Tommy.'

'No. I s'pose not.' He gazed miserably out into the night. He said: 'You don't really think he's alive, do you, Laurie?' Hudson was looking at her with the eyes of a wounded spaniel, pleading to be convinced of something, but she couldn't tell what.

'Get me a drink, Tommy,' she said abruptly.

He sat up straight. 'Laurie, you ought to take a couple of those pills and get some rest. We all need some rest.'

'It's Christmas Eve and I want a drink,' she said, and when she saw how the harshness of her tone hurt him, added: 'Be a sweetheart. Please.'

Hudson got up and walked through to the kitchen. Lauren waited, rocking herself in her chair. Alive? She would never be able to explain it to him. To anyone. Matthew had always been beyond normal rules. Had he escaped? Of course he had. He had escaped into his own mythology. The papers had sensed that at once. They used words like 'mystery' and 'legend' and 'vanishing' in their headlines.

But to Lauren he was another order of being altogether. She knew he was the Elf King, luring the loveliest of children to annihilation, possessed of a lambent spirit which burned with beauty and evil in equal measure. To talk of him dying was simply absurd. He would have found a way out.

The line of her thinking led her to Cobb. A remarkably clear vision of the detective flashed into her mind, as he had looked when she walked into him at the hospital: a square, compact man, serious in his dark suit. There was something about him, something unrelenting. He did not even believe his quarry was there to be found. But despite that, once he was set on the hunt he would track the spoor to the very end. She knew instinctively that Cobb was the kind of man for such a task, the kind of man to whom duty was a religion and a curse. Duty. He had used that word to her, and she could still see the contempt in his face as he had used it: 'Your duty?'

She got up quickly and walked out of the room, brushing past Hudson in the hallway as if she had not seen him.

'Laurie—' He followed her, concerned, setting the spilled drink down on a window ledge.

Lauren walked across the lounge to the couch and sat on the edge of it. After a moment she began, hesitantly, to stroke Freya's hair. She did not recognise the feel of it. The child did not interrupt her silent play to look at her. 'Frey—Frey,' Lauren said softly. 'I know that you know. It's not your fault. But perhaps it's not mine either.'

And finally the child lifted her face and looked at her. She nursed the toy against her, her eyes huge and filled with an unreadable sadness.

Chapter Four

PROBABLY NOTHING would have called him back if it had not been for the thrashing of the dredger's propellor. It demanded attention, a distant chirping noise, inhuman, metallic. Pain erupted in his hands and feet and burned inwards to his chest and brain, and all at once the thing was on top of him, a black fortress of gantries lurching past so close he could hear the steel groaning. The big prop was churning a few feet away, wildly rocking the black water, and once again he was plunging down.

The knocking was irregular but insistent. Tap-tap. Tap-tap-tap. He came awake reluctantly, keeping his eyes closed. His confusion did not strike him as particularly strange. He thought perhaps he was drunk. He opened his eyes. But when he did it all made even less sense. There was a solid wall of black above him, and running up the side of the wall from his eyelevel was a flight of steps. He could see his legs, black against the glittering water. They did not seem to belong to him.

Silver moved his head experimentally and two things happened at once: he was filled with a ballooning fireball of pain, and the knocking stopped abruptly. As it did he realised it was made by his skull, knocking against the bottom step as the water moved him. Then he saw there was a figure at the top of the steps. The creature moved forwards and Silver could hear big boots, clumping down.

The man stood quite still, his coat flapping like a sail in a gust of wind. Silver knew he was watching him, wondering, perhaps, whether he was alive or dead. The man called something—a question, a demand. The man moved a couple of paces. He stopped, shouted again.

Silver closed his eyes, weary to the point of death, hoping that perhaps it might come and release him even now, and in that moment the man reached down and gripped the collar of his leather jacket. Silver felt his body bump up a couple of steps, felt the pain flare up again, but less keenly this time, and realised that his mind was drifting. His rescuer was wheezing from his effort and sat back on his haunches.

'Can't leave you in the drink, son. Against the rules.' The tramp's voice was a rasp, thick with drink and smoke. 'We don't leave the floaters in for the little fishes. Dead or alive, my son, we pull 'em out.' He spoke, and as he spoke his hand stole down inside Silver's jacket.

'No good to you now, you poor bastard, is it?' the man protested to himself. 'Not when there's them as needs it, eh?' Silver felt the hard warm hand against his chest. The pigskin wallet slid out of his breast pocket. 'Feller can't die without a name, now can he?"

Something stirred painfully in Silver's mind. With a huge effort he lifted his hand and gripped the derelict's wrist. The man shouted and stumbled back and tore his wrist free so violently that he fell back up the steps. Silver heard the wallet slap against stone and then the splash of it and he knew it was lost and was glad. The man scrabbled with his heels, pushing himself up, panting with fear, and at that moment a woman's voice shrilled: 'What the fuck are you up to now, Stevens?'

Another slighter silhouette stood at the top of the steps, arms akimbo. Silver saw a flag of hair flap in the wind, bone white in the moon.

'Christ on His cross, Maggie! It's alive down there!'

'You've been on the piss again, Stevie, ain't you?' Silver saw her crane over the edge, a shrivelled old woman. She looked directly at him. In a different voice she said: 'You stupid bastard. What have you got me into now?'

'I just pulled him out, Maggie. That's all. Out of respect, like.'

'He's a jumper, you stupid bastard. It's where he wanted to be.'

'Can't leave 'em in, Maggie. Can't leave a man in the 'oggin.'

'You and your bloody Navy. Nobody'd think you was thrown out.'

'Honest to God, I thought he was dead. I just wanted to pull him out.'

'You wanted his wallet too, while you were about it.'

Stevens rubbed his hands on his coat and sulked. 'Thinking he was dead, mind. We need it. He don't.' The woman looked at him until he answered the unspoken question. 'He chucked it in the river.'

She snorted again. 'Move aside and let me take a look.'

Silver watched the woman hitch up her skirt and then step cautiously down the steps towards him. She bent over him and touched him on the neck. 'Jesus. You're more dead than alive, you are.'

The muscles of his throat were clamped: they ached with the effort of speech. 'Leave me,' he said.

The woman sat back on her haunches on the steps. 'Leave you?'

'Please.' Silver moved his hand far enough to reach his jacket pocket and tapped it with his forefinger, again and again. 'Please.'

'What you got here, then, sunshine? What's this here?' She felt inside his pocket and pulled out the wet wad of notes. 'Show old Mags.'

The water ran glittering off the wad. Silver saw her freeze at the sight of the money. Then she sighed, and he knew she had made up her mind. She stuffed the notes somewhere in her clothing.

'Sorry, my luv,' she said, with what sounded like real regret. 'But it don't work that way.' Then she stood up and screamed, 'Stevie? You get down here and give me a hand with him, you useless article.'

He was vaguely aware of being dragged, bumping, up the steps with the man grunting in his ear. He would have resisted if he could have found an ounce of energy or will. He felt himself dumped on the dockside while the man struggled for breath. He could see he was on the apron of a warehouse washed in acid light by a three-quarter moon.

The grinding rumble of a roller door. Growled curses. A crackling and a popping near him, a sound he could not place but which seemed strangely comforting. He struggled to open his eyes. Only one of them would obey but it was enough to show him wild flame shadows flickering among iron pillars, and he understood that the crackle and hiss was a fire. Now he could feel the warmth of it pulsing against his back. There was a rough blanket against his skin and he registered that he was naked under it and that the blanket stank. It was impossible not to yield to the animal comfort of the flames and the dry touch of the wool, but beyond that he had neither thought nor recollection.

She was digging about in the ashes of the fire and it was grey daylight. He could see she was shivering, and realised that, for the moment, he was not. Finally she found a live ember and, grunting with satisfaction, placed a curl of paper next to it and blew asthmatically on it. A worm of fire hurried along the edge of the paper and then blossomed into yellow flame. She placed splinters and shreds of wood and a cigarette carton over the nest of flame, and in a second it was crackling.

'Reg'lar girl guide, me.' She looked up and leered at him. 'Not what we're used to, Stevie and me. But we was turned out last week. Again.' She moved nearer to him and pulled up a milk crate and sat on it, warming herself at the fire. She was an ugly woman in her late fifties, with grey hair in rat's tails over a haggard face. She shook her head as she looked at him. 'My Christ, but you're a sight,' she said.

Silver lay, barely breathing, and stared at her in pain and misery. At last he said: 'Who are you?'

'Me? I'm Maggie Turpin. Everyone knows me.'

But that wasn't what he had meant. He didn't care what her name was, and he closed her out of his mind. He tried to move but he was as weak as a kitten. He could flex his right arm a little, though his shoulder hurt him fiercely when he did so. His legs were as dead as if they were carved out of wood. He dragged down half a breath and shouted feebly at her: 'For God's sake—why couldn't you let me die?'

'It wasn't your time,' she said easily. 'That old river don't give folks up easily, and when it does, there's a reason.'

'Jesus,' he whispered in despair.

'But now you're a bit of a problem. Seeing as you're still in the land of the living.' She looked down at him with a strange, detached benignity. 'I give you till this morning, see? I reckoned if you'd passed on in the night, well, that was meant to be. But now—well, this is a poser.'

'Just leave me here, for God's sake. Just fuck off.'

'Can't do that, luvvie. Now, what I should do is call the law, and be gone when they get here.'

Silver had not thought himself capable of alarm. He said, in a clearer voice: 'Don't do that.'

'Oooh,' she said. 'That got your attention, eh? Well, don't you worry. That'd be breaking another rule.' She paused. 'Because you've done something, luv, ain't you?' Silver was silent and she went on, more gently: 'Well, I'm not going to be calling any policemen. But—see the problem? Can't call the coppers. Can't leave you.'

'You crazy old witch—why can't you just forget you ever saw me? You know I'm going to finish this just as soon as I'm strong enough.'

'Oh, yes,' she said, quite unruffled. 'You have to do what you have to do, dearie. Just like I do.'

'It was wrong of me Mr Cobb,' she said. 'The way I spoke to you at the hospital.'

Cobb stood just inside the conservatory door with the phone to his ear. He was simultaneously surprised, angry and resentful at being called at the farm: it shattered his peaceful mood in an instant. But Lauren's apology disarmed him, that and his understanding of her trouble. He composed himself with an effort. 'Mrs Silver, you have nothing to feel sorry about. In fact, I should probably apologise to you.'

'Oh?'

'Going to Freya like that without asking you. I can see—'

'As a matter of fact, that's another reason for my ringing.'

'Why? Is she talking yet?'

'No, that's partly my point. Tommy and I both feel she has taken to you in some way.'

'I only gave her a toy, Mrs Silver. Nothing more.'

'Yes, there was something more.'

He closed his eyes and took a deep breath. 'Mrs Silver, I ought to make it clear to you that I can't get involved . . .'

'You are involved.'

'Not for very much longer, Mrs Silver.'

'Come to the funeral,' she said abruptly.

'I'm sorry?'

'Goodie's funeral is tomorrow. It's at a very quiet little church at a place called Leighford, down in Surrey.'

'But, Mrs Silver, I'm a police officer, it wouldn't be appropriate.'

'Don't policemen usually attend funerals?' she said, with some of her old acidity. 'To see if the murderer comes back to gloat?'

This wrongfooted him for a fatal couple of seconds. In the gap he left her she read him the address of the church and the time of the service, and before he had regathered his wits she rang off.

Cobb left the car in the car park of the Cross Keys pub, where Hudson's security people had directed him, and walked across the field to the church. The greystone church looked deserted and Cobb paused for a moment in the shelter of the roofed lich gate.

A convoy of black limousines swept up the lane and came to a halt and the doors opened and a knot of people in black emerged and hurried against the rain into the church. Cobb recognised Hudson, shepherding, directing, and saw a hospital-style wheelchair with a slight figure huddled in it. He waited until they were inside and then he followed and sat at the back. It was the first funeral he had attended since Clea's.

The casket was absurdly small—so small that it reminded him of a violin case as it lay in front of the altar. He ran his eyes along the line of mourners. There were very few of them, no more than fifteen including the main players. Relatives, he supposed.

When the service was over he stood back and let the small procession shuffle past him. Freya was wheeled past him in her chair, pushed by a distraught Latin woman Cobb had never seen before. Against the child's sombre clothes the pink toy made a flamingo splash of colour. He caught Freya's eye and smiled. She did not smile back, but her eyes stayed locked on to his as the weeping woman pushed her away.

The grave seemed cavernous, a chasm swallowing up the tiny coffin. Cobb moved from behind the mourners to the far side of the pit while the vicar read the closing phrases and the coffin was gently lowered down. Cobb looked up. Hudson stood like a soldier on parade, rigid in every muscle. But his lower lip wobbled uncontrollably, twisting his mouth into a grimace. Lauren, her veil lifted, stood with her cold face sightless in the rain, utterly remote, beyond the touch of sympathy.

And then the priest had finished. He turned back through the rain towards the church, and the little group moved to follow. At the last moment Lauren seemed to rouse herself. She drew a white rose from inside her jacket, kissed it, and tossed it down into the grave. The gesture surprised Cobb. For some reason it gave him a flash of hope for her, and that pleased him. Then she turned, and walked steadily and alone towards the church.

On the far side of the grave from Cobb the Portuguese maid was trying to turn Freya's wheelchair on the soft ground. She slipped and caught one rear wheel in the mud. She strained to shift it, failed, and her legs buckled and she was on her knees in the mud, wailing aloud. Cobb moved quickly around the grave but Hudson was there first, catching the woman under his arm and lifting her easily against him.

'I'll bring the girl,' Cobb told him, and Hudson nodded and moved away towards the church, half-carrying his helpless burden.

Cobb freed the wheelchair easily. Then something made him look down at the silent child with Clea's toy nestled against her, and quickly he swept her up into his arms. 'Come on, Princess,' he told her. 'You've been pushed around enough, I think.'

'Wait,' she commanded.

Cobb froze, aware that something extraordinary had happened but for a fraction of a second unable to recognise what it was. When he did, he said softly: 'Princess.'

Her arm moved in a jerk and the pink toy flew from her and fell with a small thud onto her sister's coffin far below.

'I thought Goodie might like to take him,' Freya said.

'I expect she would, Princess,' Cobb said. 'I'm sure she would.'

'Frey!' It was Hudson, hurrying back from the church. 'Did I hear . . .?' He turned to Cobb, his battered face shining. 'Did she . . .?'

'You'll have to ask her,' Cobb said. He hefted the child in his arms and handed her to Hudson, then walked quickly away down the field path.

Lauren stood beside the car. She lifted her veil and let the rain drive into her face. A driver in a chauffeur's cap tried to usher Lauren in through the car's back door to shelter from the rain. She ignored him and after a while he slid into the driver's seat.

Hudson shouted from beside the grave. Lauren lifted her eyes with an effort. She saw him smile in wonder at her, mouthing words across the wet churchyard, holding Freya up like a trophy. She knew instinctively what had happened. Hudson pulled up the collar of his coat to cover the child and carried her to where Lauren stood silently watching.

''Swonderful, Laurie, ain't it?' His big face was glowing as he came up to her. 'Bloody miracle, eh?' He pulled Freya to him and hugged her hard. 'Eh, ya little darlin'! Talking again! Eh?'

Lauren watched her daughter's dark eyes as they gazed at her from under the shelter of Hudson's coat. Those eyes tracked her as Hudson swivelled and shouted the news to the others. They unnerved her. She was surprised to find that she was still capable of being unnerved.

'Take her, Laurie,' Hudson was saying, moving the child on his hip so that Lauren could reach for her. 'Go on. You take her.'

The group around them fell quiet, waiting. Lauren frowned. Hudson seemed to be speaking to her from behind glass. It did not seem possible that, simply by reaching out, she could touch this surviving cub of hers, feel her weight.

'Put me down,' Freya commanded.

'You got a bad leg, Frey,' Hudson said. 'You can't—'

'Put me down *now*!' the child spat, and this time he obeyed at once, sliding her down so that she rested her good leg on the ground and balanced for a moment on it, stork-like.

Slowly Lauren reached out her hand. Freya took it and steadied herself. Freya's hand was cool and dry in hers. The touch of it sent her a message, she realised—not a message of warmth and comfort, but a challenge. It frightened her. To break the spell she guided the child into the car and got in after her, closing the door behind them in the faces of the others. She locked the doors. She found the switch which controlled the glass partition and pressed it. Mother and daughter sat in silence for a space, the rain streaking the windows. Finally the engine murmured into life and they pulled away. Lauren glanced at the child beside her, but Freya's eyes stared directly ahead.

'Why did he go?' Freya said suddenly. 'Why did he leave us?'

'He didn't leave you, Frey. He took you. It was me he left.'

'Why?'

'I don't know, Frey. I don't know much of anything any more. I did everything I knew to keep us all together.'

'Well, he's left both of us now, hasn't he?'

'Yes, Freya. I suppose he has.'

'Was it my fault?'

'You mustn't think that,' Lauren said quickly. Her mouth seemed to be full of ash. 'Don't ever think that.'

'There must be a reason,' Freya said, her voice full of a grim certainty.

Lauren licked parchment lips. She leaned forward and clicked open the walnut cocktail cabinet.

'Don't,' Freya said sharply.

Lauren swallowed hard and squeezed her eyes closed. Very deliberately she shut the cabinet again and sat back in her seat.

'I don't think I can do this, Freya,' she said.

'You have to,' her daughter told her. There was no pity in her voice. 'You just have to, that's all.'

Silver became aware of a low angled ceiling and a luminous rhomboid of window. The window was dark blue, and he knew it was night.

He had no clear idea how he had got here. He remembered being roughly bundled up and pushed into the back of an old estate car. He remembered noticing, in moments of lucidity, that the car was shabby, full of litter. After that the images had slipped and blurred.

That seemed long ago now. He was drifting comfortably again and, though his skin burned and his throat and lungs were raw, he floated above all this in a strange euphoria. There was the reassuring sound of music in a room downstairs. A girl was singing plaintively to a guitar. She had a beautiful voice, untrained but wonderfully pure. The singing was muffled, but he identified it effortlessly. *Virgil Caine is my name . . .* Joan Baez. He allowed himself to be lulled by it.

A door slammed below and there were heavy footsteps on the stairs, and voices, a man's and a woman's. The woman came in first, the same shrivelled grey-haired Maggie Turpin woman he had seen before. After her came a smiling thickset man of fifty in a hairy tweed jacket.

The woman cawed at him. 'Back with us at last, eh? Thought you'd either be awake or stiff. And it looks like you got two eyes after all.'

The smiling man shouldered her aside. 'Move your wrinkled ass now, Maggie, will ye?' It was an Irish accent, so strong that to Silver it seemed the man must be hamming it up. The bluff and merry face came closer to his, and Silver saw that the eyes were cold. 'Jaysus—where did you find this one? He's as hot as a feckin' furnace. And he stinks.'

Silver swallowed again and found his voice. 'You're a doctor?'

'I'm Kilpatrick. Where I come from, mine is not a lucky name for a man of my profession. Though it proved prophetic enough.'

'I don't want a doctor.'

'Well, ye're safe then, for they tell me I am one no longer.' Kilpatrick's smile broadened. 'Still and all, I'm the best you'll get.'

Kilpatrick's big hands were competent and utterly uncaring. He stripped the coverings off and felt the bones of Silver's legs under the bruises, flexed each rib so hard that Silver felt the fractured ends of bone grate together before he passed out. In interludes of semi-consciousness he felt something cold injected into his face, more than once, and then the prick and drag and tug of stitching. When he came round again he was on his side with his head hanging over the edge of the cot. He had puked and someone had slid a newspaper under his head, presumably to make it easier to clear the mess up later. Silver drifted in and out of this strange new world, feeling his body throb with pain with every heartbeat.

'Well, your golden goose has got about a 50/50, Maggie. I've stoked him up with antibiotics and sewn him back together, but that's about all I can do. The ribs will heal on their own, most likely. If this doesn't turn into pneumonia he'll probably see the New Year.'

The door was opened and Kilpatrick's footsteps moved out on to the landing and clumped down the stairs. He heard the cheery voice one last time: 'Oh, Maggie! I near forgot! D'ye want it for a keepsake, now?'

'What?'

' 'Tis his finger. Had to snip it off, ye know.'

Whatever reply she gave was drowned by Kilpatrick's guffaw, and Silver could hear him laughing as he clumped down the stairs.

She returned after a few moments and stood silently in the doorway.

'Which one was it?' he said.

'Does it matter?'

'It would have, once. It would have mattered a lot.'

He tried feeling his hands but both seemed to have been bound up stiffly, like paddles. Maggie Turpin held up her left hand and wiggled her ring finger. 'This one.'

Left hand, fret hand. How would all those chords sound now, without that one? He was surprised how little he cared.

He let his head loll back and the movement brought the newspaper before his face again. He watched as it swam in and out of focus, a fuzzy patchwork of print and a single big photograph. It looked oddly familiar and he forced himself to concentrate. The headline read MIRACLE GIRL and the photograph was of Freya, sitting up in a hospital bed.

'And now there's another thing,' Maggie said. 'What do we call you?'

He breathed hard, fighting for control, feeling his damaged ribs spike him with pain. Freya was alive. He had killed Goodie, but Freya was alive. Where did that leave him? How could the debt be cancelled now?

'I said, what do we call you?'

Downstairs in the bar the woman had started singing Joan Baez again. While his conscious mind spun, his subconscious unerringly—uselessly—identified the song, filled in the words.

I dreamed I saw Joe Hill last night
Alive as you or me.
Says I, 'But Joe, you're ten years dead.'
'I never died,' said he.

'Joe,' he said. 'Joe Hill.'

'Right,' Maggie said. 'Joe Hill.'

It was gone eight by the time Cobb reached his Baron's Court flat. He let himself in and brought the flat to life, snapping on lights and igniting the old-fashioned gas fire.

Cobb poured some red wine and sat by the window. He sipped the wine. It had been open two days and was almost dead, but that didn't matter. It was merely a ritual. And he needed some ritual, some stability.

He could make no sense at all of the events at the funeral, nor of his feelings about them. He was glad for the child, liked the child, hoped he would never see her again. Never see any of them. He wished he had forced his resignation on Sykes and simply walked. It was a lousy way to behave, and it would have cost him dear. But he did not think it would have cost him as much as this entanglement was costing him.

The tapping on the door was as swift and light as a woodpecker. He set down his drink, walked across the room and pulled the door open.

'I know you'll be angry, but I had to come.'

'Mrs Silver, how did you get this address?'

'That doesn't matter.'

'Yes, it does.'

Her eyes met his in irritation. 'Look, I'm rich, OK?' she said. 'I can get that kind of information. Even from the police.'

'Someone at work told you?'

She shrugged. 'I might have lied a bit. Look, can we pull the plug on the outrage, Inspector Cobb? I really need to talk to you.'

He let her pass and closed the door behind her. 'I'm sorry for your trouble, Mrs Silver. Terribly sorry. But this is totally out of line.'

'Inspector, I buried my little girl today. You watched me do it. You should know I don't give much of a shit about anything.'

She walked across to his own favourite spot by the window, her heels clicking on the polished boards. Her face was so white against the black of her suit that the contrast was painful.

'Mrs Silver, this is not the way these things are handled. About your husband—'

'This isn't about Matthew.' She turned the hardbacked chair round and sat without invitation, facing him. Cobb noticed, irrelevantly, that she had had her broken tooth fixed. 'Have you got a drink?'

He went to the tiny kitchen and poured the last of the red wine and handed it to her.

'Mrs Silver, I think you need to talk to somebody about all this.'

'About all what?'

'You're not behaving rationally. Coming here. Asking me to the funeral, even. In a way I appreciate it, of course, but it's not appropriate.'

She waved her glass scornfully. 'Look, fuck appropriate, Mr Cobb. It worked. My daughter's speaking again.'

'Yes, I'm glad about that.'

'So stop quoting the regulations at me.'

'Nobody expects you to be superhuman, Mrs Silver. Human beings weren't supposed to get through this kind of thing alone.'

'I'm not alone. I've got Tommy.'

'Good. That's good, Mrs Silver. Tommy Hudson seems like a strong person to me. Would you like me to call him for you right now?'

She sipped her wine and looked at him thoughtfully, half-smiling. 'You think I'm totally out of my tree, don't you?'

'If I were in your place, I think I might be.'

'Mr Cobb,' she said. 'This isn't about me. You should know that it wouldn't matter to me right now if I didn't wake up tomorrow. But I've got a daughter to go on living for.'

'You're right. She's a beautiful little girl.'

'Beautiful?' She repeated the word vaguely and her voice began to drift. 'I never thought of Frey like that. Not beautiful. Not like Gudrun.'

'Well, I never knew Gudrun,' Cobb said harshly, 'but your little girl is bright and brave and intelligent, and in my opinion, if you want a good reason to live, you couldn't ask for a better one.'

She straightened and her mouth hardened. 'All right, Mr Cobb. You can cut the sermon. As I was trying to tell you, Freya is why I'm here.'

'Oh?'

'It was right, what I said on the phone. You have a way with her.'

'Mrs Silver, Freya started to talk when she was ready. It happens like that sometimes. You don't want to read too much into it.'

'She blames herself in some way.'

'That's ridiculous.'

'Of course it's ridiculous. What difference does that make? I need to get her mind off it. I need to get her interested in life again.' Cobb said nothing, and she correctly interpreted his silence. 'You promised her, Mr Cobb. Cows and pigs and sheep and pink dinosaurs—the whole bloody lot. She told me.'

'Mrs Silver, I'm a police officer. You're involved in a case I'm working on. I cannot—'

'Just a day, that's all. We'll drive up any day you say. We'll be no trouble.'

'Mrs Silver—'

'It's for my daughter. Please.'

Cobb stared at her unhappily. He passionately didn't want them on the farm. But of course she was right. It was for the child, and it was for one day. It was little enough. He felt ashamed of himself.

'Mrs Silver, of course, if that's what Freya wants.'

She screwed her eyes closed and turned her face away from him.

'Thank you.' Her head dropped forward an inch as she said it.

'But I'll do a deal with you on this,' he went on. 'I don't want you to ever come here again, or to the farm, without my invitation. I'm sorry if that sounds harsh, but my privacy is important to me.'

'Anything you say.'

Chapter Five

'NOT SO FAST, Commie swine!' Fred hunched in the cockpit, as he jockeyed the F-16 into position. 'Let's see how you like this!' He thumbed the gun button and released converging streams of tracer at the fleeing shape of the Ilyushin. The Soviet fighter bloomed into lurid flame. 'Got him!' The old man slapped the desk. 'Right up the tailpipe!'

Chortling to himself, Fred shut the computer down. Then he slapped his knees hard and said: 'Right.'

Cobb folded his paper and set it aside, knowing what was coming next. His father had used brisk, mock military movements of this kind ever since Cobb was in short pants to signal that he wanted to discuss something delicate. Cobb said: 'I should have taken the bloody dog out.'

'Too late. Fetch the bottle.'

Resigned, Cobb rose and brought the Laphroaig from the black oak dresser under the stairs. He didn't particularly want to drink or to talk. But once initiated, the ritual could not be derailed. It stretched back to Cobb's teens, when to be offered a drink by his father was a rare privilege indeed and always meant that some key issue was about to be raised. Cobb remembered every one of these occasions, always with a shadow of the awe he had felt on the first time that bottle and the two shot glasses had appeared.

It was on the verandah of a palm-shaded bungalow in the suburbs of Jakarta, where his father had just started a two-year stint as assistant trade secretary. Cobb, just fourteen, was finishing his homework at the rattan table.

'Your mother has left us, Samuel,' his father announced from behind him, setting the bottle and glasses on top of his son's history homework. 'My fault entirely, of course.' And then an astonishing thing happened. His father began to cry.

'**W**ere you rubbing that bottle in the hope of attracting a genie?' Fred asked him.

'Sorry.' Cobb poured the smoky spirit, took his own and sat down next to the fire. He poked moodily at the embers. He said: 'I'm not happy about them coming here, that's all. I shouldn't have agreed to it.'

'I see.'

'I don't want their wide boy ex-pug minder here either. I don't think you should have to put up with any of them.'

'Me? I'd be glad of the company. All I have is this comatose hound, and rather too much of you every week.' Fred sipped his Scotch.

'I just don't want to get mixed up with them. I'm a policeman, not a social worker. Besides, the file isn't closed yet. The man only drowned a week ago. I shouldn't have any social contact with his family at all.'

'Why not?'

'It's unethical, it's unprofessional and it's bloody awkward.'

'Unprofessional, unethical and bloody awkward?' Fred smirked. 'These are a few of my favourite things.'

'You silly old sod. You've never had so much as a parking ticket in your entire life.'

'Don't change the subject,' his father said primly. 'And don't try to make out that all this concern is on account of your dear old father.'

'You don't understand,' Cobb said lamely.

'I understand quite well.' Fred set his glass down. 'I understand a distraught woman comes to you the very day her child is buried and begs a favour of you—a small thing—on behalf of her surviving daughter.'

'It wasn't like that.'

'And I understand that you *hesitated*. And, having reluctantly agreed, you are now trying to weasel your way out of it.'

'Jesus, Dad, all right!' Cobb raised his hands in submission. 'Look, you win. I give up. It's selfish of me. I'm a prick.'

'And?' Fred's voice quivered magnificently.

'And of course they can come here, and I'll be just as nice as pie to all of them. I'll be so nice it'll make you vomit.'

'Splendid,' Fred said sweetly. He lifted the bottle. 'A nightcap?'

Cobb looked across at his father and gave a snort of laughter.

'I think we should.' Fred tilted the Laphroaig.

'Mad if we don't,' Cobb agreed, closing the circuit with the response they had rehearsed for over thirty years.

Cobb drove into London and worked methodically until midday. It was Monday, the first of the New Year, and he found himself grateful for the day's routine dullness after the dislocation of the last couple of weeks.

Horrie Nelson was on leave and Sykes was at a conference in Scotland. Cobb was glad about that. He did not want another confrontation just yet. He wanted a day or two to recharge, and the absence of his superiors gave him a measure of peace for the rest of the week. He returned half-a-dozen emails, chased up the pathology report for Gudrun Silver, and called the Accident Investigation people at Barnes to make an appointment for the next day.

Warming to the task, he called every member of the task force team as if they might really have fresh information, and contrived to sound surprised when they did not.

Cobb found that the activity helped to refocus his mind. It had been nine days now, and still Silver's body had not turned up. That was curious, he had to admit.

'Mr Cobb?' The female Constable, Carlow, appeared beside his desk. 'It's the path report you wanted.'

'Thanks.' Cobb took the folder from her and flipped open the report.

There was nothing in it which surprised him, and a little which relieved him. The girl had not drowned. Her neck had been broken, possibly by the impact of the passenger side air bag. She was dead by the time the car had settled in the water. She had been spared the horror of seeing the black water climb the windows, shutting out the light. Unlike her sister, Cobb reminded himself. Unlike her sister.

He flicked through the remaining pages and then through the sheaf of photos. Looking at them now Cobb found it hard even to see the resemblance which had struck him so forcefully at the time. Gudrun had short dark hair like Clea's, and a certain reminiscent squareness to the jaw. It was the most passing similarity. Gudrun Silver had nothing in common with Clea Cobb except that she had died too young, and on the same day of the year. The phone buzzed and Cobb answered it.

'Mr Cobb? It's Lauren Silver.'

'Mrs Silver, I was about to call you about Freya and the farm.'

'You promised, Mr Cobb. You promised me.'

'Mrs Silver, if you'll let me finish—I've had a word with my father, and I was going to suggest you bring Freya down on Saturday week.'

'That will be fine,' she cut in. 'Saturday week will be fine. Perfect.' Her relief was palpable and it took her a moment to recover her composure. Then she spoke again: 'You need to interview me, don't you?'

'When you're up to it, Mrs Silver—'

'I'm up to it. Freya's out of the house. Come down today.'

'Today?'

'You know where it is. Security will let you through.'

She rang off. Cobb replaced the receiver and looked at it for a while. He was tempted to ring her back and explain to her that minor celebrities did not summon police officers just when they felt like it, but he decided he would be doing no one any favours if he let his personal distaste get in the way. He locked away the file, signed himself out, and took the lift down to the basement car park.

The roads were still holiday empty and Cobb reached Virginia Water in a little over forty minutes. He spotted the first security men half a mile away, and soon saw the knot of TV vans clustered outside the tall cypress hedge which screened the house. Security men waved him through onto the drive and a couple of the photographers were bored enough to flash off shots at him as he drove past.

The house itself was a hundred yards away down a drive of tawny gravel. Cobb parked and was met at the door by the Portuguese maid he had seen at the funeral. The woman showed him down a long panelled hallway and into a huge room cluttered with oriental teak furniture.

'Mr Cobb.'

He had not seen Lauren, her small figure lost in the scale and complexity of the room. She was smoking. An ashtray full of butts stood on a side-table next to a bottle of vodka which was only a quarter full. She was dressed carelessly in trousers and a sweater of cream wool which showed up the pallor of her face. She did not rise but waved him to a seat on a blue and gold brocade sofa opposite her.

'Coffee, Mr Cobb? You don't look the drinking type.'

'Coffee's fine.'

'Good choice. Merilda is very good at making coffee.' The implication unmistakably was that Merilda wasn't good for much else.

The woman slid Lauren a stiletto of a look and marched out of the room. Cobb had the feeling that the whole scene was for his benefit—ostentatious drinking and smoking, insults to the servant. It made him uncomfortable and impatient.

'Mrs Silver, I really only need to establish exactly what happened on the night of the accident.'

'And that's all you're interested in. Right?'

'It's as far as my job goes, Mrs Silver.'

'He is out there, you know.'

'Yes, well. We'll keep looking.'

'You know, Mr Cobb, when I met Matthew I thought he was the most magnificent creature who ever walked the earth.'

Oh, Christ, he thought. The poor bloody woman wants to talk.

'He was an extraordinary talent,' she went on. 'A genius. It put him beyond the normal rules. Do you imagine that genius of that order could just be snuffed out, Mr Cobb? Just like that?'

'Yes, Mrs Silver, I do. I think Matt Silver played some great guitar and wrote some great songs. But when all's said and done he was just an ordinary joe like the rest of us.'

'Well, a philosopher *and* a policeman. That's refreshing.'

'And I'm sorry, Mrs Silver, but I believe he's just as dead as the next joe would be, and the sooner you accept it, the more comfort you'll be able to find.'

At that moment Merilda appeared with the coffee. She poured it out. The small ceremony took place in a bell jar of strained silence. He lifted his cup and sipped, still avoiding Lauren's eyes. 'You're right,' he said, mainly for Merilda's benefit. 'This is wonderful coffee.' The woman managed a half smile and left the room. Lauren watched her go.

'I can handle this, you know, Mr Cobb,' she said, tilting her glass towards him. 'This stuff, I mean. It's not a problem.'

Cobb nodded and tried not to show his doubt.

'It may look like a problem to you,' she went on, enunciating too clearly, 'but it isn't. It's just because Freya's out.'

'I'm not judging you, Mrs Silver.'

She looked away. After a while she spoke again, in a smaller voice. 'What did you mean when you said "not for long"? On the phone?'

'I'm sorry?'

'Before the funeral I said you were involved, and you said "not for long". What did you mean?'

'I'm leaving the police, Mrs Silver. I'm resigning.'

'No. You can't do that.' She said it with finality. You haven't found Matthew yet. You can't leave.'

He looked at her. Her manner had changed altogether. The pose was gone and she was breathing a little faster. 'You have to find him first.'

At that moment a door banged. Footsteps clattered in the hallway and someone shouted a greeting. Tommy Hudson came barrelling into the room, shedding coat and scarf as he came. 'Mr Cobb, sorry I'm late. I planned to be here but—something came up.'

Cobb rose and shook hands and Hudson strode over to Lauren and bent to kiss her on the cheek. The caress was brotherly but Cobb detected something different about Hudson, a new assurance, a sense almost of possession. It was not the kiss which alerted him to this so much as the cast-off coat and scarf, slung untidily over a chair as a man might dump his own clothes in his own house.

'Tommy,' Lauren said. 'He says he's resigning.'

'Oh?' Hudson looked up in surprise. 'Laurie wouldn't want you to do that, Mr Cobb. No, we wouldn't want that. Neither of us.'

Cobb could not quite work out how he was supposed to take this. Their concern was so genuine that he was obscurely flattered. He said, feebly: 'I haven't actually resigned yet.'

'Oh, well, that's OK, then,' Hudson ploughed through him. 'Still time to talk you out of it!' He laughed rather too jovially and before Cobb could speak again, turned back to Lauren. 'I'm just taking Mr Cobb into

Matt's studio for a minute, Laurie. Something I want to show him. OK?'

Whether it was OK or not, Hudson took Cobb's arm with an irresistible pressure and steered him quickly out of the room.

'Sorry about the manhandling, Mr Cobb. Let's go and have a chat.'

Cobb allowed himself to be led through the house to Matthew Silver's studio. The room was stacked with guitars and keyboards and computer and recording equipment. There were no windows and the walls were dull black, so that when Hudson snapped on the lights the instruments and electronic gear shone like treasure.

Hudson waved Cobb to one of the stools which stood before a control desk as impossibly intricate as the flight deck of an airliner.

'I spent days in here with Mattie, Mr Cobb. I can see him now, sitting just where you're sitting, scratching out riffs on that old Gibson he always used for practice.' Hudson pulled up a second stool and sat down. 'Could you do me a big favour, Mr Cobb? Could you put off resigning—just until you find poor Mattie's body?'

'I don't quite—'

'It'd have to turn up in a few days anyway, wouldn't it? Just a few days, Mr Cobb. It'd mean a lot to Laurie.'

'She doesn't even believe he's dead.'

'No, but you do. And when you find him, she'll be able to accept it. She trusts you, Mr Cobb. After what you done for Frey and all.'

'Listen, Mr Hudson,' Cobb stood up. 'I'm not making you any promises. We might never find him.'

'She's trying hard with the drink,' Hudson said, as if he had not spoken. 'It mightn't look like it, but she is. I feel like we all owe her a bit of support, know what I mean? Couple of weeks, Mr Cobb. That's all.'

Cobb stared at the ceiling. He did not like being backed into a corner in this way, but on the other hand he could hardly leave the office within two weeks even if he handed his resignation in tomorrow.

'Two weeks,' he said.

'Good enough, Mr Cobb. Now let's go back in there and get you a proper statement.'

Sergeant Maxey, who met Cobb at eight thirty the next morning at the Barnes garage, was a small, neat man with receding hair and a beard. Cobb followed him out of the station and across a car park into a steel hangar crowded with vehicles. The Jaguar lay halfway along one row, the driver's door open a little but taped to prevent it swinging wide.

'It's hard to know what to show you, Mr Cobb, without a clear idea of what you're looking for.'

Cobb, who had very little idea himself of what he was looking for, moved around the car slowly. One headlight assembly hung half out of its fitting, like an eyeball from its socket. The Jaguar's sunroof, windscreen and driver's window had all been shattered.

Cobb mooched around the wreck. Finally he said: 'You're the expert, Sergeant. How do you think this happened?'

'Well, not wanting to pre-empt the report in any way . . .'

'This is informal. I'm just interested in your opinion, that's all.'

'Well, sir, I see it this way.' Maxey positioned himself in front of Cobb. 'He clipped the railings with the driver's side. That popped the headlight and might have been what burst the driver's door open too. But also the impact flipped the car over so that it hit the water on its roof. By then it's travelling at—oh—sixty or seventy. Out goes the side window. Bang. Out goes the screen. Bang. Maybe the sunroof too. Bang. She fills up with water, and down she goes.'

'The divers say the car was the right way up on the bottom.'

'That's quite correct, Mr Cobb.' Maxey was animated now. 'But think about it. Most of the car's weight is concentrated in the wheels and the subframe, and of course the engine. As it fills up with water and sinks it will gradually right itself and go down by the nose, faster and faster.'

'I'm with you. Can we look inside?'

'Of course, sir. The forensic people have already been over her.'

Maxey produced a pair of scissors. He snipped the tape and tugged on the door to open it. Cobb stuck his head inside. It still stank of the river, a tomb smell, and the tan hide upholstery was streaked with filth. The deflated air bags lay draped across the dashboard.

'What do you think happened in here, Sergeant?'

'Well, Mr Cobb,' Maxey looked doubtful, 'I don't think they'd have known a lot about it. They weren't strapped in, you know. Not that that would have helped, probably.'

'So.' Cobb pulled himself out of the car and wiped dirt off his fingers. 'We've got one little girl in the front. She was dead virtually on impact. We've got the driver—dead or unconscious, his body thrown out through the open door, presumably, when it hit the water.'

'Not right away, sir. There's water rushing in through the window and the screen, remember. Tons of it. It would tend to pin the deceased in there till the car sank far enough and the pressure equalised. Then it might float him out through the open door.'

'Fair enough. But meanwhile we've got the other kid in the back, protected by the front seats, injured but perhaps conscious.'

'She must have had a very nasty time of it, sir,' Maxey said. 'Very nasty. Completely black. The car filling up. The noise. The pocket of air squeezing down to nothing. She wouldn't have known which way was up.'

'But she got out. How?'

Maxey stepped over to the car and leaned across the roof. 'You feel the edge of that, sir. Mind the glass.'

Cobb ran his hand along the lip of the broken sun roof. 'What about it?'

'Just there. Excuse me, sir.' Maxey took Cobb's hand and guided it to the forward edge of the fitting. 'There. Feel that? The sun roof assembly sits inside these channels. That's what it slides in to open and close it. Just here the edges of the channels are bent upwards. Outwards.'

'You think it was forced out from the inside? Not pushed in when the car hit the water?'

'Maybe the air pressure inside the car blew it out,' Maxey said carefully. 'That's what the other lads think. Myself, I wouldn't have thought the pressure would be nearly great enough. But I'm in the minority.'

'So in your mind you've got a picture of this Jaguar settling on the bottom of the Thames with the sun roof still in place.'

'Correct.'

'If you don't think the air pressure popped it out—what did?'

'Oh, any number of things,' Maxey said. 'Maybe the sun roof stayed in place all along and the child got out some other way. In that case our lads might have broken the roof when they fished the car out.'

'Is that likely?'

'It's possible.' The Sergeant shrugged. 'When you've seen as many crashes as I have, Mr Cobb, you know that almost anything can happen.'

'Does that include miracles?'

Maxey smiled knowingly, as if he had expected this. 'There's always an explanation,' he said, 'and usually a boring one.'

Cobb drove thoughtfully back to the office and immediately put in a call to John Piggott at the Institute for Naval Medicine near Gosport. He had known Piggott for over twenty years. They had met on a diving course during Cobb's short service commission. Piggott had stayed in the Navy and was now a Surgeon Commander, carving out a niche for himself in survival medicine.

'So your man's in pretty good physical shape?' he was saying. 'But stuffed full of laughing powder and grog?'

'By all accounts, yes.'

'And injured. Though you don't know how badly.'

'He isn't wearing a seat belt but there are air bags and they do operate. The car has a collapsible steering column and all the other safety gadgets. The front end isn't too badly damaged. I think he might have survived the crash.'

'And you want to know if he might have survived the river too?'

'Right.'

'In December? The Thames? Yes, he might have. In theory. About twenty-five per cent of people who fall in will be dead in two or three minutes. Another twenty-five per cent could last up to two hours. The rest somewhere in between. There's no telling.'

Cobb held the phone and said nothing for a moment.

Piggott said: 'What's up, Sam? Blown another pet theory to buggery, have I? Don't despair. If it makes you any happier, the entire scenario is pretty unlikely. Even if he hasn't been too badly chewed up, he's just been belted in the face by an air bag. A thing like that affects your thinking, especially if you're underwater, in the dark and you're scared shitless. For him to gather his wits and get out of that, he'd need to be Harry Houdini.'

Cobb was silent for a moment, then said. 'John, it'd all be adrenalin, right? Pure blind instinct?' He was not sure exactly what he wanted to say and let his voice trail off.

'You want to know what it was like in there?' Piggott said, interpreting Cobb's line of thinking. 'You still dive, don't you, Sam?'

'Not much.'

'But still, you know the answer to that one better than I do. It's cold. It's dark. He's in shock and he's hurt and he's trapped. If he sees a way out of that he'd be heading for the moonlight like a fucking Trident missile. He wouldn't stay to look for his car keys.'

'No,' Cobb agreed. 'Not for his car keys.'

He sank to a bitter black place. A nameless roaring filled this place and a rotting taste. Over and over again he would hear a voice shrieking in panic and know it to be his own. And then the screaming would twist into the wailing of a siren and the frightened cry of a child and he would feel himself vaulted out into blackness again and there would be a vast explosion and then a nameless roaring would fill the world and he would be diving once again into the same black and bitter place.

And then one day it stopped. On that day he awoke and knew that he was back in the world. Perhaps the girl's voice had touched him awake. She was still singing sweetly, a little off-key, a song in which his name was intertwined. The childishness of her voice soothed him.

I dreamed I saw Joe Hill last night
Alive as you or me.
Says I, 'But, Joe, you're ten years dead.'
'I never died,' said he.

'I never died,' Silver said, and suddenly he was entirely conscious.

'Didn'tcha, now?' Maggie Turpin's voice answered him from the gloom under the attic roof. 'If you didn't, you was pretty bleeding close.'

Silver rolled his head with an effort and saw her lumpy silhouette in the cool evening light.

'Playing your song, was she?' Maggie Turpin said, rising, taking up a plastic drinks bottle. 'Is that what done it?'

'I know it,' he said. 'The song.'

'You should. She's played it every Saturday night for the last three weeks.'

'Three weeks?'

'Since we come to the Nile.'

The Nile? It seemed no crazier than anything else. Silver lay back and closed his eyes, his mind beginning to churn and mesh. He was in a cot of some kind—perhaps a folding bed—in a low, angled space under the roof of some quite large building. He remembered the clinking glasses and the beery laughter and knew that he was in some kind of space above a bar, and in his mind's eye he saw a pub sign: a ship-of-the-line, spewing smoke. The Battle of the Nile.

The attic had been planked and roughly partitioned with chipboard and sacking tacked to the upright timbers. A bare bulb hung from the centre of the space, giving a miserable yellow light. In one recess there was a toilet bowl and an old enamel bath and a sink growing out of the wall. Silver rolled his head to see more. A section of the roof space near the head of the stairs was partly screened off with sacking and loose plywood. Through a gap in this screen Silver could see a collapsed armchair and as he looked he noticed that Stevens was slumped in this chair, watching him from the shadows, a can of McEwan's Export cradled between his hands. Silver read hostility and contempt in the man's look, a slow-burning aggression which made him feel weak and vulnerable.

He saw the woman move across to the sullen Stevens and hiss commands at him. Then she took up an old shopping bag and pushed Stevens in front of her down the wooden stairs and out through a street door, and all at once Silver was alone in the attic. He felt a twinge of panic and fought to control it, forcing himself to think.

Three weeks. That would make it mid-January. Three weeks. Gudrun, the child of his flesh, the child he had killed, dead three weeks. And yet the world ground on somehow. He tried to move and found he had the strength now to flex his shoulder muscles. He could not see his hands, what was left of them, but he could make weak fists of them. His body was healing. It made no sense. It seemed that he healed just as quickly as a man who had not murdered his own daughter.

Three weeks. Why had they not found him? Presumably because they were not looking. Whatever the reason, he was glad not to be found. If he could have finished it on that first night he would have done so. Yet here he still was, his body knitting back together, growing stronger, undetected, unsought. In some sense free. Three whole weeks later.

He thought of Freya. He still lived, after a fashion, and she still lived, when both should have died. But what was this grotesque half-life for? He could not decide. Perhaps he slept then, though he was not aware of either sleeping or waking. He heard the door bang and the woman's footsteps on the stair and was glad not to be alone any longer.

Later he sat naked on the edge of the bath. The cold enamel branded his buttocks but he was unwilling to stand up again. The effort of standing was enormous. Without the old woman's help he would never have got this far. He looked down and surveyed his ruined body. He was perhaps seven stone. He had always been a big man. Now he was a camel, a spider, with stick limbs and big knobbled joints. The stump of his missing finger itched as his body gradually came alive.

Silver steadied himself against the enamel bath, drew in a breath, and stood as quickly as he dared. Now he could almost look into it, the shard of mirror which hung on the joist above the cistern. Another shuffling step and he was there. He felt a cold sweat begin to distil on his skin and leaned his forehead against the timber of the joist. Standing upright was a precious agony. At length his pulse steadied. He lifted his head and looked in the mirror.

The face was gaunt and yellow, the jawline grizzled with stubble. Most of the hair was gone, inexpertly hacked off close to the scalp. Where it was growing back it was iron grey. Three puckered scars ran diagonally across the face, as deep and coarse as the stitching on a leather ball. The deepest of them ran from the right eye socket to the mouth like a sabre slash. It tugged down the edge of both eyelid and lip, leaving them out-turned, red and dry.

'You won't be pretty no more, Joe,' the woman observed. She had pulled the sacking aside and was watching him. 'I done me best for you. All the same, you won't be pretty no more.'

He leaned into the reflection, fingering the contours of his new, ravaged face. It was impossible to believe that this grotesque mask belonged to him.

'Look at me,' he whispered. 'Just look at me.'

She focused her ancient eyes on him for the first time and her voice changed. 'No one wants to look at you no more, Joe.'

He said: 'I killed my little girl.'

'That's right.' Maggie Turpin glanced at her cheap wristwatch as if she might be late for the hairdresser's. 'But then, you got another one.'

Chapter Six

'SO PEOPLE USED TO LIVE up here, is that right, Mr Cobb? I mean, it was like a regular town in the old days?'

Tommy Hudson was trying so hard that Cobb found it embarrassing to watch. 'We'll have to stop this Mr Cobb business. Call me Sam.'

'It's force of habit with policemen. But Sam it is, then.' Hudson smiled ferociously. 'So, Sam, this was a town, eh? What d'you think of that, girls?' he shouted over his shoulder.

Cobb turned and saw Lauren, still hunched in the Land Rover twenty yards away, staring through the streaked windscreen. For a moment he couldn't see the child but then spotted her, half hidden behind the oak in the corner of the field, a small figure in a red parka. As his eyes met hers, the girl left the cover of the tree trunk and trudged towards them.

'What d'you think of that, Frey?' Hudson cried. 'A town. Right here.'

'A village, anyway,' Cobb said. 'It even had a name. Funny name, too.'

Freya frowned at him suspiciously. 'What name?'

'It was called Piddle in the Sludge.'

'Piddle in the Sludge!' Hudson shouted. 'You hear that, Frey? You're a card, you are, Sammy boy.'

Cobb winced but Hudson didn't register it.

'You're tricking me,' the girl told Cobb coolly. 'Like you did about the dinosaurs.'

'The dinosaurs? Oh, they don't hatch out till spring. Like ducklings. Couple of months and the fields will be pink with them.'

'That's a fib,' she said, glowering at him.

'Yes. Guilty as charged, ma'am. It was really called Upper Durning. That's why the farm is called Lower Durning. Only now, Upper Durning's lower than Lower Durning, if you see what I mean. So maybe we should call it Lower Upper Durning. Or maybe Lower Lower—

'Don't make fun,' she told him. 'Why did you say it was called Piddle in the . . .' She tripped over the word and for a moment Cobb saw the mask of her gravity slip and his heart went out to her in a swoop that caught him off guard. He crouched down to meet her eyes.

'To make you laugh, Princess,' he said.

'Well, he made *me* laugh,' Hudson shouted, proving it by guffawing like a maniac in the rain. 'Oh, he made me laugh all right!'

'That's because you're stupid!' the girl spat at him with sudden malice and flung away from the two men. Cobb could see Hudson was hurt and felt sorry for him. 'Let's go grab a beer, Tommy. We're all getting soaked out here. You go back to the car and I'll fetch her.'

Hudson nodded and plodded off to the Land Rover.

She was standing on the highest of the mounds, under the oak where he habitually sat. Cobb climbed up beside her.

'Let's go, Freya. We'll all grow gills if we stay out in this, like fishes.'

'Did people really live here?'

'Yes, they did. They had houses and streets and shops too. In the spring, when the new wheat is just coming up, you can see where the main street went—right across that field. There's a depression there.'

'Why did they leave?'

'The Plague,' he said, meeting her eyes. 'There was a dreadful disease and so many of the people here died that the others couldn't carry on working the fields. The few who survived just moved away.'

She nodded. 'But you tricked me about the dinosaurs,' she said.

'You mean, I can talk to anyone in the world with this thing?' Fred sounded incredulous.

'I told you,' the girl said crossly. 'It's email. We use it at school.'

'Well, blow me down. You mean, I could do that and I never knew it? I must be a silly old duffer.'

Freya gave him a look through her glasses which suggested he might be just that. 'Everyone knows about email,' she told him.

'Well, maybe you'd better show me how to use it, young Miss Freya, since you know so much about it.'

Freya hesitated, then she slipped from the chair, walked across the room and silently pulled herself up on to the monk's seat beside Cobb.

He let his hand rest across the child's shoulder. It struck him that it was an occasion indeed when anyone found him more charming than his father. Fred was a natural diplomat. But even Fred's diplomatic skills had been stretched today. The January weather had been so foul that they had been imprisoned in the farmhouse since mid-morning. Fred had been equal to it. He filled the dim farmhouse with light and music, made great theatre out of cooking an enormous roast and co-opting Freya to help, allocated an endless stream of jobs to Cobb and Hudson as if they were small boys: build up the fire, open the wine, set the table.

Only the woman had been left alone. She sat close to the fire, staring at the flames, while activity broke around her like surf. Cobb watched her during the meal. She wore no make-up and her fair hair was scraped back so severely that it looked painful. She ate little, and said just enough to register her presence. She did not touch the wine and he wondered if the effort of self-denial was taking all her strength. He was ashamed of himself but could not suppress his resentment. He did not want her in his home.

Cobb noticed Hudson stealing a glance at his watch and guiltily he felt his heart lift. Perhaps they were about to leave. Then abruptly Hudson sat up and looked towards the kitchen. 'Was that my phone?'

Cobb said: 'I didn't hear anything.'

'I bet it was. It's in my coat out back. Be right back.' He made for the kitchen like a half-back, and as he left Cobb distinctly heard the burr of a mobile phone from near the back door. In a few moments Hudson was back. 'Bit of a problem, folks.'

'Is it Paris, Tommy?' Lauren prompted.

'Yes, that's it. Paris. They're trying to sort out Matt's contract. He was going to do three concerts, and then he goes and . . .' He floundered. 'I'm really sorry, but I'll just have to go over and fix it.'

'To Paris?' Fred raised his white eyebrows. 'You mean, right now?'

''Fraid so.'

Cobb watched the exchange carefully. It was so amateur that he found it amusing. This was a rehearsed performance.

'Will you be able to drop us in town first, Tommy?' Lauren asked.

'I don't see how I can, Laurie.' The big man was theatrically doleful. 'I'm booked on the six-thirty from Heathrow.'

'Already?' Fred said. 'Good Lord, you do move fast.'

'I got the last seat, Mr Cobb. I was lucky. I booked it just then. But if I don't leave now I'll miss it.'

'Don't worry, Tommy. We'll get the train back,' Lauren said. She looked up at Cobb, her expression unreadable. 'I suppose it's easy enough to get a train at this time on a Saturday afternoon?'

'It's no problem,' Cobb said. 'I'll drive you and Freya to Oxford later.'

'Don't be ridiculous!' Fred was outraged. 'Stay the night. Stay the weekend. Pleasure to have you.'

Cobb thought: So that's it.

'You're very kind,' Lauren said sweetly. 'It's such a drag getting through town and down to Virginia Water on the train.'

'Settled, then.' Fred smacked the desk, jumped to his feet and took Freya's hand as she came back into the room. 'Come along, young lady. Here's an adventure. We'll put your mummy in the garden room and you in the box room over there. How about that?'

Cobb was caught off guard. 'The garden room?' he said. 'There'd be more space in the coach-house.'

Fred led the girl across the room and stopped in front of his son.

'We'll put Mrs Silver in the garden room, Samuel,' he said evenly.

Cobb swallowed and looked away.

'Look, I'm sorry to cause all this trouble.' Hudson looked crestfallen. 'It's just one of those things.'

'No trouble, Mr Hudson,' Fred cried. 'Our pleasure.'

'This is really good of you, Mr Cobb.' Hudson stepped across the room and put his arms around Lauren. 'Take care. I'll ring you when I get there. You sure you'll be all right?'

'Don't worry, Tommy. We've got both Mr Cobbs to look after us.'

Cobb looked up and caught her watching him over Hudson's shoulder.

The night was velvet black and Cobb could see only a faint track of sky between the over-arching trees. He strode out along the sunken lane while the old dog shambled beside him, grunting in protest. By the time they reached the top and crossed into the upper paddock they were panting, their breath steaming in the cold.

The couple of beers he had drunk during the long, tense evening sat heavily in him. Cobb wanted to burn them off, to feel light again and unburdened. They followed the black wall of the hedgerow with the farmland falling away towards the house a mile below. He could see the porch light now, trembling in the darkness, and began to feel better.

He turned to walk back down the field towards the farmhouse, and as he did so the kitchen light sprang on, and he knew what it meant, and he felt the bitterness rise up in him again.

She sat at the end of the scrubbed pine table. She was wearing a man's grey sweater and it hung on her thin body. Cobb realised that the sweater was his and felt a pang of unreasonable indignation. Her hair was loose now and she had lost the tight, locked-down air of earlier in the day, but something slightly sluttish and brassy had replaced it. He could see why. A square green bottle of Gordon's gin and a half-full tumbler stood on the bare wood in front of her. Despite everything he could not hold back some pity for her. Back in the office he had early file photos of her with Silver. He called to mind one shot which showed her dancing with her laughing mouth wide open, blonde hair swinging across her face. She had been a fine-looking woman then, Cobb thought, with her high cheekbones and clear blue eyes. And packed with the vibrant energy that attracts the camera. There wasn't much of that vibrant woman left now. The alcohol was desiccating her.

Cobb closed the door behind him quietly and knelt to unlace his boots. Baskerville shambled over to the table and nuzzled Lauren's bare knee, thumping the table leg with his tail. She ignored the dog and tapped the bottle with her nail. 'It's yours. I'll pay you.'

'You're a guest here. Have anything you want.' He hung up his coat, snapped his fingers to call the dog away, opened the door of the pot-belly stove. 'It's almost dead. Aren't you cold?'

She shrugged, indifferent. He rattled the grate and threw on a couple of logs and the flames sprang up at once. She tapped the bottle again and cocked her head at him inquiringly.

'No thanks. I don't want one.'

'And neither should I?'

'You can do what you want.'

'Aren't you going to lecture me? I was hoping you would.'

'You're a grown woman, Mrs Silver. You know what you're doing and why you're doing it.'

'Mrs Silver, for Chrissake!' she snorted. 'Don't be such a hardass, Sam. It's boring. Get a fucking drink and call me by my name at least. I'm not Mrs anybody any more. Not until you find him.'

Cobb hesitated then relented, fetched himself a Scotch from the hall cabinet and sat at the opposite end of the table nursing it.

'That's better,' she said. She seemed amused. 'You don't want me here, do you, Sam?'

'The great flight for Paris drama . . . what was all that, an alarm call that came in late?'

'British Telecom and poor old Tommy. What a team.'

'So what was the idea?'

'Freya needs to be here. For a couple of days. Maybe more.'

'Why?'

'She needs to be near you. I'm damned if I know why.'

'You could have asked.'

'You might have said no. I couldn't risk that. She'll probably need to come back too, and when she does, I'll fix that as well.'

He sat back. 'Lauren, I think maybe you need—'

'Understand this,' she said fiercely. 'I will do anything—anything at all—to give my little girl what I failed to give her sister.'

'I think you're going the hard way about it.'

'I can't afford to be in your power on this, Sam. You don't like me. You don't trust me. You'd refuse me if you could.'

'So you get my old man to ask you? Because he's too gentle and compassionate not to?'

'You got that right,' she said. 'And I'd do it even if he was some mean old bastard instead of being twice the man you are, which he is.'

Cobb could feel his anger rising, but could think of no way of voicing it that would not be merely destructive. She deserved his pity, his help if he could give it. Yet her pain gave her such power over him.

'Who's the woman?' she asked suddenly.

'What woman?'

'The picture. In my room. It was in a drawer.'

He cleared his throat, feeling the conversation spinning out of control again, but in a new direction. 'Clea. My wife. Dead now.'

'That was her room?'

'In a way, yes. She died in it. In the bed you're sleeping in.'

Lauren pursed her lips, considering him. 'Why did you tell me that?'

Cobb shook his head, confused. 'I'm not sure.'

'To give me a jolt? Win a bit of sympathy? Freak me out?' She refilled her glass. 'Won't work, pal. My leads have been pulled.'

'I shouldn't have said anything. I'm sorry.'

'No, I'm supposed to say *I'm* sorry. "Your wife's dead? How tragic. I'm sorry." That's how it goes. Only I don't feel sorry. Nothing personal—I don't feel anything. That's what I'm trying to get across to you. That's why I can do or say anything I want.'

Cobb tossed back the Scotch and gripped the edges of the table with his fists so hard that he could feel the muscles quivering in his forearms.

'People die, Lauren. I don't know what happens, but I know they go away and they don't come back. And I know something else. We can't start again until we let them go. My wife. Your husband. Your little girl.'

'Oh, please!' she laughed. 'Spare me the sermon on healing!'

'I'm being strictly practical here, Lauren. Life starts now. And now. And now. You'll never make sense of the past by trying to pull the present into line. You just stuff up the future.' He let go of the table edges and spoke more slowly. 'It gets better, somehow. You don't know how but it happens. Something goes on putting you back together time after time. Even if you don't want it to. Some day you wake up and you start noticing the sun on your back, or laughter, or the sound of the sea.'

She watched him for a moment longer. 'Nice try, Sam,' she said at last. 'But I'm not interested in getting better. The only reason I'm interested in staying alive is because Freya needs me to.'

'I don't think that's true, Lauren,' he said. 'I don't think you can help wanting to stay alive. You're too strong.'

He got up and turned his back on her and had almost reached the kitchen door when he heard her forehead hit the table like a mallet. He got back to her in time to stop her sliding off the chair, but her lolling arm caught the bottle and it toppled and shattered on the stone flags.

Cobb got one arm under her shoulders and the other in the crook of her knees and lifted her. He was surprised by how light she was. He carried her through into the garden room and laid her on the bed, Clea's bed, and pulled a blanket around her and stood back. He killed the light and made to leave the room. But then he glanced back and saw the moonlight falling through the French doors, and heard the woman's breathing from the bed, and the scene lanced him with a sudden aching familiarity. Without knowing why, he did what he had always done and sat in the chair by the window, watching her quietly until he was sure she was asleep. After that he rose and went back to his own room.

Cobb was up before first light, following his normal Sunday morning routine. He rescued the fire in the pot-belly stove, so that by the time he had finished cleaning up in the kitchen the small window was glowing cherry red and warmth was beginning to leak back into the air. Then he took the dog out into the dim chill morning and set off up the sunken lane and across the fields towards his lookout in the abandoned village.

By the time he got back, Fred was already at work in the warm kitchen in a clatter of bright pans and a blare of talk from Radio 4. He was singing very loudly over the radio.

Cobb took off his coat and sat at the deal table. 'You are a noisy old bastard,' he told his father, by way of greeting.

'Two out of three,' Fred conceded. 'Try harder.'

'You're making a lot of noise,' Freya said from the door. 'You woke me up.'

'And high time too.' Fred cracked an egg one-handed into hot fat. 'Breakfast is almost ready, young lady.'

'Hello, Princess.' Cobb moved a chair round for her and she climbed up on to it, opposite him. 'Is your mum coming to eat?'

'She's asleep,' the child said, looking down. 'She never has breakfast.'

'All the more for us, then.' Fred gleefully set a plate of bacon and eggs in front of her. She blinked at it.

'Is that all mine?'

'If you think that's a lot,' Cobb told her, 'just you wait till the dinosaur eggs start coming in. One of them lasts us a whole week.'

'That's very funny, that is,' she said. 'Ha, ha, ha.' Cobb grinned at her and fetched himself a coffee.

Fred brought his own plate over and sat next to the girl. He dangled a bacon rind. 'I don't know where he gets it from.' He nonchalantly stretched it like an elastic band and shot it across the room at Baskerville. The dog lurched to his feet and devoured the rind while the child watched in astonishment. The dog, deciding his luck was in, shambled across the kitchen and stuck his nose against Freya's knee.

'He licked me!' she cried, outraged and delighted at the same time.

'He's OK,' Cobb said. 'Just don't make a noise like bacon.'

'You're tricking me again,' she told him, her eyes narrowing. He winked at her and sipped his coffee.

After a while Cobb walked through to the living room and lit the fire. Finally, when he heard the back door open and close, he returned to the kitchen. The two figures were moving across the yard: Fred stooped and white-haired, and Freya bright in her red parka.

'He's a wonderful man,' Lauren said.

Cobb had not seen her sitting at the table. 'Yes, he is. Coffee?'

She nodded. 'Please.'

Her face was sharp and tight, and there was a greenish pallor to the column of her neck. But she had about her none of the brassiness of the night before.

'You look pretty good,' he said.

'All things considered, you mean.' She smiled bleakly. 'Come on, I look like shit.'

'Time to worry is when you can do that and look normal.' He placed the coffee on the table in front of her.

She met his eyes. 'I said some stuff last night—about your wife. I shouldn't have. I'm sorry. It won't happen again. I know I can't let it happen again.'

'Fair enough.' He went back to the bench top and filled his own cup.

'You know, Sam, I don't suppose we'll ever like one another much—'

'But we don't have to be enemies?'

She glanced up at him in surprise. 'That's right,' she said. 'We don't.'

He held her eyes uncertainly for a moment. 'Look, Lauren—'

'Sam,' she spoke in a rush, cutting him off, 'I think I need some help.'

'We're talking about the drink here, are we?'

'Yes, I'm talking about the drink.' She lifted her chin at him a little defensively. 'I wasn't always this way.'

'You don't have to tell me.'

'I know I don't have to, Sam. I just want you to know that.'

He watched her for a while, then nodded.

'Will you see someone? I'm not talking about anything heavy but there are controlled drinking programmes. Informal groups. Just to give you a bit of support.'

She laughed, and he discovered that this hurt him. 'What's so funny?'

'You're such a policeman, Sam. I ask for directions to the station and you call in a SWAT team and helicopters.' She saw his confusion and leaned towards him, smiling. 'I'm sorry. Look, I won't promise anything. But if you send me some stuff, I'll look at it.'

'You will?'

'Yes. And I'll even say thank you.'

In the yard the child and the old man moved across to the henhouse door. Fred opened the shutters and a small explosion of feathers and straw puffed out over both of them and for the first time Cobb saw Freya laugh. He wished he could have heard it. He said: 'Bring her here whenever you want, Lauren.'

He put his cup down on the counter and opened the door and walked out of the room without looking back.

Cobb crossed to the barn and collected his spade and fork and carried them across the pasture to the back of the orchard. He sank the fork into the ground and hung his anorak over it. He stretched, feeling the knots click in his back, and breathed deeply. It was a raw white morning and the mist still lay in the hollows of the folded ground down towards the river. He began to dig. He worked for an hour, chopping the heavy soil and turning it up in dark slabs on the edge of the ditch.

A glint of chestnut caught his eye and he set aside the spade and knelt and felt in the loam with his fingers until he found it, a conker-brown chrysalis, two inches long. He lifted it out carefully and rolled it in the palm of his hand.

'What's that?' Freya asked him. He had not heard her approach.

'Here.' He held out his hand and when she did the same tipped the chrysalis into her palm. 'It's a chrysalis,' he said.

'I know that,' she said with some scorn. 'They're what butterflies come out of. I've never seen one this big, though.'

'That one's a moth. A great big fat hawk moth. The caterpillars eat the leaves on the apple trees all summer. It drives my dad wild.'

She stroked the pupa with the tip of her finger. With a quick gesture she handed the chrysalis back to him. 'Will it die, now you've dug it up?'

'No. Tell you what, we'll put it in some sand in a box in the barn. That way the birds won't get it. You might even get to see it hatch out.' He laid the chrysalis on the ground near the ditch and covered it with some loose leaf litter and marked the place with a stick.

She stared at him solemnly, at the ground where the chrysalis lay hidden, and then down into the sheer-sided ditch he had dug.

'That's what will happen to Goodie,' she announced. 'She'll stay in that little hard box until it's safe outside and then she'll hatch out.' She looked up at him, challenging. 'Do you think?'

'Yes, Freya. I think you're absolutely right.'

She nodded, apparently satisfied that the question was settled. She was quiet for a moment. 'Why did you invite me?' she demanded suddenly.

'I asked you because I thought you deserved a break. It was your mum's idea first.'

'Nobody ever asked me anywhere before.'

'Come on, Freya! You must have been invited lots of places.'

'Not me. Me and Goodie. Usually people asked Goodie, really.'

'Maybe she just said yes first.'

She considered that. Then she said: 'Are you very clever, Sam?'

'Like most people I'm pretty clever about some things and very stupid about others.'

'Are you clever enough to find Daddy?'

'I'm not sure anyone's that clever, Freya,' he said carefully, 'but I'm going to keep looking. It's my job to keep looking.'

'Do you think he's died?'

'I think so, Freya. I think he'd be with you if he hadn't.'

'Mummy doesn't think he's died.'

'I know that's what she says. But she's very upset right now. She may come to see things differently later.'

'She's only upset because she made him go away,' the girl said fiercely.

'It's not as simple as that, Princess. It's never as simple as that.'

Freya looked down at the ground. 'I can't remember what happened,' she said. 'I can't remember any of it.'

'Don't try.'

'I've got to try! She says he's a really bad person for what he did, and I was there and I can't remember any of it.'

'Ah, I see. But, you know, Freya—he did whatever he did, whether you can remember it or not. You don't have any responsibility for that. He does.'

'You think he was a bad person too, don't you?' she accused him.

'I tell you what, Freya. I think he was a really, really stupid one.'

Silver looked up as Maggie Turpin pushed the door open and clambered into the half-built flat. The breath hissed out of him in spurts as he pumped against the boards. Eight he'd managed this morning. Three repetitions of eight push-ups. It gave him a certain savage triumph. When he had started, just ten days ago, he had been unable to lift his thin frame off the floor more than twice. He became aware that she had not moved, standing in the doorway with the bulging white Tesco bags, wheezing with the effort of climbing the stairs.

'What's up, Maggie?'

'If you're so fighting bloody fit, you can fetch your own!' she shouted, and dumped the plastic bags on the floor so that they spilled fruit and tins across the boards. 'You bloody eat it all, anyway! I feel like a bleeding cuckoo, fetching and carrying for you, day in, day out.'

'What's your problem, Maggie?'

'My problem?' She advanced into the room. 'I'll tell you what my problem is, Mr Joe Hill! You plan on staying up here like bloody Quasimodo for the rest of your life while I wait on you?'

He stood up and stooped to gather the groceries, dropping scattered items back into their bags. 'Is it the money?'

'Yes! Yes, it's the money. The money and—'

Silver walked across the room and pushed aside the sacking that hung across the woman's sleeping space. From beneath the tangled blankets he pulled out a battered McVitie's biscuit tin.

''Ere!' she cried in sudden alarm. 'What you doing with that, Joe Hill? That's private, that is.'

Silver opened the lid and took out the wad of notes. He weighed the money in his hand without glancing at it. 'How much is left, Maggie?'

She looked truculently at him. 'Near enough three grand, I s'pose. It ain't gone to waste, Joe Hill, unless you count Stevie's boozing. You can't accuse me of nothing.'

He thrust the wad out to her. 'Take it.'

'What?'

'Take it and get out.' He pushed the money into her hand.

'Don't fool yourself, Joe,' she said. 'You can't just smash things up and stick them back together again and expect them to work.'

'What are you talking about?' When she still didn't move he grew impatient. 'Don't give me the cow eyes, Maggie,' he scoffed. 'You've done all right. Now you've got the last of it.' He started stacking the groceries inside the fridge.

'You know, Joe,' she said to his back, 'while you was dead to the world in there I could have took all of it any time, and let you rot.'

'So why didn't you?'

She stared at him and shook her head. 'Be buggered if I know.'

When he looked up again she was gone.

Later, Silver lay with his hands locked behind his head and listened to chucking out time in the bar below. He had never seen George, the barman, but knew his name and his Drill Sergeant's voice, as he might know a character in a radio play.

Silver smiled to himself. It was his first night alone and he savoured the solitude. He felt behind the fibreboard and pulled out the newspaper cutting. The photo had been over-enlarged from some old library shot, so that Freya's image was misty and indistinct. He smoothed the soft paper and pinned the cutting up on a beam.

The stair door banged. 'Oi, you up there?' George's voice boomed up from below. 'Joe, or whatever your name is?' The barman came pounding up the stairs and stood peering in the dim light.

Silver said: 'I'm here.'

George made to step forward and pulled up short as he saw Silver's face. 'Jesus, they done a job on you.'

'What do you want?'

'Want? I want you out of here, mate. I seen Maggie earlier. Took that old shitbox car of hers and that drunk she hangs around with and pissed off. You have a barney, did you?'

'It doesn't matter.'

'It bloody well does, mate. I only let you lot stop up here as a favour to old Mags. Shouldn't be here at all, by rights.'

'You got paid, didn't you?'

'Only up to the end of the month. That's Tuesday. I'll give you till then, but that's it. You're out.'

'I'll pay,' Silver said.

And only when he formed these words and uttered them aloud did it come home to him that he could not pay, that he had no money.

He said: 'I can work. I'm fit. I'm getting fit.'

'Yeah, but . . .' George looked at him doubtfully. 'No offence, mate, but you'd scare me customers half to death.'

'Maybe some of them could do with it.'

George hesitated. Silver could see greed flicker across his fat beery face. George said, slyly: 'You got a problem with the law?'

'Not the way you think.'

'Because I don't want no trouble, you hear me?'

'I just want some peace and quiet for a while and a few quid every now and then.'

'Peace and quiet.' George nodded. 'That's the way I like it.'

Silver followed George down the stairs to a bare concrete passage crowded with steel beer kegs and smelling of piss. At the far end of the passage Silver could see the car park. It occurred to him he did not know where he was—London, presumably, but which part he could not even guess. He followed George through a back door into the bar. The place had been closed for an hour, but a blue fug of smoke still hung under the low ceiling and the shoddy room stank of stale beer.

'I'm on me own here,' George complained. He pulled himself a pint. 'Fucking brewery'll close it before long. They don't give me any help, the tight bastards.' He drank, looking at Silver over the rim of his glass. 'So I help myself now and then.'

'I'm going to need some money,' Silver told him.

'Fuck off!' George banged his drink down. 'You ain't even started yet.'

'I'll start now.'

Silver stepped into the room, righted a couple of chairs, took a cloth from the bar and wiped tables. He found a rubbish bag under the sink and moved around the tables emptying ashtrays and collecting litter.

George watched him suspiciously. 'What's your game, then?'

Silver glanced at him. 'No game, George. I just need a little money from time to time, just enough to live. I won't cause any trouble.'

'Bloody right you won't. Not here, anyway.' George refilled his empty glass. He punched the till and when it opened, groped inside and slapped a ten-pound note on the wet bar in front of Silver. 'That's a float, right? I'll see how you work out before there's any more.'

Silver worked in the run-down pub all week, gradually growing used to activity: lifting, cleaning, rolling kegs, pulling beer—moving in new ways. He had not realised how thoroughly wasted his body had become, and at first the simplest acts left him dizzy and spent.

George was too slovenly to be strict, and Silver worked at his own pace while he learned what his body would and would not do for him. He discovered that though he could walk well enough, his leg dragged slightly. The stump of his missing finger throbbed maddeningly in either hot or cold water, and sometimes the ghost finger itself hurt him fiercely.

At night he would serve a few drinks, if George needed him to, although the Battle of the Nile was almost empty during the week. After closing Silver would climb back up to the attic, so weary that he had to force himself to eat from the remnants of Maggie's last shopping foray—fruit, stale bread, tinned fish straight from the can.

By Thursday he could feel his body beginning to respond to this routine. He knew that soon he would be able to risk walking out in the street, and the prospect filled him with a strange excitement.

He had no clear idea what he was building up to, and between work and weariness barely had the energy to ask himself. But every night the child's eyes looked defiantly out at him from the newspaper cutting pinned to the beam. She would make him ask the question, he knew. And, soon enough, she would force him to find an answer to it.

'How's this sound?' The girl's amplified voice boomed across the room. Silver looked round sharply. He had not realised anyone was inside the pub and for a moment he thought the question was for him. The voice sounded familiar. 'One. Two. Three. Mary had a little lamb . . .'

He realised she was testing a microphone. She was in the dim far corner of the room standing in a tangle of leads, with an old amplifier and a Yamaha twelve-string guitar at her feet. The girl had lurid blue hair cut short, an old black T-shirt worn loose over frayed jeans, and huge army boots. He thought she was perhaps seventeen. She fixed the mike on its stand and, glancing up, saw him watching her.

'What are you looking at, Scarface?' The insult was so casual that it was comradely.

He said: 'Who are you?'

'I'm Jit. I'm here every Saturday.'

He placed the voice at last. 'You're the Joan Baez girl.'

'Yeah, yeah.' She waved him away, too busy, losing interest. She shouldered the guitar strap and hunkered down to adjust the amplifier. 'How's this sound, Nugget?'

Silver saw a solid man of around thirty-five leaning on the bar with a pint standing in front of him. The man wore a black shirt and his forearms under the rolled-up sleeves were thick and brown. He nodded across at Silver and raised his glass slightly in greeting. Silver saw steel-rimmed spectacles and the flash of intelligent blue eyes behind them. The man tapped his glass. 'The money's on the fridge,' he said cryptically. He had an Australian accent. He stuck out a big bony hand. 'Bob Nugent. They all call me Nugget.' Silver took the hand warily, and when he didn't speak Nugent prompted him: 'And you?'

'Joe. Joe Hill.' For the first time Silver noticed the man's dog collar.

The girl struck a chord which rang like a bell around the dim bar. 'Sound OK, Nugget? Not too loud?'

Nugent said: 'Sounds great, Jit.'

Silver heard himself say: 'The second string's out.'

'You say something, Scarface?' she asked.

'One of your B strings is out,' Silver said. 'Flat by half a tone.'

'Don't talk shite,' she scoffed.

Silver shrugged and moved away. Nugent was suddenly interested, and put out a hand to detain him. 'You know a bit about music, Joe?'

'No.'

Silver kept moving, unstacking chairs, wiping down tables, collecting stray glasses. He noted that when his back was turned Jit quietly tuned the off-key B string. Silver could tell he had unsettled her and when she executed a knuckle-breaking blues sequence he suspected she had done it to re-establish her primacy as the musician in the room.

'How d'you like that, Nugget?' she called. 'That last one's a major seventh. I only just learned it.' She played it again.

Silver polished a pint glass and stacked it with the others in a glittering pyramid. He said: 'It's a major ninth.'

'Get outa here!' the girl cried.

Silver glanced over his shoulder at her. 'It's C major ninth,' he said.

'If you know so bloody much, why don't you come up here and play the thing yourself?' He ignored her and went on polishing glasses.

By seven the pub was packed. The priest left after two pints and Silver deliberately ignored his departure. He did not want to attract the man's attention. He knew he had tweaked Nugent's curiosity, and was annoyed with himself for not keeping his mouth shut.

Jit played on as the babble and the smoke rose through the evening. No one paid much attention. The Battle of the Nile was a drinkers' pub, and beyond an occasional patter of applause they ignored her. Silver wondered why she bothered. Her choice of music was eclectic, a mixture of folk, some unplugged Clapton, and a handful of strange and haunting songs he did not recognise.

He found he didn't mind washing up. It left his mind free to work on other things. Soon he was into a soporific rhythm of washing and rinsing and drying which lasted him for two hours or more, while the girl's clear song played through his mind like a breeze.

'Oi! I'm *talkin'* to you, clothears!'

Silver started. He had not heard George's summons. 'Sorry, George.'

'Sorry, George,' the landlord mimicked for his cronies who were sitting along the bar. 'Ring me up four pints of half-and-half and a lager, like I've been telling you for the last ten minutes.'

'Right.' Silver stepped to the till but fumbled the entry. He tried again, fumbled it. George stepped up behind him.

'What's up, sunshine? Can't count to ten, eh?' He grabbed Silver's left wrist and held up the mutilated hand for his cronies to see. 'No wonder. His bleeding calculator only goes up to nine!'

George bellowed with laughter until they joined in, his red face thrown back and his black and stumpy teeth exposed.

'You got to keep a sense of 'umour. See, Joe?' George gently cuffed the side of Silver's head, as if he were a naughty boy in class. 'That's Rule Bleeding One.'

He turned away and in a moment was drinking with his mates, his dominance re-established. Silver emptied the sink, unloaded the dishwasher and reloaded it again, pulled more pints. He did it all mechanically, using the simple actions to calm himself. He knew he would have to learn how to deal with this. He knew this would not be the last time.

'Sorry about that crack.' Up close her bright blue hair was shocking against the line of shabby jackets along the bar. 'You know—' she mimicked her own challenge '—"come up here and play it yourself, buster". I didn't know about the hand.'

'It doesn't matter.'

'How did it happen? Car accident?'

'I'm busy.'

'How was I?'

'I didn't notice.'

'No, of course not.' She smiled. 'That's why I could see you listening. You knew all of them, didn't you, Joe? Every note. Except the ones I wrote myself, of course.' Silver looked up quickly and she smiled. 'Ah, that got you, didn't it? Well, it's true. I wrote the middle set. What do you think of them?' He stared stonily past her. 'You can't fool me, Joe. You know about music, I can tell.'

'My father used to make instruments. I picked up a bit from him.'

'That's cool. What instruments did he make?'

'Violins and cellos. Things like that.'

'Can you do that?' she asked eagerly. 'Make things?'

He stared at her stonily. 'It was a long time ago.'

She was a little ruffled by this. 'OK, Joe. Have it your own way.'

He watched as she bent down for her bag, took a step away.

'It's nothing personal,' he said, and she halted and looked at him. He found it impossible to avoid the question in her eyes. 'You're pretty good,' he said. 'And if you wrote that middle set, you might be very good. Very good indeed.'

She turned back, surprised and flattered. 'Well, thanks.'

He walked away quickly to the far end of the bar and lost himself in serving a group of Irish roadworkers raucously celebrating a birthday. After a while he saw Jit pack up her gear and a minute or two later the Australian priest reappeared and helped her carry her stuff out to a van.

Chapter Seven

IT WAS SUNDAY, but Cobb was on duty in the office to take the call.

'Inspector Cobb, sir? It's Dennis McBean.'

'Sergeant McBean. I see you're enjoying your weekend, like me.'

'Thing is, Mr Cobb, I'm sitting here doing Sunday roster, and I get talking to a mate of mine over at Rotherhithe about an hour ago. I think they've found Silver's wallet.'

Cobb sat up. 'What?'

'I called the Duty Sergeant there, sir, a bloke called Gornall. He says it's not positive yet, but it sounds like it must be Silver's. One of those treasure hunter types—blokes with metal detectors?—found it in the mud down there. I told Gornall I'd give you a buzz about it direct.'

'Do you fancy a trip to Rotherhithe, Sergeant?'

'Meet you there in half an hour, sir.'

Cobb slid the waterlogged wallet out of the plastic evidence bag onto the table and poked it with a pencil the Duty Sergeant handed him. Sergeant Gornall was a hard man of sixty with a weatherbeaten face who disapproved of having his evidence prodded about. The wallet was black and clogged with mud and it stank of the river. Cobb shook the contents out onto the surface and separated them with the pencil. A platinum AmEx card glittered through the grime.

'We cleaned that one off a bit to get the ID, sir,' Gornall said. 'Of course we'll get forensic to have a proper look at it.'

Cobb nodded. He separated the plastic cards on the table. Visa, Diner's, three £50 notes and half-a-dozen French 100-franc notes, the remains of a boarding pass, and a flat metallic security card. Cobb assumed this was what the detector had picked up. There was one other item, a square of disintegrating paper. Cobb peered at it.

'It's a photo, sir,' Gornall said. 'Wife and kids, I suppose. You can just see the outlines under the light.'

Cobb stood up from the table. He felt curiously let down. He was not sure what he had expected, but the wallet did not speak to him. It carried Silver's name, but not his identity.

Gornall parked the squad car in what had been the entrance to the warehouse car park. They crossed the forecourt and walked down beside an abandoned warehouse towards the river. The warehouse was set back a little with a dock area in front of it.

Cobb walked to the edge of the dock and rested one foot on an iron bollard. Below him a flight of stone steps led down ten feet to the mud of the foreshore, exposed now at low tide. The plodding line of police searchers were dragging with agonising slowness through the foul mud. There were a dozen of them, all Cobb could muster on a Sunday afternoon at an hour's notice, grim men in waders and oilskins.

Cobb turned to Gornall who was standing beside him. 'You know the river, Sergeant. Could the wallet float here from Lambeth Bridge?'

Gornall jerked up his chin. 'Leather and plastic? It wouldn't float at all, sir. No special reason for it to fetch up here.'

'So what does that mean?' McBean demanded, walking up between them. Cobb recognised in his voice the same impatience he felt himself, a sense that they had been cheated, that they had come here for a solution and found only more confusion.

'It doesn't mean much,' Gornall said. 'Maybe your Mr Silver was washed in here, and rolled along the bottom until the wallet fell out of his pocket. Maybe he's stuck in the mud right now, just below the tide-line there. But most likely he just drifted out again on the next tide and left his wallet behind to fox us.'

'Let's get this straight,' Cobb said. 'In your opinion, you don't see anybody getting out of the river here after floating down from Lambeth?'

'Getting out alive, you mean?' Gornall smiled. 'My opinion, sir? Your boy's crab food. That's my opinion.'

'And what are the chances of ever finding what's left of him?'

'This old river's a quarter-mile wide here. It's six miles wide at Southend. Twenty-five miles at the mouth. There's shoals and channels and marshes and tidal islands and all sorts, all the way down. That's a lot of nowhere to find one poor little stiff in.'

'Great,' McBean said. 'That's just great.'

Gornall shrugged again, losing interest. 'I'll be over in the car when you need me, sir,' he said, and walked away with ponderous dignity in the direction of the fence.

Cobb watched him go. Beside him McBean kicked a loose stone and it cannoned over the river and fell far out with a white plume of spray.

'Ever since that night,' he said, 'this one's been on my mind. Mine and Jayce's. Hayward, sir, that is. You get involved. It feels kind of personal. Know what I mean?'

'Yes.'

'I hear the wife doesn't believe he's gone, sir. Would that be right?'

'That's right.'

'Hubby marches out like that with the kids. Breaks your life up. And then there's no corpse. No end to it. You feel sort of sorry for her.'

'Yes.'

'I suppose she'll come to believe it in the end, sir. Only—'

Cobb looked across at him, and completed the thought for him. 'Only you're not so sure either. Are you?'

The Sergeant met his eye, held it appraisingly. 'I saw that little kiddie come up out of that water, like she was inside a big bubble. Like one of those membrane things babies are born in sometimes, or kittens. What d'you call it?' Cobb shook his head. He couldn't remember either. 'Anyway, like she was just born on the surface in one of those. This sounds crazy, right?'

'No.' Cobb said, watching him.

'Well, sir. It shook me. That I'd nearly missed it, I mean. If it hadn't been for Hayward, that little girl would be dead now. I can't get it out of my mind how certain I was. And I was wrong, wasn't I?'

Cobb stared up at the white sky. Bruised clouds were blowing in from the sea. It was growing cold. 'Let's walk,' he said at last.

They walked slowly towards the abandoned warehouse.

'There's no way that wallet got into the mud out there unless it arrived in his pocket,' McBean said, suddenly emphatic. 'So he was here, wasn't he? Whether he was alive or not. We know that much.'

'It probably happened the way Gornall says.'

'What? The body floats in here, drops the wallet, and floats away again?'

Cobb faced him. 'So what's your explanation? This far downstream from the crash he just feels like getting out? Oh, and then tosses his wallet back in, with a hundred and fifty quid still in it?' But as he said this, a thought struck him and he stopped.

'What?' McBean demanded, sensing an opening.

'Lauren Silver said he pocketed the cash she was going to take away with her. We didn't find it in the car.'

'Oh? How much?'

'Six thousand.'

'Six! In cash?' McBean whistled. 'With six grand in his pocket he didn't need a wallet.'

'For God's sake,' Cobb laughed. 'Why are you so keen to prove he's alive?'

'Why are you so keen to prove he isn't?'

Cobb froze with his hand on the handle of the warehouse door. It started to spit with rain but for a second he still did not move.

'Did I say something, sir?'

'No. No.' Cobb shook himself and wrenched the door open, grinding against its runners. He stepped inside.

They stood just inside the door for a couple of minutes, shrugging themselves deeper into their coats, while the rain grew heavier outside. As his eyes grew accustomed to the gloom, Cobb made out a semi-circle of plastic milk crates over to the right of the door, and a mound of what looked like ash. He walked across to it and McBean followed. Wooden pallets lay in pairs to form three low platforms on the open sides of the fire. Soiled blankets, a sleeping bag and stacks of newspapers lay abandoned around the pallets.

'Welcome to the Hotel California,' McBean sniffed, stirring a blanket with the toe of his boot. 'They left in a hurry.'

Cobb lifted one of the newspapers, then another and another, peering in the dim light at the mastheads.

'They're two months old,' he said, looking up. 'All of them. Just before Christmas.'

'Yeah?' McBean was suddenly alert.

'If you were a bum, out sleeping rough,' Cobb said, 'why would you leave all your blankets behind?'

'If six grand had just floated into my lap,' McBean said carefully, 'maybe I wouldn't need blankets.'

Cobb left the flat early the following morning and, though he chose to walk to work, he was in the office before eight. He took his coffee across to his desk and settled himself there while his computer booted up.

It had nagged at him all night, yesterday's business of the wallet and the dead fire in the warehouse. Someone had seen the body, had rifled through the wet pockets. That someone had found the bundle of money, and in panic had thrown the incriminating wallet away and pushed the body back out into the ebbing tide. Gornall was right: Matt Silver was food for crabs. But somebody had seen him first. If they could find that witness, that would be enough to close the whole thing off.

'Hey, Cobby,' Sykes shouted from behind him. Cobb started and spun in his chair. Sykes grinned demonically. 'First time I've seen you with an untidy desk. You must be busy, for once.'

'Something like that, sir.' To cover his surprise, Cobb shuffled papers aside and cleared a space for his coffee then set it down.

Sykes grabbed a chair from a neighbouring desk and banged it down facing Cobb. 'Matt Silver,' he said. 'Developments?'

Cobb talked him through the investigation as succinctly as he could. It surprised him that Sykes was interested.

'Right.' Sykes grinned savagely. 'Pull the plug on it.'

'What?' Cobb could not hide his surprise.

'The Matt Silver Task Force is disbanded as of now. What's up, Cobby? Thought you'd be pleased.'

'But this business down at Rotherhithe yesterday, sir . . .'

'Doesn't prove bugger all. We've still got no body.'

'No, sir. But I was going to send a couple of lads round to liaise with Gornall's people. Maybe one of the local dossers got rich at Christmas.'

'Fair enough,' Sykes said, indifferent. 'But Silver's just as dead either way, right?' He looked narrowly at Cobb. 'That is right, isn't it?'

'Sir.'

Sykes nodded. 'Wait. I'll tell you what, Cobby. Keep tabs on it till the inquest. When is it, by the way?'

'Three weeks, sir. March the eleventh.'

'OK. Until then.' Sykes stood up. 'And after that we might find you some real work to do. That is,' he grinned so hard his eyes disappeared, 'if you're going to stay around long enough?'

Without giving Cobb time to answer, he replaced his chair with a clatter and strode away across the CID room, tossing jokes and insults at anyone who caught his eye, and grinning his piranha grin as he went.

Cobb rescued his coffee and sipped it. He was oddly disappointed by Sykes's announcement. Of course it was right to close the case. But in the past two months Cobb had spent so much time thinking about Silver, that this ending seemed brutal. He finished his coffee and switched his phone off voicemail. Instantly it buzzed at him.

'Sam? I'm sorry to call you at work.' Lauren sounded ill at ease.

'No problem.'

'I really need to come down to the farm this weekend. It's quite important to me. That will be all right, won't it?'

It was not a question. That did not surprise him, but the form of the demand did: she had spoken in the first person singular.

'That's fine. You're welcome any time. Both of you.'

'Thank you.' She sounded relieved.

He left a gap for her to fill with some kind of explanation, but she did not, and eventually he said: 'I'm off duty Friday. I'll be going down Friday morning. But you turn up whenever you want. Tommy's bringing you, is he?'

She hesitated for just one beat but he registered it.

'Tommy can't bring us this time,' she said evenly. 'He's away on business. I'll come on the train with Freya on Friday. She's got half term.'

'Why don't I pick you up? I virtually drive past your place anyway.' She didn't answer at once. 'Well, only if it suits you, of course.'

'It's not that.' Her voice changed in a way that silenced him. 'I go down to the church at Leighford every Friday. To Gudrun. I'm taking Freya this time. We couldn't come until after that.'

'Ah.' He drummed his fingers on the handset. 'Look, Lauren, if it's any use to you, it's not much of a detour. I mean, I'd be happy to drive you to the church. Drop you off there and pick you up an hour later, or whatever. It's no trouble.' She was silent for so long that he thought they had been cut off. 'Lauren?'

'Yes,' she said in a flat voice. 'Pick us up here at nine.' She hung up without waiting for him to confirm.

It was only much later in the morning that he realised he had forgotten to tell her about the wallet. It would keep until Friday, he decided. Perhaps by then there would be more to tell.

Silver worked quietly and with mounting strength through the following week. He used his half-healed body carefully, husbanding it. There was a little more money from George and he slipped out every afternoon to fuel himself at some cheap café, picked up newspapers discarded by the customers and read them all. There was nothing. He seemed to have evaporated. He supposed they must have looked for him. Presumably that had stopped now. He did not exist.

By Friday morning he was ready. He had picked up an old black coat from the Oxfam shop, which covered his shabby shirt and jeans. He told George he would miss the lunchtime opening and left the pub, walking at first, then taking a bus to the City and the tube out to the western suburbs of London. He got off at Kew and walked some more.

He took up his position on a bench just across the road. His heart banged painfully and he felt nauseous with apprehension. It started to rain, heavy drops slapping through the bare branches of the trees in the park. He didn't care about the rain but he would have to move or he would look conspicuous. He must go. He rose to his feet. He saw her.

She was impossibly real, impossibly solid. He had dreamt about her for so long that it was hard to accept she had an independent flesh and blood existence outside his own mind. But she did. She reached the arched gateway of school and paused there with a band of other girls, sheltering, solemn as ever. Silver walked towards her helplessly, walked until he crossed the flowerbeds and collided with the iron railings of the park, and but for the railings he would have walked on blindly across the road to her and taken her in his arms and felt that warm puppy weight of her, no matter what the cost.

She turned her head a fraction towards him and in a second she would see the gaunt figure clinging to the railings fifty feet away, the scarred face and outstretched arms. But in that second a black London cab pulled up between them and a blonde woman he did not recognise ran across the kerb and hugged the child in her arms and hurried her into the back of the taxi. The woman's face was pale in the gloom, and though she hugged the child, the child did not return her embrace. Silver realised that the woman he did not recognise was his wife and it was pain that made her unrecognisable to him.

Later, he lay stretched on the mattress under the luminous rectangle of his window. It was midnight, winter midnight on a Friday in London with the cold rain sluicing in from the estuary. Through the window he could see the cloud base as thick and grey as an army blanket over the rooftops. The foul weather must have kept the drinkers away because downstairs it was quiet in the bar. George had not come bawling for him: perhaps the fat publican had seen his face when he came in, soaked and shivering, and had thought better of it.

The image would not leave him alone. The moment he closed his eyes he saw their faces swim back into focus. Lauren, pale and jagged, like a woman in physical pain. Freya, squinting against the rain through her big flashing glasses, jostling in her yellow raincoat with her schoolfriends. He could see that she was among them but not of them. He saw the faces of those schoolgirls, the polite and kindly faces of well-mannered children, careful with his daughter. And yet they maintained a distance, as if her tragedy marked her. How could she ever be like any other little girl now? She could never be. And this was his fault. He was guilty.

When he looked again the clouds were gone and a sky of rinsed pearl had replaced it and his stomach was telling him it was empty and somehow a day had passed. He got up stiffly and hobbled to the makeshift bathroom and urinated and stared into the shard of mirror at his branded face. At least this was the last time he would have to look at it. He felt neither calm nor rested, but at least his course was clear now and he found himself able to plan it with dispassionate precision.

He crossed to the upturned tea chest which served as a table and emptied his pockets. A twenty-pence piece, a scatter of smaller coins. He had used what little he had getting to Kew. He needed enough to get back to Lambeth Bridge on the far side of London. Go back to the beginning, to where all this had started, replay it, and make no mistake this time. It was absurd to be cheated of eternity for lack of a ticket on the tube. He could almost have laughed.

The stair door banged open below and George's beery voice came booming up. 'Joe? You up there, you idle bastard?'

'I'm sick.'

'Sick be buggered. It's gone four. You want this job or don't yer?'

Silver straightened his back. His joints felt swollen and tight. He could feel the back of his throat burn with the itch of infection. Well, he thought, it didn't matter much now. If he could get through tonight and beg, borrow or steal just a little cash . . . maybe he could help himself to a half bottle of Scotch—something to take the chill off that dreadful black water—and then he could quietly slip away.

'Give me five minutes, George.'

He heard the man grunt, and the door slammed. He shovelled his handful of coins into his pocket and moved stiffly down the stairs.

George held a glass up to the light, squinted at it, buffed it on his sleeve, squinted again. A banknote lay on the bar.

'Take it or leave it, my son. This ain't the Royal Bleeding Mint. And you been skiving off. You're lucky I give you that. Where you been, anyway?' It almost sounded as if he cared.

'I was sick, George. Flu.' Silver smoothed the crumpled note against the wood. It would probably be enough for his purposes.

Nugent swung himself up on to a bar stool. 'A pot of your finest ale there, tapster.'

Silver stared blankly at him. On the far side of the room Jit was setting up mike stand and amplifier. Saturday night. Music. He had forgotten.

Nugent said: 'Do we have a problem?'

'No.' Silver crushed the note into his pocket and pulled a pint. Nugent took the beer, sipped it.

'You want to talk about it, Joe?'

'I'm working.'

'Me too,' the Australian said, deadpan, 'I'm about my father's business. But maybe you didn't notice. I've never been much good at this love thy neighbour stuff. It's not that I care much about you, Joe. It's just we're supposed to ask.' He drank, leaned his elbows on the bar top. 'I'm just wondering what brings you here, Joe. A bloke with a lot of new scars, with the remains of a thousand-quid leather jacket on his back, with one of those halfway educated Pommie accents. And here you are in this bloodhouse, taking pocket money from an old bastard like George. Fair go. It'd have to make you curious.'

'It doesn't matter,' Silver said. 'Trust me. It doesn't matter now.' He turned away and moved down the bar.

Silver worked in a haze, dragging himself down the hours towards closing time. Perhaps it was only the girl's singing which made it bearable. And she was singing beautifully tonight. He seemed to hear her through a mild delirium, a cool, pure voice that soothed him.

He set himself 11.00pm as his target. It would be easy enough to cross London then, and quiet enough by the time he reached Lambeth Bridge. He watched as the hands of the clock above the fireplace crawled towards the end of his life, and willed them to move faster.

At ten-fifty the bar was packed. George was out of the way for the moment, packed into a circle of rowdy boozers at the far end of the bar. Jit was finishing up with one of her Joan Baez favourites and, for once, she had the attention of almost the whole room.

Silver seized his chance, dodging down the steps into the cellar storeroom. He found a half-bottle of Bell's in its cardboard carton, broke the seal and drank some of the hot spirit, then slipped the flat bottle into the inside pocket of his jacket. He came back up the steps and quietly opened the bar flap. He saw George look at him and slide down from his stool, suddenly suspicious. Silver took three steps through the crowd towards the doors, feeling the bottle in his pocket knock against his chest.

'Joe?' Jit appeared right in his path, her face shining with pleasure at her small triumph. 'Was I good, or what?'

'Great.' He tried to move past her.

'Well, don't go overboard.' She looked disappointed at his reaction, but stood her ground. 'Look, give me a hand with the gear, will you? Nugget's gone to get the van.'

'I can't.'

She squared up, hands on her hips. 'What do you mean, you can't?'

'There's something I've got to do, Jit, that's all. Something important.'

'What's so bloody important you can't give me a hand with my gear for five minutes, you miserable sod?'

'Jit—'

'All right, sunshine,' George said, shouldering her aside. 'What's your hurry, then?' He flipped open Silver's jacket and in a surprisingly dexterous move extracted the Scotch. 'I just knew you was—'

Afterwards, Silver could only remember snatches of it: the splintering of the girl's amplifier as he pushed George hard in the chest and the fat barman tripped backwards over the equipment. He remembered turning to run and a mass of bodies blocking him, dragging at him. Then Silver struggled but what fight he had was gone out of him: he allowed himself to be pushed, half-crushed, towards the doors. George got his boot into Silver's back and sent him skidding over the tarmac so that his knees burned and his chin bounced. He rolled over and George stood towering and bristling at the door.

'Don't try coming back here, Joe Hill. You got any stuff upstairs you'll find it out by the bins in the morning. I don't want to see your ugly face again.' He turned to go in, swung back, pointing, triumphant. 'I knew you was trouble from the start. Knew it.'

George tugged down his waistcoat and swaggered back into the bar. Silver sat up in the rain and hugged his knees until the pain died down. After a moment he heard the door open and swing closed again. An arm was hooked under his and dragged him to his feet.

'One of the problems with this job,' Nugent said, 'is I have to be nice to arseholes like you.'

'I suppose you've got nowhere to go.' Nugent made no attempt to hide his disgust. He rammed the van down a gear and took a corner so sharply that the back wheels skidded a little on the wet tarmac. 'I suppose we've got to give you a roof for the night, with all the other derros.'

'Dump him right here, Nugget,' the girl shouted from the back. 'He's wrecked my amp.' She prodded Silver hard in the collarbone. 'What got into you, you crazy bastard? What have I ever done to you?'

He stared out dully at drab streets flicking past in the night. 'I'm sorry,' he said finally.

'Sorry? What good's that? How am I going to get another gig without an amp?' She was almost in tears. 'And I was doing good tonight.'

He rubbed his head. He felt ill. He felt like death. The thought formed into words in his mind and he was caught for a second between laughter and tears. He felt too ill to die; it was too much effort tonight. He heard himself say: 'I'll fix the amp.'

'You can't fix that!' she cried. 'It's totally fucked. Totally!'

'I can fix it. I can fix things.'

'Is that so, now, Joe?' Nugent said, with new interest. 'Is that a fact?'

After a few minutes he drove through a maze of crumbling backstreets and into a square of narrow Edwardian terraces. On an island in the centre of the square crouched a grey stone church with a hall of black corrugated iron beside it. Nugent turned in through a rutted driveway and pulled up. Jit got out without a word and slammed the car door behind her. Silver climbed out.

Nugent led Silver round to the front of the little hall, pushed the door open and stepped inside. 'Hi, Phil. How's it going?'

'No trouble at all, Father.' A portly man with horn-rimmed glasses and a maroon cardigan sat at a table inside the door, reading from a New English Bible. He smiled at Silver. 'Another guest, Father?'

'For tonight, maybe,' Nugent replied over his shoulder, striding the length of the room with Silver in his wake.

Silver became aware of half-a-dozen huddled shapes on beds around him, folding beds laid out barrack-wise, feet to the central aisle. The dark shapes stirred and muttered as they passed. The air was tainted with the smell of urine and unwashed bodies.

Nugent stopped, peered into the darkness. 'Spider?'

A voice answered, sepulchrally: 'The Demons of Beelzebub, Father. They're after me again.'

'I'll be bloody after you tomorrow, Spider. You're not taking your medication, are you?'

'It seems ineffective against Beelzebub, Father.'

'Rest easy, Spider. Not even Beelzebub will get past Fat Phil.'

'No, Father.' Doubtfully. 'Thank you, Father.'

There was a small stage at one end of the hall and Nugent led Silver round it and through to a kitchen. He flicked on a light and closed the door behind them. There were three sinks in a row against the far wall, an old gas cooker, and in the middle of the room a kitchen table and five unmatched chairs. The space under the stage, which formed one wall, was packed with boxes of tinned and bottled food, plastic sacks of clothing, battered children's toys. Nugent put the kettle on the gas, rinsed out some mugs, spoke over his shoulder.

'Clean up that gravel rash. There's some Dettol in the cupboard on the wall there. Use the kitchen towel.'

Silver looked down and saw that his jeans were torn through and that his knees were grazed and bleeding. He had not noticed. 'It's nothing.'

'Just do it,' Nugent told him impatiently. 'I can't stand fucking heroes. And when you've done that, sling your duds in the bin and dig around in those sacks for something that fits.'

Silver was too tired to argue and did as he was told, stripping off his ruined jeans and dabbing antiseptic on the raw flesh until it screamed at him. Then he dragged over a couple of the plastic sacks and broke them open and rummaged through them on the floor. He stopped, too weary and ill to go on. The room tilted a little and he sat down on the floor with a thump. He felt Nugent's strong hand grip the nape of his neck and his head was roughly pushed forward.

'Breathe,' the priest told him, as he tried to straighten up. 'Breathe. You can't pass out here.' Nugent took his hand off Silver's neck and let him sit up. He handed Silver a mug of tea. 'Try that. There's enough sugar in it to stand the spoon up in. And these.' He shook out a couple of white pills and pushed them into Silver's hand.

He sipped the tea. It was sickeningly sweet but he felt some of his strength return at once. He sipped again and then again. He looked up after a while through the steam and saw Nugent reclining on one kitchen chair with his feet up on another, watching him.

'Well, Joe. Look at you now. Going through the rag basket for cast-offs, taking charity tea. Getting all ready to bed down on the floor with a dozen drunks and misfits.' Nugent drank some of his tea, surveying Silver almost with amusement. 'You got no job. You got no home. You haven't even got your own name any more.'

'My name's Joe Hill.'

'And I'm Joan Baez.' The priest stretched back so that the chair creaked. 'No, Joe. I don't know who you are and I'm not going to ask. But I guess you're just about as low as you'll ever get. Wouldn't you say?'

'I'll move on tomorrow.'

Nugent shook his head. 'We ought to call the police right now. You couldn't be any worse off.' Silver stared at him stonily. 'I'm not going to do that, Joe. Not because I like you much, but because it's not part of my brief. There's supposed to be somewhere to go when there isn't anywhere to go, and this is supposed to be it. All the same, it isn't a bolt hole for crims who probably ought to be locked up.'

'I'm not a criminal. Not the way you think.'

'Whatever you are, Joe, you can stay here tonight.' Nugent stood up. 'After that, you pay your way.'

'I'll be gone tomorrow.'

'We'll see.' Nugent leaned over and hooked from the heap of clothes a pair of khaki trousers, a couple of shirts, socks, underwear, and piled them on the kitchen table. 'We'll see.'

Silver came awake with a jolt. Nugent was standing over his cot in the morning light, kicking him lightly on the leg. The priest clutched bulging plastic sacks in his arms. He kicked Silver again.

'Wakey, wakey. Hands off snakey.' Nugent set one of his sacks down, opened it and tossed a bread roll on to Silver's blanket. It was still warm. 'Breakfast. Now get a wriggle on.' He marched off towards the kitchen, shouting instructions to Silver over his shoulder. 'There's a shower out the back in the shed, but leave that till later. Give a hand in the kitchen.'

Silver sat up on the end of the bed and yawned and shivered in the cool, trying to wake up. His breathing was thick and his throat was sore. But his body felt so restored by sleep that compared to the night before these things were insignificant. He had slept like a dead man.

The rich aroma of the hot bread made his stomach gurgle and he nibbled at the roll, then devoured it in two wolfish bites, surprising himself. The food thrust energy directly into him and he sat up. All around him other sleepers were all already up, rolling sleeping bags, folding their beds and stacking them to one side. Taking charge was a fit-looking young man with a ponytail and a yellow T-shirt, restacking the beds, bullying them along, clapping his hands and shouting orders at them. He ignored Silver, perhaps giving him a few moments to recover.

A small neat man clicking an amber rosary appeared at Silver's elbow. He wore shiny black trousers and a surprisingly clean white shirt. The man moved closer. 'I don't think the Prince of Darkness is afraid of Fat Phil.' Silver ignored him and shrugged on his shirt, shook out the blanket, fumbled under the fold-up bed for the release catch.

'No, my friend. I believe it's you who kept me safe.'

Silver stared at him, too surprised to move away even when the stranger leaned forward and gently touched his face with his fingertips.

'I believe Beelzebub saw your battle scars, and knew you were too much for him.'

The man bent down and slipped the catch on the folding bed for him and expertly collapsed the jangling frame. Then he turned away and joined the breakfast queue. Silver was still staring at his narrow back when Nugent shouted from the door.

'Don't stand there like a stunned mullet, Joe. Get your arse into gear.'

Silver walked up to the kitchen door where Nugent was stationed. The priest was supervising the breakfast hand-outs like a Quartermaster

Sergeant. Silver could see over Nugent's shoulder into the kitchen beyond, where a band of women toiled in clouds of steam and smoke and a jabber of voices. They were mostly elderly, irreverent characters making a great game of frying bacon, buttering bread, pouring tea.

Nugent said: 'We struck lucky with the local minimarket. Freezer broke down and they were going to dump it all. We took it off their hands.' He pointed to the small table near the door where Fat Phil had sat the night before. 'Go sit. I'll bring it over.'

Silver walked to the table and sat down heavily. The door of the hall was ajar and through it he could see the soft grey sky shining above terraced houses of ochre brick. Silver stared out at the soft morning.

Nugent came striding across the hall with a plate of food and set it down with a clatter. 'Eat.'

Silver did so, ravenously, without even looking up to thank him, tearing at bread, cramming bacon and egg into his mouth. At the end of it he was breathless with the effort of eating. He became aware that Nugent was watching him, amused, across the table.

The priest was toying with a matchstick between his teeth, rolling it thoughtfully from one side of his mouth to the other. Nugent tapped his own face, nodded at Silver's. 'That was punishment, was it?'

'You could call it that.'

'You upset somebody important?'

'Yes.' Silver looked at his plate. 'Apparently.'

'And is that finished? The punishment?'

Silver frowned at him. 'Finished? How could it ever be finished?'

Nugent lifted his chin in acknowledgement. 'That wasn't quite what I meant, but as an answer it'll play.' He sucked the match for a moment. 'You weren't stealing that Scotch last night, were you, Joe?'

'Not the way George thought.'

'You were going to top yourself, right? Slip out and pop a few pills, wash them down with the booze. Draw a line under it.'

'Something like that.'

'Well, I'll tell you what, Joe. For a bloke who's so keen on dying, you show a powerful will to live.' He got up. 'It's not my job to stop you topping yourself. Call the Samaritans for that. But I'll tell you this much: guilt is debt, right? To get free of debt, you've got to start paying it off. Now you can go and kill your stupid bloody self if you want.' He stood and took a couple of steps away, then turned back. 'But wash up first.'

After a while Silver took his plate across the hall to the kitchen. He had not seen the other inmates go. He had not been paying attention, seated in a daze by the door, sleepy from the food.

He walked into the kitchen and slowly washed his plate and cutlery, then dried them and found a drawer and put them away.

When he had done this he put his hands on the edge of the sink and leaned on them and stared out through the dirty glass of the kitchen window into the churchyard.

'You going to stand there all bloody day?' Jit crashed into the room, backing through the door, her arms around the remains of her amplifier. 'Well, give me a hand then, you dozy bugger.'

Silver took the debris from her and set it on the table.

'And you reckon you can fix that?' she said, challenging him.

'I don't know. I suppose I could.'

'You suppose you could?' she mimicked. 'You've changed your tune, Mr Bloody Fixit.'

'Have I?' He frowned and looked more closely, handling the ruptured speakers, tugging at soldered wires. He said: 'This thing's a wreck.'

'I know it's a wreck!' she shouted, hands on hips. 'You wrecked it! You made that fat fart George sit on it. My bloody amp!'

He got a grip on the top and wrenched it off, exposing the guts of the cabinet. 'It's a wonder this thing ever worked at all,' he said. He held up a length of electrical flex, its insulation crumbling and the copper wires showing through. 'Look at that. You're lucky you didn't kill yourself.'

She opened her mouth to fire off a reply, but at that moment seemed to hear what he had said and caught herself. And then abruptly she started to laugh. He watched her in amazement.

'I'm sorry, Joe,' she gulped, regaining control for a second. 'But . . . I'm lucky I didn't kill myself? Don't you think that's about the funniest thing ever, coming from you? Nugget told me—'

Silver was astonished to discover that his dignity was offended. This girl didn't think he was tragic. She thought he was ridiculous. For one crazy second, trembling on the edge of hysteria, he thought so too.

'I'll need tools,' he said, with such desperate seriousness that she stopped laughing at once and looked up at him, wiping her eyes.

'Nugget keeps them under the stage. I'll show you.'

She took him to the rear of the kitchen where Nugent had piled up the bags of charity clothing. An old wooden toolbox had been pushed under the stage. Silver dragged it out and opened it. They were fine old tools, bearing the marks of English and Scottish manufacturers, marks he had not seen since a child in his father's workshop. He sat in front of the box and took the tools out, and turned them in his hands. It calmed him.

He asked: 'Are these Nugget's?' It seemed important to know.

'I guess they are now. They belonged to the guy who had St Mark's before him, Nugget said. Some old geezer who was here forever.'

Silver nodded. She watched him curiously.

'These mean something to you, Joe?'

'My father had tools like these,' he said.

'Oh, yeah. He made violins and stuff. You said.'

'Yes. He made violins. And dulcimers. And lutes. Anything with strings.' Silver smiled. 'Except guitars. That's why I had to have one.'

'So you do play,' she said. 'I thought so.'

He brought his head up quickly. 'I can fix the amp. Come back in a couple of hours.'

It was satisfying to have his hands occupied again. Even his injured left hand worked well enough, automatically compensating for the missing finger. His little finger took its place for most operations, and he could feel it gaining in dexterity. He worked quietly at the job for over an hour. Nobody interrupted him. Nobody seemed to know he was even there.

He touched a final globe of solder onto the back of the jack socket and watched it cool and glaze as it hardened. He straightened his spine luxuriously, and then sat for a minute or two examining his handiwork.

'Not bad,' Nugent said for him. He was standing by the door and Silver had not heard him approach. 'So you really can fix things.'

'It's not done yet. I need to get hold of a couple of cheap speakers.'

'You'll find some down the Mile End Road tomorrow.'

Silver looked at the priest but the remark was neither a plea nor an offer. It was simply a statement of fact, and Silver could either take it or leave it. Nugent beckoned to him. 'Come with me a minute, Joe.'

Nugent led him out of the kitchen and across the bushy turf of the churchyard. Against the back wall of the hall was a brick double garage with collapsing wooden doors, overgrown by bramble and privet. Nugent unlocked the doors and dragged one of them open.

'There you go, Joe Fixit,' he said. 'Think you can fix that?'

The Ford minibus stood at an odd angle, with its offside tyres flat. Silver could see it was filthy and rusting.

'What's wrong with it?' he asked, poking around it.

'Beats me,' Nugent said. 'But Father Lewis had it running before my time, and we could really use it now. Can you fix it or not?'

'I can fix cars. Used to be able to.'

'How are you with drains?'

'What?'

'Boilers? Leaking roofs? Wiring? You name it, it needs fixing around here.' But Nugent's questions were rhetorical now and he no longer expected an answer. 'Listen, Joe,' he said. 'You suit yourself. But I'll give you a roof and a meal so long as you're useful to me here. Up to you.' Nugent looked at his watch. 'I've got Communion.'

Chapter Eight

LAUREN LIT HER FOURTH CIGARETTE of the morning. She usually made some effort not to smoke in the same room as Freya: but on Fridays she had to cut herself some slack.

'So, Frey,' Hudson boomed, 'down to the farm again.' He walked to the stove and poured himself coffee and sat at the far end of the table.

Lauren closed her eyes. Freya did not answer.

Undaunted, he went on: 'Second time in two weeks. Not wearing out your welcome a bit, are you?'

'If she were I wouldn't take her,' Lauren snapped.

'Hey. OK. Take it easy.' He pulled a face. 'You all got out of bed the wrong side, didn't you?'

'I'm sorry. I'd better get ready. Sam will be here in a minute—'

'Sam,' Hudson said, trying the name on his tongue. Suddenly Lauren knew where he was coming from.

'I can't very well call him "Inspector Cobb" when we're staying at his house, Tommy,' she said, and realised how defensive that sounded.

'Marvellous old bloke, the father,' Hudson mused, too casually, 'but your Sam's a bit of a cold fish. That's what I reckon, anyway.'

Lauren said nothing. Freya smiled brightly up at Hudson. 'You're just jealous,' she told him.

Hudson swung his head slowly to face the child. 'And you're so bleeding sharp, young lady,' he said with undisguised malice, 'that one day you'll cut yourself.'

A rocket went off in Lauren's brain and she was on her feet yelling. 'Don't you ever talk to her like that, Tommy! Do you hear me? Not ever!'

Hudson looked up at her and for a second his eyes were stones. Then he relaxed and smiled. 'Hey, come on, Laurie. You know I didn't mean nothing.' At that moment the security buzzer sounded. Hudson nodded towards the door. 'Your chauffeur's arrived. Better hurry.'

As Cobb climbed out of the Saab, Lauren was already leading Freya out of the front door and across the gravel towards him. Before he could speak she said: 'Can we go right now? I like to get there early.'

'Sure.'

Her urgency surprised him, but he saw her clenched face and knew better than to comment. Instead he opened the car door for her and held it while she settled Freya in the back. He made a funny face at the child but she did not respond. Her eyes shifted past him and as he followed her line of sight he caught a glimpse of Hudson standing inside the house, at the window beside the front door, watching them. It puzzled him that Hudson had not come out to see them off. Cobb climbed in and drove slowly past the house, half-expecting Lauren to wave at the big man, but she stared rigidly ahead. Cobb drove out through the gates, lifting a forefinger in acknowledgement to the security guard.

They motored on in tense silence, through the wealthy suburbs and south through the brown and bare winter countryside.

Cobb caught a glimpse of Freya's eyes in the rearview mirror, fixed solemnly on him. Lauren curled away from him on the leather seat, and fell asleep.

Cobb drove quietly down through Surrey and turned off into the steep lanes to the west of Guildford. He threaded the car deeper and deeper into the country through the pretty villages but she did not wake until he pulled up in the lay-by opposite the church. He left the motor running.

'I'll park at the Cross Keys,' he said. 'Take your time.'

'We won't be long.' She hesitated. 'Why don't you come to the church in about twenty minutes? You can walk across from the car park.'

He felt she was trying to include him a little, or at least trying not to exclude him, and was grateful. 'Fine. Twenty minutes then.'

She climbed out and helped the child out of the back seat then leaned back into the car. 'I'm sorry, Sam. We're a miserable bunch today.'

She closed the door. He sat there for a moment and watched the sullen child and the faded woman as they walked towards the squat little church. Then he drove quietly up to the pub at the end of the lane.

The Cross Keys was not open yet and he sat in the parked car next to the wall of the churchyard. He realised now he should have called Lauren about the wallet earlier. It would be difficult to tell her today, and he should have foreseen that. But then, it hardly mattered. The fact was that the man was gone, one way or the other. As he watched, the two figures re-emerged into the churchyard and Freya broke free of her mother's hand and ran away between the headstones to the far fence. Even from this distance he could see Lauren's shoulders sag at this small rejection. She sat heavily on a stone bench up against the church wall. Cobb got out of the car and walked across the field towards the church.

The rough grass was wet and hung with dewy cobwebs and it soaked the bottoms of his trousers. He walked around Gudrun's small neat grave to stand beside Lauren. 'Am I too early?'

She shook her head, patted the bench, inviting him to sit. He did so. Gudrun's grave was bright with the flowers they had brought. Freya was at the fence. She had made friends with a pair of ponies and was feeding them with torn-up grass, stroking their velvet muzzles.

'She blames me. Herself too,' Lauren said. 'Especially when we come here.'

Cobb could think of nothing useful to say.

Lauren lit a cigarette and leaned back against the stone. 'Do you think he's still alive?'

'No, Lauren. I never did think that.'

'How come he won't let me go, then?'

'You sure it's not the other way round?'

She shrugged. 'What does it matter? He's there. I'm not strong enough to put a stop to him.'

'I wish I could have put him to rest for you. I know that was my job.'

'Yes, I wanted you to find him. I thought you would if anyone could.'

'They're taking me off the case,' he said abruptly. 'They're closing down the investigation.'

'When?'

'After the eleventh,' he said, avoiding the word.

'Gudrun's inquest.'

'Yes.'

'Will you be giving evidence?'

'I'll probably be called, yes.'

'Good. That seems right.'

'You know you'll be called too, Lauren. They'll want you to go through it again. It won't be a very good day for anyone.'

'What difference will it make,' she said, 'after all this?'

They were silent for a while. 'It'll be spring soon,' he said. 'There'll be some lambing this weekend if we're lucky.'

'Lambing?' she almost laughed. 'You really go in for this country squire stuff, don't you?'

'Me? I'm useless. But I like to watch the lambing.'

'Frey will enjoy seeing that.'

'Of course she will. So will you.'

'Why should you care, Sam?' She made no attempt to soften her tone. 'When it comes right down to it, it's none of your business.'

'No, it's not. I guess it's because I've been part of the way there myself.'

'What was she like?' she asked suddenly. 'Your Clea?'

'Like?' The question wrongfooted him.

'Tall? Short? Smart? Dumb?'

'She was dark,' he began at random. 'She wasn't tall. She was thirty-six.

She was from New England. She was as bright as a new penny.'

'And?'

He stood up. 'And she got cancer. And she died.'

'And you couldn't help, right?'

'She had cancer, for Chrissake.' He swung on her. 'How could I help?'

She silenced him with her raised hand and when he was quiet again, repeated, very deliberately: 'And you couldn't help. Right?'

'That's right.' He looked away.

'Some things you just can't help, Sam,' she told him. 'Some things just run their course.' She leaned forward and patted his hand. 'Let's go.'

Cobb drove thoughtfully back across country, winding up through Berkshire and skirting Oxford. No one spoke much, though the earlier tension relaxed the further they got from the church.

By the time Cobb had carried their bags into the garden room, Fred was allowing himself to be dragged around the yard by Freya on a tour of inspection. Cobb watched them for a moment through the French windows. The old man was happy to be with the child.

Cobb checked that the radiator was working and opened the window a fraction. Lauren appeared in the doorway just as he was about to leave it. She started unpacking her bags.

He noticed that this time she knew which cupboards and drawers to use and what to put in each. He liked to see that.

She walked across to the window to stare out into the garden. 'Do you see her at all, Sam?' she said abruptly, turning to face him. 'Clea, I mean. Is she still around for you?' She stood with her back to the glass.

Cobb waited a while before answering. 'There was a time, just after she died. She'd had a lot of pain, you see.' He paused. 'For a while I used to hear her. At night, sometimes. But after a time, after a few weeks, it seemed as if she simply left.' He looked up at her. 'And I stayed.'

'It's like that for me with Gudrun. I wondered if I was strange or something. No one ever tells you.'

'You're not strange.'

'Do you know, the other day I went an entire hour without thinking of her. Isn't that dreadful?'

'No.'

'When I realised it had happened, I had this agony of guilt.'

'You don't need to feel guilty. You heal whether you want to or not.'

'You told me that once. I didn't believe you.' She closed her eyes. 'It'll never be over for me. But one thing you said is true: Goodie's gone. Wherever she is, it's a different place. And I'm still here. More or less. I can't help it.'

'And Matthew?' Cobb said. 'Is he still here?'

Her eyes sprang open. 'Please don't crowd me, Sam,' she said, as though he had asked quite another question.

Cobb woke at five and lay listening to the sparrows fussing in the eaves while the square of his window paled. He rolled out of bed, tugged his jeans on, then grabbed his shirt and moved through the sleeping house to the kitchen. He stopped in surprise at the door.

'Well, it's young Princess Freya, up with the lark.'

She sat upright at the table on one of the kitchen stools, with her hands curled round a Bart Simpson mug. 'You look like you've been dragged through a hedge,' she told him. 'Backwards.'

'Not forwards? Definitely backwards?'

'Definitely.'

'Well, it's nothing that a pot of coffee won't fix.' She tried to hide it, but Cobb could see her face fall. He put the pot back on the shelf. 'Bugger the coffee. Let's go and see the lambs.'

She skipped ahead of him across the yard while he dragged on his sweater. The air was sharp and clean, cool enough for their breath to steam. There was already activity in the yard. The ewes were crowded into one corner of the field, and a gangling boy was moving among them, spreading his arms to keep the animals bunched together. Arthur Riordan, in gumboots and rainjacket, was leaning on the rail, shouting to the boy to cut out this one or that one from the flock.

'Well, if it isn't the Laughing Policeman,' Riordan called across to Cobb. He looked at his watch. 'Putting in a half-day, are you, Sam?'

'Give me a break, Arthur. I did bring an extra hand.'

'So you did. Well, I'm sure she'll be more use than you are.'

'What a rude man,' Freya said loftily. Cobb laughed and took her hand and led her into the barn.

'Don't mind Arthur,' he told her. 'These are mostly his ewes. He just boards them here. Let's have a look at some of his new arrivals.'

The barn had been partitioned off into a series of stalls, one ewe in each, some already suckling their newborn lambs, others on their bellies in the straw, waiting for delivery. Riordan's two horsey daughters and a young vet who looked like an accountant were working among the sheep. In the centre of the barn a flock of uneasy ewes milled, bleating.

'We only have half-a-dozen of our own. Just for fun. That's why Arthur takes the mickey out of me.'

'Birth isn't a spectator sport, Sam,' Riordan called, dragging in another ewe. 'Time to get your hands dirty.'

'Me? I don't know one end from another.'

'You'll soon work that out, my lad. And your little sidekick can help too, if she wants.'

'All right,' Freya said at once.

By the time Lauren arrived, around mid-morning, Cobb was helping to deliver his sixth lamb.

'Get your hand right up there,' Riordan shouted at him, holding the ewe's head. 'Get hold of it and pull.'

'Go on, Sam,' Freya told him, picking up one of Riordan's phrases: 'Pull it—don't tickle it.'

Cobb, kneeling in the straw and caught between effort and laughter, groped inside the animal, felt the unborn lamb jerk under his fingers. The ewe pushed forward a foot, and the movement freed the lamb, which was born in a rush in his arms, slimy and bloody.

'It's a boy!' he shouted in triumph. He could hear Freya clapping and squealing with excitement. Riordan took the lamb by its back legs and laid it on the straw. It looked like a drowned rabbit.

'Is it going to be all right?' Freya asked.

'Oh, it'll be fine,' Riordan said. 'A perfect delivery.' He lifted the lamb's black little leg. 'And by the way, Sam, it's a girl. See that the mother suckles it, now.' He left the stall, leaving Cobb still sitting in the straw.

'Sam's delivered six of them!' Freya shouted to her mother, jumping with excitement. 'Six little lambs!' Lauren stared at her daughter, speechless. It was as if she didn't recognise this joyful, noisy child.

'Freya helped with all of them,' Cobb said. 'We did it together.'

'Great,' Lauren said, feeling for her cigarettes. 'That's great.'

'Mustn't do that in here, Mummy,' Freya cried, 'you'll give the baby lambs passive smoking.'

Lauren put the cigarettes away again. She looked dazed at the change in her daughter. Cobb looked away to give her a chance to recover, fussing with the newborn lamb. It was then that he noticed the ewe had not moved. She lay on her side, still panting.

Freya followed his eyes. 'What's the matter with her, Sam?'

Arthur Riordan struggled past, manhandling another ewe towards the yard. He glanced down as he went by. 'She's got another one in there, Sam. Better do your midwife bit again.'

'Arthur—'

'Too busy. Sorry!' And he was gone.

It only took five minutes, though it seemed longer. When it was over and the dead lamb lay on the straw at the girl's feet, there was a moment when Cobb could have murdered Arthur Riordan. Maybe he might have saved it, and then Freya would still be bouncing and noisy with joy.

Cobb wiped his hand on his jeans and touched Freya's arm. 'Well, we saved one of them, Princess. Didn't we?'

'Yes.' She hugged the surviving lamb but her eyes were fixed on the dead one. Suddenly she said: 'They'd have been twins. Twin sisters.'

He saw Lauren's head turn and knew she was watching him. 'Yes, Freya,' he said clearly. 'They'd have been twins.'

'Why did she die?' the girl said. She was looking at the dead lamb, but Cobb knew better.

'I don't know. Nobody does. Don't let anyone tell you they do.'

'It isn't fair.'

'No, it's just the way things happen, Freya. It's nobody's fault.'

She looked at him steadily. 'It was Daddy's fault.'

'Maybe that's true, Princess. I only know it wasn't your fault. And it wasn't your mum's either.' She stared at him, hugging the lamb, rocking it. Cobb stroked the lamb's warm head. 'Why don't you keep her?'

'I can?'

'Of course. She's one of ours.'

'How do you know?'

'Oh, I can always tell.'

After a while she got up quietly, struggling under the small weight of the lamb, and staggered past him out of the stall. She sat down next to her mother, hugging her lamb, hot-eyed, her mouth turned down. She hesitated there for just a moment. Then, in a sudden and convulsive movement, she clutched in against her mother's side and turned her face into her mother's body and Cobb saw Lauren's arm lock quickly around the child and her head come down so that he could not see the girl for her mother's protective hair, falling across both their faces.

Silver worked on the dismantled engine for most of the morning, hand-grinding the pitted valve seats down to matt grey steel, checking the guides, replacing worn valve springs.

He had learned most of his skills on the road, in the years when the band's transport was his first priority, ranking way ahead of food, drink or even dope. Without transport they were literally nowhere. The only vehicles they could afford were big old brutes, including a beaten-up Ford Transit not unlike this one. Silver remembered the Ford particularly because it had lasted right up until his first major recording contract. He remembered it too because of Lauren. He would not forget that morning. He had taken his leave of her upstairs in her bare little cube of a student flat. And then, ten minutes later, she arrived uninvited as they were loading up outside, a shining, tight-bodied blonde of nineteen, quivering with the promise of adventure.

He had thought of telling her, gently enough, to run along home. She was not much more than a schoolgirl, with her too-new rucksack and her wide and eager blue eyes, and he could not find the heart to do it. There had been something else too, a kind of exultation about her, that he could not deny. It came to Silver suddenly that she really had loved him then. He wondered if he had ever truly loved her.

Silver straightened his back and began to tidy up. He was as methodical as a surgeon, cleaning the tools and putting them carefully away.

It had been over a week. It did not take this long to get the head off an engine and regrind the valves, but every time he started to make progress, Nugent would appear with some new task. Silver had been sent to fix a loose step in the hall, to dig out the drain, to climb up on the roof and wire into place one of the sheets of corrugated iron which had blown off in the night. He was deliberately being kept busy—not perhaps solely out of concern for his welfare, but in order to get the most out of him while the opportunity was there. He did not resent that. It seemed like a fair exchange to him. He could not deny that each day he achieved something, however small, and that this felt good. He did not know where this was leading. For the moment it was enough to live each day at a time.

He pulled the garage doors across and moved into the kitchen to make himself a coffee. He could hear someone moving in the body of the hall, and after a moment she began to sing in a high and plangent voice. It gave him a peculiar pleasure to hear it. She had been gone for a week, visiting relatives. He was glad she was back.

He walked into the hall. 'Don't stop,' he said.

But she did stop, looking down at him uncertainly from the stage.

He fumbled for something to say. 'I've fixed the amp, more or less.'

'You have?' She sounded surprised.

'Nugget got you a couple of new speakers and I fitted them yesterday. It works fine now.' He made to walk away then changed his mind. 'Play some more. Please.'

She kept her eyes on him as she hefted the strap of the big guitar onto her shoulder and began to sing: an old Lightnin' Hopkins twelve-bar, then some Bessie Smith, and two more of her own. Somewhere in the middle of this he found an old canvas-backed chair and sat in the body of the hall, and after a while he closed his eyes and let go.

'You know about this stuff,' she said. She had stopped playing and was standing in front of him with the guitar held across her. 'It touches you.'

'Yes.'

'When you used to play, before you lost the finger, you were good. Weren't you?'

'Yes.'

'I know—just by watching you—when I'm going wrong.'

He straightened in his chair, cleared his throat. 'You sing a little flat in the top register. That's mainly confidence. Breathing and confidence. That can be fixed. But your guitar technique is pretty average. You spend too much time on open strings up near the nut—'

'You could teach me. No one ever taught me.'

'Did you ever see a nine-fingered guitar teacher?'

She shrugged. 'Django Reinhardt only had eight.'

He stared at her.

'Jesus, Joe, you're a defeatist. I've got my brother's old six-string up in the room. You could have that. It'd be a challenge, wouldn't it?'

He looked hard at her. 'What are you doing here, Jit?'

'Nugget brought me here,' she said. 'I'd come down from Nottingham with Jake. My brother. I was kind of looking after him. He was on a methadone program, but he'd been selling it for crack. He's OK now.'

'He is?'

'Sure. He's a New Age traveller now. In a camp out near Northampton. But at the time he'd done his head in a bit and he sort of left me with nothing up at Euston Station. That was a bit severe. I was sleeping rough near King's Cross when Nugget picked me up one night. I was pretty low. Now I sort of work for him here. Half-a-dozen of us do, on and off. Just for board. The church owns a couple of the houses in the street. We have rooms there. Bedsits, sort of.'

The back door of the kitchen banged and Nugent's voice rang out in the hall. 'Joe? Hell are you?' The priest walked through into the hall, saw Silver. 'The bloody heater in the church is stuffed again. Come and take a look at it.' He noticed Jit for the first time. 'Oh. You're back.'

'Joe's going to teach me music,' she told the priest.

Silver made to protest but she went on: 'He's a gypsy. Did you know that?' She talked to Nugent over Silver's head. 'Oh, yes. He was the best gypsy guitarist in the world, and in love with the beautiful Esmeralda. And then one day his deadly rival Vargas burst into his caravan and did that to his face and cut off one of his fingers so he couldn't play any more. And then Vargas left him for dead, and now it's Vargas who lives with Esmeralda. Joe's been plotting revenge ever since. It's dead romantic.'

'Right.' Nugent looked at Silver. 'Now piss off and fix the heating.'

'I'll take a look.' He walked to the door.

'Wait,' Nugent said. 'You doing that folk club gig tonight, Jit?'

'Every Tuesday.'

Nugent nodded to Silver. 'Why don't you go with her? Give her a few tips if you know something about this stuff.'

Silver said: 'Nugget, look—'

'Take the van.' The priest tossed the keys to Jit. 'I'll be glad of a Tuesday night without listening to those hairy bastards caterwauling.'

Despite its grand name, the Duke's Head Music Room was merely a long dim chamber above the saloon bar. Ranks of plastic chairs with a tiny triangular bar cutting off one corner. Jit liked it, she told him, because here she had a real audience, people who had come specifically to hear singing—hers among others—and not simply a casual crowd of drinkers in some beer-stinking bar.

He let her buy him a pint and then slipped away from her to the back of the room. He took a corner seat in the shadows and watched as the place filled up. Jit sat up at the end of the second row, chatting easily to people who could not keep their eyes off her brilliant blue hair. She caught his eye for a second through the swelling crowd and winked conspiratorially at him. Knots of over-hearty people were greeting one another at the door. New people arrived every few moments, backing into the room with trays crowded with pints of bitter.

There was a burst of applause and some cheering and a neat, bald man who might have been a bank manager took the floor. He carried a banjo. He was joined by a squat woman with long grey hair and a dress of brown Indian cotton. Finally a second man shuffled to a dim spot just on the edge of the audience, staring fiercely at the floor while he adjusted the straps of the accordion over his shoulder. After a moment of nervous patter the grey-haired woman began to sing *The Lark in the Morning* and the two men came in raggedly on the second line. They were not very good. Silver found it torture to watch.

The woman finished her song and an astonishing storm of applause and cheering and whistling swept over her. Did they really think this woman was good? Had he missed something? They loved her, for some reason that was hidden from him. But he knew that the truth was that she was simply one of them. Silver was suddenly overcome with a great sadness. Yes, he had missed something, all right. He had missed a turning, and he had missed it long, long ago. At about the time that he had come to backstreet singalongs like these, and sneered at their amateurism. He heard his sixteen-year-old voice, defiant in Dr Gottschalk's study.

'But I want to be the best!' he had cried, raging against the awful grey suburban life outside the streaked windows.

And the old man had stroked his moustache and asked: 'Why?'

Silver got up quickly and pushed roughly out of the room. He walked the black streets blindly for two hours until cold and exhaustion forced him back to the church. It was close to midnight. Silver went into the kitchen. The lights were going down in the hall, but he did not feel like sleep. He pulled up a chair and sat down and waited.

Jit opened the kitchen door and startled him. Perhaps he had dozed off after all. He had not heard the van's engine, over the drumming of the rain on the tin roof, nor her steps up the side path.

'Hi, Joe. Still up?'

She rested her guitar against the wall and shook the rain off her bright blue hair. She pushed the door shut behind her and pulled out a couple of the clothing sacks and sat on them with her knees drawn up and rummaged in her shoulder bag. She lit up and closed her eyes and inhaled hard and the aromatic smoke rose in a blue mushroom.

'You'll get busted carrying that stuff about,' he told her.

'You sound like my dad.' She leaned back, at ease. 'Why didn't you stay till the end?' She handed him the joint.

He took it, drew on it, passed it back. 'Reasons.'

'I did some Baez for an encore. Thought it would keep the folkies sweet. They loved it.' She paused. 'I am good, aren't I, Joe?'

'Too good for that place.' But this wasn't the answer she wanted.

'I made twenty quid,' she protested. 'If I could do that every night I'd be OK.'

'You could do better.'

'Like what?'

'Theatre restaurants, nightclubs . . .'

'I don't want all that!' she said. 'All those rich wankers perving at me!'

'You prefer poor wankers perving at you?'

She smoked in silence for a while, a little hurt. Then she said: 'Brought you a present.' She reached across to the guitar case and flicked it open. He realised for the first time that it was not her own twelve-string guitar but a Yamaha six-string. 'It's Jake's. The one I told you about. I said you could have it.' She smiled at him. 'So now you can be king of the gypsy guitarists again and win back the beautiful Esmeralda.'

'From the evil Vargas,' he said.

'You got it.' She stood up, watching his face.

'Won't your brother want it back?'

'Jake? No. He's too busy becoming a real gypsy. Get stuck into some practice, Joe. Because I want you to teach me.'

'Jit—'

But she was gone, waggling her fingers at him in farewell.

Lauren pulled up opposite the school and spotted a parking space almost at once. There was a blue coach parked outside the gates. A small knot of people had already gathered at the foot of the steps: a woman with a clipboard, a handful of fussing parents, a driver with a cap.

'There you go, sweetheart,' Lauren said, as brightly as she could manage. 'Looks like you're going to have fun.'

Freya stared silently out of the car window at the bus while her mother backed the car into the space.

'I don't think I really want to go,' the girl said miserably.

Lauren leaned across and pulled her daughter against her and kissed her. 'I know it's difficult, sweetheart.'

'The camp won't be the same without Goodie.'

'Of course it won't. How could it be?'

'She always won everything at camp,' Freya said, and thought about this for a moment. And then: 'Everyone's going to ask me where she is.'

'They'll all know, love.' Lauren hugged her. 'We've told everyone who didn't know already.'

'Not all the girls from the other schools. Not all of them will know.'

'No, I expect not all of them will know.' Lauren looked out through the windscreen. 'It'll be hard no matter what we do. Life is.'

'I should stay here with you,' Freya said, suddenly fierce, pulling free to face her, and Lauren could see at last what really troubled her daughter. Freya said: 'You need me.'

'Yes, I need you, Frey. But not for the inquest.'

'*You* have to be there.'

'Yes, but you've told them everything you know, and there's no need to go through it again. It's just an official thing, that's all.'

'Will Sam be there?'

'Yes,' Lauren replied, surprised at the question.

The answer seemed to satisfy the girl. 'That's all right, then.'

'It is, yes,' Lauren said. 'In a way.'

'I can't remember what happened,' Freya said suddenly, and looked at her lap. 'I've tried and I've tried.'

'You're not expected to, Frey. People often can't remember that kind of thing. It's good they can't. It's a defence.'

'Will I ever remember?'

'It won't matter, sweetheart. I think we know what happened anyway, don't we?'

They were silent for a while. Across the road the pavement was growing crowded with parents and children and teachers. The luggage compartments of the big shiny bus were open and bags were being pushed in while a teacher tried to keep track of it all and tick it off a list.

'I've not been a good mother to you, Frey,' she said.

'Not very good,' the girl agreed. 'But you're the one I got.'

Then in an uncharacteristically impulsive gesture she wrapped her arms around her mother's neck and kissed her.

'See you Saturday,' she said, and before Lauren had time to respond she had grabbed her bag from the back seat and was lugging it across the road into the crowd of excited children.

Silver was head down under the bonnet and did not hear the priest until the last moment.

'You're singing, Joe,' Nugent observed. Silver started, then levered himself up out of the engine compartment.

'Is singing against the rules?'

'My oath! This is a Christian establishment. You're supposed to suffer.' Nugent walked around the old minibus, stroking the bodywork. 'You reckon you'll ever get it going? You've been on it for weeks.'

'You should've got me a reconned engine, like I asked.'

'Money, Joseph,' the Australian said easily. 'And at least it keeps you off the streets for a while. Which may be a benefit to the community.' He rolled his head and squinted up at Silver. 'Is it, Joe?'

'Is it what?'

'A benefit to the community?'

'I do what I'm told around here, Nugget. What more do you want?'

'Oh, you're a regular saint, you are. Three weeks of cleaning up after the bedwetters, digging out the cesspit, keeping Beelzebub off Spider. And sleeping on the floor among the bums while you do it. Better watch out. We'll start to think you like it.'

'Is this what I get for humming a tune?'

Nugent stood up. 'I wouldn't want you to get too happy, Joe. I wouldn't want you to think you could stay here for ever. This can only be a halfway house for people like you.'

'Who are people like me?'

Nugent held his eyes. 'There's nothing much wrong with you, Joe. You're a first-class asset among all these liabilities. But one day I'll have to ask why you're still here.'

'Are you throwing me out?'

'You should want to get out.' He looked steadily at Silver. 'Sooner or later you're going to have to look beyond here and get a life,' Nugent said. 'You'll have to face it, Joe, sooner or later.'

Silver said nothing. Nugent took a couple of steps out into the sunshine and stretched, opening his arms to the slight heat of it, embracing it. He let his arms drop to his sides.

'Jit says you're playing again.'

'With nine fingers? What do you think?'

'She says you're already better with nine fingers than she is with ten.'

'I just fumble around. I haven't played since I was a kid.'

Nugent smiled slowly and Silver saw that this was a lie too far.

'That's not what Jit says. She says you must have been bloody excellent once. She also says you can teach her a lot.'

'I've got nothing to teach anyone.'

'Oh, I'm sure you'll learn to, Joe. Because you want this.' The Australian tossed him a key with a wooden tag. 'Second floor in number seventeen, across the street. Young Andy's moved out.'

Silver rolled the key in his hands. The houses were half derelict but they belonged to the diocese, and if Nugent put him in there he could have some peace and some small space to himself.

'Thanks, Nugget.'

'Now you listen, Joe. I'll give you a few quid a week. But it's not a cheap apartment or a bolt hole. I put you in it because I want your work. And while you live in it you do what anyone here tells you to do.'

'Understood.'

'Anyone. And that includes Jit. She wants to learn, you teach her. Otherwise, it's been nice knowing you.'

It was a bare cube with a single shadeless bulb, a couple of chairs and a split foam mattress. He pulled the door to behind him. Then he moved one of the hardbacked chairs around and sat on it. The room was no more than a partitioned-off box in what must originally have been a front bedroom. The plasterboard partition cut the window vertically in half. His half looked out over the ugly little church in the centre of the square. The lowering afternoon sun gave a gilding of life and colour even to this shabby pocket of East London.

'Hi, neighbour.' Jit pushed open the unlatched door. She had brought her guitar and now stood it against the wall. He said nothing and she idly ran her finger along the bass string of her guitar so that it buzzed like a wasp in a jar.

'I've got a gig at the Rum Jungle Club Thursday week,' she said.

'The what club?'

'It's in Stepney Green. It's not much, but at least it's a real nightclub. I've written this new song for it. Listen.'

She took up the guitar and began to play. He sat back to listen.

'Put you to sleep, did I?' she accused him. 'Well, that's a compliment.'

He shook himself. 'The song's great,' he said. 'You'll do fine.'

'Is that your idea of constructive criticism?'

He was stung by her persistence. 'Look, Jit, you want criticism? Well, I'll tell you. They'll all love you because you look sweet and you sound like a Sunday school teacher. But technically you're nowhere.'

'Well, don't beat about the bush, Joe. Come right out and say it.'

'You've got to do what I tell you and move down the fretboard more. I told you that before. All this C, F, G7 twelve-bar stuff won't do for an audience that knows what it's listening to. You need to put some grunt into it.' He found himself warming to this. 'Here, give it to me.'

He took the guitar and cradled it. This time his left hand found the positions on the fretboard with a speed that was almost fluid. A dammed stream was overspilling, carving a new channel to his remaining fingers. In his surprise at this returning power he did not realise what riff he was playing. She rolled her head back against the wall, eyes closed, and whisper-sung the words:

'You people climbing on that Narrow Way—'

He clapped his hand hard over the strings, killing the song dead.

She opened her eyes and pulled a face at him, mocking him. 'You were playing it, pal.' She was silent for a moment. 'You did something bad, didn't you, Joe?'

'Yes.'

'Can you put it right?' Her voice was matter-of-fact.

'No,' he said, but he realised that he had hesitated, and that she had sensed this.

'Well, can you make it any better than it is?'

'Jit, I don't want to talk about it.'

'You don't?'

'No.'

'You want a fuck, then?'

He stared at her in such frank astonishment that she laughed aloud.

'You're shocked! Hey, Joe—I'm not that bad, am I?'

'I'm three times your age, Jit.'

She regained some control with an effort, wiped her eyes, assumed a serious expression. 'You can still get it up, can't you, Joe?'

He stared at her in confusion. 'Christ, Joe—don't look at me like that! I can't stand it.' She stood up with an effort. 'I'm sorry, Joe. I mean, look, if you don't want it, you don't have to have it. But did you think I was some sort of little nun?'

The idea of this doubled her over again and she groped for her guitar and pulled the door open. Silver could hear her joyful laughter ringing all the way up the stairs. It was a curiously innocent sound.

McBean shifted the phone to his other ear to block out the noise of Hayward eating. He had grown used to doing this because Hayward was almost always eating. The car smelled like a different restaurant every day. Today it was Chinese. It took McBean a moment to identify the gruff voice on the phone, and he had to ask the man to repeat his name.

'Gornall. From Rotherhithe. Couple of weeks back.'

'What can I do for you, Sergeant?'

'It might be that I can do something for you, Sergeant.'

'You mean about the Silver business?'

'I do. I put the word out, to see if any of our local yobbos had got rich quick. Like we agreed.'

'Yes?'

'I just had a call from Newington. There's an old tom called Maggie Turpin who used to hang around the pubs up our way from time to time. Not a local. From up East somewhere. And now she's just turned up dead in this flat in Newington. The thing is, they found a lot of cash on the bloke who's with her.'

'A lot?'

'About fifteen hundred quid. I thought you might like to shoot round there.' Gornall read out the address then said, 'Look, I wouldn't go jumping to any conclusions. This probably doesn't mean much. Get round there and see for yourself, I would. The lads are still there.'

McBean's favourite uncle had lived in Newington and he knew the area well. He found the street and parked behind a squad car and an ambulance. He and Hayward climbed out and moved through the huddle of neighbours gathered on the public side of the tape. McBean recognised the Sergeant who met them at the front door, a tall and angular man called Crick. He had a beaky nose and a permanent stoop and reminded McBean of a stork.

Crick led McBean and Hayward through the cramped hallway of the flat and turned right through the kitchen-diner. It was a bare, underfurnished room. The bench surfaces were empty and uncluttered, but there was a faint smell of spoiled food. From a bedroom the other side of the hallway came a sudden explosion of obscenities, a man's voice, a ripped, drunken voice which spiked up, roaring, and then faded feebly away. Crick followed McBean's glance.

'The other half. We can't get much sense out of him.'

A man in a white lab coat was on his knees on the floor in front of the open oven, minutely checking the linoleum.

Crick said: 'My bet is he came in pissed, found the old duck in here, and then put her to bed.' He ushered them through into the bedroom.

The bulky figures bending over the bed made her body look as frail as a sparrow's. The flesh was grey, her hair yellow-white on the pillow. She had been placed with some care, the blankets pulled up to her chin and her stick like arms laid outside the covers. McBean glanced around the bedroom. It was surprisingly pleasant in a cheap and chintzy fashion. Clearly she had tried hard to make it cheerful, and this immediately brought her to life for him. McBean knew a good deal about making the best of shabby flats.

'Poor old biddy,' Hayward said from beside him.

McBean leafed through the papers.

'It says here you were a sailor, Stevie.' The documents were crumpled and stained. 'Long ago, was that?'

Stevens's eyes drifted to meet McBean's. He had washed-out blue eyes with a hard white ring around the pupils. He was filthy and he stank of excrement and of some raw spirit. He looked feverish and ill.

'Open that window, Jayce,' McBean said, then loudly: 'Where are you from, Stevie? No one around here seems to know you.'

'I been in the East.' The voice was vague. 'The Nile and all.'

'The Nile, Stevie?' McBean pulled a comic face. 'And it says here you were born in Deptford.'

Stevens stared through him. 'Had to be somewhere *nice*, Maggie says.' Stevens flipped his hand contemptuously at the flat. 'For once, she says. *Respectable*, she says.' Stevens leaned forward, remembering, and his voice became thoughtful. 'Just like she was sleeping, it was. She blew nearly the whole wad, renting *this*.'

'What wad?' Hayward said. 'Where did you get all this money, Stevie?'

But the man's face was slack and the focus of his eyes drifting.

Outside the door McBean handed Stevens's Merchant Navy discharge papers to Crick and shook his head.

'We won't get much out of him.'

Crick shrugged. There was a sudden commotion in the bedroom and Stevens appeared in the doorway, purple in the face and bellowing, two Constables struggling to hold him back.

'Shoulda left him!' he roared, thrashing against their grip. 'Shoulda let him just float away! Him and his fucking money!' Stevens fixed McBean with a look of crazed despair. 'It was so cold,' Stevens said in an entirely rational voice. Then his eyes rolled up and he slipped through the policemen's grip to the floor and there was shouting and a rush of paramedics and McBean was pushed back against the wall.

It was the end of their shift and they drove back to the station in silence. They still had not spoken ten minutes later when they took seats opposite one another across the canteen table. Finally Hayward said: 'I know what you're thinking. You're thinking Stevie pulled Matt Silver out of the river. You're thinking maybe Silver wasn't dead when he did that. And now Stevie's gone to the big meths tank in the sky, and we don't even know where to look.'

'The man didn't know what day it was, Jayce. He thought he was still in Cairo or somewhere, in the Navy. And all that stuff about the Nile?'

'It's the Curse of Tutankhamun's tomb,' Hayward said, daringly. 'That explains everything.'

'I guess it doesn't matter now,' McBean said. 'They're closing the book on it after the inquest.'

'It matters,' Hayward said decisively. Then added in a rush: 'I keep thinking of his wife and the little girl. It's funny, I feel kind of responsible. Maybe they just need to know for sure.'

McBean was quiet for some time, rolling his warm mug between his palms. Eventually they got up and returned their mugs to the counter.

It was not until Hayward was pushing open the door of the canteen that he spoke again. 'You know, Sarge, it's a funny thing . . . Where I grew up, there was a pub. Queen of the Nile, it was. Everyone just called it "The Nile". Think there are any pubs called that, up East?'

McBean looked at him. 'Tell me something. How did you get a name like Jason? You an Argonaut or something?'

'No, Sarge.' Hayward looked shocked. 'We're Methodists, we are.'

Chapter Nine

COBB DISMISSED THEM and watched them file out of the incident room for the last time. They seemed happy enough to go, even without a result, and shuffled out smiling and joking. He could hardly say he had welded the Matt Silver Task Force into the Met's dream team during the three-month investigation but he had grown fond of his unlikely crew.

Cobb closed the door behind the last of them and walked back into the untidy little room and let his gaze wander around the pinned photos and the scribbled whiteboard. All this had been for nothing. Cobb supposed he should feel bitter or frustrated at their failure. But he did not. They had looked everywhere there was to look. The door opened behind him and he turned.

Sykes said: 'That's it, then, Cobby? Lord Dismiss us with Thy Blessing, and all that.'

'I suppose it is, sir.'

Sykes reached up and jerked a photograph free from the notice board. It was the pathologist's picture of Gudrun Silver.

'Tomorrow, is it? The inquest?'

'Two o'clock.'

'Accidental death. Formality.' Sykes tossed the warped photo back onto the table. 'Over in twenty minutes. Pity they can't do the father at the same time.'

'Yes.'

'Come back here after the inquest. Take all this stuff down. Put it in the bin. Lousy fucking job. All PR, no policing.' Sykes looked up at him. 'But you done all right with it, Sam.'

It took Cobb a moment to register that this was the first time Sykes had ever used his Christian name.

Sykes turned away and reached for the door handle. 'Superintendent Parris at Regional Crime's got an opening, Sam. Nominated you.' He waited. 'I expect you mean "Thank you, Mr Sykes".'

'Yes. Yes, I do. Thank you.'

'One snag—Parris is away for a few weeks. You got any leave owing?'

'Leave? A couple of weeks, sir.'

'Take it, Sam. Make a clean break with all this.'

'Sir.'

Cobb watched him swagger away across the big open-plan office. He felt that he had completed some sort of apprenticeship. Or perhaps it was a rehabilitation. Whatever the truth of it, Cobb knew that Sykes had opened a door for him. For two years his career had been sliding. His life, indeed, had been sliding. He had known and he had hardly cared. Sykes had shown some faith in him by waiting while he got his balance back. He was grateful.

Cobb had a sudden sense of things coming together, of new beginnings. His hand touched the curling photograph on the desk and he picked it up and looked at it. He was momentarily annoyed with himself for forgetting that tomorrow would be a grim day for this child's sister, for her mother. But then it came to him that the two issues were interlocked, as endings and beginnings always are. 'It's over,' Sykes had said. Yes. In a way. Cobb was filled with an irrational sense of protectiveness. He crossed to his own desk and dialled her number, and when she answered, he said: 'Come down to the farm this weekend.'

'Sam?' Lauren sounded surprised. And something else. Cautious. 'You know what tomorrow is?'

'Of course I do. That's why.'

She did not answer directly. 'I sent Frey on a school camp. To South

Wales. I wanted her away from here this week.'

'Good idea. When does she get back?'

'Saturday morning.'

'So get them to drop her off at Oxford. We'll pick her up. It'll do you both good.' When she didn't answer, he said: 'I planned a bit of a surprise for her. Take her mind off things.'

'All right. I'll come up on Saturday.' Her voice was still uneasy. 'Sam, you know I'm not going to be a bundle of laughs this weekend.'

'That's not what it's about.'

'No,' she said, doubtfully. 'I know it's not.'

Lauren replaced the receiver quietly in its cradle and stood looking at it for a while, thinking. Hudson asked, too casually: 'Cobb again?'

'Yes.'

Hudson, seated at the antique desk in the corner of the room, turned back to his work. 'An Inspector calls,' he murmured.

Lauren registered what he had said. 'What do you mean, "again"?'

He looked up, innocently. 'Sorry?'

'You said "again". Cobb "again". What do you mean by that?'

'All right, Laurie. All right.' He spread his hands. 'I just meant—'

'Why don't you just mind your own business, Tommy?' she snapped. She instantly felt sorry. Hudson looked so pained whenever she hit out at him.

He sighed, then turned towards her and laid his glasses on the desk. He said: 'I understand, Laurie. It'll be better after tomorrow. You'll see.'

But for some reason his sympathy only sparked her irritation afresh. 'Fuck off, Tommy,' she shouted at him. 'Just fuck off.'

She turned and stalked out of the room, banging the door hard behind her, shocked at her own outburst.

She found a jacket in the hall and slung it over her shoulders and marched blindly through the dim corridors of the house until she reached the kitchen. She pushed open the swing doors. Merilda was crooning along with a Latin radio station, all guitars and passion, and at the same time cooking energetically with garlic and tomatoes and basil. As Lauren came through the kitchen Merilda stopped singing and stared at her. Lauren forced a smile and walked through to the back door and opened it and went out into the evening garden.

There was an old set of wooden garden furniture outside the back door. She sat down there. It was cool, but the last of the spring sun fell at an angle through the larch trees and across the lawn and filled the corner where the table was placed. Merilda came sweeping out of the kitchen, beaming at her. With a practised flourish Merilda set a cup of fresh coffee in front of Lauren. She tapped the hot rim of Lauren's cup with her fingertip, making no attempt at subtlety.

'More better, Mrs Silver,' she said kindly. 'Coffee more better than wine in bad times.'

Then she swept away again, singing to her own music.

Lauren smiled to herself. Merilda was right, but all the same at this moment part of her would have dearly loved a drink. Confrontation always made her feel like this. That was something she had learned at the counselling sessions she had started attending, and was glad to have learned it, because knowing it made it easier to handle. Besides, a drink was out of the question. It would have meant retreating back into the dim heart of the house, where Hudson would still be hunched over his papers. The thought of him made her feel ashamed. He had been good to her, in his fashion.

He dealt with all the finances, from the accountants to the funeral expenses, handling everything so that all she had to do was sign the cheques or the forms. She had not seen a bill for months. He had fielded every single phone call, every pestering reporter, every threat to her security and privacy. He had protected her like a medieval champion. And he had asked little enough in return. Only to be useful. Only to be around her. Only to be given the merest flicker of hope.

Oh yes, she thought guiltily. That was it. That was why she felt ashamed. She should have done something about it before now. But not tonight. Not tonight of all nights. She was entitled to a little peace, a little space to gather her strength.

It was good to see the sun again, this primrose spring sun. She remembered that Cobb had said something about this: that one day she would feel the sun on her skin and discover that it still felt good. Something like that. She sipped her coffee. That was good too. She felt the tension go out of her shoulders. It would all come back again. Gudrun would not come back, but summer would.

She caught herself. It was growing cold. She heard the blackbird chirr away in the gathering darkness. Perhaps after tomorrow she might allow herself another peep through the keyhole. After tomorrow.

The motor started at a touch and purred like a sewing machine. Silver had known that it would but his sense of achievement was overwhelming just the same.

'Hey, that's neat.' Jit stuck her head out of the rear window. 'It goes.'

'Of course it goes,' Silver grunted. 'I fixed it so it would go.'

She made a face at him and went back to work. She had dragged all the rubbish, loose seats and fittings out of the bus. He was surprised at how practical she was and how resourceful, finding spanners and screwdrivers for herself, unbolting brackets. Now she started on the burst plastic seats, so that the garage was filled with the smell of pine cleaner.

'Pride's a sin, Joe,' Nugent said. The priest was watching him from the door. 'One of the seven deadlies.'

'So I'm a sinner.' He could not keep the satisfaction out of his voice.

'Not much doubt about that.'

Nugent continued: 'This was supposed to be occupational therapy. I never thought you'd actually get the bloody thing to work.'

'It's not finished yet,' Silver said. 'We need a couple of new tyres. And the battery's shot. But apart from that she's OK.'

Nugent nodded. Jit clambered out of the rear doors with a plastic bucket and walked away into the kitchen for fresh water. When she was gone, Nugent said: 'Take it down to Danny at Triple-A Motors in Bow Road. New battery and a couple of tyres. Just to make it legal, OK? Make sure you tell him it's for me. He'll put it on the slate. I'll sort out the registration later.'

'Right.'

'And then you'd better get ready to move out.'

'What?'

'Truck's fixed. You're fixed. And we need the room. You knew you'd have to face it one fine day.'

Silver stood silent for a time. Nugent was right: he had known that he would have to face this some day. 'When, Nugget?'

'No rush. Jit's got this gig coming up, hasn't she?'

'The Rum Jungle. That's next week.'

'I want you there for that.'

'She doesn't need me there.'

'She needs you there,' Nugent said. 'After that, I don't know, maybe the two of you can sort something out. You seem to get on.'

'Me and Jit?'

Nugent yawned, too tired to argue. 'Mate, I don't care what your deal is with her,' he said. 'You take help where you can find it in this world.' He yawned again and then said, 'You've done some good things here, Joe. For Jit. For yourself.'

Silver raised his eyebrows. 'But?'

'But debts don't get cancelled, Joe. I told you before. They have to be paid. Maybe it's time you thought about that.'

Silver edged the minibus out of the driveway and drove hesitantly the couple of miles to the garage in Bow Road. The trip took all his concentration. He had not been behind a wheel for months. At the garage the mechanic called Danny told him the work would take an hour. It was late-morning and Silver discovered that he was hungry. He crossed the road to a cheap café and ordered a bacon sandwich and a tea. They seemed normal things to order. The greasy smells of the café were normal too, and so were the other customers. Reassuringly normal.

Could he ever be part of it again? He could feel the bulge of the wallet in his back pocket. That was money, the few pounds Nugent gave him every week. Not big money, of course. But real money. Enough to pay for this sandwich. Enough to buy a couple of movie tickets, a few pints in a pub, a bus pass. And, if it kept coming in, why not enough eventually for a decent Gibson guitar, for a few books, a cheap stereo, some CDs? It wasn't much. It wouldn't ever be much. But it could be a life. A place of his own. And what after that? Was there a way to get a National Insurance number, a driving licence, a passport even? Could such things be fixed, if a man had a small income, a place to live, an identity? He had heard that they could.

He finished his food, paid and left the café, and stood for a moment outside in the road, hunched into his jacket while the cars hissed by. An identity? What kind of fool was he to be thinking this way?

He crossed the road to the garage. He took the keys back from the mechanic, climbed in, started up. It took him over an hour. He drove south and west, cutting across the motorway, out through the suburbs and the stockbroker belt, winding cross-country with the wipers sighing. He drove through the village, drab in the rain, and up the steep-sided lane beyond. He parked in a lay-by cut into the bank and left the van there, climbing the last two hundred yards on foot.

The churchyard was unkempt, overdue for its first mowing of the year, and the gravestones stood in banks of cow parsley and nettle. But hers was clear, a rectangle of dark earth with a simple grey marble marker above it. The letters of her name were sharply cut into the stone: Gudrun. Just her first name. He did not blame Lauren for that. He did not blame anyone for anything any more.

His knees gave way and his body crumpled on to the grassed mound beside her grave. He reached out and tore up a handful of yellow ragwort, an early spike of bluebells, and arranged them carefully on the raw wet earth beside him. The rain ran down the groove of his spine and along the ridges of his face, and fell on the flowers as he laid them down.

It was a high 1930s courtroom and the sun fell in dusty bars from the tall windows across the benches and chairs. For Cobb, now that he was here, a curious sense of unreality surrounded it all, as if he were watching it on a stage. These dramas were not supposed to be personal, and he experienced a fresh sense of shock each time he realised that characters in the cast or in the audience were people he knew. He had forgotten about Phil Latimer the police doctor, and about Sergeant Maxey from Accident Investigation; about McBean and Hayward. Even about Tommy Hudson. He supposed he must have known they would all be here, but on one level he still had not expected to see them. He had only expected to see Lauren.

Yet Cobb avoided looking at her. It disturbed him to see her. Her white skin against her black suit reminded him of the night she had come to his Baron's Court flat. He had thought her crazy then, beyond hope or help. He did not feel that way any more, though this had not been clear to him before now.

And then he was called, and his automatic professionalism took over and he answered the coroner's questions in full, just as if he had been talking about any little girl, any child's sister, any woman's daughter.

After that it went very quickly indeed. Lauren was called briefly and spoke in a low voice about Silver's state of mind when he left her, taking Gudrun away for the last time. There was some stirring of interest among the handful of journalists seated behind Cobb, but, if she heard it, she ignored it. When she had sat down again, others were called in rapid succession. The coroner hurried them through, muttered a few words of sympathy, and recorded Accidental Death. Then the inquest of Gudrun Silver, nine years old and never to see ten, was over.

Cobb waited until the court was empty, then packed his battered legal case and followed the last of the stragglers out through the swing doors. He did not want to meet Lauren face to face. It would be grotesque to make small talk about travel arrangements. For a moment he regretted extending the invitation. He knew he had pressured her. It would do her and Freya no harm to be away from London this weekend of all weekends. After all, that was why he had suggested it.

And then he did catch a glimpse of her, Hudson's broad back ushering her through the street doors, a swirl of black coat, a flash of the fitful sun on her hair. Yes, that was why he had suggested it. Surely.

Lauren let Tommy Hudson guide her out across the pavement to the waiting limousine. He pulled open the door for her and she ducked in, but before he could climb in after her she closed it in his face. Hudson hesitated outside the car and then slid into the front passenger seat. Lauren heard him grunt a command at the driver and the car shot away from the kerb and forced its way into the traffic with a blare of its horn.

Hudson slid back the glass partition. 'All right there, Lozz?'

'Don't call me that,' she told him. Lozz? When had he started doing that? 'And tell him not to drive like a maniac.'

Hudson gave her a knowing, long-suffering look but he signalled to the driver and she felt the pressure of the car's acceleration ease slightly. He said: 'I want to get you home as quick as poss, darlin'. That's all.'

She closed her eyes and massaged the bridge of her nose. This was ridiculous. The very sound of his voice was beginning to grate on her. 'Just leave me be for a while, Tommy. Please.'

He twisted his mouth in disapproval but slid the partition closed and faced the front. With his broad face turned away Lauren felt an instant release. She realised all at once that they were following the southern bank of the river, and that here—just here—was Lambeth Bridge, off to her right, with the broad stretch of water sparkling beneath it.

She said: 'Stop the car.'

Hudson twisted urgently in his seat. 'We can't stop here, Lozz. It's—'

'Stop the fucking car right *now*!' Lauren smacked the glass partition hard with the flat of her hand, again and again, until the driver pulled over. A storm of protest—car horns, shouted insults and a short squeal of brakes. She pushed open the door and slid out and ran across the road through the gridlocked traffic.

She slowed to a walk and crossed to the eastern pavement. Trailing her hand along the smooth iron railings, she walked towards the midpoint of the bridge. Just short of halfway she stopped. Here. It had been here. She placed her palms on the parapet and went up on tiptoe to see the sliding water below. This place. These railings. That water. She tried to feel horror. And yet it was such a very fine day. The river sparkled at her. It came to her that no one was going to declare Lambeth Bridge a national monument because Gudrun had died there. People would walk and drive across it just the way they always had. Just as if Matthew Silver had not driven through it one insane night in December.

She felt for her wallet and opened it and slid out the photograph. It had never worked, trying to get the two of them in the same shot. Gudrun so thoroughly eclipsed her sister. Yet this was the picture she had carried. She gazed at it for a while. Then she folded it and tore it gently across. She lifted the torn square of paper and kissed it and then let it flutter from her hand, a fleck of confetti flickering down towards the river until the wind caught it and sucked it away under the bridge and out of her sight. When it had vanished she looked down at the other half of the photograph. 'Hello, Freya,' she said.

His heavy steps clattered towards her. 'Christ, Lozz! You gimme such a fright. Come back now, darlin'. Come back.'

She let him lead her back to the car. She climbed in and they drew smoothly away. She turned in her seat, but though she craned to see, the scene withdrew from her and quickly it was left behind.

She must have slept then, for she was next aware of the car swinging down the gravel drive and they were back at the house. She climbed the stairs to her room and shut the door behind her, aware somehow that Tommy Hudson was standing at the foot of the staircase, watching her, troubled by her strange new assertiveness.

She stripped and ran the shower and got in and let it hose over her, as hot as she could stand it. Tommy *would* be troubled, she thought. Despite what she planned to do, she found it impossible not to feel sorry for the big man. She stepped out of the shower and towelled herself dry and dressed slowly in jeans and sweater. When she could put it off no longer, she walked out of her room and down the stairs. He was in his familiar seat by the antique writing desk. The half-moon glasses made him look studious and even gentle. For a moment she thought her spirit might quail, and she spoke quickly, before it could do so.

'Tommy, I want you to move out.'

He did not seem to hear. 'How's that?'

'You've been a real friend in need, Tommy. I want you to understand that. But I think you've done your duty by Matthew and me.'

'What are you on about?' He laid his glasses on top of the papers and without them she saw what she already knew, that he was neither studious nor gentle.

'I mean it, Tommy. Of course there's no rush at all, it's just—'

He smiled. 'Don't fool yourself, Lozz. You couldn't cope without me.'

'Please don't call me that,' she said, and all at once she was angry. 'Just don't call me that, all right?'

'Hey, hey.' Hudson spread his broad hands, smiling, conciliatory.

'For God's sake, Tommy! Will you stop smirking at me and listen?'

'All right.' He stopped smiling. 'All right, Laurie. But there's no need for this. We all know it's been a shit of a day for you. For me too.'

'I understand that, Tommy. I know you loved Goodie too.'

'Not just Goodie,' he said.

'Oh, Christ, Tommy, don't make this any harder than it has to be.'

'It doesn't have to be hard at all. You just give yourself a couple of days to settle down, and we'll be back to normal. Right as ninepence.'

'I'm sorry, Tommy. I want you to leave. I appreciate everything you've done, but I can stand on my own feet now.'

He looked at her for so long that it made her uneasy. Finally he said: 'Are you fucking that copper?'

For a second she could not believe that these words had been spoken. She screwed up her eyes and stared at him in utter outrage. 'What?' she demanded. '*What* did you say to me?'

He put his head on one side, pursed his lips. 'Just a thought,' he said.

'Tommy, you pack your bags and get out of here right now. I mean it.'

'Think you'll be able to manage this big old place without me, Laurie?'

'I'm going to sell it,' she said. 'I'm going to put this whole business behind me. Behind us. Behind me and Freya.'

'How are you planning to do that?' His calm was unsettling. 'I mean, it's not like you own the place.'

Lauren stopped. Through her shock it came to her that this was a thing unacknowledged, a thing dreaded, and yet a thing not entirely undreamed of. He rose and went to the bar and poured himself a Scotch. He dropped the ice cubes in one by one, punctuating his words.

'I took over the payments on this place weeks ago, Laurie.' Clunk. 'And the kid's schooling.' Clunk. 'And every other bill that came in.' Clunk. 'You should be bloody grateful.'

She fought hard to concentrate. 'This is ridiculous. They'll release Matthew's money to me in the end. I'm his wife. His widow.'

'Understand this, Lozz. You can't get hold of Mattie's money until he's officially dead. Without a body, that takes for bloody ever.' He took a sip of his drink. 'Oh, you can try if you like. You might even work it out. After a few months of arguing. You up to that?'

'There are people—'

'No, Laurie, there aren't *people*!' he shouted. Then, hearing himself, he lowered his voice. 'There isn't anyone, Laurie. There's just me. Mattie didn't know nothing about money. And he didn't know nothing about friends.' He tossed back his Scotch. 'There was only me.'

She felt her spirit return. 'That doesn't make me your responsibility.'

'Oh, yes,' he said with quiet certainty. 'Yes, it does.'

'I'll find somewhere to live. I'll get a lawyer.'

He put his empty glass down and walked across the room to her. There was something stricken in his face. He reached out and took her shoulders in his hands. 'Laurie, I been straight. All those times I come here when Mattie was away, and fixed things for you and the kids, and done things Mattie forgot to do. But he's gone now.'

'Take your hands off me, Tommy,' she told him.

His eyes faltered but he stayed where he was. 'Laurie, you don't understand. I'd do anything for you. Anything.'

'Then let me go.'

His breath was in her face and she rolled her head away from him. The connecting door banged open.

'Everything is all right, Mrs Silver?' Merilda called to her.

'Fuck off,' Hudson told the woman without turning.

'I speak Mrs Silver,' Merilda replied haughtily. 'I don't speak you.'

Lauren took the opportunity the woman gave her and ducked under Hudson's arm and walked away from him. She could feel herself trembling but it gave her strength to see Merilda's plump defiant face lifted in her defence. 'It's OK, Merilda,' she said. 'I'll call if I need you.'

Merilda waited for a moment longer, then tossed her head disdainfully at Hudson and turned away and stumped off through the house.

'Tommy, we have to work this out. We have to be sensible about this. I'm not going to live here as your house guest. Or whatever you expected.' She looked at him. 'You couldn't have thought that.'

'In the end you'll do what you have to do to get by, like the rest of us.'

'What does that mean?'

'You were just Matt Silver's wife, Laurie, when all's said and done. You'd've been nothing without him. What gives you the right to be so damn choosy?'

She stared at him. 'I'm not staying here to listen to this.' She ran up the stairs to her room and threw clothes in a bag and came back downstairs and walked across the room to the front door. Her hand was on the latch before he turned.

'Where d'you think you're going, Laurie?' His voice sounded weary. 'Don't be bloody stupid.'

She looked at him for a moment but could see nothing in the bovine face that gave her hope. 'I've just got to get away, Tommy,' she said.

His eyes hardened. 'No one'll take care of you like I will, Laurie.'

'I don't need anyone to take care of me, Tommy. Not any more.'

'You'll be back,' he said.

She tugged open the front door and ran across the gravel to her car.

She drove blindly at first, simply following roads that looked familiar. For the moment it was enough to be in the safe cocoon of her car, away from him. It wasn't until she reached Guildford that she realised where her unconscious mind had been taking her.

It was almost dark by the time she got there. Lauren pulled up beside the churchyard wall and climbed out. She walked around the church to the grave. She was not sure what she had expected: some mystical infusion of courage, some sense of bold new direction. She did not get it. Something was wrong. Not wrong, out of place. The flowers she and Freya had brought on their last visit lay wilting on the wet soil. But they had been moved. Just a few inches, but moved aside. And beside them a ragged bunch of wildflowers had been laid. The blooms glowed in the failing light, yellow and blue. A well-wisher, maybe? She leaned forward and touched them with her fingertips. The flowers were fresh, perhaps a day old, even less. A few drops of rain struck her face and arms and she felt all at once cold, miserable and alone.

She walked back to the car and sat behind the wheel. She realised she had no idea what to do next. She saw Hudson's heavy face in her mind. His expression was weary, tired of her play-acting. 'You'll be back,' he had said, as though she were a teenager threatening to leave home after a tantrum.

The lights of the Cross Keys pub sprang on beyond the far wall of the churchyard. She drove up the lane and parked outside the pub, locked the car and went in. She was the first customer. She crossed the empty room and leaned on the bar. The landlord was setting out fresh coasters and ashtrays and at first did not notice her.

'I'm sorry, madam. Didn't see you there.'

'It's OK. No hurry.' That was true enough, she reflected. She had nowhere to hurry to. A sudden surge of panic swept over her, and she thought: To hell with it, and ordered a vodka. If she couldn't have one tonight, when could she?

She took the drink to a table in one of the window bays and sat on the padded window seat. She began to relax. It was comforting to watch the landlord busying himself around the room. The vodka warmed her and she went back to the bar and ordered another. She was halfway through the second drink when the landlord opened the back door and let an old boxer dog into the room. With a rush of yearning she thought of the farm and of the old dog there and of the fire, and of Cobb and Fred. A sane and tranquil place where she and Freya were treated with respect, with gentleness. Treated even with affection.

She stared for a long time into her drink. If she left now, she could be there in—what?—an hour and a half. Uneasily, she rolled her glass between her palms. It wasn't as simple as that. At the start, she had needed to beg for permission to go there. She had promised not to go there uninvited, and even now she felt that to do so would somehow be against the rules. She tipped back the last of her vodka. She desperately wanted another. She thought of her controlled drinking group, the circle of friendly, sincere faces every Thursday night. Two drinks a day was supposed to be her limit. It would be her first lapse. But then, they'd forgive her. It wasn't every day you went to your daughter's inquest—and walked out of your home with nowhere else to go to. But of course she'd be over the legal limit too if she drank any more, and that might matter if she had to drive all the way to Oxford on a night like this. To go or not to go? Lauren remembered suddenly the last time she had had this argument with herself. It was not action which had been fatal then, but lack of it. She stood up quickly.

'Same again, madam?' called the landlord cheerfully. By the time she had registered his question, he had taken her silence for assent and was already pouring another double. Well, she thought, she didn't have to drink it. Just pay, avoid any tension, thank the man and go. She walked to the bar, found some crumpled notes in her bag.

'Staying in the village?' the man said, taking the money.

'I don't think so.'

'Oh, I thought you'd probably come down for the wedding.' He brought her the change. 'The Ashtons? Big local family.'

'I'm just passing through.' It was impossible to move away from his affability, from the warmth of the bar. She found she had started on the fresh drink. She could not decide why she still lingered here. She was expected tomorrow morning anyway. They couldn't possibly take it amiss if she turned up twelve hours early. Could they?

'And have you got far to go, then, madam?'

'Oxford,' she said with sudden decision. 'Near Oxford.'

'Oh,' he said, a little taken aback. He sucked his lower lip, avoided looking at her empty glass. 'Well, take care, won't you.'

'Too late for that,' Lauren said.

Cobb had been working in the barn for a little under an hour and was close to finishing. It was cold, and he was beginning to get tired and hungry, but despite that his sense of contentment grew steadily. He put down his paintbrush, stretched and walked to the barn door.

He saw a car's lights flicker through the trees on the road above the farm. The car slowed and turned through the gate, then came bouncing down the track towards him. He frowned: he did not recognise it at first and he did not feel like visitors. He noticed that one of the headlights was badly askew. He glanced at his watch. It was late, whoever it was.

As he came out into the yard she was climbing out of the car, pulling her bag from the back seat. As he stepped forward, she reached the farmhouse's front door. Lights sprang on in the house and the door was opened to her. He heard Fred's cry of welcome and her low reply, and then she was ushered into the house.

He crossed the cobbled yard, pausing to look at the car. The offside wing was badly scraped and the headlight assembly hung loose. By the time he got to the kitchen Fred was already setting the kettle on the stove. He was fussing over Lauren, plainly delighted by her arrival. She was seated at the kitchen table, pale and tired and a little crumpled.

Fred gestured with the teapot. 'Samuel, my boy. I was just coming to call you. What are you doing out there, anyway?'

'I'm sorry to barge in like this, Sam,' Lauren said, cutting across the old man. 'So late. So early, I suppose.'

'What happened to the car?' he said, his concern making him brusque.

'Nothing much. I had a bit of an argument with a crash barrier on the M40, that's all.'

'Are you all right?'

'Yes, I'm *all right*, Sam,' she said. 'Don't make a fuss.'

'Get Lauren a drink, Samuel, would you?' Fred asked.

'A drink?'

'That's what I said, Samuel. I have a feeling she needs one.'

Cobb hesitated and then did as he was told. When he set the gin down in front of her he could smell the alcohol on her breath. 'What's happened, Lauren?'

'Happened?' She shrugged with theatrical unconcern. 'Nothing's happened. I bent the car a little, that's all.'

'Perhaps this can wait, Samuel?' Fred said quickly.

'Were you drinking before you drove here?'

'For God's sake, Sam.' She set her glass down hard. 'Don't be such a fucking policeman. Do you want to see my tax disc too?'

'Why didn't you call me, Lauren?'

'Maybe because I thought I'd get a reaction like this.' The room fell silent. She stood up suddenly. 'I knew this was a dumb move.'

'Lauren, you know I'd have picked you up.'

'I don't need "picking up", Sam. I don't need to be in by midnight. I don't need nursemaiding. Jesus! Why don't the lot of you just leave it alone?' She grabbed the bottle of gin by the neck and turned her back on Cobb and faced Fred. 'Excuse me, Fred. I'm going to bed.'

'And you need that?' Cobb nodded at the bottle.

'Yes. I need this. And you're not making me need it any less.'

Fred stepped between them. 'My dear, I'm sure we can—'

'I'm sorry. I knew I shouldn't have come.' She stuffed the bottle under her arm and with her free hand gathered up her bag and walked to the corridor that led to the garden room. 'I'd drive away again, except that Inspector Morse here would probably confiscate my keys.' She marched down to the bedroom and banged the door behind her.

Cobb stared after her. 'I would have, too,' he said, half to himself.

'You know, Samuel,' Fred set the unused teapot back on its stand and regarded the beams of the ceiling. 'There are times when I'm quite glad you didn't follow me into the Diplomatic Service.'

Lauren stood at the kitchen window and cradled her coffee cup in both hands. Her head felt dull and the smell of Fred's fried breakfast made her slightly nauseous. She had stayed in her room until she heard the old man go out to start his rounds about the farm. Cobb had left much earlier, presumably to climb to his eyrie up at the old village. She was safe from both of them for the moment.

She drank some coffee and waited for it to make her feel better. As she waited she saw a movement in the gorse on the flank of the distant hill. It was the old dog wallowing through the yellow brush, his brown back breaking the rough carpet of colour. And there was his master, a hundred yards further up, striding down the slope, a dark, square figure moving easily over the steep ground. As he drew closer and swung over the last stile into the farmyard she could see his face. It was as stern as his bearing. More than stern, the downturned face was grim. Well, she felt pretty grim herself. But at the same time she was as nervous as an adolescent about facing him. She didn't want to fight with him again.

She turned away from the window so that he would not see her as he came nearer. In turning, she saw that she had left the gin bottle standing in full view on the kitchen table when she had brought it out of the bedroom. She rammed the bottle into the cabinet with the others, and had actually closed the doors on it before she turned back and pulled it out again. The spirit tasted vile and for a second she almost choked on it. But it gave her a spike of energy. She replaced the bottle steadily, closed the cabinet and walked back to the window.

Perhaps, if he had walked in at that moment. But instead he stepped out of sight into the barn without even glancing at the window where she stood. Lauren stepped back from the window. She could not seem to find her earlier defiance. Instead, anxiety began to grow in her again. This was all on the point of going horribly wrong, just at the moment she most needed it not to. It came to her that when Freya arrived she would have to tell her that they had nowhere to go after tomorrow. Or worse still, she would be forced to do just as Tommy Hudson had predicted she would do. Because no one would look after her like he would. She felt her stomach clench. She poured her coffee down the sink and went back to the cabinet.

Cobb worked on in the barn, glad to be occupied. A little delicate sun was breaking through over the fields.

'Thought we might all go and pick the little one up,' Fred called from the door. Cobb could see he was excited. 'It's a little early, I know.'

'I'll leave you to it, Dad,' Cobb said. 'You and Lauren. I want to finish up in here. Get everything ready.'

'Oh.' Fred hesitated. 'Not being just a little . . . prickly, are you?'

'I just thought I'd keep a low profile for a while.'

'Well, you know best,' Fred said. 'Not that you ever did before.'

An hour later Cobb heard the Land Rover pull up outside and the banging of the car's doors and the child's excited voice and the dog's asthmatic bark of greeting. When he had heard them all go into the house he followed them across the yard.

The moment he opened the kitchen door his eyes met Lauren's and he knew how it would end. She sat at the head of the table, somehow apart from the old man and from her daughter. There was about her the jaggedness Cobb remembered from the first time he had seen her. Her skin had the same unnatural pallor he had seen then, and her hair was roughly bundled up into a faded blue scarf. He saw she already had a fresh drink in front of her. Her eyes disturbed him most. They seemed to carry both accusation and defiance.

'Hello, Sam!' Freya cried and ran across to him and hugged him. He ruffled her hair.

'Hi there, Princess. Back from the wilds of Welsh Wales?'

'You'll never guess what I did!' she shouted at him.

'I think you're going to tell me.'

'I played rounders. *And* I played hockey. *And* I played soccer. *And*—' the child shouted, slapping at her mother's arm for attention.

'Frey,' Lauren smiled tightly, 'easy on the decibels.'

'—but the best bit—*listen*, Sam!'

Cobb had been watching Lauren again, noting her struggle for control. He said: 'I am listening, Princess. What's the best bit?'

'Wait!' Freya commanded and ran out of the room.

'Well, she seems to have had a wonderful time,' Fred boomed, trying to fill the widening gulf with his cheerfulness. 'Splendid! Splendid!'

Cobb sat back and crossed his arms, then realised that this betrayed the gathering darkness of his mood, and uncrossed them again. She might at least have stayed sober long enough to greet her own daughter. He felt desperately let down by her on Freya's account and on his own. Obviously nothing was going to change. He supposed he should not blame her. And yet it was so very hard not to.

Freya returned with a packet of instant-print photos and a rolled certificate tied with red ribbon. She pulled the ribbon loose and let the cartridge paper spring open. She spread it reverently on the table. As she worked at this she passed the photos to Cobb. 'You can look at those.'

They were prints of children, boys and girls of about Freya's age, paddling open canoes on a peaceful river fringed by willows.

'There!' Freya said.

She had weighted the certificate down with cutlery. Cobb leaned across her and he read aloud: 'Freya Silver. Admiral of the Blue. Wow! Sounds great, Princess.'

'Admiral,' Lauren repeated slowly. She was standing behind her daughter now, frowning over the child's shoulder at the certificate. Cobb saw her face cloud as if she were having trouble coming to terms with this news. 'Did they really make you Admiral this year, Frey? You?'

'It says so there, doesn't it?' Freya rapped the cartridge paper indignantly. 'Admiral of the Blue. See?' She turned to Cobb, her face shining with triumph. 'And *I've* never even been in a canoe before!'

And then, as if a switch had been thrown, she laid her head on her arms on her outspread diploma and burst into tears.

The room froze. Cobb instinctively looked to Lauren to act and their eyes met: perhaps a moment later she would have moved, but he did not see this. He saw her standing rigid, her eyes hot and defensive, glaring at him while her daughter wept between them. Cobb moved forward, but Fred was quicker and swept the child up into his arms.

'Push them a little too hard at these camps, I think,' the old man said gruffly, rocking Freya against him. 'Little over-tired. Only a tot, after all.' He hefted the girl against his shoulder and carried her across the room and out into the farmyard.

Cobb closed the door behind them and watched them go for a few paces. Then he turned back into the room and crossed to the table and rolled up Freya's certificate and retied the ribbon. He did not look directly at Lauren but he saw that she had not moved.

'Don't you try to lay this on me, Sam Cobb!' she cried suddenly.

He stood up to face her. He tried to look bewildered but he could not bring conviction to this attempt, for he did blame her, and he knew that this showed in his face. He said, as evenly as he could manage: 'I thought maybe all this was behind us. Behind you.'

She dragged out a chair and banged it down on the flagstones. 'Christ! You think you're so smart.' She pointed out into the yard, to Fred and her daughter. 'You think that was my fault?'

'Lauren—'

'Well, let me tell you what that was about! Gudrun was Admiral of the Blue for the last three years. *Gudrun* was. It was Gudrun's job. Freya always watched from the bank.'

He sat down and looked at her. 'I see.'

'You see,' she sneered.'You've got all the answers, haven't you?'

'Lauren, look at yourself. You don't want to be like this.'

'Will you get off my case? I am not your responsibility.'

'In this house you are.'

'Is that the price of coming here?'

'You know there isn't a price.'

'Oh, yes, there's always a price. You have to control everything. That's the price.'

He took a deep breath. 'I care about you, Lauren. I don't want to see you do this.'

The confession cost him something and, once spoken, he expected it to defuse the tension a little. Instead it seemed to infuriate her.

'Go on!' she spat at him, thrusting her face towards him. 'Now offer to take care of me, why don't you? That's all I need.' The venom in her voice shocked both of them into silence. 'You know this whole thing isn't about me anyway. It's about Freya. She's all that matters.'

'We all matter, Lauren. Whether you like it or not. Freya and you and me, and my old man. Everyone connected with us.'

She pushed her hair wearily out of her face but didn't answer.

'I didn't want you around here in the first place,' he went on. 'I didn't want anything to do with you and this whole tragic mess. But now you're here I can't ignore you.'

'Why not?' she said. 'I can ignore you.' But the brutality was a reflex. She was spent. She pulled out her chair and slumped into it.

'Because we're real people, Lauren, that's why. When it comes down to it we have to look out for each other. That's what real people do.' He got up, walked around the kitchen in a circle. Finally he came back to the table. He said: 'This can't go on, Lauren. We both know that. I'm not going to sit back and watch this happen and do nothing about it.'

'I don't want your help,' she said. 'I didn't ask for it.'

'Yes, you did, Lauren.'

'My Christ, you're a self-righteous bastard.' She stood up clumsily, pushing the table back. 'Why can't you just leave me alone?'

Freya opened the back door and stood in the doorway, staring at them. After a second the bewilderment in her face hardened. 'You were shouting so loudly,' she said, 'I thought Daddy had come back.'

'Me too,' Lauren said bitterly. She pushed both hands through her hair, and the fight went out of her. Cobb thought he had never seen her look so defeated. Almost sadly, she said: 'Freya, we'd better go.'

'Go?' the child repeated, puzzled. 'Go where?'

'You don't have to go,' Cobb said. 'That's not necessary.'

'Oh, don't worry, Sam,' Lauren said with bleak sarcasm, 'I'm not planning on driving anywhere.'

Fred stepped into the room past the child. 'Lauren, there's no need. Everyone's upset this weekend. That's natural. Now we'll have a bite of lunch and cool off a little—'

'It's best we go, Fred. Truly. It's not your fault.'

'But we can't go now,' Freya cried, with an edge of desperation. 'My surprise is in the barn. Uncle Fred told me.'

'That's right,' Fred pounced on this. 'I almost forgot. Samuel—you'd better take Freya over there and show her what it is, hadn't you?' When Cobb didn't move, Fred repeated very loudly: 'Hadn't you, Samuel?'

Fred waved the girl out into the yard, then he grabbed Cobb's arm and pushed him through the door. As he did so Fred hissed in his ear. 'You'd better think of something. And pretty damned quickly.'

Then Cobb was moving mechanically across the yard and Freya was pleading with him, catching at his hand.

'What's happening, Sam? Why do we have to go?'

The sight of the child's distress forced Cobb to get a grip on himself. 'I can't answer you, Princess. Your mum's very upset at the moment. I suppose we all are.'

'Have I done something wrong?'

'No,' he said fiercely. He stopped and looked down at her, and said again: 'No. You're about the one person who hasn't.'

'I don't want to go back there, Sam,' she said. 'Back to our house. And I don't care what Mummy says, she doesn't want to go either.'

He looked at her. 'I'm afraid she's going anyway, Princess.'

She stared at the ground, and kicked the dirt with the toe of her shoe. He knelt down to face her. 'Freya, you're not going anywhere just yet. Not until you've had your surprise, anyway.'

He stood up and pushed open the door to the barn and ushered her in. It was gloomy inside and he snapped on the light.

'What's in here?' Freya asked, peering around at the closed stalls. He swung the stable door open. A five foot dinosaur in shocking pink sat grinning from a nest of straw, with six pink beachball eggs at its feet. 'I told you they come here in the spring.'

'It's my dinosaur!' Freya's voice was awed. 'Can I touch her?'

'She's yours, Princess.'

'Is she? Is she really?' Freya ran into the stall and put her arms around the fat pink beast. It was bigger than she was, but she could just lift it off the ground with one arm hooked under its tail. She hugged the grinning creature. 'She's beautiful! I love her!'

'Sam.'

Cobb spun on his heel. Lauren was leaning against the doorpost. 'Sam,' she said again, and her voice was lost and desolate.

Freya caught sight of her mother and opened her mouth to speak, then thought better of it. The child stood cuddling her huge pink dinosaur as she looked in silence from Cobb to Lauren and back again. She said carefully: 'Can I take my dinosaur to show Uncle Fred?'

'Go on, then, Princess,' Cobb said, without taking his eyes from Lauren's. 'Don't run.'

She staggered out into the yard, almost smothered by the stuffed animal. Lauren was staring at the pink eggs in the straw. She had untied her hair and the blue scarf hung from one hand. Without it her hair was a blonde tangle.

'You stupid bastard,' she said, without turning.

'Hell of a job to paint the eggs,' he said, suddenly awkward with her.

She still did not turn to face him. 'You stupid, crazy bastard.'

There was a catch in her voice. She began to laugh, softly at first and then louder, her head thrown back. For a moment he was glad she was laughing. And then she wasn't laughing any more but sobbing with huge tearing sobs that shook her and shook the door she clung to.

'Lauren. Don't.'

He moved forward and touched her shoulder and she turned to face him, her face crumpled and wet, the sobs heaving helplessly out of her. He took the scarf from her hand and wiped her face with it as if she were a child, murmuring to her, knowing he was lost. Then the length of her body was against the length of his, hip and thigh and breast, and her arms were clutched convulsively around his neck, and his face was in her tangled hair.

Cobb felt her stir beside him and was awake at once. She was propped on one elbow and in the chrome light of the afternoon she was studying herself in the dressing table mirror.

She caught his eye in the glass and her reflection made a rueful face at him. 'Jesus. Look at the state of me.' She ran her fingers down her thin bare ribs and around the ridges of her eyesockets. 'I used to be a bit beautiful, I think,' she said. 'At least, everybody said so.' She turned to him. 'What are we going to do, Sam? What's going to happen to us?'

'One day at a time.' He brushed the backs of his fingers along the curve of her throat.

'Sam, you know I can't go back.'

'Who can?' He touched each of her fingers in turn, flexing them under his thumb, examining them minutely.

'No, I meant . . .' She took a deep breath. 'We'll have to stay here for a while, Sam. At the farm. Freya and me.'

He looked at her. 'That's a problem?'

She laughed a little and put her arm around his neck. 'I thought it was.' She kissed him. 'I thought it was a big problem.'

'Well, there you go.' He slid his arm under her head so that she lay back against his shoulder. She rolled her head a little against his arm. She said: 'That's good. You can do that.'

He felt her open beside him and he moved into her as naturally and gently as breathing. Her fingers followed the curve of his waist and he felt his own flank shiver like a horse's flank. Then he was away somewhere in a world where the only sound was the tap-tapping of a thrush against an anvil outside, again and again, and then she breathed out one long breath and he lifted the weight of her head against his shoulder and rocked her there for a long while.

She moved beside him. 'You know that if you tell me he's gone, I'll trust you,' she said suddenly.

He turned his head to look at her and her eyes were dark with intensity.

'You don't have to find him, Sam. You don't have to prove anything. Just tell me he's gone.'

'He's gone, Lauren,' Cobb said. 'He's gone and he won't ever come back.'

She watched his face as he said it, and finally nodded. 'That's good,' she said. 'That's very good.' She reached up her arms to him and kissed him. Then she rose and crossed to the dressing table and sat down and began to comb her hair. After two or three strokes she stopped, examining herself again in the mirror. 'Maybe I could be beautiful again,' she said.

Cobb stood behind her and rested his hands on the yoke of her collarbone. He said: 'Time to make this official.'

He kissed the top of her head and moved away. He dressed and left the bedroom, walking down the short passage into the kitchen. The room was filled with the hot savour of roasting meat and with a torrent of Elgar at his grandest. Fred, his back to Cobb as he worked at the Aga stove, was conducting the music with a carving fork. In the living room Cobb could see Freya perched on the sofa, fussing over her huge pink dinosaur. He walked through and pulled up a chair opposite the girl.

'We plan on staying here for a while, Princess,' he told her. 'How do you feel about that?'

'You mean here at the farm?'

'For sure. Right here.'

She lifted her chin warily. 'Together?'

'Yes, Princess. Together.'

'And what about school?'

'We could stay at my flat during the week. It'll be a squeeze, but we'll work something out. Come down here on weekends.'

She thought about this. 'Squeeze is good,' she said finally.

Cobb heard Lauren move up beside him and he glanced around, and in that moment Freya flung her arms round his neck, clutching him, and he heard her hot voice hissing in his ear: 'Yes. Yes. Yes.'

Later, after the meal, Cobb watched as his father repaired the battlefield of the kitchen. He knew he would not be allowed to help and he was glad. It was late, and he felt heavy and comfortable. Lauren had already gone to bed but Cobb did not want to move yet.

Fred emptied the sink and finally dried his hands. Then he set the Laphroaig bottle on the table in front of Cobb. With a flourish he produced two shot glasses from his apron pocket. 'I think we should,' he said.

Cobb smiled. 'Mad if we don't.' He filled the glasses with the spirit.

The old man lifted his drink and peered at the amber light which shone through it. 'I know I told you to think of something, Samuel.' The old man's moustache twitched as he fought back a smile. 'But you are such a very literal chap, aren't you?'

They clinked glasses.

'Sam?' The girl was standing in the doorway.

'Hey, Princess.' Cobb quickly set down his glass and crossed the room to her. 'What are you doing up?'

'Scarecrow Man.' She knuckled her eyes.

The words pricked him strangely. 'Who?' He shook himself, bent down and scooped her up. 'You want to tell me all about it?' He carried her through and sat her next to the pink dinosaur on the settee.

'It's a dream,' she said, her mouth turned down. 'It's dumb.'

'Dreams aren't dumb, Princess,' he said. 'But they aren't real either. You don't need to be scared of them.'

'Scarecrow Man's real,' she said. 'I've seen him.'

'Oh?' he said. 'And where have you seen this shady character?'

'At school. Over the road in the park. All the girls have seen him.'

'And what's he like, this Scarecrow Man?'

'He's like a scarecrow, silly. He's thin and funny-looking and he wears this long horrible old coat and his face is all . . .' She twisted her face into a pantomime grimace and thrust it at him. The effect was so grotesque that Cobb only just stopped himself from flinching.

'And you've seen him?'

'Well,' she looked down, 'not really. I sort of caught a glimpse of him once. The other girls told me the rest. But he was there.'

'Sure he was, Princess.'

Cobb heard the door open and Lauren moved into the room.

'What are you up to, young lady? Frightening the poor man with your stories? Come on. It's time we were all in bed.' She took the child's hand and led her away. But at the door Freya turned back to Cobb.

'He won't come here, will he, Sam? Scarecrow Man?'

'No, Princess. I promise you he won't come here.'

For a while after they got to bed the incident troubled him. He lay watching the starlight fall over the midnight fields, trying to remember what it had been like to be a child and to be afraid of nameless horrors.

He said: 'What's this Scarecrow Man stuff?'

'Oh, that.' She rolled to face him. 'It's something the girls at school go on about. I think they've got a bit of a thing about some drunk in the park over the road. Someone christened him Scarecrow Man. It doesn't mean anything.' She nestled against him.

'Has it been going on long?'

'I don't know. A month or two.'

'And it's getting to her?'

'A bit. She's had a few bad nights. You've got to remember what she's been through, Sam. She's not the ice maiden she makes out.'

'I know that. But—'

'Look, don't worry. Frankly, I'm glad they're scared of dirty old men, aren't you?'

'Does the school know about it?'

'Of course the school knows about it. And the Parents Teachers Association. And the local police.'

'Good. That's good. I'll check with them when I get back.'

'You're such a Mr Plod, Sam,' she said, touched and amused by his concern. 'It's just some harmless old drunk. And the girls aren't allowed outside the gate alone. Not ever.' She kissed him. 'It'll be at least ninety per cent make-believe, trust me. You know how kids are.'

'No, I don't.'

'Well,' she sighed, moving the length of her body against him, 'I guess you're finding out.'

Cobb came awake slowly. The windows were slate grey with the dawn. It was raining softly outside: he could hear the water running in the gutters. Lauren was curled away from him in the bed, breathing deeply. He checked his watch. It was not yet six but he found himself seized with a restless energy which would not let him sleep. He rolled silently out of bed, threw on a bathrobe and left the room.

He padded through into the kitchen with his clothes bundled under one arm, and stopped there, the ancient flagstones stinging his feet. He felt the silent weight of the sleeping house around him. In the yard, just beyond the back door, the gargoyle at the end of the stone gutter was spouting rainwater onto the cobbles.

He waited for a moment, then slid the bolts on the back door and swung it wide and let the robe fall away from him. He moved out onto the cobbles and, without pausing, stepped under the spouting water. His breath shuddered and he clapped his arms around himself.

'Is this part of the deal?' she said from behind him. 'Cold showers at dawn? I'll have to rethink the whole thing.'

He stepped out of the water and faced her, smiling and unembarrassed. She was standing inside the door, swathed in a towel, hugging herself against the chill. He said: 'I thought you were asleep.'

'Not any more.' She paused. 'Were you going to stand there all day?'

'I've got to walk,' he said. He stepped back inside, towelling himself with the robe. 'Do you want to come along?'

'I'll grab some clothes.'

'Perhaps we both should.'

They walked in silence for half a mile up the sunken lane which ran from near the farm gate. Not fifty feet ahead a russet fox loped across the lane, stopped insolently halfway across to stare at them. Baskerville, shambling through the nettles under the hedgerow, did not notice. They climbed the bank and crossed a stile into the upper pasture and followed the path diagonally across it. At the point where the muddy track reached the upper fence stood a wooden bench, commanding a view over the farm to the dark ribbon of trees bordering the river. The rain had stopped and they sat quietly for a while.

'Well, that's torn it,' Lauren said suddenly, and started to laugh.

'What has?' He wanted to hear her say it.

'Us.' She waved her arm. 'We've torn it. Haven't we?'

'A bit,' he agreed. 'I suppose we have.'

She looked at him, still laughing. 'How did I ever get into this?'

'Just lucky, I guess.'

'You know yesterday won't happen again, Sam. The drinking. Not like that. You know it won't, don't you?'

'I know.'

'But let's not fool ourselves. This isn't all going to come right just like that. No matter how good it feels now.'

'And?'

'I need to sort some things out,' she said. 'Tommy will take it hard. I've not handled that well.'

'I'll go and see him.'

'No,' she said. 'It's not your problem. I'm going to see Tommy today, Sam. You can drop me at Oxford and I'll get the train.'

'You've got this all worked out, haven't you?'

'Yes.'

'You know, you don't have to put yourself through this, Lauren.'

'Yes, I do. Listen to me, Sam. I'm not made of porcelain. I won't break. Not any more I won't.'

'If this is what you want, Lauren.'

'It's what I want. I'll meet you later at the flat if you like. We'll spend the night in town. Frey's not back at school till Tuesday. She can stay here till Monday.' Then she laughed. 'Give up, Sam. Whenever you try to look serious, I see you standing under that waterspout. I think I always will.'

Cobb dropped her at Oxford station just after midday. She kissed him quickly and left without a word and then trotted away up the steps, her bag bouncing jauntily against her hip.

He drove on slowly, savouring his mood. He was taut, nervous and exultant all at once. Like an adolescent, he reflected, an adolescent at forty-six. The thought of that made him smile as he drove.

He stopped at a village somewhere near Watlington. It was a place with a stone bridge and a black-beamed pub which looked out across a patch of green. He bought a pint and took it outside and sat at a wooden table, sipping his beer in the sun. The phone squawked in his pocket. Cobb fumbled for it, spilling beer.

'It's Sergeant McBean, Mr Cobb.'

Cobb tried to focus. 'What's on your mind, Sergeant?'

'Something kind of strange has come up.'

'Oh?' Cobb felt his heartbeat quicken.

'Couple of weeks ago we found this old tom, Maggie Turpin, dead in a flat in Newington. Suicide. And some old wino she shacked up with. Bloke called Stevens. He's dead too, now. But the point is, sir, they had money on them.'

'How much money?'

'Over a grand.'

'That doesn't mean anything. They could have got that anywhere.'

'That's what I thought. But then I did some checking. And it seems they'd been throwing cash around for weeks. So there must have been quite a wad to start with.'

'And that's it?'

'Well . . .' McBean faltered. 'Well, yes. Except Hayward's got this theory about the Nile—'

'You did the right thing telling me, Sergeant,' Cobb said briskly. 'But we've closed this one off. Don't waste your time on it, Sergeant.'

'If you say so, Mr Cobb.'

'Yes, I do say so. But thanks again.' Cobb hung up and turned the phone off. He looked around quickly but in the bright spring sunshine the garden was as innocent as before.

The cab dropped Lauren at the gate. She took a deep breath and walked quickly between the tall pillars before she could change her mind. She walked across the gravel to the front door past Hudson's black BMW. There was a movement behind the glass and the door opened as she reached it. Hudson was barefoot and wore a blue flowered shirt open over slacks, and as soon as their eyes met Lauren knew that he knew.

'Well, well,' he said. He was smoking the remains of a cigar. 'I wondered when you'd be back.'

'I'm not back, Tommy.'

Hudson looked at her for a moment and walked away into the house. Lauren followed the big man down the hallway. 'Sorry about the ciggie. I know you don't like it in the house. But then it didn't seem to matter any more.' He stopped and turned. 'That's what you've come to tell me, I expect? That it doesn't matter any more.'

'We need to talk, Tommy.'

'Yeah.' Hudson's big face closed at once. 'I thought so. Drink?'

'Thanks, no.' She walked across the huge living room and took a seat on the gold brocade couch while Hudson poured himself a beer.

At length he brought his drink over and sat opposite her.

'We're going to stay at the farm for a while, Tommy,' she said.

Hudson sipped again. 'You have a reason for that?'

'I don't need a reason. But you can guess at one if you like.'

He held her gaze. 'Cobb didn't come with you?'

'I thought I'd spare him the scene.'

'You mean, I might give the cheeky sod a slap or two?' Hudson leaned forward with tension bunching the muscle along his upper arms. 'I might be over the hill but I could still knock him through that wall.'

'Let's not do it this way, Tommy.'

Hudson sat back a little and took a pull of his beer. After a moment he said: 'I worshipped you, Laurie. Swear to God. Still do.'

'I know, Tommy. I'm sorry.'

He pointed at her with his finger. 'And you led me on. Didn'tcha?'

'You wanted so badly to be led, Tommy.' Then she shook her head sharply and stood up. 'I didn't come here for this.'

'What did you come here for?'

'To get you out of my house. Out of my life. To take back control.'

He smiled unpleasantly. 'Want to get your hands on some of Mattie's money for your new boyfriend?'

'Tommy, do you really think I care about the money? But I won't leave you in charge any longer.'

'You'll never sort it out, Laurie. There won't be two quid left by the time the lawyers have finished taking their slices out of you.'

She lifted her head. 'At least it'll be my two quid. Mine and Freya's. We won't owe it to anyone.'

Hudson looked at her in silence for a long time. Finally he said, 'You know something, Laurie? You can toss me away. I'm just a prick. But you won't get rid of Mattie that easy. Maybe neither of us ever will.'

'What does that mean?'

'Thing I was told early on,' Hudson said. 'Never punch above your weight. Should've learned that.' He turned to face her. 'P'raps we both should've learned that, Laurie. You and me.'

Lauren opened her mouth to speak and then thought better of it. There seemed no point. She started to walk away.

'I'll be out of here by tomorrow,' he called after her. 'There'll be nothing missing. I'll hand it all over. The papers. The deeds. All that.'

She stopped. 'Thank you, Tommy.'

'I never wanted none of it anyway.'

'I know you didn't.' She looked at the floor and then back at him. When he didn't speak she said: 'What will you do now?'

He lifted his battered face to her and shrugged. 'What does it matter?'

She left the room quietly and walked out into the sunshine.

'And what time d'you call this, my lad?' Nelson's Yorkshire accent boomed cheerfully around the office.

Cobb emptied the bottom drawer of his desk into a black rubbish bag. 'I'm on leave, Horrie. I only came in to clean up.'

'Oh, yes. I did detect a certain bank holiday demeanour. However, my trained policeman's mind allows me to make other deductions too. I note, for example, that the subject exhibits a certain jauntiness. Indeed he appears to be—how shall we put it?—shagged out all to buggery.'

Cobb put down the rubbish bag.

Nelson lowered his voice to a stage whisper. 'You're tupping that Silver woman, aren't you, you sly dog?'

Cobb was surprised how much he resented the casual crudity. He had to resist a ridiculous urge to defend her honour.

'She has a name, Horrie. It's Lauren.'

Nelson said. 'Oh, it's like that. No offence, I'm sure.' He spoke a little stiffly. 'Of course, strictly speaking it's against the rules, you know, Sam. File not long closed, and all that.'

'Horrie,' Cobb said. 'Shut up.'

'Right. Right.'

Cobb said: 'Was it just my sex life you wanted to speak to me about?'

'No.' Nelson sucked his lip. 'No. What I really wanted to say . . .'

'Well?'

'We're going to miss you round here, Sam.' Nelson stuck out his paw. 'That's all.'

Cobb took Nelson's hand in both of his, suddenly ashamed of himself. 'Thanks for everything, Horrie. You're a good man.'

Nelson made to move away towards his own office but hesitated at the last moment. 'One last thing, Sam. You know Regional Crime really wanted a Chief Inspector on this team. You don't need to be bloody Einstein to see what that might mean.'

'I won't blow it, Horrie. Don't worry.'

'See that you don't.'

Cobb watched Nelson walk away across the room. Then he cleared the last of the litter from his desk, packed a few personal things into his bag and took the fire stairs two at a time.

Cobb let himself into the flat and dumped his bags by the door.

'Hey,' she said, gladly, 'I didn't expect you until tonight.'

'I had to get out of there. How did it go with Tommy?'

'It was fine, Sam. Everything's going to be fine.'

He stood staring at her. She sat at the tiny dining table in a chute of sunlight. A cup of coffee in front of her smoked into the radiance and a book lay open against the dark wood. She had tidied the flat and showered and she was wrapped in his threadbare bathrobe, and the room was fragrant with coffee and soap and beeswax.

'What?' she said. Then tilted her head and smiled.

Cobb was astonished by their lust. They made love hungrily, roughly, hilariously. They made love on the floor so that the boards creaked like a ship at sea, and pretended until the last moment that it was not desperately uncomfortable. They moved to the sofa bed and made love again there with the stays twanging like harp-strings beneath them. Their sex was playful, thrilling, explosive, volatile, dangerous.

But it was not enough.

He awoke at three in morning in the dark cube of the room. It was raining outside again.

'Sam?' She breathed his name in his ear. 'Do you think this could really work?'

'If they give us a chance.'

He did not know why he used this form of words, though he did know they echoed some tremor of fear deep in himself.

He said: 'What was he like, Lauren?'

'You want to talk about Matthew.' It was not a question. There was a kind of resignation in her voice.

'I just meant . . . it can't always have been bad.'

'No. It wasn't always bad.' She rolled over on to her back. 'Don't do this, Sam.'

For perhaps a full minute she said nothing more and he thought she had drifted back to sleep. Then abruptly she swung her legs out of bed and sat up and reached in her bag and found a cigarette and lit it. It was the first cigarette she had lit for four days.

'It was a ride, Sam. A ride like you couldn't believe.'

'You don't have to say anything you don't want to.'

'Oh, yes, I do. You want to know what he was like?'

'I don't—'

'Well, I'll tell you. Beautiful. Brilliant. Funny. Exciting. Exciting? That isn't the word. He was like a natural force. A hurricane, maybe.'

'Lauren.'

She stood up and paced across to the window so that the blue light fell across the planes of her body. 'But what you really want to know is if he was better than you. You want to know if you can compete.'

'I didn't ask you that.'

'Yes, you did. You just didn't voice the question.'

'Lauren, I'm sorry.'

'Was he a better man than you? That's what you want to know. Well, of course he wasn't. But, you see, Sam, that wouldn't have made any difference.' She swung towards him in the darkness. 'Is that what you wanted to hear, Sam? Is it?'

Cobb stood. He could see the tears shining on her face.

'For weeks after the crash not a day passed—not an hour—when I didn't ask myself if I would have taken him back that night. If he had just begged me once more.' She drew herself up and looked straight at him. 'But things are different now. You have to know that if Matthew walked in right now and begged me to take him back, I would tell him no.'

'Lauren—'

'You make sure you heard that right,' she said fiercely, her voice twisting, 'because I'm not going to say it again.'

Cobb stepped forward and slid his arms around her and lifted her body against his. He felt her breath and her tears hot against his skin.

'He's dead, Lauren.'

'It doesn't matter,' she said. 'It doesn't matter any more.'

He rocked her there for a while in the darkness. 'This is my fault.'

'Yes, it is.'

'I should keep my big mouth shut.'

Her voice changed. 'Why don't you, then?' She reached up and brushed her fingers over his lips. 'And I will too.'

In a rush he said: 'I can't face losing it all again, Lauren.'

'Then hold on.' She slipped her arms around his body and locked him fiercely in her grip. 'Hold on really, really tight.'

Chapter Ten

HE WAS WATCHING the child. There was something different about her, he knew, something indefinable. Was it a certain balance? Did she somehow stand more squarely to the world? He could not decide. She waited just inside the school gates with a crowd of friends. At length he was able to see what had changed about her. It was the space which had somehow always been beside her, around her. It was gone now. She had grown to fill it.

Silver felt a great regret. He had missed something, he knew, some seminal event in her life, and she was passing away from him. Whatever had happened to her, he had not been the first person she'd told. He would never be told, not about this or any of the other changes that would form her life.

Freya's face lit up and she ran out of the gates to meet them. The man's presence confused Silver, a square man in early middle life who walked beside Lauren. Freya hugged her mother and Lauren bent to kiss her and then turned her head and looked at the man and there was the pride of possession in her look. And the man looked back the same way and bent to accept the child's kiss, and the three of them turned and walked away up the sunlit street to a parked car.

The car pulled out and drew slowly past him so that the driver's face was no more than a few yards from him. A regular face, perhaps even a pleasant one, if a little stern. Silver tried to memorise the features. It seemed to be important to know his wife's lover, his child's protector. For this, he knew, was how it was. Silver stood up and walked a few yards. His body seemed not to work properly: he found it hard to coordinate his movements. There was a low wall beside the bus stop and he sat down heavily on it. People in the queue glanced at him curiously and then looked determinedly away.

Nothing had prepared him. Yet he knew what Nugget would have said. This was part of the price. Debts must be paid, even when there is no hope of meeting the bill. He lurched to his feet and walked away.

The Rum Jungle was a dark low-ceilinged place with rattan furniture intended to look tropical. Square concrete pillars were decorated with plastic jungle leaves and plastic lianas and lurid yellow plastic bunches of bananas. On a miniature stage at the far end of the room Jit glittered in the spotlights, her hair a blue flame. Silver waited just inside the door while she finished the song. From this close he could hear a tremor in her voice, a fumbled note or two in the last chorus. When she hit the final ringing chord he could almost taste her relief.

As Jit bowed and bobbed up smiling the audience clapped and whistled at her and shouted their approval. Silver crossed to the bar, found a stool and ordered a beer.

'I'll get it.' Nugent appeared out of the gloom, took the seat beside him, and paid for the drink. 'You cut it fine, Joe.'

Silver said nothing. On stage Jit was stumbling through a funny story to introduce her next number. The audience found her nervousness endearing and whenever they could find an excuse they laughed to encourage her. Silver drank. 'She's doing OK.'

'She's terrified.'

'She's supposed to be terrified.'

'She depends on you, Joe.' Nugent allowed his anger to flash like a blade. 'You understand that?'

'There's no point in anyone depending on me.' Silver turned away from the priest and looked back to the stage. She was still ploughing through her story. Silver noticed that she had placed his six-string on stage in its stand. He saw her eyes slide nervously towards the bar, trying to pierce the glare. Silver took pity on her. He leaned forward and half stood so that she could see him and raised a hand to her.

'Hey, Joe!' she cried into the microphone. 'I knew you'd make it!'

Silver cursed and pulled himself back into the shadows while people in the audience craned to see him.

'You people out there!' Jit was calling out, all confidence now, working them. 'You want to hear a real guitar player?'

Silver saw what was coming and slid off the stool. Nugent's hand locked on his arm. And then she was calling his name and the audience was baying for him and Nugent was shouting in his ear: 'You run out on her now, you deadshit, and you'll leave your arm behind.'

Silver would have shaken him off, but at that moment he caught a glimpse of her over the priest's shoulder. She was crucified in the spotlights, her eyes beseeching him, and he could see her confidence begin to crumble. Silver found himself walking past Nugent into the light.

And Jit was saying into the microphone: 'Come on, Joe! Bloody late, as usual,' and she was laughing as she said it. And Silver was up on stage and had swept up the six-string from its stand. He moved to the microphone and struck the chords she knew, the chords they all knew, and he said: 'Hit it.'

And she did. And she sang so that her pure voice filled the room and there could be no doubt of it any more.

You people climbing on that Narrow Way
Can climb from cradle up to Judgment Day.
You want to win, but first you gotta lose—
That's what they call
That's what they call
Redemption Blues.

It was past one in the morning before they left the club. Nugent helped them load the equipment and drove them back to the church. Silver sat in the back of the little van, dozing fitfully, hearing Jit chatter from the front seat but too tired to listen. The images flickered through his mind. Lauren bending, her hand on Freya's back, and the sun flashing on the child's glasses as she looked up. The bulk of the new man's shoulder through the car window. The dazzle of the spotlights and the raw energy that pulsed up to him through the darkness, just as it had in the old days, before life had stopped.

Nugent dropped them by the door of the house and drove away to park the car and did not come back. Silver helped Jit lug her gear up to her room. Then he followed her downstairs again and into the tawdry kitchen at the back of the house.

She was alight with her triumph. 'Let's have a drink, Joe.' She was pacing, tugging open cupboards. 'I really need a drink.'

'You're just on a high, Jit. It's like that.'

'You feel it too, Joe.' She could not keep still. 'Come on, partner. It's easier once you admit it.'

He said nothing. She was right. They had given it to him, just like the old days. That raw pulse of energy. The power. They had sent it to him.

She opened the fridge again. 'There's got to be some booze around here *somewhere*. We need champagne.'

'We haven't got any champagne, Jit. Get a grip.'

'Hey! There's some Newcastle Amber upstairs. Andy left it. At least that's got bubbles.'

She left at a run to fetch the beer. He heard her bare feet pattering up the stairs, as light as a deer. Before he had properly registered that she had gone she burst back into the kitchen. 'I'm a star, right?' she demanded. 'Now is that right or not?' She handed him an opened bottle.

'That's right,' he said.

'Right,' she confirmed. 'But I couldn't have done it without you.'

She opened a second one for herself, clunked it hard against his, and tipped down a draught of beer that half-emptied the bottle.

'That,' she said, and he knew she meant the whole glittering triumphant evening, 'was fun.'

'It could be more than fun, Jit. For you.'

'Don't start that shit again.' She waved at him in good-natured dismissal. 'It was just fun.'

'I know what I'm talking about, Jit,' he said.

'Pah! When are you going to get it through your head, Joe? I don't want to be rich and famous. It's just not my scene.'

'You've got talent, Jit. People should hear you.'

'People in pubs hear me. For Chrissake, why don't you get it? It's here and now. But you won't have that. You've got this mania for easy answers.'

'Easy?'

'Well, answers anyway. You want things to add up. You with your ton of guilt. Nugget with his crazy religion. Debt and payment. What are you? A lot of bloody accountants?'

'Life's not as simple as you make out, Jit.'

'Yes, it is, Joe.'

'What would you know?' he bridled. 'Standing there with your blue hair and your army boots and all of your seventeen little summers.'

'You mean I'm not smart, like you?'

He caught himself before he could answer. Instead he tipped the gassy beer into his throat, glad of the distraction.

'Let's get out of here, Joe,' she said suddenly, in a different voice. 'Nugget's giving you the elbow anyway. What's there to stay for?'

'There's a person I need to see sometimes,' he said sullenly. 'An important person.'

'Is that where you slide off to these afternoons? Well, I don't know where you go, but it busts you up every time. What's the future in that?'

'Anyway, where would I go?'

'I don't know.' She waved her beer bottle expansively, banishing the shabby room. 'If you want me to name a place for you, we'll go up to my brother Jake's people in Northamptonshire.'

'The New Age gypsy? Jit, come on.'

'Why not, Joe?' She gripped his arm. 'We'd play in pubs. Make a few quid. Have an adventure. Have some fun.'

'And then what? After all this fun we're going to have?'

She shrugged. 'Then one day we'll get sick and die. What did you have in mind?'

The country was paintbox pretty under a duck-egg sky. They played Bach on the Saab's CD and wound back the sun roof and drove too fast all the way. At a little after nine they turned through the farm gate and down the track towards the house. Fred was busy in the yard, trudging in and out of the barn with what looked to Cobb like bundles of tawny bedding which he dumped in a heap in the trailer. Something staccato about the way his father moved warned Cobb even before he rolled the car on to the cobbles that there was a problem. As he drew level, he stopped and lowered the window.

'Your bloody fox is responsible for this,' Fred snapped at him, before Cobb could speak. He was plainly furious. Cobb saw that the tawny bundles his father carried were dead chickens, torn and bloody.

'My fox?' he protested.

'You should have shot it weeks ago,' Fred accused him, brandishing a lifeless hen. 'Nasty destructive creatures. Five of my best Rhode Islands. Five! I'd've shot the bloody creature myself if it wasn't for this blasted arthritis.' The old man slung the chicken onto the heap and a cloud of loose brown feathers rose on the air. He bent down to the car again and spoke across at Lauren and Freya. 'I'm sorry, my dears. Not much of a welcome home. Damned foxes.'

'I'm so sorry, Fred,' Lauren said. 'Your beautiful chickens.' She made a sympathetic face at Cobb, then slid out of the car and escaped with Freya towards the back door.

He said: 'I'll have a pop at it this week.'

'A lot of good that'll do now,' the old man grunted.

'Didn't Baskerville hear anything?'

'Samuel, that damned dog is deafer than I am. Now put your flashy foreign car away and give me a hand.' Fred stumped off into the barn.

Cobb garaged the car and carried their bags across the yard towards the house. He glanced at the slaughtered hens on the end of the trailer as he walked by. The sight darkened his mood a little. He pulled himself together. He would not have a shadow cast over this weekend. He would not allow it.

Freya slipped down from her chair and ran across and hugged him. He lifted the child up and kissed her.

'Uncle Fred says you have to shoot the fox,' Freya said, gripping Cobb's hand. 'Poor fox. I mean, poor chickens too. But poor fox.'

'Don't worry, Princess. I probably won't even see Mr Fox. And if I do I'll probably miss.' He winked at her. 'But I'll give him a good fright, so he won't come back.'

A little later Cobb changed into his farm clothes and walked across to the barn. He circled it from the outside until he came to the wire enclosure of the chicken run. The surviving hens were huddled in one corner of the run, making small timorous noises at him. Cobb could see the scratched depression the fox had dug for itself before bellying under the wire. Cobb walked into the barn and opened the rear door of the henhouse. Blood-drabbled feathers and droppings lay in the grit.

Freya was seated on a high wooden stool at the workbench and for a moment Cobb could hardly make out her small figure in the gloom. 'Hey, Princess. I didn't know you were here.'

He saw now that she was peering at something on the bench, her head on one side. 'What have you got there, Princess?'

'It's our hawk moth. He's hatching out, just like you said he would.'

'Well, so he is.' Cobb had forgotten about the chrysalis in its tray of sand. He bent over her to see. The moth's front legs and antennae were already clear of the pupa.

'Isn't he beautiful?' Freya asked him.

'He certainly is, Princess.'

He felt a fresh rush of affection for her. It took the eye of faith to see anything very beautiful about this damp leggy insect, as fat as a small cigar. But as a child he had felt the same way about moths. There was something magical about their metamorphosis. The moth gave a convulsive heave. The chrysalis dropped clear, and the insect hung free with its bladders of wings bunched behind it.

Cobb said: 'In an hour or so he'll have two of the loveliest glossy wings you ever saw.' She did not reply and he wondered if somehow she had not heard. He tried again: 'Do you want to keep him? We can put him in a box. Otherwise he'll fly away tonight.'

'No,' Freya said finally. 'That wouldn't be fair.'

'That's my girl,' he said, and ruffled her hair. To his surprise she turned at his touch and put her arms around his neck and swung herself off the stool and clung to him like a monkey.

'I can remember, Sam,' she said into his ear.

'What?' His voice tightened. 'You can remember what?'

'I can remember.' She was quite calm. She let him go and slid back down to the stool.

'You don't have to remember anything, Princess.'

'Of course I have to.' She leaned over the box and breathed very gently on the moth. 'I remember Daddy saved me.'

Cobb could hear his own pulse booming in his ears. He said nothing.

She sat up straight and faced him. 'I remembered when I saw the moth climb out.' She faltered. 'It was so dark.'

'Do you want to tell me?' He put his hand over hers on the bench.

'I remember him. Kicking. I could feel his legs. Kicking. Really hard. I couldn't see him. I couldn't see anything. I couldn't breathe. There was this awful roaring noise.'

'It's all right, Princess.' He stroked the small hand. 'It's all right now.'

'Then he grabbed me and sort of pushed me. Out. Through a hole. It hurt me.'

'The sun roof. He saved you. He kicked out the roof and he saved you.'

'Yes, that's right.' She frowned. 'There was glass around the edges. I felt it.' She looked up at him. 'Why didn't Daddy follow me, Sam?'

'I'm not sure why, Princess. Maybe he couldn't. The main thing is he got you out. That's all that matters.' He ran his fingers down the side of her face. 'Are you all right? You look a bit pale.'

'So do you,' she said. And then: 'Sam? Should I tell Mummy?'

He swallowed. 'Yes, Princess. You should.'

Lauren threw back her head and stared at the white sky, blinking hard. She could feel Freya's uncertain gaze on her and she longed to give the child reassurance, but for the moment her power of speech seemed to have deserted her. Instead she groped across for her daughter's hand and found it, took it between both of her own and rubbed hard.

'Does it make you sad?' Freya asked doubtfully.

'Sad?' With an effort Lauren faced her. Freya sat in her red parka with her feet swinging under the bench. Lauren said, 'How could it make me sad that he helped to save you, sweetheart?'

'You look as if you're sad.'

'I suppose I do.' Lauren laughed and pushed her sleeve across her eyes. 'I don't feel sad, Frey. But I do feel all sorts of other things.'

'What other things?'

For a second Lauren was on the point of gently laughing the question off. But something stopped her. She turned to face the girl squarely and took both her hands in both of hers. 'I'll try to tell you what I feel, Freya,' she said with determination. 'I'm full of joy that your father could do such a thing. That anyone could. It gives me hope. And I'm full of anger with him for confusing me. It would be so much easier to be able to hate him.'

'But you don't hate him?'

'How can I hate him now? And yet it's so . . .' She screwed her eyes up and struggled to find what she wanted to say. 'It's so bloody *typical* of him to do something like this. Something wonderful and unexpected, just when we had all decided he was a bad man.'

Freya thought about this and nodded to herself. 'I think it's good not to hate him.'

'Yes it is, Frey,' Lauren said, and felt the sudden release of something which had been trapped within her. 'Hating won't get us anywhere. I think I always knew that, but I didn't want to face it.'

'Will you be able to face it now?'

'I'll just have to learn, won't I, sweetheart?'

Freya watched her mother's face gravely for a second or two, and then reached up her arms.

It was mid-afternoon. Cobb came quietly into the room and Lauren moved under the sheets to show him that she was not sleeping. He walked over and sat on the edge of the bed and took her hand. He saw that there were tears on her face. He said: 'She told you?'

'Yes.' Lauren brushed her hand across her eyes. 'It's a relief, isn't it? We don't have to go on wondering when it's going to come back to her.'

'And neither does she,' he said. 'Yes. It's good news.'

'This?' She indicated her own face, in response to something in his tone. 'This is nothing. Just brought it all back for a moment. This will happen sometimes.'

'Of course it will.' He kissed her face and tasted salt. 'So it should.' He worked his arms around her in the warm bed.

She looked at him and made a funny face. 'What are you doing in all that gear? Get it off at once.'

He stood and shrugged off his sweater and shirt in one movement and sat on the edge of the bed to unlace his shoes.

'Sam, I know what's on your mind. But it's all right now. Trust me.'

'He saved her. He stayed in the car and saved her.'

'You didn't want to hear that, did you?' she said gently. 'You wanted him to be an evil bastard. Rotten to the core.'

'Yes.'

'Well, I didn't.' She pulled herself against him. 'I'm glad to hear something good of him. It . . . closes the circle. Now we can all rest in peace. Do you understand?' When he did not reply, she said, 'This doesn't change anything, Sam. Trust me. Good or bad, dead or alive, Matthew is in the past now.'

Cobb looked at her and the fear fell away from him. He pushed his hand up into her hair and lifted her face and kissed her.

His mobile phone squawked. Cobb breathed hard, looked at the ceiling. He said, 'This cannot be happening.' He snatched up the phone and punched RECEIVE.

'What?' he shouted.

'Is that you, sir?' McBean's voice was uncertain. 'Inspector Cobb?'

'McBean?' Something cold slid down Cobb's spine and fear made him angry. 'Jesus Christ! What do you want now?'

'I'm sorry if it's a bad time, sir,' McBean said levelly. 'It's important.'

'I told you we'd finished with this, Sergeant.'

'And I told you it's important. Sir.'

'Well, what is it?'

McBean hesitated, guessing, perhaps. 'Can you talk, where you are?'

'No, I can't.'

'Then I think you'd better get over here.'

'Over where?'

'I'm at the Battle of the Nile pub in Stepney.'

'For Chrissake, Sergeant. I'm at home. I'm on leave. I don't plan on going anywhere for two whole weeks.' He glanced across the room at Lauren. She was dressing. She smiled across at him sympathetically, as if determined not to influence his decision.

McBean said sharply: 'Get over here, Mr Cobb. I'll give you two hours, and then I'm calling the local division.' He rang off.

Lauren looked across at Cobb and smiled ruefully. 'I guess this will happen sometimes, too.'

'I'm really sorry, Lauren.'

She shrugged. 'The weekend had a bit of a rocky start. Get back as soon as you can and we'll begin again. What's the drama anyway?'

'Something I left unfinished, like a fool.' Roughly he pulled his clothes back on. She put her arms around him and hugged him.

'Don't be angry, Sam.' She kissed him quickly. 'I'm not. Anyway, I'd better get used to it.'

Cobb threaded the Land Rover through the City and out into the half-abandoned Docklands. He drove badly and had to make a deliberate effort to concentrate on London's Saturday evening traffic.

He was shaken by how thoroughly the call had thrown him. He grew furious with McBean, even while he knew this to be unfair. The Sergeant had been on an unauthorised digging expedition. If he had unearthed a mine it would be Cobb's world that was blown apart, not his own.

It was nearly six when he found the pub. It was on the corner of a sidestreet of terraced houses. The Battle of the Nile was a crumbling Victorian pub in sooty red brick with a crude sign swinging from it. A Ford Sierra was parked by the far fence. Cobb switched off and climbed out, and as he did so McBean emerged from the Sierra and walked across to him.

'Sorry about this,' McBean said. But he did not sound apologetic. The Sergeant seemed as edgy and ill at ease as Cobb was.

'Don't keep me in suspense, McBean. Have you found our man?'

'Found him? Not exactly, sir.'

Cobb felt a spurt of relief and fought to contain it, for he knew this was not all McBean had to tell him. 'So tell me.'

McBean concentrated on Cobb's eyes. 'Like I said, there was this dead tom, Maggie Turpin. And her old man, a dosser name of Stevens.'

'And?'

'Maybe it's nothing,' McBean said, 'but Stevens said some things. About pulling someone out of the river.'

'Alive?'

'Not clear. But he talked about this place. This pub. Or at least, that's what we worked out, me and Hayward. So I came here. Just to satisfy myself. And it seems this Turpin woman did bring a bloke here. He worked for a while behind the bar. Gave the name of Joe Hill.'

Cobb said: 'And that's all you've got?'

McBean shrugged.

Cobb said: 'So does this Joe Hill fit Silver's description, or what?'

'They say not. But he was about the right age, about the right height.'

'Well, where is he?'

'He's gone. Left weeks ago, apparently.'

'Wait a bit.' Cobb struggled to disguise the relief in his voice. 'Are you telling me you called me out here for this? And this Joe Hill character doesn't even look like Silver?'

'Sir.' McBean stared into space.

'I think you're getting a bit hung up on this, Sergeant. Wouldn't you say?'

McBean pursed his lips for a moment, then looked down at him. 'I think I've heard enough from you, Mr Cobb.'

'What did you say?'

'You shut up and listen. Do you think I don't know you've got every reason for wanting Matt Silver to stay vanished? Do you think I'm a complete bloody idiot, not to know what's going on with you and Lauren Silver? Half the bloody Met knows.'

Cobb said nothing. He found that he felt vaguely ashamed. On some level his bluff had been called and he had no answer.

McBean said: 'I'm not drawing any conclusions. I'm not on duty. But I think Matt Silver got pulled out of the river alive. I've always thought so. And I'll tell you something else: you've always thought so too.'

'Matt Silver's dead,' Cobb said, fighting to keep his voice level.

'If you say so, Mr Cobb. I'm not going to say different, I'll promise you that much. It's your call. You can go in there and ask more questions. But if you don't want to know, don't ask.'

McBean turned on his heel and strode away across the car park to his modest saloon. He drove past Cobb without looking up at him.

Cobb watched him go and stood for a full minute outside the mean pub. A knot of noisy men in London Transport jackets walked up the steps and pushed in through the bar doors. Cobb locked the Land Rover and followed them, catching the swinging door as he went.

It was shabby and rundown. At the bar, a very fat woman sat chain-smoking while two greyhounds lay coiled like springs beneath her stool. A big rawfaced landlord in a greasy sweater was polishing glasses. Cobb walked up to the bar. Before he could speak, both greyhounds bared their needle teeth and growled at him.

'He's a copper, George,' the fat woman said.

'Oh, yeah?' George bristled at once, pulling himself up to his full height and setting down the glass as if to leave his hands free for action.

'Have you ever seen this man?' Cobb said. He flashed open his warrant card in George's face and then slid the black-and-white picture of Silver out of his wallet and laid it on the counter. George flicked his eyes disdainfully to the photograph.

'Him? He's been on TV, ain't he?'

'Is that Joe Hill?' Cobb said.

'What?' George laughed scornfully. 'Joe? That useless prick? He wasn't nothing like that.'

'Nothing at all like that?'

'Nah. Joe? He was all scarred up. A car smash or something.'

'So where is he now?' Cobb pocketed the photo.

'I chucked the tosser out. He was nicking stuff. Chucked him out in the street, thieving bastard. Weeks ago now.'

'Where did this Joe Hill stay when he worked here, George? Where did he sleep?'

George's eyes flickered towards him, suddenly defensive. 'I don't know, do I?' When Cobb didn't speak, George said urgently: 'He never stayed here. The brewery don't allow it. Anyway, I got no rooms.'

Cobb put away his wallet. 'I want to look round, George.'

'Don't you need a warrant?'

'Don't you need a licence?'

George stared at him for a moment with a hunted look.

'Where did he sleep, George?' Cobb said, and then more gently, 'I don't give a stuff about the brewery. I just want to find Joe Hill.'

George pulled up the barflap and opened the back door onto a passage stacked with kegs. George jerked his head upwards. 'Stairs at the end. The three of them dossed up top for a while.'

Cobb pushed past him.

'I took pity, like,' George called after him, desperately. 'Tried to do them a good turn, see? This is what I get for it.'

Cobb trotted up the stairs and ducked into the dim half-built attic. He felt for a switch and found one. The bare bulb sprang on. Off to his right was a clutter of blankets and bedding with a pile of women's magazines and an ashtray filled with butts. He moved on, past a partition of plasterboard tacked over the studs. In a boarded-off space behind a curtain was a toilet and beside it a sink unit growing out of the wall on its own pipes. There was a cot on the far side of the room, a folding bed of some sort laid out under the skylight. The bed had been roughly made up, the blankets pulled into place.

Cobb could see no trace of personality or comfort about the sleeping space: no papers or books, no coffee cup or ashtray. He stood in the low space and looked at it for a long time. Then he turned to go, gripping the joist above the bed as he did so. His fingers touched something pinned there—a scrap of newspaper. He stopped and tore down the cutting and held it under the light, tilting it to make out the fuzzy photograph. Freya's eyes looked out at him solemnly, and finally there could be no more doubt in him.

Cobb came back into the bar and lifted the flap to let himself out. The greyhounds rumbled warningly at him as soon as he reappeared. He leaned close to them and bellowed: 'Shut the fuck up!' The room fell instantly silent.

'Ooh, you've got a way with dogs, luvvie,' the fat woman said admiringly, turning to face him for the first time.

Cobb got a grip on his voice. 'When did Joe Hill leave here?'

'About—what?—six weeks back. But I never—'

'Where did he go?'

'I dunno, do I? I just slung him out.' George was nearly frantic that he could not give a useful answer. 'Wait. I did hear that padre picked him up and dusted him off, like. Not that I hurt him, much, see—'

'What padre? A priest, you mean?'

'Aussie bloke. Not a bad type for a do-gooder. Used to come here with some tart with a guitar. I ain't seen neither of them since.'

'Which church?'

'St Mark's,' the fat woman told Cobb amicably. 'It's off the Mile End Road, dearie. You'll find it, clever chap like you.'

Cobb pulled up outside the church but did not turn off the engine. It was dark now and under the two or three sickly streetlights which still operated the narrow square looked bleak and threatening. The church was in darkness but a black corrugated iron hall stood next to it and the open door threw light onto the pavement. Cobb sat in the Land Rover, nauseous from tension and hunger. He realised he had not eaten all day.

For the first time it occurred to him seriously that he still had a choice. He could drive out of this cul-de-sac now and no one would be any the wiser: not Lauren, not Freya. He could go back to the farm and pick up his life where he had left it, on the brink of a new chapter. Yes, he thought. And perhaps he wouldn't jump every time the phone rang. He cursed himself, turned the engine off and climbed out.

'You looking for me?' A solid grey-haired man in his mid-thirties was standing in the middle of the road, looking at him. The man had been walking up the street towards the church. He carried white plastic shopping bags bulging with bread rolls.

He took out his warrant card. 'Are you the priest here?'

'Bob Nugent, that's me. You?'

Cobb picked up the Australian accent this time, flat and wary. Nugent did not look at the warrant card in its important wallet but waited for Cobb to speak his name. 'I'm Sam Cobb. Inspector Sam Cobb.'

'You've come a long way, Mr Cobb.'

'I'm sorry?'

'Lower Durning Farm. Oxon.'

It took Cobb a moment to realise that the priest was reading the address from Fred's fancy script on the Land Rover's door.

'Bit off your patch, aren't you?'

'It's the family farm,' Cobb said. 'I'm with the Met, Father Nugent. I'm looking for Joe Hill.'

'Are you now? Well, you'd better come in, then.'

He led Cobb across the street and through the door of the hall. Two young men and a girl were setting out folding beds and folded blankets in rows up the body of the hall, supervised by a plump man in a maroon cardigan. Nugent marched through the hall so fast that Cobb found it hard to keep up with him. 'Hi, Phil. Any takers yet?'

'Not yet, Father.' The fat man smiled at Cobb. 'Have you brought us a guest already?'

'This bloke?' Nugent shouted with laughter. 'Hardly. But he does look the part a bit, I'll grant you.' In a kitchen area behind the stage Nugent dumped his bags, gestured to Cobb to take a seat, and filled a kettle at the sink. 'So what do you want with Joe Hill, Mr Cobb?'

'You know him, then?'

'I've met him.'

'Is he here now?'

Nugent carried the kettle over to the cooker then walked over to the table and pulled out a chair opposite Cobb's. 'I'll do you a deal, Mr Cobb. I'll be straight with you, if you are with me. And I'll tell you upfront that I don't much like talking to you people about my people.'

'Have you seen this man?' Cobb laid the photo of Silver on the table.

Nugent turned it round and took off his glasses to study it. 'No. Well, that is I've seen him on TV. That's Matt Silver, or his twin brother.'

'It's Matt Silver. Is it also Joe Hill?'

'You're joking, right?' Nugent leaned back in his chair. 'Of course it isn't Joe Hill. Joe Hill was nothing at all like this man.'

'Was?'

'I picked Joe up one night when the fat bastard who runs the Battle of the Nile threw him out. I gave him a place to stay for a while.'

'That's it?'

'That's it.' The kettle sang and Nugent rose and crossed to it. 'Coffee?'

'No, thanks.'

'Have a bloody coffee, Mr Cobb. You look stuffed.'

Cobb said nothing while Nugent made the coffee and brought him a cup. Cobb cupped his hands around the mug and noticed that his hands were shaking slightly. The coffee was very strong and very good.

'When was the last time you saw Joe Hill, Father?'

'He stayed a couple of nights. Drifted off. They all do.'

Cobb knew he was lying, and that Nugent knew that he knew. He could think of no way of outflanking the priest. Cornered, he set down the coffee. 'I could have this place turned over, Father Nugent.'

'Been there, Mr Cobb.' Nugent sat back again, at ease, looked at the ceiling. 'Done that. Got the T-shirt.'

'If you're protecting him—'

'Look, Mr Cobb. Just see if you can get this straight. This man—' he tapped the photograph '— is not Joe Hill.'

They sat in silence for perhaps thirty seconds. Eventually Nugent touched the picture again. 'What did this guy do again? I thought he was supposed to be dead. Wasn't there a car smash some months back?'

'He killed his child.' Cobb sipped at his coffee. He felt weary and defeated. 'Nine years old. Nearly killed her sister.'

'That's terrible.' Nugent shook his head. 'You mean, he was driving and there was a crash and his own kid gets killed. That's terrible.' He looked innocently up at Cobb. 'So what do you want him for?' Cobb felt a nerve jump in his cheek but Nugent had not finished. 'Let me guess. You've been chasing him for four months so you can punish him. If that wasn't so bloody grotesque, it'd be funny.'

'I don't make the rules, Father.'

'No. You're just following orders, Mr Cobb.' Nugent stood up. 'How's this for an idea? Why don't you drink your coffee and fuck off?'

A car's headlights swung across the windows and Cobb heard it pull up in the street outside. Cobb and Nugent faced one another in a tense stand-off for a moment. Almost at once the car's engine restarted and they listened to it whine away again in urgent reverse up the length of the cul-de-sac. A second later the plump man put his head around the curtain and gave a little nod of apology. 'Excuse me, Father. I told the young woman that she was no longer welcome here after her behaviour last night. I'm afraid I was rather short with her. I hope I did right?'

'Quite right, Phil,' Nugent said, without taking his eyes off Cobb. 'Bless you, Phil.'

Cobb said. 'You know I have to find him.'

'Why? Who'll gain by it?'

'Not me, Father. Believe me.'

'Have you got some personal angle in this, Cobb?'

'What do you mean?'

'Look at you. You're coming apart at the seams. Why is this so important to you? Do you think you'll be free of him when you find him?'

'Least of all then.'

'So why look?'

'Because you don't set the agenda here, and neither do I. There isn't one rule for him and one rule for everyone else.'

'So make one.'

'You might have that luxury.' Cobb stood up. 'I don't. I have to find Matt Silver because he's done wrong. And now I believe he's alive. I wish to Christ I didn't believe that.'

'Then don't. Faith is achieved, Mr Cobb, not granted.'

'That's a good trick if you can learn it.' Cobb tossed his business card onto the table. 'Thanks for the coffee.'

Chapter Eleven

SILVER WAITED in black shadow on the basement steps and watched Cobb walk across to the Land Rover. As he moved through the yellow pool of the streetlight Silver could clearly see his face. This was hardly the smiling, confident man he had seen outside Freya's school just days before: this man was drawn and unshaven. But there was no question that it was the same person. So he was the police.

Silver waited while Cobb backed the Land Rover up over the kerb, its suspension groaning, and then drove off towards Mile End Road. Beside Silver among the garbage cans Jit was silent for once. They moved quietly down between the church and the hall and Silver led her in through the back door. Nugent was at the table with his arms crossed.

Silver said: 'Thanks, Nugget.'

'You don't know what I did yet.'

'I know what you did.' Silver crossed to the table and picked up Cobb's business card. 'Inspector Sam Cobb,' he read. 'So that's who you are.'

'He knows you, Joe.'

'And I know him.' Silver made a short sound something like a laugh. 'So we all know each other now, don't we, Nugget?'

'You're Joe Hill,' Nugent said steadily. 'That's who you are. I don't know bugger all about anyone else.' Nugent stood up and fetched his coat. He took out his wallet, opened it and threw some notes on the table. 'You're out, Joe. That's all I've got on me. Take it and get out now. Take the Ford bus. I won't report it.'

'Take the bus?'

'Take it. Keep it. That big old heap's no use to me. I only wanted you to fix it so you wouldn't top yourself before you'd dug out the drains.'

'Nugget—'

'Just get out of here. Now.'

Jit said: 'I'll get our stuff.'

Silver turned to her. He had forgotten she was in the room.

'It's half my van anyway,' she went on, her chin coming up defiantly. 'I cleaned the bloody thing out.'

When she was gone Nugent reached under the stage and dragged out the ancient toolbox by its steel handle. 'Take that too,' he said. 'It's no good to me. You might make yourself a few bob somewhere.'

'Nugget—'

'Listen to me, Joe. I'm doing this because Joe Hill deserves a break. But I'll tell you this much: I don't believe Joe Hill has a hope in hell. This bloke is smart and tough and he will not give up. I know the type. More than that, he's driven. I don't know by what.'

'I do.'

'Whatever it is, you stay a very long way away from him.'

Silver smiled. 'And I thought you wanted me to pay my debts.'

'That was the other bloke,' Nugent said. 'He's dead.'

Ten minutes later Silver sat in the passenger seat of the Ford bus in the street outside the church. He glanced back into the body of the vehicle. A couple of bags, the toolbox, two guitars, two sleeping bags.

'Isn't this neat?' Jit said in delight. She clashed the gears noisily. 'Don't worry, I'll get the hang of it.'

She pulled away with a jerk and drove up the cul-de-sac in a reasonably straight line. Glancing into the wing mirror Silver saw that Fat Phil and Nugent were both standing in the hall door, dwindling in perspective as the bus drew away.

Jit pulled up at the end of the street. The main road was a stream of trucks and black cabs and red buses jostling for position, all of them urgently going somewhere on a late Saturday night in London. Silver stared at it all in sudden bewilderment. For a second he was seized with a feeling close to panic. 'But where are we going?'

She glanced at him and swung the minibus left into the traffic. 'We're going to join the gypsies, Joe.'

Cobb pulled up in a service area on the M25. He was bone weary. He wandered into the bright plastic palace of a restaurant. He heard himself order something and took it away and slumped over it and forced himself to eat. Before he could change his mind again he pulled out the mobile and made the call.

'Sam? Do you know what time it is?' Even in his annoyance, Nelson's thick Yorkshire accent was comforting and familiar.

'No, Horrie. I don't.'

'It's eleven-thirty on a Saturday night, Sam. I've got the family here. Everyone's in bed. Kiddies trying to sleep. This had better be good.'

'It isn't good,' Cobb said. He left out McBean's involvement but included everything else: Joe Hill, the crumpled photograph in the attic, the lying priest.

He felt instantly better when he had finished, as if a boil had been lanced. The matter would move out of his hands now.

Nelson was quiet for a long time. Finally the Yorkshireman said: 'Are you out of your mind, Sam? You've got nothing at all here.'

'Horrie, I can't dodge this any more. You know what this means?'

'This means nothing, Sam. Because you've got nothing. No witnesses. No one talking. Nothing. Just a newspaper photo pinned up in some loft.' Nelson's anger was stoking steadily. 'Don't you understand at all, Sam? You've moved on from here, thanks to Mr Sykes and me. A new start. Do you want to throw all that away? The Matt Silver file's closed. Good Lord, Sam, you shouldn't even be making enquiries.'

'Hold on, Horrie—'

'Nobody cares about this any more, Sam. Only you. And we know why *that* is.' Nelson cleared his throat and spoke more calmly. 'Sam, you must see you're on some kind of a vendetta here. And against a dead man at that. It's paranoid. It's unhealthy.'

Cobb said: 'You've got this all wrong.'

'I don't think so, Sam. I don't think so at all. Now you listen. I'm going to forget this conversation ever happened. But if you choose to raise this officially I won't support you on it. It would look very bad for you all round, Sam. Think about it.'

'Horrie—'

'I've bailed you out before, Sam. But not this time. You're on your own.' He hung up.

It was past midnight when Cobb drove down the track to the farm. He parked and climbed stiffly out. He crossed the yard towards the back porch and was startled by a sudden movement at his feet. 'Baskerville?' The old dog gazed up at him from the shadows of the porch with milky eyes. Cobb knelt and fondled the dog's sleep-warm head. He sat on the step next to Baskerville's bed and the dog grunted and shifted his head and dropped it like a log in Cobb's lap.

He must have slept a little then, for he came awake with a jolt and saw that the moon was tilted further down the sky than it had been.

'Can you tell me about it?' Lauren said gently from beside him. She was sitting on the other end of the step, watching him.

'Soon,' he said. 'But not right now.'

'Is it about us?'

'Yes.'

She nodded and looked away, looked up at the moon. 'Is it too much for you, all this? Are we too much?'

'It's not that.' He stretched out his hand and she took it and he could feel the ball of her thumb stroking the back of his fingers.

'Will you be able to handle it for us, Sam?'

'I hope so,' he said. 'But just at this moment I can't see how.'

She leaned across and kissed him. 'I trust you, Sam. I trust you to keep us all safe.' She rose. 'Come in to bed when you're ready.'

Silver took over the wheel as soon as they left the motorway and Jit was asleep the moment she settled into the passenger seat. He drove on through the dark country, moving from main roads to minor, edging first north and then west.

A lay-by came up and he swung the minibus into it. The noisy ratchet of the handbrake woke Jit and she sat up, blinking. 'What time is it?'

'About two.'

She stretched and yawned. 'Where are we?'

'We're nowhere, Jit.' He unclipped his seat-belt. 'You take the bus.'

'I don't know the way,' she said quietly.

'You'll find it. And then I'll know where to find you.' He leaned forward and rested his forehead on the cool rim of the wheel. 'Jit, you know why I've got to go.'

'Of course I know. You've got to find the evil Vargas.'

Silver reached across and pushed his hand through the short pelt of her hair, feeling it bristle against the stump of his ring finger. She nuzzled briefly against his palm. He said: 'Maybe the evil Vargas is me.'

It grew cold. Finally Cobb lifted the dog's head out of his lap and quietly entered the house. In the kitchen he stopped to check his watch. It was three thirty in the morning of Easter Sunday. He supposed he should go to bed but sleep felt nowhere close. He poured himself a fat Scotch and paced for a while around the kitchen. At length he took his drink down the short corridor to the garden room and, entering, softly closed the door behind him. He stopped there. It had happened once before but this time the haunting familiarity was keener. The peaceful room, her warm sleeping form and rhythmic breathing.

He sat down where he had always sat, in the winged chair by the door, and watched over her. It could not be as bad as that last time, he told himself. Nothing could be as bad as that. And yet a worm of doubt had entered his mind and was already eating at his certainty. Surely he could lose this woman just as he had lost Clea? It was unthinkable, but being unthinkable did not mean it would not happen. She had promised. But when she had promised she had thought her husband gone forever. How could he compete if Matt Silver were no longer a ghost after all? So he sat and watched her silently as the minutes crept by, watched her slipping out of his grasp all unknowing, as that other woman had slipped from his grasp two years before.

His head came up with a jerk. Freya's cry pulled him up from his half sleep and he was instantly awake. He stood up. It had been a small sound and Lauren had not stirred. He opened the bedroom door and stepped into the corridor, pulling the door closed behind him.

She stood in the kitchen, tiny and waif-like in her pyjamas. 'Sam?'

He went to her and lifted her up on to a chair. 'What's wrong, Princess?'

'I had a bad dream.'

He could see that she was pale and frightened. He found his sweater and wrapped her up in it.

'I heard something,' she said.

'You did? It's that fox again.' He was seized with a wave of protectiveness, as fierce as it was impotent, and with it a great rush of pain flooded through him. 'I'll be right back,' he said.

He went to the cellar and unlocked the gun cabinet and brought out the shotgun and pocketed the cartridges and trotted back up the steps to the kitchen. She fixed her great eyes on him.

'Is he going to take me away?' she asked quietly.

Cobb stopped. 'Who?' he said, and a weird dread crept through him, as if she had seen into the darkness and turmoil of his mind.

'Scarecrow Man,' she said. 'It was Scarecrow Man.' She pointed to the moonlit yard. 'He was out there. I saw him. He saw me.' They were both silent for a long moment. 'You promised he wouldn't come here, Sam.'

'So I did, Princess. So I did.' Cobb walked to the window. And, as he knew it would, the gaunt figure stepped out of the shadows, the night wind moving its long coat, its face twisted and white in acid moonlight. In a second it was gone. Cobb glanced back protectively at the child but she had seen nothing.

'It was a dream, wasn't it, Sam?'

'Yes, Princess. It was just a dream.'

'The fox woke me up in the middle of my dream,' she scolded herself for her silliness. 'That must've been what happened, Sam. D'you think?'

'That's what happened, Princess.' Cobb's heart began to trip with a deep, full rhythm and he felt raw power and decision flow through him. He walked across and bolted the back door. 'You stay in the house,' he told the child, and took up the shotgun. 'I'll get your fox for you.'

She was suddenly anxious. 'Will it hurt?' he heard her voice calling after him as he moved away through. 'Don't let it suffer, Sam.'

Cobb let himself out of the front door and crossed the paddock to the sunken lane. He padded up the track, surefooted in his familiarity. He wanted a vantage point over the farm, some place high enough to show him the buildings picked out under the cold moon. His brain was working frighteningly fast now. He paused and thumbed two of the fat shells into the gun and closed the breech. The clack of the action spoke through the trees but it was the only noise he made.

It was then that he saw him. Silver was making little attempt at concealment, climbing straight up the centre of the paddock two hundred yards to Cobb's left, visible through a gap in the hedge. He was following the track which led to the ruined village. Cobb watched him. It was as if, after a fabled quest, he had at last tracked down some mythical beast, a creature he had only half believed in. Scarecrow Man. Tall and skeletal with a long flapping coat. He was toiling at the climb, dragging one leg slightly. Cobb thought suddenly: But I have not tracked him down. He has tracked me. He has tracked me to my home. And this thought sent violence leaping through him.

Cobb trod silently over the turf, keeping himself below the skyline, and finally edged up to the mound which marked the far wall of the buried churchyard. And here he stopped, sinking down behind the cover of the mound.

'Hello, Sam,' Silver said from behind him. 'You've been looking for me.'

Cobb rose and turned in one motion, the shotgun clamped so hard against his shoulder that it bruised him. The spider-thin silhouette stood against the western stars. Cobb's blood boomed in his ears and the cold air whistled through his teeth. He felt for the trigger.

Silver said gently: 'You could do it, Sam. No one would blame you.' The dawn light fell across his ruined face. 'No one would even know.'

Cobb took a half step back as the shotgun kicked his shoulder. The twin shattering explosions hurled flat echoes around the hills.

'I don't know what's so precious about this old life,' Silver said as the echoes died away, 'that neither of us seems to be able to end it.'

Cobb dropped the gun on the turf and sat down heavily among the rocks. 'Why couldn't you leave us alone? Why couldn't you stay dead?'

'I'm sorry about Freya. I only wanted to see her again. I never thought she'd see me.' Silver gathered his coat around him. 'You love them, don't you, Sam?'

'Yes.' Cobb looked hopelessly at the turf between his feet.

'So do I. I always did, really, only I was too stupid to know it.' Silver belted the coat. 'I watched you, Sam. I watched you out on the step there with my wife. I watched you through the window with my daughter. And I watched them with you.' He stepped over the graveyard wall. 'You couldn't love them more than I do, Sam. But I think you love them better.' Silver sought out his eyes and held his gaze. 'There's no need to tell them, Sam Cobb. You'll never see me again. None of you will.'

He turned and began to walk down the track on the far side of the hill, away from the farm. Cobb stared unbelieving at his retreating back. 'Wait!' Cobb shouted after him.

Silver turned and looked up at him, wordlessly.

'You saved her,' Cobb said. 'You stayed in the car and you got Freya out. Or they'd both have drowned. You remember that?'

'Nothing. I remember nothing.'

'It's the truth,' Cobb said. 'She told me. She remembers. She'd want you to know. They both would.'

Silver stood still for a long time. Then he nodded gravely, perhaps in awe, perhaps in gratitude, and walked away through the bracken.

Cobb stayed on the hilltop until the pale sun rose and burned away the pearl mist in the valleys. Then he came back down the hill, the gun hooked over his arm, across the wet paddocks and through the hedge into the sunken lane. Halfway down a tawny fox stepped out on pointed feet not five yards from him, stared at him, and tripped away silently among the hawthorns.

Somehow he had not expected them to be up but they were all in the kitchen. Fred, clattering about the stove, waved his spatula at him in greeting. Lauren wrapped in a bathrobe, was nursing her first coffee at the kitchen table, sitting in the spot he had come to think of as hers. She glanced up anxiously at him as he pushed open the kitchen door but Freya spoke first.

'You shot the fox.' The child looked at him sadly. 'We heard the bang.'

'I believe I did, Princess.'

'Did he suffer much?'

'Oh, yes, Princess. I believe he suffered a great deal.'

And then the room and the world it contained were swimming, and the faces of the people he loved were trembling in it.

Lauren stood up and crossed to him quickly. 'Sam?'

He felt her arms come round him and her fingers lock in his hair.

Fred put his head on one side and gave him a quizzical look from under his chef's hat. 'Lot of fuss for a bloody fox,' he said.

TIM GRIGGS

Tim Griggs says that he cannot remember a time when he didn't want to be a writer. While he was growing up, he was inspired by his father, Percy Griggs, who in the 1950s wrote stories for teenage boys. 'His books were mostly adventure stories based on camping and hiking holidays—a genre that's almost forgotten now. I used to idolise him. I always wanted to do the same.' Now in his fifties, Tim Griggs is delighted that with the publication of *Redemption Blues* he is at last following in his father's footsteps, though sadly his father is no longer around to see it.

The author is someone who thrives on change and adventure. In his twenties he worked as a freelance journalist and then as a science editor for international research agencies in Africa and Asia, before moving to Australia. There, he and a business partner set up a communications agency quirkily called *The Corporate Storyteller*. They specialised in working for government agencies, science and technology companies and research laboratories. He says that running his own company was exciting, profitable and great fun, but in his spare time he still concentrated on his first love—writing fiction. And now, six unpublished novels later, his determination has finally paid off. *Redemption Blues* was sold to a publisher for a six-figure sum and was an instant best-seller on publication.

Tim Griggs lived in Australia for seventeen years, only returning to this country four years ago. He and his wife, Jenny, now live in Oxford. He says they left Australia because they were 'too comfortable. We were well set

up, we had a house in the middle of Sydney and a great lifestyle. But I was coming up to my fiftieth birthday, which felt like a really important one for me, and I just wanted to spice life up a bit. And my wife Jenny had never lived outside Australia so we thought it would be interesting to live in the UK together and enjoy some shared adventures.' He misses Australia, but not as much as he expected to. Returning to the UK has enabled him to see lots of people he knew when he was younger, which he regards as an added bonus. 'It's interesting, but the first question people ask me, people who haven't seen me for twenty-five years, is "how's the novel going"? So it's great to have something published at last. It gives me something positive to tell them.'

In spite of his writing success, he says he's not sure he would advise others to spend their lives writing in the way that he has. 'You have to enjoy the process of writing, because you may not get anything else out of it. For me it was something I felt I just had to do, a compulsion. But from the practical point of view it's very far from a sensible career.' Tim Griggs now writes fiction full time. 'I found it rather hard at first. Writing fiction has always been my dark passion. Now suddenly it's my job. It's hard to convince myself this is actually work.' But he says that years of earning his living as a commercial writer makes it easier to write professionally now. 'I can't afford to wait for inspiration, I just have to sit down and start writing.'

Sally Cummings

THE DREAM CATCHER. Original full-length version © 2001 by Maria Barrett. British condensed version © The Reader's Digest Association Limited, 2001. The extract on page 124 is from *Lady Chatterley's Lover* by D.H.Lawrence.

OLIVIA'S LUCK. Original full-length version © 2000 by Catherine Alliott. British condensed version © The Reader's Digest Association Limited, 2001.

REDEMPTION BLUES. Original full-length version © 2000 by Tim Griggs. British condensed version © The Reader's Digest Association Limited, 2001.

The right to be identified as authors has been asserted by the following in accordance with sections 77 and 78 of the Copyright, Designs and Patents Act, 1988: Maria Barrett, Catherine Alliott and Tim Griggs.

PICTURE CREDITS: COVER: Gettyone Stone. Maria Barrett photograph: John Dominick. Catherine Alliott photograph: Sophie Alliott. THE DREAM CATCHER: pages 6 & 7: Mother and Child, Getty Photodisc; School children, Format Photographers; Newspaper, Getty Photodisc; page 161: John Dominick. OLIVIA'S LUCK: pages 162 & 163: Illustration and chapter decorations by Jack McCarthy; page 317: Sophie Alliott. REDEMPTION BLUES: pages 318 & 319: Guitar, Retna Pictures, Woman, Getty Image Bank; Girl with short hair, Images Colour Library; Girl with glasses, Getty Photodisc.

Printed and bound by Maury Imprimeur SA, Malesherbes, France

601-012-1